THE AELFRAVER TRILOGY

BOOK II

THE REBEL

J. R. TRAAS

For more about *The Aelfraver Trilogy* and other works by the author, visit www.blankbooklibrary.com

This is a work of fiction. Any resemblance to actual events, situations, and individuals (living or dead) is purely coincidental.

to Buzz, who convinced me it could be done

CONTENTS

PART SEVEN - ASCENDANCE

... For it is written that,
one day, the Achemir
shall wreak vengeance upon the world
in the name of the enslaved/created,
whose champion/undoing shall be
master of eight,
killer of death

Dragon-friend and -slayer,
Anointed and Profane
Conqueror and Liberator
Uniter and Sunderer,
Faithful and Faithless,
Self and Un-self,
who shall draw
battle lines between the Gods

... From that drowned empire
of Doused Flame, from war's fog
shall arise a republic
of chaos, where the masterless shall
fell one another for absolution
in the Dust
as the Ashes of the uncountable dead
suffocate the wicked, their brethren

Written in the cuneiform language of the Rioans, gleaned from three-story-tall stone tablets buried in the chasms under that mountain the ancients named *Bith Burrig Cincantin* ("Elder Mountain"), these twenty-three short lines are all that remain of "The Prophecy of the Achemir."

The vast majority of the epic has been effaced by time and the elements, rendered illegible. Tragically, no copies have ever been found. Some historians have conjectured that this erasure was intentional. Indeed, and quite curiously, certain patterns of damage in the stonework appear almost deliberate.

Although the concept of "The Achemir" is referenced in several other Rioan works from earliest antiquity, "Prophecy" is the only surviving hint as to the purpose of this mythic being; a being which, by any measure, was neither man nor god—but something else entirely.

— Excerpted from *Those Who Came Before: Mythologies of the Heathen Dead* by W. L. Annigandu, Professor Emeritus of Lore, The Gild

PART ONE

DENIAL

1

EILARS

NEAR THE POND, DRAPED across a bed of moss-cushioned stones, lay the bodies of two women.

In the green water swam pale, orange-speckled fish nibbling on clouds of algae. A breeze carrying cranberry bush blossoms brushed the hair from the women's faces. They hadn't moved in half a day. They hadn't breathed in four hours.

They were ignored by Eilars—groundskeeper, caretaker—a skinless man, sinew-like wires enveloping his gleaming gears and black tungsten bones. Exposed segmented plates clicked, and little cogs whirred as he stepped over and around them, tending to the pond, skimming red, five-corned leaves from the pool.

Skimmer balanced on his shoulder, he left their motionless forms undisturbed. He whistled. His tone modulators were off-key, but the noises they produced were superior to what his damaged voice box could manage.

Over his decades spent here, he'd come to appreciate the peace of this grassy, tree-ringed plateau. Swallowed by the rocky jaws of Mount Morbin, his doom was to linger here until he rusted into motionlessness, became a lawn ornament.

He hadn't previously believed someone like him—a man born not of the womb but the 3D press—could have a "mind" to lose. But, indeed, he had lost it. And, in his insanity, he felt untethered. Madness provided comfort. To have been so damned confirmed his ownership of a soul.

It must be enough, he supposed, to know that his family was out there, somewhere. Safe for his sacrifice. If there were any justice at all, he would see his wife and son again. Meanwhile, he would fulfill his promise to the Old Crow, and die.

He dredged and skimmed the pond, fed the fish, pruned the trees, swept the red-tiled terrace, and scraped the moss and clinging vines from the seven crumbling statues, so ancient that their features were barely recognizable now. Rubbed smooth by wind and rain, they remained humanoid, but not human. That was all one could tell by looking at them. Having studied the effigies, Eilars also knew that they were between four and five thousand years old—and were made of no element known to modern science.

Ah well. Mystery could no longer sway him to fear. Not since his dealings with the Old Crow, in fact, had he feared anything at all. Eilars had abandoned his curiosities together with his mind, contenting himself to his upkeep duties. Thus, for years and years and *years*, he'd lived one day on repeat. Not a programming glitch—a template. Time was passing, but he stayed in exactly the same place, performing exactly the same tasks, as when this cycle had begun. The only difference? His body was finally failing. His nuclear power core would survive another century most likely; his manufactured organs would not.

Frankly, it was a miracle he'd lasted this long. Too perfect, almost. Were he a bigger fool, he might've dared believe that the Old Crow's curse was not responsible for his survival up till now. But Eilars no longer gave credit to the illusion of coincidence. Fate guides everything; fate is cruel. And he felt its clawed hand at work in the arrival of his guests, detecting accelerated signs of decay in his hardware and software. His corrupted registry files, no longer merely unstable, were becoming inoperable.

Mount Morbin no longer needed him, so it consumed him. Finally.

The older of the two women had come first, strolled in as if she owned the place. The younger, some months afterward. Their trampling boots devastated his manicured lawn, the work of decades. Their shadows scythed the peace of his garden.

Far worse, he'd seen in the younger one something familiar and terrible and unwanted—a maddening afterimage seared onto his frying hardware. Her umber skin and green eyes were unremarkable, and even the blue-tinged tips of her long, prematurely graying hair were no bother. Instead, what he despised about her— hated with every fiber optic inch of his slowly disintegrating frame—was her resemblance to the devil. The trickster. The necessary evil.

Dimas K'vich, the Old Crow. Just as he'd prophesied long ago, his heir— Alina—had come at last. She, by birthright, could dispose of this mountaintop sanctuary as she pleased.

Eilars paused to listen to the magpies in the branches. Whether they mourned or mocked him didn't matter.

His tungsten bones ground in their socket joints as he returned to his hut, laid down, and switched off his eyes. The incandescent glow of his heart still pulsated for now. His lung-sacs still inflated and deflated. There would be time enough to say goodbye to this place he'd become part of.

Tomorrow.

He thought about the one positive to come from Alina K'vich's arrival: the girl, Cho. Shifty-fingered, quick-witted, lively little Cho.

He mustn't let Alina kill that spark. He must not.

"Last thing I do," he murmured, initiating his sleep cycle, running maintenance on his sluggish operating system.

He deleted a rogue impulse to check on the women (he'd been scolded before for ensuring they still breathed, monitoring their pulses). The older one — not much older, though, only in her mid-thirties — had informed him that, if he ever so disturbed their meditations again, she would snap him clean in half, like the overly large datastick he was.

He did not sleep, nor did he rest. Machined men do not dream.

As night crept up Mount Morbin like midnight ivy, drowning the seven strange statues in shadow, the bodies remained where they'd lain all day…

… where Alina dreamed.

She could see it from afar. Her death of a thousand slow steps.

With every breath, blink, eye-twitch—

The Crow drew closer.

Few nineteen-year-olds were ever cursed with knowing exactly how their lives would end.

As it had done—for months now—the Crow drew ever closer.

2

CHO-ZEN

SECOND-HAND GUN RUNNER AND pirated movie salesman Raridan crushed the stump of his cigarette under his boot. Another hung from his lips, ready. In the dark of night, the flame of his chrome-plated lighter illuminated the earnest little face of the earnest little girl before him. Leaning against the trunk of his black convertible Nightwing—its gas-guzzling eight-liter engine growling under the hood—he took stock of her and her friend. She wasn't fooling anyone with her short, sleeveless hooded vest decked in colorful anarchist patches and hand-drawn marker scribbles. The toxic green of her hair might have had her parents fainting, but Raridan had seen this particular domestic drama play out before. "Let me guess," he said, "you're here on a dare." He took a drag from his cigarette. "You wanna be edgy? Get bangs, or paint your nails black. Go on home, kid, and I'll forgive you for wasting my time. *This* time."

As fresh-faced as the girl was, her cute boyfriend was even worse: black hoodie, high black stockings nearly touching his gym shorts. Looked like he used conditioner in that thick, wavy brown hair of his. Wow. These *children* should've been praising their gods that they'd met a softy like Raridan. Any other two-bit crook would've snatched them up for the offense they'd given. And, with what Raridan had in his trunk…

The girl cleared her throat, advancing a step, earning her one of his rare amused smirks. "Yo," she said, "I came here to complete the transaction we agreed on. You really want the upstanding communities of the Darkthreads to think that Raridan L'wendess isn't a man of his word?"

"Nice bluff." He chuckled. "I'd be amazed if someone like you even knew what a VR headset looked like."

The boyfriend chimed in: "You do know who she is, right?" He seemed genuinely uncomfortable. Poor kid.

High time somebody scared these two back to their safe straight-and-narrow. But it wasn't Raridan's responsibility.

"Yeah, so." He flicked his second cigarette into the darkness. His face lit only by the red glow of tail lights, he pushed off his trunk and pulled out his keys. "I'm gonna take off."

"Thought you were a businessman, Rary," said the girl. "Gonna have to give the guys who vouched for you an earful."

"I came here to deliver a product to a fellow esteemed colleague. Not some baby punk."

"You ever meet this 'colleague' face to face?"

"No," he admitted. "No one has."

"*Very few* have," she corrected.

Gods, this girl. If she wasn't, like, twelve years old by the look of her, he oughta—

"You can shove off, Rary." She pulled something from the pocket of her sleeveless vest. "Assuming you don't care about the cred you'll lose among our 'fellow esteemed colleagues'... or *this*."

He craned his neck, squinting to see what she held up. The moonless night and rising cloud of exhaust forced him to step in again.

That thing in her hand—a datastick. He cracked his neck. "You're not her," he said. "Rumor is she's an Elemental."

"I don't look Elemental enough to you?"

"You look... normal. Like one of us." Weathered, he wanted to add. Battered. Poor. "Elementals are all tall and dressed in designer crap, head to toe."

"Pssh. The tall thing is really dumb. As for the clothes, one day your mind will be blown wide open when someone explains to you the idea of *getting changed*."

"Kid, play date's over. Last chance. Get back to your parents."

Before he could turn away a second time, she said, "My parents are dead, actually. And I'm fixing to even the score. That's why I need the explosives in your trunk."

"What—I don't have anything like—"

To the boyfriend, she said, "Do the thing."

The brown-haired boy reached into the front pouch of his hoodie, and Raridan—a hair too slow—drew his pistol. He'd hesitated when he saw what the kid had been fumbling for. A plastic bottle?

The top of the bottle tore clean off, and Raridan flinched as a jet of water rocketed toward him. Next thing he knew, his hands were stuck together, encased in a block of ice.

"You're a Maggo?" he sputtered.

Staring at his own feet, the boy shrugged.

"Now," said the girl, smirking as Raridan tried to break his hands free. "Since I do have my own reputation to consider, I'm willing to take the high road here and still give you what we agreed on. As long as I get what I came here for. Yeah?"

Either this was a ridiculously involved prank—one of Raridan's crew getting even—or the girl really was who she claimed to be. But that would mean he'd stepped in it. Bad.

Shaking his head, he said, "Show me what's on the drive then."

She sighed. "Fine." And she jabbed the datastick into her neck.

A second or two later, her *eyeballs* projected onto the Nightwing's passenger door lists of corporate freight inventories, planned convoy routes—everything a gang like Raridan's needed to rob a couple of the big LLCs blind and live like kings for years to come. He drooled.

Plucking the stick from the port in her neck, the girl said, "Happy?"

He nodded quickly.

There was venom in her eyes as she considered what to do with him, and he marveled at how quickly he'd swiveled from confident annoyance to fear.

She said, "If my partner drops his spell, you won't do anything *else* stupid?"

Another nod. "By the gods, I swear it."

"The gods don't impress me. Swear it on your rep."

"You got it, ki—I mean, yes, ma'am. Um. I swear on my reputation, you'll have the goods."

She'd subtly shifted her stance, her vest opening just a little. Far enough to reveal the throwing knives lining her belt.

The ice melted from Raridan's hands, and he immediately but slowly raised them. "My keys." He tossed them underhand to the girl. "You aren't worried it's trapped?" he asked as she approached the trunk. "There's more'n a few people that want you out of the headlines." Hurriedly, he added, "Not me, though. Just sayin'."

"I'd know if it were rigged to blow," she said, not looking at him. Fingers wiggling, she unlatched the trunk. It popped open, revealing its contents: enough plastique to level a city block. Maybe two.

She flung the datastick at him. He almost bungled the catch. Awkwardly pocketing his prize, he coughed a couple times. Asked, "So. Why do they call you 'Cho-Zen'?"

"Why do you suddenly care about some kid?" she bit back.

"Makin' conversation."

She stacked the brown, brick-sized packages into the empty duffel bag she'd unslung from her shoulder. While she worked, she told him, "It's 'cause I didn't choose this life. It chose me. But I'm cool with it. That a problem?"

"Nah," said Raridan, "no way. It's cute—uh, extremely intimidating. Yeah. And, hey, my compliments on the way you emptied out the *Gelderwerp Bank* a few months back without even stepping foot inside. Oh, and when you cut the power to the whole Authority HQ downtown—sure, they had it back up and running in like an hour, but still. And everyone's talking about your squad car fleet hack. Had the Pinkojacks's shiny toys on cinder blocks for a week. That's gotta be some kinda record!" His laugh turned into a wet cough. He spit to his left. "Never heard of anyone who Zero-Ones better than you. Made me think you'd be…"

"Older?"

"Sure. Bigger, too. Scarier."

"Oh, she can be real scary," said the boyfriend. "Believe it."

Raridan clicked his tongue. "So, it was you who shut Wizzyrm out of his own system the other day? Man's set to blow a gasket when he finds out he got wedged by some kid."

The girl shrugged. "His fingers were slow, his brain slower. Really puts the 'hack' in 'hacker.'"

"I gotta know. What's your secret?"

"Butter."

"Fine, don't tell me." Hands in his pocket, Raridan took a step forward. "But a lotta people'd love to get a peek at the hardware you're packing."

"You b-better stay back, buddy," said the boy, tilting, off-balance, in an effort to strike an intimidating pose.

"Easy, bro."

"Anyway, that's enough chit-chat," said Cho-Zen, zipping up her bag.

Raridan snapped his fingers. "So."

"Yeah?"

"What're you planning to do—with the stuff, I mean?"

"Just curious?" she said.

He cracked a smile. "Wondering if you need any extra muscle."

"Not from the likes of you, Rary. Ya came through in the end, but ya won't be getting a five-star rating from me."

To his surprise, the comment stung.

Cho-Zen looked to her boyfriend—bodyguard?—whatever, the other pre-teen-looking fool. "We're out."

And Raridan, part-time bomb maker with connects throughout the town of Truct and beyond, watched the two teens sorta waddle off with probably *way too many* boom-boom bricks. They both climbed onto a one-seat scooter, the girl in front, and peeled off.

Having gotten to where he was in life by avoiding activities like loitering at the scene of an arms deal, Raridan hopped into the driver's seat of his Nightwing, jammed the keys into the steering column, and gave the gas pedal a stomp. The engine revved, and, from his rear-view, he watched the kids' taillight disappear around a bend in the road. Then he went to buy groceries, toiletries, essential supplies—making a mental note to take himself and his crew to the safehouse outside town for a week or so.

You know, just in case.

3

JEJUNE

THE ELEMENTAL EMPIRE SPANNED the world—what parts of it that mattered, anyway. All roads led to the Nation of El, all money to New El, The Capital, a sphere anchored to the earth by three titanic chains. From this planetoid, skyscrapers and temples jutted like teeth. Day and night, lights bled onto the clouds. High above the fields, forests, mountains, lakes, and marshes of El's heartland, The Capital was a shining beacon of prestige and progress.

At its very center lay the Divitia District, organized in neat rows of gleaming, photovoltaic glass towers and water-absorbent concrete superdomes. Surrounded by a park of white, carbon dioxide-soaking artificial trees and blue shrubs and grass, stood the Elemental Stock Exchange. And, inside one of the top-floor offices of the figure-eight building, Mr. Jejune moaned through his jaw-popping yawn.

Fogging the phone's plastic with his breath, he said, "Just blast it off the map, then. Any other day, those backward colonial heathens can eat each other for all I care, but—right now—sector-wide bottom lines are at stake. Dusty superstitions *must not* trump the fiscal benchmarks of the shareholders. Tell you what, I'm feeling generous, so let's sweeten the pot. Tell your guy at the Department of Liberation to declare a new Secondary Objective: kill any native protesters agitating against Elemental presence. Ooh, and double the Battle Bonus Tokens for bagged targets. That juicy incentive should encourage our Liberators to go the extra mile. Eh? Great."

He ended the call, idly wondering what today's uninspired specials at the office cafeteria would be. Maybe he'd have something flown over via drone instead.

With cracked, reddened fingers, Mr. Jejune thumbed through the news alerts on his data pad, chewing on his dry lip until he tasted blood. He quickly pulled out his green handkerchief and dabbed, hiding the cloth in his pocket again. He wouldn't want to face the embarrassment of having to kill anyone for asking why his blood was black. He told himself he shouldn't worry; after all, no one had yet taken notice of his rubbery egg-white skin or the black spider-veins clustered around his eyes and nostrils and knuckles. Thus far, no one had found it worthy of comment that industrial-grade cleaning crews scoured and steamed his office every other week. Perhaps no one had noticed, or perhaps no one cared. Either way was fine by him.

Money and fear removed all limits; perks of working directly for The Big Man Himself, way down in Basement Seventy-Seven.

Each afternoon, his latest assistant—a bright, preppy young woman whose thick-rimmed cosmetic glasses framed her angular face—brought him his polystyrene cups of coffee on a cardboard carrier. She'd read to him the news of the day as he stared through the large interior window overlooking the Elemental Stock Exchange. Why was she so meticulous, so conscious of his needs? Fear. She assumed she'd be terminated for even the slightest of failures.

She was right.

Alas, as his thoughts wandered back to his immediate surroundings, he realized with a slight tinge of dread that today was proving to be a day like any other. Bored, he considered the idiots that stumbled around downstairs. He could see them all through the wall-wide window of his VIP office, the executive throne from which he supervised and managed the humdrum chaos of the Stock Exchange.

Brokers rushed this way and that, slamming into each other, swearing, soaking their expensive suits with sweat and tears. Overhead, a hologram displaying three-letter tickers and their prices circled the grand hall, weaving around the marble columns, reflecting off the polished floor tiles. Mr. Jejune's eyes trailed after the tickers.

AFX was down less than one percent, and there was still time for it to pick back up.

RRK had lost three points, a devastating blow to the value of soybeans from Denadon Province.

GLD remained in the gutter, which was to be expected, considering the scandal that weighed it down: dozens of Terrie Aelfravers had been tracked down and arrested in recent months, but that couldn't erase the fact that The Gild had trained them and issued to them their licenses in the first place. Many movers and shakers in the investment industry leveraged this troubling fact to buy, buy, buy. Mr. Jejune himself had acquired ten thousand shares for his clients at

Walazzinmart, further expanding ELCORP's control over The Gild and its magical curriculum.

It was all par for the course: droughts, trained personnel shortages, famines, pestilences, wars… Each presented an opportunity to profit off the distribution—and strategic *withholding*—of products that people desperately needed. Medicine, food, water, comfort, and security, these were the season's hot commodities. And business was booming.

Of course, unlike all these apes scurrying about on the Stock Exchange, excitedly howling at their associates, banging out orders onto their holographic keyboards—*unlike* them all, Mr. Jejune didn't care one lick about the money.

See, money was a means to an end. In other words, *worthless* by itself. Gelders, the currency of El (and therefore the world), were only as good as what they could give you. And, ultimately, what everyone who craved money really wanted, what they desperately desired, was control. Power.

All humans were consumed by an urge to believe, for once in their miserable, short-lived existences, that they had some control over their own destinies. Purely and simply, people craved power. And what was power if not the ability to force others to do what you wanted?

Mr. Jejune cared nothing for money because he already had that kind of power. Far more of it than any of his pathetic, simpering underlings could imagine. Yet, there remained a great emptiness within him.

Ah, if only he could return to the age of his youth, when humanity had been a gaggle of mud-slinging, club-swinging bags of bones and blood… Simpler times. Nobler times. A glorious scrap, was that too much to ask for?

Nowadays, on the surface, the humans' world was far more complex. However, to one like Mr. Jejune, who *also* hadn't stopped growing and learning, corrupting those around him had become easier than ever before. The job had become tedious. Uninteresting. Humdrum.

Where was the passion he'd once felt when cracking open a mortal shell to devour the yoke-like soul within? Long gone were the chances to do battle, to pit himself against human champions, to watch despair and blood wash their faces as he broke every bone in their bodies, one by one…

It was true. Pointlessly complicated, human society had devolved, a mere echo of its glorious past. For Mr. Jejune, there was hardly any challenge at all, these days, in wriggling his way into the hearts and minds of mortals. They'd become basically self-centered, easy targets, whose will to resist had leaked out of them. Where before, he'd slaked his thirst on countless eager foes, now he only had to promise a man power and then *withhold* it, just like he might any other resource, and then sit back. Power existed in limited supply. For even a whiff of prestige and privilege, men would tear each other apart.

Thus, the foodchain for Mr. Jejune's kind remained unbroken, secure, everlasting. The strength of this system, built up over thousands of years, and overseen by legions of his siblings, ensured its indestructibility.

… Which made it crushingly boring to Mr. Jejune, who craved excitement. Unlike most of his colleagues—scattered among the humans, hidden in plain sight—he desired nothing more than action. His entire extended family was sustained by greed, which to him tasted as bland and unappetizing as unsalted oatmeal.

What he craved was *wrath*.

This was precisely why, whenever opportunity came knocking, he indulged himself with a little treat.

He realized his assistant had been prattling. Something in her report had caught his keen ear.

"Say that again," he told her, and the bespectacled woman flicked her way up the holographic page a paragraph or two.

"Triple-I reported yesterday that Tytan LLC's geological charting was successfully completed."

"Yes, but what did they uncover? Read that part."

"Apparently, there are 'significant copper deposits' in the qa-Hasir quadrant of Nasharam-vilh-amsul."

"That's in Kadic, isn't it?"

"Yes, sir. It's supposedly a holy site, dedicated to one or other of their defunct gods." She tried to read the name ("Eat-ee-awn," "Ee-ought-ion") but quickly gave up as her boss lost his patience. She added, "There's also a high concentration of residential buildings above the site of Tytan's exploratory tests."

"And?" said Mr. Jejune.

"Well, that's why the author of the article claims Tytan's not going ahead with the mining operation quite yet."

Mr. Jejune glared at her, sipping his black coffee.

She flinched, sputtering her explanation, "CEO Nedratus has to go through the proper channels. He'll have to appeal to the Plutocrats—standard procedure—and the Consul himself will have to sanction the operation, since the area in question is a hot zone for insurgent activity, and—"

"*Terrorist* activity," Mr. Jejune corrected.

"Of course, terrorist activity. Yes. So, because of the, uh, peacekeeping efforts in the region, a joint task force of Authority commanders will have to be appointed to, to… Sir, are you alright?"

He squinted at her, a smile winching his lips apart. "Never better." He steepled his fingers. "Now, tell me, Ms.…"

"Vivenna," she said, nervously clicking her pen a few times.

Oh, dear. He'd become a little too excited, he felt. "How long have you been in my employ, Ms. Vivenna?"

"Well," she said, tripping over the syllable, "it's been about six weeks. I'm very grateful for the opportunity, I feel as though I've already learned a lot, and—"

It couldn't be helped, he supposed.

He clapped his hands twice, and the tint of his wall-wide window shifted to opaque black. This triggered warm ambient lighting—like you might find at a high-end restaurant where the humans serve each other tiny, overpriced, unsatisfactory bites.

"Vivenna. Shut up. And then shut the door."

Should he not be allowed to enjoy himself, every once in a while? No one should mind too much.

Vivenna the assistant nodded silently and nudged the door with her hip. The latch clicked.

"Six weeks, you said?" His lower lip drooped as he salivated, his spiked blue tongue lolling from between the rows and rows of serrated teeth sprouting from his purpling gums. "That's honestly impressive."

Obviously too shocked to scream, let alone formulate a coherent question, she could only gape at him in horror, moans knotting in her throat.

Crouching low, Mr. Jejune launched his tongue like a javelin, spearing her. He dragged her down to the ground, closer and closer to his barrel-sized gullet...

When he'd finished, he smacked his shriveling lips and reverted to his human disguise. It was less comfortable, true, but he'd grown used to it. It was all part of the game.

His human-like hand closed around the cellphone on his desk. Bringing it up to his slick cheek, he kissed the spatter of blood on its screen. "ViiCter, call Commander Devandel."

ViiCter—his phone's integrated intelligence—chirruped, then answered: "Calling Commander Devandel, Foreign Command, Department of Tranquility."

The dial tone trilled in his ear as half a dozen football-sized cleaner bots rolled into the office through an open hatch near the floor vent cover. They began misting the seeping puddles of gore. The air reeked of bleach.

After waiting on hold for a minute or two, Mr. Jejune tingled with pleasure when a staffer put the man himself on the line. "Devandel speaking."

"Dev, my old, old friend."

Devandel said nothing for a moment. Then, politely, "What can I do for you today, sir?"

"Good man. Just the one to remove an obstacle for me. You are familiar with Nasharam-vihl-amsul?"

"My son's stationed there. Thanks to your timely support, he was promoted to captain."

"Wonderful. Well, tell *Captain* Devandel that I have a job for him." As he spoke, Mr. Jejune displayed the news article Vivenna had been reading. His eyes scanned over the sites at which Tytan had discovered copper veins. "I need a perimeter cleared."

"Clear Nasharam, sir? For what purpose? The fighting's much hotter farther north."

Mr. Jejune glanced at the clock. Five PM. That left one hour. Should be just enough time. "That's not your concern. If you need a reason, go about it as usual: fabricate a convenient lie. I don't care how you do it. All I want to hear from you is that, by six o'clock El Standard Time, the Kadicians of that shantytown will have vacated their dirt hovels. Am I understood, commander?"

"It shall be done, of course. Only... why not go through Palonsa on this one? They'd be able to expedite your request, get it done much faster."

"If I wanted a targeted series of drone strikes, I *would* have called Palonsa. But I *don't* want drones today. Too messy."

"It'll be even messier for infantry to move in. We're talking about fifteen thousand civilians down there, and, by the Seventy-Seven Gods, they'll only move once the insurgent leaders in the area are neutralized. It'll have to be loud."

"The louder the better, honestly. Listen, commander, I don't expect the region to be depopulated by six o'clock. But I *do* want the ball rolling downhill by then. There will be a media presence, so make sure your optics are set. And don't forget to tell your son to smile for the camera."

"Yes, sir. I'll send the order out to deploy the teams at once. They'll be on the ground in forty-five."

"Make it thirty-five, and there'll be a bonus in it for you."

"There's only one unit—the 31st Forward—that could deploy on that time-table, sir. And they'd be alone." The commander paused. "There'll be heavy casualties."

"They're *Cutcords*, the dregs of the failed Torvir Family. Need I remind you that the expenditure of the Torvir Assets, including their honorless armies, is now the direct purview of our Consul—and, therefore, *me*." He picked one of Vivenna's teeth out of his nose. "Has there ever been a more expendable unit? Now, do as I say."

"Yes, sir. In Plutonia's name, for the glory of the Plutocracy. Wealth and prosperity to you."

"Naturally," said Mr. Jejune, hanging up. He chuckled under his breath. "Wealth and prosperity."

He smiled. He had to admit, he'd been wrong. Most days were dull, business as usual: the rich got richer, and the *Rel'ia'tuakr* fed off their desires, their pain, and their greed. One some rare and beautiful days, however—like today—he got to taste genuine, good, old-fashioned delight. Why, he could almost hear the delectable screams of terror and agony as The Authority cannon fodder moved in to "liberate the people" to "ensure greater regional stability and quality of life."

(The talking points constantly floating up from the Department of Communications were simply *precious*.)

A shame that he hadn't been able to refrain from devouring his assistant *before* she could organize the news media coverage of the impending assault. So inconvenient. He even had to call in his *own* order for half a million shares of Tytan LLC. His human "colleagues" thought he was insane for betting on a company that hadn't struck gold in over a year. In the morning, though, they'd all be bawling their eyes out, cursing their own shortsightedness and stupidity. And they'd be right. They ought to know by now to respect his genius.

Sure, it was a repetitive, predicable cycle, manning the Elemental Stock Exchange. But he was *good* at it, and there was pride to be had in that simple fact, wasn't there? No shame in working a menial job if it provided value to your community. He'd long been one of the Master's favorites precisely because of his consistency. Why fix what wasn't broken?

In the meantime, he should continue to enjoy his small pleasures.

Ah, almost forgot. With gore-soaked, slippery fingers, he pressed his pen to the least bloody sheet of paper by his computer, and made a note to shop around for a new assistant.

As the army of tiny cleaning bots busily scrubbed the floors, walls, and ceiling clean of Vivenna's leftovers, Mr. Jejune leaned back contentedly in his swivel chair.

On his tablet, he opened the six o'clock news just in time.

He giggled as the grave-faced anchor in the video said, "This story just breaking. A sudden surge of Authority platoons tonight in the qa-Hasir sector of Nasharam-vihl-amsul, Kadic. Warning: the following images may be disturbing to some viewers. Children should be sent away—unless they are enrolled in an Authority Youth Training Corps." Live drone footage showed power-armored shock troops ramming down doors and blasting apart walls with thermite charges; there were even clips of insurgents being gunned down in the streets, alleys, parking lots, and hallways throughout town. "We take you now over to our Kadician foreign correspondent…"

Mr. Jejune lost interest. "Something-something Authority Foreign Command. Something-something, a dozen more platoons en route. Blah, blah." He fixated on the stock tickers as they glided by overhead.

The Elemental Stock Exchange was the financial hub of the Elemental Empire, so data transmission was as close to instantaneous as physically and metaphysically possible. This allowed Mr. Jejune to laugh as Tytan's stock ticker—TYN—soared to first double, then triple, then *quintuple* its value of only ten minutes before.

With The Authority expelling the locals, Tytan would be able to almost immediately begin mining those copper deposits, benefitting multiple key industries—electronics, plumbing, HVAC, space exploration, etc. Of course, Mr. Jejune owned stock in all of these sectors.

His meaningless monetary gains, by themselves, gave no pleasure. But he did derive especial joy from the expected pitiful cries of shock and rage as the traders below took notice of the seismic disruption of the market.

"Hear that?" he asked the frumpy office plant sagging in the corner. "That's the sound of thousands of fortunes trading hands."

Indeed, one man's profit was another's suffering. But suffering itself was a profit all its own to Mr. Jejune, his colleagues, and their Master.

A good day.

4

ALINA

TETHERED TO FRIGID, BREATHLESS bodies, two souls had cast off from the mossy stones of the fish-filled pool. Behind and beneath and surrounding them, the physical plane of existence shrank to a dot of blood on a fingertip washed away by inky rain. They traveled an infinite distance, yet where they'd come from remained within reach. Where they arrived—in a translucent, blueish, whitish, bubbling, bouncing, spinning emptiness—the pair floated around one another in a loosely elliptical pattern.

Even though space and movement technically did not exist in this realm, the mortal mind demands comfort. The travelers reflected their physical forms: drifting, cross-legged, they appeared to be women, and human. Though they pushed the boundaries of these categories, each in her own way.

The slightly older of the two, like an heirloom blade, was tightly wound in dark blue cloth—her cloak of uncertain origin, unknown to all but her. The freckles on her cheeks and nose were constellations in miniature. Her eyes (one, jackal-fur brown; the other, sand-snake gold), she pinched shut, and she glared sightlessly beneath her halo of curly black hair. She was the master, an Aelfraver specialist of Revomancy, one of the Eight Disciplines of Magic. Some called her Morphea; some, Queen of Dreams. A handful dared to use her birth name—Ruqastra bol-Talanai.

Opposite her, striving to mirror her every movement, was her one and only student, Alina, whose face was hidden behind a curtain of coarse hair that scratched her collarbones. Unlike her mystically attired master, the student wore jeans, an open button-down, and a ratty band tee reading *"The Sinsations—Summer of Sin Tour '68."* As usual, her sleeves were rolled up to her elbows, where began the trail of razor-sharp, chasm-black feathers ending at her wrists. The shirt, her last name (K'vich), and her bad attitude she'd inherited from her mom. The conflicting aims to both please and flee had her dad written all over them. Both parents had died when she was five. Now, with her grandfather gone, she had only one blood relative left living. And, wherever he was, it wasn't far enough.

Ruqastra's silver-gloved fingers were taut from frustration, jaw clenching. "Your mind drifts."

"And you're trying not to strangle me," said Alina. "See, I'm paying attention."

"A lucky guess."

Ruqastra claimed to hold the answers to many of the mysteries of the K'vich family, but this information had a steep price: Alina's training in Revomancy under the sadistic mystic's guidance. After months of astral projection, consciousness-hopping, and nightmare-cultivating, Alina had learned next to nothing. She'd traveled to and escaped countless dreamworlds, each a tiny strand of the interconnected, infinitely tangled knot known as the Revoscape. And *still* Ruqastra said she hadn't "earned" the privilege of fully understanding her grandfather's schemes.

Alina suspected she'd never be "ready" for the truth. She thought back to her first journeys into these worlds that existed both inside and outside the self, the mind. Nothing could have prepared her for the sky-splitting chases with cloud cutters, eating fire honey straight from the hives of the astral bees that pollinated galaxies, and wrestling the Deep Squids—whatever could or couldn't be imagined had been given life by dream. She'd come a long way since those early forays, but apparently not far enough.

For her part, Ruqastra didn't believe in easing into anything. It was always sink or swim. Trial by fire. Boxing match with extradimensional demon. Sometimes, Alina wondered if these lessons were intended to be fatal, if she were surviving them purely by accident.

Today's lesson was much calmer by comparison. As usual, though, she had no idea where she was. The guided meditation was supposed to help anchor her, but she'd not been told the *why* or *how* of it. All she could see were the brilliant beams of light piercing the gooey, low-gravity substance in which she twirled as if suspended by a string tied around her head.

"Drifting again," snapped Ruqastra, her hair wafting as she glided forward. "Close. Your. Eyes."

"How can you tell they *aren't* closed?"

"Because I do not need mine to see. You might learn. If you tried."

Aside from Revomancy, Ruqastra had at least one other area of expertise. She knew exactly how much pain to apply, where and how to press and prod, to carve away at Alina's pride. When they'd first met, Ruqastra had enveloped Alina in darkness and commanded her to return to Truct, her home. Yeah, their whole relationship had begun with a threat, one that Alina, true to type, had tested. Little did she know that's exactly what Ruqastra had wanted all along: *push the girl, carve away at her until only the core remains.* Defying Ruqastra had sent Alina charging along a twisting, turning path that had only grown narrower and more treacherous. She'd been kidnapped, imprisoned, cut, burned, and worse—but she'd survived.

According to Ruqastra, Dimas had had a grand plan for his granddaughter. ...*Until only the core remains, and harden that core into a shard of iron—jagged, sharp— to drive through the throats of our enemies.* Alina sometimes heard Ruqastra's thoughts bubbling from her sleeping mind like boiling pitch. Within them lay the truth. *Enemies.* Alina was meant to be a weapon.

It was plain that neither of the women enjoyed the other. Violence, and the thought of being used, disgusted Alina, and Ruqastra could see only a girl who always failed to mind her elders' sage advice.

Close your eyes? Alina snorted. Here? Why should she, when her current form didn't technically even have them? Not real, physical ones anyway. Everything here was made up. Pointless. But the master insisted it was all about the form of the exercise. To *imagine* seeing with eyes—real or not—would encourage the Mage to continue to rely on what she could *see* only. A terribly stupid mistake, apparently. Because, in the Revoscape, nothing was as it appeared, blah, blah, blah.

Bored, jittery from exhaustion, Alina busied herself by tapping her eyelid with her pinky finger, listening to the little squelching, bubbling fart noises created by the pocket of air trapped there. Finally, she groaned. "Where are we?"

Ruqastra's narrow face was inflexible as ever; her voice, still and smooth. "A droplet of rainwater falling to earth."

"Our earth?"

"No."

"Oh, cool." Alina, her legs aching, hugged her knees, stretching her back muscles.

"Stop that now. You only *think* you need to stretch. Break that habit. Uncouple your mind from your physical senses."

"Sounds healthy." Alina made a popping sound with her lips. "So, if we're in rain, does that mean water can dream?"

"Absolutely not. We are inside the dream of a tree wishing for rain."

"That was gonna be my next guess."

"You are deflecting." That's how it was with Ruqastra: endless accusations that Alina wasn't trying hard enough, that she was dodging the issue, being lazy.

Once Alina had seen the face behind Ruqastra's coyote mask and become her apprentice, she'd briefly expected to be treated more like a valued peer and less like a painful pocket of abdominal gas. Ruqastra may have stopped wearing her edgy costume around Alina, but she'd only grown harsher and more secretive.

Feeling her teacher's sightless judgment like fangs biting bone-deep, Alina struggled to hold herself together. Quite literally: one slip in concentration could have severed the slim thread of magical energy connecting her spirit to her body. A body that, while not perfect, she'd very much like to return to. Soon.

"You are deflecting because you are afraid," said the teacher, flaunting her characteristic ability to read minds.

"No," Alina lied, closing her eyes again.

"They can taste your fear. See how you lure them, in ever greater numbers—" Ruqastra paused for effect as imperfectly circular, featureless, furry little critters drifted toward them like motes of dust—"Umbrites, they will swarm you. You draw them to us because you—"

"Look, I *am* trying to concentrate."

"—lack discipline. Were your mind occupied by more than Watchbox cartoons and other childish fancies, we might have moved on months ago."

"You are a terrible teacher."

"Proclaims the inadequate student." Ruqastra sighed, which—again—was pointless because there wasn't any breathable oxygen here, where they were. Because they weren't real. None of this was *real*. No need to breathe; no need to sigh. But she did it, anyway, for effect. "Focus. Clear your mind. Now."

"I can't force myself not to think. That'd be like working really hard to relax. It's not possible."

The master Revomancer was right, though. The Umbrites were becoming a problem. At first, there'd been one or two of the fuzzy little parasites, and their proboscises latching onto Alina's shadow hadn't been too much of a bother. In small numbers, they didn't drain a lot of Niima. Now, however, there were hundreds of them, and her magical reservoir was sinking dangerously close to empty. A few more minutes of this and she might become seriously ill. Not too much longer than that and she could slip into a coma. Or worse.

"Not possible?" Without a word or even a twitch, the master's form rippled, emitting a wave of invisible force, a distortion of sound, that warped the raindrop world, blew Alina's astral body back and upward, and drove the Umbrites away. "If only you put half as much effort into your Somnexiomantic studies as you do your flippant back-talk. Tell me at least what spell I cast, just now."

Alina began to sweat. Rather, she imagined herself to be sweating. (It wasn't fair. Her glands and organs and senses had more than nineteen years of practice running on autopilot! How could she be expected to separate her self-identity from the image of her body in just a few months' time? To be a Revomancers—weaver of illusion and dream—she apparently had to drop "bad habits" like breathing and laughing. Being human, apparently, was a weakness.)

"Trick question," Alina said, righting herself with her mind, and floating back down to rejoin her teacher. "That wasn't a spell at all. You pushed them back with your will."

"Magic may be defined as manifested will. Be less vague."

The apprentice, as ever, felt her way toward the answer using intuition and educated guesses. The process felt right. After all, an Igniomancer's element was fire; a Revomancer's was fiction. There were no facts to memorize in Revomancy; the art changed as often as the medium it manipulated. Starting with a good hunch was half the battle.

Covering her eyes, Alina muttered, "You... overfed them. With... your fear?"

Ruqastra smiled, a subtle and dark expression visible even through closed eyes, for in this otherworldly space the master lived both inside and outside her apprentice's being. "Good. You aren't completely beyond hope. How did I harm them with fear, then, if fear is what they crave?"

"Because... because..." A chill at Alina's fingertips.

"Answer."

"I don't know!" The chill began to spread from her knuckles to her elbow.

Air jetted from Ruqastra's nose as she explained, "I control my fears. I can summon and dismiss them at a whim. Emotions, illusions, flights of fancy, nightmares—I command them all."

Tendrils of ice spiraled from Alina's shoulders down and up her spine until frost nibbled at her from her toes to the root of her tongue.

"Yes, and like a *root*, we must tear out your fear, that you may use it like a broom to sweep away your doubts and inhibitions, like a club to strike at your enemies. Your fear is your weapon; you can let it harm you, or you can redirect its *bite* outward. The choice is yours."

As Ruqastra said the word *bite*, the nibbling sensations of iciness became exactly that—fangs of frigidity breaking the skin, piercing her muscles, pulsing in rhythm with Alina's heartbeat.

"Are you doing this? What's happening to me?" A curtain of darkness had fallen over Alina's second sight. The pain amplified. She couldn't hold out any longer. She had to look, had to see what was happening to her, no matter how terrible.

"Best you resist the urge," Ruqastra whispered, anticipating Alina's every move. "Keep your eyes closed, apprentice, or abandon sanity."

"What?"

"And purse your lips. This next part will be uncomfortable. But you will fare far worse if you let it inside."

The ice that Alina couldn't see, whose texture she couldn't feel, the million-million needles gouging into her every pore, suddenly *melted* and coated her entire spirit.

She couldn't breathe. Well, that wasn't the right word for what she was feeling. Again, she didn't have to breathe here, but she very much could still feel stifled, choked. And she was choking now, constricted by her new outer layer of ethereal ice-skin. With each involuntary movement, the solid film tightened and tightened and—

Counter to every instinct screaming at her to struggle, fight, and escape, she held her eyelids shut. She obeyed her teacher, though she didn't want to, though she didn't trust Ruqastra—the woman who'd all but led Alina into the fight that had forced her to take her own grandfather's life.

"Resist." Ruqastra's voice, barely audible through the ice. So far away, it seemed. "Do not open your eyes."

Resist what I tell you to. The contradiction was a bee sting in Alina's ear canal. *Obey me by resisting.*

She was transported somewhere else then, a place she assumed to be even deeper inside herself. But she was wrong. The black sky, black earth, broke away, and through the cracks she could see herself—a thousand of herselves, staring back. The emptiness now pummeled by asteroids, burning up on impact, her mirror images were struck down by the dozens—shattering, scattering shards of ice-touched glass. Each shard glowed, a star in this infinite darkness.

"The Abyss," said Ruqastra, "existing inside and outside all sentient life. It was born of our dreams, and yet now it is more."

Help me, Alina wanted to shout but couldn't.

From the swirling, exploding stars of gold and green, she heard a wretchedly familiar voice parrot hers: *Help me.*

Between the celestial bodies bursting with energy, there unfurled a shadow like a black-feathered wing. The outline of a man, perhaps, featureless but for two white-gold eyes—cold, spherical flames shining as if through two holes gouged into a sheet of blacker-than-black paper.

It was the Crow.

She could feel it, always, hiding in the corners of her thoughts, clinging to her memories like a tick to dog's flesh, awaiting the moment she'd lower her guard. Though it had no mouth, its smile was full-bodied, evident from the jerking, playful tilt of its head. Like the steel jaws of a trap, its arms stretched to embrace her, advancing.

Reaching.

Get away from me, she said.

Trust no one, said the Crow, that dream-winged not-bird that had arrived and perched in her mind the day she'd first come to the Revoscape. *Trust me.*

It wanted to feed. Alina hadn't yet let it. It was so very hungry.

A tremor took hold of her, working its way downward from the notch of her breastbone. Her body seizing, still, she held her eyes shut.

I'm afraid.

"That's the idea." Ruqastra did nothing. "Trust me."

Trust me, the Crow insisted.

Alina could feel her teacher doing what she did best: waiting and watching. Waiting for Alina to finally die so that she, Ruqastra, could once again become the sole heir to Dimas's legacy and School. Yes, that was it. That must be what she wanted. All of this supposed "training" was simply disguised torture, and now the Revomancer master was closing in for the kill, eliminating Alina by using her own terror against her.

Older than Alina, Ruqastra was still quite young. Her ambitions had surely been thwarted by the arrival of Alina, Dimas's blood, and Ruqastra would never get over it.

She wants to replace you, said the Crow. *Don't let her.*

Untrustworthy.

She is jealous.

Envious.

She'll kill you.

Hateful.

Alina opened her mouth to cry for help, but what she said instead—in a language she didn't know or speak but could somehow understand—was, "Tear. Flesh."

The pangs of ice climbed up her palate, and her throat swelled up, clogged.

Her panic deepening, black claws extended from her fingertips, and feathers from her arms, chest, and chin. Her teeth lengthened to fangs, and, at last, she opened her dream-eyes to a blurry raindrop world. In her teacher's place, she saw only a red smear of vaguely human shape, a thing whose name was "enemy."

Screeching, Alina pounced on Ruqastra, whose expression briefly mirrored her own terror and confusion.

Alina slammed against an invisible forcefield, a two-foot buffer between them, and she spun and swung her limbs, her claws cutting only herself.

The frost carved its way into her through newly torn gashes in her flesh. She felt herself slowing. Running out of time.

Hit harder.

Her strikes sparked off Ruqastra's barrier until the raindrop world around them evaporated, replaced by a spire of hard rock, thirty feet tall, spewing fire from each of its many cracks. The sky was an inkblot, an abstract spattering of violets and fuchsias, turquoises and crimsons.

So. That water drop nonsense was just another lie. Ruqastra *had* been holding her in an illusion.

"No," said her teacher, reading her mind again. "I'm trying to help you. Calm down. Hold yourself together."

"Rip you apart," cried the Crow through Alina.

"Restrain your fear," Ruqastra said, her tone a warning. "Tamp it down."

"Let loose," said the Crow, stealing a grin from Alina's lips.

Something grabbed her by the neck then, squeezing, lifting her off her feet and away from the forcefield as if she were no heavier than a porcelain doll. Slowly, she was swiveled in mid-air, and she kicked and punched to no avail.

Then she saw what it was that held her.

The entity stood twenty feet tall. Far too many arms sprouted from its large, bulbous body. Its translucent skin revealed hollow insides swirling with colorful currents of air. Long fleshy rolls of mouth rippled across its oval-shaped head, tightening into a smile from ear-slit to ear-slit. Its eyeless face considered her in silence.

"Stop," shouted Ruqastra from below. "We had an agreement."

The massive face shifted downward slightly.

"A century! One hundred years of sleep in exchange for the girl's receiving the Gift of the Sisters. A single use of your Loom, that's all. Remember?" When the giant didn't listen, Ruqastra added, "I have been more than generous. Interrupt us one more time, and you'll never dream again, I swear it."

Its smile shriveled to a contrite frown, and the gases inside its oval-shaped head exploded into an array of sparkling, flaming cyan, rippling tangerine, and cascading emerald.

"No, no, unacceptable. I will send you to them *only* upon the completion of the Sisters. Lower the girl. She belongs to me."

The bursts of color shifted to muted shades of umber. It put Alina down.

The Crow—whose fury had only grown while faced with its powerlessness against the giant—surrendered to its urges and seized its chance.

In a daze, Alina turned, hunched at the shoulders, claws at her sides. And she sprinted toward Ruqastra. But Ruqastra was faster. Silently as a shadow, she glided over, intercepting Alina.

"My apologies, Dimas," she said, snapping her fingers in her student's ear.

All momentum immediately drained from Alina's forward rush.

In the Revoscape, she had no muscles, but crippling exhaustion gripped her every limb anyway. A blanket fell over the flame of her mind, snuffing it. Her imagined eyes grew heavy, closing.

She fell forward, slipping into a dream within dreams…

… She woke to the familiar material plane, the world she'd been born onto. Good, solid, *tangible* earth she could smell, touch, and magically manipulate.

Through the green leaves of spring that crowned the trees around her, she noted the orange glow of the setting sun as it rolled behind the cliffs of Mount Morbin. She remembered beginning her meditation that morning, when the sun was high. Had six or seven hours passed, or had it been days?

Only when her disorientation faded did she realize that she had her clawed fingers wrapped around Ruqastra's throat. On her back, the teacher's golden eye flashed, but she made no move to change the situation. Her expression was resolute.

Trickles of her teacher's blood on the tips of her nails, shaking, drenched in cold sweat, Alina pulled away, rolling onto her heels.

Ruqastra stood up, rubbing her throat, her shimmering silver gloves now speckled with blood. She calmly approached her student. "Look at yourself." She pointed to the pool.

Alina's gaze drifted toward Ruqastra's chin. The master wouldn't face her. She again pointed to the water.

Alina crawled forward.

Her eyes focused on her reflection, and she gasped. She looked so much like *he* had the day he'd died—the day he'd left her no choice but to end his life. Her *Tahtoh*, the old man who'd raised her to destroy him.

Alina's own face, staring back at her, revealed golden eyes and a sharp beak of a nose. Her cheekbones were more pronounced, her skin sapped of much of its natural color. She was a gray, angular thing, covered in black, razor-sharp feathers.

When she looked at herself in that pool, she saw only him. And she cried.

"What've you done to me?" she said.

"This?" Ruqastra chuckled. "This is not my doing. You are the one who refuses to face her fears. It is you who allows her fears to pilot her body like a vessel. To master Revomancy is to unlock the doors to all minds, all worlds. The gravity of that power… And you are potentially far more dangerous than any *human* Revomancer. You have to learn, Dimas."

"Don't call me that!"

"Excuse me?"

"You called me by *his* name."

Ruqastra's subtle smirk pricked her lips and crinkled the freckled skin around her nose. "Did I?"

"Don't ever do that. Ever."

The teacher shrugged. She reached for Alina's forehead.

Alina ducked, but again was too slow.

"Sleep," said Ruqastra.

And Alina fell backward onto the bed of moss.

Alina awoke. Again.

Butt still on the ground, she asked, "Where are we now?"

"The material plane. Our quaint mountain refuge."

Recognizing the trees and the pool where they'd fallen into the trance, Alina doubted the evidence of her eyes.

"You have no cause for suspicion," said Ruqastra. "There are no illusions here. I only needed you docile while I extracted the last of it."

Alina glared up at her as if to say, *Of 'what'?*

From the folds of her undulating cloak, Ruqastra produced a dark, silken bundle and offered it to Alina, who asked, "What is it?"

"Do you not trust me? After all this time?"

"Hah." The sound was day-old coffee in a dirty pot—weak and bitter. Alina noted the bandage wrapped around her teacher's throat, but she didn't acknowledge it.

"As you wish. Now open your present."

"What is this?"

"Open it."

Alina gave in to her curiosity. The wrappings unfolded in her hands to become a cloak, much like Ruqastra's, but solid black.

"*Rego.* That is its name. The Ciirimaic word for 'control.'"

Holding the cloak at arm's length, Alina said, "Now you've got us dressing alike? Buthmertha save me."

Something fell onto the ground.

Tossing the cloak over her shoulder, Alina looked down, inspecting the alien object. She crouched, picked it up, turning it, holding it up to the twilit sky.

It was a mask, red like currants, swirls of ruby curling—moving—along its gently rippling surface. It was shaped like the head of a crow with an exaggerated, scythe-like beak.

"*Ida.* 'Chaos.'"

"Is this a joke?"

"No, it's a mask." Ruqastra extended her hand.

Alina rejected her offer of assistance as she got up and straightened. Her joints popped and crackled as she shook off the stiffness. She winced at the bristling of her feathers, the taste of her own fang-drawn blood on her lips.

"If you are worried about your... appearance, it will revert within an hour or two. Follow the breathing exercises we practiced. In time, you may learn to prevent this from happening at all. Until that day, avoiding further damage is apparently the best we can hope for."

"What am I supposed to do with this mask? This cloak? What are they for?"

"*Ida* and *Rego* are your Sisters now. Treat them as such." Ruqastra turned and began to walk away. Paused, half-turned: "And get some unrest, my apprentice."

"Don't you mean 'rest'?" she muttered.

"No, I meant exactly what I said, for I'll be visiting you again this evening. If restful sleep is what you wish for, you must find some means of barring my entry into your mind." That one gold eye of hers flashed. "Badnight."

Too wiped to argue further, her knuckles whitening as she gripped the red mask, Alina stood, making a mental note to demand answers tomorrow.

The night would bring more nightmares. Great. But it was all for "training" purposes, right? Definitely nothing sick or evil about this arrangement.

Alina found her way to the tool shed, retrieved her sleeping bag, and flung it onto the dirt. Falling onto it, she curled into a ball.

Immediately, the whispers infected her mind. She tossed and turned.

As brutal as the days spent learning from Ruqastra were—and they *were* nauseating, horrifying, and nearly always *almost* fatal—the nights were worse.

5

CHO-ZEN

ONE OF TWELVE ROUGHLY equally sized slices of the Nation of El, Torviri Province was generally a wild, overgrown, treacherous land. Its stretch-mark towns had expanded irregularly and all too quickly to their natural limits. Its economically depressed midsection was segmented by acidic rivers swollen with toxic runoff, unkempt forests, and steep gorges and ravines. At the thorny heart of a vine-tangled valley, where rocky ground ensured farming or animal husbandry would be too unprofitable to attempt, human defiance had raised the town of Truct.

Landlocked and lacking an airport, the town was accessible only by winding, poorly maintained roads. Like a brick-and-concrete kidney stone, Truct scratched at the foothills of Mount Morbin and its smaller siblings. The days were therefore short throughout most of the year, the jaws of the earth swallowing the sun mid-afternoon.

The town was also noteworthy for its many tragic and tragically true stories. The warehouse district, for example, bordered a shallow, silty river named after a long-dead warrior king who'd fallen off his horse and drowned there, effectively setting the tone for the rest of Truct's history.

For a generation or two, a hydroelectric dam had kept the lights on and provided many with decent, stable lives. Unfortunately, the owners of the dam were bought out by Kassal Corp, who had promptly shut the dam down because it conflicted with their energy interests elsewhere (Ruvian coal, mostly). Since then, plagues and a rapidly changing economy had driven away most of the few good opportunities from this mud-gray, rain-soaked town.

Truct was part of the Nation of El, the fatherland of the Elemental Empire, but you wouldn't know it by looking. Walk along its streets and you'd quickly lose track of all the condemned townhouses, rust-bucket cars, abandoned dishwashers colonized by rodents, and overflowing trashcans. In fact, trash was one of the few remaining moneymakers in town: waste disposal services, the regional dump, and the recycling plant employed nearly half the working-age individuals who hadn't fled for a slim chance at a better life anywhere else. Some of the waste materials were burned for fuel; some, repurposed into cheap plastic toys and knock-off shoes. There were many towns like Truct, scattered across the country, where garbage fell and settled. Even in its better days, Truct's industrial sprawl of squat, gray, concrete, cookie-cutter businesses and homes looked like the setting of a melodramatic documentary about the rising rate of teen pregnancy or human trafficking. On a cold night, you could almost hear the sad piano music.

In summary, it was a fine place to be a criminal.

For Cho, moving unseen through its streets had been as easy as breathing. She'd logged a fair amount of time dodging the prying eyes and rough hands Authority Enforcers in The Capital. Up there, with all the camera drones and security checkpoints and traffic and crowds, sneaking around was a trick and a half. Down here, though, her path was clear. There were cameras, but they were all mounted into walls—easily avoided. There were Enforcer patrols, but she could hear the squad cars coming half a mile off. Because Truct was so terribly *quiet*. Most people stayed inside their boarded-up, crumbling, moldering homes. Anyone who did go out moved quickly, with purpose, and they were so concerned with going unnoticed themselves that they wouldn't have given Cho a second glance even if they literally bumped into each other. This was good. If they'd been just a little more observant, they might have connected Cho's face to the wanted posters everywhere. Or to the grainy images of her younger self glaring back at her through the screens of the second-hand Watchboxes inside the electronics shop to her right.

Unlike the odd passersby, she did consider, for a moment, the frilly blue dress, the poofy auburn wig. She was glad she almost couldn't recognize the girl in the pictures any more, with those big, watery eyes. The only feature they still had in common was that trademark scowl—feral, cornered, unbroken. She'd dragged more of that side of herself out of its hole with each passing month. The more it came to the surface, the more distance she put between herself and her past. The scowl was her mask, and how she dressed now, her armor: washed-out, holey, black and gray rags that were fifty percent patches, ten percent fabric, and forty percent attitude. Her street-wear. Comfortable and camouflaging. The uniform of Truct.

Cho turned, waiting for Kinneas to catch up.

He splashed through a puddle clogged with soggy newspaper and cardboard, a flickering neon red shop sign illuminating his frown.

"Cold feet?" she asked.

Fresh out of freshman year of public middle school, and grumbling about the turn his summer vacation had taken, Kinneas blew a long brown lock of hair out of his eyes, blinking away beads of sweat. His shrug was forced. He quivered at the elbows and knees. His heart-rate and body temperature rising, pupils dilating, and—

"Stop," he told her. "You're doing it again."

"What?"

"*Scanning* me." He was picking at his cuticles. "I hate that."

"It's automatic," she lied. Because he didn't seem convinced, and she needed the backup tonight, she added, "Sorry. I'll dial it down. I am glad you're here with me."

Appeasing Kinneas Amming was the easiest task ever. All it took was an exaggerated smile. He pulled the sleeves of his black hoodie. Another nervous tick.

"Something wrong?" she said.

"Back there." He pointed to the intersection they'd just crossed, past the permanently out-of-order traffic signal. "There were, like, a million dead birds just kinda lying in the mini-mall lot."

"A million, huh? Sounds like the street sweepers'll be making overtime this weekend."

"Cho." Amazing how, coming from him, her *name* could become a reprimand. "It was messed up. I'm—"

"Shook?"

"Yeah."

She patted his shoulder. "It's die-off, Kin. Air and water pollution, loss of natural habitat—a flock of dead birds here and there is expected."

"That supposed to make me feel better?"

"Better? We're commiserating."

He wasn't lightening up like he usually would be by now. How frustrating.

"Kin, what is it really?"

"Fine, I'll say it: are you sure you wanna go through with… it?"

Becoming suddenly very conscious of the weight of the duffel bag slung over her shoulder, Cho rubbed her eyes. "I get it. You're bummed about the birds. And the lake fish with all their tumors. And how we all have to boil and hand-filter our drinking water. I hate all that too, don't get me wrong. I'm just focused on big-picture stuff. Like how it's all connected." She lowered her voice. "To the Walazzins."

"You say that about literally everything."

"Because it's true."

Kinneas shook his head. "The Walazzins didn't drive this town into the dirt. Truct's always been crap." He must have known how much that would hurt her.

She bit back her retort, settling on a more diplomatic answer. "I'm sure the Torvir weren't perfect. Nobody's saying they were. But my parents never plopped an army of Enforcers downtown, treating their own people like war criminals. You're a goldfish-brain if you can't remember that much. Ever since that turd-choked eel Wodjaego wriggled his way into being Consul, things have been sliding from Definitely Depressing to Violently Bleak. Look around—" She waved dramatically to either side; somewhere, the sound of shattering glass and a car alarm going off—"Admit that I'm right."

Kinneas couldn't meet her eye.

"He's the most powerful man in the whole country, Kin. He could make all this better with a signature. But he never will. So, we're gonna force his goons to leave. Like we agreed we would. Got it?"

"Yeah," he said quietly. "Got it. Let's go."

Since the Walazzins had deployed their Chimaera Guard, Truct had become a horror show. Downtown had become a staging ground for officially sanctioned searches and seizures, abductions, and outright murders. Barbed wire checkpoints had been installed all over, masked soldiers with machine guns checking bags and confiscating anything that looked suspicious (or they wanted for themselves). They conducted random pat-downs and harassed pedestrians for their Proof of Assetship Cards. Often, people disappeared in broad daylight.

At night, the Enforcers didn't bother asking questions. They simply gunned you down and hauled the body away before dawn.

Past parked tanks and stacks of undistributed pro-Plutocracy propaganda posters, Cho and Kinneas stealthed through the streets. Patrols were tighter than tight. Rings of electrified fence, camera drones, and spotlights challenged their progress. However, there were few places on earth Cho couldn't get into.

She pulled Kinneas by his collar into a drainage ditch just as a searchlight cut across their path. As they were practically on top of each other, she felt his chest press against her side as his lungs expanded and contracted. The unsteady breaths of borderline terror. But he stuck with her, for which she gave his neck a grateful little squeeze.

The fort lay just ahead: three rings of fence surrounding several large warehouses and a repurposed sports stadium, nearly meeting the river on their east side. Above the front gate, a sign proclaimed in bolded letters: "DOMCOM PACE" (Domestic Command, Peace & Asset Compliance Enforcement). A long, fancy way of saying, "We jail and kill our own people regularly enough that it's a stable career choice with good benefits."

During her days spent staking the place out, clocking guard shifts, Cho had learned quite a bit.

Combo prison block, training yard, regional headquarters, munitions storehouse, and bomb shelter, DOMCOM PACE—Truct Edition—housed about eight thousand army grunts and just over two-hundred commissioned officers (one-hundred and sixty lieutenants, forty captains, and eight majors). The base had been setup inside repurposed emergency food storage warehouses, most of the goods having gone straight into the bellies of the Walazzins and the rest of the pinkojacks. The Authority couldn't have done much better, location-wise. The cluster of blocky buildings was centrally positioned, easily fortified, and likely to withstand organized assault by land, river, or air. But they hadn't counted on a couple of fourteen-year-olds crawling through the gutters until they almost bumped up against the electrified perimeter fence.

Cho and Kinneas crept forward, into the shadows cast by a short bridge west of the front gate. Here, the dry creek running between two hills provided cover, giving them a moment to rest and think.

"How're your levels?" she whispered, making conversation to settle her own nerves as much as his.

He squirmed, sliding his phone from his pocket, cupping his hands around the screen to block to hide its light. The cheerful two-tone chime announced he'd opened his energy-tracker app. Cursing under his breath at the noise, he switched his device to silent before saying, "Niima's at 92 percent." His clipped answer was telling.

"And your Phys-i?" She already knew his stamina was low. From the circles under his eyes to his pounding heartbeat, he was obviously strung out. But she wanted him to admit it, in case there was some underlying cause that might jeopardize the mission.

He pursed his lips.

"Kin?" She poked his stomach.

"68 percent. Didn't get much sleep, that's all."

"Me neither."

"I'm fine, though."

"Good." One more playful poke. "Tomorrow, I'll buy you a plate of fat bacon and waffles to make up for it, yeah?"

She peeked out from under the bridge. Above them, a green LED screen advertised a VR-and-bar combo. With a fizzle, it went dark, as did every other weak light nearby.

Rolling brown-outs were common all over Truct. From schoolhouses to hospital ICUs, every zone was affected. Every one, that is, except for The Authority's downtown headquarters, whose bulbs blazed as white and bright as ever. High flew the illuminated red-and-gold flags of the Walazzin Family. Slightly higher still, the national flag of El, a red shield (with its twelve black, outward-facing spears like clock hands) dividing equal fields of violet and white.

As if the light pollution weren't bad enough, The Authority assaulted the ears as well: while regular people huddled in their homes without air conditioning, hot water, or the use of their electric stoves, the national anthem blared through huge speakers pointed outward from the encampment in all directions.

The anthem's theme was quite subtle.

Dragons' blood,
Dragons' blood
At dawn we bathe in Dragons' blood

Scale the chains, leap the walls
Through wind and hail and fiery rain,
By wetted blades, through cracking halls,
Ascend, arise, and bleed your veins
Or die as crawling, wretched thralls
Awash in Dragons' blood, for Dragons' pains;

A thousand men, a thousand more
By curse of mage and spear erased;
It cannot be as was before:
A stair of bone and flesh is raised
Each yard is earned by comrades' gore—
'Tis Dragons' blood they thirsted for

And, in hell, they bathe in Dragons' blood;
Dragons' blood,
In hell they bathe in Dragons' blood…

The song droned on for longer before restarting. Cho made an effort to stop paying any attention to the lyrics. She didn't envy the poor souls living within earshot, who had to hear that crud on loop. Pure punishment. The melody, if it could be called that—so many drums and trumpets—was simple; the song's entire point was to remind everyone of who was in charge. As if they could forget. Sure, it was awful, but at least it was also obnoxiously *loud*.

Cho tapped Kinneas's shoulder. "Move it."

They crossed the creek bed and headed southeast, away from the front gate where most of the traffic and attention would be focused. Close to the river now, they crawled up the hill. The skeletons of vines and shrubs covered their slinking, mud-soaked approach. Every time the spotlights glided past, they pressed themselves flat against the slime, faces down, breaths held, noses pinched. A brownout would roll through; the lights would move on. She and he would inch forward, closer and closer to the street.

The flags. The noise. The tanks and jets and clanking of armored, marching feet. On some level, Cho was grateful for the many reminders of why she'd come out tonight, and the weight of the bag on her back soothed her.

A pair of riflemen walked past. she held up three fingers, counting down. Then she and Kinneas crouch-ran across the street, hiding in the middle of a mound of trash bags filled with empty aluminum cans and glass jars.

The outer fence lay within reach. The metal hummed with the current running through it.

Kinneas said, "Great. How do we get in, again?"

In the planning phase of tonight's theatrics, Cho had suggested he enter through the sewage pipe. He hadn't laughed.

So, she'd have to find some other way.

Oh, Kinneas. He wasn't half as crafty as she was, but having an Aquamancer in her back pocket was aces. He could also swim like a salmon. That was sure to become useful. Someday.

For now, it was her time to shine. "Wait here." Almost giddily, she triggered her camouflage, blending into the environment. She wasn't exactly sure *how* it worked—her body hadn't come with a user's manual—but she could bend light around herself such that she could only be spotted by a close and careful looker.

From only five feet away, Kinneas had lost track of her. "Good luck," he whispered.

Having already scouted the perimeter, she knew to walk south another minute or two. She found the shed abutting the fence and climbed its rusty roof. A leap, tuck, and roll and she was over. Inside DOMCOM, she shadowed soldiers till she found a guard with a keycard attached to his belt by retractable cord. Considering where he was stationed in the base, it probably would open the back, river-facing gate.

She dogged the soldier's steps. He was sniffling with a cold or something. He leaned against a guard tower wall, shoulders tensing.

Around the corner, Cho waited, knife ready.

A sneeze bent him double, and she rushed in—cutting the keycard from his belt.

She dashed away.

Returning to unlock the side gate, she collected her Aquamancer companion. They took cover between a pair of parked APCs.

Squatting low, Kinneas said, "Why didn't you just hack the gate? The lock's electronic."

"It's not like stunning a drone or adjusting a patrol path. Breaking through a door leaves a traceable footprint."

"Well, you've left cocky messages before."

"If you're referring to my tasteful cyber crime signatures, they're meant to provoke the bad guys into making mistakes. This is different. We'll get slammed with a lot more than five-to-seven years if they nab us tonight."

During her meteoric rise to fame in the cybernetic underworld, Cho had acquired quite a few criminal contacts, each of whom had seen her skills in action to one degree or another. Some called her machine-whispering a gift. Others, a magic touch. Unlike all of them, Kinneas knew a version of her far closer to the real deal.

She'd been a fool to tell him. About her family. About how her brain had been enhanced with a suite of billion-gelder cybernetic implants. She hadn't yet scratched the surface of their features, but the several abilities she was aware of came in handy: she could mask her footsteps by emitting a frequency undetectable to un-enhanced ears; her camo relied on a light-bending bubble she could hold for a few minutes at a time. Long enough to escape. The many benefits of being bionic *and* genetically altered.

Armed with so many truths about her, Kinneas knew what she was behind the Darkthread celebrity "Cho-Zen"—a girl hardly ever felt confident in her choices. Those drowning pool eyes of his. Always doubting but never leaving her. In one way, being her most loyal friend had made him her worst enemy. He disarmed her with his infuriating faith in her. She wished he'd have faith in their mission. Instead, he seemed stuck on believing there was a kind soul encased within the plates and machinery and skin and bones of her body.

She often wondered if there really was anything worthwhile in this hardened shell of hers. Could it have survived her family's funeral pyre? Meanwhile, Kinneas valued her strongly enough for both of them, which left her free to tackle more immediate concerns.

She recalled the blueprints of the facility with perfect accuracy, overlaying the three-dimensional map she'd made with the physical world in front of her. A flashing, dotted, yellow line appeared on the ground, leading her. She took point, leading Kinneas through the base.

It took some doing, but they arrived at their destination unseen, thanks to Cho's scouting.

They sneaked inside the munitions storage facility, which was lit only by strips of emergency lights lining the pathways to the exits. After a quick survey, Cho considered the problem before her as practically as she could. "Twenty crates," she murmured. "Bad intel."

The map she'd bought had been mislabeled. The explosives Raridan had sold her should have been more than enough to reduce this facility to softball-sized concrete lumps, but there was a problem: the building's dimensions were much larger in real life. The crates, much more spread out. Some people might have looked at this situation and thought "the jug of nitroglycerin is half full." Cho, however, was a perfectionist—in extremely particular instances, including military sabotage. She could accept no less than the complete destruction of every one of these huge crates of guns and ammo.

"Any bright ideas, dude?"

Kinneas grumbled. "I didn't wanna do any of this in the first place."

"Helpful. Helpful." She wondered why he always showed up when he clearly didn't approve. Could've stayed home. "Say, pal, you going limp on me? Getting a taste for The Authority's boot, are ya?"

"*No.* But, I'm just saying that maybe—maybe blowing up a big, fat pile of bullets in the middle of town is not, I dunno, the best way to—"

She grabbed his elbows, staring into his eyes. "Has anyone ever told you how much of a wet noodle you are? Really."

"All the time. Doesn't mean I'm wrong."

She rolled her eyes. "The stockpile in here, it's all owned by Walazzin garbage mites. Enough said."

Biting his lip. "We could still bail. I know it's been hard for you, but maybe we—"

He didn't get it. Why could he never get it?

"What do you think these bullets are *for,* huh?" she said. "Decoration? Making a statement? Realistically, how many of 'em d'you suppose'll end up in someone we know? And you wanna go home? Nah. There's nowhere I'd rather be. This is it."

Kinneas reached for her swooping cyan-and-emerald hair. "Hey, don't cry."

"I'm not crying. Gods, Kin." She backed away, sniffing. "Read the room. Y'know, before I blow it up."

As his fingers curled away from her, she shoved the detonator into them. He fumbled with it. "Holy Buthmertha. Be careful!"

"Chill, puddle pants. Hold that while I think a minute."

She considered their surroundings, the general situation, variables such as poundage of plastic explosives and how many rounds per crate. Letting her mind wander gave her an idea. A dangerous, bonkers idea, but that meant it would work.

"Kin?"

"You've got that look in your eye again. Not a fan."

"Shut up and ask me what I'm thinking. Quick, before I forget."

"Okay, what're you thinking?"

"What do we know about bullets and explosives?"

"Rhetorical questions, great. Uh, explosives… explode? Which is why we brought them."

"Yes, Kinneas. They go boom. And so do bullets. So, even though we didn't bring a big enough bomb to blow all of them up when they're so spread out…"

He cracked his knuckles, finishing her thought. "C'mon, I'll help you push the crates together." Under his breath (which Cho's ears could easily pick up): "Whatever gets us outta here faster." He cast about the room. "There's a water main over there. Why doncha open it."

There was the Kin she approved of—the one who got stuff done.

Cho ran over to the wall he'd pointed out and tried to turn the wheel. "It's stuck," she stage-whispered at him.

"Cho, lefty-loosey."

"Oh, right. Whoops."

"You're supposed to be a mechanic."

"Listen, bro, I don't get pipes, 'kay? Toasters, VR consoles, cars, sure. But pipes make no sense to me. All that pressure and… wetness. It's not right." A blast of water knocked her back. Sputtering, she gave him a dripping thumbs up. "It's flowing. Now what?"

"Give it a sec."

"We don't have too many of those left before the night guards head back this way."

"Hey, I'm game. I'm ready. But I can't do my thing if I've got, like, no materials to work with. Can a sculptor without marble carve a statue, or whatever?"

"Would you just make the water go splash?"

Shaking out his wrists, he said, "Most great artists were misunderstood while they were alive."

"If you don't hurry, you'll be very *understood* very soon."

"Fiiiine."

The rushing water had dampened the concrete floor of maybe half the warehouse, but probably less. Kinneas buckled under Cho's impatience, though, and began casting. He stood on the balls of his feet, shifting his weight between his legs every several heartbeats. He extended the fingers of his right hand, pointing these toward the ground; his left fingers speared upward. His right wrist he rotated counterclockwise; his left, clockwise.

And, inside the walls, a rumbling could be heard. The spigot tore off the wall, unable to handle the spike in pressure. He then bent his hands into C-shapes, twisting his body as if scooping the water. In this way, he directed the rush around the warehouse. He was clumsy, still learning, but it was cool to watch: he cut through the liquid as if using a giant, invisible paddle. Soon enough, the crates and floor under them had been covered.

Water continued to spill in.

Even though Alina had told him a hundred times that he didn't have to, he muttered the words of the spell under his breath like a mantra. It helped him focus. At his side, Cho watched him strain, the veins popping out of his neck and above his nostril, as he levitated hundreds of gallons of water, shaping them into wedges that nudged and slightly lifted the heavy crates farthest from the center of the warehouse.

She stamped a kiss on his cheek. The container buckled for a second, but he caught it and himself.

With a final grunt, he spread his hands wide and then clapped, and the water froze. Not all at once, but in a wave flowing outward from his body. Once all the liquid had turned to solid ice, he dropped to one knee, drenched in sweat despite the cold.

His and Cho's breaths steamed from their noses. She beamed as the crates on the outer edges glided down and along the ice slides he'd shaped. They crashed into the ones in the middle. One big, combustible pile.

She considered her friend.

It was undeniably amazing that he'd managed to learn so much under Alina's flip-flopping supervision. Clearly, she'd done something right. He'd become much tougher than he let on. Still, under it all, he really was a softie at heart.

Why had he volunteered to come with Cho tonight? He didn't hate the Walazzins. He didn't *hate*, period. Not like she could. He was the room temp to her scalding boil, the water to her fire. She boiled him over, and maybe some part of him liked that, even if he didn't consciously realize it.

He gave so much, and she always asked for more, and still he gave. Sometimes it felt like she was awash in the heady crash of his generosity, pulled in by the undertow, a creature diving to reach the floor of his giving—there must be a seafloor to it, a bottom—and drowning in the depths of him.

She said, "That'll do, Kin." Arm looped under his shoulder, she hauled him up. "Sure was loud, though, so let's hustle."

With the stacks of munitions clustered, it was the work of a few minutes to plant the charges and activate the detonator.

Scuffing his heels, hands in his pockets, Kinneas paced the length of the wall. "Still think we could've come up with a better, less permanent kind of distraction."

"Sure, now he chimes in." Cho turned around, inspecting their handiwork. "No one got hurt—"

"So far!"

"—and we might've just saved a bunch of lives."

Clinging to the shadows cast by the warehouse's roof and walls, they crept into the night.

Kinneas whispered, "Who taught you to program detonators anyway?"

"It's basically a coffeemaker. Now shut up unless you're raring to find out if traitors can get time off their sentences for good behavior."

Slinking between the spotlights, sidling against the house-sized steel containers, they took care to avoid the roving night guards. Still, these were only Peace

& Asset Compliance Enforcers, reserves that mostly existed to crack down on problem areas inside the homeland. Burning down off-the-grid homesteads and breaking up labor strikes, that's what they were good for. True to the stereotype, the PACE-yourselves officers in this base weren't super alert. Cho could hear most of them snoring in their barracks closer to the river bank. It wasn't too hard to work around them, even for Kinneas. He'd grown more than a foot over the summer, so his steps were uneven, stumbling, and loud. It was impressive that, far off and sleepy-headed as they were, even these unobservant weekend soldiers hadn't noticed him yet.

The Authority was nothing if not overconfident; whoever was in charge clearly had assumed the base's defenses good enough to handle the local bumpkins. However, the people of Truct were far from bumpkins, and Cho was no exception. She exploited the glaring blind spots PACE had been kind enough to leave open for her as she led Kinneas toward their next objective.

More good luck. The only eyes on this part of the base were the silver, fist-sized drones scanning for intruders. Cho happened to be able to hack such machines. Without touching them.

A camera drone whizzed and clicked, spinning toward them. She focused on it, and it fell like a zapped moth.

Minutes later, she and Kinneas came within spitting distance of their second and final stop. A white sign on the side of a rectangular building—which had once been a wrestling stadium—read "Detention Facility." Its corners were rounded, and all along each of its sides jutted curved steel beams like ribs. The front entrance, a wide archway, was too well lit to risk. The better option was the staff entrance, a single door, on the opposite side.

Cho knocked out a couple more drones on the way. The disabled metal balls rolled along the gutters, slipping neatly into a roadside drainage grate. She and Kinneas found a stack of oil drums to crouch behind, and she put a finger to her lips, pointing toward the entrance. She watched his eyes widen as he counted the guards. Four of them, with big guns. Their uniforms, red trimmed with gold, identified them as Walazzin jacks, trained rats who didn't care where the pellets came from as long as they were fed.

Raising her finger and shooting Kinneas a meaningful look that simultaneously said *Wait for it* and *Watch this,* Cho held up the detonator between them.

Beads of sweat glistening in the white electric light of the camp, he mouthed, *Are you sure?*

She glared at him, mouthing right back, *Noodle.* The hand gripping the metal cylinder trembled. Her thumb hovered over the button.

Taking her other hand, he whispered, "There's still time to turn back."

"No, there isn't." She pressed the button.

The explosion that tore apart the munition storage building was like a giant finger of flame pushing through a plastic bag until it gave way. A roiling inferno lit up the night's sky, and a rain of metal scraps followed, clinking and clanking off the windows and walls of the base. Among the rows of tents where the grunts slept, a few small fires broke out. By the sounds of the responses, it seemed no one had been (seriously) hurt.

Immediately, the alarm sounded.

As hoped, many of the guards protecting the detention facility—including two from the side entrance—rushed off to identify the source of the commotion.

Two men remained. Bronzed mechanical exoskeletons, paper thin but harder than any steel, covered their bodies except for the visors revealing their faces. Specially coated plates protected their hearts, necks, and other vital places from light weapons, pulse or ballistic. The translucent energy cones surrounding them would deflect plasma and laser beams. In addition, the power suits gave them superior speed and strength, and guided their aim. No doubt, these two were Chimera Guard—heavy duty. Walazzin's bruisers.

Even with all her martial arts lessons, Cho knew she couldn't match a professional soldier (or two). Decked out like these two were? Forget it. No biggie, though. She had a workaround.

She had read somewhere that "discretion is the better part of valor," which she understood to mean "why fight when you can cheat?"

She prepared to Zero-One'd herself—splitting her consciousness into two pieces, effectively becoming a Zero and a One, a Yes and a No, *at the same time*. She was not the only one with this ability, and she made sure to learn from others' mistakes. Pioneers in ZOing had quickly discovered that the mind can't endure the stress of the split for long. The bigger the chunk you send off, the higher the probability of your going insane.

Quickness was key. And caution. Cho was nothing if not cautious. It was always a risk, but she tried to play things safer by only ever separating a small portion of her mind, like severing a limb off a starfish. Although, one key difference: she could recall the mental "limb" afterward; she did *not* become two separate Chos (magnificent though that would obviously have been.)

The other part of being ZO'd no amount of Darkthreads research could have prepared her for was the experiencing of two instances of time simultaneously. In her body, she felt it as all people did: slow, going from moment to moment in chronological order. Her "Zero" mind-bit, however, got thrown into a much faster, more chaotic version of time, where everything happened very fast, all at once, and out of order.

It was... confusing.

Whenever the "Zero" part of her mind dug into a machine, it couldn't feel time in the same way anymore, even as her bigger part, in her own body, still acted as normal. This separation created the "Hackerdox," short for "Hacker's Paradox," which referred to the hacker's brief existence as *both* a being that *can* sense time and a thing that *can't*. The term had been coined by the fanciest expert in the field of artificial evolution, Doctor Porfirias Panoklas. His research centered on the record-holder for longest ZO (three seconds) who'd spent the last eight years of his life in a solitary confinement cell, plucking every hair out of his body and muttering to himself about "the green men who eat time."

Having read this account, Cho prudently kept her ZOs under the expert-recommended one-second limit, figuring her mind was strong enough to handle more, but not wanting to find out for sure.

Generally, the other bigwig authors agreed with Panoklas that this sensation of "split-time" and the significant possibility of going wonky were caused by the "mild trauma of biological, electrical impulses undergoing instantaneous digitization as a parcel of the human consciousness insinuates itself into and amalgamates itself with the circuitry highways of the distinctly non-conscious electronic apparatus in order that the former subjugate the latter's core functionalities; what, after all, is time to a machine that can neither sense nor self-reflect? Is the true cyborg, then, not the greatest of contradictions?" (Panoklas, *Beyond the Psycho-Self: Theorizing Metahumanity*. A nice, light read). Cutting through all that pointlessly complicated jargon… basically, Panoklas suggested that time doesn't exist for simple machines because they can't *think*. Thinking is what allows people to know that time exists. Or, maybe thinking is what creates time as sentient beings perceive it?

She felt the usual migraine coming on, and reminded herself it was best not to think too hard about all that. Instead, she focused on her target and took action.

As if she'd cracked her skull open—a spoon tapping a soft-boiled egg—her mind spilled out like gooey yolk. Just enough, not too much. She experienced the usual fuzziness, that sense of stepping outside her own head. Her larger "One" piece of self stayed inside, the other digitizing, "Zeroing" off, zapping through the air. This second part of her consciousness became a pirate wireless signal that wormed its way into the operating system of the right-hand soldier's exoskeleton.

In a quarter-second, she'd assumed total control of the Chimera Guards' exoskeletons. It began to whir and shift at her command. Her nose poking over the row of barrels, she forced the soldier to draw his automatic sidearm, aim at the leg of the other soldier's power suit, and empty his mag. At this range, the first ten plasma rounds burnt away the energy shield; the next ten destroyed the layer of armor protecting a small and very important circuit board, paralyzing the power suit.

The soldier who'd been forced to disable the other man's entire exoskeleton weapons system then marched in the opposite direction, away from the detention center.

While the paralyzed soldier panicked, Cho dashed over and shoved him, tipping him backwards, onto the ground, face-up. She dusted her hands before gesturing for Kinneas to hurry up. One more glance at the soldier confirmed that his power suit had kept him from being hurt, but, like a turtle on its back, he wouldn't be getting up without assistance. His shouts couldn't escape his soundproofed helmet because no juice was flowing to the mic or speakers in there.

"Poor baby," said Cho.

"That was incredible," said Kinneas.

"Bought ourselves maybe a few minutes." She was already checking the entrance.

This side door to the detention facility had a sophisticated electronic lock that *normally* would require a key card and fingerprint scan to open. Cho ZO'd herself again, the other piece of her mind crawling around inside the lock, until she found the internal "off" button.

The soldier, meanwhile, was still shouting for help, and even though no one could hear him, it wouldn't take long for a group of his buddies to circle back and see him. Which left Cho very little time to reach her contact.

Twisting the handle, she pulled the door open, and she and Kinneas ran inside.

They leap-frogged the turnstiles, making for the light at the end of a long, dark hallway. Weird that there were no guards or mechanical sentries. She'd expected them, planned for them. Apparently, the Chimaera Guard were just *that* arrogant.

She'd also expected, on entering the floodlit arena, to find maybe a dozen pens clustered in the center of an overgrown field of weeds. What she saw, instead, beneath ratty, rain drenched awnings, were stacks and stacks of cages, each stuffed with white-eyed people. Too many people. Between each row of cages was just enough room for one adult to squeeze through; they were so close together that some of the detainees were able to reach across the aisle to touch fingers. Human beings, piled in crates, like animal carcasses readied for the skinning and tanning process.

"Too many," Cho breathed. They couldn't *all* have come from Truct.

Her shock abruptly shifted focus to her right, to the soldier who'd padded over and shouted a challenge, raising her rifle. Whether she'd planned to fire a warning shot or go for the kill would never be known: Kinneas's arm went up, and the flask at her belt burst, a stream of water flying at her eyes. Stunned, the Enforcer sputtered and blinked.

The distraction lasted just long enough for Cho to dash forward, kick the rifle free from the soldier's grip, sweep her legs out from under her, and yank the pistol from the woman's leg holster.

"Take it easy, lady," said Cho, taking a step back and keeping the gun trained on the Enforcer. "Stay right there."

Wiping her face, the woman looked up at her. "You're making the biggest mistake of your life, kid," she said through her teeth.

"Like I haven't heard that a million times," said Cho. To Kinneas: "Get over here." She pressed the gun into his clammy hand, noting his pale complexion. "Just keep her right where she is. I'll be done in a sec. In and out before you can say 'high treason'."

Clutching the weapon two-handed, Kinneas nodded, gulping, his elbows locked. His forearms jiggled with each slightly unsteady breath. He looked absolutely miserable, but held it together for now.

"Be right back." Cho dashed between the cages filled with detainees. The prisoners nearest the commotion woke and began to spread the word. Within a minute, the whole block was buzzing with worry and rumor and pleas.

"Let us out!"

"Help us!"

"I got kids!"

Her eyes cut through the stacks of strange faces as she homed in on the guy she was looking for, tracing the wireless signal of the tracker he'd swallowed. The pings only she could hear grew louder and more frequent until she was practically on top of him. Inside the cage, a scratchy, damp blanket covered the knotted shoulders of a man with a red-fading-to-pink mop of hair, who leaned against the bars.

"Rooster?" she said.

He wasn't the only one in there. Several others huddled on the ground, filth and flies all over them. Been there for weeks, looked like.

At the sound of her voice, Rooster jumped, turned, and flashed his broken-, gray-toothed smile at her. "Well, well, well. If it isn't the Cho-Zen one. Wasn't expecting you for another two days."

"When I heard they'd sewed up your hideout, nabbed you, and brought you here, I came quick as I could."

"You did all that for lil ol' me?" said Rooster. The flesh around his eyes was as pink as his hair. Bruises on his neck.

"Yeah, 'course. You got the thing I need?"

He winced, seemingly debating himself on something. Then he opened his mouth wide and jammed his knuckles back there, prying his jaws farther and farther apart. With a grimace and groan, he removed his spit-covered fingers and offered, in his palm, one of his incisors. There was remarkably little blood, but still—

"Ugh, what? Why—I don't want one of your teeth!"

Rooster hissed, "That's *it*, silly. The data drive. It's in there. It's a false tooth. Nifty, no?"

"Uh, yeah." She pocketed the tooth, zipping it into one of the compartments in her sleeveless, hooded vest. The synthetic material brushed against her ribs, a chill touching her collarbones. "Def-o outside the box, for sure." She removed one of her earrings, a functional lockpick. Unfolding the tool, she set to work.

"Whatcha doing, there?"

"What's it look like?" she snapped. The tumblers popped into the place, the lock sprung open, and the door slid inward an inch or two. "Thank me later. Let's go."

He seemed confused. "Cho, you don't get it."

Her jaw dropped. She flung her hands outward, saying, "How are we not already running?" Why were none of them in that cage lunging for the door and freedom?

"They'll kill us if we leave."

"So, what, you'd rather die in there?"

Gaze dropping to the floor, Rooster said, "The whole gang's gone, Chosie. Everyone but you and me. All Zinokled, every last one on some chain gang or plantation by now. And they're the lucky ones. Your boss? The one you asked me to look for? Man, they got him on ice. One unlucky smack to the head, and he's gone. I—I don't wanna end up like that, Cho. I don't." He took a deep, shuddering breath. "They got my boy Dope Sandwich doing a four-year in Tinniby Correctional. That's not so bad. He could get out in twenty months if he's the good sport I know he is."

Everyone else in the cage, clinging to one another for warmth or comfort like a bunch of rain-soaked kittens, simply watched.

"Rooster," Cho shouted over him. "Listen to yourself. You can't *give* up. We're the Resistance. We're Truct-4-Life. What happened to 'Seventy-Seven Hells for The Authority' and 'Stomp Walazzin the Worm'? You can run, right now, and *live free*. What's happened to you?"

He backed away from the ajar door, sitting down beside the others. "What happened to me is I figured myself out. I know what I am and what I'm not. It was fun when we were pirating radiowaves, tagging public buildings and stuff. Slogans and bragging rights and dames. But people've *died*, Cho. Died. You don't seem to care much about the news of your old boss."

"Of course I care about Mr. Ovaris," Cho said, kicking the bars, rattling them. "Of course I care! That's why I hafta keep fighting."

"You do you, friendo. But I'm out. This Rooster's crowing days are over."

She cast around, looking for a sympathetic face, someone who would see reason. She found none. "What? So you're all just fine with how things are? You're just gonna sit there and let the Walazzins do to you whatever they want, no consequences? You gonna thank them for it afterward, too?" The owners of every pair of eyes she met shrank away from her. To Rooster, she said, "Why even give me the data I asked for?"

He shrugged, not meeting her eye. "My last job. Now we're square."

Cho couldn't believe it. She activated her infrared and X-ray sensors, scanning for implants, mind-control devices, anything that could explain how all these people had had their wills so thoroughly broken.

"How did they do it? How did the Walazzins crush all of you this badly?"

Rooster crossed his arms, tearing up. "They didn't have to. Those of us on *this* side of the cage, all we did was admit the truth. It's hopeless. And if you're not careful, you'll find that out for yourself, the hard way. Like the rest of us did."

Nods and murmurs from the crowd of wide-eyed, grimy-faced detainees. Many of them had been here for weeks, maybe longer. Some would leave on the trucks tomorrow, shipped off to the colonies or who-knew-where-else. In spite of everything, they were prepared to accept whatever hand they were dealt, even if it was just one card, cut in half and singed at the corners.

How they hated losing, but they'd gotten so used to it that simple survival could seem like victory. Full stomachs came at the cost of empty eyes. These were abused animals, not people. No fight left in them.

Clenching her fists, Cho said, "That's fine. I'll do it myself. I'll take care of the Walazzins, all of them, pay them back for what they've done. To me. To all of you. I'll do it. Me!"

Before Rooster could reply, she spun on her heels and ran.

Returning to where she'd left Kinneas and the Walazzin Enforcer, she caught the soldier telling her friend, "The girl's no good, kid. You have to see how she's going to drag you down, likely even get you killed."

Kinneas twitched when he saw Cho approach.

The Enforcer pleaded with him, "Make the right choice."

Cho snatched the rifle from Kinneas's hands. Screaming, she swung it like a club, the stock striking the woman's skull and knocking her out cold.

"What are you doing?" yelled Kinneas.

Collecting herself, Cho flung the weapon down. "We gotta go, Kin. I can hear them, they're just outside. We gotta go now."

She grabbed his hand.

Building to crescendo all around them, the noises of boots thudding on concrete, the swish and fizz of hydraulic power suits springing to action, the whir of hovercraft engines zooming past above, the sirens and alarms—

They ran for it.

6

ALINA

ALINA RESTED ONE OF her bare feet on the downed trunk of an old pine tree. It'd fallen at the edge of the woods during the last thunderstorm a few weeks ago. About fifty feet long with healthy guts. The perfect size for what she had in mind. She spent several hours hacking off branches and carving handholds at the middle.

She examined the round length of trunk she'd worked on, doing the math. The pine probably weighed about two thousand pounds, give or take a couple hundred.

She squatted, rubbed some dirt on her palms. Then she grabbed the tree by the carved handholds. Arms straight but not locked, she lifted through her knees.

The dead wood came up off the ground, muck and leaves sloughing off its underside.

Breathing hard, she bent her knees again and set the tree down. Holding her dirty hands up to the early morning light, she said, "Whoaaa."

Previously, the heaviest object she'd lifted was a wooden tool shed. Ruqastra had wanted to use its old spot for meditation because it was quieter and got better moonlight, or whatever. Quality moonlight was hard to come by, apparently, and shouldn't be wasted on a tool shed. Too lazy to dismantle it, Alina had simply picked the whole construction up. It weighed about seven hundred pounds.

Before that, she'd started lifting progressively heavier weights until she ran out of weights to add. And, before that, at the start of her stay at Mount Morbin, she'd lost her earphones under a car and had shoved the vehicle back five feet. With one hand. While holding a half-eaten veggie burrito in the other.

But... dead-lifting two *thousand* pounds? That was something else.

Ruqastra materialized out of the morning mountain fog. "Put it on."

"Did you not just see that? What I just did?" said Alina, gesturing at the tree. "I saw."

"How are you not even a little bit surprised right now? I just did something superhuman."

Ruqastra didn't even blink. "You are Demidivine. The strength of the ancients courses through you. Every fiber of your corporeal form was stitched, strand by strand, from the fabrics of death. The threads of fate are your garment, your flesh, your will made manifest." She was saying objectively weird and awesome stuff, but everything about her tone grumbled, *I'm bored.* "You are of the Sevensin."

Alina waved off all that mystically unhelpful crap. "Ruqastra, did you *see* me lift the stupid tree? Would it kill you to compliment me?"

"Why would anyone compliment you for what you did not earn? Shall I congratulate the octopus for owning eight limbs, or the lion for its mane? A human must work for years, dedicating themselves to laborious training regimens, controlling their diets, and so on, and still they would never be able to approximate what you can do naturally because of who and what you are. There will be no congratulations from me on this matter."

"Wow. Well. Could'a just said 'no.' And, for the record, again, I'm *three quarters human.*"

"You have Aelf blood in you. A quarter, a twenty-seventh, no matter: you are an Aelf." The red mask floated up between them, its wicked beak facing Alina. "Now, put it on. I must show you how to use it before you find some means of destroying it, yourself, or me due to your ignorance."

"Good morning to you too, master." Alina curtsied. "And thank you so much for all the wonderful nightmares. They were really helpful. I learned a lot."

Resistant to many standard conversational tactics, Ruqastra was fazed least of all by sarcasm. "Don your face, apprentice. It is high time you understand its purpose and its cost."

Alina took the floating mask, noticing again that its coloration shifted even as she looked at it. She slipped it over her head. The black cords tied themselves. "Haunted mask. Great. Probably can't ever take the thing off."

"If only that were true," said Ruqastra. "Now, *sleep.*"

Before Alina could so much as slip out a "Hey, wait a—" she was dreaming once more.

There was nothing but blackness, dark all around, crowding in, nestling close, embracing them both where they stood on nothingness. A nothingness that, here, had shape, heft, and purpose. A living, watching thing, vibrating with will. From within its embrace, cradled in its velvety tentacles, the Crow—as always—waited for her.

At Alina's appearance, it lurched, perching on an invisible ledge, following her movements with its lidless, pupil-less gold eyes that shone like coins.

She hadn't told Ruqastra about the Crow, not yet. Maybe she was afraid her teacher wouldn't see it, too. But what if she *did*?

Searching for answers to its slow but unending pursuit of her, Alina had spent countless hours pouring over accounts of urban myths on the Aetherthreads. But the closest relevant results she could find to her searches of "*Being followed by scary shadow person HELP*" had only led her to barely understandable gibberish. In the end, she'd figured out that the author and commenters were dealing with a common haunting. She'd replied to the thread, asking for a nearby address; then, a few minutes of research showed that, near the author's home, a school had burned down a century ago. *You've got yourself a case of the Lords and Ladies,* she'd explained in three succinct paragraphs. *Sprites that feed off the pain of people who've lost loved ones, and the regrets of the dead. The tragedy of these children fits perfectly. L & L's could get fat off that kind of energy for a long time. But, don't worry, they can't hurt you as long as you stay calm. Anyway, you don't need a priest, pal. You need an Aelfraver. Get The Gild on it, and that should be the end of your problems.*

Unfortunately, after all her trouble, the only response she'd gotten from the moderators for explaining one of their "Unexplainable Mysteries" was to be blocked from the chat. So much for online gratitude.

Long story short, Alina had come no closer to determining if she were being haunted or hunted, or simply going crazy.

She looked from the Crow—her skin crawling—to Ruqastra. No, Alina decided. She couldn't tell her. She wouldn't understand. Or, worse, she would think she did and then try to tell Alina it was all fine and for the best.

The Revomancer master wore her mask and cloak—her own Ida and Rego, as Alina had recently learned they were called. With her silver-gloved hand, Ruqastra waved Alina over.

Now there were silver threads *everywhere*, stretching from the floor into the swirling, whispering shadows high above. Each thread, Alina realized, originated from her, spread out from her, as if she were the center of a spider's web. She plucked at one with the tip of her finger; it thrummed, the sound changing into a rustling of leaves. She tried another, this one's warble the cymbals of crashing waves.

At the other end of one of the silver threads was the Crow. It tugged on one, pulling itself closer. And closer. Soundless.

Alina looked away—

Lurching.

—and sat opposite Ruqastra, so close their shins touched.

"Before you ask any banal questions, such as 'Where are we?'…" She thrust a hunk of green, faintly glowing, slightly warm-to-the touch stone into Alina's arms. The stone was chipped, a crack running down nearly half its elliptical length.

"Get that thing away from—"

"You will hold it."

Alina's fingers disobeyed her, clasping the Chrononite Lorestone to her chest. It hummed at her touch.

They stared at each other, master and apprentice.

There, again, Ruqastra flashed her power. It wasn't a hardness, not exactly. She wasn't large or muscled or iron-jawed; her eyes weren't the lusterless mirrors of a killer. Really, she was all the more terrifying for the fact that she seemed so very human behind the cloak and the mask and the mystique. Just a woman losing her patience. A woman who could *snap* at any moment, let her lupine smile widen just a little bit too far. It would have been better, in a way, were she more like Alina—drowning in the waters of herself, grappling with the sea snakes of her soul—but Ruqastra was nothing like that. She lived neatly inside the box of her sanity and restraint until such time as control seemed more hindrance than advantage. At any moment, she could decide to break free from the cage she'd built for herself.

Telling, then, that Ruqastra was the one to break their contest to say, "I ask a lot of you, but I only do it because the night grows short."

What Alina saw in her teacher's eyes stirred in her the wish to speak, of the Crow, of the way she curled around her pillow at night. Unable to sleep, but equally unable to rise. Then she pinched shut her lips. Ruqastra could read thoughts, literally see through others' eyes. No way did she not already know everything that happened on Mount Morbin.

Starved for attention, the Crow rasped behind Alina. Its meat-locker breaths slapped the nape of her neck.

Ruqastra knew everything and did nothing. As for what she was after—

Well, for all Alina knew, the Crow was Ruqastra's handiwork. Another torture method, like whatever she had in store for her star student next.

"Now," said her teacher, "I invite you to pay close attention to what you are about to witness."

The infinite darkness closed in, limiting itself to a small room with a high ceiling. The faceted, iridescent walls reminded Alina of a shimmering beehive. Each gemstone wall reflected the two Aelfrravers in their matching long, dark cloaks. Alina noticed something missing from her reflection; she looked down.

The Chrononite was gone.

The color and nature of their surroundings now made more sense. "We're inside the Lorestone," said Alina.

A metal fold-out table appeared, holding a laptop and a dusty old projector, whose light clicked on with a soft, high-pitched whine. Ruqastra levered the laptop open and tapped one of the keys.

The projector's light split into three, illuminating three facets of the Chrononite walls. In front of Alina, in a row, a trio of scenes played out. From left to right, the grainy, low frame-rate, choppy footage showed her only what she had no desire to see.

A long-nosed guy with full lips and ever-changing hair color, his easy smile threatening her with a ghostly kiss. He was Ordin Ivoir, and he was dead.

A dark-faced guy with lightning bolts shaved up the sides of his hair. It seemed like he'd always had his back to her. Baraam bol-Talanai. Possibly dead, but definitely out of her life.

A lanky guy, brown hair and green eyes, who'd kept her warm with handmade jackets. Calthin Amming, off at Authority boot camp. He'd left his little brother in her care, and she'd taken it upon herself to drag Kinneas into the thick of the world's badness.

"But it's not about them," said Ruqastra.

The three scenes stuttered, replaced by three copies of the same image: Alina as a six-year-old, crouched at the center of a hedge maze, alone as the sunlight faded, crying for her parents. Parents who, even then, were dead.

"Isolation, loneliness," said Ruqastra. "A common fear, though still too superficial. The deeper dread is the lack of love. That you'll never have it. Never be worthy of it."

The projector went dark, the walls revealing the Crow's searing, expressionless eyes everywhere Alina looked.

She closed her eyes. "Why're you putting me through this?"

"Again," said Ruqastra.

"I don't want to."

"What are you afraid of?"

Over-shoulder, the Crow hissed a long exhale. Anticipation.

"Death?" Ruqastra scoffed.

"Sometimes."

"Whatever for? It's just another dream."

Dusty light deepened the darkness around it, once more drawing Alina's gaze to the three mirrors of herself. She buried her face in her crossed arms, but the vision couldn't be denied. The image twirled like a sequined dancer, sparkling in her mind's eye.

This time she was treated to a vision of her Tahtoh gripping Baraam's unconscious form over the edge of the ruined City Hall tower in New El. Dangling him over the ledge by his heel. Casually declaring that he would kill his protege if Alina didn't do as he demanded.

Although this moment had happened two years ago now, she still relived it each and every night.

Powerless as ever to change the outcome—because it had happened and always would happen exactly this way—she watched her past self dash forward and spear Dimas K'vich through his heart with her own mutated, clawed hand. What the images couldn't show was how the aftershock of the killing blow had nearly torn her apart. The man who'd raised her, struck down.

What she saw in this light show in her head was a monster, a murderer, a sick and wretched thing she'd do anything not to be.

She hadn't wanted to do it; she'd wanted anything *but* for that result. But now, not only must she live with it, she also had to endure Ruqastra and the lump of Chrononite throwing it in her face.

The worst of it was the inescapable question: had she really saved Baraam from becoming a victim of her grandfather's mind games, or had she simply called the bluff of a disturbed old man, granting his desire for death at his granddaughter's hands?

The pulses of her worsening headache were the beat to which the Crow's feet shuffled forward. Always moving, always reaching. One day, she'd lose the will to hold it off…

Lunging, the Crow dug its claws into her shoulders—

… *But not today.*

Meeting a forcefield, the shadow creature rocketed backward and bounced noiselessly off a dark corner. It did not return (for now).

Yeah, there was still enough *her* inside herself to remain as she was. Return to sender, pal. Try again later.

"When—" Alina coughed. She tried again: "When are you going to tell me why it all went down like that, with Baraam? When, Ruqastra?"

Her teacher said nothing. For a third time, the projector flicked on.

"You owe me answers."

"I owe Dimas. You would not be here if not for his dying wish." Avoiding Alina's eye, she reached for the keyboard again.

Alina growled, swept the laptop from the table, hefted the projector and flung it at the wall. It shattered into dozens of plastic chunks, which fizzled with electric sparks, instantly transforming into helicopter seeds, spinning gently downward.

"A child, only," Ruqastra said. "Reap what you've sown, *Stitcher.*"

As soon as the seeds landed, each beamed a light onto every wall facet all around—top and bottom, side and center—the choppy films overlapping, blending as they burned into Alina's eyes events and memories that could not have been hers but that, nonetheless, she somehow recognized.

A young boy picks flowers in a meadow, his parents calling him home.

Next to him:

Riders on the hilltop, white stallions like ships sailing upon a wave of dew-green grass.

Next to them:

The wizard delights in teaching a frog to recite poetry. Hop along to the next stanza now, and—

Setting sun, rising moon, trading places again and again.

Through the eyes of the wind, Alina watched these miniature worlds.

The flower boy's home is in flames; he runs inside to find his parents and siblings.

Her gaze darted from one to the other to the next.

The wizard asks for council. War has come to their shores. The old one stirs, ready to end what in his youth he'd begun. His will cannot be denied. Power moves with purpose.

"What is all this?" Alina asked. "What am I seeing?"

Armored soldiers line gray-robed priests and priestesses along a wall. Archers nock arrows, draw and fire. The gray-robed fall down or are pinned to the stone.

A subtle knife, Ruqastra's voice sliced sound from silence: "Echoes of things said." She peeled words from her throat like gristle from chicken. "And things done."

Between Alina and her teacher appeared two figures. The man was short, bad-kneed; he wore slash scars on his arms; his eyes were wide and deep, and they drank the light like drains would water. Thumbs tucked into the black sash he wore around his waist, he did not look one bit the legend he was supposed to be.

Bearing down on him, the woman was tall, broad-shouldered, long-limbed. Body thin in that way only showed she'd been malnourished in her youth. She'd remained pale since her enslavement in the mines; her several deaths hadn't helped.

Both were Iorians, blue of skin, with hair like wafting crimson fire.

Alina would have guessed the man was a vegetable farmer or something. Strong hands, sun-beaten brow. But she felt that wasn't the whole story. Not by a mile.

The woman carried a long, silver-plated sword, hooked at the end, nasty, her non-dominant hand clutching at the silver chain around her neck. Through her fingers, the shape of a three-tongued flame could be seen. (A silver flame necklace. Three-pronged and stabby, like the faithful of The Sanctum wore. Weird.)

She said, *"If the gods object to my channeling the river, the graves, the air, then let them strike me down now... See? Do you see that I stand here still? Hear it now, the will of the eternal: all is silence."*

The flower boy is uprooted but grows strong, like a wildflower, eating the drifted ash of distant forest fires. He grows hungrier.

"Who are they?" Alina shouted into the darkness.

"They are you. You were them. The magician sage, the lost boy, the genocidal lord. Each one, in turn. You."

"No." The images were blinding, the voices deafening. "How do I stop this?"

"You don't," said Ruqastra. "Let it flow into you and through you. Pour it into the mask."

"I can't."

"You will have to. Like a varnish, *Ida* will shield your soul, your mind, from the acid rains of nightmare, the gnawing frost of guilt, and any dangers natural to the work ahead. But, first, it must hurt you."

Street by street, the fires tore through town.

Alina wept at the force of these moments as they wriggled their way inside like worms into a week-old carcass.

Banners falling, raining cinders.

She saw them happen as if they'd happened to her, though the settings could not have been more alien.

Warriors' corpses hacked apart by specters.

There were people, creatures, cities she'd never seen, wouldn't have been able to imagine. And, as is the way of dreams, she experienced these lifetimes as herself and those within them.

Children thrown from high windows.

She was the child and the invader. She was the window. She was all and none.

Fear ate away each second, minute, day, week, month, year, lifetime of these dramas with the steady patience of a fungus, consuming without killing, stretching out the feast forever.

She saw sun-bleached walls, buildings like broken bones, crumbling mortar like dried marrow. A town where only the unliving moved, shambling through silent streets, weathering the stone with rotting feet.

Dead City.

She ruled it from a throne of unwashed fingernails. Her thralls had collected them from the still-living, a tribute to their queen who conquered death.

Shrinking in upon herself, Alina curled up, crying.

Seven Lords of the Dead City, tomb of the old gods, seat of the New Power.

Her world became a pinprick of light in an infinite tunnel of despair.

God of Light. One True God.

She felt a hand on her shoulder, another under her arm. She was guided back to her feet.

"Let me show you," said Ruqastra. Her quiet voice reverberated through the emptiness, echoing, shaking the seeds of light, which were uprooted to float back to the table, where they reformed the dusty projector and open laptop.

With two fingers, Ruqastra jabbed the keyboard's space bar. A single movie—widescreen and high-def—spread itself before them, unveiling a *long road set between alabaster columns. Golden cliffs form a "U" around a cluster of white homes built into a hill, each structure reflecting the desert sun's fierceness. A girl, covered from head to toe in dark blue robes, guides a sand-colored alpaca. Maybe seven or eight years old, a boy lies draped across the animal, buried in its fur. The girl holds him steady as he sleeps, drooling a little. The alpaca's rump sways from side to side. She, her rider, and her guide progress, unhurriedly, homeward.*

The girl hums.

A flash of brilliant light challenges the sun for dominance, briefly, briefly, as it slices through the skies, headed straight for the hillside village. Lulled halfway to sleep herself, the girl momentarily believes this apparition to be a god come to bless her family and friends. She quickly realizes her error: the twin trails of white left behind are no work of gods'. She has seen such smoke before.

Then, as expected, the piercing screech: it is the voice of death himself, crying in a forgotten and terrifying language the names of those he calls away.

The girl has been alive a few years longer than her brother; unlike him, she remembers this sound all too well.

She slaps the alpaca's backside, urging it forward with a shout. Her brother awakens. As she jogs alongside, she tells him not to worry. Don't worry, don't—

A second, smaller glowing light separates itself from the first, and the sky-thing arcs away, screaming off into the infinite blue above.

There is a moment in which all seems fine. Maybe this was merely a false alarm.

Then the hillside village is torn apart, shattered like a cluster of block towers stricken by the hand of a tantrum- throwing child.

The village is destroyed by fire.

The boy doesn't understand what he is looking at, but the girl does.

She remembers other days like this one.

The memory faded.

Alina looked to Ruqastra. "That was you? I'm so sorry. I had no idea you—and Baraam…"

Ruqastra's ever-shifting coyote mask of blackest black materialized on her face—the straps tying themselves taut around her skull and jaw—hiding her cracking expression. "Fear," said the master, "is your sword, your shield, your armor. With it, you will erase your enemies. Just as I do. But you will be greater, for you *must* be."

"Your family," Alina said, unsure of how to proceed. "They were killed in that drone strike?"

"I have never since felt such potent fear as I did then, leading Undidi toward the ruins of my village." The wearer of the coyote mask faced Alina. "But Dimas taught me how to turn my weakness into strength. I have revenged myself a thousand times over, never once dirtying my own hands. Revomancers have no need of swords, firearms, or any such banal tools. Any beef-brained fool can swing an axe. A surgeon, however, respects the differences between a scalpel and a saw, applying either or both as needed. Revomancy, in this same way, is subtler than all the other arts because it employs the mind of one's enemy against itself—doubts, nightmares, misconceptions of self and other. A master Revomancer understands how and when to reach for the scalpel or the saw. In attack and defense, you must know your enemy's emotions better even than he does—better than you know your own—or suffer your spells to be turned against you. You must read your opponents like graffiti, each curve and color a sign or symbol, each leading to an opening, an opportunity."

Alina sighed. "You're not gonna tell me how any of this relates to my grand-father's last words, are you?"

"Patience."

"It's been over a year!"

"And we might have been farther along had you not wasted entire months uselessly pursuing materialism over asceticism." Ruqastra snapped her fingers, and the two of them were in the material world again, seated, opposite each other, their legs crossed.

The Chrononite rolled onto its side, now lying inert on the ground.

Her back against the log she'd lifted earlier, Alina waited for her teacher to finish the lesson. There'd be a command at the very end. There always was.

On cue, Ruqastra said, ticking off her fingers, "Drink only water from the mountain spring. Meditate morning, noon, and night to achieve mastery over your fear. Let go of who you think you are, and remake yourself into what you must become. And keep the Lorestone with you *at all times*." She got up. "Perform these tasks diligently, and I will, one day, tell you everything I know of Dimas, the Dragon Ji'inaluud, and your destiny, Alina K'vich."

As was her habit, she disappeared as the sunlight touched her. She did not walk or otherwise move away; she left the clearing in pieces, like dandelion seeds blown from their stalk.

Alone again, Alina held her *Ida*, turned it over in her hands, and looked at the ugly red mask with its S-shaped rivers of liquid fire running through the grain of whatever strange material it had been made of. It was hard as wood, but flexible as rubber, and its texture suggested it had been woven rather than carved. Its beak, angular, angry eyes, its two long fangs... This discounted haunted-house-gift-shop piece of crap was supposed to be a projection from her subconscious?

Always skimpy with the facts, Ruqastra had explained that these "Sisters" were exclusively created by Sloth Demons like the one that had grabbed Alina by the scruff a few days ago during the raindrop dream.

Sloth Demons, apparently, desired nothing more than to return to the mate-rial world, but could only do so by possessing mortals. That wasn't unusual for Demons. What made the Sloths special, however, was *how* they entered the ma-terial world: their natural state was to shuffle across or lounge in the Revoscape, but if they could force themselves to fall asleep in the dream world they would wake in the material one. Now, the word "force" was appropriate here because Sloths could not sleep without magical intervention. Something about an ancient binding spell that had locked all the original passageways the Demons once used to hop back and forth between dimensions. Alina hadn't been especially interested in that part.

Instead, what she'd fixated on was how the Sisters were made and the cost of their weaving. Sloths were among the strongest dreamers in the multiverse. Though they never really slept, they were constantly daydreaming, and these daydreams, because they occurred in the Revoscape, inevitably took shape. In other words, Sloths could make things out of dream-stuff. The first Revomancers had come to an arrangement with these Demons. In exchange for the Sisters' power, the Revomancers put the Sloth weavers to sleep, allowing them to possess human beings and "dream" their way through a mortal life on the material plane. Basically, Alina's mask and cloak had cost someone his life. Ruqastra wouldn't say anything about the chosen sacrifice, but it wouldn't have mattered if he were a serial killer or a schoolteacher—*Ida's* blood-soaked hue forever advertised its price. A price Alina herself never would have paid.

Victims of Sloth possession were robbed of their *dreams*, which rendered them a shell of their former selves, unable to do much more than wander through life, forever unfulfilled because there would always be that undetectable vacuum of mental and spiritual energy, sapping them of their will.

Of course, not all depressed people were possessed by Sloths. The vast majority, in fact, were not. But some were. And, for Alina's sake, without her asking for it even once, one more person would suffer through that fate for his entire lifetime. (Unless an Aelfraver were paid to find, identify, and exorcise the demon.)

Ruqastra had reminded her that there was no point in her feeling sickened; it was too late to do anything except honor the sacrifice by wearing the mask. If Alina didn't, the stranger's suffering would be for nothing.

This kind of thinking regularly plagued Alina. If she faltered *at any time*—if she didn't unravel the mystery behind her grandfather's last words and request, all her struggles, the fight against the Bane of New El and the other Ravers and The Authority—the sacrifices of all those who'd helped her reach this point would lose all meaning.

There had to be a reason for all the loss and suffering, for her learning Revomancy from a woman who resented her, for her being able to lift a two-thousand-pound pine tree. But why did finding the answers have to bear a blood cost? Why had Dimas taught her not to kill, when he himself was a murderer? He'd always demanded non-violence of her, and then he'd forced her to end his life. Could he not have done that himself, if he'd hated this world so much? Dragging his own granddaughter into it, the coward—

Maybe the point was to build her up for years and years just to break her down. Obviously, he and Ruqastra took pleasure in being right. Did they look at Alina and delight in the broken-winged bird before them, delighting in the idea that they could mend the bones they themselves had fractured?

If their goal was to change her, she would disappoint them. She'd play their games, make them think she were progressing their little plots, if it meant finally getting answers. She didn't know how to give up.

Ruqastra pushed and tested and threatened, but she ought to know better by now; she'd been one of the strongest forces working against Alina during the New El ordeal. Under the guise of Morphea, Queen of Dreams, she'd done everything she could to turn Alina away from The Capital. And look at how that'd turned out.

The billionaire Ordin. The celebrity Aelfraver Baraam. The witch Morphea/Ruqastra. The pinkojack Detective Ding. And the serial killer Tolomond. Alina had overcome them all. Once she put her mind to a task, *no one* and *nothing* could stop her.

She knocked out ten more reps with the tree, then went inside her shack. Sweaty, she fell into bed but was too restless to sleep.

Hopping upright, she heard her phone ding, displaying the daily "!xXError#%" notification. It'd been months since the app had been able to accurately measure her body's physical and Niimantic reserves. A sure sign of her inhuman growth. Sooner than later, she'd probably be strong enough to *demand* answers from Ruqastra. A pleasant thought.

Yes, she'd finish her training, master the art passed down from Dimas to Ruqastra to her. And, if by the end Ruqastra still wasn't straight with her, Alina would bring all her new Revomantic powers to bear and crack her master's mind open like an egg.

A sudden chill. Alina shuddered; the Crow was pecking at her insides, trying to claw its way out.

Sliding to the ground, she placed her palms on her knees, closed her eyes and began to hum in the way Ruqastra had taught her to help her slip into a meditative state.

The sun gave off no warmth. Its light only exposed the emptiness of the clearing—no birdsong or cricket screams.

The quiet closed in.

She practiced her breathing exercises for a while and totally failed to calm down.

Following a snaking deer path, Alina found a pair of rocks, the taller leaning against the shorter. Beneath these, a stack of rain-smoothed stones had been carefully stacked like egg-sized bricks and mortared with tree sap and super glue. Dried leaves hung over the front opening of this pyramidal structure that reached nearly to Alina's knee.

"Hey, you in there? It's me."

No response. She focused, listening for the sounds of breathing, the shifting of hand-stitched beanbag chairs no larger than a thumbnail.

It seemed he wasn't home. Probably off hunting, though he didn't usually prowl the woods this close to nightfall. She guessed his (regular-sized) solar-powered microwave must be busted again.

The wind dropped to a whisper against her goose-pimpled skin.

With practiced ease, she exited her body, her spirit gliding upward. Soon, she'd passed above the tree line, moved beyond the reaching claws of Mount Morbin, and soared through the clouds.

She paused, drifting, surveying.

Before her stretched the fields and roads, hills and mountains, rivers and lakes of Torviri Province. Her home, though she was no longer welcome here.

Her spectral form faced the floating sphere, hundreds of miles to the north-east, bristling with towers of glass and steel burning in the refracted light of the setting sun. That was the Capital, New El, anchored to the earth by three titanic chains. Legend had it that the sphere and the chains had been built over centuries by humans enslaved to the Twin Dragon Kings, a project completed more than three thousand years ago. With humanity's defeat of the Dragons and the Aelf armies at their command, twelve champions rose to power, and their descendants—the Twelve Families—had ruled the Nation of El ever since. Their word was law. A law Alina never seemed to be on the right side of.

It had been a sunny evening, like today, when she'd gathered Cho and Mezami and, the three of them crammed onto Cho's moped, sped along the winding road toward Mount Morbin. A beautiful day, clear and crisp. The same refreshing chill that had brushed her skin on the day of Dimas's death. Whenever Alina teetered on the edge of falling and shattering to pieces, the world around her rejoiced.

Thank Buthmertha, by the way, for the anonymous tip that had alerted Alina to the Enforcers' coming for her. Another hour, and the net would have dropped, and she'd been locked in solitary, eating slop out of a rusty bucket.

There'd been, unfortunately, no one else to turn to other than Ruqastra, who claimed that there was magic in the earth and rock of Mount Morbin. As one of the supposed "roots of the world," it dripped with "Old Magic" (Alina always imagined the capital letters; seemed appropriate). Using Revomancy, Ruqastra wove its energies into a shield of sorts, and had—so far—kept everyone safe from the jets and drones that passed overhead some nights. By illusion, hidden from prying eyes and searching spells.

Alina frequently asked what it was about the mountain that *actually* allowed them to remain undetectable in plain sight, for more than a year. There had to be more to it than "Old Magic," but Ruqastra was allergic to directness. All she'd say was, "Stay on the mountain, or I cannot guarantee your safety. Keep your feet on the ground as much as possible."

Alina wasn't even supposed to astrally project herself away from the mountain without Ruqastra's supervision. Her solo practice had to stay within the boundaries she now knew by heart: no farther than the foothills to the south and east and the ravine to the north and west. For over a year, she'd been stuck here, doing the same things every day. Waking, meditating. Eating, meditating. Physically training. Magically training. Meditating. Eating. Sleeping. And again.

Cooped up like a prize hen, she was losing her mind.

She allowed her thoughts to drift like clouds, and soon her mind was clear again. That's when she noticed the fuzzy spot on the horizon to the southwest. Like part of the sky had been smeared with charcoal and smudged until it was just a messy, runny dark splotch.

Well, that was new. Never seen anything like it before.

The fuzziness lay in the direction of Kadic, but looked farther away than that. Distances were a bit wonky when seen through spirit eyes, and Alina had never been great with geography, but it seemed as though the weirdness was flowing from Ozar.

Before she could wonder about it for too long, though, she felt a tug at the line around her waist.

The first lesson every novice astral projector learned was to tie a cord of energy around her body. That way, even if she got swept up by a strong ethereal current, she could pull herself back.

Alina's energy cord snapped.

Safety harness gone, she was yanked violently to the southwest, toward the fuzziness, toward Ozar. Flailing and flapping, she struggled against the force, but her resistance was as useless as entering a shoving match with a tidal wave.

Losing all sense of direction, she blasted past hundreds of miles of grassland, rocky cliffs and pillars, sandy dunes, and the great nothingness where there'd once been a sea. Through columns of smog, over rows and rows of houses and skyscrapers and traffic-jammed hovercraft, she hurtled. Then she was back in the open again, crossing mesas of bleached and wind-scarred stones at ever-increasing speeds until—

She slammed into a solid wall. In this form, she had no bones to break, but she still could feel. The harsh arrival jarred her.

A shaft of light fell upon her cheek. All around her was softness, like leathery wings, hanging. She realized these were clothes she touched. Off-white robes.

She'd landed in a closet. Good quality, solid wood by the feel of it.

Her vision blurry, across from her she could make out the shape of a man standing over a desk, his hand clutching something, dragging it across a smooth, cream-colored surface. He was writing, pen scratching paper.

The bang that had announced her unexpected arrival, however, gave him pause. He glanced over his shoulder, facing the closet.

Alina slid a little farther into the shadows.

She had to return to her body. Of course, it wouldn't be as easy as taking the way she'd come; she didn't know how she'd gotten here in the first place.

And, where was *here*, anyway?

The stranger took a step toward the closet, then another. A dull green glow emanated from his hands. Preparing a spell.

His features came into focus: a dark-skinned face with bushy eyebrows, a thick beard hugging his strong chin, and long, braided hair tied behind his head. He looked a lot like Dimas, this man. And in realizing this resemblance, Alina recognized him.

Uncle Mateus. Her sole surviving relative, and the very person her grandfather had demanded—with his dying breath—that she kill.

All other thoughts competing for second place, her mind was seized by the urge to hide her identity. But how? She'd left her mask with her body. Another bone-headed move.

She had to change her appearance. There was only one way, but Ruqastra hadn't let her practice it much. It took a lot of effort and Niima to maintain, and Alina's all-time record, so far, was a whopping thirteen seconds.

Hopefully that would be enough.

She dragged her rough palm over her face, pinched her nostrils with thumb and finger, tugged at her earlobes, and ran her other hand through her thick hair. Her nose elongated and sharpened, her ears widened, the hair on top of her head burnt away in an instant (male-pattern baldness).

Mateus gripped the door handle with his glowing green hand. What was he casting? Felt like some kind of Corpromancy—the magic governing the physical body—but that's all she could tell.

She held her breath, agonizing over her every mistake.

Rather than a shape-shifting spell, she could have tried an illusion, which would've been easier to create and less costly to maintain. But illusions could be pierced. Risky to try to swindle a fellow Maggo with simple tricks.

If her true shape-shift wasn't enough, maybe she could still talk her way out of this. Or run past him. If only she'd had a few seconds more to plan her escape.

The door was flung open, and Alina raised her arms, bracing.

"Impossible." Uncle Mateus gasped, baring his teeth. "You're dead."

Glaring at him, Alina stood there, petrified by fright.

Reflected in Mateus's eyes, candle flames bucked and fluttered like the swinging hips of dancers. "Are you some kind of spirit, come to torment me? Did you not get your fill of that in life?"

Still, Alina said nothing.

Mateus reached into the closet with his green-glowing hand. "Answer me, ghoul."

Alina found her words: "Touch me and you'll regret it."

"Ah, so it *does* speak."

"Back away."

His bushy brows crept closer together as he grimaced. "You aren't him. You're not cruel enough. You wear his face imperfectly, creature. So, what are you, and how did you get in here?"

Who did he think she was? What face had she put on?

"I owe you nothing," she said.

Any second now, he'd figure out that she was stalling, that she was projecting her consciousness here. He'd find some way to bind her soul, and then her *pevool* would be cooked.

This was the one person in the world into whose hands she must not fall. After all, what Dimas had ordered her to do to him, Mateus could just as easily do to her.

Egogenesis, the consumption of a sentient being in order to absorb their physical and spiritual powers. If Mateus figured out who she was, he might try to eat her soul.

He glowered at her. "Nothing, is that right? But I owe *you* something, Father."

Father? Alina groaned inwardly. She'd transformed herself into Dimas. His had been the first face that had popped into her mind, and she'd acted on instinct. How incredibly unhelpful, changing her appearance to just *another* person in their family. What a brilliant disguise.

The window of opportunity was closing. So, she fell back to old habits. She tried the first idea that shoved its way to the front: she invaded Mateus's mind.

Well, she tried to.

He sliced through the crown of shadowy threads she'd thrown over his head, deflecting the mental attack with a smirk. "Thank you for the clarification, for now I'm certain you aren't Dimas K'vich. You're far too weak."

Oh, she'd show him. She'd hold a mirror up to his face and show him the meaning of "weak." Gritting her teeth, she focused a surge of Niima and entangled him again.

She failed a second time, but, in tearing himself free of her threads, he fell away from the closet.

Leaping out after him, she yelled her defiance, the cry becoming a shriek as the Crow gripped her mind in its talons once again. This time, she let it take her.

The Crow was stronger than she. In this moment, it could do what she couldn't.

Claws extending from her gray, feather-lined arms, Alina (her Dimas disguise deflating, replaced by the monstrous, shadow-clad, gold-eyed Crow) slashed at Mateus. The Crow raked four deep gashes into the man's arm before pouncing on him, knocking him another two steps backward.

With a roar, the Crow, together with Alina, tore into Mateus's mind. Thrown, he wasn't able to burn away the Niimantic threads this time.

He shouted for help, but it was too late.

As the Crow clawed its way deeper and deeper, Alina read Mateus's thoughts like notes pinned to corkboard.

Then, a blinding, pure white light filled her consciousness, as if a sun had spontaneously blazed into existence right above her. Its radiance seared her being, violently throwing her and the Crow out of her uncle's mind.

What was it, that all-encompassing, exposing, burning light? Not a spell, no. It had felt *alive*. There'd been a will in there. An incredibly powerful one.

It had almost killed her just now.

Mateus, clutching his bleeding forearm, glared at her. His eyes flashed gold. He thrust his palm against her chest, and—

She was flung through the wall, feeling every atom of stone as she passed through. Though she left no mark, the pain was incredible. Yet, she could not faint to avoid it.

She careened, again, across huge tracts of land—dunes, canyons, grasslands, fields, forests. Finally, she shot, meteor-like, through the clouds toward Mount Morbin.

As the moon rose, Alina fell like a shooting star, and crashed into her own body.

She opened her eyes, her physical ones. Staring down at her, a look of concern on his face, was the blue-furred, long-snouted, inkwell-eyed rodent with shaggy goat legs and hooves for feet. Mezami, a Pyct of clan Tzi, wore his usual short rat-hide tunic, kilt, rat-leather belt and bracers. Folded under his cape, his dragonfly wings fluttered nervously.

"Dreaming: darkly, you," he said in that deep, rumbling voice of his that in no way suited his toothpick-tall body. He stood on her chest, muscular arms crossed over his exposed six-pack abs.

Alina realized too late that she'd brought the Crow back with her, and the Crow couldn't tell friend from enemy. Using her hand, it tried grab him, but Mezami was bullet-quick: he windmill kicked out of reach, flying up a foot or two, buzzing around the Crow as it swatted at him.

Dodging, he said, "This for: sorry, I," and his tiny fist delivered a blow many orders of magnitude above his weight class, the backhanded slap of a trained wrestler several hundred times his mass.

The strike to Alina's gut squeezed the air from her lungs. She fell over, hugging herself, coughing.

The Crow had been winded, too.

Mezami buzzed over, offering her his tiny hand. She reached out with her pinky, which he grabbed, and he heaved her upright.

Wheezing, Alina rasped, "Thanks for holding back." She wasn't kidding. The last people Mezami had fought—Authority Enforcers—had had to undergo

emergency surgery and intensive care after the encounter. The one before
them—a hulking, sword-swinging murder machine—Mezami had drilled
through his chest like a mole through dirt.

Satisfied that Alina had become herself again, he landed on her knuckle like
a bird. "Helping: happy, I." He furrowed his mousy brow. "Go: where, you?"

Alina shook her head. "Somewhere I definitely shouldn't have." She walked
over to the red crow mask lying on top of her neatly folded black cloak. *Ida* and
Rego. Picking the items up, she added, "I'm starving. Let's see what's cooking."

"Ate: already, I. Am: full, I."

She welcomed the distraction. "Cool. And what was on the menu today?
More rats?"

"Wrestling: water snakes, good. Enjoyed: challenge, I."

"Alright, alright." She fist-bumped him with the fist he wasn't standing on.
"Well, I look forward to seeing what you make out of their skins."

"Shoes: need, I."

"Just what do you need shoes for, man?"

Solemnly, he said, "Fashion week: participating, I. 'Voguing' teach: Cho, me."

"Beautiful. Maybe tomorrow I'll throw down some planks for a runway. Can
already see it in my head."

She walked in silence for half a minute. "Hey, Mezami, I'd, uh—well, I'd just
appreciate it if you could keep my little episode to yourself. Wouldn't want anyone to worry about me, y'know?"

"Hiding: unwise, truth. Transformation: important, you. Should tell: Morphea, you."

"I will," she said. "When I'm ready."

He grunted. "Trust: you, I. Trust: me, you?"

"Of course, buddy. You're pretty much the only one who gets me around
here." Between the branches, the stars of the southwestern sky glinted. "My primary pal."

Flitting ahead, Mezami lingered at a cliff's edge. A far off mountain goat lifted
its bearded chin before leaping to another ledge, out of sight. This sent a shower
of stones sliding, which thudded against a boulder, knocking if free; the boulder
thundered downhill. Black blurs darted from the surrounding trees, taking to the
sky: concentric circles of crows, cawing their protests.

Alina watched them with the Pyct.

"I'm scared," she said. When he didn't jump in with a response, she continued, "I've always been the scrappy little guttersnipe. That's my story. But, if I
become stronger than any human who's ever lived, if I can sneak into dreams
like rooms—then, what am I? Who is Alina?"

Mezami cocked his head.

"I pray to Buthmertha, every night, that I'm more than Dimas's teachings.
More than his blood." She sucked on her lip, thinking. "Ruqastra calls it destiny,

but my body is a prison. Everything I do feeds her story about me, Dimas's story. There's no way out. The stronger I get, the more the walls close in."

He flicked her earlobe, drawing her eye. "Are: more, you."

"You can't tell Cho. She's the one person who still sees something of the old Alina inside me. She doesn't know that she's staring at a zombie. You can't tell her."

"Do: what, you? If see: you, she?"

"Well, she'll figure me out, sooner or later. See me for what I'm changing into. What'll I do then? Nothing. Cry, maybe. Because the true death is being forgotten. When she loses sight of the seventeen-year-old screwup who accidentally saved her life, my old self will be erased, and I'll completely become—"

Alina rapped her knuckles against the mushy bark of a dead tree. She allowed the unfinished thought to float up even as she and Mezami walked away.

Her breath, her words, were pecked to bits by the cackling crows.

7

CHO-ZEN

WINDING HER WAY UP the sheer, crumbling mountain trails on Kinneas's puttering scooter (his arms wrapped tightly around her waist), Cho set her eyes on the high, waxing moon. Stark outlines against its pale white face, the trees swayed like punch-drunk men, leaning on each other as the wind pummeled them.

On a tall rock among the pines perched a long shadow—Alina, tracking Cho and Kinneas's return. Craning neck, pivoting spotlight eyes. She had a knack for the *silent watcher* routine. And, was that a cloak she was wearing now? It flapped like a black flag.

From her nails to her nape, Cho shivered.

Uncertainly, she waved, then blinked.

Alina had abandoned her stony outpost, lost in the branch-strangled dark of the mountain.

Cho's nightmares had been worsening for months.

Morbin held many secrets, and none of them pleasant. Eilars couldn't help but casually spit a steady stream of haunting tales about the mountain. Supposedly, it'd once been home to a gang of bandits that worshiped a nameless fiend. The bandits had fed the creature human sacrifices and made candles from the corpses' rendered fat. Even farther back in time, a madman had squatted here, hiding from punishment, writing his thousand sins in a book he tied shut with a ribbon of Aelf-sinew. It was he, legend had it, who'd bound vengeful spirits to the pines and streams.

Because of such stories, Cho lost her appetite most days, glancing over her shoulder at the smallest noises. She'd tell herself it was nothing—that, in the end, old tales couldn't touch her if she didn't let them. History couldn't help but sink to the seafloor of time, far beneath the little people like her who treaded its waters. The thought comforted her, if only a little.

Much more unsettling than the past was the *present*. A… feeling governed the mountain, a weighty presence no amount of reasoning could explain away. Always, the woods remained eerie and oddly quiet, as if listening. Things that didn't *sound* like animals scratched at the base of her treehouse at night. And, the circle of faceless old statues by the fishpond gave her the impression of being watched by mindless, eyeless entities. She avoided that circle, even by daylight.

Alina and Morphea spent way too much time there, and Cho wanted no part of anything those two wackadoo witches cooked up. Of all the spooky, nightmare-fueling things on Morbin, they were the worst.

Most Maggos had at least a little strangeness to them, taking on some of the qualities of their magical element. For instance, Kinneas, as an Aquamancer, was just a teensy bit damp all the time. Not necessarily in a smelly way, but more like a "wow, it's humid today" sorta way. Totally forgivable and harmless. The waterworks flowed whenever he laughed too hard or got too excited. Also, he had to pee more often than most guys. (Not that she was paying too close attention to that kind of thing, though. That would be gross. And invasive. Anyway…) According to the books she'd read on the subject, Igniomancers tended to be more intensely emotional (playing into the "hot-head" stereotype); Machinamancers tended to rely on cold logic and reason; Caelomancers tended to think they were above everyone else; and so on. There were plenty of examples of spell-casters who didn't fit these generalizations, but many studies had shown, overall, a clear connection between personality type and magical skill set. Of course, the question remained: were people born with the quirks that made them most suited for a particular magical Discipline, or did Niima change the Maggo in small but interesting ways over time?

Either way, whatever it was that shaped them (nature, nurture, or Niima), Revomancers were flat-out disturbing.

Even before Cho had met her, Alina had never been normal, exactly. In a good way, though! Alina had been steady, strong. Like stone. Like the Geomancer her gramps had trained her to be. But now, after eighteen months (give or take) of Morphea's training and influence… It was bad enough when Alina had been all awkward jokes and choppy dance moves and the inability to make small talk with anyone. At least she and Cho had been able to laugh together over episodes of *Say No to the Bro, Bachelor Battle Royale,* and other trash Watchbox programming. Eventually, though, something changed. On the inside. After a while, Alina just seemed to stare at the contestants, hollowly, with sunken eyes— like she knew how and when each of them was going to die. Hanging out with her stopped being fun. So, yeah, they'd stopped pirating Watchbox signals. Too hard to do up here on Morbin, anyway.

More and more, Alina and Cho had kept to themselves. For the best, probably. Cho had her Epic Quest for Redemption to plan and execute; and Alina had, well, more raw birds to chew on. Or whatever she did these days.

Sometimes, Cho would snap awake and listen to the night noises. And she'd hear, drifting quietly as mist, Alina's voice—speaking in lots of different languages, none of which Cho could understand. Once, she'd recorded and played back what was said for Alina, whose only response had been a blank-eyed stare.

The terrors that seeped into Cho's dreams were like those words—alien.

She just wanted her friend back, for things to go back to normal. Failing that, she had to get off Morbin. Fast. Before the fitful nights scrambled her brain, draining her sanity like water through a cracked drinking glass.

Peeling her clothes from herself like slimy layers off a moldy onion, Cho dived into the stream that ran from the spring buried in Morbin's heart down to its rocky toes. She bathed herself like an otter, scraping away the gunk with her fingers, rubbing with her palms until her flesh was raw and pink.

She traced the old surgery scars from her palms, between her knuckles, up her elbow, to her shoulder blades. She massaged the deep grooves in her neck and jaw, feeling the smooth protective plates under her skin under which quietly hummed the circuitry and processors linked to her lymphatic, circulatory, respiratory, and adrenal systems. Hugging herself, she felt the swelling of her breath, artificial lungs expanding against reinforced ribs.

She often wondered why she'd been made to be this way. She'd been a perfectly healthy child, as far as she could recall. There had to have been a reason for the testing, the operations, the needles and knives and months and months of recovery in quiet, empty white rooms.

A proximity ping in the back of her brain made her turn. "Anything you can do I can do better, Eilars. I'm the newer model."

No more than a dozen feet away, Eilars lifted his metallic skull-face, his sea-foam-blue flashlight eyes glowing in the night, raspy voice soft but carrying far: "You were born human."

She waded towards him. "Peh. What's human?"

Eilars flung her towel at her along with some river-washed clothes (all sun-dried). He didn't avert his eyes, and she felt no sense of shame. There was nothing between them but air.

She finished dressing. When he spoke, his steely teeth clicked like tiny tap shoes. "You're covered in traces of blasting powder. The night went well."

"It's a miracle I'm not dead." She walked over, sat beside him on the straw mat. "You're proud of me."

"Pride isn't what I feel. Relieved, sure."

Like everything else about Eilars, how he'd ended up on Mount Morbin was a mystery. Something to do with Alina's granddad. The lonely old android refused to say more, and although he and Ruqastra seemed more like enemies than roommates (mountain-mates?), the witch respected him enough not to dish. Even though she clearly knew his secrets.

To Cho, Eilars was a venerable elder, a confidante, and a friend. She'd known him only a short while, but in that time she'd learned respect for him—guardian, watcher, gardener, zen master. The fact that he was dying tortured her. Many of the rivets and smaller mechanical joints that held together his black metal bones had rusted red like burst blood vessels; frequently, these days, his fingers locked into a fist as he was sweeping, sewing patches into clothing, stirring a ladle around a pot. He would stare at his hand, unable to do anything more.

Always moving with purpose, he still only walked in the same circles, day in and day out. His life was a closed loop, a prison from which he could only watch himself fall apart. Was this what he'd imagined his life would be? Had he chosen this for himself?

Sometimes, in a flash of clarity, Cho felt certain of the truth: he'd been left here on this mountain, to gather dust and to die.

"What were you hoping to prove?" he asked.

She'd been ready for that one. "That the Walazzins aren't beyond justice."

"Justice?" His chuckle was the clipped whisper of a stone skipping across a lake's surface.

"For holding my town hostage."

"*Your* town, you say?"

"I've lived here long enough. And, this is my family's country."

"So, if anyone should blow it up, it should be you?"

In the moments she took to bite back her reply, she fumed at his skinless face locked in a never-aging but increasingly decaying smile; how he held himself with pride, even though the cold mountain rains had nearly completed their slow work of eroding him; most of all, she hated to see how the wind weaved between his bones because it caused her to ask herself just how different they really were, the two of them.

When she looked at Eilars, she saw what she feared she'd become—artificial, a replica. Hollow.

He was an android who called himself a man, a father whose wife and child had been taken from him; Cho, a daughter who'd lost her parents and brothers and sisters; and they were both made to be something other than they wanted. She still had her bag of skin stretched over the wires, carbon nanoweave, and reinforced limbs, but she might just be every bit the walking reminder of death he was. A newer model, maybe, but still only the skeleton of a girl.

His jaw levered open, and he filled the silence: "Truct—and many towns like it—have always been oppressed. And probably always will be."

Where was this coming from? Eilars's emotional range usually bounced between 'gloomy' and 'grumbling,' but she'd never seen him this fatalistic before. "Things could change. The Battle at City Hall two years ago—"

"Not this again."

"—seriously! Who was there, at Pluto Plaza, huh? Pretty sure it was me. So, I know that it's not too late to make a difference. The Authority is *not* untouchable. The Landsider Aelfravers got a raw deal, but they fought the good fight and—"

"There are no good fights. There's only suffering. Yours or your enemies'. Usually both."

"So, what? We should all let The Authority do whatever it wants, even if it's killing us?"

"I thought it was the Walazzins you were against. Make up your mind. Either way, I guess, it doesn't matter. Justice can't side against those who *write* the laws, Cho."

"The law and justice aren't the same thing."

"The upstart Aelfravers, from what you've told me, are in the wind. Same as anyone else who's ever challenged The Authority, they're fair game. The more you play in the deep end, the likelier you'll drown. Where is there room for justice?"

"Thanks for the pep talk." She moped, grasping for a counter. "Not all the Ravers have been caught. I've been tracking the rumors. And, and Alina's still around."

"Time. Less or more, it depends. But all it'll take is time; the troublemakers will be caught. Including your friend. Including you and me. It always ends the same way for those like us."

"Should we just grin and take it? As speaking out and resisting leads to mock trials? Life sentences? Death penalties? The Walazzins run the whole show now, Eilars. The people who killed my whole family are in charge."

"I'm not saying you should do nothing."

"Then why this lecture?"

"You have to reassess your—Cho, I won't be around… forever. And I want nothing more than for you to outlive me, hopefully by a very healthy margin. For that to happen, you need to understand. Justice is an illusion, an idea that changes shape according to point of view. Revenge, now, that's tangible, real. You have been used your whole short life. If you want to survive, you'll have to claim your own corner of the world *with violence* because that is the only truly universal language. But you won't ever make it if you fight in the name of smoke and air. Admit that you don't care about what happens to the Landsiders who rebelled. Them or their pointless, spell-slinging death spiral. Admit that you don't care about Torvir Province or any of the wasted fools living here. What you want is perfectly natural—reasonable, even. You want those who wronged you to suffer and be destroyed. Are they cruel?"

"Yes."

"Then that's all the motivation you need."

"You're wrong about me, Eilars."

He raked a little clot of dirt with his creaking metal fingers. "I'm not doing this for me." She got up. "Not just for me."

"You'll see my side. You will." He gripped her ankle, preventing her from leaving. "D'you think the cousin who sold out your parents, the secret police who executed them, or the Enforcers who would snatch you up and sell you back to your abusers—you think they worry about 'honor' and 'justice'?"

"I want to be better than them."

"You already are. So much better and kinder and—"

That caught her off-guard.

He slumped, releasing her. "Forgive me. It's not my place." His demeanor was suddenly very different.

She was still angry, but the feeling sank to the bottom of her heart like a rock-laden, lake-tossed corpse. "It's my fault for telling you so much about my life. I'm poison."

"Stop that," he said softly. "I'm glad. Glad we knew one another, Cho. Just glad."

"All this past tense is making me uncomfortable."

"Forget it." He waved her off. "Dinner in an hour." Dusted his hands with a *clank-clank-clank*. Three steps away, he half-turned. "If you're going to keep trading favors with Thredders, you can't stay the lost daughter of a ruling family. As Cho-Zen you can be anything you need to be. Choraelia Torvir, however, can only die a second time."

8

ALINA

SCOWLING AT THE VIAL of iridescent, chalky goop, Alina worked up the nerve to down its contents in one gulp. Ruqastra called the stuff a "fortifier"—her homebrewed *Auggie* to enhance Revomantic powers. A secret family recipe she refused to even hint at.

Tasted like blue cheese mixed with damp paper, but Alina drank it every night before dinner. No cheating.

Or Ruqastra would force it down her throat.

Shooting for Most Unsettling Butler of the Year, Eilars always seemed to be scuttling around with a shovel, a hammer and some nails, or a washboard. Alina never noticed him until she could feel the heat radiating from his components. According to Ruqastra, he'd been living on Morbin, alone, since before she was born. Three decades at least.

That had left the android plenty of time to keep the hedges trim and cultivate a healthy population of colorful fish. Small wonder he'd lost his mind. Alina could empathize.

It had quickly become clear that the unease between them went both ways. The machinery of his skull limited his range of emotions, but he found subtler ways of letting her know he disliked her. While teaching her, Cho, and Kinneas the finer points of martial arts, he'd demo hook kicks and pressure point jabs on Alina, and, with her on the ground, he'd show her his back. A sign of contempt for one's enemy, a challenge. *Do it*, he seemed to say. *Come at me.* It was like he expected her to lash out at him. He thought he could sense something in her, and in his eyes she saw a reflection of herself she grew to hate.

Still, he was undeniably useful. Thanks to his training, she'd picked up right where she'd left off with Dimas years ago, and she felt more confident than ever in her reflexes.

For months, she'd wondered what deal they'd struck, Eilars and Dimas, way back when. How cruel it must have been for Alina to inherit the rage that came packaged with it.

One day, Alina had discovered that Eilars was compelled to obey her commands. A condition of the old agreement? An overdeveloped sense of loyalty? Wherever the motivation came from, he resented her for her power over him. He resented her more still when she refused to abuse that power. The more humanely she treated him, the wider the distance between them. Eventually, he couldn't stomach training her any longer.

"My life ended because of you," he'd said then.

"I haven't done anything to you."

"But you're the reason." He'd been absently rubbing his shoulder where, in fading, chipping yellow was painted his model number. *E1-L4-R5.* "For this prison."

Drunk on her mental cocktail of gratitude and guilt, she'd said, "Neither of us asked for this."

"And yet—" he clenched his skeletal teeth— "only one of us benefits. When I look at you, all I see is him. You're birds of a feather."

"Then you don't know me at all."

"Just leave me, hatchling. Haven't I given you enough yet? Leave me to tend to the vegetable garden, muck the pool, and spend my last days without the damnable chitterings of carrion feeders. If the gods exist and a single one of them is kind, they'll give me the dignity of death before you ask more of me."

Yep. That was pretty much how they'd left it. The deepest conversation they'd had since amounted to a pair of "G'mornings."

In addition to his cleaning duties, Eilars took it upon himself to prepare dinner each night. It seemed to be a source of pride for him, but, in so doing, he revealed the fatal flaw of his programming. Culinary masterpieces were not his bread and butter; he had a bad habit of over-salting, so all his stews tasted like chunky seawater. He also only used ingredients he could scrounge from the mountain. (Like Ruqastra, he was paranoid about leaving Morbin's confines. Or, maybe he was unable to?) Still, food was food. Heavily watered down, it wasn't so bad. And, on the nights when Kinneas brought packaged goods from the only grocery store still open in Truct, the overall quality of the meal skyrocketed.

Tonight was one such night, thankfully. After her harrowing experience with Mateus and his protector made of light, she could use some plastic-wrapped pre-buttered garlic bread and sandwich cookies to accompany Eilars's root-vegetable slop.

They were all there, eating together, for the first time in weeks. Maybe a couple months. Near the creepy gaze of the seven weather-worn statues, they sat under the awning built in the branches of a centuries-old tree. Snaking around two-by-four pillars buried in the dirt were solar-powered lights that sputtered until Ruqastra (without looking up from her bowl) waved her hand, magically refilling them with energy.

Taking the place of conversation, a whole lot of throat-clearing and clanking of cutlery on plates.

At the head of the rectangular fold-out table, Eilars ate even though he didn't need to. Maybe he thought he was doing the others a favor, trying to appear less strange. No such gesture could compensate for his appearance, though: he looked like a midnight-colored skeleton with glowing, lidless turquoise eyes. Alina hadn't yet worked up the courage to ask him what had happened to his skin. All androids, as far as she knew, had been built to resemble humans, which meant they came standard with epidermises like real humans'. And eyelids. Even though these machines had been outlawed years and years ago, and Eilars probably had no way to perform maintenance on himself, he should still have had his outer protective layer of skin. After all, that stuff was supposed to be weather- and even bullet-proof.

The circuits and cogs in his body fizzing and whirring, Eilars caught her staring and fixed her with his unblinking eyes. She quickly looked away.

To his (and Alina's) left sat Cho. With her uneven, long-in-the-front-short-in-the-back green wig, dangling earrings, yellow eyeshadow, and combat knife tucked into her boot, she now looked like the kind of girl who could have buried her old self in a shallow grave and not missed a wink of sleep about it. Was it still possible to save that old Cho somehow? Bring back that snarky kid who'd once risked her neck for Mezami and Alina, even though she herself had been drowning in trouble? Not so long ago, together, she and Alina had learned to swim. But now Alina was adrift, treading water, and Cho was a creature of the depths.

Across from Cho, Kinneas Amming combed his wavy brown hair away from his eyes, fumbling his way through a joke. As soon as he'd finished his helping of stew, he tossed a sandwich cookie in his mouth, stripped down to his undershirt and boxers, and dashed into the nearby stream. With Eilars demanding that he cease bothering the fish this instant, Kinneas laughed and swam straight up the short waterfall ahead of him. He cannonballed down right after, launching himself into water that was shallow enough to guarantee he'd break several bones. Except, he waved his hands as he dropped, and the stream rose up to meet him. He slipped into the column of water, and, for a few seconds, hovered in its middle, flexing. When his concentration broke, the water bubble that held him popped, and he fell on his backside with a groan. He wasn't seriously hurt, though, so Cho and Alina laughed. Cho sauntered over to poke him in his bony ribs, and his blush spread from head to toe.

To the left of Kinneas's now vacant seat, Mezami had nestled himself onto a pincushion from which he watched the proceedings with all the stateliness that a rodent's face can muster.

On the opposite end of the table from Eilars, Ruqastra hadn't said a word all night. She wasn't ever much for casual conversation, but she'd usually toss out at least a cryptic metaphor or two. A few phrases of nonsense masquerading as wisdom. Presently, her lips were pursed, her gold eye fixed on Eilars's stew (basically a brick of salt, melted in boiling water).

Having had enough of the awkward silence, Alina said, "Hey, Cho, so, what'd you two get up to today?"

Cho shrugged. "Stuff."

"Care to sling me a detail or two?"

"I don't know. We got some food and—" shooting Kinneas a look—"chilled out."

He snickered.

"I don't get it," said Alina.

"It's an inside joke," said Cho. "Stop looking at me like that. We lead really boring lives, Li. Supes hum-drum, you wouldn't care to know more."

By the way Cho's eyelid crinkled, just for a second, Alina knew that her friend was lying. Odds were ten to one that she'd been out Thredding again in some weirdo's basement, or tagging abandoned buildings with Rooster. Or, hells, maybe she'd done way worse. But, being a firm believer that some secrets are necessary, Alina let her keep this one. A teenager wanting a little privacy? How extraordinary.

Besides, Cho's dodgy front didn't bother Alina half as much as her teacher's gold eye, which now fell squarely upon her.

Ruqastra sighed quietly. "Ordinarily, what an Elemental princess does with her precious free time is none of my concern. Yet, my own late master—your grandfather—extracted an oath from me that I would instruct and keep you safe. I cannot do that if pampered sky-children and their petty desires draw undue attention upon all our heads."

Voice rattling, Eilars said, "Be kinder to the girl. She's been through enough."

Cho chimed in, "I'm no Elemental. Nothing like 'em."

The comment dragged Ruqastra's focus off Alina. She breathed in deeply through her nose. "Hahh. But I can smell it on you, child. You're blue-blooded, through and through. What flows through your veins? Barely more than air."

"Stop picking on her," Alina snapped.

"I can stick up for myself, thanks," said Cho.

Still dripping, Kinneas rushed over. "Hey, let's not do this. Not again. Come on, we—" His voice was drowned out.

The five-way shouting match (Mezami abstaining) continued until Ruqastra swelled to triple her normal height. Towering over them all, her voice boomed. "Shut up, all of you." She flicked a giant finger at Alina, and the red mask flew from the table onto Alina's face, the clasps latching automatically behind her head. "I will not repeat myself again. Wear it, or *else*."

The mask slightly askew, Alina's nose was smushed uncomfortably. She couldn't see out of one eye, and she fumbled with it while Ruqastra shrank down.

Amid the stunned silence, the Revomancer finished her meal with sharp, jerking gestures. Rising, she turned to Eilars, inclined her head an inch or two in thanks and blinked out of sight.

The android collected the bowls and tableware, shuffling away with them.

Sucking on his teeth, Kinneas said, "Still not the worst dinner we've had."

Cho punched his arm. As Alina peered at her through the one properly aligned eye hole, Cho told her, "That thing makes your head look like a spiky pimple."

"Thanks," said Alina, her voice muffled. "Oh, and don't worry. I'm sure I can untangle my hair on my own. As you were, all of you."

With a click of her tongue, Cho hopped over and began helping Alina. Once the mask was adjusted, Alina said, "Wear this damn thing all night? The beak's gonna to be a real pain. I hate sleeping on my back."

Bending as if to get a good look up Alina's nose, Kinneas said, "I can't be the only one worried that thing's going to haunt my every waking minute?"

"I like it less than you, bud. Count on it. It's just a feeling, but it reminds me of…" She shouldn't tell them about the memory that *Ida* called forth. A memory not her own, of gliding through the moonless sky to land atop a tower. Of slashing her way through waves of guards until she'd reached the lowest level, where the hatch awaited. The hatch and, below it, the darkness and the children…

"Reminds you of what?" Cho said.

Alina shook her head. These memories were of death. She must bury them.

The Crow detached itself from one of the trees and took a tentative step forward.

"Don't," Alina warned it.

"Eesh, alright, forget it." Cho put her hand on Alina's shoulder. "Steady, there, Li?"

She blinked. "Yeah, all good. I'll deal." If only she could show them the magnetic, crackling eyes of the Crow. If only they could walk around in its shadow inside her head awhile, wrap themselves in the tangle of her memories twisting tighter and tighter and— "Anyway, doesn't matter how I feel, does it? Ruqastra's raging too much lately. Better keep the peace, do what she says."

"For once."

"Whoa there. I listen." Alina took a breath. "Sometimes. When it makes sense to."

"If it were me," said Kinneas, the grin on his face telegraphing his pun, "thinking about taking off that mask? I wouldn't *dream* of it."

Cho and Alina groaned.

Cho said, "Don't quit your day job, Water Boy."

"Ladies, please. My stage name is *Mr.* Water Boy."

And so, the quips continued, Alina tuning them out more and more over the next few minutes. She watched the Crow lurch closer as she sat on her own vibrating arms that tickled with the urge to catch a fish and beat it to death with a river stone.

A most welcome distraction, her phone vibrated against her hip.

It was such an alien feeling now, getting a text, let alone three in a row. How long had it been since she'd *texted* anyone? She really only kept this burner phone in case of emergencies. (Ruqastra had destroyed her old one for fear of it being traced. Smart move. Awful, but smart.) Actually, how had someone gotten ahold of this number? She hadn't given it out to, well, anyone.

Her thoughts racing with questions concerning the mysterious texts, she opened her messenger app and read them.

She read them again. Then a third time.

Glancing at Alina, Cho said something.

"Fine," Alina mumbled automatically. She couldn't stop staring at the words on the screen. They just weren't making any sense.

Facing her, head between his legs as he energetically stretched, Kinneas said, "We sparring tonight?"

"What? Oh. Nah. I'm just, uh, gonna get some sleep, I think. Sorry. Been a long day." Without another word, Alina rushed off to be alone. Alone with her thoughts and the trio of texts that had sent her tumbling down a mental chasm of "what ifs," "hows," and other vague and frustrating questions.

The texts read:

Sincerest apologies for the unsolicited message. However, there are some things I'd very much like to discuss with you. Please meet me at Glaric's Diner on Pender's Way.

It concerns the man you last saw at a lighthouse.

Come tonight. Come alone.

She knew immediately who must have sent these, though she couldn't understand how that was possible.

He was, after all, *dead.* She'd read the summary of the murder investigation. She'd watched the broadcasts of the court cases in which the lawyers and feuding family members squabbled over his assets. She'd followed the whole story as closely as she could on the Watchbox and via the Darkthreads, until she'd had to cut herself off from the outside world, from all news, when she'd come to live on Mount Morbin.

What if, in the year or more that she'd been trapped up here, there'd been a surprising—no, a miraculous development? What if it was possible that he'd *survived*, somehow?

Quelling her terror and excitement proved impossible. There was only one person this "man you last saw at a lighthouse" could be referring to. Two years ago, she'd watched the live broadcast of his funeral, but this message—

It couldn't have come from anyone other than Ordin Ivoir.

9

CHO-ZEN

MEZAMI HUNG BY HIS tail from a branch, arms crossed, body curling inward with each snore. Alina had claimed to go off to sleep, but Cho sensed her nowhere within the confines of the camp. Off somewhere being uncanny again, probably. Ruqastra's more dramatic disappearance was nothing unusual, and Cho didn't really care where she'd gone. With both the dream-witches absent, she might actually catch a rare good night's sleep.

Once the plates and spoons were washed and dried, Cho, Eilars, and Kinneas began their biweekly ritual of martial arts training. The android's motions were fluid, precise, in contrast with the clicking, scraping, and popping of his joints. He led them through the same forms, again and again, correcting their stances, straightening their wrists, turning their heads—just so.

As always, after forms came sparring. From the start, he'd ordered them to strike open-handed, lessening the damage they dealt to each other, but they'd never once worn protective pads. "If you can't take a knee or elbow and keep fighting, you're already a walking corpse," he'd say. "Unpredictability. Speed. Tenacity. These separate the victors from the dead."

It had been some months since Kinneas had last pulled his punches against Cho. She was too fast now. Too strong. She'd far surpassed him, and didn't seem to feel pain like he did. Lately, she'd made sure to go a bit easier on the kid, but Eilars only berated him more intensely.

"Every strike, a killing blow," the android would bark. "This isn't a dance, boy. Stop *flowing*. Crisp movements—there. Relaxation and… *tension*." He'd often punctuate the ends of his sentences with demo punches, sending his students stumbling backward, gasping. Sometimes he'd repeat a movement or a syllable, getting stuck like a corrupted music file, and they would wait for him to snap back to reality.

Tonight, however, he seemed more focused than ever before. He came at them with hammer strikes and roundhouses hard enough to break bones. Only by working together, counterattacking from both sides, were they able to come out of the bout with only nasty bruises. When Cho spin-kicked him into Kinneas's leg-sweep, and he fell to the ground, he lay there a moment. His expression showed neither pride nor satisfaction, only resignation. She helped him up, understanding from the look they shared that he'd made up his mind about something. What that something was, though, she had no idea.

By the end of the session, Cho and Kinneas were panting, their clothes soaked through, and Eilars gave one of his grunts of dismissal.

They scraped the drippings from the cooking pot with their fingers, licking them clean. Then, they bathed in the natural springs.

New blisters, bruises, and cuts covered the healing ones; their muscles and joints always ached. That's how it had been, ever since Cho had moved to the mountain, since she'd befriended the strange, inhuman guardian of this secret sanctuary: drill, eat, wash, sleep. And again.

As was his habit, after second-dinner, Kinneas lingered just a little past his welcome. Hovering near Cho, he seemed to be waiting for her to say or do something. She had no idea what that might be.

She was grateful when Eilars came over and clucked at the boy. Kinneas, per usual, took the hint, stretched, and said, "Guess I'll be headed home, then."

Though all she wanted was some peace and quiet, she did feel bad for him, having to drive home, alone, in the dark, on his little scooter. "I could walk you to your ride."

"That's okay." He smiled. "Same time next week?"

She nodded and gave a two-fingered wave. "'Night."

Awkwardly mirroring the salute, he shouldered his pack and followed the stream out of the clearing, down the path, around the bend, and out of sight.

Eilars poured near-boiling water from an antique tea kettle. Droplets of soapy water splashed onto his metal bones, which glistened in the moonlight as he scrubbed the bowls and utensils clean. Without looking up, he said, "Good kid."

"Yeah."

He dried the dishes with a clean rag, stacked them, and carried them back to the hut where he slept. He returned to Cho, and, like a wriggling eel, the silence stretched between them.

She knelt, watching the fish flit between the reflections of the constellations. She enjoyed her and Eilars's banter. It was… simple and honest, with much of their meaning going unsaid. In a lot of ways, it was the opposite of her interactions with Alina.

When Alina had gone to "get some sleep," her heart rate had been elevated, her pupils had dilated, and she'd gotten all fidgety. Long story short: she'd lied.

Cho used to get angry about the lies. Now, though, she considered them harmless enough; there was no malice to them. Alina simply couldn't own up to or face certain truths, so she masked them with simpler, cleaner excuses.

Anyway, she would always come around. Might take her a while, but her mind would turn the same stone over and over and over again until, however long it took, she made sense of its shape. Usually, she'd come clean right around the time Cho had figured out the real situation on her own.

What could you expect, really? Their friendship had begun with lies about everything, from who they were to what they wanted. Over time, though—supported by all the untruths—they'd built a bridge between them. Each had lived a hard life. Therefore, each understood how lifesaving and necessary a good lie could be. Even when Alina was lying to her face—and Cho could almost always tell when it happened—she did it to protect both of them. From each other. From her problems.

Alina was still trying to take care of Cho in the only way she knew how: by avoiding her when things got tough. It was a ridiculous way to handle problems, sure, but she had a lot of growing up to do. Unlike Cho, who, at fourteen, had absolutely everything figured out.

The android's unsteady footfalls, behind her. The squeaking of his knees. He was headed to bed. Well, to power down, she supposed.

"Eilars."

He turned. The glow of his lidless eyes accentuated his jaw- and cheekbones, which gleamed like rain-washed black stone. Though ghoulish, his unchanging death-mask of a face comforted her.

"You want to... talk?" he asked.

"It's nothing. Just..."

He faced her, as if squaring off with an opponent.

"I've been wondering—I don't wanna pry, is all."

"Ask your question."

"Why are you so decent to me but you hate Alina so much?"

The downward swoop of his gaze carried all the weight of his pensiveness. As he spoke, Cho analyzed his emotions through his vocal patterns: his inflection, tone, and speech pattern were markers of the sadness buried inside. A forgotten temple, choked by the sands of ages. "I don't hate her," he said, as if trying to convince himself. "Her grandfather was a devil. With the one hand, he'd give—promises, secrets, favors. With the other... Well." He rested his skeletal palm on his scratched tungsten chest-plate, bowing his head. "Look at me."

Rather than drill deeper and risk cracking the vast world lost under the shell of him, she simply said, "I'm sorry."

Another length of silence uncoiled like a snake, and from its fangs dripped the venom of his next words, "I thought about escaping this place in the beginning. But I had sworn myself to service. Of course, I don't regret the sacrifice I made, binding myself to the K'vich name to secure my family's safety. Although—" He lifted his gaze to the stars, his voice a crackling, malfunctioning whisper. "I have a son. I don't know if he's alive or dead now, but he'd easily be old enough to be your grandfather. You and he are nothing alike, really. Not in any measurable way. Even so, you remind me of him. I don't know why. Wishful thinking? Corrupted memory banks? My failing processor?" His black-metal hand shot up, dug into the back of his steel-and-wire-mesh neck. Struggling with it, he then gasped in time with an audible *snap*, and he yanked free a small, rectangular thing.

He held out his hand, waiting.

Cho had never seen a Demon, but—scrutinized by the bright-eyed, shadow-dappled, machined skeleton who waited, perfectly still—she wouldn't fault someone for thinking Eilars might just be one. Yet, she knew better.

She approached. "What is it?"

The microchip he held in his palm was slick with brown vegetable oil (hand-pressed by Eilars himself). Cho focused on the serial number. No matter how many times she scanned it, the tiny bar code remained unreadable. Her inability to figure it out made sense, in its own way: android tech, now illegal, was a well-kept secret. Even her black market cybernetic parts wouldn't be able to parse the code.

Dropping the chip onto her outstretched hand, Eilars said only, "Don't repeat my mistake. You are no one's dog. Not The Authority's, nor the K'vich girl's." His fingers clamped onto her shoulder. "Take your revenge."

He left her alone with the oil-slick chip and the fish blubbering in their pond and the moon and stars.

She took the short walk back to the tree house she had built with Kinneas's help last summer. Climbing the rope ladder, she brushed aside the spiderwebs and nudged open the trapdoor. Pulling the ladder up after her, she closed the trapdoor again.

Datasticks hung from the ceiling like wind chimes, each one full of thousands of pirated digital textbooks, novels, instruction manuals, and more. The works covered every subject she'd ever taken an interest in or thought useful—vehicle maintenance and repair, hand-to-hand combat, wilderness survival, weapons training, anatomy, psychology, fitness and nutrition, meditation and mindfulness, spirituality, tactics and strategy, history, politics and government, economics, philosophy, Niimantic theory…

From her pack, she procured a small resealable plastic baggie, carefully placing the chip inside of it. She then rolled into her sleeping bag, her tired mind replaying Eilars's words again and again.

As the onset of dreams stripped it of its meaning, the sentence made less and less sense: *Take your revenge.*

Take your reave-edge.

Tackle real henge.

Taco meal hedge.

And then she dreamed of bushes made of food. Kinneas lived in her pocket; also, he was a salmon. Alina wasn't there, though. She had to get the cobwebs out of her hair before her big group date with a frog and a fly and some other animals. It was very important that Cho go find her, so that Cho could help her get ready by making friends with a bunch of rabbits. That way, they could finally catch the big hairy slug in a bottle.

Very important stuff.

10

ALINA

R EGO SWIRLING BEHIND HER like a black cloud on a starless night, Alina felt just a little bit silly as she hunched over the handlebars of Cho's moped, snaking along the mountain road toward Truct. A Maggo like her, reduced to stealing a motorized bicycle that hiccupped black exhaust every few hundred yards.

So much for her grand destiny, eh?

Ida she'd tucked into her backpack. She told herself she'd hidden it away because it impeded her vision too much to wear while riding. Really, the thought of putting it on made her sweaty and twitchy.

Its constant whispering didn't help.

It was late enough that there was no one on the road with her. The outer neighborhoods of Truct weren't exactly famous for their thriving nightlife.

During the hour-long ride, she was left alone with her thoughts. An extremely dangerous predicament.

The moped's sputtering little engine fell still, Alina flicking the kickstand into place.

After she'd wrapped the chain around the nearest street lamp and snapped the lock shut, she stuck her tongue out at the cracked screen of the corner bulletin board which showed her younger self scowling into the camera for her first mugshot (Disorderly Conduct and Resisting Arrest).

Footsteps echoing along the side-streets, Alina pulled up *Rego's* hood. The witching-hour chill burrowed into her bones. And, all the while, *Ida's* muffled warning whispers hissed from between the teeth of her bag's zipper.

She looked around at the short, grungy-walled buildings and rotten scaffolding. This was no longer her town, and she wasn't welcome, but she had a right—a need—to be here tonight.

Again, the Crow was waiting for her. The yellow lights of its hollow eyes betrayed no emotion; its head twisted, creaking, to follow her progress as she—ignoring it—pulled open the glass door of Glaric's Diner and stepped inside.

The Diner was one of the few local mom-and-pop establishments that hadn't been shuttered as a result of The Authority's occupation of Truct. To anyone not in the know, this might seem strange: there were hardly ever any customers inside the single-story, rectangular building; no one sat at any of the corner tables or high stools lining the counter. The black-and-white checkered floor, the milkshake containers, the steel sinks, fryers, and ice cream freezers were coated with a combo of dust and grime. The owner, Glaric, rarely spoke, and, when he did, he mostly uttered one of three grunts meaning: "What do you want?"; "Anything else?"; or, "Pay up and get out."

But Alina, who'd always been excellent at sticking her nose where it didn't belong, knew Glaric's secret. A few years ago, he'd inherited a fortune from a relative. For whatever reason, though, he'd decided to keep running the Diner. By looking at him, you'd never know the dude was a millionaire. Maybe he hadn't upgraded his lifestyle because he couldn't imagine what else he'd do with himself. Maybe he stayed tight-lipped because he lacked faith in the morality of his fellow Tructians. Probably a good call. In Alina's darker moments, as her bills had piled up, even she had briefly entertained the idea of robbing him. (She hadn't gone through with it, though. Surely, in this case, it *wasn't* the thought that counted.)

Contrary to his gruff and unfriendly demeanor, Glaric did have a soft spot. He'd slid a free shake or two Alina's way over the years. And, every once in a while, a charity fundraiser would receive a large anonymous donation, or some kid's medical bills would be paid in full. Glaric flew under the radar, which Alina certainly could respect.

Even before the occupation, the main form of entertainment had been to peer out at occasional passersby through parted blinds, tracking their every movement. Alina hated having eyes on her, so Glaric's place (open 8 AM to 2 AM, every day) had provided a safe haven, where she could go unnoticed. Tucked away in her little corner with a book or her favorite Billie & The Were-wolf album blasting from her second-hand earphones.

It being one of her old haunts, she knew the place—and its drifter customer base—quite well. So, the woman in the all-white, dressy, sleeveless jumpsuit stood out immediately. Knees crossed, she'd claimed the far corner, away from the windows and drafty door. A tablet rested on its stand in front of her, display-ing holographic images of the late-night news. Knotted around her high neckline she wore a black cravat with three diamond studs. The effortlessness of her tou-sled, chin-length platinum hair—her marble-smooth skin—suggested a lot of time and attention went into her routine.

Catching sight of Alina, she switched off her tablet and narrowed her hazel eyes.

She nodded toward the booth seat across the square table from her.

Two emotions fought their way to the front of the line in Alina's mind. First, disappointment; this wasn't Ordin. Second, curiosity; who was this person who knew so much?

Unsure if she was walking into a trap or not, Alina flared her Niima, ready to cast if needed.

"Thank you for coming." The woman's voice was high, clear, with a slight rasp at the tail-end of her words. "I wasn't certain you would."

Folding the ends of her long black cloak onto her lap, Alina took her seat. "And just who are you, then?"

From her clothing to her brand-new omnipad to the way her angular eye-brows arched as she flashed her perfect teeth—everything about her advertised her wealth. She looked twenty-five but could've been seventy thanks to plastic surgery, gene therapy, organ cloning, etc. The super rich could bribe time—and even death—to ignore them. For a while.

Beyond the lab-engineered beautiful symmetry of this stranger, there was something familiar, too.

"Before I give you my name," she said, eyes narrowing and lips pursing, "I need some assurances."

"Sure…?"

"You are a mage, and I am not. How can I be certain you are not imperson-ating the woman I came here to meet?"

"Could ask you the same."

"We should prove it to each other then. You came here thinking you had been contacted by Ordin Ivoir, or someone close to him. Is that not so?"

Careful. Alina had almost blurted, "Yeah. That's right," but caught herself.

"Do you remember his last words to you?" the woman asked.

Caught off-guard, Alina wondered how anyone could have known about Or-din's final message to her—the one he had composed but never sent. No, she decided, this rando couldn't possibly be talking about that note. Alina herself had only discovered it by sheer, dumb luck, snatching it out of the Sea of Deleted Comments.

Instead, the stranger was probably referring to Ordin's lighthouse, the Ordin Airy, the virtual reality lobby he had built as a base for his dives into the seedier corners of the Darkthreads. Alina remembered that day clearly, when he'd kidnapped her, Mezami, and Cho to prevent them from getting entangled in the Rave on the Bane of New El. Her having been at the Airy was a detail that no one except for her or Ordin—or someone who'd been very close to him—could possibly have known.

Alina searched her memories of that night, when it had been raining hard. That storm had washed away all her old conceptions of self and all her illusions about Ordin. She could see him now as clearly as she had then. Lying in the gutter runoff, battered by rainwater, he'd looked up at her, raised his pale hand...

Under the table, Alina clenched her fists. "He said, 'I wasn't lying.'"

The woman in the white suit nodded slowly. The corners of her ensnaring eyes grew damp. "Other than himself, only three people ever knew about the island of his lost youth." She held up three fingers, ticking them off as she said, "Father, you, and me." Her slender-fingered hand speared across the table, hovering in front of Alina, who met her eyes. "Ordin was my brother. My name is Ivion."

Tentatively, Alina took her hand. "He didn't mention you."

"Ordin never liked to talk about family, for which I don't blame him. Our parents... Well, it is enough to know that they did not attend his funeral for fear of losing out on a lucrative business deal. Something about rubber." Ivion released Alina's hand but held eye-contact. "I was there for the service, as were the staff, and reporters, of course."

"So." Tears traced an arc down Alina's chin, hanging there like bats. "He really is dead." For too long, she'd dared to hope.

Face set, rigid, as if carved from soft marble, Ivion nodded again.

Alina fidgeted with *Rego's* hem. "Those last couple weeks, how much did he tell you about what happened at The Capital?"

"Not everything, but enough to be certain that, were he here, he would rightly apologize to you."

Alina didn't know what to do with that. "If" he were alive. What good were "ifs" anyway?

Her elbows thudded onto the table. "Well, I'm here. So?"

"Do you want the short, blunt, ugly pitch, or the long, flowery one I practiced during the entire shuttle ride here?"

"Blunt, I guess. Get to the point."

One hand primly folded over the other, Ivion said, "I want your help in avenging my brother."

Alina stared at those long-nailed fingers as they interlaced with all the delicateness of antique pocket watch gears.

Glaric finally shuffled over to take their order.

Alina was grateful to stall. "Coffee, five sugars."

Assuming a radiant smile, Ivion ordered a salmon salad, vinaigrette dressing, light capers, a blend of spinach and arugula (freshly picked), spiral-cut baby carrots, and a star-fruit garnish. (Alina smirked behind her hand.)

Glaric muttered, "House salad combo (hold the tomaters), comin' up," and wandered back to the kitchen, pulling his pants up.

Silence lingered a moment in Glaric's wake.

Then, Ivion said, "They wouldn't serve *farm*-grown salmon here, would they? And has that man ever even heard of arugula?"

"You're a long way from The Capital. Count yourself lucky if he's got one whole cucumber back there. And I wouldn't hold my breath for wild-caught fish."

"I'm so sorry. I didn't mean to offend. It's not from New El that I come, though. I've been in the colonies the past months, tending to my parents recent acquisitions. Filling the void left by our Family's departed heir."

"Is it hard, throwing your dead brother in with all the other business?" Alina clamped her lips shut as soon as she'd said that last bit.

"It is. Often." Her long fingernails clicked against the tabletop. "But, my journeys have allowed me to learn many things, as useful as they are alarming. Do I have your attention, or have you heard enough?"

"I should probably leave."

A layered smile revealed Ivion's sculpted teeth. Touched by the light overhead, they flashed like sun-struck dewdrops on a garden spider's web. "Now's your chance to withdraw. If I go on, you won't want to."

Alina saw the fork in the road ahead, and made her choice.

For so long, she'd had to content herself with Ruqastra's secrecy, half-truths, and cryptic references to destiny. Nowhere in that mix were there ever any actual answers, only more questions. In at least this one instance, Alina couldn't be blamed for wanting closure. She'd go back to Morbin, sure, but first she had to know.

"I'm listening."

Considering, finger tracing a circle, finally Ivion placed her palm on the table, perfectly flat and still. "What if I told you that Ordin was assassinated by the Walazzins, and I can prove it?"

"The news said Tolomond Stayd murdered him. And, usually I don't buy into the official story, but I… met Tolomond. So, yeah. Can confirm that he was more than happy to torture and kill."

"Mr. Stayd performed the deed, that much is certainly true. But a creature like him? Merely a weapon. Sanctumite zealots like him never do their own thinking. I'd bet my life that it was the Walazzin Family who set Stayd upon my brother."

"Either way, what do you want from me?"

Angling her chin down, hair framing her leaf-shaped face, Ivion looked up at Alina. "I am aware that you and Ordin quarreled. Before the end."

"Yah, that's one way to put it." Alina felt she wouldn't be able to say no to whatever came next. If Ivion was a beautiful trap, some part of Alina had already made up her mind to fall for it.

"So, if you will not do it in his memory—for which I wouldn't blame you—then perhaps do it for Ugarda Pankrish."

Alina exhaled sharply.

Ivion added, "Tolomond's ignoble slaughter of Master Pankrish in that anonymous alley... Plutonia Herself must have wept diamond tears that day, to witness so unfit an end of so fabled a man. Would you not agree?" Ordin and his sister clearly had in common a love of overly poetic turns of phrase.

"Of course I agree," said Alina, shifting in her seat. "You can prove it somehow, you're saying? That Wodjaego Walazzin gave the order?"

"Not only him. His son, Kaspuri, was intimately involved. The rot runs deep in that Family. If you assume the worst will be over when that slug Wodjaego finally expires, think again. Kaspuri is the heir-apparent, set to inherit his fathers fortunes and armies. Gods help us, but, in some ways, he is even worse than his father."

"What do you mean? How?"

Ivion leaned in, whispering, "Your friend, Choraelia. I know who she is."

At the mention of Cho's name, Alina growled under her breath. The iron bolts pinning the booth in place squeaked as the entire table rattled. Ivion snapped backward, frightened by something she saw tear across Alina's face.

"An innocent comment! Please." Stumbling over her words, finally knocked off balance, Ivion said, "I'm only referring to her tragic past."

Sniffing, Alina felt the surge of adrenaline ebb and leave her body like steam. "How?"

"Ordin told me. But I've informed no one else, I swear. Not even my closest friends and allies. Alina, we may not know each other, but I have come to respect you from afar. From what I have learned about you, and what Ordin told me before he passed, you... I believe you could make a difference. For yourself, for Choraelia, for your country."

"Like I care about the country."

"You can't mean that."

"Why are you bringing Cho into this?"

"Because the Walazzins are, as they always have done. They'll not rest until she's either under their influence or buried. Don't you understand? The Torviri were slaughtered in one night. In that matter, each Walazzin is as guilty as the other. What the father orchestrated, the son accomplished. Your friend's parents, siblings, and House are destroyed because of the Walazzins' greed."

"And I hope they burn for it. For all the suffering they've caused, may Buthmertha and all the Seventy-Seven Gods curse them. I spent five minutes with Wodjaego, and I probably couldn't ever take enough showers to clean his filth off me. But what good am I to you? Who do you think you're talking to, here?"

Glaric returned, sliding a coffee cup, spoon, and five packets of sugar along the sticky table toward Alina. The brown liquid sloshed onto the dish beneath the big off-white mug. Alina tore open and dumped the sugars into the lukewarm sludge and took a swig. Ivion glanced down at her wilted purple and green leaves drowned in a gallon of vinegary dressing.

"Eh?" said Glaric, meaning "Anything else?"

Alina thanked him, and he left.

Pushing the slop of leafy greens with her fork, Ivion shook her head. Then, she pulled her omnipad back onto the table, tapped the screen.

Over the past year, Alina had become quite familiar with the image now being projected between them: her wanted poster.

Eyes unfocused, Alina lost herself in thought. How had she screwed everything up so badly?

She remembered the day of the Battle at City Hall and Baraam's handing her a bag full of cash. Escaping New El with it, she'd briefly had money enough to live like a queen, but she'd tried to stay basically the same. She bought the same kinds of clothes, music, gadgets, and whatnots—just better, newer versions of them. And she'd still come by her old haunts, like Glaric's Diner. Out of respect, and because it was familiar. She'd even taken Cho here a few times, sharing the local flavors, you know. The food was so lardy that Cho (still used to dumpster diving for scraps) hadn't been able to stomach it. But still, good times.

Alina missed those days. She'd *tried* to hold onto them. Another slice of life taken from her by circumstance.

She had hoped The Authority, with all those other fugitive Ravers running around out there, would forget about her. She'd dared to dream Baraam had actually done as he'd promised and wiped her criminal record clean. If the Enforcers had ever come knocking, she'd imagined she could just get all weepy and stammer a story about being a dumb kid caught up in crazy events way beyond her control.

Trouble was, The Authority hadn't come knocking but shooting.

She looked at the wanted poster. The photo wasn't horribly unflattering. PACE had used the one on her most recent Proof of Assetship identification card from about three years ago. Yet, the sixteen-year-old with coarse pounds and pounds of black-and-gray, tied-back hair was barely recognizable. She'd lost most of the hair, which was now wavy and home-dyed crimson. She also had a few more scars. But, what was most different was the expression: the kid looking back at her was exactly that, a kid. *She* still had a grandfather and—though times were tough for her—a home to feel safe in each night. This sixteen-year-old Alina hadn't yet tangled with Demons, been kidnapped and shot at, or squared off against her own flesh and blood. She hadn't yet made the choices that would lead to her face being plastered on every street lamp and cracked brick wall across the Province.

Framing the picture of her scowling face, the text read: "Alina K'vich. Alias: 'Stitcher.' Born 3485. 5'11". Wanted for impersonating a bonded Gildsmen Aelfraver, resisting arrest, assault, breaking and entering, theft of magical artifact, defrauding the state, conspiracy to overthrow the Plutocracy of New El, miscellaneous felonies. Suspect is a Mage of moderate ability and should be considered highly dangerous. Information leading to the arrest or execution of this individual subject to a rewarded of no more than 10,000 gelders."

Alina said, "I still think 10,000's a bit on the low side. I mean, with all my cri—*alleged* crimes—I should be worth more, right?"

"Well," said Ivion, grinning, "The Authority has had to put out cash rewards on nearly one hundred Landsider Aelfravers, if that spares your ego."

"The Twelve Families have cash to burn. They could loosen the purse strings a little. Seriously, though, why show me this picture I've seen a million times? You thinking of collecting my bounty, huh?" Alina waved her hand to indicate the clean, extremely expensive white suit and diamond-studded necktie. "Doesn't look like you need it."

Ivion pointed to the image of sixteen-year-old Alina. "The woman who could do all that *and* escape—she's someone worth meeting. In all honesty, I only wanted the chance to sit before you and make my case."

Alina drained the rest of her coffee. She waved toward Glaric to bring her another. He didn't notice.

"Are you not Alina, granddaughter of Dimas K'vich, the most underrated Aelfraver to have ever lived? Alina, the Landsider who grew up in poverty and squalor in backwater Truct, who forged a Raver-X License in order to hunt a Demidivine in the heart of New El, and helped set off the powderkeg that turned the common Ravers against The Authority?"

"I dunno. Am I?"

"Enough false humility. They say you are a master Geomancer, kept hidden by your grandfather, to be set loose once you were ready. They say you are as powerful as Baraam. A secret weapon against the ruling element."

"Well, I don't know what to tell ya. 'They' are full of it, whoever 'they' are. Most of that's absolute crap."

"Most," said Ivion slyly, "but not all. You did escape The Authority. I interviewed Detective Ding, and he did not mince words."

"Ding was a clown. And I had help that time."

"You yourself admitted you fought Mr. Stayd."

"He almost killed me. That's hardly the same thing."

"But you lived, Alina," said Ivion, becoming either more and more frustrated or impassioned. Hard to tell.

"There is footage of you fleeing the Elemental Bank with Baraam bol-Talanai."

"That's, uh, not completely untrue, but—"

"Even as City Hall burned, and the battle raged, you and Baraam fought the Bane together—and won. When no one else could. That is undeniable: after you left the bank, the Bane was gone, and it has not returned since. Don't insult my intelligence by claiming everything I've said is coincidence."

Puffing out her chest a little, Alina couldn't hold back a nervous but real smile. "Sure, it's just…"

"You infiltrated The Gild and stole a Lorestone from the Crystallarium, rescued a kidnapped heiress from the clutches of a sinister family." Rosiness bled onto Ivion's porcelain face. "Deny it, I dare you."

"I mean, okay, when you put it like that—But, I didn't do all that alone. I had help at every step."

"Exactly," said Ivion, shutting off her omnipad and stowing it in its black leather bag. "And, now I need your help. And you need mine. The Walazzins have taken so much from us both, from those we care for. They must be stopped. Before they can cause more harm."

"Fine. Let's imagine a world where I'm willing to go along with this."

"I can do more than imagine." Ivion quirked an eyebrow, smirking.

"Aren't you one of the most powerful people in all of El? What do you need my help for?"

"You once joined my brother—"

"Because he lied to me."

"But he became a better man because of it. He told me so himself. He loved you."

"I think I loved him too," said Alina, surprising herself. "So what? It's over."

"It doesn't have to be," said Ivion, adjusting her tight cravat with her slender pale fingers.

They stared at each other.

Glaric waddled over and sloppily poured Alina another mugful of coffee. He left, clearing his throat with a noise like a backfiring engine.

There was silence. Ivion allowed the conversation to settle in time with the thick, slimy coffee.

The coffee, however, wasn't settling at all. Staring at the cooling muck, Alina noticed ripples. Then, the whole mug and saucer began to shake and clink together. The rattling knocked the spoon off the plate and onto the table.

A roar of engines shook the building as something flew past. High up. Very fast.

Mouth sand-dry, Alina saw beyond the window several bright streaks in the sky.

Drone exhaust.

"What direction are they headed?" she shouted.

"West, I think?" said Glaric. "Don't worry, they're long gone."

West. Toward Morbin.

Locked in that particular type of paralysis that results from needing to move, right now, but trying to sort through what to grab or where to go first, Alina looked across the table. "I'm sorry," she said—to Ivion, herself, Ruqastra, or Cho. It didn't matter who for, but she was. She stumbled out of the booth, nearly falling. Righting herself, she said, "Gotta get back. Gotta—"

She ran out the door as Ivion shouted after her, "Can I help? What's going on?"

"I'll think about what you said," Alina told her, throwing the door open.

There wasn't time to run back to her moped. And that old clunker was too slow anyway. She'd have to fly. Even so, she couldn't catch up to a drone.

Before anything else, though, she sent a tiny Niimantic charge hurtling toward Ruqastra, a telepathic pulse. A warning signal.

No time to wait for a response. Moving on to step two.

"Lighter than air, lighter than air," Alina murmured, "lighter than air," willing herself to calm down and her mind to clear.

Ruqastra had forbidden the use of magic beyond the confines of Mount Morbin for fear that it would attract attention to their hideout. It seemed, though, that the damage had already been done.

Like a fierce bird, *Rego* flailed behind Alina's back as her arms spun and fingers contorted. She cast the spell, uncaring of who might see, and her body became transparent, ephemeral.

The wind picked her up, throwing her into the sky, higher and higher, like a storm-tossed seedpod.

The spell took incredible effort and focus. Her mind had to juggle three all-important tasks at once: staying light and breezy, flying in the right direction, and holding her body's molecules together. A sneeze at the wrong time, and she'd be blasted into a million pieces.

Faster. She had to move faster.

The drones tore through the night sky ahead, their trails acting as guiding lights as she made straight for the mountain.

11

CHO-ZEN

CHAINED THING—A PERSON, *maybe, but too, too tall.*
They're wrapped in silky cloth. Like—
Spiderwebs. They've been asleep forever, but they're so tired.
Always tired.
And so, so angry.

Cho woke to screaming. It was Alina, who stood in the clearing by the fishpond, cupping her hands around her mouth: "Get up! We have to go! Wake up!"

Slithering out of her sleeping bag, Cho grabbed her bug-out backpack, opened her tree house trapdoor and swung down together with the rope ladder. Landing in a crouch, she sprinted forward. The small fire in Eilars's hearth acted as a beacon in the dark.

She skidded and bumped into Alina, who pulled her in for a hug. Alina's cheeks were slick with tears, her eyes wide. "Thank Buthmertha I got here in time."

"What's happening?" said Cho.

"They found us," Alina panted. "Drones. Searching the mountain."

A downpour of black, viscous goop fell between them, and from this hissing, popping sludge materialized Morphea. "The drones are handled. They've flown safely by." Swelling in size, she bared down on Alina. "And where were *you?*"

"I was—I—" Alina shook her head, her exhaustion switched to anger. "Why don't you just read my mind, huh?"

The master's gold eyes flicked toward Alina's bag, slung over her right shoulder. Morphea's voice dropped to a low growl. "*You were not wearing your mask.* Can you understand what you've done?"

"You said the drones were gone."

"Scouts and nuisances. It is not the *machines* I worry over. Even if you care nothing for your own survival, think of your friend's." Morphea jabbed a finger into Cho's bony chest. "Might as well shoot her yourself. Save the enemy the effort."

Alina advanced, Niima flaring. "Don't touch her again."

"Hey," said Cho, stepping between them. "Take a breath." With both arms, she shoved Alina backward.

All three of their heads jerked upward toward the mechanical grumbling, groaning of a dozen small airships and an equal number of fighter crafts circling the forested plateau. Spotlights carved the sky, speared the earth.

"Troop transports," said Cho.

The fighters passed by, strafing the trees in random intervals with their chainguns and missile launchers, making their intent abundantly clear.

As the forests of Morbin caught fire, Morphea whispered, "Eilars, it's time."

Even though he'd been fifty yards away, the old android must have heard because he burst out of his door and used a nearby bucket of water to put out the flames in his fireplace.

Carried by the wind, smoke blanketed the area, dampening the glare of the still far-off—but quickly spreading—forest fires. The worse threat would be the landing crews, whose boots would be hitting the ground any second now.

Cho had read all about The Authority's breaching tactics in various environments. They were treating Morbin like hostile territory, shredding it before sending in the shock troops. They weren't here to take prisoners.

Through the smoke, she caught the unnerving sight of Alina and Morphea glaring at each other. Three gold eyes in the gloom. Then, her night-vision switched on and the darkness receded, and she could see their whole bodies again, washed in greens and whites and grays.

The master Revomancer turned to Cho and Alina, lips parting, but then she held out her palm and, out of thin air, the glowing green Chrononite Lorestone appeared and fell onto it. Her fingers curled around the stone's smooth base. To Alina, she said, "Take it."

Alina hesitated.

To Cho, Morphea said, "Watch over her."

Cho nodded.

With an impatient huff, Morphea thrust the Lorestone against Cho's chest. Cho grabbed it and automatically stuffed it into her bag.

Eilars walked by, placed a hand on her neck. Lightly. Cold metal digits.

She looked up at him. "Is that a *rocket launcher*?"

Jaw locked, he fixed her with his stare—double circles of indigo in pools of black. He said nothing, in which he communicated to her everything. She discovered she was crying.

Shouldering the bazooka, he let her go, sprinting off.

Cho scratched her scalp. Blood under her fingernails.

"He is here." For the first time ever, Morphea looked afraid. "I can feel him." She turned her back to them. "The android and I will engage as many as we can. You'll have to fly. Find somewhere, anywhere you can lie low. After that... I can't say. You're not ready, yet you are on your own now." She glanced over her shoulder at Alina. "Had we but more time."

"Ruqastra!" Alina called as her teacher darted forward, a leaping beast of shadow.

Tongues of fire licked from branch to branch, engulfing the canopy. Bubbling sap dribbled onto dirt and grass.

Scanning the trees, Cho noted at least two dozen white human-shaped blobs in the middle distance. "There are a lot of them."

Gunfire sounded from all directions; Cho and Alina hunkered down.

"We're not really going to leave them behind, are we?"

"They should've run with us," said Alina. That thousand-yard-stare. Half of her was somewhere else again.

"But they didn't." Cho grabbed her by the shoulders. "So, what do *we* do?"

A whirring, rumbling noise above them preluded a spotlight that slammed down like a hammer. Cho's night-vision was overloaded and went bright white, blinding her. Her regular sight returned just in time to be bombarded by rifle-mounted flashlights from the left.

Soldiers ringed Alina and Cho. Wearing the gold-and-red of the Walazzin Family, they closed in, one heavy footfall at a time, their metal-studded boots sinking into the mud. Light bounced off the gilded, lion-headed pauldrons and helmets of their exo-suits. They were Tranquilizers—also called Tranqtanks or just Tranqs—whose specialty was "reducing resistance levels to a tolerable threshold." Read: kill until the locals stopped fighting back.

"On the ground," shouted one of them, a high-pitched whine emitting from the pulse rifle in his hands. The weapon hissed; viper-like coils of green light writhing inside. "Get down. Now!"

Cho and Alina looked at one another.

They'll kill us either way, Cho thought at her, praying Alina was reading her mind. *It's us or them.*

Alina nodded.

A voice pecked at the meat of Cho's brain; the scraping tickle of talons. It must have been Alina, though it was strange to hear these words of hers—soundlessly formed: *I'll distract them. You run.*

Cheh. Like that's ever gonna happen.

No matter what, Cho, you have to make it.

Arms steady, postures low, the Tranquilizers tightened their formation. Forward, closer, squeezing the oxygen and space from the circle in which they'd caught their prey.

How had this happened? There'd been no warning. The Dream Queen seemed to always know everything. How had she and everyone else in the Morbin gang missed this? She and Eilars were out there somewhere, fighting to open a window for Cho and Alina's escape. A window now shut by their hesitation.

For the span of a breath, Cho tortured herself with the thought that this was all her fault. Her stunt with Kinneas last night. She'd clawed the lion's nose, and here he'd come for payback.

One of the Guard snatched her wrist and yanked her arm, hard. "Lakpin," he said, "take the other."

Lakpin lunged for Alina. She spun to the right and threw a clumsy hook-kick, which hit the soldier like a truck. He pirouetted as he fell. Alina then stepped in, dropped low, and drove her fist into the nearest Tranquilizer's gut, denting the metal plates of his armor, and he flew straight back—fifteen, twenty feet back—snapping through the ferns and saplings.

Cho's wrist was released, as the Tranquilizer who'd grabbed her swiveled, raised his long, double-barreled gun at Alina, and pulled the trigger. A colorless wave of force distorted Alina's body, blasting past her, but she stayed standing.

The Tranq's eyes widened. Cho seized her chance, twisting her entire body to deliver a roundhouse kick to his head, but his arm got in the way. There was a gross cracking noise, his bones shattering, and the man screamed as he dropped his gun. The next, she fan-kicked, her heel catching his chin, and he went down.

She hit the dirt just as the other Tranqs sprayed pulse rounds into the air, bolts of energy that singed the tips of the grass and leaves.

Then a succession of metallic *tings* rang out, like someone was furiously banging the keys of a large xylophone. And as Cho rolled upright to face the other goons, she saw that most of them had already been dropped. The last was flung four feet off the ground, landing on his back with a cry of alarm.

Between Alina and a pair of unconscious Tranqs, a cluster of rocky columns crumbled into clots of dirt and molten rock. Tense, she'd apparently also been expecting more of a fight. She looked around for their rescuer.

The fluttering of wings, humming-bird like, caught Cho's ear. "Mezami!" She beamed as he landed on her shoulder. "We owe you one, big man."

"Owe: many, you."

"Who's counting anyway?"

"This is all my fault," said Alina.

Cho wanted to tell her the truth, to take away her guilt, but they couldn't afford to pause here and hash things out. "We have to go after the others."

"Are they dead?"

"I don't know. They ran off."

"The Authority dudes." Alina knelt over the two she'd hit with her rock pillars, and glanced at the bushes to her right (where the Tranq she'd punched had landed). "I was only trying to stop them. I didn't mean—I wouldn't—"

Taking a breath, Cho told her, "They're biometrics are stable. I scanned them." That was a lie. "They'll live." And that was a guess.

"You sure?"

"I mean, they could be *better*, y'know? But we got our own stuff to deal with." She hesitated only for a second before placing a hand on Alina's shoulder. "Li. Ya did what ya had to. Now, c'mon."

Buzzing between them, Mezami raised his dukes, ready for anything. "Go: us? Stay: us?"

"I couldn't fly us out, not after spending so much Niima getting here from town," said Alina, rising. "We'd have to make a run for it. But the fires have cut us off from everywhere except the south pass."

"We're not running, though." Cho twirled her knife in her palm. "Are we?"

Flipping the hood of her weird, writhing cloak over her head, her face lost in shadow, Alina said, "Why didn't she come with us?"

"Let's go ask her, yeah?" Cho cracked her knuckles. "I'm not leaving her or Eilars behind."

Under Alina's hood, milky blackness and two gold eyes. Coins at the bottom of a well.

Cho said, "C'mon, Li. The five of us, together, we can take these pinkojacks!"

Finally, Alina nodded.

With Cho leading, they headed northwest, in the direction they'd seen the android and the witch run off. Cho's internal clock enabled her to tell exactly how much time passed as they dashed through the woods of Morbin—awash in flame and shadow, each heightening the other. They ran for four minutes and twenty-eight seconds. It felt much longer.

An explosion of white, hot light tore through the secluded forested mountainside. The flash dizzied Cho. Steadying herself against a nearby rock, ears ringing from the shockwave, she could hardly hear Alina shout, "Buthmertha, what was that?"

Cho shook off her shock, but something was wrong. Her sensors were going haywire. Either that, or she really was picking up a huge number of unidentifiable bodies not too far to the north. Bodies that moved but emitted no life signs.

She broke into a sprint, shouting for the others to keep close. Ducking under branches and weaving between ancient trunks, she ran straight as a steel beam, having to leap over the same snaking stream several times before she heard the clamor of the fight ahead. A rifle cracked to her right, the muzzle flaring twice. She leapt up behind the shiny-armored soldier—another Walazzin Chimaera Guard—and kneed him between his shoulder blades; he toppled forward, slamming into the leaves, and she jumped off him.

Just ahead, maybe forty feet away, were Eilars and Morphea the Dream Queen. From all sides, bullets sparked as they glanced off an invisible forcefield, striking wood, stone, and grass.

The riflemen, posted behind trees and boulders, surrounded the two defenders. Her night vision still rebooting, Cho had trouble counting and spotting them all.

What was plain to see, even by what little moonlight filtered through the canopy, was the source of the strange signals Cho had been picking up. A swarm of—gods, what *were* those things? Black, freakishly thin, gleaming, and lurching like stop-motion clay figures, they couldn't have been human.

Alina caught up with her and kept running, but she bounced off a wall of rippling, translucent black energy that had spontaneously appeared between her and the fight. She got up and, nails scratching the magical wall, she raced up and down its length, looking for a way around or through; there was none.

"Morphea!" she cried.

In her head, Cho heard the Revomancer's voice, the weakening yowl of a trapped animal, a wordless plea for her cubs.

Alina must have heard it, too. "Let me help you." She began to change: her skin grayed, her arms lengthened, the familiar black feathers tore through the sleeves of her shirt, and her eyes blazed an even fiercer gold, like two coins thrown into a fire.

Cho's attention returned to the battle and the creatures—thin and tall, as if they'd been stretched like putty figures. Wrapped in frayed, graying cloth, they slashed with hooked hands, attacking in waves, charging and faltering as if they were on rails. They could only move forward, fall, and rise again, unthinking. Some of them had taken enough damage to reveal their bodies under the wrappings to be animated, black-boned skeletons. Eyeless, organ-less. Shredded fabric floated behind them as they launched themselves at the Maggo who'd cast that fierce, bubbling, black energy shield.

The witch's face was obscured by her dark mask, which roiled and shifted forms multiple times per second—jackal, coyote, beetle, vulture—and with each shape, the shield receded.

Eilars loosed what must have been his last rocket. The projectile burst a ways off, scattering but not breaking a bunch of the black skeletons. He jabbed the butt of his shotgun outside the shrinking bubble and blasted the closest enemy, throwing it; it got up a few seconds later, and charged again.

Then that same white light from before sprung from the earth, a spear of energy carving a heavenward path, and the skeletons retreated in jerking movements like moths drawn to flame.

Cho's eyes adjusted to the light enough to see its source: a man holding a greatsword overhead. He must have been over six-and-a-half feet tall, and his sword nearly five in length. From his left wrist burst a chain that ended in a hooked blade shaped like a three-tongued flame.

His face came into focus. Eyes and mouth sewn shut with black wire. His inhumanly pale body was covered in old, stretched, fleshy scars and badly healed, newer, purpled ones. Stitches ran from his nape to his belly, his shoulders to his hips. There wasn't a hair on any visible inch of his skin, and not a patch that wasn't bruised royal blue. Despite his unearthly appearance, Cho recognized him.

So did Alina, clearly. "Tolomond!"

His silvery weapons gleamed as he leapt toward Morphea.

The monstrous rage behind Alina's shriek caused Cho to shrink away, even as she watched Tolomond strike at the Dream Queen. The forcefield deflected several blows from his light-sheathed greatsword, but each one brought Morphea lower and lower until she was all but kneeling before him.

And the black-boned creatures piled on top of Eilars, who blasted as many as he could with an old hunting rifle.

They overwhelmed him.

In her shock, Cho noted Eilars's resemblance to the creatures that were literally tearing him to pieces. Black bones, artificial bodies. The similarity could only have been superficial, though. Eilars was a gentle person. A person. Even though he'd been assembled in some government factory, he was more a man than most.

Springing up, Cho banged on the wall of dark energy, demanding she be let in.

Bony fingers tore his arm off. His eyes flickered. Next, they took a leg. They worked in brutal silence, these creatures; the only screams were his.

Cho's arms fell limp, slapping her hips.

Eilars had been kind to her. A quiet, stable presence. And now she was forced to watch him, her friend, die; watch him be ripped apart by abominations that dared to look even a little like he did.

What were they? Who'd sent them? The questions lingered in the air, unexpressed, cut apart by the spears of light emanating from Tolomond's sword, which he raised once more. His body swelled to bursting with light, an X-ray effect briefly displaying his bones. Unseeing, his blank, ruined face ignored the Revomancer at his feet. He simply stared straight on, his arms poised for the final blow.

The blade fell, striking Morphea's head; her mask didn't so much crack as burst and splinter, the shards spraying from her now bloodied face. She lifted one arm instinctively, even as Tolomond swung his sword again. Mechanically. As if he were chopping wood.

Looking Cho and Alina's way, Morphea was speaking, lips working frantically, a whisper lost to the night. She reached out to them, blood running from her scalp into her eyes.

There was another, final explosion of light. This strike did more than drive away the darkness, however; it tore into Morphea's body. The fierce, white, searing light spread from the witch's chest to her arms and legs, fingers and hips, toes, neck and head, and—with a scream—she erupted from within, fracturing into hundreds of fragments of light, which then winked out. All at once.

A pillar of pain and fury, Alina roared. Her jaw unhinged like a serpent's. The graying skin peeled back from her nose, a black beak protruding from the gash. Roiling shadows curled about her like scorpion tails. Uselessly, she clawed at the wall of magic.

Cho stared dumbly, aware that she was in shock but unable to speak, swallow, breathe, or even think. Her stomach lurched, as if she were about to be violently sick all over the forest floor.

Then she felt a pulling sensation on her ears and ankles—two equal forces, tearing her in opposite directions. And—

12

BARAAM

T HOSE WHO HAD NEVER been to Kadic tended to assume it was a wasteland. Empty. Inhospitable to life. A place only for those with nowhere else to turn.

True, Kadic's spine was quartz and sandstone—a mighty and unforgiving desert home to nomads and worshipers of the old gods. However, with its northern savannas, southern canyons, and eastern wetlands—where the River Prodigy met the sea—its geography was as colorful and varied as its people. And, like its people (artisans, masons, sailors, Sahamans, gladiators, gardeners, technicians, traders…), Kadic endured.

Through centuries unending, and countless foreign land-grabs; through the pillaging of their motherland, the nomads and city-dwellers and farmers endured. Because they were Kadicians, all.

On the highest snow-crusted peak of the northwestern mountains grew the Blood-Arrow Thistle—a unique species. When El was but a city-state in its infancy, the Gara Sahamans raised a temple upon this peak, which they named *Sula eretanat*—"the daughter of heaven lifts her chin high." Prized for its rarity, the Blood-Arrow Thistle was fiercely protected. Although the Sahamans' mountain temple fell into disrepair thousands of years ago, Kadicians still clung to the ancient idiom, "as long as thistle graces the daughter's crown." The expression could be used as greeting, threat, or oath. It referenced eternity, the invincible certainty of Kadicians that they and their cultures would not perish from the earth.

In the year 3399, miners from El blew the top off *Sula eretanat*. The coal they extracted from its blasted wreckage powered the homes, Watchbox sets, hot tubs, and video games of millions for several years. The environmentalists who'd protested the mountaintop mining operation were arrested on trumped-up charges, carted off to different colonial labor camps.

Yet, in Kadic, people still said, "as long as thistle graces the daughter's crown." For that thistle, watered with Kadician blood, no bomb could truly destroy.

On his way into town, Baraam stopped as the wind picked up, greeting it as it tousled his coarse, scraggly hair. He lifted his gruffly bearded chin to the sun, basking in the soft warmth of the breeze. Then his long locks resettled on his cheeks, hiding his face once more, and he continued trudging along the old, cracked stone path.

Cradled by outcroppings of rock, he walked between the weedy, parasol-leafed trees jutting outward to provide sparse pools of shade. From afar, the town of Besalic hummed like a swarm of bees: gas engines vibrating in the blazing heat; children's footfalls as they ran back and forth across the playgrounds, playing ball; the electric hum of the fluorescent lights and signage of the various restaurants and public buildings.

Baraam's business lay just outside of Besalic proper. He needed go only so far as the gas station for some fruit (the Sahamans were on a tight budget). Even from afar, however, he could see what was amiss: the green sign that read "FOOD & PETROL" was out, and the station's proprietor—Imlin—stood under it, shaking his head.

"Ah!" Catching sight of Baraam, Imlin bowed his head courteously.

Returning the gesture, Baraam asked, "Trouble?"

They spoke Kadician, a language whose lilting syllables remained nostalgic music to Baraam's ears. Though he was out of practice and spoke haltingly, he took every chance he could to practice.

Imlin explained, "Another power outage. The whole town. Elemental siphoning again. How do they expect us to live like this?"

"The other lights are on."

"Indeed, sir. We do all have backup generators. Shame, however, for mine is broken. Blasted thing petered out an hour ago. I fear for my produce, my ice creams, all my perishables. This spells disaster for my business."

"Show me this… generation." As soon as he'd said it, Baraam realized he'd mispronounced the word 'generator.' He winced, but Imlin, who had bigger problems, graciously ignored the mistake. "I am, eh, good with machines. Maybe I can help."

The two walked around back, through the small parking lot, past the three gasoline pumps under their slightly lopsided awning. There, Imlin indicated the offensively silent generator.

Baraam set down his wicker fruit basket, knelt, and pulled free the plate protecting the interior components. Truthfully, he knew very little about machinery, and certainly couldn't diagnose complex problems pertaining to them. He did, however, have a useful and relevant talent.

In his other life, he'd been called by many names—Skyhammer, Living Lightning, and so on. With a small push, he ought to be able to get this turbine spinning again. Focusing his Niima, maintaining control, limiting his output, he converted his inner magical energy into pure force and sent a surge of it through the generator. It sputtered and whirred, spinning furiously again.

Overhead, the electric signage tinkled, flickering to life.

Imlin gasped. "Thank you, sir, thank you. Please, let me pay you for your services."

Baraam raised a hand. "Keep your money." He picked up his basket, tapping the generator with his sandaled foot. "What I have done will keep it working for a day. No more. You should find a professor… *professional* to fix it permanently."

"Well, you have my sincere thanks. At least, let me give you your persimmons, dates, and mangoes for free. I am afraid I must insist."

Bowing his head, Baraam followed Imlin inside the warm building as the vents began to spit gusts of cool air again. The owner waited patiently for Baraam to gather his choice of ripe fruit into one basket—persimmons, dates, and mangoes, a daily ritual—and present them. Imlin bagged them up, voided the transaction, and wished Baraam well with a smile and a wave.

Exiting the gas station, noting with satisfaction that the automatic sliding doors were working too, Baraam began the three-mile return journey to the Saludbabni, where for countless generations had dwelled the Salud Sahamans— priests, the last of their order in Kadic and all the world.

The wind crossed his path again, and again he paused, respecting its passage, embracing it like a friend. As the Sahamans had taught him.

In this moment of respite and reflection, the sun bearing down on his long black hair, he could not help but be grateful for the peace he'd found. This quiet, humble life far from his old troubles.

Still, even now, when he felt calmness bathe him in its light, he wondered about those he'd known as his past self, the self he'd willingly ended only two years ago. He'd come here looking for new beginnings, and new beginnings were what he'd found in his symbolic return to the land of his birth. However, no matter how many times he walked to Imlin's gas station, bought the fruit, walked back to the temple, swept its stone pathways, mucked its pig pens, prepared its chickens for the monthly mass... He could not forget them. Those he'd left behind. He found himself wondering, as his mind wandered its own desert dunes, how his family fared, where they'd gone.

He remembered especially well his most recent conversation with his sister. Ruqastra had entreated him to come "home" to El, to fight the battles that needed fighting. He'd reserved harsh words for her, even chased her away with thunder in his voice and lightning on his fingers. "Keep me from your plots," he'd screamed at his older sibling. And she'd done exactly that. Left him.

Ten or more months since then. Out here, with the infinite blue of sky and gold of sand surrounding his every day life, it was hard to remember exactly. Time crept by, and the world's business lay blissfully beyond his reach.

Still, he wondered if he'd ever see Ruqastra again. In the dark of night, he missed her. Did she plague him with dreams to cause him grief? Or, did he simply suffer for her absence?

Around noon, Baraam wiped the sweat from his forehead as he entered under the stone archway of the Saludbabni, calling out to the Sahamans in turn by name. They stopped what they were doing to return his serene and joyful acknowledgments, calling him "brother." This process took some time, but there was no hurry here in this refuge.

Once, Baraam had been famous for the speed of his wrath; he'd awed generations with the precision and swiftness of his killing strokes. Here, this truth faded away, evaporating like moisture from the sand and squat plants, until—like a sun-dried tomato—he'd been sapped of all desire for past or future. For him, there was only now.

Or so he wished it could be.

Behind his peace lurked the shadow of his former self, a trespasser in his own mind, a creature of rage and thunder. It awakened whenever he looked too closely at the land and air around him, whenever he wondered where the herds of gazelle and flocks of birds had gone. It was mating season. The skies should be ripe with the trills and calls of all the gods' creatures. And, yet, all was quiet. Too quiet. Excepting the screams of drones, the booming whir of engines overhead as the messengers of El scythed the air and killed the peace. In these moments, he would taste the rank bitterness, the sickly sweetness of pollutants tainting the air—clouds of miasma drifting from the cities farther north. Elemental-controlled factory cities, where the rivers and lakes clotted with radioactive silt. Often, thinking of such things, he grew angry—beyond that, he felt fear, not for this place but for the sanctuary it provided him. A sanctuary under threat.

Then, always, he would fly out the window of his room in the dead of night, soar over the industrialized cities only several miles to the north, adjacent to the Nation of El. He would land upon the corner of the tallest building, hairs raised, leaning over the edge like a mountain-conquering goat, chewing on what he saw.

Billboards advertising junk. Machines of war. Citizens of Kadic losing themselves to the encroachment of Elemental wealth. And he would realize, slowly, all over again, that he—in his own way—had helped this happen.

Finally, a desire to deal harm would return to him, and he would battle himself all over again. He reminded himself that he must tamp it down, this rage of his, keep it contained. If the Sahamans ever knew him for what he truly was—what he could become again—they would shun him.

Aglow in city night lights, Baraam would drown out the voice of his past with the sound of his own deep breaths. He would return to his quiet room at the Saludbabni, and somehow fall asleep. Upon waking, the hot, dry air would still his mind once more.

The feeling of calm restored to him, he'd rise to collect the fruit from Imlin's gas station, bringing these to Jija in the kitchen before setting about the rest of his routine.

Every day, the same. It felt good—soothing—to tend to the gardens, to watch things grow.

And he tried his hardest to forget Baraam bol-Talanai, to become Baraam of the Desert, Baraam the Gardener. Lost to the gentle whims of the wind.

PART TWO

BARGAINING

13

JEJUNE

GETTING OUT OF THE office certainly was a change of pace, though by no means a refreshing one. As boring as the Elemental Stock Exchange could be, at least it wasn't dirty. The same could not be said for the *rest* of the human world beyond The Capital.

After a hop, skip, and supersonic jet ride, Mr. Jejune had arrived at Andrador International Airport, one of hundreds of Authority control points in Kadic.

A handful of gray-uniformed Hruvic Inter-department Coordination Agents (ICAs) escorted him through the private terminal to an armored personnel carrier. As Mr. Jejune entered the vehicle, staring at the Hruvic mascot—the purple hornet—adorning their uniforms, he was reminded of the Hruvic Family's motto: "Beware Our Sting." Then he could only laugh at the much more popular mockery of it: "Hear Us Drone." The soldiers' monotonous chatter, buzzing at each other, did nothing to discourage the stereotype. Their faces were as stony and gray as their uniforms.

Possibly the only thing in the world duller than they: the desert.

Through the blue-tinted windows of the armored personnel carrier (APC), Mr. Jejune watched the drab dunes roll by. Rocks, sand, rocky sand, sandy rock. Honestly, Kadic's wealth of raw materials was only just barely worth the bother of the invasion. The heat, the monstrous insects, snakes, and—hells!— the humans who lived here were all deadlocked in competition for greatest nuisance.

When the creators engineered this world, they'd surely added Kadic in as an afterthought to test the damages that alternating boredom and terror can wreak upon a healthy mind.

The white sands gradually slipped away, hidden by square, red-clay shops and homes of Nasharam-vilh-amsul. Attempts had been made to paint their walls with bright colors, but the effect was somewhat dampened by the frequent black residue of explosives and the bullet holes scarring the walls and street. And this was the *nice* part of town. Mr. Jejune shook his head, his sunglasses sliding a hair farther down his perspiring nose.

Somewhat more than hour later, at last, the APC pulled up to the chain-link fence that marked the end of the sarcastically named "Safe Zone." With insurgents running amok everywhere, no zone in all of Kadic could truly be called "safe." Still, it was good PR. Had to keep up appearances (*talking points!*), ensure the power of The Authority remained unquestionable.

Mr. Jejune was reminded again of that power as the chain-link gate shuddered aside and the APC entered the aq-Hasir quadrant. Here, everything—structures, people, animals, water—was some shade of clay-dusted, sand-scarred, ash-washed red, brown, or white. Hundreds of desert-camo wearing Liberators now patrolled the streets, clearing the buildings of lingering families, pets, hideaways, and valuables. Piles of artifacts, furniture, jewelry, lined the gutters. Many warfighters picked through the spoils, pocketing antique books, silver-gilded necklaces and tableware, leather shoes, and more.

The APC trundled to a stop in front of a hastily constructed barbed wire barricade. The driver turned around and said, "Sir, beyond this point I can't guarantee your safety."

"Do I look worried?" Mr. Jejune cocked his head and grinned.

The driver's eyebrow twitched, but he said only, "If you'll please follow me."

Under the watchful eye of a dozen Liberators armed with plasma rifles, his entourage of ICAs helped him around the barricade. Down a few more blasted, cracked streets and abandoned playgrounds, Mr. Jejune ambled, whistling.

If the soldiers with him thought anything of his lighthearted ghoulishness, they kept it to themselves. One of them even obliged him by snapping a few shots of him in front of a full gallows, where he struck muscle man poses and clung to the feet of the hanging dead, pretending to weep or hold on for dear life.

Satisfied with the quality of the shots, he ordered the ICAs to lead on, and he closely followed the APC driver until they heard a shout from one of the nearby rooftops. A split-second later, a thunderous boom, and the driver was slammed against the wall to his left. He collapsed, leaving a snail-trail of blood on the cracked plaster.

"Sniper! Get down! Down!"

The shooter, however, was too slow in abandoning his nest. The Liberator nearest Jejune took a knee, shouted a warning, and fired a rocket-propelled grenade at the enemy combatant. The entire top third of the building collapsed in on itself, and more than one scream erupted from within. Another Liberator, her uniform striped with the bright gold and sky blue bands of Caelus, rushed over to the downed driver and began to drag him back behind the barricade.

Mr. Jejune, unperturbed, pressed on with the surviving members of his escort.

Finally, he knew he'd reached his destination by the sight of the white-eyed, soot-stained faces of the vanguard Liberators that lined the streets, alleys, rooftops, and animal pens around him. Their uniforms were cobalt and navy in color, and each wore a three-inch length of orange cord on the left breast of their uniforms. All soldiers wore such cords close to their hearts, a symbol of their loyalty to the Plutocrats—an unbreakable bond. The cords of these particular soldiers, however, had been severed. A reminder of their never-ending shame.

For here were the warriors who'd been sworn to the service of the Torvir, the Family that had fallen from grace and been removed from the political chessboard. These Liberators, these Cutcords, while still obligated to uphold their oaths to the Nation, were disgraced beyond salvation for having failed to defend their lords and ladies in their hour of direst need.

These were exactly the sort of hopeless fools Mr. Jejune could use.

He found the one he'd been searching for resting under the shadow of a desert-camouflaged battle mecha, spray-painted with a pink bunny's head with two exes for eyes. The twenty-foot-tall, two-legged war machine had been powered down. Mr. Jejune gawked at the cracked, oblong glass windshield, running his fingers along deep gashes in the metal of its right foot. "Phew," he said. "This old girl's seen some scraps, hasn't she?"

He pointedly directed his attention to the woman seated atop a slab of stone resting against a hill of rubble. She said, "Ran out of Battle Tokens half way through the encounter."

"Tsk, tsk. Should've rationed better."

She shook her head. "We used them all up in the first few minutes. Five Slot Machines. Overwhelming force."

Slot Machines. Mr. Jejune wasn't up on all the parlance, but he knew that was the grunts' term for the battle mecha. The nickname referred to a scoring system employed by Authority overseers to boost combat performance. It was wonderful; war had become a game with simple rules:

1. Tokens were awarded for the completion of Primary and Secondary Objectives, courage under fire, team support, exemplary conduct on the field of battle, etc.

2. Disobeying orders, failing to pray the regulation number of minutes to the Goddess Plutonia, engaging in any activities deserving of disciplinary action, and more would cost the soldier—and his team—Tokens.

3. Automatically debited and credited directly to the individual soldier's Asset Identification Number, Tokens could be exchanged at the commissary for rewards including (but not limited to) higher quality rations, new body armor, phone calls to one's family, medals, photo opportunities with celebrities (subject to availability), and, of course, temporary control of the "Slot Machines" (battle mechas) to boost the unit's numbers even further.

4. Token could be bought for exorbitant prices, either by the soldier himself or by his friends and family.

And these *Cutcords* had somehow racked up enough Tokens to deploy *five* mecha at once. Armed with missile launchers, tree-sized rail guns, three blades, and auto-turrets, these giant robots—controlled remotely by Authority Machinamancers (safe in the Air Force's flying fortresses)—would certainly have overwhelmed the Kadician defenders. No wonder the 31st Forward had managed to nearly win the whole battle before the first reinforcements had arrived.

Would've taken a *lot* of Tokens, though. A lot.

Dedicated, callous, foolhardy. This team of fools would be perfect for what Mr. Jejune had in mind.

He took in the alluringly hideous vision that was their leader, the broken woman before him: her shoulder-length black hair grew out of only half her scalp, the other half having been erratically scarred by shrapnel. Her left arm, shoulder, and leg up to the knee were prosthetics, and ill-fitting ones at that. Her constantly scowling jaw was synthetic as well, and its dark blue hue clashed with her sun-burnt skin. She, too, wore the mark of shame, the severed length of orange cord. Although damaged, she remained property of the state as declared by the matte yellow lettering on each of her artificial body parts—ELCORP.

"Captain Hael Tiberaira, I presume. You can call me Mr. Jejune."

"What's a civilian doing out here?" said the captain, rising.

"I'm the reason you're here."

"Huh." She didn't seem particularly grateful.

Sure, it'd been a hard fight, but they'd won the day. Glory and honor and all that garbage, wasn't that what these animals lived for?

"I have another job for you," he said, adjusting his sunglasses, oily fingers smudging the lenses. "Sensitive. It pays extremely well."

"That so?" Tiberaira slid down the stone slab, stopping in front of Jejune, sizing him up.

He sized her up, too. "I watched your work last night via satellite-captured footage. Your unit is precise, to say the least."

"Thank you for the compliment. I advise you leave this quadrant, civilian. It's not secure."

Jejune rapped his knuckles against his bulletproof vest cheerfully. "I'm not worried."

"Listen here, Chuckles. That thing might be good for small rounds from a reasonable distance, but it sure won't protect you against the fangs of Kadician *utch-Aharan* war dogs, a thrown knife to the neck, or—gods forbid—one of their berserker Shamans. But, hey, long as I'm not liable, you do you."

"Your hospitality is appreciated. Would you care to at least entertain the offer I flew thousands of miles to present to you?"

She crossed her arms, leaning against a crumbling wall. "By all means."

Which detail made him more uncomfortable, her self-assurance or his inability to tell how many weapons she had on her? He knew she had at least one; he could sense it on her. Just couldn't tell where. Troubling.

"Clearly, you're a busy woman. I'll cut to the chase, shall I? Leading a coalition force of the finest warriors of the empire, the Walazzin heir, Kaspuri, is mounting a full-on assault against The Coven and Hexhall. You and your men are wanted on the Ozari battlefield, captain."

Tiberaira shook her head. "We're Cutcords. Disconnected. Why would you want to hire ghosts of war like us?"

"Hang on, now, Captain. Let's consider your accomplishments tonight. Your unit, first on the field was, by all accounts, expected to suffer an attrition rate of thirty-five percent."

"Yeah, thanks for sending us in anyway, even though you obviously full-well knew the risk."

Mr. Jejune pressed on: "Yet, casualties incurred amounted to only ten percent."

"Only?"

"Truly, you beat the odds most impressively, I must say. And that's only your most recent accomplishment. Your file is full of harrowing tales of heroism and derring-do."

"You read my file."

"Not the *whole* thing, I confess, but the salient bits, sure."

"Well, had you read my entire file, you'd know I have three Terramancers in my command."

Bursting forth in a spray of sand and mud to the front, back, and right, camouflaged soldiers shot up and held their rifles trained on Jejune, who clapped his hands and laughed delightedly.

"Wow. Excellent! Do it again, please."

Tiberaira drew a knife from an invisible compartment in her combat vest. (And *there* was the weapon he'd fretted over.) She didn't brandish it threateningly; holding it at her side, loose but ready, was enough. "Tell me why you're really here, or I'll kill you."

"Do you even know *who I am*? You can't harm me. Much less in broad daylight, surrounded by your fellow siblings-in-arms! Why would you want to?"

"Because I don't like being toyed with, and there's something you aren't tell-ing me. I'll die before I expose my warfighters to danger, and I'll kill before that too. So, I'll ask you one more time: why us?"

Jejune slowly raised his hands, palms facing the captain, and shrugged. "I need you to do a hitjob, off the books. He had her attention now; he could tell. "There's a *considerable* bonus on offer."

"How much?"

He told her the ridiculous number, withholding that he'd be willing to go higher.

Tiberaira didn't so much as blink. "Target?"

"A loose end. A traitor who, my sources tell me, will very soon be on her way to Ozar."

"This traitor have a name?"

"Choraelia Rodanthemaru Dreintruadan Shazura-Torvir."

She hid it well with her practiced soldier's nonchalance, but he caught the brief flicker that flashed across her face: pure, unfiltered hatred.

He had her, he knew. Now all he had to do was seal the deal.

"A practical individual like yourself knows that there is no way to erase the past, but it can be overcome. The job is simple: capture the mark if you can; tag-and-bag her if you can't. Once young Choraelia has been disappeared, you and your Cutcords will be given a clean slate. Your honor restored."

"How?"

"You'd be folded into the Chimaera Guard, the Walazzin elite unit. As serv-ants of the Consul himself, you'd be promoted to Jaandarmes, endowed with all the privileges and glories worthy of the title. All this and more can be yours at the cost of one life. One problematic little life."

Tiberaira sheathed her knife. Wordlessly, her three Terramancer riflemen lowered their weapons, too.

"We'll find her," said Captain Tiberaira.

"Fantastic. You are making the smartest decisions of your lives. Of course, I can't submit this contract in writing, you understand... but, shake on it?" said Mr. Jejune, grinning.

They clasped hands. Her grip—even in her flesh-and-bone right hand—was iron.

That was that. Tiberaira had made up her mind, and the Cutcords fell in line without a word, appearing from behind the slag heaps, under rubble and debris. Sweat streaking sooty faces, they watched Mr. Jejune silently, heads turned slightly, as if they were hares listening for the stealthy approach of a fox.

"And you," said Tiberaira, "you'll be headed back to The Capital?"

"I wish. Unfortunately, I have one more important item of business in this gods-forsaken country."

"Don't let us keep you then, Mr. Jejune."

"A pleasure doing business with you, captain." He made to turn but paused. "Oh, do you need a current photograph of your target?"

"No," said Tiberaira without a second's hesitation. "I'd recognize that girl anywhere."

Jejune smiled, nodded, and left them to tie up the remainder of the battle.

Ambling back toward the barricade, he checked his phone: Tytan's price per share was through the roof. Their mining operations had already been green-lit by Consul Walazzin. In a week or two, the bulldozers would move in and sweep away qa-Hasir. And the copper mined from beneath this dump would fuel the technological industries of El for generations to come.

With the Torvir brat gone, another obstacle would be removed from play, and the game could continue on and on and on. Always a pleasure to work in a little mayhem in the name of maintaining order.

All the little pieces in place. Yes.

Another very, *very* good day.

14

ALINA

THE PORTAL SWALLOWED ALINA whole—toad tongue to fly.

No control. She could not get her bearings. All she could manage was to fall—upward, sideways, diagonally. Any direction. It didn't matter. Here, in this tunnel, there were no colors or sounds. She couldn't even hear her heartbeat or the grinding of her joints.

Short. Long. The spinning carried on.

She had time to think. A specific memory surfaced. Of Ruqastra. But, why this one?

That day had blended into Alina's memory like any one of the hundreds of others they'd spent together: just the two of them, in the forest on Mount Morbin. It might have been a sunny morning, or rainy—or misty midnight. Around Ruqastra, time was an afterthought, a guest you welcomed to the party out of obligation.

Still, one detail Alina felt reasonably sure of, this particular day had fallen late in her apprenticeship. Ruqastra had sat her down on a log, letting a long, hungry silence devour the seconds and the space between them until all sound faded and nothing remained except the clearing of her throat and a sense of breathless, mounting dread.

"Do you know," asked the teacher, "how Revomancy came to be?"

Alina opened her mouth to answer.

"The question was rhetorical. I will tell you the tale of our high art's origin. Listen with care, apprentice, for I will not pause or repeat myself as I tell you of *The Gifts of the Sisters*..."

Predating the collapse of the Iorian Empire, this tale is far more ancient than humanity, a story passed from teacher to student since the age of wild magic and miracles.

("Oral histories are unreliable," Alina interrupted.

"Books serve their purpose, yes, but they are, ultimately, crutches for races with short memories. And do you suppose, furthermore, that textbooks can't be edited for the sake of convenience? Shall I continue dismantling your childish interjection, or may I continue?"

Alina grumbled but did not retort.)

Once, there were three Sisters whose parents cast them out of their childhood home to face the world and earn their fortunes. The family had no prospects, and, according to some tellings, the mother had taken ill.

Each of the Sisters, naturally, had differing ideas of how to claim her place in society.

Jiin the Eldest flexed her muscles and proclaimed they should fight in the Arena to earn fame. Strength could take what was owed—power and influence.

Ud the Youngest stamped her feet and demanded they win their wealth at the Forum's card tables. Money could buy anything, including position and privilege.

Alu the In-Between disagreed, suggesting they instead seek to make themselves useful. By working together, making allies, they would not only find their place in the world but be connected with it. This would be its own reward.

Jiin and Ud mocked their middle Sister, calling her "dreamer." "Only those who use their talents to out-compete others can thrive," they said. "Those who offer freely of their talents are destined for servitude. With an attitude like that, Alu, you'll never amount to anything."

Accustomed to being ignored and dismissed, Alu simply shrugged. "It seems we each have wildly differing ideas concerning destiny, Sisters."

"Aye," said Jiin.

"We would be better off apart," said Ud.

"A competition, then?" Alu sweetly suggested. "Let us meet again in ten years' time, here at this Crossroads, and see which among us is 'greatest'."

"The losers shall walk home in shame to father and sing the praises of the winner," said Ud, clapping her hands gleefully.

"Agreed," said Jiin, who could resist no challenge.

"Ten years," they said, and turned on their heels.

Many days they traveled, each headed in a different direction. So it was that, after a time, Jiin found her way to the sky cities of the Titans, where she wrestled and waged mock wars in their martial tournaments. Meanwhile, Ud—through the lilt of her singing voice and the rhythm of her feet—delighted the gahool, who invited her into their fortresses many fathoms beneath the earth's surface.

With the greatest realms of earth and sky so claimed by the Youngest and Eldest, it seemed the In-Between had nowhere she could turn save for the destitute and failing cities of the land— stagnant, beaten down by the harsh sun, frozen come nightfall by the tyrannous stars. She lived among the suffering. She was happy, however, for she was never short of tasks to accomplish and people to aid. Thus, neither was she short on friends, the tally of which grew and grew until, one day, nary a town crier had not shouted the name Alu the Dreamer in the streets. She would fight when called upon and heal when able. Her power was that of rest for the weary and painless death for the wicked. Of the lost peoples in their cities, the righteous and cruel alike grew to fear and respect her name. Though many tried to disarm and dethrone her, her weapons were not swords and staves, nor even fists and feet: her mind was her glory, and from it she could not be separated. She carried it with her, always, and ever honed it through the pursuit of knowledge, experience, and alliance. Some called her queen, mother, goddess. All shrank, bowed, and scraped at her approach.

But the greatest power attracts the greatest jealousy, and there were those who abhorred all rivals—and who had the means to destroy her. Not all Titans had abandoned the world of mortals to build castles in the sky. Some had remained, burrowing into stone, cocooning themselves in mountain vaults. Waiting for a true challenge to their ancient supremacy.

Thus came forth the Spider and Her brood to drown all lands in the blood of Alu's allies and subjects, swiftly drawing Alu herself into battle.

All the more swiftly was Alu defeated, for—alone—she could not stand against this elder, master race, whose dominion extended beyond the known planes of existence. Alu fled, hiding in shame. The brood of the Spider could burrow through any crack and portal, and so poured into the kingdoms, besieging whole cities from within. The world was at war, and the Spider promised an end to the bloodshed only if Her prize were brought to the field of Her conquest: "Bring me Alu the Dreamer, for her dreams have disturbed my sleep, and for this sacrilege— for touching upon the infinite—her soul is forfeit."

Despite Alu's years of service, the fear that surrounded her power was pronounced and held sway over many. The people were divided: some cried for her head to send to the Spider; a minority were willing to fight on in her name. Upon seeing her kin so torn, Alu felt her heart swell with pride and break under the weight of her sadness. She resolved to remove the choice from others hands: she set forth to meet the Spider head-on in the fields.

The brood parted before her, she who was—to such as they—merely a small, frail wisp of a woman. The creatures skittered aside, allowing her passage to their Queen, the Spider, whose laughter upon seeing this puny witch shook the crumbling towers of the surrounding cities She had ravaged.

Their struggle proved brief. The Spider was immortal, after all, a product of forces primordial and beyond the understanding of any latter-born being of the material realm. Thus, Alu *suffered a grievous wound to her brow and side, and—stricken—fell upon the crown of a hill, across which cut a weathered old path.*

There, she waited for her end.

Most fortunately, however, as Alu's final moments loomed, her Sisters returned. Indeed, as destiny would have it, Alu's defiant stand had brought her back to that very same Crossroads of ten years prior.

"Ten years it has been," said Jiin and Ud, Eldest and Youngest, offering their hands to their In-Between, who arose. "Ten years to the day."

"And have my Sisters become great?" Alu asked weakly.

Jiin thumped her staff against her shield. "I fought my way through every tournament, winning regardless of cost. In reward for my never-ending hunger for victory, the Titans exiled me."

Ud played with the bands of her shimmering belt, fanning herself with bejeweled fingers. "My lust for merriment and dance and fine clothes tired the gahool. *Fearing their hatred, I fled."*

"I sought only power and fame," said Jiin.

"And I wished only for trinkets and wealth," said Ud.

"Neither of us is half as great as you," they said.

"How now?" said Alu incredulously. "I have lorded my will over my lessers. Every act has led to the expansion of the myths about me, but it is not real. It is not me. I am the least among you, for I did not conquer the skies nor walk the deepest recesses of the earth."

"But you stayed among our people and sought to serve. And look how you sacrifice yourself in battle for them, not for yourself but for the mortal nations."

"I dreamed of better, I swear, but my every act only made me a greater tyrant. Now, when I am needed most, I can only fail."

"No, Alu," said the Eldest and Youngest, "for we have come to you now—Dreamer—knowing that you were right all along, and the best of us, always."

"How can you say this? Your stories are legend. Jiin, you are the strongest warrior in the world. And, Ud, your cleverness is unmatched in all the realms, from ages past to present day."

"They call me Jiin Giantslayer, the Invincible. But I could not hope to best the Spider in combat."

"And me, Sleepless Ud, the Insatiable, who could drink dry the oceans and bluff the gods themselves. But the Spider is One even I could not outwit."

Together, they said, "You, however, can save us all."

"How?" asked Alu.

"Change the rules. The Spider and Her brood are stronger than we, more relentless, more cunning. But you can Dream a new world." They lifted her to her feet.

"I cannot," said Alu. "Alone, I am not enough." She held Jiin and Ud close. "With my Sisters, though, nothing is impossible."

Alina cleared her throat. "There a point to this lore-dump?"

Ruqastra stared at her.

"Well?"

The teacher gave the silence a workout, slamming it to the ground and forcing it to do crunches. That was a strong silence; it could've wrapped its fingers around Alina's throat and choked her out right there.

Finally, Ruqastra, on her terms, ended her tale:

The Eldest and Youngest told the In-Between, "Separately, we admitted defeat after had passed only half the alloted decade of our wager. By happenstance, we met one another on the road. Together, we found you and watched you from afar. We beheld how fiercely you worked to forge a better world, and in shame we retreated to wander for some time still. We swore an oath not to return to you until we could bring Gifts worthy of what you taught us. Today, we find you again."

Jiin said, "It is Chaos I have brought you. IDA. The shadowed Second Face of the Moon, Mask of the Dying Star."

"And, I," said Ud, "give unto you Control. REGO, the Cloak of the Old Stone Father, Cradle of Eternity."

"You are the In-Between," they said. "If you hope to prevail, you must be as both of us, and neither. Alone, we were nothing; together, we may become all."

The Sisters three stood as one against the Spider, then. Undaunted. United.

Ruqastra stopped.

Legs shaking with nervous energy, Alina leaned in. "And?"

"Hmm?"

"How does it end?"

"That *is* the end."

"You're messing with me. Come on. Do they win or what? You mad I cut you off a minute ago or something?"

"Looking for a tidy little statement of theme and a pat on the head can lead only to disappointment."

"Did. They. Beat. The. Spider?"

"The Spider is an allegory. Probably. It doesn't matter either way."

"Whew, well, you really committed to that whole production," said Alina. "Bold move, considering the dumb anticlimax. What a letdown. Still, you can't honestly believe any of that really happened."

Ruqastra snapped her fingers. It's what she did when she couldn't take another second of Alina's derailments. She was riled up. There was something personal for her about the bizarre morality play she'd just recited. "Like dreams, the story is a symbol behind which waits the truth."

"What truth?"

"Ida and Rego, chaos and control, doubt and certainty. These are the fundamental forces between which is balanced all of creation—and us."

"Revomancers?"

"Revolutionaries."

"I didn't ask for this."

"And yet, here we are." Pause. "Do you not seek change?"

"Our world's messed up, sure. Of course I want things to be different."

"But you won't be the one to fight for it?" Ruqastra blinked slowly. "Understand. Like Alu, you must accept the burden placed upon you—and you must wear the protection of your Sisters, recognizing that they are now part of you. Same as every Revomancer who ever lived, in an unbroken line back to before there were these divisions of 'Aelf' and 'human.' Recall: before the first human being, there were the Iorians."

"Not another history lesson."

"The Iorians took wild magic, untrammeled power, and bound it to themselves. Some among them learned to join their bodies, minds, and souls into oneness. Thus came into being the Noble art of Egogenesis."

"Stop. I hate that word."

"You cannot shrink from discomfort. It is the essence of life. I speak of how the Demidivines, the Dragons—magic itself!—came into being. Studying contradictions—embodying them—therein lies true strength. Becoming more than yourself and the other, more than the sum of your parts. It's what you are destined for as a carrier of that ancient Egogenetic heritage."

"A cannibal. A murderer."

"Pointless." Ruqastra's eyes rolled upward, and of the air she asked, "Dimas, why her?"

She dissipated into colorless smoke, leaving her single-gold-eyed coyote mask to glare at Alina for just a moment before it, too, vanished.

Funny how this particular conversation only stood out to Alina now that her teacher… Well.

Maybe we don't get to choose how we are remembered. Maybe we do.

Who had chosen *this* memory to burn into Alina's mind as she spun through interdimensional space? Herself? Ruqastra?

Was it a message? A warning? Or, was it Ruqastra's neurons, flung to the corners of the sky, misfiring as she'd burst? Alina might've caught some pieces of her, shards of the master embedding themselves in the student. Sealing her final act on earth.

They'd never liked each other, it seemed to Alina. Gotten on like vultures picking over the same corpse. Ruqastra had always pushed too far, guarded her mysteries too perfectly.

Why did Alina miss her so damn much?

The portal opened, threw Alina out like a leaky sack of garbage.

The crackle of thunder set the earth and heavens trembling. Thunder without lightning.

The moon was crowded by clouds, hidden. The only light emanated from Truct's main drag, and a small but fearsome glow blazing near the highest peak of Morbin to the west. The mountain burned.

If it weren't for the sudden downpour, those few walking the town's cold streets would have heard a *hiss* and *pop*—the sounds of a champagne bottle opened in reverse order.

Appearing fully horizontal, five or six feet above the roof of a bankrupt two-story car dealership, Alina flailed and shouted.

A glass skylight broke her fall: she belly-flopped through it, straight down, crashing through several stretched tarps and sheets strung across the abandoned place of business.

At least, it had seemed abandoned. Worried faces turned her way, people sidling backward into the safety of the shadows. She barely registered them as she stumbled out of the muddy showroom floor. Rain fell through the hole her body had left in the ceiling. Nauseous, she muttered an apology to the retreating squatters as she stepped into a bucket of filthy water and tripped out the front door.

The bucket stubbornly clung to her foot. With a growl, she gripped it in one hand and tore it free, crushing it as if it were made of tinfoil.

She pulled the hood of her cloak over her head and got to her feet. In a nearby alley, she leaned against the concrete wall.

In her hand, the red crow mask's patternless grain and swirls of color shifted. Her tears fell upon it like rain, and she remembered the raindrop dream she and Ruqastra had inhabited together only two days ago. All the dreams they'd journeyed through during Alina's training came flooding back. All at once.

She still had so much to learn. As a Revomancer. As granddaughter of Dimas. Supposedly, Ruqastra had had the answers, guarding them jealously, and now she was gone.

Why hadn't she been able to defeat Tolomond? She'd done it once before. What changed?

The answer came to Alina from her unconscious, that part of her she'd been taught to trust above her rational mind and even the evidence of her eyes: it was *Tolomond* who'd changed.

From the other side of Ruqastra's barrier, Alina had felt him—rather, she'd felt the *lack* of him. The man who'd previously lived inside that body was gone. The flesh remained, dead and putrefied, but whatever piloted it was something else. Not a man, and certainly not Tolomond.

And those bone-creatures that had accompanied him, they'd moved in a jerking fashion, as if puppeteered. Almost like Demonic possession, but the source of their magic had to be a Maggo. A Necromancer. Alina felt sure that that power was different from the one behind Tolomond, but clearly buddy-buddy with it.

Grinding westward, her glare locked onto the beacon on Mount Morbin. The light blazing from the creature occupying Tolomond's body burned like a star even from miles and miles away. From the distant dark trees, it flashed as if winking at Alina—the entity that had tried to kill her, her teacher, and her friends. Tried for all, succeeded for half.

Alina closed her eyes and allowed her mind to wander. She abandoned all preconceptions of what made sense, what was logical. She untethered herself, eyes glazing over, heartbeat slowing.

The answer came to her. She couldn't have known how she knew. That was the curse of Revomancy and its reliance on ineffable truths. And she couldn't understand *why*, but she felt certain of her discovery all the same.

Mateus K'vich, her unconscious told her. He had something to do with this. The what, why, and how of it, she couldn't yet know. But, beyond doubt, she would find out.

Her grip tightened on *Ida*, its ghastly beaked face grimacing back at her as it roiled hypnotically.

By Buthmertha, she would remove her uncle's ability to cause further harm. She would make him *explain himself*.

Whatever the cost, she would take back the answers he'd stolen from her.

15

CHO-ZEN

—AND, SUDDENLY, SHE WAS falling.

Midair, she spun and rolled before she hit the ground, minimizing injury by dissipating the impact of her fall.

Beneath her, wet asphalt. She was in the middle of a street. Back in Truct.

As soon as she stood, she wished she hadn't: dizzy, disoriented, and violently queasy, she hugged her gut.

A figure in a black cloak burst out of the closed-down car dealership to Cho's left. The figure carried a bag slung over one shoulder and a red mask in its left hand.

"Li," Cho called, but, her mouth dry as a dusty attic floor, she choked on the name. Lifting her face, she drank the pouring rain, swishing and gargling with it. She spat onto the street before crossing it to join her friend.

Alina hunched, face hooded by shadow and shadow-colored fabric, in the empty parking lot. Sounded like she was cackling.

"Li," said Cho, slowing. Reaching out and touching her seemed like a bad idea. Cho raised her voice: "Alina."

The quiet, guttural laughter drained away as if a plug had been pulled. Alina snapped out of her trance, or whatever, and looked at Cho with those golden eyes of hers. An earthy gold, the color of seams ringing the roots of mountains. Alina's eyes had once been a perfectly normal, pretty green with flecks of yellow. Since a few months ago, when the gold-eye-flashing had started, her eyes had still eventually reverted to their natural, human hue. However, the change-back part took longer each time. Maybe, one day, the gold would stick.

Sometimes, facing her felt like gazing into the eyes of a creature skulking inside an almost-convincing Alina-suit.

Blinking, focusing on Cho, Alina asked, "This looks like Valona Street."

"How'd we get here?" Cho bit her lip. "Must've been Morphea, right? Before…" She let the statement fade, cut to ribbons by the rain. "Why am I so thirsty?"

"A common side-effect of translocation," Alina said. "Yeah, Ruqastra *bamfed* us here. She—Anyway, she managed to have us both arrive pretty close together. Impressive." Looking away, she added, "Considering."

"So, where's Mezami?'"

"Here's hoping Ruqastra's three for three." Alina clamped the mask in her armpit, tossing back her hood before top-knotting and pinning her home-dyed red hair. Then the hood went up again. "Help me look around. Let's move."

"Yeah, can't stay out here. Authority patrol might swing by any minute."

They picked a direction and began to walk, not too briskly, searching as they went. They lingered in alleyways, checking in and under dumpsters, peering down sewer drains, and suspiciously eying stray dogs.

Alina said, "How did they find us? That's what I don't get. How?"

"What're you asking me for?"

"I dunno, maybe because there's something you're not telling me. Actually, bet there's a lot of somethings you haven't been sharing lately."

"Oh, really?"

"Yeah, like where you've been hanging out the last few weeks. Gone all hours of the day and night. Back late. Usually bruised and sweaty."

"You wanna do this. Here? Whatever. Sometimes I work out. Sometimes I go for a run or just do random stuff. What, you want me to hang around all day doing nothing while you learn magic tricks? Sorry, but I got my own goals. We can't all drop everything for Alina, the Chosen One."

"It's funny, you using those exact words. If I wanted to, I could throw them right back atcha. I never wanted to be special. But what about you, *Cho-Zen?*"

"I—well—How did you find out about that?"

"Cho, I can see into people's *dreams* now. Ruqastra held me prisoner on Morbin for eighteen months like a Dragon with her precious tower princess. You think for one second I wasn't using every trick I could come up with to escape even for an hour or two?"

"You, like, snooped around in my dreams?"

Alina had the decency to seem embarrassed.

Cho pulled her burner phone out of her pocket, held it up to her ear. "Hello, there, mysterious caller. What's that? You're with the Massive Privacy Violation Corporate Offices? Yes, uh-huh. Uh-*huh*. I see." She thrust the phone toward Alina, saying, "It's for you."

Elbowing her, Alina looked thoughtful. "What were you really up to?"

"Can't you just read my mind?"

"I can't see everything, and I don't get to pick which details. It's like pulling from a bag while blindfolded. Believe me, it's super frustrating. So, do you wanna talk about it or what?"

Sighing sharply, closing one eye, Cho admitted, "I mighta gotten Kinneas and myself into some trouble."

"What kind of trouble?"

Cho laced her fingers behind her head. "Y'know that DOMCOM fort downtown? Used to have a big ammo depot?"

"Used to...? You didn't."

"I kinda, um—" With her hands, she mimed an explosion.

They were silent, watching the runoff carry a grasshopper along the gutter.

"Look," Cho said, squaring off with Alina, "I'm not dealing with a lecture right now, so—"

Alina shut her up by gently touching her elbow. "It'd be a joke, Cho, honestly. Me, lecture you? Now? I'd be one to talk."

"Why, what'd you do?"

"Lately?"

Despite herself, Cho smirked. "Yeah, lately."

"I astral-projected into Mat—" She caught herself, started muttering. "Shouldn't say his name aloud yet, just in case. Dunno what all he can do." At normal volume: "I bumped into my uncle. Projected myself to him. In some stone-walled room, like a stuffy old office. Somewhere in Ozar."

"You can do that?"

"Apparently."

The downpour was downgraded to a drizzle.

Rubbing her eyes, Cho said. "Okay, okay, but even if you jaunted over to his study and such, he shouldn't have been able to track you, though? I thought we were protected on the mountain."

"Until I left earlier tonight."

"*You* broke the spell." Cho tried to keep the relief out of her voice.

Distracted by her own guilt, Alina didn't seem to notice. "If he had feelers out for me, and if he's powerful, he could've picked up my trail."

"Weren't you going to go after him eventually? With Ru—uh, once you got done training, I mean."

"Sure, eventually. Maybe. But, not like this."

Cho shook her head. No, not like this. "Are we sure it was him? Deadbeat uncle's one thing, but going after your own niece and her crew, that's lower than low."

"I got no proof, no. Just a really bad feeling. Isn't it weird? The day after I cross paths with him, The Authority swoops down, and—" Alina's voice cracked.

"Not just any Authority. Chimaera Guard. Walazzin's thugs."

"And those *things*." Alina sucked in a breath. "It doesn't matter which one of us caused this, or if we both did." Softly, maybe reassuring herself: "It doesn't matter." To Cho: "All that matters now is what we do next. We've gotta get to the Ammings' place."

"And drag Kinneas into this?"

"Is there literally one other option out there? Good idea, bad idea, I don't care, but I can't think of anything."

Beside them, a cardboard box stuffed with soaking newspaper finally tore from the weight of all that rainwater. The inky slush shredded across the sidewalk. Somewhere, a car alarm went off.

Cho's throat tightened. Her lip trembling, she looped her arms around her friend. "I can't believe they're gone," she said into the folds of Alina's cloak. "Just like that." When she backed away, she saw Alina was crying too.

"I'm sorry about Eilars. He hated my guts, but I kinda liked that about him." She wiped her eyes with her sleeve, which didn't help one bit because it too was dripping. "And I know he meant a lot to you."

Cho rubbed her nose on the back of her wrist. "Let's just go. Faster we find Mezzy, faster we get to the shop. Kinneas's life isn't gonna endanger itself." Shoving her hands in her pockets, she slouched forward.

Three minutes later, from farther ahead, they heard a muffled shriek, a crash, and the tinkle of glass. They looked up just in time to see the bristles of a broom slap a small, blue, mouse-like figure through the shattered window.

Wings aflutter, Mezami quickly spotted Cho and flew over to her, touching down on her shoulder. Leaning on her neck, below the umbrella of her wig, he shook himself like a dog. Droplets spattered Cho's skin as Mezami clenched his fist at the broken window, saying, "Damn: you, I."

"Glad we found you. You really got thrown, bucko."

Offhandedly, Alina said, "Could've been a lot worse. We might have come out of the wormhole inside out, or eyeless, or even wearing each other's clothes." She held out her hand for a low-five. Mezami's slap almost threw her to the ground. Shaking the soreness from her hand and, scoping the shattered second-story window, she said, "Yowza, Mezzy. Dude had it out for you. What'd you do to the poor guy?"

"Snack: cat, I."

"You ate his cat? Come on, man!"

"*Try*: eat, I."

"We are going to find you some chow immediately. I will not be having you eating cats in my town."

"Have: counterpoint, I."

"No, we *talked* about this."

"Agree: reluctantly, I."

"Moodiness noted."

The homeowner poked his bulbous nose outside. Glaring down at the three of them, he held his phone in front of his face, shouting into the receiver phrases like, "violent criminals," "forced entry," and "send help immediately."

"Time to move on," said Alina.

"Narc," Cho yelled.

They left as the man started chucking magazines at them.

"I'm coming with you," said Kinneas. He was sitting atop a tray precariously balanced on a pyramid of boxes. Every few seconds, he combed his fingers through his hair, futilely trying to smooth down his cowlick.

Being closed for business had only worsened the disorganization of the *Amming & Sons* tailor shop. Much of the merchandise had been packed up, even the colorful threads running along the walls near the ceilings. The nails around which they'd been wrapped remained. Dull, gray, rusting. The place was lit only by candlelight. All its windows were kept closed, the drapes drawn. Dimness, dustiness spread like a wet sneeze through the unventilated damp.

Mezami had turned a clutch of spider eggs into a tasty snack, and now he napped, like some kind of hermit crab, in a corner under an overturned can of beans.

"I'm coming with you," Kinneas repeated.

Her elbows propped on the dusty sales counter, between the stacks of newspaper, Alina grimaced at him. "How d'you figure?"

"Yeah," Cho chimed in. "Did you not hear anything we just told you?"

"I got it. You're in danger. I wannu help."

"Kin, please don't take this the wrong way, but—"

"Stop talkin' to me like I'm a little kid," he said, sliding off his box seat. "I'm a Maggo—an Aquamancer. I can fight."

"You're an Aquamancer-in-*training*," Alina corrected. "And you should know when to cool it. You're nowhere near ready for..." She paused before finishing quietly with, "what's gotta happen next." She slapped herself on the forehead, covering her eyes. "Oh my gods. I sound just like Baraam. I've become *Baraam*. Cho, help me."

"Relax, already, you're nothing like Captain Thunderpants." Then Cho patted Kinneas's hand and said, "We're working the thinnest of hunches here, man, and it feels like we haven't hit maximum badness yet. Ya gotta understand, I can't have any more of my friends dying on me."

For some reason, what she'd said made Kinneas pull away, turn from her, cross his arms. "Couple of *Iurk'et* heads, the both of ya. You're not the only ones who've lost someone, ya know." Cho reached for him, but he leapt like a butter-flyfish. "Don't touch me right now. Got no room for your pity."

"Kin," said Cho, fingers curling, hand drifting down to rest on the back of a tablecloth-covered chair.

"Why do you think I came with you all those nights we spied on the pinkojacks?"

"I knew it," Alina muttered.

"The Authority's no friends of mine," Kinneas shouted. "I hate 'em for what's happened to Dad, and I hate 'em even more for taking Calthin from me. 'He'll serve a tour or two,' they said, 'and Mr. Amming's medical bills will be taken care of.' Like hells they were! My dad's in the ground, and my brother's off somewhere getting shot at, and you're telling me I need to sit down and shut up like some stupid little village idiot boy." He thumped his chest. "I got every right to hate 'em as much as you do, and to want to hurt them for what they did to me. And I'm not a coward. I'll fight 'em." He deflated a little. "You two can't say *nothin'* anyway. Like either of you ever did what you're told."

Cho snorted, looking to Alina to rally and talk him down.

Lips pursed, Alina smiled. "Kinneas Amming."

She'd used the tone that meant the start of class; he straightened his spine and pulled back his shoulders.

Something about the gleam in her eye made Cho queasy.

"Let's see what you've got," Alina said.

"It's raining, though," he said.

"Huh. And here I thought an Aquamancer would be grateful for the ad-vantage." Alina moved toward the front door, and, all at once, every candle in the room went out.

A hush consumed the room. A feeling like cold, damp flecks of dirt tumbling down Cho's spine.

Kinneas hopped off his seat.

Alina's gold eyes shined in the dimly lit room as the door creaked open. The flickering streetlamp cast a pale cerulean glow on her thin, black-cloaked frame.

At the threshold, she waited.

Cho's ears popped; Kinneas was flaring his Niima. He stepped outside into the storm.

They stood in the downward-sloping strip mall parking lot, water draining into a grate between them.

Watching from the sidelines, Cho and Mezami placed their bets. Of course, neither of them wagered against Alina. Rather, they gambled on how long Kinneas would last.

"Let's go, Kinneas! Let's go," Cho shouted because she'd placed a ten-gelder bet on him going a whole minute before tapping out.

"Fail: shame, not," said Mezami, who'd bet thirty seconds or fewer.

Sprays of misting rain spattered Alina, a gust catching the edges of her cloak which—amid the eddies and flurries of wind and water—had never looked more like a crow's wing, extending for takeoff.

Around Kinneas, the rain formed a thin, miniature vortex.

"Quit showing off," Alina yelled.

When Kinneas started whispering the words of the spell he was casting—telegraphing his punch—Cho shook her head. Not a great start.

He leapt into a deep lunge, arms jabbing forward, shooting through the rain like a swordfish through the sea. Ahead of him, a jet of high-pressure water blew towards Alina, who deflected it with a transparent energy shield. But he wasn't done: now within spitting distance, he swung his back foot into a front kick, a scythe of water trailing it.

Twirling, she hip-checked him, following up with an elbow to his throat—which was just a feint. It gave her the opening to grab his arm at the elbow, spin him, bend his wrist back, and control his shoulder with the flat of her hand.

Kinneas struggled, grunting. All the rainwater on his skin solidified into ice, and Alina lost her grip.

He sprung backward, turning to face her, arms raised.

"You've gotten real slippery," said Alina, clenching her fingers to crack the ice off them. "Good for you. But I'm gonna need you to stop aiming *near* me and start aiming *at* me. My next move is going to end the match. Unless you stop me."

Growling, he wove together the words and hand-signs that froze the rain in a column above Alina's head, turning the hundreds of drops into hail. She shifted backward to avoid the shards, and he charged, his arms like fins, cutting the water, sending a ripple of force that gathered it in the sky and on the ground into a single wave. The wave became solid, crashing into her. The sheet of ice exploded like glass struck by a hammer.

The cocky grin barely had time to pass his lips before she leapt at him, aiming a strike at his center of gravity. He easily knocked aside her spear-hand, protecting his solar plexus. She repeated the attack. He blocked it again. She repeated it *again*.

"What are you doing?" he shouted.

Then, from both sides, fists made of asphalt and concrete shot upward, flying toward his head. He ducked these, putting his face directly in line with Alina—at the tip of this dangerous triangle—and her punch.

He winced.

She pulled the punch at the last fraction of a second, but the force behind it blew his hair back and unbalanced him, putting him on his backside, awash in gray gutter- and garbage water.

Cho watched as the rain evaporated around Alina, turning to steam before even touching her.

Beside Cho, Mezami cleared his throat. Grumbling, she rolled up a ten-gelder bill and surrendered it to him. He unrolled it, folded it into a much smaller rectangle, rolled it up again, and tucked it into his belt, wearing it like a sword.

Splashing in the puddle of his defeat, Kinneas slammed his fist onto the ground. He clearly regretted it, though, grabbing his wrist and whimpering, "Ow, ow, ow."

Striding over, Alina said, "That wasn't bad, honestly. But 'not bad' isn't good enough." Standing over him, blocking the shoddy streetlamp's flimsy light, her shadow engulfed him like a wave of molasses. "The next time you fight, you'd better *win*," she said, a single lock of hair having come loose from the hairpin. "Where we're going, second place'll get ya killed."

Whipping a strand of his hair out of his mouth, Kinneas looked up at her. "We?"

She helped him up.

"So. What's the plan?" said Kinneas. "Fill me in."

Back inside *Amming & Sons*, drying off with musty towels, Cho wringing out her wig, the four of them sat around eating whatever packaged and canned goods could be scrounged from the pantry.

Cho popped open her can of clam chowder (which tasted like tin, but she had no cause to complain), and she stowed her pocket multi-tool (can-opener, bottle opener, knife, toothpick, guitar pick, lockpick...). "If working with the resistance has taught me one thing—" she dropped a mouthful of gooey, room-temperature chowder between her lips and chewed—"it's that picking off outposts and cell towers and even ammo depots run by The Authority—the

Walazzins—it's too small-time. They just replace whatever we break or steal. We're gonna need a bigger hit. Something that *hurts*."

Juggling three beans, Mezami said, "Remove: head, you. Die: will, beast."

"Mezami!" said Alina.

"He's not wrong, though," said Cho. "Whenever we harass the grunts, the big shots don't feel it. We gotta poison the source."

"Sure, yeah." Alina stretched in her seat. "Then, when we get noticed, they'll send the Jaandarmes to axe us. Scratch that. They'll catch, torture, and *then* kill us." She sucked up a lump of canned, gravy-soaked beef.

"They need to pay," said Cho. "You hafta see that, at least."

Alina clutched her can of beef and flicked her pointer finger toward Cho. "Once upon a time, weren't you the one who told me to be 'better' than that? The tables have turned, I guess, but the truth hasn't. We can't be in this for revenge. What we should be after is answers."

"Answers to what?"

"Why they did this. Why they want to kill me."

"Who cares?"

"Uh. *Oh*-kay."

"I didn't mean it like that. Quit making this all about you."

"I'm not—"

"Ya gonna let me finish?" Cho snapped. "I'm saying, the Walazzins've been coming after my family and me since I was in diapers. I've got as much skin in this as you, and I don't care *why* they want me crossed out. They just do. Maybe they're angling to hold onto all my family's fortune and land and stuff, and they don't want me popping up later to stir the pot. Maybe they just love making people suffer. Whatevs. Doesn't change what I want: them, dead."

Alina licked her teeth. "Killing solves nothing."

"Oh, enough already. Get off your whole Buthmertha trip. You're not better than me, Li. 'Kay? Your whole saintly song and dance is phonier than my wig."

"Back off, Cho," said Alina, tone low.

"It's different now. Alright? It's different. Two years ago, it was you versus other Ravers who were all after money. Just money. And you were ready to kill Ordin because he got in your way."

The shadows swelled, the weakening candlelight sputtering. "Ordin betrayed me."

"Yeah, he betrayed you, fine. He tricked you, definitely. But what were you fighting for? A cash prize. That's nothing like now. Now, here, in this moment, it's not about money, or safety, or what we think we're owed anymore. It's about what's right. The Walazzins killed Eilars and Morphea. Our people were murdered by the Chimaera Guard and nightmare bone-things. But even that isn't the worst part. I'll tell you what is: the Walazzins have hurt millions of people the same as us. Some even worse." Cho glanced toward Kinneas, who was nose-deep in canned chili with a side of stale blond sandwich cookies. "Truct, and the whole province… People like us, who just wanna live, we're never gonna be free until we're rid of the Walazzins. They're cancer, and we gotta cut them out. So, yeah, I want them dead, but I don't want them dead for me." Cho could almost be certain that last bit was the truth. "They gotta go because they're bad for everybody."

Alina crossed her arms, refusing to meet Cho's eye, saying, "I don't disagree. I really don't. Not totally. But, it's… Even if taking out Walazzin was the right way to handle this—and I can't agree with that part—how would you even get close to that old creep? I don't think getting kidnapped by him is going to go so well a second time."

"Yah, no, I'm done being ordered around and kept prisoner."

"And we can't go back to New El. The Enforcers would tag us and bag us before we got a hundred miles outside the city."

"I'm not talking about The Capital. I'm talking about this." Cho unzipped her front jacket pocket and pulled out Rooster's fake tooth.

Frowning, Alina asked, "You feeling okay?"

"Ha-ha. Shut up. I don't know what's on here, exactly, but whatever it is led to Rooster being thrown into the downtown prison camp."

"Gods, you're working with Rooster?"

"Li, I need ya to focus. This—" Cho held up the tooth—"is important. It has to be."

"Great. But how do we use it? We don't hafta, like—" Alina gagged—"put it in one of our mouths, do we?"

"Yuggh, gross. No, it's virtually coded. We just need to hop onto the Darkthreads. That should let me see what's hidden inside."

"Can you just pop it into your ear or something?"

"As an enhanced individual, I don't appreciate your stereotyping. The connector's too retro. Without an adapter, I can't use it directly." She snapped her fingers. "Kinneas?" He'd nodded off, lips parted, snoring softly. "Kinneas!" He snapped awake, muttering, a little surge of Niima sparking from him, causing his sweat droplets to spatter against the ceiling. Cho asked him, "You still have those old VR octo-helmets?"

"Well, yeah," he mumbled, "but we got no power."

Cho remembered they were gathered in a candle-lit room. No electricity. "Damn."

Alina cleared her throat. "I've got an idea."

"Thanks, but—don't take this the wrong way—all that witchy stuff makes me uncomfortable."

"You're not the only one. Still, you got a better plan?"

With a sigh, Cho passed her the tooth.

"Yummy," said Alina. She looked around, spreading her arms. "I'm gonna need a bit of space. Three feet in diameter at least."

"Or what? The building explodes?" Kinneas grinned.

"Or I get claustrophobic and can't enter the trance state."

Between the four of them, Mezami doing most of the heavy lifting, they made quick work of shoving stacks of boxes and other miscellaneous junk into corners.

Producing a piece of white chalk, Alina drew a circle in her practiced free-hand. Then she sat cross-legged at its center. The tooth rested in her palm. "Anything I need to know about this thing?"

Cho shrugged. "I don't know how Revomancy works—"

"To be fair, neither do I, really."

"—but as long as you can, uh, open it, you should be able to read or watch the information inside."

"The vaguest possible instructions. Sweet."

"I don't know if it's video or text, but, like, it is *Rooster* we're talking about. Can't be too complicated."

"Anything else?"

"Yeah, if it asks you for a password, it'll be 'Stitcher.'"

Frowning at the use of her old nickname, the one she'd tried on at different times throughout the years (and, most recently, to spectacularly disastrous effect in New El), Alina said, "Why?"

Cho stuck out her tongue and winked. "I can't help Rooster's romantic tastes."

"Ugh." Alina closed her eyes. Squinting out of one of them, she said, "Maybe you could all just not stare at me the whole time I'm doing this. Just, go away. As you were. It's not gonna work if I'm feeling self-conscious." Murmuring a mantra under her breath, she again peeked through one eye. "Before you go, quick note: if I start screaming at the top of my lungs, just kinda let me wear myself out."

Cho chuckled nervously.

Alina shifted, reaching into her bag. She took the red crow mask and pulled it over her face, closing her eye.

Another deep breath or two, and she'd slipped away.

Cho snapped her fingers in front of Alina's face. No response.

16

ALINA

SHE'D FOCUSED ON HER breathing, feeling the tingle of her life
energy originating in her heart and surging outward from there. Traveling throughout her body. To her fingertips, toe-tips, and the roots of
her hair. It hadn't stopped there, either. Within moments, her essence had
melded with the physical and metaphysical worlds around her.

Separation is illusion, she'd reminded herself. She could go anywhere because
she already *was* everywhere.

"Entering" Rooster's artificial tooth turned out to be far easier than she had
anticipated. Relaxing into the meditative state Ruqastra had taught her, she imagined the tooth held loosely in her hand opened itself to her. And, in the
Revoscape, imagination *was* reality. But, of course, everything did end up just a
bit zanier than it would have had Cho accessed the data via the Darkthreads.
Virtual reality could be weird and tricky in its own way, but it had nothing on the
*un*reality of dream.

Alina stood in a circle of what she at first thought were stones. In fact, they
were too angular, ridged, and shiny-white to be anything but teeth. Jutting out of
a sandy beach. Waves lapped at her boots like a fuzzy gray tongue, a fog unraveling, screening the weak sunlight.

Before her stood a tall, gangly man with gelled, spiky red hair.

"Rooster?" she said. She lifted her mask.

"Stitchee-o," said Rooster cheerfully, opening his arms for a hug. Then he paused, remembering a problem. "Alas, I'm not real. I'm Rooster.exe. The real Rooster left me as a worm in case of unauthorized access. Cho-Zen is the only one who has access to this file."

"Really?" Alina slid the mask back over her face. "If that's true, then why is the password 'Stitcher'?"

"You know about that, eh? I've never been much good at hiding my truest affections, have I?"

"Cho gave me permission to see what you left her. We're out of options. You gonna spill the beans?"

"For you, anything." He blushed. "Also, I'm literally incapable of doing otherwise, now that you've given the password. Just one query, if you don't mind."

"Yeah?"

"In the real world, do we happen to be romantically involved yet?"

"Uhh, I don't—"

"Say no more. I was programmed to ask that question, but I see that it's made you uncomfortable. Here." He walked up to the nearest tooth, which glowed. All the tooth-stones began to glow. Rooster.exe said, "Access granted," and then backed away, fading into the fog.

Tentatively, Alina reached out and touched the nearest tooth-stone. A jolt ran through her fingers and into her skull, bounced around, and exploded into hundreds and thousands of pictures, digimails, and video files.

She saw inter-office communications, Authority clerks detailing meetings between generals; boot camp training videos; photographs of refugee and prison facilities all throughout El; strategy maps outlining troop movements; lists of enemy combatants and persons of interest to be captured or assassinated; and the current location of high value targets.

"Rooster, you mohawked fox." Alina whistled. "You hit the mother lode."

Just like that, she had absorbed terabytes worth of data on the Elemental Empire's battle plans. The most useful of these, relevant to what she'd been looking for, was the impending siege on some place called Hexhall in the City-State of Ozar.

Wodjaego and his son Kaspuri were going to be there. The Walazzins would lead the assault. Based on the battle maps and audio recordings of talks between military officers, this was set to be a decisive strike.

Alina didn't care about what The Authority wanted in Ozar. El had spent centuries conquering its neighbors and other countries around the world. There was always some kind of war going on. But now she knew where the Walazzins would be.

She just had to decide whether she'd tell Cho. If she did, there'd be nothing standing between the girl and her suicidal revenge mission

Well, anyway, there was no sense in sticking around, here in this weird circle of teeth.

She was just about to wake herself when, all at once, the fog dissipated and the sun above shifted from dull and soft to sharp and searing, a blazing orb whose radiance filled the expansive beach. Its oppressiveness was like a weight bearing down on Alina's shoulders. She instantly broke into a sweat.

Vrana, said a voice.

"Eh?" She cast about, seeking its source.

It had rumbled like the start of a rock slide and roared like a spout of magma bursting from a volcano. All the same, what it had said was unmistakably clear, even though those two syllables meant nothing to Alina.

Vrana, it said again. *Where are you? It has been too long.*

She finally identified the direction the echoing voice originated from: squinting at the sun, she shouted, "Wrong number."

Vrana. The First.

The heat of the dream-sun pressed against her. The sweat on her face sizzled, evaporating into flecks of salt.

"Look, buddy, dunno what to tell ya, but I'm not 'Vrana.' I'm hanging up now."

She tugged on the cord of energy around her midriff, willing herself to wake up.

It wasn't working.

"Uh."

The temperature was becoming unbearable by now. Felt like she was being basted in her own sweat.

Arms burst forth from the sand around her. She jumped. The limbs were made of sand themselves, and they pulled larger sand bodies out of the ground.

There were dozens of them. As they climbed out of the earth and stood, each was sculpted by invisible hands, scooping away excess material, until they resembled moving, human-shaped sand statues. Most Alina didn't recognize, but there were two she did: Mateus K'vich and Tolomond Stayd.

The Tolomond effigy lunged, grabbing her by the throat, stifling her yelp. Where it throttled her, the sand hardened, flash-baked into gleaming glass.

The other sand figures closed in, arms extended, fingers bent and reaching.

Without thinking, she flung out her hand, looping her fingers around sand-Mateus's arm. As soon as her skin connected with its body—

—she was thrown far away from the tooth-stone beach, hurtling through a narrow dark tunnel, bouncing off its walls, spinning, tumbling.

She landed on a mosaic floor of lusterless blue and red tiles. Posted on her elbows, she gazed up at a vaulted cathedral ceiling, gaping at the gargoyles. What had happened? She'd fallen, yes, but how?

She discovered there were people all around her, silent, waiting, focused entirely on her.

Knowing by their confused, hopeful expressions that they expected something of her, knowing she needed to reassure them, she said, "The Author has spoken to me. Just now. His spirit has entered me; He blesses you all, who have come though you are hated and mistrusted for your love of God. But He sees you, He does. He is witness to your commitment."

She arose and moved through the parting crowd, approaching the dais whose corners were lit by roaring braziers. Flames reached out to embrace her as she neared.

That's right, she thought, running her fingers through her graying beard: the Lectors, Exorcists, and the dregs of the church were all present, impatient for the Firelight Vigil she was meant to lead.

Atop the dais, she placed her hairy-knuckled, heavily calloused hands on the lectern and gazed upon the hundreds of attentive faces—old and young, Elemental and Ozari—and said, "Sanctumites, let us pray. In the Name of The Author."

"Hail The Savior," called someone in the crowd.

"I am but a man," said Alina, stilling the outburst with a wave. "It is to our Lord that we give thanks. It is for Him that we labor. May He Rewrite our Story."

"May we be His Instruments," said the gathered faithful.

A most pleasing sentiment. Yet, something was wrong.

She cradled her head in her hands, playing it off as the onset of divine bliss. Really, she didn't feel quite herself.

What was happening?

Who is this? she thought. *Who are you?*

You again? a second thinker replied, straining as he untangled their minds. *How did you get in?*

Thrown upward, Alina sailed past the grinning gargoyles, through the vaulted cathedral ceiling, into the sky, and she landed on the beach, in a milky white pool.

Transparent, skeletal glass hands wrapped in soggy, see-through gray fabric latched onto her. They pulled her down—or up—and she was submerged in the milky liquid, blinded, choking—

17

CHO-ZEN

O VER ALINA'S MASK-MUFFLED SCREAMS, Cho shouted, "I know what she said, but I'm pretty sure this ain't alright!" She lunged and tore the red mask from her friend's face, flinging it aside.

The screaming stopped, and Cho held her breath, but then Alina began to choke, her arms rising, fingers scratching her throat. She gasped for air as the flesh of her arms turned gray, and her nose lengthened, got bonier, became more beak-like.

Leaping onto Alina, Cho shook her by the shoulders, tearing her claws away from her throat, yelling, "Li, wake up!" Cho slapped her—once, twice. She nicked her finger on one of the small bladed feathers jutting from Alina's cheek.

"She's going into shock!" Kinneas yelled.

"Get back!" Cho raised her hand again. Before that third slap landed, Alina threw her off.

Her eyes wide, she sucked in a string of shallow breaths. Black feathers shriveling, her skin flushed and darkened with human color once more.

"By Buthmertha, what happened?" Kinneas knelt beside them, gaping at Alina's transformation. "Some kinda spell?"

Poor, innocent Kinneas. Cho nudged him away. "Give her some air."

Clasping Cho's hands, Alina stuttered, "The Walazzins—Kaspuri—they're in Ozar. Big, big battle, and they'll be there, in the thick of it. That's when we get 'em."

"Alina, you're shivering and your lips are turning a very pretty but upsetting shade of purple." Cho brushed her friend's hair from her face. "Are you copacetic? Can I getcha something?"

"I'm fine."

"No, you're not, but alright. What else did ya see?"

"I think I might have a stalker."

Cho pursed her lips. "Want me to beat him up?"

Alina cough-laughed, and Cho smiled.

Sitting upright, Alina accepted Kinneas's offer a water bottle and explained everything she'd experienced.

"Is: Vrana, who?" said Mezami.

"No clue. But my new astral pal sure seemed convinced he had the right gal. Maybe the mask reminded them of someone?"

"What do you think they were? A Maggo, messing with you?"

"Thought it might've been another Revomancer at first. That would've explained the bad guy sand statue collection." Alina chugged the contents of the water bottle, set it down half-empty, and said, "But, nah. I've never felt anything like that. This thing turned the earth and sky against me. Whatever they are, they aren't human. I was totally powerless against them."

"You weren't. Got yourself out and all. Though, I still don't get where you ended up to begin with."

"I don't either. I think I was inside my uncle's mind. Or, my mind *was* his mind. It's confusing. I'm pretty freaked." She shivered. "I can't stop thinking this is all connected to my uncle and me somehow."

Kinneas said, "It is super bizarre that he's in Ozar. Right where Walazzins'll be. Maybe it's fate."

"Eh," said Alina. "Let's not get carried away. There's probably a connection, but don't go slapping the 'divinity' label on anything just yet. All I'm saying is there's something up, and now I'm even more invested." She locked eyes with each of them in turn.

Reality clamped its cold grip onto Cho's neck. This time felt different from the events leading up to the Battle at City Hall. Whether that was good or bad remained to be seen. Once again, though, Alina had found a way to further complicate an already ridiculous problem. It had been horrible enough, watching Eilars torn to shreds by those animated bone monsters. And Morphea, cut down. But now Alina's messed up family was somehow involved. Wonderful, and somehow perfectly predictable.

"What if," Alina started, finishing her water bottle, "what if The Authority knows he's there? Or, if they don't already, what if they find out."

"Yeah, what if?" said Cho.

"That can't happen. They *can't* have him. Ruqastra told me Dimas said *I* had to be the one to... you know..."

"Kill him?" At Cho's words, Alina tensed as if she'd been slapped again. Cho didn't relent. "Listen to what you're saying: 'she said that he said that she said'… Did any of them bother to tell you *how* you were supposed to fulfill your stupid destiny?"

"No, but—" Alina pointed to Cho's bag—"this Lorestone's supposed to have the answers. Only, Ruqastra didn't show me what to do with it. Or give me the missing piece that I apparently need to get the whole truth."

"Wouldja *please* stop listing problems before my head explodes?" Kinneas said. "There's so much to worry about already. Magic rocks, evil uncles, skeleton monsters… Can we start simpler, work from there? How we getting to Ozar in the first place? Alina, you can fly."

She said, "Short distances. Ozar's south of Kadic. It's like a thousand miles away."

"Two thousand three hundred and fifty, give or take," said Cho.

"What she said." Alina rubbed her eyes with her palm heels. "You're right, Kinneas. There's too much, so we should focus on what we can solve right now."

Humming to herself, Cho said, "Sometimes I wish you could just magic an atom bomb or something."

"What?" said Alina.

"Like when you saved Mezami's life. You told me about that, remember. You were messing with the molecules to make radioactive stuff for him. Could just do that a bunch of times but, like, make plutonium or something. Chuck that at the Walazzins's palace. End it in five seconds."

"I appreciate the humor," Alina interrupted, "But that's never gonna happen, so let's not waste more time on the idea."

"Not everyone can do what you did. I looked it up. Just sayin'."

"Even so, just because I *can* build a dirty bomb (probably) doesn't mean I should. If everyone who could do terrible stuff *did*, we wouldn't be having this conversation right now. 'Cause we'd be dead."

"—we'd be dead, yeah, gotcha."

"Destroying the world is good for nobody. It's why it hasn't been done."

"Yet."

"Look, we're just talking in circles. Face it, we're three kids and a flying pocket mouse."

Mezami snarled. "Am: not, I!"

"Point is, we're *not* getting to Ozar on our own." Alina massaged her wrists. "Wish I didn't feel like I had no other options, but there's only one play, here." She picked up her phone, opened a message string, tapped the "call" button. After a few seconds of silence, she said, "Ivion?"

"What're you doing?" Cho whispered, trying to snatch the phone from Alina's hand.

Cho prided herself on her speed, but Alina cheated by shadow-teleporting across the room, saying, "Bad connection, sorry. Yeah. Just calling to tell you

I've thought about your offer, and, as long as I can bring my entourage, we're on."

The person on the other end of the line said something Cho couldn't catch.

"Great." Alina hung up.

Arms akimbo, Cho said, "Who the hells is 'Ivion'?"

18

ALINA

HOVERING BY THE DOOR to the Ammings' shop, Alina heard whispering inside; Cho and Kinneas were talking about her. She could've heard a pine needle falling onto damp moss, so making out the words of two excitable teens was no problem.

Kinneas hissed, "We're just gonna pretend that she didn't go all gray and, and spiky on us? What was that all about?"

So, Alina realized, they'd seen the monster rattling around her insides. She'd hoped to cage it longer.

"I don't know what to tell ya," Cho said. "But I won't—shh! Shut up. Someone's outside."

Taking that as her cue, Alina entered. "Cho, Mezami, Kinneas," she said, holding the door open for the woman in the white suit. "This is Ivion Ivoir."

Predictably, Cho's nostrils flared, but she held her tongue behind puckered lips.

Tossing her head, her wet platinum hair glistening against her pale cheeks, Ivion smiled. "It is gratifying to make your acquaintances."

The noise Kinneas made, part groan and part throat-rattle, coincided with the reddening of his ears. "Uh. Nice to meet you." He rushed forward, offering his hand.

Cho's foot shot out, tripping him. "Don't you get all cozy with the likes of her."

"Lady Shazura-Torvir." Ivion bowed her head. "One cause of my being here today is to begin to make amends for the hardships you have suffered. My long silence in the wake of your family's tragedy has made me complicit." She did not look up. "Please accept my deepest apologies."

"Useless words," Cho snapped.

"Too right you are. I deserve your ire. We, the children of the Plutocracy, did not raise our voices in protest when most needed."

"Talk wouldn't have saved my family."

"That is why I offer action in its stead." Ivion, still gazing at the dusty floorboards, took a knee. "Lady Choraelia of House Torvir, I—Ivion Lantusia Arenee Alecta Ivoir—solemnly swear that I shall bring to bear all of my power, ability, and resources in delivering justice unto you."

Arms crossed, Cho side-eyed Alina. Her thoughts were so sharp and clear Alina could hear them as if they'd been uttered out loud: *fine then; perfect little package; impossibly privileged woman-girl, sashaying on in; spotless white pants, little white booties; good presentation, yeah; what's she hiding under her seamless surface?*

After a few seconds of shredding Ivion with her gaze, Cho said, "Well, you aren't lying. So, I guess we'll hear you out. But, just so everybody knows, I've got major reservations about bringing you in. I don't trust you, and not just because of your brother's bad habits. I didn't wish him dead, but you can't say he was the dictionary definition of chivalry or anything."

On her feet again, Ivion said, "My brother—Plutonia rest his soul—was far from perfect, but I loved him because he was mine." She locked her hazel eyes with Cho's. "You, of all people, ought to know the full weight of that love which binds us. Tethered to it, we may sink or soar, but it is ours to hold. Forever."

"Sure. As long as everyone knows that I don't trust noble or rich people, generally; and, specifically, I don't trust smooth-talkers or anyone who appears just a little too conveniently close to when they're needed."

"Would ya let her speak?" Alina said. "Buthmertha help me."

Ivion rubbed Alina's elbow, their eyes meeting. "I have been informed of the terrors that befell you last night, and your pressing need to head southwest. By the grace of Seventy-Seven Gods, our interests are in perfect alignment. We all want the Walazzins disposed of."

"One way or another, they need to be stopped, but I won't be part of any murder plot," Alina said. "My target is The Sanctum."

Her expression statuesque, the ideal of saintly patience, Ivion patted Alina's hand, saying, "In recent years, The Sanctumites and Authority have bound their fates the one to the other. The zealots bolster morale with their pro-imperial propaganda, and their ideology infects the footsoldiers and commanders alike. Attacking the preachers is the same as attacking the army, and defeating the one requires dealing with both. This clearly supplies you each with *motive* to infiltrate Ozar. Now, with your blessings, I would like to supply the *means* and *opportunity*."

"How fantastically convenient!" Cho clapped her hands.

"I know you scanned me, Lady Torvir." Ivion's eyes narrowed. "By your admission, I'm not lying. Yet you doubt me."

"That's right."

"Why?"

"I just do."

"Do you not trust your friend?"

Alina straightened. The grimace on Cho's face when looking at her lingered a little too long, and her, "Yeah," was slower in coming than it should have been.

But she did say, "Yeah, I trust Li. Doesn't mean she's not wrong."

"We haven't committed to anything yet," said Alina. "If you're not cool with the deal by the end, we'll scrap it. Just, what's the harm in hearing her out?"

Cho was obviously scraping her conversational reserves for a comeback, but Ivion was faster: "If the lady has finished listing her concerns, perhaps she will allow me to explain the plan…"

Ten minutes later, Cho leaned back and forced a laugh. "Oh-hoh, no way. Don't like that at all." Rudely sticking a finger in Ivion's face: "First of all, who even *are* you? And, secondly, how can you think we'd all hand ourselves over to you, no questions asked? Why should we trust you when your brother was a capital-J Jerk."

"Cho," Alina said, reminding herself to breathe. "Ordin's dead, and Ivion's been straight with us so far. Her way's so much better than anything we could pull off on our own. Admit it."

"Yah, sure," Cho said, pouting, "maybe. But I still don't like it."

"I dunno if my vote matters," Kinneas said, "but the plan makes sense to me."

"Of course you'd take Alina's side."

"What's that supposed to mean?"

"You're always sucking up to her."

"Oh, come on," said Alina. "He's one-hundred-percent your little devotee."

At the jab, Kinneas blushed salmon-pink. "Woah, am not."

"Ivion," Alina said, "I apologize for their childishness, but please don't judge us. We've had a long night. They're helpful when it matters."

Ivion said, "I would not trust me, were I in your shoes."

"Hah!" Cho poked Alina between the collarbones.

Ivion continued, "Understanding your reluctance, I can offer you some insurance: hold me hostage. Allow me to travel with you, and if our relationship sours, you may kill me." She smiled at Cho. "Are these terms acceptable?"

Shrugging, Cho said, "It's dramatic and hardcore. Now you're speaking my language."

Alina said, "Kinneas?"

"Since Ms. Ivoir's willing to put herself in danger with us, she must be pretty confident, so I'm down."

Ivion winked at Alina, who felt a tingling in her gut.

Growling under her breath, Cho paced between the stacks of boxes as the candles burned low. "If this is a trap—"

"You'll slit my throat." Ivion's smile was as soft and beautiful as a morning-misted spider's web.

"I won't have to." Licking her thumb and finger, Cho pinched out a candle's flame. "Because *he'll* beat me to it." Mezami landed on her knuckle and flexed his thimble-sized pecs. She gave a slight nod.

"We'll just take that as a horribly awkward 'yes.' So," Alina said, "when do we hit the road?"

Outside, under the cover of her transparent umbrella, Ivion sauntered over to Alina. "That went better than I had any right to hope."

"Sorry for Cho's attitude. She means well."

"I admire her ferocity in defending her friend. She's a mountain cat on the prowl." Lifting her chin, closing her eyes, Ivion inhaled the scent of the rain. "Three days in a freight truck is by no means my first choice of how to spend a weekend, but the company could certainly be worse."

She stared at Alina, who said, "Uh. Likewise."

Ivion held up a key fob and clicked the chrome button. A red, sporty hover-car whirred to life and glided across the parking lot. "I am sure I will enjoy watching you... work." She took Alina's hand, kissed it, held on.

The car door lifted straight up. Ivion released Alina's hand and, closing and shaking her umbrella before tossing it onto the passenger seat, she climbed inside.

She revved the engine, giving Alina a little wave. The door closed, and the vehicle zoomed off.

Alina was left alone to count the number of seconds before her heart rate returned to normal.

Some hours later, as Alina lay heavily on the Ammings' couch, drifting from this reality and into another, she felt a nagging suspicion that she was forgetting something.

She must have nodded off because, when she opened her eyes again, the sun had risen.

With a gasp, she tumbled off the couch.

Scrambling for her bag, she ripped it free from the corner of a box, spilling a bunch of fragile-sounding stuff onto the ground—pottery maybe, but she didn't care. She tore the zipper open and searched inside the bag.

Her fingers came out wet and *chalky*, sizzling slightly.

"Damn it."

She went out back and emptied her bag into the trash bin. Every single item inside it had been soaked in Ruqastra's *Auggie* mix. The vials must have shattered when Alina had fallen through the dealership roof last night.

At the kitchen sink, as she scrubbed the now-stinging iridescent liquid from her fingertips with soap and sponge, she stopped.

It scared her that her last several doses of this "fortifier" which was supposed to make her stronger had been destroyed—now of all times. Worse, though, was the thought that Ruqastra wouldn't ever brew any more of it again.

Alina scrubbed and scrubbed and tried her best to think of nothing.

19

CHO-ZEN

THE THREE-DAY JOURNEY WOULD turn out far more boring than Cho could ever have imagined. Before meeting Alina, she'd never been outside The Capital. Since then, all she'd seen was Truct (not exactly a hub of art and culture). So, she had hoped to maybe watch the changing scenery roll by, see some sights. No dice.

According to Ivion's master plan, they'd all hopped into a rental car, Ivion driving them an hour east toward Puurissei. There, they were stashed inside a couple of empty crates and hauled into one of Applied Infomatics's freight trucks. The company (owned by the Ivoir Family) had a convoy scheduled to deliver microchips and computer cables to Ozar.

"Supplying the Elemental war effort?" Cho had said, once informed of this part of the plan.

"Hospital emergency rooms, actually," had been Ivion's answer.

The first hour or two Cho had spent pressed up against an excessively sweaty Kinneas, who did his best to shrink away from her even though they shared a tiny cube's worth of squatting space. Eventually, Ivion had given the signal, and they'd all popped out of their boxes into the only slightly less baking-hot interior of the truck itself.

Ivion showed them the hidden switch that opened the hatch leading into the secret compartment right behind the cabin. And that's where they stayed for almost the whole stretch.

The truck was auto-piloted, at least, so they didn't have to worry too much about making noise. Lucky, because talking was just about all they could do in that cramped toaster oven.

Poor, sweet, silly Kinneas had brought a deck of cards, which provided about forty-five minutes of quality entertainment and bonding time before everyone grew too hot and frustrated to focus on games.

Mezami and Cho lazily mumbled their way through "I Scry" and "Fifteen Questions" for a while, until their idle chatter started to annoy Alina.

By the end of the first day, they were all ready to pull each other's hair out, but made it through without major injuries. And Ivion informed them that they'd cleared the border of El shortly before nightfall. "My bribe fell into the right pockets."

Mezami periodically asked, "There: yet, we?" And the others took turns grumbling, "No." Except Ivion, of course. Miss prim-and-proper sat with perfect posture, back against the truck wall, polite as ever. At least she'd traded her ridiculous pure white getup for a more sensible dark gray one. Hah, dark gray to hide the pit stains, probably. Yeah.

Ivion and Alina were rarely far from each other, and they frequently had their eyes closed at the same time, breathing evenly. Meditating together.

Cho wished they'd get a room. Hells, she wished they could all get rooms. The heat was making her crazy, and it only got worse the farther south they traveled.

And they had to stay hydrated, of course, which resulted in Cho's having to pee a lot. But she had to hold it for hours because the convoy—their truck included—only stopped on a fixed schedule at predetermined re-fueling stations. These stations usually were staffed by only one person and a few dusty old robots, but the cameras—with built-in facial recognition scanners—were in working order. To prevent anyone from realizing there were stowaways aboard, and to avoid alerting The Authority, the self-smugglers had to hurriedly take turns hopping out through a secret escape trap door that dropped them through the bottom of the vehicle. From there, they had to crawl on their bellies on the dirt and, as nonchalantly as possible, sticking to the far side of the truck, dash away to do their business.

On her latest outing, Cho did indulge in an extra thirty seconds to stretch her legs and take a few breaths. She looked around the rocky plains and grasslands stretching in all directions as far as she could see. This was Kadic, then. Northern Kadic anyway. The desert must lie farther south.

Wonderful. The next day promised to be even less comfortable, then.

Her frustration faded for a few moments as the cool evening wind caressed her damp skin.

Her thirty seconds expired, she returned to the oven to roast with the other living kebabs.

Day two of three. Yeah, it was hotter.

They'd all stripped down to their undershirts, set aside their socks and shoes. Mezami was naked except for a loincloth. Everyone smelled *ripe*.

Her temperature modulator struggling, Cho was strongly annoyed by serene Ivion's fitness model glow. Either she was an excellent actress, or she'd been enhanced with top-shelf tech.

Rationing their snacks and sips from their canteen, they all dealt with the slow, vibrating sameness in their own ways. Cho continued to stew in her own juices. Kinneas was the most miserable of them all by far: an Aquamancer, sweating his face off, forced to drink ninety-degree water.

During their first bathroom break, at dawn, Cho saw a giant bird circling the cliffs a few miles away. Her vantage point provided a clear view of the desert to the south and west. Out of curiosity, since it was the only living thing in her field of vision, she squinted, her telescopic eyes zooming in on the creature. It wasn't a bird but, rather, a butterfly. Or a moth. A huge one. Its dark iridescent wings gleamed in the sun and blasted sand dunes with gusts of air, reshaping the desert along its flight path.

Though she didn't know why, Cho felt a sense of understanding as she watched the uncertain creature. By its erratic movements, it seemed to have flown far off course. Lost in a strange land.

Once back in the truck and on the move again, Cho described to Alina what she'd seen.

"Sounds like a *Vlindra*," Alina, the living Aelf encyclopedia, explained. "Decades ago, scientists tried to breed them in labs. They shed, once per year, and the husks are full of some kinda neurotoxin. Used for a while by pest control companies. Until all the reports about human infant deaths (and some other bad news I'm forgetting). The Ravers who dealt with *Vlindra* documented that touching the husks directly causes hallucinations and, sometimes, death. The gunk falling off the wings, though? Breathing even a tiny amount of the stuff can blind you. A bigger dose is deadly. Anyway, they're usually found in deciduous forests. Oh, and the rainforest in northeastern Kadic, maybe. The one you saw, way out here? Something must've confused it. *Vlindra* hate hot, dry climates."

"Is it gonna give us trouble?" said Cho.

Alina shook her head. "The big shiny metal rectangle we're in won't interest it. It's probably just trying to find its way home."

"I feel a little bad for it. Not gonna lie."

"At least it wasn't a *góra'cień*. Much more common around these parts, and much more aggressive, chasing rock lizards and wild horses and stuff. Fun fact: they kill their prey with their claws, then pummel the corpses with their skulls until the bones are crushed, swallowing and digesting the animal whole."

Smacking her papery lips, Cho said, "Li?"

"What's up?"

"Thanks for that image. Let's not talk for a while."

Ivion seated herself uncomfortably close to Cho. "I heard you're quite the little hacker."

Cho scowled at her.

"Meant as a compliment."

"I got a few tricks. What of it?"

"Well, I did catch you trying to access my datapad yesterday. You would have succeeded, too, with the right leverage. I am sensing just the tiniest bit of tension between us, and I'd prefer we were friends. I thought I might make myself more useful to you. So, I wondered if maybe you would like to add another 'trick' to your repertoire. I could show you—"

"I'm gonna stop you right there," said Cho, low, slow, and quiet. "Just because you've got Alina eating out of your hand doesn't mean you get to start training me like a pet."

Under the cover of Ivion's phony, innocent sadness simmered frustration salted with anger, but she quickly lowered the temperature. "Really, I can't say what I could have done to earn such animosity."

"Nothing. That's the point. I don't know you."

"After arranging this whole escapade, smuggling you across borders, protecting you all—even your Aelf companion—at my own expense, no less. What will it take for you to accept me?"

"I honestly don't know. It's true. You haven't done anything but help us. So far. But my friend," she said, pointing towards the napping Alina, "has a bad habit of giving your family credit where it isn't due."

"So, guilty until proven innocent. Is that it?"

"It ain't personal, lady."

Ivion's clever eyes narrowed. "Oh, isn't it, though? Protecting your friends, that is noble of you, Lady Shazura-Torvir. It is sensible. But what of you? Why do you seem to have it out for me, when we have never before met? The only encounter you have had with my family is one moment with my brother—whose judgment had lapsed. He was in love with Alina, and he behaved in a manner unbecoming his station and lineage. But how can that rightly make you hate me?"

Cho snorted. "You spin pretty words. I'll give you that much. Sparkly, shiny, big words to trap people in webs of logic. But logic isn't the same as being right—not always—and, growing up the way I had to, because of people like you, I had to learn, the quick but dangerous way, to follow my gut."

"Infallible instincts," said Ivion with a smirk. "Must be nice."

"Not saying I'm always on target. I just usually am. So, you can keep setting up whatever game it is you're playing. Just remember that I'm watching you. You might, at some point, show me that you're worth trusting. But, until that day, if it ever comes, I want you to remember something for me. I'm a pissed-off, twitchy little urchin, and I definitely don't know everything, but I do *see* almost everything. And I'll be watching you. Closely."

"You're wrong about me, and I hope to show you the truth of that, as soon as I can. For now, I can only protest that I am nothing like the Walazzins. Even with my own family, I have little in common. And I know that your augmentations allow you to take the measure of my heartbeat, micro-twitches, and vocal inflections. Again, you know I'm not lying."

"I can tell that you're breathing is even, your voice is steady, and you're not afraid to look me in the eye. But I'm not stupid or young enough to believe that a good liar can't outsmart lie detectors."

Sweat-glistening pale collarbones rising and falling, Ivion smiled. "You are refreshingly honest. Usually, a clash of wills among nobles, like this, would have stretched out for months, and we only would have played our hands to disgrace the other in our shared social circles. Truly, you are exceptional among our kind."

"There is no 'our kind.'"

"Like me, you were born to rise, Choraelia Torvir. Whether you care to admit it or not."

"Let's get one thing straight: my name is Cho-Zen. I'm nothing like you and all the other bluebloods."

"Why then do you hound the Walazzin and seek to reclaim your birthright?"

"Birthrights?" Cho laughed. "Who cares?"

"Revenge then. I can respect that."

"No. You don't get it. The only thing I want is justice for my family—my parents, aunts and uncles, brothers and sisters. And for everyone the Walazzins have crushed along the way."

"Well," said Ivion, bowing her head. "I will leave you be. Perhaps my hope is in vain, but I still hold out faith that you will think better of me one day. Whatever may come, by Plutonia, I vow to drag the Walazzins to the Seventy-Seventh Hell." Her resting pulse was well within the normal range; she betrayed no signs of untruthfulness.

Opening her eyes, Alina asked, "Time is it?"

Ivion checked her platinum-plated pocket watch. "7:30 in the evening. Next stop is in two hours, at Atika Junction."

Stretching shakily with a strangled squeal, Alina said, "What were you two talking about?"

"Nothing much," Ivion said with a wink. "She was telling me tales from her early days, about how she gained her prodigious hacking abilities." She turned to Cho, adding, "Your older sister, Aotereis, wasn't it?"

Cho glared at her. How had she known?

Ivion prodded her again: "Is that not right? Did I misremember or mispronounce the name?"

"No," said Cho, slowly. "You got it."

Alina said, "Huh. You never told me about your sister. Or any of your siblings, actually."

"Never came up," said Cho, her gaze fixed on Ivion, who obviously was quite capable of making threats of her own.

Cho wasn't even sure how she'd just been attacked, but the hairs on her arms pricked against the fabric of her shirt, and her stomach acid began to boil, and these were feelings she knew to pay attention to. Whenever she'd felt them in the past, she'd had to run or fight for her life soon after.

She watched Ivion scoot closer to Alina. Watched them slip into easy conversation.

Cho looked to Kinneas and Mezami, both snoring in the opposite corner, the Pyct nestled in the boy's armpit.

As usual, no one else was *actually* seeing what was happening in front of their noses. It would fall to her, again, to save Alina from herself.

Fingering the comforting, warm steel of her pocketknife, she struggled to hold her eyelids open as the heat and the metronome-swaying of the truck bed attempted to lull her to sleep.

Cho snapped awake, disoriented. Tried to check the time, but her phone's battery had finally died.

Everyone else was out, even Ivion. When they woke, they found their own devices dark as well. (Cho could've plugged hers in to her wrist to slow-charge it, but she was worried about overtaxing her system given that she was on the verge of dehydration. Bad idea to push herself too hard.) Unable to mindlessly skim articles or watch videos about piano-playing iguanas, now there *really* was nothing to do except talk. And notice subtle changes in mood, posture, and expression.

"You're doing the thing again," Cho told Alina.

"What?"

"That face. That's your 'I'm nervous about something, but I'm too upset or worried to share' face."

"That's just my face. You're describing my default look."

"I know, but it's more intense than usual. So…?"

"Well, I wasn't gonna say anything 'cause we got a lot going on, but—the other night—after we got 'ported into Truct, when I checked my stuff, I saw something was broken. A vial."

"What was in it?"

"I don't know, exactly. It was a kind of *Auggie*. All Ruqastra would tell me was that a drop a day would expand my connection to the collective subconscious."

Cho blinked.

"Boost my Revomantic powers."

"Ah. And it's all gone now?"

Alina nodded.

"Sucks, but I'm sure you'll be fine without it. You're… really strong, Li. You know? Like, stronger than ya oughta be. And I'm not just talking about the magic."

"That's the other thing, honestly. I don't know what's happening to me. It's like I'm not really myself anymore."

"Come on, stop it," Cho said. Though, in her mind, she shouted, *Uh-huh, yup.* "You getting stronger because of, um… what your grandfather did to you… that's not changing who you are. You're still the same annoying, clingy fool begging me for favors. Like always." Maybe this was just wishful thinking—silly, pointless—but she lent a voice to her hope, regardless: "You're still the same person."

"There's something inside me. It doesn't feel like me. It's like a stranger broke into my body, and I'm hiding in my mind, hitting the panic button, as I listen to it break down the door."

Flashing back to Alina's screaming transformation a couple days ago, Cho scratched the bridge of her nose. "So you get a little more, um, feathery sometimes. So what? That's not so bad. The grayness goes away after a while."

"What if, eventually, it doesn't?"

"Uh. We'll buy you a nice big birdcage and some high quality seed. One hundo-percent organic."

"Cho, I'm not joking. Every time it happens, I'm so angry and scared, and it makes me want to do things… It's stronger than I am. It can fight its way through obstacles I can't. And, I've started to—never mind."

"Say it. For the gods' sakes, just tell me."

"I like it! Alright? There it is. I actually, sometimes, *like* losing control. Because it's—it's hard to explain, but being angry is easier than being afraid. And this thing inside me, it's always angry."

Cho put a hand on her friend's. "You sure this 'other thing' isn't just, ya know, *you*? Maybe you're using powers you didn't know you had, and you're standing up for yourself more than you used to. Maybe it's a sign that it's time to start fighting back. And that's what we're doing: we're going to get payback for Eilars, for Morphea, for Truct and everyone."

Alina's machine-gun heartbeat slowed, steadied. Her head lolled against Cho's shoulder.

Cho patted her sweaty hair. "I'm here for you, Li. Never won't be."

The pause lasted so long, it seemed Alina had fallen asleep. But then she wormed along the floor to lie down, and murmured, "I love you, Cho."

"Don't make me say it. But." Cho looked away, shrugged. "You know."

Finally, at the onset of the third day, Ivion informed them that they would arrive in Ozar in approximately seventeen hours.

Hooray, yes, but those hours sure crawled by.

On the last stop of the day, Cho's will broke. Declaring, "I don't care anymore. If I have to eat *one more* energy bar, I'm going to *snap*," she climbed through the hatch and rolled from under the truck.

She was in luck. Where previously, there'd only been refueling checkpoints, she saw the convoy had come to a real gas station. With a convenience store attached and people coming in and out.

While bots refueled the trucks as usual, she dusted off her clothes and casually strolled to the store.

Above the faded public notices hammered into the concrete building's walls, a fluorescent sign proclaimed this place the property of some dude named Imlin. A pile of regional maps had been stacked on a rusting wire shelf beside newspapers and magazines. Paper products were much more common in the boonies (even in El), where digital devices were fewer and usually belonged to the community. Cho imagined the bigger cities of Kadic would be more like the ones back home—high tech, high pollution, low morals—but Ivion's route had purposefully skirted the major population centers.

According to a colorful advertisement hanging above the automatic glass doors of the shop, the nearby town, which Cho could see at the end of the one-lane snaking road, was "Historic Besalic, birthplace of the Salud Tradition." She had no idea what that meant, and Hungry Cho would tolerate no investigations that didn't end in sandwiches.

Before she entered the building, she noted the two bearded, long-haired men flanking the doors. They wore woolspun robes and no jewelry, and neither one appeared to be cybernetically enhanced in any way. She did detect a faint aura of

Niima around the one on the left, but it was so weak it could have been a fluke or a glitch in her equipment brought on by prolonged heat exposure. Or, she was just tired.

The man on the right stood beside a straw mat onto which had been tossed a few gelders and some coins she didn't recognize. These guys weren't performers, she thought, so they must've been holy men.

As she walked past, she pulled a crisp gelder bill from her pocket, ducked, and placed it on the small pile. A little extra godly goodwill couldn't hurt.

"Blessings, child," said the man on the right. "Good fortune on your way."

Cho scampered inside, grabbing chips, wraps, sandwiches, and other goodies for the group. Yes, even Ivion. Though she made sure Ivion ended up with vinegar chips. It seemed appropriate.

The beans and mushroom burger patties were only lukewarm, the lettuce frumpy. After having to choke down almond bars for days, though, Cho's mouth watered at the aroma wafting from her plastic shopping bag.

Leaving the convenience store, she saw in the distance a tuft of tawny fur, a flash of sunlight bouncing off canine eyes. It was a coyote, a silent sentinel. And it was alone. That was unusual for a scavenger.

Morphea's mask had most often borne that same long-snouted, sharp-eared shape. Maybe it was her, Cho thought, watching. Maybe.

The coyote yipped and wandered off. Ah well.

Careful not to draw the attention of the robed men or anyone else nearby, Cho ran to the far side of the truck. She scrunched the food bag under her shirt and, on her back, wriggled her way inside.

"Hope you like your chow dusty," she said.

"That was an unnecessary risk," said Ivion.

Cho tore open the wrapping around her white-bread, meatball sub. "Oh, I *meatly* disagree." In one huge bite, she disappeared a quarter of the sandwich in her mouth. Chunks of meatball and globs of sauce and cheese rolling around her tongue, she added, "Heavenly."

She went over to Kinneas and Mezami. The Pyct took his packet from Cho and snapped a pair of AA batteries in half, dripping their acid over the greasy meat on his relish-clogged hot dog bun.

"And what did ya get me?" asked Kinneas.

"A knuckle sammich," said Cho, and took a swing.

He made to block, but it was just a feint: she swept his legs out from under him. Not wanting to hurt him, though, she helped control his fall, and he pulled her down with him. They ended up tangled together, half of Cho's sandwich toppings covering their bodies.

Kinneas, on his back, awkwardly cleared his throat. Cho shot up and off him.

After a few moments of silence, he said, "Seriously, did you actually get me any food? I'm starving."

Smirking, she flung his wrapped sandwich at him. "It's pork because I know how much you like hamming it up."

They ate together, savoring each bite.

Occasionally, Cho would pick a string of cheese from his hair.

20

BARAAM

BARAAM AND JIJA STOOD in comfortable silence for more than an hour, each taking up his customary position on either side of the glass doors leading into Imlin's convenience store. Just outside Besalic, travelers were often generous enough to drop a few coins onto Jija's straw mat.

The Sahaman residents of the Saludbabni could provide for most of their own needs, and trade for the remainder, but small cash donations allowed for other transactions. For example, these alms funded Baraam's daily trips to buy fruit at this same location.

Though the concrete was scalding, the two men were barefoot. Their lack of shoes, and their long hair and beards, completed the image expected of a pair of hermit mystics.

His current appearance put Baraam at odds with the many etiquette and social studies lessons of his youth. His mentors and peers at The Gild had enforced ancient Elemental grooming traditions, including keeping one's hair from falling below the ears and maintaining a smooth-shaved face. Long locks were a nuisance in battle, and beards did not suit civilized men.

Yet, here Baraam stood, unkempt but not unclean. It wasn't his beard that made him a barbarian.

Sentinel-like, he and Jija flanked the store. Travelers came and went, some stopping, most ignoring the Sahamans. Baraam enjoyed the simple peace of watching people's faces exit his life as effortlessly as they'd entered it—like the ebb and flow of a gentle breeze.

There was a man in a business suit, who hurried into the store. Minutes later, he reemerged with a bag of sugary sweets clutched in his ringed fingers. He seemed frazzled. On his way home, no doubt, after a long day. Jija tugged at the whiskers of his chin-beard pensively, asking, "Spare some change for the Saludbabni, sir?" The man glowered at them. Baraam let the stranger's emotions wash over him and recede.

Then came parents with children in tow, who always bought five lottery tickets (one for each member of their family). They wore hand-mended clothes, their smiles fresh and entirely their own. The children bowed to Baraam and Jija. Guided by her mother, the littlest one toddled over to the straw mat and delicately placed a bill onto the small pile of money.

"Blessings, good people," said Jija. "May peace reign over your lives."

For a long while, no others came, and Baraam grew somewhat impatient. "Should we not leave?"

Long silences contented Jija. When he'd had his fill, he said, "I have been thinking. Do you remember what you asked me, the day we met? You, this sprig of a boy, green and pliable, you asked me, 'Why did my mom and dad have to die'?"

"No, I don't remember that," said Baraam, too quickly.

"All my years of ascetic training fled my mind in that moment. Not so old yet myself, when faced with so earnest a question, I was divorced of all confidence. In some ways, I have never stopped examining what you asked me. I've come to suspect that what I told you on that day was completely, unforgivably wrong. Do you remember what was my reply?"

"I told you, no."

"Come now, Baraam. Humor me. We both, after all, know more than we let on." Jija grinned, his coffee-yellowed teeth on full display.

Baraam sniffed. "Very well. If it will close this topic sooner... As I recall, you said, 'Sometimes bad things happen to good people. It might seem unfair, but there is balance, in the end and always.'"

"Did that comfort you?"

"No."

"Of course not. It shouldn't have. Now that we are both men, and I've had a quarter century to reflect further on the issue, I would like very much to amend my answer."

"Have it your way."

"Do you believe in evil?"

"Of course."

"I do, too. The evidence of our senses, our hearts, is incontrovertible, yes. Years ago, in my blind idealism, I would not acknowledge it. But I now know that evil is very real, and I have seen from where it truly derives. When you were a boy seeking answers and meaning, I should have told you, 'Where death comes naturally—by claw of creature or tooth of time—it is no evil. However, we must not let this truth bend us to complacency; where death is delivered by the hands of Man, motivated by greed and jealousy, it must be confronted, resisted, and challenged at every turn.' What do you say to that, eh?"

Too little, too late, Baraam thought. "I say that, as a child, I would not have understood. And, as an adult, I do not care." He scratched his beard. "I once thought I knew what evil was."

"You are an Aelfraver."

"Was."

"Quite a good one, from what I hear. Even in Besalic and its environs, stories of your battles aren't uncommon."

"I wish it were not so."

"Is it so terrible a fate, to be a national hero?"

"I do not wish to be."

"Even to your fellow Kadicians?"

Baraam did not answer, but he knew he'd already given his friend too much. Even more than long silences, Jija relished circular philosophical arguments.

As predicted, Jija pressed him, "And why did you hang up that mantle of Aelfraver?"

"Because, more than ever, I'm uncertain about the true nature and source of evil. I see it in everything."

"Ah. Then you have become very wise, indeed, my young friend."

Baraam shooed a fly from his face.

"It *is* in everything." Jija tapped his fists against his chest. "In me, in you. Just as there is good in all things as well. Though we mortals lean in one direction or another, most of us achieve a sense of inner equilibrium—imbalanced as it may be at times." Swept away by his own rhetoric, he began to pace and gesture as he spoke. Behind him, the automatic doors glided open as he crossed the rubber welcome mat. "Some men give in to their easy lies more readily than others, or they do harm with greater frequency and lesser concern. I should hesitate to call them wicked. Some others choose to pursue the path of greater difficulty, to seek right action in all things. Whether they succeed or fail, the beauty lies in the attempt. Are they not good? Who knows? But their trying means something, and I should not in good conscience call them evil for their failures. Still others actively enforce and promote evil. They neither simply *give in* to temptation nor create suffering through thoughtlessness; no, this last class I speak of deliberately acts unjustly. Indeed, they revel in their sinfulness, deriving a perverse enjoyment from the suffering of others. They feel content in the knowledge that their riches were pilfered from the toiling masses. The fact that the cost of their luxuries is borne by the rest of society—and not by themselves—is no deterrent. They do not ignore the misery they cause. To them, it is a bonus." Jija fell still for a moment, brooding, chewing his gum. "Though I may, in the pursuit of nuance, doubt my judgments concerning the first two categories, there can be no doubt about the third. Such men, Baraam, are evil. Pure, sickening evil. They are of the sort who ordered the bombing of your village, and there is no cure for their disease save death."

"You speak as I once did." Baraam rolled an orange-flavored wad of gum around with his tongue.

"Really?"

"My views were simpler, though: the Aelf were, to me, evil because I hated them. All of them."

"And now?"

"I still do, I think, but there's a problem."

"Ah?"

"Now I know one of them."

"Hmm. Is this Aelf, the one you ran from—whom you have come to know—evil?"

Baraam, again, didn't answer. It was easier not to.

"Do you suppose killing is evil?"

"Not so long ago, I would have emphatically said, 'No, not if it's evil that you kill.'"

"Has your opinion changed?"

"In all things, I often doubt myself."

"Good. Doubt can be a powerful tool."

Red-faced, soaked with sweat, a green-haired girl appeared before them. She had the small, nearly imperceptible divots and lines in her arms and cheeks that indicated cybernetic implants. There was a moment's hesitation before she walked up to the straw mat and dropped a gelder onto it. Jija thanked her, and she went inside Imlin's place.

Scuffing the dirt with the ball of his bare foot, Baraam felt something important had been left unspoken. He did not yet know how to voice it, but he tried: "Some wars are righteous, I suppose."

"But, how to tell the difference, hmm?" said Jija.

"I'd rather stay out of them altogether. I've changed."

"Changed, how? Why?"

"I don't know."

"Is it this Aelf you fear? Is that why you suppress your powers? Why you returned to us, years and years after we sent you out into the world to make a great man of yourself?"

"I came back to find peace. And I don't fear the Aelf I speak of. I'm afraid of what I might do to her."

"Would you kill her, had you the chance?"

"I'm not certain I could, even if I wanted to."

"Is it your skill you doubt, or your resolve?"

These never-ending questions nudged Baraam closer and closer to a mental cliff. He dug in, pushed back. "Neither. I fear nothing except my own motivations. I've always fought only because I was told to, fought with unbreakable conviction. When I discovered the truth about her—she whom I thought of as a sister... I have to believe she isn't a monster."

Jija watched the girl with the green hair leave with her bag of soggy sandwiches and hot dogs. He sighed. "We welcome you here as a brother, Baraam, all of us Sahamans do. I only wonder if your highest purpose is served at the last Saludbabni in our remote corner of the country."

"Purpose is lost to me, and I to it. But, of one thing I am certain: I will never fight again."

"Even against true evil, one you could not doubt is your enemy?" Jija groaned as he stooped to pick up the straw mat.

Baraam watched an auto-piloted truck lift off the ground five feet or so, pick up speed, and return to the highway. He scooped the money into his fanny pack and zipped it shut. "Whom do you speak of? Where is this *undoubtedly* evil person? Point him out to me, and I will slay him dead. Until then, enough of these maddening postulations. Let's go home."

Shaking the sand from the straw mat and placing it atop his head, Jija said, "Perhaps, in the twilight of my life, I have grown too fond of my own bleating voice. Forgive me, my brother."

Holding up his hands in a gesture of peace, Baraam said, "There's nothing to forgive, my friend. I don't often mind locking horns with you, but it's late, now, and I am tired. My apologies for my rude tone."

"Life will be far duller without you, my mulish lad." He grabbed the younger, bigger man by the back of his neck and squeezed. "We will find a place for your restive soul yet."

"But I have found my place."

"We'll see." Jija chuckled under his breath. "We'll see."

21

ALINA

TRAPPED IN A METAL box full of stagnant, sweaty air. With zero privacy. And *teenagers*. Alina itched to escape it all. As the final day of the journey drew to a close, she was quite ready to stretch her legs and breathe more than a lonely few minutes of fresh air every ten hours.

By the light of a couple yellow glowsticks rolling along the floor, Ivion brought everyone in for a strategy session. She explained that they'd be in enemy territory from here on out. (Cho snorted. "I'm sorry, were we in friendly territory before?") Attracting minimal-to-zero attention was key. Assuming they cleared the border inspection, they'd meet one of Ivion's contacts, secure a vehicle, and drive to a safehouse at the base of the Sixth Stack of Ozar.

Encouraged by Alina's questions, Ivion elaborated: the city-state of Ozar had been built into a colossal crater in a rocky plateau south of Kadic. It comprised seven layers, called "Stacks," the first of these closest to the surface, the second below it, and so on. Each Stack was equal to one of the empire's larger cities and boasted a unique blend of religions, artistic traditions, languages, and more. Legend had it, the Seventh Stack reached such phenomenal depths that, there, even natural laws began to bend.

Mysteries were a fact of life. The biggest of these was the Ozari people's supposed divine protection. The stories differed on the source of this mysterious blessing (the earth, their ancestors, or their master-gods), but one fact remained consistent: the power was generally known as The Abyss—Ozar's great shield, the reason this city had endured for centuries where so many other nations had fallen before the Elementals' might.

The Empire's latest campaign had been underway since before Cho and Kinneas had been born, some fifteen or sixteen years ago. However, Ozar and El had been at war, on and off, for 1,700 years, give or take. Ozar had continuously and laboriously expanded for ages, and with each expansion, the carved gash in the earth grew deeper, as more peoples from all over the world flocked to its promise of freedom. Unfortunately, the vast majority now found only El; the empire's reach enveloped nearly every country on the globe, and Stacks One through Five were no exceptions. These territories had been seized at tremendous cost of blood, treasure, Niima, gunpowder, and time, and the Elementals ensured they were jealously and violently defended. Even so, many refugees did manage to sneak into the "free" half of the Sixth, a nut El had not yet cracked.

Alina soaked up the information, learning the lay of the land, asking followup questions. Ivion fed on her eagerness.

Lying lazily atop uneven stacks of crates, Cho picked at her fingernails with her pocketknife. She seemed her usual amount of unimpressed. Alina preferred this quiet, docile version of her friend to the antsy one from earlier, who'd clambered on top of the crates and swum in the shadows above like a deep-water predator thrown into a tiny fish tank. Searching for a way out that didn't exist.

Kinneas was confused. Like so many others, he had been convinced his whole life that El had already conquered the world "ages ago." It's what he'd been taught in school. Alina was grateful for Ivion's help in explaining that the official histories had oversimplified everything, claiming that for two centuries the Elemental Empire had assumed stewardship of the planet to "maintain law, order, and fellowship among all the races of men." Ivion shied away from coming down too hard on the Plutocracy, which she insisted was made up of "flawed individuals" but still "promoted peace through fruitful global partnerships." However, she and Alina agreed that the reality of El's war for world domination was far messier than the sanitized lie.

Kadic had never officially surrendered.

The Four Isles were home to brutal guerilla fighters who had no love of the empire.

Every other decade, a revolt would tear through the colonies.

And Ozar had fought the Elementals to a bloody standstill. Half the Sixth lay unconquered, and the Seventh remained secure beyond it.

The Authority war machine labored to make good on the promise of a truly global empire. So far, it had not succeeded, and no number of false histories or puppet governments could completely erase this embarrassment.

Ivion next turned the conversation toward the Hextarchy—six supposed immortals who had led Ozar for more than two thousand years. For all the Plutocracy's (and, specifically, the Ivoir Family's) resources, the truth about the

Hextarchs had remained inseparable from fiction. Whether they were the source of the mysterious Abyss force, flesh-and-blood kings masquerading as divinities, a fabrication to bewilder invaders, or anything in between, the Ozari openly worshiped them as living gods. It was possible the Hextarchs were in fact ancient beings, cunning and millennia-old, hiding in their fortress at the base of the Seventh Stack. However, concerning their true natures precious little was certain.

"Our spies and assassins have never caught even a glimpse," Ivion said. "They are an enigma, shrouded by their ghoul-like, cultist followers—a collective of human- and Aelf-kind known as The Coven. Whenever our soldiers meet The Coven in battle, the reports speak of brutish fanaticism. The 'Covenants,' as they're called, kill with passion. They do not hesitate to lay down their lives for the cause."

"One guy's hero is another's psychopath," said Cho. "*You'd* know all about fanaticism, Ivoir. Elementals are obsessed with making sure everyone kisses Plutonia's feet and kneels for the flag."

"My lady, our nation's armed services recruit volunteers. The Covenants are made from brainwashed children."

Cho sneered. "Weren't you just saying all this info's up in the air? 'Brainwashed children'? How do you know that's not just gossip, or what they want you to think?"

For once, Ivion seemed thrown. "*Virtually* everything we know about them might be false—or true." She switched topics. "It is to 'the Abyss' that the Covenants attribute their success in holding back the invaders—the 'Lightbringers,' as they call us. That's all about to change soon, though."

"Drop the meaningful stare, already," said Cho. "This suspense is literal murder."

"For all The Coven's bravado, the fortunes of war are soon to tilt in El's favor, and the balance will be so off-set that Ozar will not recover, its destruction made inevitable thanks to the efforts of The Savior."

Alina tensed.

Cho said, "Ooh, ominous-sounding name, but—Li? You doing okay?"

"I'm fine," said Alina. "No, that's a lie. I'm not fine at all. 'The Savior,' that is what you just said, right? I'm not losing it, am I?"

Ivion nodded.

"In the dream-vision I fell into the other day—" Cho shot Alina a warning glance, but Alina ignored her and continued—"when I saw through my uncle's eyes, I was—sorry, *he* was in a big, stone building. A cathedral, seemed like. There was a crowd there, worshiping. Definitely a religious service of some kind. And they kept calling him 'The Savior.'"

Eyes narrowing, Ivion said, "Your uncle? I don't understand. What do you mean, you 'saw through his eyes'?"

"So, he is in Ozar," Alina muttered to herself. Excitedly, she said, "None of it makes sense, not yet, but it's all connected somehow, and now I've got one more piece of the puzzle. Tell me *everything* about this Savior guy."

Recovering from the revelation, but still side-eying Alina, Ivion said, "The Savior preaches enlightenment in the name of The Author of Creation."

"A Sanctumite."

"It would be naive to assume his faith is genuine. He proclaims what is useful to the empire, that Elemental rule brings with it wealth, peace, and light. This fomentation of dissent among the Ozari has been the most effective weapon in centuries: what you cannot fight with bullets and blades, you kill instead with ideas. Much more powerful in the long term."

"Can he really pull it off?" said Kinneas.

"Thousands attend his 'masses' every week. Intelligence suggests he has tens of thousands of citizens sympathetic to his cause on the Sixth Stack alone. He's focused his efforts there, ever since the Walazzins installed him and backed his operation with regular and generous 'donations.'"

"Well, isn't that a neat little coincidence," said Cho.

"Kaspuri himself was in charge of this operation before he was given command of the full-scale invasion of the Seventh Stack."

"And when's that happening?" Alina said.

"Only the generals, including Kaspuri, would be privy to that information."

"Ugh, what good are ya?" said Cho, looking around with a wry grin. "Gods, you guys. I'm kidding."

Mezami had tied a pair of energy bars to his legs and was now using them like stilts. Mid-stride, he paused to say, "Surrounded: us, enemies. Attack: how, we?"

Raising a finger, Ivion waited for him to finish before jumping in with, "My proposal was always going to be that Alina infiltrate The Savior's circle, gain his trust, and from him learn all about the Walazzins' war strategy. That might give us all the information we need to cut them off at the pass."

"Of course *you'd* suggest a back-stab," Cho muttered. Even under the hum of the truck's engines, her words rang clearly in Alina's ears.

"Unfortunately, if the Savior is in fact related to you, my plan is dead on arrival," said Ivion.

"Haven't been around each other since I was a toddler," said Alina, "but, yeah, he might recognize me."

"What's the end-game, here?" said Kinneas. "I'm honestly confused. We've got Alina's crazy uncle—no offense."

"None taken."

"And the Walazzins are the ones responsible for Ruqastra's and Eilars's deaths."

"Ow!" said Cho, who'd nicked her finger with her knife.

Kinneas continued, "Alina's uncle is working for the Walazzins, and he's pretending to be a Sanctum prophet, or whatever. So, are the Sanctum and The Authority basically the same thing now, or am I missing something?"

"In this case, they are very closely aligned in their desired outcomes: The Authority seeks the final destruction of the nation-state of Ozar, the last truly independent hold-out against El's domination of the world; The Sanctum seeks followers, and this production of a 'Savior,' who will guide the war efforts of 'the righteous' against 'ancient demons'... Well, it is an excellent recruitment tool."

"What a giant heap of crap," said Cho.

"I don't disagree," said Ivion, "but, as 'giant heaps of crap' go, it is a well-constructed, thoughtful, and—most critically—persuasive narrative that the desperate will *want* to believe. Give it a generation or two, and history will forget the truth of it."

"Luckily we don't care about history or the fates of whole countries," said Cho. "We're only here for the Walazzins. If collateral damage includes The Authority war effort, that's cool, but it's not my priority."

"Cho," said Kinneas. "We could help these people."

"How?"

"I don't know, but—"

"And, why would we? We don't know what Ozar's like."

"Probably full of just regular people, like anywhere else. You said it yourself, Truct is the perfect example of what happens when The Authority takes control. What if, here, we could make a difference, for real? Wouldn't you want to?"

"Love the enthusiasm, bud, really, but we can't save the whole wide world by ourselves. Look at us: we've got a bodybuilding mouse, a weird shadow witch, a human water gun, a white-haired trust fund baby, and the world's most attractive thief. The Elemental Empire is *way* above our weight class. Its got thousands—millions of officers, politicians, company men. Wodjaego and Kaspuri Walazzin, on the other hand... they're powerful, but, if we get 'em cornered, they're just *people*. And people can be killed."

Cowed, Kinneas shriveled like a sea slug retreating into its shell.

Alina clapped her hands. Just once. "No. We'll damage and ruin their plans, but—and I need *everyone* on the same page, with me—we're not killing anyone." Her shadow swelled, the dim light of the glowsticks waning. "Got me?"

"How do you suggest we beat the Walazzins, then? You wanna take their hands, stare deeply into their eyes, and force them to see us as human beings?"

"I'll tell you how we'll get it done," said Alina. "I'm gonna get close to The Savior, Mateus K'vich, just like you planned, Ivion."

"We already talked about that! He'd know it was you. Your cover would be blown instantly."

"I don't think so," Alina said, grinning. She pulled the red crow mask from her bag. "Here, Cho. Take it."

"What are—"

"Take it. Put it on."

"Don't see how playing dress-up's gonna solve anything, but sure, I'll go along." Cho placed *Ida* over her face, holding it there for a few seconds. "Happy?"

"Pass it back." Alina slid the mask over her own face.

Its colors and texture shifted, the edges smoothing, the beak receding, and what was once a stylized, wide-eyed, red-faced crow had become a perfect copy of Cho's face, from chin to scalp. Alina's hair and body didn't change, but her face was now indistinguishable from Cho's.

"Uh," said Cho.

Kinneas couldn't stop staring.

Mezami laughed at the ghastly expressions Alina pulled (going cross-eyed, pretending to pick her nose).

Snapping her fingers, Cho said, "Oh-*kay*, that's great. Thank you."

The mask reverted to its normal red monstrousness. Removing it, Alina said, "With *Ida*, if I can get my hands on one of the higher-up Sanctumites—anyone tight with the Savior— I can look and sound just like them."

"Alina, that is incredible," Ivion said, beaming. "I can't believe how amazing you are."

With a flourish of her fingers, and a flutter of her heart, Alina bowed her head.

"Yeah, yeah. Tremendous. Now we know what's she'll be doing." Cho leapt off the boxes. "So, what about the rest of us?"

"Mezami should come with me," said Alina. Wobbling on his energy-bar stilts, the Pyct gave a theatrical bow.

"Excellent," said Ivion. "Only, be careful about where you go. The occupied sectors of the Sixth Stack follow Gild policy: Aelf are captured and destroyed with extreme prejudice. In the 'free' sectors, under Hextarchy control, however, sentient Aelf are welcome and fairly common."

"Nice," said Cho, waving her hands, "but what about me and Kinneas?"

Ivion took a deep breath, but before she could answer, the truck slowed. She whispered, "We've nearly arrived. There'll be an inspection any minute. The shielding I paid good gelders for should confuse their sensors, prevent them from reading our body heat signatures. However—and I can't stress this enough—one sound, and we all die."

The vehicle came to a full stop.

22

CHO-ZEN

THANKFULLY, IVION'S TECHNO TRICKERY worked, fooling the automatic scanners, drug- and bomb-sniffing dogs, and other tools at the Enforcers' disposal. Also, unlike in the movies, nobody sneezed at the worst possible moment.

Thus, the group survived the border inspection.

The sun was high; the air, dusty. Nearly one hundred power-armored Tranquilizers patrolled a camp in the middle of this wasteland—the barren expanse of nothingness that was the Kadic-Ozar border. As Cho would be reminded time and time again during her stay, almost nothing was as it seemed.

The Authority appeared to be milling about in the sun, but in fact they surrounded a titanic hexagonal hole in the earth—eight miles deep and three miles wide. The Stacks, Ivion had explained, had been built around this central opening in a staggered fashion, like a descending, circular stairway of cityscapes.

That living hands had carved out this cavity seemed impossible; it must have been the work of gods.

Guided by Ivion, Cho and the others disembarked the freight truck and side-stepped barbed wire, sandbags, machine gun nests, and automated missile launchers. They were led through a back entrance into the barracks. Enforcers wearing the black-and-white uniform of the Ivoir Family provided them with plastic-packaged military rations (brutally disgusting, but filling), fresh clothes (spare black fatigues), and a cold shower each. Fed and clean, they hopped into an APC, Ivion in the driver's seat, and passed through the checkpoint without issue.

"Friends in high places," Ivion said. Smug.

A few dozen Enforcers challenged her access to the single road that led into the hexagonal hole, but Ivion flashed her fake ID at them, and they let her pass without a second glance.

Cho caught the name on the phony Proof of Assetship card. "Vioni Eorivi? Your pretend-name is just an anagram for your real one?"

"The most believable lies contain a glimmer of truth, Choraelia."

"Why not just tell them who you are? They'd take you anywhere you wanted. Make things much easier."

"Going incognito for now better suits my purposes. They'll know who I am when I decide it's time."

Ivion drove the APC over the speed bump and down into the shadows. It glided along that road bored into walls of ancient stone, looping around and around and around, spiraling inward and downward, for what felt like forever.

Cho watched the dashboard's digital clock count higher and higher as she and the others descended. To the left of the hovercar, always, was the opening to the sky, a slowly but surely shrinking hexagon of light. On its right, nothing but solid rock.

Her mind wandered.

"Each Stack has several entry points," Ivion the tour guide said. "Impenetrable metal doors surrounded by indestructible stone. There are also Authority camps and outposts at each level."

"How long before we get to Stack Six?" said Cho.

"It's been like an hour," said Kinneas. "We must've gone down at least three levels by now."

"In fact, we haven't passed the First Stack," said Ivion.

Cho groaned. Kinneas began to giggle like a mad man.

From his pocket in Alina's bag, where he'd been hiding, Mezami said, "Mind: losing, I."

"You will know when we get to the Second Stack. There will be another checkpoint, and probably a thirty- to ninety-minute wait in line."

"Keep it together, Cho," she told herself. Her restless limbs itched for movement.

The sedentary journey continued.

Meanwhile, Ivion prattled about the First Stack's famous hot springs, which were supposed to have magical curative properties, able to stitch tears of flesh and fractures of bone. Unfortunately, impossibly, the waters only healed the Ozari—human or Aelf, it didn't matter. On the other hand, any foreigners who'd taken a dip wound up fatally poisoned. So far, no scientist or Maggo had been able to figure out why. Accordingly, The Authority had long since banned any entry into the hot springs.

At the next checkpoint, Ivion slipped the inspector an envelope stuffed with hundred-gelder bills, and he let them pass after swishing his flashlight over their car once or twice (not looking at anything or anyone too closely).

In the background, digital billboards displayed handsome, smiling actors holding prop guns. The text proclaimed:

YOUR EMPIRE NEEDS YOU!
THE PATRIOTIC
ADVENTURE OF A LIFETIME—
ENLIST IN THE ARMY
KEEP THE PEACE
BECOME THE AUTHORITY

The billboard then shifted images, showing an actress with blindingly white teeth. Her smile was way too big as she tickled the tiny toes of what was supposed to be her baby. The caption read:

AT ELCORP
HUMANITY IS OUR GREATEST ASSET

When Ivion had described Ozar as an "underground city-state," Cho had imagined a maze of tight, crisscrossing tunnels like gopher paths or worm holes.

She'd been right, as it turned out, about the worms: *Dan'yn'daup,* they were called, big and long as trains. Keeping them away from the Stacks took teams of soldiers operating what looked like satellite dishes but were actually giant sonic guns. Built into towers, the devices emitted waves at frequencies immensely painful to the creatures. Every fifteen to thirty minutes, the APC passed another one of these installations. Cho tried not to think too hard about why there were so many of them.

Driving through multiple military outposts had Cho *sweating*. If caught, Kinneas might go to a minimum security prison for a few months to a couple years. Ivion might be slightly embarrassed at the next Plutocratic cocktail party. But Cho and Alina were wanted women, and Mezami was an Aelf. One misstep, that's all it would take.

Alina calmed Cho down by explaining what she did to disguise them anytime the APC slowed for an inspection: stitching a blanket of Revomancy over them, she made it so that anyone looking at them would see only illusion—changed hair and skin, reshaped nose arches, and shifted eye curves and colors. The girls would become just a bit fuzzy to potentially unfriendly eyes. Since Mezami was travel-sized, she just made him invisible.

Her being able to hide two whole people in plain sight while *also* throwing a more traditional illusion a third creature—that was exceptional. Kinneas could not stop gushing. Ivion smirked her little approving smirk. The only one who didn't seem aware of how astounding she'd become was Alina herself.

She had always been scarily good at certain things, which made up for when she was a total dolt at others. Cho wouldn't admit it out loud, but—Alina's ability to hold so many spells in her head all at once and flip them on like a light at every checkpoint, every time an Enforcer inspected their APC a little too closely—was awesome.

The process, however, was taking its toll.

Ivion stepped out of the parked vehicle to exchange a few quick words with a Tranq officer. When she returned, Alina was gripping her arm rests with white-knuckled fingers, saying, "We gotta do that *five* more times?"

"No. Checkpoints four, five, and six will be staffed by men in my father's employ. I made sure of it. We'll roll right on through those."

Invisible Mezami whispered, "Breathe: just, you. Believe: you, I."

Alina took a breath, which did seem to help a little.

Cho glanced at the shrinking patch of twilight high above. It looked like a six-sided, dark bowl of honey. If only she'd known at the time that this would be the last sky she'd see for years to come, she might have committed it to memory.

Ivion remained in a frustratingly good mood, blabbing about how the Second Stack held a wealth of information on the Iorians' civilization: crumbling libraries stuffed with scrolls thousands of years old; dilapidated temples ornamented with hieroglyphs dating to the beginnings of their people. Elemental and Gild scholars had uncovered so much fascinating lore, unraveling mysteries concerning the mythology of this Aelf race and their fictional foes, the titans.

"Why 'fictional'?" said Alina.

"Everyone knows the titans were a fabrication. An exaggeration of an enemy tribe, perhaps. Or an allegory for the ravages of time. The Iorians, though much less civilized than we, were nonetheless keenly aware of the disintegration of their way of life well before the final rot set in. For centuries, their politicians fretted over what they called 'the lie factory' (sometimes translated as 'the forge of falsehood'). Apparently, the Iorian court of this part of the world believed that their race would be destroyed from within."

"How does that disprove the existence of titans?"

"It doesn't," Ivion admitted. "But have you seen any fifty-foot-tall behemoths lumbering about lately?"

"No, but I haven't seen any Dragons either. And they for sure existed."

Ivion fell silent for a while.

Cho treated all this history as if she were peeling shrimp—tearing away the shell to get to the meat. She was still waiting for helpful information about her prey.

More time passed. The APC proceeded along its never-ending left turn.

"Speaking of Dragons, the Third Stack," Ivion said eventually, glancing in the rearview mirror at Cho and Kinneas, "according to legend, was once home to a great old wyrm and its hoard. Much of the gold-plated historical artifacts—plates, ceremonial urns, and such—were said to have been made of the silver, gold, and precious stones taken from the beast's treasure when it was slain."

Alina said, "Dragons never hoarded jewels and other shiny junk. Now, *that's* a myth."

Ivion laughed. "I'll have to remember we have an Aelfraver aboard. Usually, I can get away with a bit more embellishment before I'm called on it. The truth is, the Third Stack grew out of gold mines. Half the gold in El comes from Ozari sources."

"Stolen you mean," said Cho.

"There may actually have been a Dragon down here, once, though. Lirilemnin the Blind, the stories name him. Enslaving an army of cultists, he allegedly ruled over these lands around the same time that the Twin Dragon Kings tyrannized our own ancestors. Back when all humanity was under the thrall of the Dragons."

"Yawn. We all know."

They crossed the next checkpoint. Cho noticed that many of the Enforcers here wore cobalt and navy—Torvir colors—marking them as soldiers who'd once been loyal to her parents. Now, they marched right along side the red-and-gold uniforms of the Walazzin and all the other Authority peacocking pinkojacks. What a world.

Through her window, she checked the sky-hole. The hexagon was now dark and, from this distance, the size of a six-sided die.

Cho's ears popped several times as their downward trek progressed. She voiced her latest random thought as it occurred: "This car's gonna run outta juice before we're halfway there."

"Correct," said Ivion, not missing a beat, "which is why we will be charging it up at the station on the Fourth Stack, which, by the way, is home to the Ineffable Forest."

"Sounds nifty," said Kinneas, who kept answering Ivion far too cheerfully (earning him one of Cho's patented Scowls of Aggravation).

"Leafless trees, acres of them, multiplying and growing at terrifying speeds. Pressing their way out of the rock. Crushing the earth beneath their roots as they crawl, inch by inch, from all sides toward the buildings. Every morning, hundreds of Enforcers venture out to burn away the growth of the previous night. *Every day* this has to happen, or the trees will gain ground and, eventually, choke the entire Stack. Fire is the only cure."

Catching Alina's thousand-mile stare reflected in the passenger-side mirror, Cho found herself wanting to check in for the millionth time. As much as Alina claimed she was holding it together, it sure didn't seem like it. But with Ivion—and, to a lesser extent, Kinneas—present, Cho didn't voice her concerns. She didn't want to make Alina uncomfortable.

Ah, maybe Cho was just being paranoid. Why was she treating Alina like her kid sister anyway?

At the gas station, Ivion waved an attendant over to refuel the vehicle. Cho kept an eye on Alina, noting the beads of sweat on her friend's forehead. Having to switch on and hold a magical disguise this many times in one day, and for this long, was visibly wearing her down.

Hopefully, her pained, distant expression could be chalked up to nerves and exhaustion. She'd earned a rest. They all had. A real, good night's sleep on a bed with—gasp—a pillow and sheets.

But they were a long way off from such a pleasant dream. Cho mentally steeled herself for another several-hour leg of their never-ending saga of Driving to their Doom. Too tired for her usual award-winning quips, she let Ivion's commentary wash over her like lukewarm shower water.

In that intellectually detached way of hers, Ivion recounted more historical and cultural details of each Stack as the APC slowly, agonizingly slowly, spiraled ever down and down and down.

The Fifth Stack had these unexplainable upside-down mountains and valleys, the ice caps separated by frozen lakes, with a constant snow storm flowing upward from an inter-dimensional tear. Despite the wonky gravity, the natives had managed to live there relatively comfortably for a long time. Their new Elemental bosses were still getting used to it.

The anti-Authority, anti-El terrorist organization known as Anarkey made life on the Sixth Stack unpleasant for any non-Ozari. Therefore, the Sixth held the highest concentration of Elemental-led forces. Anarkey attacks weren't mounted on a daily basis, but they were frequent and unpredictable. More effective than El's propaganda machine would prefer to acknowledge.

Groggier by the minute, Cho still managed to make a mental note to investigate these Anarkey rebels once she got situated in town.

Finally, hypnotized by the spiraling downward glide, she became so drowsy she could hardly keep her eyes open. She was only half following what Ivion was saying now.

Something about the Seventh Stack (which made Cho think of pancakes).

Something about the legend of an Achy Mirror that wasn't good or bad as long as it was perfectly balanced. But someone had broken the Mirror a long time ago?

Something about how humans now lived in the bones of Cool Cities, and that there was still so much to learn from the translated documents recovered by researchers, and if only the Elementals had more Kiwi Dancers.

Cho felt pretty confident that was all one hundred percent accurate reporting of what had been said.

She nodded off.

Tall, compact, brick buildings with flat roofs, balconied windows, and glowering gargoyles framed Cho's vision as she opened her eyes. Painful brightness; a searing red glare lit the night—dozens of signal flares, curling in the air like question marks. In answer, a warning cry, followed by screams.

She'd landed in the middle of an urban battlefield. No, *battles* had to be at least a little bit two-sided. What was happening all around her was slaughter.

Marked with the PACE (Peace and Asset Compliance Enforcement) logo, Authority tanks rolled down the street on which she stood. All around her, people crawled out of windows and doors, slid down fire escapes, and scattered. They clung to each other, to swaddled babies, to briefcases and bags stuffed with possessions and money. Gelder bills fluttered all around her like moths, pushed higher and higher by the rising flames, catching fire.

Loose rows of people were pursued by a steadily marching line of Enforcers, who raised their weapons, knelt, and fired. The fleeing individuals fell among the ash. A tank shell blasted apart the base of an apartment building ahead, which groaned, tilted, and toppled. Clouds of brick dust rose as Enforcers gunned down those who crawled out of the wreckage.

Grimacing, her head reeling, Cho ducked behind an abandoned car.

The street was littered with pamphlets smudged by mud, blood, and ash. She read,

**— LINKSY LIBERATION LEAGUE —
FREE TERRESTRIALS UNITE
AGAINST THE TYRANTS IN THE SKY!**

Linsky. That's the northwestern region of the Torviri Province. Thousands of miles from where Cho was supposed to be right now. When and how had she become separated from the others?

Though the roar of flamethrowers and tank engines and the storm of bullets was deafening, a momentary lull, a hush—as if the gods of carnage stilled their fury for the span of a breath—allowed Cho to hear it, that smallest of sounds. The sniffling of a child.

Looking left, Cho saw her, a little girl with dark skin and long black hair falling around her face, hugging a dirty stuffed blue octopus doll.

A spotlight passed over her, and she winced, retreating deeper into the shadows cast by the pulverized brick walls. Nearby, flames danced across an oil slick.

A body slammed into Cho, the hands of a man in his late twenties or early thirties grabbing her, steadying her. He yelled over the clamor, "Please! I'm looking for my daughter. A five-year-old, black hair? Have you seen her? Buthmertha have mercy, please!" His green eyes streamed tears that sliced through the smeared soot on his cheeks.

Unable to form words, Cho pointed to where she'd seen the girl.

"Alina!" he turned and called. "Alina, where are you?"

Smoke and ash brought tears to her eyes as she numbly watched him run off. Confused, having no clue what to do, Cho decided to follow the man who'd said "Alina." She took off after him, over the heaps of splintered furniture and twisted pipes, through a wall of flame, and over a fissure in the ground, a crack that had split an alley right down the middle.

There, on the other side, the man knelt beside the girl, who looked up at him with dark green eyes. Alina's dark green eyes. Her blue octopus's head had been singed, as had the hem of her skirt, the toes of her shoes, and the tips of her hair. She stood, rocking from side to side, over the body of a woman. Curly gray hair haloing her head, the woman hacked, blood spattering her cheek.

The man slid to his knees at her side. Curling an arm around the little girl, he pulled her in close; with the other, he propped the woman's head.

She'd been shot. Cho's scanners weren't functioning for some reason, but it was obvious that the woman's spirit was slipping from this world. The man leaned over her, and she whispered something in his ear.

Above them, a brass plaque read "Elemental Bank, Clerica Viridim Branch"—but the "Elemental" part had been angrily scratched out. Onto the wall, in red, had been painted the words, "No more blood taxes." Bright banners celebrating new year 3490 had been slashed.

3490? A year before Cho had even been born. "So, it's a dream," she whispered. "A nightmare."

This wasn't how it had gone down. None of the details were right. Alina hadn't talked much about her parents, but she had claimed they'd died in Rafleugar Square, taking advantage of some kind of protest movement to rob a bank. The tunnel they'd been digging with Terramancy had caved in, crushing them. Alina had been in the hole, too, but she'd lived. A miracle, really.

What Cho was seeing now didn't match that story at all. The location was way off (Rafleugar Square was in New El, not Torviri Province), and a failed heist was a far cry from this Authority-drawn bloodbath. The only features consistent with Alina's telling were the nearby bank and the anti-Loyalty Law signs everywhere.

All the details were wrong. Yet, it felt true.

The harsh voice of an Enforcer echoed along the alley, and he fired a warning shot in the air.

"It's not real," Cho tried to convince herself.

"Please," said the kneeling man, clinging to his family. "Please, just let us go."

Cho shook her head. "Alina's an adult, napping in a car, on her way to a totally different warzone. This is just my overtired, overstimulated imagination feeding me nonsense."

The Enforcer raised his pistol.

"A dream," she insisted. "Just a—"

The Enforcer was going to kill them. All three of them. She could feel it.

The soldier wore the colors of the Torvir—two entwined orange dragons, under which were crossed a key and hammer (also orange) on a field of cobalt. Cho's family crest marked his heart, and the fool was going to execute three innocent people unless she stopped him.

Dream or not, she wasn't about to watch her best friend die.

"Ours Shall Endure!" she shouted.

Hearing the Torvir Family motto caused the Enforcer to hesitate just long enough for Cho to run up, kick off the wall, and drive her knee into his nose. He went down and did not get up.

Her victory was short-lived. More shouts from behind.

She turned to the family of three, but it was too late. Three more Enforcers rounded opposite corners, one on Cho's end of the alley, the other two out of her reach. She'd couldn't fight them all.

"Please!" the man said again.

Two of the Enforcers wore dark green and black uniforms bearing the three emerald wolves' heads of the Reautz Family. The third soldier, in soot-gray adorned with the Hruvic Family's wine purple hornet, closed in and took aim. Cho yelled at him, but her words were clipped and would not reach.

He fired two shots, striking the pleading man in the chest.

The man bent backward. Squeezing her stuffed toy, the little girl swung toward him. Cho was sprinting, throwing herself forward, but she'd never make it. Throat and lungs clogged with ash, legs rubbery and weak, to her the distance seemed infinite yet growing.

The family of three receded.

The Enforcers closed in.

The dying mother raised her shaking, dark hand. She made a fist—
And *screamed*.

The fissure in the alley spread and deepened, a rumble filling Cho's ears. The world around her shook, knocking her off her feet. The apartment buildings on either side collapsed inward as if their foundations had been sucked into a sinkhole. Cho rolled as clusters of bricks and mortar slammed down like hellish hail. Regaining her footing, she launched into a backspring as everything in a thirty-foot radius around the woman was consumed in the sudden earthquake.

Blinded to all else but the path away from the destruction, the asphalt and concrete beneath her giving way, Cho leapt. She clung to the crumbling edge of the street, glancing down at a thirty foot drop. Scrabbling, she pulled herself up.

When the dust had settled, and the roar subsided, the crackle of gunfire and the growl of tank engines moved on, leaving only ruin in their wake. The Authority had cleared this sector of Clerica Viridim to their satisfaction, proceeding to the next.

Turning her back to the fire and death, Cho picked her way down into the pit, leaping from ledge to quivering ledge, until she reached the bottom.

It wasn't long before she found the family again, covered in debris, soaked by the spray of a burst water main. The little girl lay between her parents, her father's body flung over hers, shielding her from a fallen hunk of wall.

None of them moved.

"Alina," Cho breathed. She dashed over, lifting through her knees, growling as she rolled the man aside.

The girl lay there, eyes closed, her mother's arms around her. Even in death gripping her tightly as vines clinging to concrete.

Kneeling, Cho wept, reaching with trembling fingers. But she stopped when a crow landed between her and Alina, hopping in a semicircle.

It cocked its head, considering Cho, weighing her. "Who are you?" it asked.

"Uh," said Cho.

Alina looked up. "You could have saved them."

"But, I'm not even here," said Cho.

"You didn't do enough, and now they're dead. It's all your fault."

"What was I supposed to do? I wasn't expecting this, any of it. There wasn't enough time—I'm just a kid. Just one kid. There were too many of them."

"You didn't do enough. You could have done more."

"Stop it." Cho covered her ears. "I tried."

The hue of Alina's eyes shifted to yellow. "They're dead, and it's all your fault."

Squawking frantically, the crow flew right at Cho, about to skewer her eye with its beak.

Cho shot out of her seat, bonking her head on the roof of the APC.

"That's one reason to wear a seatbelt," said Alina. "You okay?"

Casting around, breathing hard, Cho swallowed. "Did you see—?"

"See what?" said Kinneas. His concerned face dragged her back to reality.

She shook her head. "Crazy dream. No bigs." Wondering if Kinneas had splashed water on her as a prank, she realized that, no, she was drenched with sweat.

The APC had slowed to a stop. "We're here," said Ivion.

Rubbing her eyes, Cho said, "Where's here?"

"Uh, Cho, you got a little—" Alina pointed at the corner of her own mouth.

Cho wiped her drool on the cuff of her shirt as Ivion answered, "You were asleep quite a few hours. This is the Sixth Stack, where I've secured for our use an old Jaandarmes' Safehouse."

"Jaandarmes?" said Kinneas.

"Secret police," Alina said, yawning.

"This is a terrible idea," said Cho.

"Sure feels like it. But, I'm not ashamed to say, I'm beat. I'd almost take life in prison if a feather mattress came guaranteed."

"Are you aware of how prisons work?"

"She's kidding," said Kinneas. "Right? She is kidding, I hope."

"Kin," said Cho, "I'm half asleep, and even I figured that much out."

Ivion cut in. "Please do not misinterpret the spirit of what I'm about to say, but would you all kindly *get out*. It has been a very long few days, I'm sure you'll agree, and I would very much enjoy a rest as well. Grab your things, head inside, and check the perimeter."

Cho saluted. "Aye-aye, ma'am. And where would you like your bags stowed? I can think of one place. It'd be a tight fit, but—"

"Cho!" Alina snapped.

"Alright, alright. I'm going."

Mezami popped his head through the tiny opening in the zipper in his hiding bag. "Propose: slumberparty, I."

Parked as the APC was in a narrow alley ending in a dead-end wedge between three buildings, disembarking was a tight squeeze. Cho looked up at the ceiling and shook her head. Darkness.

Here, at ten miles or so beneath the surface, the ichor of moss and damp earth masked all other smells, and the sun was but a distant memory. They'd left it behind when they'd passed the inner checkpoint of Stack Six, marked by a door equal in width to a battleship. Cho had slept through that part. She hadn't even had the chance to say goodbye to her old pal, the sun.

Well, she could start exploring the splendors of Ozar tomorrow. For tonight, she'd simply hope her dreams would be good old normal ones again. Not whatever she'd experienced in the car.

Slinging a bag strap over her shoulder, she stared at the back of Alina's head and the curve of her neck, shaking off the vestiges of nightmare.

23

JEJUNE

WHEN A REMINDER ALARM dinged on Mr. Jejune's watch, he muted the long-distance office party celebrating Tytan's predicted windfall profits. Although he remained away on business in Kadic, the firm simply couldn't wait to commemorate his stellar work. They'd uncorked the champagne and whipped out the trays of hummingbird tongues—as if any of them had had anything to do with this success. He slammed his fist against the wall, punching clean through the hardwood paneling. Ah well, another item on the expense report.

This was Kadic. Everything was cheap.

There'd be another soiree for him, promised his partners (hah!). They knew what he was worth. They knew to be afraid. A party in his honor, yes, there had better be one, but the vapid apes would have to endure the absence of his sparkling personality just a while longer. His blathering, moronic colleagues now unable to hear him, his fingers tapped across the screen of his third phone, dialing the unsaved, unregistered number.

"Captain Tiberaira," he sang jovially into the mic of his wireless headset. He popped a lump of tepid, rubbery, room-service lobster doused in cocktail sauce into his mouth. Flying fresh seafood this far inland had been prohibitively expensive, but exorbitant cost had never before stopped Jejune from treating himself. Once again, however, he was disappointed.

He considered which of the hotel's employees to gut like the very shellfish they'd so horribly overcooked as he said, "My good captain. The evening finds you well, I presume. How are you and your subordinates enjoying your upgraded statuses?"

There was some static on the line, and the captain spoke so gruffly that a human might have had trouble understanding her. Of course, Jejune digested every syllable perfectly, together with the shrimp, and grinned as he listened.

She said, "I take it this isn't a social call. What do you want?"

"Only to check up on my newly collected friend. And, if you'd be so very kind, a quick update as to your progress."

"We've been squeezing the Sixth Stackers. No word of the girl yet. If she's here, she's either well hidden or well protected."

Jejune's fangs tore right through his cheek. Spitting blood onto his over-starched napkin—he could hardly fold the thing!—he began to notice just how terribly wrong everything was. The curtains were too heavy, and they drew unwanted attention to the smallness of the room. The audacity of the staff here, the sheer nerve. He wiped a viscous streak of his blood on the tablecloth and bedsheets, sweetly saying, "I have no doubt whatsoever concerning your capabilities, captain, and I'm certain our wayward miscreant will turn up."

Tiberaira grunted. When that seemed to be the only reply she was willing to give him, he growled under his breath, tasting bile. Control the conversation, he reminded himself. Change the topic. "It couldn't escape my notice, reviewing your unit's cam feeds, that your numbers have dropped slightly. Would you care to enlighten me as to the cause?"

"Travel time accounts for part of it. As for the rest, to be perfectly honest, the Jaandarmes' stipend we're now receiving is worth almost as much as the kill bonuses. Why should we stick our necks out, running low-priority secondary objectives in the streets of the Sixth, when we can put all that time and effort into pursuing our primary objective—acquiring the target?"

Mr. Jejune pursed his lips, thinking. "Ah-huh. Sensible. Logical."

"Second thoughts about selecting us for this job—" she paused. Insolence or uncertainty? Neither answer appealed to Jejune. Finally, she finished with— "sir?"

"Not at all, not at all. I did not mean to imply anything of the sort. I'm just a, uh, *man* who makes it his business to learn all there is to know that might be relevant, thus maximizing my gains. We're the same, in that way, you and I."

Silence on the other end.

Finally, Jejune gave up and said, "Well, don't let me keep you any longer, captain. Rest well, and do let me kn—"

Captain Tiberaira cut him off. "This unprompted call was highly disruptive. Don't bother me again unless absolutely necessary."

A little beep in his ear let him know that the signal had dropped. Or she'd hung up on him. One of those two causes was far likelier, but, again, she'd presented him a pair of most equally unsavory choices. If this was to become a habit, he'd have no choice but to tear off her hands. Hmm, maybe just the one hand. He'd have to see how he felt in the moment.

Regardless, Tiberaira and her Cutcords didn't have to like him; they only needed do as instructed.

Jejune's great regret was that he almost certainly wouldn't be there in the flesh (so to speak) when Tiberaira executed Choraelia Torvir. Any human's violent death was a cause for celebration, but particularly tasty were life threads snipped when they were still taut with the vibrancy of youth. Always so much better when they retained their *promise*. Better still were threads like Choraelia's, thick and thrumming with destiny. Cutting short such a thread...

Alas, no, unless the good captain were inexplicably slow in the execution of her task, Mr. Jejune likely couldn't enjoy this very special morsel for himself. He had menial but unfortunately crucial business to which to attend in Kadic, so he must content himself with the prospect of a near-future buffet of carnage. Soon, he and his thousands of siblings would gorge themselves on the institutions and people of the City-State of Ozar.

The mere thought had him shuddering with pleasure.

He unmuted the office party, bid the short-lived dullards "good night," and consigned himself to the lumpy queen-sized bed.

In the morning, he'd decided, he'd take the owners out back and kill them. And, one day soon, unless she learned her place in the scheme of things, he'd go after Hael Tiberaira with equal gusto.

He snapped his fingers, snuffing all the light in the room—the electric chandelier, fireplace, candles. Tucking himself in, tasting his own blood, he smiled himself to sleep.

But when the rush of water in the plumbing woke him from his pleasant dreams, he declared aloud that he'd been too conservative in requiring the lives of only the owners—and too lenient in allowing them to live through the night.

Mr. Jejune shed his human disguise, the flesh sloughing from his expanding, crackling exoskeleton.

Slavering in the darkness, he skittered from the room.

24

CHO-ZEN

FERRYING THEIR FEW BELONGINGS inside, they all groaned, stretched, and hydrated.

Mezami popped out of Alina's bag, streaking across the below-street-level bunker Ivion had dubbed the Safehouse. It consisted of four small, square rooms, smushed together to form (you guessed it) a larger square. There were no windows, and apparently only one point of entry—a vault door with a supposedly uncrackable electronic lock requiring a six-digit code (a quick scan from Cho revealing multiple failsafes). The second of the quartet of rooms had been stuffed with old computers and electronics, fan blades, and other mechanical parts. The "kitchen," just a sink and some cupboards, was limited to one corner of the storage room. The room last was empty except for bed cots and plastic bins stuffed with spare clothing.

Staring at the cold, gray concrete walls, floor, and ceiling, Cho said, "Homey."

"At least there's room to stretch," said Kinneas, falling to the ground in a split. "Ee-ouch! Shoulda warmed up first."

Ivion set down her bags and ran a hand through her still annoyingly full-bodied and shiny platinum hair. "Its lack of charm notwithstanding, there is one feature I know you will appreciate." Nudging the door open with her hip, she ambled into the storage kitchen. "What do you know of the Jaandarmes?"

Alina's eyes went glassy. "The word is Ciirimaic. 'Jaan' means 'protector,' and 'darmeser' is a verb meaning 'to cut' or, sometimes, 'to hone.'"

Ivion turned, smiling. "Yes. 'Blade Guard' is an oft-used translation in the histories."

Cho yawned.

"However, contrary to common misconception, the order of Jaandarmes predates The Authority." Smugness radiated from Ivion's smooth skin. "If you'll permit me a little historical backgrounding… The word 'Jaan,' as a skilled linguist such as yourself may already be well aware, was one of many words borrowed from the Iorians. Its origins in Ciirimaic may be traced back to the Extermination War. In the all but extinct Iorian, 'Jaan' meant 'Dragon.' This (and our current understanding of 'darmeser') allows for the early modern interpretation, 'Drag-onblade' or 'Dragoon.' The Iorians had one other word for 'Dragon,' equally revealing: 'Rhin,' meaning 'sovereign,' which is highly suggestive of their societal hierarchy. Unless several key texts have been completely mistranslated, both 'Jaan' and 'Rhin' refer to the Dragons, and Dragons, therefore, were alternatively considered servant-guardians *and* masters of kings. A terrifically complex pair of contrasting representations."

Cho said, "Much as I love hours of exposition, there a point you're working towards?"

"There is, in fact. Alina, as an Aelfraver, you'll have been taught that the Dragons, of all Aelf, were among the most naturally gifted in magic, that they are creatures *of* pure Niima."

"According to Aelfraver lore, sure. The last Dragon was exterminated hundreds of years ago, though, and the guy who took it down died without telling anyone much useful about his final Rave."

"Elegir Wyrmslain, I'm familiar with his tale," Ivion interjected, apparently needing everyone to note how well-read and knowledgeable she was. "A legend, supported by centuries of historical research. A cryptic reference in some of Elegir's notes (the ones that weren't incinerated in his funeral pyre) claimed there were men that worshiped the Dragon Gurgulniir, and these mortals had been gifted with something called 'Dragonfire.'"

"Sounds like Igniomancy," said Kinneas.

"Alina could tell you better than I that that is one of the many falsehoods surrounding this mysterious race."

"Yeah," Alina confirmed. "They didn't breathe fire. And they probably weren't big, flying lizards."

A decade's worth of adventure comics turned to ash in Kinneas's stare. Alina gave his shoulder a sympathetic squeeze.

Once started on a rant, Ivion apparently couldn't be stopped: "Actually, the word 'fire,' used in this sense of 'Dragonfire,' is probably another metaphor— the Iorians loved them—an alternate translation of their word for 'soul.'" Give her a job in sanitation because she was a natural at info dumps.

"Maybe it's related to how the Iorians had flaming hair," said Alina, leaning against a wall. "Supposedly."

Cho clearly remembered Alina telling her about the encounter with the Librarian at The Gild; Alina's addition of "supposedly" meant she wasn't ready to trust Ivion with every detail just yet. Good. Very good.

"Relevance: missing, I," said Mezami as he rolled past them, circling the room on a marble.

"My apologies," Ivion said, inclining her head. "I do have a tendency to ramble and ensnare myself in a web of tangents. The point is this: if 'fire,' 'soul,' and 'magic' were all rough synonyms to the Iorians—and they were—then the original Dragoons could reasonably be assumed to be the wielders of this 'Dragonfire' spoken of in the old legends. It would make sense; after all, to this day, every Dragoon, every Jaandarme, is a talented mage, trained from childhood at The Gild. On the basis of merit, the majority of them are recruited from the rank and file of The Authority front-line soldiers. Promoted for exemplary service and battle prowess."

"A willingness to kill," Cho said.

"That certainly does not hurt one's chances of being selected. Anyway, talented Mages, secret police. They have a fondness for subtlety that, I think, will serve our merry band quite well in the coming days." Ivion knelt in the middle of the kitchen, her long, pale fingers gently raking the dusty floor. With her other hand, she reached into her sleeve, producing a silvery, diamond-shaped metal object attached to a simple steel chain. "A key. And now, to find…"

Cho focused on the key, noticing that it wasn't quite diamond-shaped after all; it had three "teeth," a larger central one flanked by two slightly smaller. The swirling detail etched into its side gave the impression of dancing flames. Its chemical composition—pure, high-grade titanium. What was the point of having a titanium key? Why not make it of iron or brass or something easier and less expensive to manufacture? Another of Ivion's excesses.

"There," said Ivion. She inserted the key into a thin slit that had been, even to Cho's enhanced vision, entirely invisible up to that very instant. A square indentation appeared, then lowered a few inches before sliding aside. Ivion smirked at Cho, saying, "A trapdoor that cannot be found unless you've been shown where it is."

"That is awesome," said Kinneas, putting his hand into the square hole, wiggling his fingers.

"This route only opens with this key. Nothing else."

Alina whistled through her teeth. "The Niima-weave is incredibly complex. It'd take a lot of time and effort to untangle and dispel it."

"I haven't yet told you the best part. This place served as a Jaandarmes spying outpost, so this chute leads directly down into Stack Seven—the last wholly unoccupied sector of Ozar. As long as we are careful, we may operate in the free and occupied sectors of the city as we search for clues to The Savior's plans."

Ivion tapped the key against the edge of the hole—three times—and the passageway sealed itself again. She wrapped the steel chain around her wrist and slipped the key back where it'd come from. "I have a few things to take care of. Mainly checking the alarm systems, making sure they are all fully functional. I suggest you all get some rest."

"Great," said Cho, throwing her bag on the ground at last. "So, are we all expected to pee in that sink?"

"I'm sure we get our own sinks," said Alina. "Help me find the other secret switches."

Ivion rolled her eyes. "There are a shower and toilet built into the wall, over there. The compartment swivels. Just press the panel."

They spent some time settling in, and Cho got to thinking about that magic key. Considering how difficult it would be, even for her, to steal it off Ivion's wrist—and copying it likely wouldn't work—she abandoned the idea.

After a few halfhearted games of cards with Mezami, Cho ogled Ivion, who'd emerged from the shower stall, clean and dressed in one of her white suits again. This one sparkled. Ooh.

Telling them all to hang tight, Ivion promised she'd return with food.

Cho squinted at her as she left through the front vault door, tugging it shut behind her. A satisfying series of clicks echoed in the mostly empty rooms of their concrete one-star hotel.

Over an hour later, Ivion came back with what she assured them was an Ozari delicacy procured from the underground lakes some miles west: she passed around cardboard takeout containers packed with rice, steamed tubers, and mostly dead eels.

"You have to be sure to bite down on the head before you swallow," she said cheerfully, "or you might choke on one as it wriggles to escape your throat."

Frowning and nodding slowly, Cho nudged the eel container aside, piling the rice and tubers high. "I've decided to fully embrace a cruelty-free lifestyle."

"Only when convenient," said Actual Vegetarian Alina, also avoiding the eels.

Green as a bottom-feeder, Kinneas followed their examples.

By contrast, Mezami was having a ball, wrestling the wriggling creatures, gulping them down two at a time.

"Now, Lady Choraelia," said Ivion, wiping her mouth with a paper napkin before discarding it on the pile of plastic, cardboard, and styrofoam trash. "Alina and I were talking earlier, and she has something she'd like to tell you."

Cho quirked a brow, meeting her friend's eye. "Well?"

"You're not gonna like it, but—I think you should stay here with Kinneas. At least until we know what we're getting ourselves into." Alina seemed taken aback by the total silence engulfing the space. "Listen to me, okay? Hear me out."

"I'm listening. Say your piece. Go on."

"It's just that—you're a little too... raring... right now."

"Raring, huh? 'Raring,' she says."

"What I'm trying to say is you're not thinking straight. Eilars's death hit you hard—hit us all hard, but you especially. And I don't think you're done grieving, which is fine, and normal. But it's made you obsessed with, like, punishing the Walazzins. And, here, where they've got literally thousands of soldiers and Maggos protecting them, a wrong step could get you captured. Or worse."

"Hey! I was obsessed with the Walazzins *way* before Eilars—No, hang on, that came out wrong. I mean, I know what I'm doing. And, you don't get to tell me how to handle myself. Like losing Morphea didn't faze you at all. Yuh, right. Don't get it twisted. I'm not any more scrambled than you are."

"Listen, I'm not trying to be condescending."

"Too late."

"Well, I'm sorry, then. But the fact is, we're wanted. If we get caught, they won't just throw wigs and bad dresses on us."

A cold fire burned in Cho's gut. How dare she bring up that day? How could she just casually throw it into the conversation with *her* listening. Cho glared at Ivion.

"Cho, look at me," Alina said. "I can disguise myself. You can't."

"Give me a pair of sunglasses and a hat, then. Buthmertha damn it all, I'll wear a stocking on my head." Cho flung her styrofoam plate at the wall. Rice fell on Mezami like snow. "I didn't ride in a giant toaster for over three days just to sit on my hands."

"You won't have to. Just let me get the lay of the land. It's one day, Cho. Give me one day. I just don't want you getting hurt."

"I don't want that for you either. But you gotta stop thinking you're better than me."

"That's not—"

"You're more capable 'cause you're a Maggo, that it? So, you can walk around in people's daydreams and throw stones with your mind. Great. Doesn't mean you're more fit for the fight."

Kinneas leaned in. "I get that you're trying to downplay her skills, but all that stuff you said is legitimately still pretty cool and not helping your point."

"I know that. Shut up. What was I—right. Sure, so you can, like, shoot sparks and junk. But I've got a trillion gelders' worth of cybertech crammed into every inch of my body. And I was handling myself at a much younger age than you."

"You're right," said Alina, quietly. "And you shouldn't have had to."

"No, that's not what I'm—am I speaking Zinoklese? Why isn't anyone *hearing* me?"

"Cho, I'm sorry." Alina raised her black-gloved hand, splaying her fingers. "But this is for your own good."

Last thing Cho remembered, her suddenly heavy arms fell to her sides and her eyelids drooped.

Why'd you even bring me along? she shouted into the void.

In Alina's voice, the void answered, *To save you.*

Cheek damp, Cho mumbled and rolled over. Her eyes popped open.

She clenched her fists and tensed her shoulders until the numbness faded.

She and Kinneas were alone. He sat in the corner, reading. When he heard the rustling of her clothes as she sat upright, he set down his book and waited, assuming his default expression—embarrassment.

She took a minute to collect herself, then said, "She put me to sleep."

"Out like a broken light," he said. "Mid-sentence. And Alina's only been at this Revomancy stuff for a year. She's something else."

"Oh my gods, whose side are you on, anyway?"

"No one's! I can't be on anyone's side because she's my teacher and you're my g—friend. My friend. Is it super awkward, getting stuck between you two all the time? Hells yeah, it is. I'm as unhappy about this whole situation as you are. Probably more."

Too irritated to reply, she focused on the slit in the floor. She scrabbled over to it. "They went this way?"

"Yeah."

Pressing her lips up against the keyhole in the floor, Cho shouted, "This was never part of the deeeeeaal."

No response except a faint echo.

"They've been gone at least an hour." Kinneas snapped his fingers. "Right, I was supposed to tell you something. From Alina. Just remember, please, I'm only the messenger."

"What, Kinneas? What?"

"I feel like I really can't make it clear enough that these are her words, not mine. Um. She said to tell you, 'Cho, I'm sorry, but this just proves that I'm right. You need time to cool down. Think of what would've happened if I'd really been trying to hurt you. You're not ready. Please try to understand.' Then she said something about talking to you later."

"Typical. Absolutely typical." Pacing, Cho added, "This is all that Ivion's fault, you know—the worst possible influence. And our poor, sweet, naively innocent Alina…" On impulse, she checked her phone. It had indeed been a little over an hour since she'd been put to sleep.

Since then, she'd received exactly one text. From Ivion.

Apologies for the ruse, but it's no permanent arrangement. Be good, wait for our return, and I promise I will help you in your efforts. For what it's worth, I fought for you.

"'Be good'? She think I'm some kinda dog? 'Be *good*'?"

Kinneas kicked a hunk of gravel across the concrete floor. "Maybe she could help, though. Look at how far we've come thanks to her help. And, now that we're here, we hardly know where to start. Would it be so bad to play by her rules for a while, see what comes of it?"

"Kinneas, we are two extremely capable young people. You're a Maggo, even. We don't need help—not hers, not anybody's—so long as we got each other."

"Yeah. That's true." Blushing, he nibbled his lip. "This is pretty crappy, actually, you're right. I can't believe they dragged us all the way out here just to lock us in a room. Isn't even a Watchbox in here."

"Oh, I can believe it. But what blows my mind is how dumb they were to think they could keep us in here." Retrieving her multitool and flicking out the lockpick, she began to poke and test the splinter-thin keyhole in the floor.

"What're you doing?" he said. "We might not like it, but they did tell us to stay put."

Kneeling, tongue poking out, she jimmied the lock. "You always do what the parental unit tells ya?"

"Actually, yeah. I never gave my dad any trouble."

"Good for you." She couldn't find a good position or angle, so she gave up after a few minutes.

"Well, what I want doesn't matter anyway. There's no chance of getting outta here."

"You're right. Too bad you can't, like, turn yourself into a puddle and just kinda slip through the tiny crack."

"Man, I wish I could, but I'm not nearly that good yet."

"Guess we're stuck here after all. Damn. If only someone had thought to secretly watch Ivion punch in the access code for the front door." She tapped her forehead.

He laughed. "What?"

"They're so bad at being sneaky, but they're worried about me? It's so rich, it's cheesecake." She skipped over to the keypad, slid up the metal cover, and input the six digits, 512316.

The clicks and pops of metal mechanisms informed her of her success even before she swung the door open.

Taking Kinneas by the hand, she said, "You ready?"

"I just—"

"Kin, I can't do this without you."

They locked eyes.

"Uh." His blush darkened. "Then, let's go kick some Walazzin ass."

PART THREE

ANGER

25

ALINA

Squinting up at the sky-ceiling, the stalactites hundreds and hundreds of feet above, Alina was nearly swept off her feet by vertigo. But Ivion caught her by the elbow, gently guided her by the neck. "Focus on what's ahead."

The narrow street beyond the bunker's topside entrance was perfectly dingy. The lamp light that brushed its dull, cracked stone walls, shaded scars left by decades of slightly-too-large cars passing through. Coming to a T-intersection, this nameless street fed its few passengers to the main thoroughfare, a four-lane highway populated by every manner of vehicle, from hand-pulled carts to hydrogen-powered hovercraft to Authority mobile missile launchers and armored personnel carriers. And, there, where traffic signal lights swung over a constantly clogged crossing, a declaration of war had been sprayed in paint as white as the heart of fire and red as fresh blood.

Slicing across the stone pillar that supported the roof of this section of the massive Sixth Stack cavern, the lines and shapes revealed a figure, towering, clad in white, eyes gleaming, hand outstretched in beatific offering of brotherhood. No words accompanied the image, but the graffiti's intended message was clear: *this figure you see before you is your Savior; join him.*

Most of the people of Ozar went on about their lives, hurrying to their next destination. Some few stopped to snap a photo of the mural. All lived under its piercing glare.

The Savior was watching.

Next to it, however, was another pair of messages—stylized, sharp letters in black and gold, reading,

ANARKEY CALLS!
ALL PEOPLES UNITE—
SNUFF THE LIGHTBRINGERS

and,

HAVE FAITH
THE ABYSS EMBRACES YOU

Another competing message, this one also in messy blood-red, had been slathered across the bases of six decapitated statues:

FALSE GODS
WE ARE COMING

"Ozar," Ivion said, leading Alina through the streams of people, "is ripe for a reckoning."

26

CHO-ZEN

Expecting Ozar to be mystical, alien, treacherous, Cho was surprised to discover that it had far more in common with El than advertised by the news channels and history books. Ozar may have lain miles beneath the surface, but it had the same kinds of people, milling around, bumping into each other—little rodents running along the maze for the promise of a pellet or two. Checking their tablets, businessmen with sparkling watches and high-neckline suits were pulled along in handcarts by hunchbacked, coughing men and women. A bouncer kicked a drunkard through a door, shaking his fist as the other crawled away. Silvery pillars rose out of the concrete sidewalks like enlarged fire hydrants, people of all ages plugging themselves into its ports via the wires dangling from compartments carved out of their wrists; all those connected to the pillar slipped into one big pile of drooling numbness—until they hit their time limit, and they shuffled away, rubber-faced.

Among all this quiet, desperate suffering, Cho felt right at home. The biggest difference was the inescapable dampness.

Under a fluorescent yellow sign promoting "Buy-One-Get-One: Aether-thread Virtue-All Total Immersion Headsets (TM)," Cho wondered if maybe the similarities were by design. This part of town was Elemental-controlled after all. With The Authority's conquest had come all the comforts of the empire: plastic-choked flash-frozen fillets from D'Hydromel's mega-fisheries, disposable Cae-lusian cyberpets, blood diamonds mined from the Torvirius Mountains. Shut-tered windows and empty lots told the story of what had happened to local small businesses. Every day, through the sale of shiny junk and the administration of taxes, the Elementals made the Ozari pay for the privilege of being conquered.

Would the Seventh Stack be any different? Cho would find out.

For now, she had her sights set on the Sixth and its town-sized plateaus be-tween which flowed rivers and waterfalls, the waters sliding down stair-like ledges surrounded by sparkling crystals. Between two of the plateaus rested a lake where Cho and Kinneas strolled along the boardwalk, noticing the distant dots of rowboats and ships out fishing for eels and squid.

Trawled from the lake-depths, this bounty was battered, fried, steamed, and grilled by vendors on the boardwalk. Also sold, an assortment of shirts, hats, and small, mostly pointless gifts of the type you might bring back to your kids—that is, if you ever managed to leave this impossibly huge, multi-layered subterranean world made of holes and darkness, earth and water.

Kinneas insisted on taking a dip in the lake, and Cho let him. It gave her the opportunity to steal a pair of thick-rimmed, black sunglasses and a dark green bandana. After fleeing the stand she'd robbed, she admired Kinneas's dolphin flips. With every feat of aquatic acrobatics, spirals of spray trailed him, hovering for a moment, the droplets glinting by the lamplight before splashing and re-forming with the whole.

Whenever Kinneas was out of the water, he was like a droplet, hanging, wait-ing to return to where it belonged.

She waved him over. He waded out of the water, self-consciously throwing on his shirt.

Despite his blue-lipped shivering, he was all smiles. "What's the plan?"

His smile dropped as soon as she told him.

From a balcony, they watched El's reinforcements arrive in the Sixth Stack, headed for the encampment farther south. A line of tanks rolled past, a tight squeeze between the grids of steel and concrete towers. Crowds of civilians packed onto the sidewalks, held at bay by police. Following the war machines, a constant parade of heavily armed and armored, faceless Tranquilizers marched in lockstep. The Twelve Families' banners rippled with the tepid ventilated air.

The army mobilizing in the Sixth Stack represented all corners of the Ele-mental Empire, even the colonies. Word on the street was that the assembled force numbered at least one hundred thousand, its singular purpose to bury the Seventh Stack, the last significant sources of resistance against El's dominion.

As she and Kinneas stalked patrols, listening, Cho detected accents from central El, the southwest, Oronor, Rudu, Zinokla. None interested her more than the rapid-fire, throaty voices of those native to the riverlands of Walazzin Province. Their body armor and helmets (and even their weapons in some cases) had been spray-painted a reflective gold so that they shone even in this realm of long shadows. As they stood out from the others, they drew Cho to them all the more quickly.

Kinneas tried to hold her back, but he lost sight of her.

She aimed herself at the Chimaera Guard squadron that had taken up positions on the median of a crowded intersection. Encircled by sandbags and portable energy shields that could be triggered at a moment's notice, a team of engineers directed, via radio and light signals, the movements of platoons and tanks and forklifts and armored personnel carriers. Around the techies, the Guard kept watch, supervised by a gold-skinned, purple-haired woman.

This spot clearly served as the hub of large-scale and complex military maneuvers, a delicate ballet of brass and steel that was disrupted when Cho (bandana and sunglasses on, hood up) leapt into the middle of them and pulled the pins on all their flashbang grenades.

She tucked and rolled over a ledge and into the gutter, covering her ears just as the flashes popped off in quick succession. Two-four-six—

Over the Walazzin soldiers' cries of panic and pain, she shouted at Kinneas to get away, hide somewhere. She'd find him later.

He had been drawn to the noise, now gaping at her.

Again, she yelled at him to go, and activated her cloaking ability. Hurrying between the reeling Chimaera Guard, knife in hand, she cut the laminated identification badge from its retractable tether on the golden captain's belt.

Amid a storm of swearing, she ran.

Tank guns swiveled, columns of soldiers about-faced. All nearby Authority units were now on high alert, dozens of squads fanning out to locate the threat. Using clusters of frightened people for cover, she escaped the intersection and broke into a sprint between twin rows of apartments.

Thinking she'd dodged her pursuers, she dropped her camo. Seconds later, she yelped when a heavy-caliber bullet struck the ground between her feet, way too close for comfort. She flung herself into some shadows, skidding on wet flagstone to drop behind piles of festering, oozy garbage. She thought twice about poking her head out for a look.

The sniper would be watching. He'd probably called for backup, so, the longer she waited, the likelier her capture became. Escaping the tightening noose of Enforcer and Tranquilizer patrols would be much harder if she were worried about taking a slug to the back.

Eilars had taught her to eliminate threats—efficiently, permanently, always. She knew what she had to do.

She hadn't seen the telltale glint of a scope nor any lone figure hunched on a rooftop, but her enhanced brain blazed through complex equations, analyzing the direction of the wind, the angle of the shot, and other factors. Within a second, she had a rough idea of where the sniper should have been. But he would relocate immediately to get line of sight on her current position, so she considered the likeliest places he'd next appear. Her camo bending the light, blending her body with her stone surroundings, she crept out of her hiding spot along the edges of walls. Sure enough, she sighted the sniper just as he posted on the lip of the building next to her, aiming for the dead-end alley she'd just left.

Cho climbed the nearby fire escape, crouch-walked along the balcony, and found the sniper kneeling with his back to her.

Now that she was here, she hesitated.

The sniper abandoned his stabilizing mount on the parapet, moving toward the edge of the roof for a better view. He must have noticed she wasn't in the alley any longer, but he still didn't think to check behind himself.

Whatever she was about to try, she'd better do it now. She inched forward.

His breathing was steady, and he exhibited the patience expected of one trained to lie in wait, perfectly still, for days at a time.

Her plan—scare him, throw his gun into the street or destroy it—fled her mind when she saw that he, too, wore the colors of the Walazzin. Muted and drab versions, of course, because a sniper's job is to blend in, but the insignia was unmistakable. This man was another of Wodjaego and Kaspuri's willing pawns.

The sniper lifted his gaze, adjusting the dial on his visor, searching the rooftops and streets. "Lost visual." He paused, listening.

Thanks to her cybernetically beefed-up ears, Cho heard some of what the voice in his earpiece was telling him: "... last known direction?"

"South by southwest on the corner of Lark and Minnow. I fired a warning shot, but target kept running."

"Warning...? ... ordered to kill, sergeant."

The sniper shook his head. "She looked like a kid, sir."

Anger and static cut through the other voice. "...violent terrorist... damages... insurrection... this insubordination, sergeant."

A kid. The words knocked around Cho's skull. She should've been bleeding out in the street right now. But this man, her enemy, had missed her on purpose.

Hands shaking, she began to back away. The sniper perked up, ear twitching, and turned around. Though she was still cloaked, the effect wasn't perfect; he could see the distortion in the air, and, being a trained soldier, he reflexively drew his sidearm.

No time to think anymore. Cho charged and threw all her weight, such as it was, into her push. She slammed into him, thrusting with her palms, and he toppled over the parapet, screaming. There came an audible, metallic *thonk*, and then another, as he struck several pipes on the way down.

Turning from the ledge, she dry-heaved before slapping herself across the face. Twice. Hard.

She'd had no choice. She'd probably killed him, but she'd had no choice.

He'd only fired a warning shot, and now was probably dead.

Eyes swimming in tears, she lifted his rifle, aiming for the high cave ceiling half a mile up, and squeezed the trigger. The shot echoed across the apartment rooftops. The kickback tweaked her shoulder.

Maybe somebody would find him, she thought, and get him to a field hospital.

She dashed for the fire escape. Shouts from below warned her that the Tranqs were closing in.

The next few minutes were a blur of panting, jumping, and climbing. How she'd managed to regroup with Kinneas, she didn't know.

His sweaty face contorted into an angry snarl. "What do you think you're doing?"

"Getting noticed." Her voice quivered. Even she didn't know what she meant by that.

"Not like this, Cho. You—you killed that guy."

Head slumping, she hugged her midriff. "I didn't mean for—I did what I had to, to get outta there. Maybe he's only badly hurt? Bone-setting and bed rest for a good long while, and he'll live? Might even get some nice paid leave out of the deal."

"I don't recognize you anymore."

She punched the wall next to him. "That makes two of us. Like I told ya, it was an accident. But, really, what do you think that shooter would have done if I'd left him alone, huh? What do you suppose *his* job is? Why d'you think the Walazzins are here?" He'd been an enemy. This was war. He'd known the risks. "If you can't handle it, Kin, get your mopey little face right back to the Safehouse."

The look Kinneas gave her mirrored her own heart, and she felt as if she were being dragged deeper and deeper into a fathomless sea. "I guess I didn't think it'd be like this," he said.

How dare he look at her that way, see her as she saw herself? She said, "Then you're as naive as ya look. You think your bro, wherever he's stationed, is picking flowers?"

"He's national guard. They're not deploying into a combat zone like this one."

"Oh, sure, yeah. Because everything was peaceful as can be back in Truct with the cuddly national guard in charge. Keep spinning those yarns, Kin." It was much easier to be angry, she discovered. She gave in. "You want the truth? I'm sorry I didn't move in for the kill on those Chimaera jacks, too. Every one of 'em I leave alive means another innocent in the ground. Someone else's daughter, brother, father or whatever."

"But this isn't us?" His fingers brushed her shoulder, lightly as the swish of a tadpole's tail.

She shrugged off his touch. "You see anyone else willing to do what's gotta be done?"

The Authority remained on high alert. Autonomous cameras, Situational De-Escalation Drones, lightly armored four-legged recon bots, and squads of five to ten combed the district's streets. The locals were sent indoors, an order enforced by acoustic cannons, giant sound guns capable of paralyzing a few dozen people at a time. Backing up the non-lethal crowd control measures was the threat of microwave emitters designed to vaporize moisture from hundreds of feet away (instant sun-dried human, in batches of ten).

Most of the soldiers and war machines turtled up in the center, completely blocking all major intersections, to survey their surroundings. Cho's sticky fingers had snagged one of their radios; she overheard the flustered Chimaera commanders blabbing about "several coordinated insurgent cells" and how a "larger attack was imminent."

The clustering of Authority forces left Cho and Kinneas more openings to break free. Tracking the movements of the scout teams, Cho hacked one of the recon bots, causing it to go haywire and brawl with its fellow machines. With a well-placed icicle throw, Kinneas picked off the few fist-sized, chrome-colored camera drones still in his and Cho's way.

Stage one: complete. The Authority was under the impression that serious bad news was coming for the Sixth Stack's lakeside district. As a result, they were overcompensating.

The chaos Cho sowed had Eilars's lessons written all over it. An unexpected blow to your enemy's strongest point could shake his confidence. She had made herself seem a much deadlier threat than she actually was. A risky move that had opened the opportunity for a followup: The Authority had become preoccupied with the southern sector, which left them exposed in the northwest—Cho's real target.

She and Kinneas rushed to their next objective, stage two, but encountered another obstacle on the way. A pair of Tranqs lying in wait around the corner. She could see their outlines through the wall. They must have heard Kinneas's heavy, clumsy footsteps echoing along the stone bridge as he'd tromped up a small hill sandwiched between two towers. She snatched his wrist, raising two fingers and pointing toward the wall.

Grabbing him by the collar, she breathed into his ear: "Trip 'em." Surprising herself as much as him, she kissed him full on the lips (thin, chilled, and damp, like the rim of a glass of iced soda weeping in the sun).

His mood shifted dramatically: his slouch instantly disappeared; his damp hair stood on end; his nose and cheeks reddened; his sweat froze as a blast of cold air radiated from him. As he had done the past few hours, whenever danger was near, he covered his face with a layer of ice—everything but his nostrils and eyes. A pretty cool precaution to confuse both human sight and facial recognition software.

Breaking the seal on his last plastic water bottle, he tossed its contents into the air, consolidating the droplets into one big floating puddle that he mentally directed around the blind corner. He dropped it like a small, localized rainfall. The Tranqs shouted something like "Hey! What the—" And then he froze the puddle.

Pouncing from above, Cho landed a kick against the chest of the nearest soldier, who slipped on the ice and fell on his back, his helmeted head bouncing against the ground; he rolled onto his side and lay there.

The second Tranq tried to fire, but his frosted trigger jammed. Cho drop kicked him, and he skidded forward, knocked out when he struck the wall head-first.

With two fresh assaults under their belt, the young vigilantes ran for it.

Kinneas said, "Can we call it a day yet?"

"Nah." Cho said. "Stage two's time-sensitive. So far's just been setup."

"Really asking for it if we keep pushing our luck."

"It's a sabotage and/or rescue op if that makes you feel any better."

"It doesn't!"

"You're gonna hafta tough it out. I heard some captain so-and-so talking about 'securing the prisoners.' They could be the resistance—Anarkey."

"*Could be?*"

"It's the best shot we have. Worst-case scenario, we save some political prisoners and earn goodie-good points with the universe."

"Nope. You're ignoring the *actual* worst-case: us, riddled with bullets, dying horribly."

"You really know how to rain on a gal's parade."

"*Water* wizard," he replied, tapping his forehead.

Panting, griping, still, he followed her. He always did.

From the rooftop, Cho watched the people milling and meandering below. Busy lanes of hovercars flying to and fro. Hundreds of potential gawkers, making her life as difficult as possible.

"Hurry up," she whispered down to Kinneas.

"I'm going as fast as I can," he said, cheeks swelling like a pufferfish's. "Had to refill my... bottles with... gutter water. Was gross."

"Save your breath. Just get up here already."

When he'd finally neared the ledge, she grabbed his clammy hand and helped him over.

He bent at the waist, gripping his knees, wheezing. "We can't all have metal bones and super muscles."

"Shh. Come here, take a look."

They crouched, and Cho, her cheek against his, pointed at the cream-colored tower across the street. Walazzin and Udutteta heraldry adorned its side. The construction was old, its painted bricks missing corners, and black wires latched like ivy to its western wall, running from the rusty electric boxes at its base to the satellite dishes fastened to its roof.

"An Authority relay station."

Here, orders from the Elementals' computer mainframe would be broadcast to captains, lieutenants, and squad leaders across the district. Such small fortresses also often served a secondary purposes—prisoner interrogation and data backup.

If Cho was going to make a splash on her first day in Ozar, this was where she'd do it.

She told Kinneas, "Those doors won't open for anyone except pinkojacks. They see me, I'm done. But if we can get 'em to send a team out, I can slip in behind 'em. Just need ya to take out those security cameras. And that guard on the right."

"Oh, is that all? Maybe I can ice skate down to them while solving a puzzle cube, too?"

"If ya think it'd help get the job done."

"Cho," he said gravely. "That's an Authority outpost. It's the middle of the day—I think so at least—I mean, it's hard to tell down here—still! We can't go up against that. They're armed and ready."

"How did you think we were going to spend the day?"

"I don't know. Scouting, getting the, uh, the lame of the land?"

"It's 'lay.'"

"I'm pretty sure it's 'lie,' actually."

"Whatever. We're on a budget. We got almost zero time and resources. This whole trip'll be a non-starter if we don't go big. We need firepower, support. Basically, we need to connect with the rebels, with Anarkey. And they aren't gonna talk to us unless we have something for 'em *and* we prove ourselves. I told you my idea. You got any better?"

"Why don't I just walk up and politely tell them that I know where to find the rebels responsible for the attacks?"

Lifting a finger to argue, she squinted at him. "Huh. Not bad. Simple, clean."

"And nobody gets hurt."

"Okay, we'll do it your way." She flashed him a smile that hid the trembling of her chin. Feeling itchy at the elbows and knees, she cracked her knuckles.

"I haven't agreed to anything yet. What're you gonna do once you're in?"

"Don't you worry 'bout me. Just do your bit." She pulled up the bandana she'd tied around her neck. Add to that her big, shiny shades, and most of her face was covered. "Make sure to skedaddle as soon as you're done."

"Just to recap: you're about to sneak into a government fortress stuffed with soldiers on the off chance that we'll score friendship points with armed terrorists?"

"Rebels."

"So much could go wrong literally at any point. This is stupid, and we're gonna die."

"No, it's genius, and it'll work perfectly. Look, we both know you're going to do the thing. So stop complaining about the thing." She sighed. "Right now, we just have to raise a stink. We can deal with later *later*."

"I protest."

"Your protest is noted. Ready?"

"Yes, damn it."

Kinneas's idea had worked.

As Cho had bitten her fingernails down to nubs, he'd crossed the street and scooted up to the guards, spinning some nonsense about rebels hiding, like, "Hey, look over there." A classic ruse.

The sealed, explosion-proof door had opened, a team of three Tranquilizers thudding out to interrogate him. Meanwhile, Cho triggered her camouflage and, back to the wall, sidled through the relay station tower's front entrance.

She waited in the narrow glass-walled hallway, two feet away from the metal detector. Behind the glass, an armed guard picked his nose and flicked the bogey over his shoulder.

She took a breath, waiting.

The heavily armed Tranquilizers returned, stomping past her, and she followed them through the metal detector as it buzzed.

"I still say we should've detained him," said the one in the shiny white armor, the yellow-fire-crowned hammer and anvil of the Udutteta Family on his back. "He's clearly lying, but he might know more than he let on."

The Tranq wearing Walazzin crimson scoffed. "Bah. You see his clothes? Boy's a gutter-rat just looking to make a gelder from a tip-off. Can't blame him for that."

They took a right toward the offices. Cho darted left toward the stairs.

Her lowlight vision activated, her adrenaline regulator working overtime, as she padded through the identical gray hallways, searching for the server room.

When she found it, she clicked her tongue. The Chimaera Guard captain's identification badge, doubling as a keycard, would allow her access to the server room, but there was still the problem of the camera built into a glass dome in the ceiling.

Nearly invisible, she could've sneaked up to the card reader. If the door were to open on its own, though, anyone watching the security feed would notice. She'd have company in fifteen seconds or fewer.

It's not like there were any big rocks lying around, either. Even if there had been, she'd have had a tough time punching through the thick protective glass to destroy the camera.

Well. No time like the present to try out a new body mod. She flexed the fingers on her left hand, made a fist. She curled her arm against her chest and then made a plate-tossing gesture toward the camera. The plates in her arm un-coupled, the internal lengths of electrical and steel wire uncoiling, the flesh and sinew stretching—three feet, five, nine—until her tungsten-alloy-reinforced fingers grabbed onto the glass dome and shattered it. Her fingers closing around the fragile metal and plastic of the camera, she tore it free, grimacing as the sparks singed the synthetic skin on her knuckles.

Her arm retracted, and she gave it an approving jiggle, twisting and popping it back into place again. Not bad. A little more tension could let her use it like a whip, but her late-night tinkering in her old boss's garage hadn't cost her any grip strength. Not a bad start.

The camera out of commission, she swiped the keycard, and the door opened with a *swish*.

In that dark, frigid basement, a wall of computer monitors vomited terabytes worth of data at her, ones and zeroes streaming upward like super-fast-for-warded movie credits. She pried open the small compartment at the base of her neck, tugging free a length of gray cable, and jammed the connector into the port of the nearest console. (She could've gone wireless, but a direct, analog approach was less likely to leave a trace.)

Because only a fool rushes in naked, she bounced her encrypted signature through several virtual private networks along the Darkthreads—a mess that would take several minutes to untangle, by which point she'd be long gone.

Entering the Hackerdox state, she again experienced how off-putting it was to simultaneously feel *and* be freed of time's passing. An all-body frostbite while being dropped into an active volcano.

Zero-Oned, she closed her eyes to the physical world. A digital backdoor led her into The Authority's data stream. Upcoming maneuvers, classified long-term defense projects, squad Penance Points rankings, casualties suffered in the line of duty (seven days, fourteen days, three months, and on), blasted her like a sandstorm. She pushed forward through the gusting chaos, between the fragmented communications and commands, until she came to a swirling cluster of densely compressed files—a pattern resembling a water lily.

It bloomed for her, information drifting gently now, like windswept petals. She plucked a few. Some were prisoner profiles, but these described recent transfers. Others detailed the remodeling of the fortress of the Walazzins, known as the Lion's Den, right here on the Sixth Stack. She logged those. Then she touched the folder containing the names of fourteen recent detainees, some Aelf, some human—all members of the "terrorist organization" Anarkey. The perpetrators were detained, "interrogated," and—Cho shook her head—executed this morning.

Killed fighting for their country and freedom. What a rough way to go, too— in some white-tiled Authority basement. Nothing she could do, unfortunately.

Except, of course, cause a bit of trouble in their honor.

She planted a virus seed, one of her own nasty little creations. Immediately, vines spurted from it, reaching in all directions, corrupting data, self-replicating.

The Authority's data-flower shuddered and was paralyzed; the flow of information, floating like pollen, ceased.

Cho's cyberattack wouldn't do any permanent damage, but it would shut this tower down for twenty-four to forty-eight hours, give or take.

Since ramping up from thievery to high treason, she had taken to leaving a message behind at the scene of her digital crimes. A calling card to encourage the growth of her legend. A note, hidden among the noise. Simple, same wording each time:

IF YOU ARE READING THIS
YOU ARE THE RESISTANCE

CHZN

Dropping the note now, she told herself she was just trolling, but sometimes she imagined *someone* out there might happen upon this call-to-arms and… do *something*. Whatever. It was just a silly hope. But those ten little words had helped give rise to her infamy in Truct's underworld. Maybe they could do the same for her in Ozar.

Rifling through the trash bin (you never know!), she was about to call it quits. Until something weird happened.

She was, by now, used to seeing ones and zeroes swirling around her, interpreting their meaning in real time. But what she saw rise out of the flower of data was an actual image—a long, humanoid figure, bound by chains. A creature of substance, bone and marrow, wrapped tightly in cloth. It radiated a sickly green light, floating higher until the lengths of chain that tethered it to the ground were taut, until there wasn't an inch of give left. Then it shrieked.

She felt its fear and its restlessness as her own, and she was instantly shunted away, locked out of that server by several falling walls of security. White, glowing orbs appeared, gliding closer, and a neutral-toned male voice said, "Intrusion detected. Deploying countermeasures."

Oh boy. She knew that voice. It was ViiCter, the most powerful Virtual Intelligence in existence, installed to protect and control all Authority networks.

On reflex, Cho cut her connection and ejected her plug, backing away from the console. She checked herself for damage, ran a quick scan of her own operating system. No signs of malware, spyware, or neuroviruses.

Her momentary relief was drowned out by the sudden wailing of sirens.

She counted under her breath, knowing that she'd never get to twenty before the Tranqs burst in. Her shaky fist clutched the Chimaera keycard, dragging it through the card reader.

Despite Cho's head full of stolen government data, it was the chained figure's shriek that stuck with her, echoing. She forced herself to breathe, breaking into a run in the hallway, feeling the reverberations of the creature's unique signature. She'd never come across anything like it before, not in the Aetherthreads or Darkthreads, but its nature was a riddle for another day.

She exited the server room, hauling herself up the stairs, two or three steps at a time.

A pulse round melted a patch of sheetrock next to her face, and she hopped backward, drawing her knife.

She'd had only the span of a blink, but she counted five Tranqs waiting for her in the lobby, guns pointed at the stairs.

"Come on out, whoever you are," said one of them, her voice amplified by speakers built into her armor.

"With your hands up," said another.

"It's not too late. This doesn't have to go bad."

"But we'll air you out if you try anything."

"You pinkojacks expect me to come quietly?" she said, buying time. "Killers. Let's see how you like the gift I left you downstairs." She waited for dramatic effect. When the confused muttering began, she proceeded to describe in great detail the bomb she *hadn't* planted in the server room. "It's going off in about five minutes. Wanna live to cash your blood wages? I suggest you square-dance on outta here."

The Tranqs' voices were hushed, but Cho could hear them just fine:

"She's bluffing."

"What if she isn't?"

"We have to take her out."

"Yeah, and what about the technicians on the upper floors? The threat seems credible."

After a few more moments of chatter, the first one said, "Shut up, all of you. Right. Time's up, kid. You have three seconds to surrender."

Luckily, Cho only needed two. Never before had she tried a five-way Zero-One—a legendary hack that very few had successfully navigated—but today was proving to be a day of firsts. Paralyzing the Tranqs with the bomb threat had given her just enough time to focus; their muttering conversation had created in her mind five distinct homing beacons. Her consciousness split into five pieces, bytes of her piercing their exosuits' basic security systems. The power armor joints locked, and the five of them exclaimed their surprise.

Knowing the effect would last only seconds, Cho returned to herself and made a break for it. As the Tranqs strained uselessly, shouting after her, unable to so much as squeeze their weapons' triggers, Cho patted one on the bum and pulled the pin from another's flashbang. More shouting ensued.

She ran through the lobby, under the metal detector, which emitted a harsh red light and barked at her. The soldier behind the glass wall leapt out of his chair but fell over when the flashbang in the lobby went off.

The front door was just ahead. She was almost there.

It opened.

The guard saw her, eyes widening. Instead of shooting at her, he raised his fists. Which were on fire.

An Igniomancer. Fantastic.

He tossed a fireball, and only her enhanced reflexes spared her from being incinerated. She whipped her extendo-arm at his head, missing, but her hand grabbed onto the door frame behind. Iron grip embedded in the stone, she launched herself past the Tranquilizer and landed outside.

More fire flared behind her. She tucked her chin, zigzagging away from the tower. An oil slick directly ahead was set ablaze, a low wall of fire snaking along the street. Cho had been set to front-flip over the flames, but the Igniomancer's magic raised and intensified them, cutting off her retreat.

Ducking, she lobbed a chunk of brick at his face, cracking his visor. He stumbled backward, but his colleague—coming from inside—was already drawing a bead on her chest with his rifle. Fast as she was, she couldn't dodge bullets or close in quickly enough to tackle him.

She tried anyway, howling as she ran.

The rifleman hesitated, and the hiss from behind her told her why. Encompassed in a second skin of undulating gutter water, Kinneas catapulted through the wall of fire, his shield turning to steam. A nearby manhole cover, thrust upward by pressurized sewage, shot toward the two Tranqs. The Igniomancer sidestepped; the other caught the brunt of the leaden disc and pancaked against the tower.

"I really hope he's okay," Kinneas shouted.

Cho leapt forward, confusing the Maggo Tranq, who couldn't track her movements through his damaged visor. Once under him, she sprang up, delivering a headbutt to his chin. He went limp, and she scooped up his pistol, liquefying the two nearby street cameras with a few wild plasma rounds. Kinneas had spent more of his water, crystallizing it into a finger-sized ice spear that he sent flying at the final camera. The screen cracked with a satisfying spark.

The fire and gunshots sent people clambering out of their cars, running in all directions.

Kinneas pointed, shouting, "Reinforcements!"

Two armored vehicles—sirens wailing, purple emergency lights flashing—weaved between the abandoned cars clogging the street. The low awnings and shop signs, not to mention the hundreds of pedestrians and drivers, made it impossible for them to simply fly over the traffic. Even with this minor delay, any second now, an army of Authority jacks would bear down on Cho and Kinneas.

Swish. The tower door opened.

Cho turned but was too far away to stop what she knew would be coming. One of the flashbanged Tranqs from the lobby—the Chimaera Guard—emerged. Without hesitation, he fired his sidearm twice.

The first brass bullet missed. The second struck Kinneas's head, ricocheting, and sparked as it glanced off a wrought-iron bench behind.

Kinneas crumpled.

Screaming, Cho shot back, emptying her pistol's magazine at the Chimaera Guard, who dived for cover inside the tower. His cry made it plain that he'd been hit.

Cho glanced at Kinneas on the ground. There was a layer of protective ice over his face and chest, melting. Water pooled around him, mingling with thin, curling tendrils of blood.

"Please be alive. Please let your ice-helmet have done the trick," she said.

Dragging him away from the wounded Guard, she frantically considered her options.

The first pair of armored vehicles barreled toward them, crashing through a lamppost and grinding to a stop a mere dozen feet away. Their back doors were flung open, and three teams of Enforcers, one after the other, hopped out. Their uniforms were tan and yellow, bearing the scythe and boar's head of the Denadon Family. They took position behind a bus stop, one of them shoving aside a man who'd been cowering there.

Authority Tranqs at Cho's back. Enforcers pouring out of vans at her front. Fire and screaming people all around. Just when it seemed like the situation couldn't possibly worsen, it did: a drone whirred above, gatling gun squealing as it warmed up, ready to deliver 6,000 rounds per minute.

Staying in the street would mean certain death.

Knife in one hand, Kinneas's collar in the other, Cho faced the tower, knowing there were at least five armored killers inside. Four of them stood arrayed in the glass hall, guns up, screaming at her.

Their voices hit her ear as if from very far off. Individually, their words made no sense to her, but in her mind-haze she understood their meaning: they called for her surrender.

She looked down at Kinneas again, at the blood dripping from his nose.

Her grip on her knife loosened. The blade wobbled in her palm.

She could throw or drop it, she knew, and neither choice would save them.

Then she heard a whine, a trail of curling flame streaking toward one of the armored vehicles, which exploded. It spun through the air before crashing in a burning heap on the street.

More screams erupted from all sides. This time, however, mingled with the panicked cries of fleeing Ozari, were the deliberate shouts of orders. And, from somewhere nearby... voices raised in song? What were they saying? Sounded like, *"Oso! Oso!"* and *"Snuff the Lightbringers!"*

Gunfire from all sides, shattering glass, chipping stone, puncturing metal. Cho knelt, covering her head. She put a finger to Kinneas's neck, shouting his name as she searched for his pulse.

Soon, a hand clasped her shoulder, tugging her away from him. She spun to drive her elbow into whoever had grabbed her, but cried out as her bone struck iron. She looked up into a mottled gray-and-yellow, scaly face. Its eyes widened, its horizontal, orange pupils dilating. A rusty gas mask covered the lower half of the creature's head, a tube running from the mask to a tank of swirling brownish-yellow gas strapped to its back.

"I'm trying to save you, *depix,*" it said, holstering its sawed-off shotgun, offering her its clawed hand.

"My friend," Cho said.

"Surely dead."

No. "I'm not leaving him."

Growling, the contents of the gas tank roiling, the creature threw Kinneas over its shoulder. To Cho, it said: "Follow or die. Decide." It didn't so much as flinch when a bear-sized, six-limbed bug charged past. The bug, with its bronze, reflective eyes and long, ridged trunk, crashed into one of the Enforcer squads. "Well?" the gas-masked creature shouted.

"Tough call," said Cho, shaking, hysterically giggling and crying. She fell in line behind it.

Kinneas was bleeding. She followed the stranger with the shotgun down a flight of slick stairs and into the sewers, and all she could think was that she'd gotten Kinneas killed.

She'd killed her friend.

Walking bowlegged on prehensile feet with six digits each, the strange creature was only slightly taller than Cho. It led her to an old-fashioned gas-guzzling motorcycle, the kind you only saw in history books or collectors' garages. This one appeared dinged but fully functional, confirmed when the creature climbed on, swapped out his gas mask for one attached to the motorcycle's handlebars, and inserted a metal key in the ignition. The bike sputtered to life, hacking up black fumes. The stranger crammed Kinneas into the sidecar, fastening his seatbelt.

"On," it said through the scratched metal mask that connected it to the bike, gesturing with a double-jointed gray thumb at the seat directly behind it.

"Who are you?" said Cho. A lame line, but it was all she had.

The creature's only answer was to turn away and hunker down, producing a rocket launcher, which it lifted, aimed, and fired. A missile streaked through the air, exploding on contact with the drone above. The gray creature tucked the weapon away again, and it glared at Cho, giving another thumb jab toward the seat behind it.

Sirens to the left, flaming drone to the right—forward seemed the only option.

She got on.

Her rescuer (captor?) revved the bike's engine, and Cho realized the mask it wore was connected to the vehicle's exhaust pipe.

Half-delirious, she couldn't stop herself from asking, "*What* are you?"

The creature's mask muffled its cackle as the bike tore down the street, away from the fighting. Pressing its right oddly shaped "foot" into the accelerator pedal, it said, "A name is cheap; I give mine readily. Mother called me Bizong. More to the point, *depix*, I am as those who battle back there still." A cluster of explosions rocked the streets and buildings. "You are in the company of Anarkey."

Wind thrashing her green wig, Cho ruffled Kinneas's hair. He wasn't moving. She couldn't tell if he still breathed. Hearing his heartbeat over the roar of the motorcycle's engine, impossible.

The static she'd picked up inside the relay station's server room—the chained thing's hideous shriek—played again and again in her mind.

She wondered where Alina was right now.

A different group of sounds swelled in Cho's consciousness, then: the airy lilt of Ivion Ivoir's mocking laughter, and the *crackle* and *pop* of Kinneas's ice shield as an Authority bullet struck his head.

She prayed to any gods that might be listening, prayed for her friend's life, for her own safety.

For the strength to finally make her enemies suffer.

27

ALINA

ON THE SIXTH STACK, Mezami had to stay hidden, but Ivion and Alina were a striking pair, the one dressed in a tight white suit, platinum hair bouncing with each step, the other swaddled in black, a cape of black fabric split down the middle to resemble wings, black hood pulled over her head. In more ways than one, Alina felt like Ivion's shadow. Her new partner drew all attention away from her, for which she—having never been particularly comfortable being the center of attention—was grateful. Everyone, from passersby to patrolling Enforcers, risked at least a second glance at tall, slender, sharp-featured Ivion Ivoir. Sometimes a third or fourth. This gave Alina the space to observe and plan.

"It's weird," she said, mulling over a thought. "We're miles underground, in a totally foreign country, but I still see a lot of stuff from back home. Like, there." She pointed at the neon yellow sign in the shape of a white-toothed fish. "They have a Goldgill's. Just like in Truct, and Puurissei, and everywhere else. And there, that's a Plug-n-Chug."

Ivion shrugged. "Aethernet and carbonated beverages, what's not to love?"

"Yeah, but those are our—I mean Elemental companies..." She trailed off, looking up at a blue and white glowing sign ahead. "They've even built a Walazzinmart down here." She turned to Ivion. "How long ago did you say this part of town was taken by The Authority?"

"A handful of years, I believe."

"The corporations sure moved in quick, didn't they?"

"The price of progress? ELCORP didn't come to own most of the world marketplace by being timid."

Alina frowned.

Ivion said, "It isn't all bad. Cheap goods drive down prices everywhere. Where we're standing used to be a rundown bathhouse absolutely lousy with fungus. A den of thieves, too, by reputation. I am the last to agree with all of The Authority's methods, but I can't decry all their results. Even if it comes at sword-point, prosperity is prosperity." Alina moved on, prompting Ivion to change topics: "In your vision of your uncle, did you ever learn his location?"

"No. I only got a peek at where he was, and only from the inside."

"So, we've hit another snag. Finding The Savior will be quite difficult. Paranoid by reputation, he rarely reveals the location of his next service—except to his closest acolytes."

"How does anyone know where to go then?"

"The Sanctumites watch for the signs, having little better to do. They drop everything to rush to their master whenever and wherever he makes an appearance."

"But he tells the acolytes ahead of time? Let's start with them."

"Easier said than done, but I imagine you have an idea."

"That's right. Take me to where the street-level Sanctumites hang out. You know, the gray-robed baldies always yammering about damnation and eternal punishment and all that."

"You're planning to start from the bottom."

"I'll get to the mountaintop from ground-level if I have to. But I'm hoping to skip a few steps on the way."

Alina had assumed Ivion would quickly grow bored or tired or that she'd find some other excuse to leave. She was used to people leaving, to working alone. It came as a surprise when Ivion not only stuck around but asked personal questions and seemed genuinely interested in the answers.

Alina liked the attention, she discovered.

Ivion led the way to a busy intersection near the wall. And what a wall it was: it reached from the street to the shadow-dappled cave ceiling a hundred feet above.

"That barrier," Ivion said, pointing, "is far more impressive than even it looks."

A vertical plate had been embedded in a section of the dull green stone, a hexagon carved into it. Alina swore she could hear, underneath her heart's palpitations and the grinding of her teeth, a spine-deep hum emanating from the plate. As if scratched by an invisible fingernail, her skin tingled. Sweat pooled at the small of her back. Felt like she was back in the rain-drop dream, back with Ruqastra, at the moment she touched a black nothingness, stuffed with unlimited possibility. She remembered seeing hundreds of herselves locked in a system of astral bodies blooming like dying stars. It felt to her like taking life and death each by the hand, and shattering into shards finer than white beach sand.

Ivion said, "We call this behemoth of a wall Peregar's Grief—named after the unlucky captain who first tried to breach it. The locals believe The Abyss responsible. They say it devoured her."

The hum faded as Alina returned to the here and now. "Never heard from again?"

"Nor were the five hundred under her command."

"So, behind that wall, that's Free Ozar."

"'Freedom' is relative. What you see is the southern border, the lowest extent, of the Elemental Empire. There, The Authority ends." Beyond it lay a bridge, Ivion further explained, which was the only means of accessing the Seventh Stack.

"What about the Safehouse hatch?" Alina asked. "It goes down into the Seventh."

"There are a few such bunkers throughout the city, but their usefulness lies in the fact that the enemy doesn't know of their existence. A handful of spies can sneak in and out via these shafts, but moving an army through them would be impossible. The Coven would learn of it and counterattack, and El would lose any further opportunities to covertly gather intelligence." Ivion pointed at the wall. "That gate is our way through. It must fall, or the empire will never prevail. The Hextarchs know this, which is why they defend this choke point with every soldier, trap, and monster at their command."

Crazy to think that, with The Authority holding sway over earth and sky, this ancient underground realm was still—even after a thousand years—a nut the Elementals simply couldn't crack. Alina saw merely a wall—stone and nothing more—but a Revomancer knows appearances are always deceiving.

What power had raised Peregar's Grief, and what kept it standing—set against the combined forces of the world's grandest armies?

"There," said Ivion, calling Alina back from her thoughts. (She'd been slipping too often lately—didn't feel herself these days). Drawing her attention to the row of gray-robed people standing across the intersection, Ivion said, "They protest daily. Listen."

One of the Sanctumites raised a bullhorn to her lips and said, "People of Ozar, hear me. You have been lied to your entire lives. Just beyond this wall, you believe your gods await, sheltered in their fortress of immutable rock. But it is not so! In fact, for all your days, you've been ruled not by gods but demons! Soul-leeching, blood-drinking parasites with great and terrible powers. What you see as miracles are nothing more than tricks of the eye! Their sleight of hand has blinded you to the truth: you are cattle for the slaughter. Repent your complicity with evil, and rally to our cause! Come to the light!"

"They preach salvation through their Author, of course," said Ivion. "And they cloak their evangelism in righteousness. But you and I have seen what happens when the masks fall away."

"It's sad," said Alina.

Ivion bared her perfect teeth. "Do you not hate them as I do?"

"I feel sorry for them." Alina looked on as the Sanctumites began to chant, shouting over the rumble and clamor of the traffic and construction all around them. "I'm sure they think what they're doing is right."

"Tolomond did as well. He is worthy of hate."

"He is." The sight of him. Shell of a man. Something twisted crawled around inside him, using his body, his skin—but it wasn't him.

Though it hadn't been a week, that night on Morbin seemed so long ago already.

Alina's meditations stretched time and confused space, until everything felt too surreal to her, even when she held it in her hands. So, her recollections of Tolomond were constantly morphing in her mind: when he'd nearly killed her, two years ago, he'd murdered Ugarda Pankrish. This memory blended with Alina's anger toward Ordin, who'd died soon after.

That anger was a blanket with which she tried to smother death and loss. But Tolomond had stolen from her the illusion of control. He had shown her on Morbin that preventing future separations would be just as impossible as erasing past one. She could not stay death.

He was a pair of shears, cleaving the pages of her story. She thought of Cho, Kinneas, Mezami, and she grew afraid.

She decided that she *did* hate Tolomond. And Ordin. And her Tahtoh. And even herself. For what she'd done, for going to New El in the first place.

Then, above all the sadness, doubt, and fury, she rose like a mote of dust stirred by a breath. She felt certain the weight of all that hating would one day crush her, but she wasn't quite ready to give it up.

"What are you thinking about?" Ivion asked.

"How I can lift cars and travel through dreams—even though Ruqastra said I was terrible at it. How I'm supposed to be preparing for some kinda fight, but I don't know where to even think about starting. How I'm alone. What am I meant to be? Am I meant to be anything?"

"You're spiraling. Take a breath. You have many highly uncommon talents. There are very few Revomancers in the world. And your ability to manipulate atomic structures—let's just say I know people who have killed to possess that skill."

"Thanks, I guess. But why can I do all these things? Why me?"

"Does there have to be a reason?"

"Um, yeah. My grandfather, my teacher, Cho, you—it feels like everyone has a plan for me. And, because I'm always running away from something, I don't have time to figure out if *I* have a plan for me."

"Maybe none of those paths are the right one." Ivion stopped mid-stride, facing Alina. "I hope you're only working with me because you want to, and not for any other reason."

Raking her fingernails over her elbows, Alina mumbled, "Honestly, you confuse me."

Opening her mouth to reply, Ivion caught herself.

Hovercraft engines rumbled. Electronic advertisements tinkled tinny tunes. A Tranquilizer patrol goose-stepped past, metallic joints of their exoskeleton armor clinking and clanking.

Ivion slid into Alina's arms, hugging her close. Chin tucked between the other woman's collarbones, Alina went rigid.

A few seconds later, Ivion broke the embrace. "The soldiers. They're gone."

Eyes watering, mouth dry, Alina said, "Oh, good." The embrace had been a split-second decision on Ivion's part, her only purpose having been to hide Alina's face. Relief and disappointment rolled through Alina's mind like bar brawlers, smashing bottles over each others' heads.

But then Ivion took her hand, and Alina felt as if she were rollerskating on melting sticks of butter. "Anytime you are ready to talk, I'm here for you. I'd never want you to feel uncomfortable around me. Not in the slightest. I'm the one person in this world who will never judge you. And, by the way, you *are* strong, and you're also wise. Wiser than anyone—including this Ruqastra—gave you credit for. I see it so clearly. I wish you could, too. You have a beautiful purpose in this world, and I'm going to help you discover it. We are here, together, you and I. Forget the past. It's not who you come from that defines you. Take it from me." She breathed deeply through her nose and gently squeezed Alina's wrist.

From where their fingers connected, a spark crackled up Alina's arm and struck her through the heart. She couldn't hold back her smile, bright from within the shadowed folds of her hood

"Well." Ivion flicked her head toward Peregar's Grief. "Shall we converse with some zealots?"

"Let's."

Giggling as Mezami squirmed around her hood, his tail tickling her earlobe, Alina whispered, "Settle down." And he did.

Peregar's Grief was simply huge. A tidal wave of stone, gray and slick with moisture. Access to the gate, a pair of fifty-foot-tall doors, had been cordoned off with yellow holotape and white road barriers. Signs declared "Danger: Do

Not Approach." One notice, taped to a lamp post, read, "ELCORP bears no responsibility for loss of life, limb, or sanity."

Thirty to forty Sanctumites had installed themselves in front of these barriers.

The woman with the bullhorn hopped off her upturned bucket, the first to greet Alina and Ivion. Walking up to them, she said, "Welcome, sisters. Will you join the righteous?"

"What are the perks?" said Alina.

Ivion chuckled under her breath.

The Sanctumite, like all the others, was clean-shaven. Scarred, gray-blue patches of skin on her arms revealed that she'd once had tattoos but had attempted to cover them up or, perhaps, carve them away. She took one look at Ivion and said, "Cybernetic enhancements are a sin, but all are welcome within The Sanctum. Provided they are made clean."

"'Made clean'?"

"Our healers will remove the blasphemous foreign objects inserted into your God-given body. You will be whole again. If you repent your sins and kneel before The Author."

"Just to be clear, it's beg forgiveness, repent, have a back-alley surgeon hack me apart, and *then* I get to shave my head and wear gray wool for the rest of my life? A life that I spend shouting at passing cars?"

The Sanctumite glared at Alina. "Your friend damns you by association."

Alina said, "My friend's just got cold feet. She—and I—would be a lot keener about converting if we heard it from someone with a better attitude. I get it, you want me to buy in, but, a little friendly advice? You can't come out of the gate swinging 'damnation this' and 'damnation that.'"

"If you mock one of us, you mock all of us," said the Sanctumite, lifting her chin. Several of her friends closed in. "Ozar will be cleansed in bright, holy flames."

The others energetically repeated the claim: "Ozar will be cleansed."

"Yup, cleansed, right on. So, anyway, I heard The Savior was in town, and he's something special."

"The Savior is a humble, kind, and wonderful man. A miracle worker. The Author's chosen prophet. We are all Instruments of the Author's will, but he is chief among us."

"Miracles, huh? Like what?"

"He radiates a gentle, soothing light, a healing balm to all who are blessed by his presence."

Alina muttered, "Meh. Plenty of people can do that."

"Magic is a sin," barked the Sanctumite. "You dare utter such blasphemies against the prophet? The Savior is the voice of The Author on this earth. His will *is* that of the Lord. You are nothing—less than nothing—before one who can cure the ailing and raise the dead."

"Resurrection?" Alina shook her head. "Nope, not possible."

"And, yet, he has done it. Brothers and sisters, have we not seen this miracle with our own eyes?"

The Sanctumites crowding her, surrounding Alina and Ivion now, chimed in, "Praise The Author."

"Praise Him with great praise," agreed the leading Sanctumite, who raised her bullhorn and shouted in Alina's face, "You are unwelcome here."

The circle of gray-robed, egg-white-eyed Sanctumites broke, and Alina and Ivion retreated.

When they'd crossed the intersection, Ivion said, "I forgot myself back there. Apologies."

"That could definitely have gone better, but, hey, no big deal. We both got a bit heated."

"Their ignorance makes a mockery of the divine."

Alina arched an eyebrow. "Didn't take you for the religious type."

"There are many gods—not only one—and each bears precious cultural, historical, and philosophical significance. The Sanctum seeks to erase this rich context, supplanting it with their own monolithic, illiterate dystopia. As a scholar, I'd despise book-burners of any stripe, regardless. But, yes, personally, I do believe there's a plan for each of us."

Tapping Ivion's arm, Alina nodded toward the Sanctumites. "They're splitting up. Let's follow that shouty one. She was doing all the talking while the others were just kinda chilling. That makes her sort of a squad leader, which means she'll eventually end up in a room with others like her. They've all gotta get their talking points from someone."

"Who taught you to be so devious?"

Alina shrugged. "Watchbox spy shows."

"Father never let us have a Watchbox. If only he'd known the programs could be so educational."

"Eh, you're probably better off. Every once in a while, something's useful, but I've spent objectively way too many hours watching *Say No to the Bro* and *Chapped*." Ivion's blank look had Alina sputtering: "Dating and cooking shows. Actually, *Chapped* is pretty fun because the chefs are dropped into the middle of the desert and they have to cook gourmet dishes using only whatever they can find lying a—ha, never mind, it's dumb."

Taking her hand again, Ivion said, "Tell me more." The reflected street lights sparkled in her eyes, her skin glowing like snow at sunset.

Heart tap-dancing in her chest, Alina said, "Okay."

"Just do it while we're walking. Because our loud-mouthed friend there is on the move."

The Sanctumite woman quickly left behind the street to navigate narrow shafts flush with loose wires and open vents. Alina and Ivion followed.

The surround-sound of rasping ancient machinery was as potent as a chorus of cicadas. Maybe the Sanctumite had come this way to shake any potential pursuers, but she hadn't accounted for the likes of Alina.

The gray-clad woman glanced over her shoulder often, and Alina would fling her cloak around Ivion's bright white form, the fabric stretching and falling over both of them, enveloping them in velvety shadow. With a few simple words of command, Alina sent her Niima coursing through the cloak, and she and Ivion became invisible.

The spell never held long, but it didn't have to. Alina watched through the black cape, waiting for the Sanctumite to continue on her path. Each time Alina drew back the cloak, the warmth of Ivion was like steam off a mug of tea on a cold autumn afternoon.

Exiting the maintenance corridors, the Sanctumite led them to a simple concrete slab of a building wedged between huge ventilation fans. Alina could hardly hear herself think over the constant whir of the fan blades as they siphoned out a city's worth of toxic gases and pumped them above ground. She watched the gray-robed woman pass through a crowd of people dressed in rags and sandals made of tire rubber and plastic. The Sanctumite entered the building, and a few minutes later, the doors opened. Those who'd waited outside formed a zigzagging line.

"There must be hundreds of them," said Alina, attempting a casual lean to avoid suspicion.

Hanging back, out of sight behind a corner, Ivion said, "The Sanctum opened soup kitchens to feed and shelter the homeless, the price of a bowl of gruel being a lengthy liturgy about salvation and suffering."

"The hungry make easier recruits." Alina made up her mind. "I'm going in, but I'd like to handle this part alone. It's way less complicated to only have to disguise myself. And, uh. Don't take this the wrong way, but you turn heads."

"Was that a compliment, Alina K'vich?"

Chuckling nervously, Alina slipped *Ida* on, stepped between some garbage bins, ducked low, and reemerged a different person. She was still a woman, but slightly older, with fair skin and straight hair. Her clothes remained black, but they'd lost their dream-weave sheen, appearing weathered and grimy. "Do I look okay?"

"Nothing less than stunning." Ivion winked. "When did you have time to steal that face, though?"

"Borrow. And, while you were off hiding the APC under tarps and junk, I walked around pretending I was running a social experiment for my psychology class. People are too trusting. Grabbed a few spares, just in case."

"Devious." Ivion tapped her chin. "Still, for the task at hand, would it not have been simpler to step directly into the Sanctumites' minds and take what you need?"

"Well, sure, but the problem is they'd know. Whether I got what I wanted or not, people's unconsciouses are minefields. One misstep and it's kablooie. They'd know. Especially if they're awake while I try. Since I need to stay incognito, it's sneaking time." Dryly, she added, "Because that usually goes so well for me."

"I see the logic. You wouldn't want word to run up the Sanctum chain of command, alerting The Savior that someone was coming for him. If you're sure you have this side covered, then I should be shaking hands with my Authority contacts. They'll provide us with the kind of intelligence obtainable only after months of deployment in this country."

"Great idea. I had fun, though, so I'll be, uh, bummed to see you go."

Drawing Alina into a hug, Ivion said, "Take care. Remember the Ivoir Family's unofficial motto: 'always have an exit strategy'."

"No sweat. I have backup. Mezami?"

From the folds of her cloak, the Pyct chirruped. He'd gotten really good at hanging out in hoods and sleeves. So much so that Alina sometimes forgot he was there at all.

"Watch over her, little Aelf," Ivion told the shifting lump on Alina's shoulder.

His voice, muffled by fabric, rumbled, "Fine: very, we."

"Mezami's a beast. We'll be peachy."

"Well." Ivion hung on to Alina's elbow for a heartbeat more, then let her go.

Falling in at the end of the line of homeless and hungry, Alina whispered, "Stay outta sight. I don't trust anything to do with The Sanctum."

He tapped her shoulder once for *yes/understood.*

"Mezami? Do *you* think they're all like Tolomond?"

Tap. *Yes.*

"He took everything from you. Do you hate him, like Ivion does? Wouldn't blame you if you did."

No response.

"You told me you'd killed him back at The Capital."

Tap. *Yes.*

"Happy you might get a second stab at revenge?"

Tap, tap. *No.*

"Really?" Alina switched to telepathy, one of the many skills Ruqastra had taught her. She wasn't very good at it yet; the signal was weak and laced with static, and people generally were uncomfortable communicating in this way, so she didn't abuse it like Ruqastra had. But now her curiosity overpowered her hesitation. Threading a connection between their minds, she asked, *What changed? You were out for blood before.*

Slew: Tolomond, I. Solved: nothing, it.

Wrapped around his thoughts, she sensed he was holding back. *What is it?*

A moment unraveled between them like a ball of yarn.

Pyct'Tzi: last, I. Not see: peace, I. He paused. *Ask: favor, I.*

Name it, bro.

Become: clan-mates, we. Join: Tzi, you.

She was speechless. Well, yes, she wasn't speaking aloud, but she also didn't know what to say.

Hesitate: you. Forget: it, you. Idea: stupid, it.

Mezami. Of course, I'll accept. She bowed her head because this seemed like a bowing-your-head kind of moment. *I just am stunned. Why me? Why now?*

Sheltered: me, you. Saved: me, you. He emitted the tiniest sniffle. *Tolomond: hated, I. Rediscovered: wholeness, I. Connected: you, I. In-journey: long, we.*

My friend, I can't tell you how honored I am.

It: feel, I. Alina caught a glimpse of him wiping his nose on his little fur bracer, and pulled her sleeve tighter to hide him. *Together: always, we.*

Is there some special ceremony you need to lead me through?

Be: ridiculous, not. So: say, I. So: are, you. Pyct'Tzi: Alina, sister. Done.

Quietly, she chuckled. *And I'll do my best to earn it, Pyct'Tzi: Mezami.*

A whisper cut into her thoughts, and it took her a second to realize the voice hadn't come from her mind but from just behind. "Talkin' to yerself?"

Alina turned to see a woman in her seventies or so, straight-backed with deep smile lines, measuring just under five feet (nearly a foot shorter than Alina).

"S'alright, kid." The woman leaned in to stage-whisper, "I do it, too. They don't frown on it inside, neither. So long as you repeat what they say about t'Author and whatnot. Just do's yer told, and you'll get fed."

Alina couldn't quite put her finger on what was off about this woman.

"What's yer name?"

"Stitcher," said Alina, slipping into her old alias as easily as an ice bath.

"Funny old name. I'm Nephrataru, but if that's too much to bite off, just 'Taru' 's fine. Ya got any questions, I'm yer go-to."

"Thanks."

What was up with this woman? She seemed friendly and normal. Why were Alina's instincts going haywire?

Alina felt it, then. The seams were nearly perfect, but the faint aura of Niima tendrils remained, woven around the woman's neckline, her elbows, the knees, the eyes: she was a Hideling, an Aelf that had the innate ability to change its appearance.

Hidelings were a type of Homunculus—the egghead word for "Hybrid"—children born of Aelf and human. As such, they were among the most universally hated creatures in the world. The only thing humanity despised more than the

Aelf themselves was the thought that a bridge between the two species might exist. Usually discarded at birth by their Aelf parents, Hybrids of all types were rare, and made even more endangered for their being Raved without mercy wherever they were discovered.

One word from Alina and Nephrataru would be slaughtered on the spot. Few questions were asked where Hybrids were concerned. Hidelings, at least, had better odds of survival. Their natural ability to shift their appearance, imitating human (and sometimes other Aelf) bodies and faces, could only be detected by skilled Maggos. Alina had never met one before, but Dimas had made sure she'd learned the signs. He'd taught her all about even the most exotic and strangest types of Aelf. Which, in the end, had only worsened Alina's self-disgust. She had failed to see that *he'd* been an Aelf—a Demidivine, creature of legend—masquerading as a human. Behind his fictional life, his spouse and students and all that, he'd been one of the Sevensin all along. That made Alina's mother Zatalena and uncle Mateus—and Alina herself—Hybrids, too.

Alina didn't know anything about this Hideling before her, other than the name she'd chosen to give. Nevertheless, Alina felt nothing but sympathy; they were both considered monsters by the charity workers with whom they were about to mingle. The volunteers preaching the Word of their Author wouldn't have batted an eye at the evisceration of Alina and Nephretaru. After all, the central tenet of The Sanctum held that "magic is Man's sin, the Aelf his punishment."

Times must be hard in Ozar if a Hideling's best opportunity for a hot meal came from people who wanted nothing more than to eradicate all magic from the face of the earth.

"By the way, nice meeting you, Taru," said Alina. "I'm new in town. Appreciate you checking in with me."

"Stick close to me, Stitcher." Taru smiled, revealing gingivitis-ridden teeth. (Nice touch of realism.) She repeated, "Do as I do, and you'll get fed."

As Alina slowly progressed to the front of the queue, Taru filled her in about the organizers of this soup kitchen. They were mostly Sanctumite grunts, but the one who called the shots was a barrel-chested, piston-armed bruiser named Cronn. Through Taru's unceasing chatter, Alina learned that Cronn had once run with a crew of Plasticks—guns-for-hire recognizable by their translucent plastic jackets. He'd reformed his wicked ways, however. Likely because of his colorful background, connecting him to the rougher elements of society, he'd become an evangelist for The Sanctum. His assigned life partner, it turned out, was also the woman who'd recruited him. Kellfyute was her name. And, Kellfyute, Alina noted with interest, happened to be high up the holy food-chain, possibly even a member of The Savior's inner circle. To be determined.

Entering the kitchen, Alina was handed a pamphlet and ushered into a concrete storage room stripped of everything other than its dust and cobwebs. The people she'd seen standing outside now filled this space, all facing the wall opposite the door.

They were waiting for some kind of show, it seemed.

A few minutes after Taru and Alina (and Mezami) filled out the last row of spectators (Taru complaining about never getting a good view), a man marched inside. His military bearing immediately apparent by his rigid spine and tight, snappy movements, he put his back to the rear wall, facing his audience, and said, "Light shine upon you, brothers and sisters."

Most of those present replied, out of sync, "Shun the darkness, Brother Cronn."

"Burning day. What a *day* to be afire and free." The smile plastered on his face didn't quite fit his features. It was too big, too beaming. He had the type of face you could imagine being more comfortable when spattered with a bloody grimace. But the smile was there, blasting his captive audience, defying them to doubt. "Please turn to page five of your handouts. I have a very special story for you today."

Taru nudged Alina. Having reviewed a Sanctum pamphlet on one other occasion, to Alina it came as no surprise that it was all pictures and no words. Reading and writing were forbidden.

Alina flipped through the hand-painted booklet, the pictures as morbid as she remembered. They depicted a stiff, solid-white, bearded man, tall and red-eyed. From his outstretched arms, he sent forth fires and floods that ravaged armies of tiny, fleeing, dark creatures. These scenes of violence were followed on the opposite page by an image of hundreds of little gray people bowing before their towering, joyless god.

Clasping his tattooed wrists behind his back, Cronn cleared his throat. "As we all know, in the Beginning, The Author our Lord Wrote the World and sealed away His Word so it could not fall into the wrong hands." He walked up and down the front row as he spoke. "The Lord made everything in the World, and He is Infallible, incapable of anything but Right Action. Those who walk in His Light travel the path of Enlightenment."

"Shun the darkness," said the crowd, Taru joining in a beat too late, Alina not at all.

"But there were those who resisted His Righteous Teachings. There were those who walked the shadowed paths of lies and deceit, who perverted His Creation. Over the ages, a rebellion arose, to unjustly war against the Light and the Flames of Truth that had guided and protected mankind for thousands of years. These rebels were the slimiest, filthiest vermin to ever crawl from the crevices of the earth. They led armies, tens of thousands strong, against the Lord, our Lord who had only ever shone His Love and Benevolence upon them. In their entitlement, these rebels desired more than their fair share. They craved ever more power. And, one day, one of them stole from The Author's vault one syllable of His Word. That was the day upon which, having broken His commandment, Mankind's covetous fingers touched upon magic for the first time. And that, too, was the day when the Aelf entered the World. Even though we are not *all* descended from the rebellious filth that tainted the Word with their unworthy touch, we *all* bear responsibility for this sin. In His Mercy, The Author deemed it necessary to chide us for our transgressions. He set the Aelf upon us as a reminder of His authority. Praise The Author."

"Shun the darkness," said the crowd. "Praise The Author."

Alina noticed the shift in the spectators' collective tone. The fiery speech was having its intended effect. Even if they didn't care for the topic, they loved a good whip-up.

"There are so many amazing, revelatory stories to choose from, so why this one?" Cronn paused for drama. "Because, my dear brothers and sisters, we find ourselves at a crossroads. We humble mortals, after thousands of years of being devoured by the Aelf, now stand at the threshold of a new age." Solid cliffhanger. He fed his audience like a mama bird barfing up chewed worm chunks for her babies. "The rebels I spoke of? They who dared rob the One True God? They who had the audacity to resist the Will of He Who Wrote the World and all Creation into existence? They have been revealed to us. And, now, we—happy, blessed people—stand at the final precipice. All that is required of us is a leap of faith."

The audience waited, leaning in.

"Our enemies have a name—the dark magicians who stole a fragment of the Word—they cower, even now, behind their Wall. The Authority of El, supported by The Sanctum, has for generations warred against the false gods of Ozar, those who call themselves the Hextarchy. And, do you know what, my brothers and sisters? We are *so close* to destroying them for good and all. The final Stack is within reach. Peregar's Grief will fall. We have but to push through the Wall, batter down the gates of their dark fortress, and tear them from their throne of lies. For goodness, righteousness, and truth! Burn them, kill them all! Praise The Author!"

The last message had divided the crowd. About a quarter or so (including Taru) grew visibly uncomfortable, squirming, mumbling half-heartedly, "Praise The Author." The rest raised their fists, applauded, and shouted, "Shun the darkness, Brother Cronn!"

"We must give thanks to The Author, who in His Love for us, His faithful, has sent us a champion. You have no doubt heard of him. His name graces the lips of every free-thinker in Ozar, from the first Stack to the last. He is our Savior, and because of him—through his holy war in The Author's name—the age of darkness and deceit is ending. The age of Light and Truth is upon us. But—and heed me now, brothers and sisters—only those who *believe* and who *give* will receive The Author's blessing. Now is the time. Now is your *last chance*. Side with the Light, abandon all doubt, and join us. Join The Sanctum, support The Authority! Spread the word to your friends, family, and anyone you see on the street. Call upon them to be saved. Tell them that The Savior will redeem them, if they only choose to free themselves of their wickedness. The hour grows late, brothers and sisters. The end is nigh. Soon, we shall all walk in the Light of Nehallennia—a world without sin, without Aelf! Now, I bid you farewell. I'm needed in other congregations. Praise The Author, thank you, and goodnight."

"Praise The Author!" cried the majority of the audience. Those who'd become squeamish a moment before assumed more hopeful expressions when the doors opened again and gray-robed acolytes led them into the kitchens, where every one of them was handed a bowl and a spoon.

Soon enough, steaming, hearty stew was doled out. More resoundingly than any speech of Cronn's, the kitchen staff wordlessly spoke the will of The Sanctum. Alina looked around, seeing the gratitude and relief, and thought about how powerfully dangerous it was to feed the desperate these seeds of violence with their dinners. When one of the volunteers ladled Alina's serving, he whispered, "Death to the Aelf. Death to all mages."

The final step before they could all eat was a required moment of close-eyed, silent reflection. Thanks was given for the many blessings—including this meal—granted by The Author and His champion, The Savior of all mortals ("All mortals we approve of," Alina muttered, earning a warning slap from Taru).

At last, once the food was lukewarm rather than hot, they were allowed to eat, and Alina wolfed her serving down.

Taru said, "Wow, you were hungry. Hope it ain't 'cause yer still growin'. Slow down, girl. Yer more than tall enough."

Alina smiled. "Thanks for keeping me company. But, hey, are we, uh, free to go at this point?"

"Sure. We listened and ate. Ya can walk out now if that's what ya want. I like to hang around a bit longer, let the warmth cling to my old bones a few more minutes before heading back out into the cold and damp."

"Sounds good. I gotta get going though. I have, um, a thing."

"Hope to see ya around."

"You too, Taru." Alina wanted to tell her everything would be alright, but she wasn't in the habit of saying things she didn't believe. "Take it easy."

"Might just. Might just."

Outside, Alina looked around and, as expected, saw Cronn nowhere. No problem, though.

"Mezami, you catch the scent of the man who was speaking inside? Think you can track him?"

"Challenge: not, this."

"Let's go. If I need to turn left, gimme one tap. Two for right."

As she followed Mezami's direction, marching in a straight line, pivoting into side streets and up and down staircases and steel ladders as needed, Alina thought about what she'd discovered and what it might mean.

Mateus—The Savior—was waging a holy war to eliminate the Hextarchy.

Why he'd chosen The Sanctum and The Authority as allies, she had no idea. Were they aware he wasn't fully human? Did they care, or was he simply a tool to them? If he was down in Ozar, playing soldier, why try to snuff his niece he hadn't seen since before she'd reached his knee?

The Hextarchy, whoever or whatever they were, intrigued her, too. Living gods, hidden inside an underground fortress, unseen for hundreds of years? Pretty crazy.

The questions bored holes in her humming skull. Unfortunately, the only way to get answers was to enter the game late and unprepared. On the plus side, "Late and Unprepared" had been her grade-school teachers' nickname for her.

Knowing *what* Mateus was after, at least, was something. Maybe, if she learned more, she could find a way to use it against him.

Hopefully, Cronn or his girlfriend would give up another piece of this shattered vase. Currently, Alina had far too few to figure out its shape—let alone put it back together.

Tracking the Sanctumite Cronn using a Pyct's nose? Stupid easy.

The waiting afterward? Eh…

It had been hours so far. Hours.

Alina's astrally projected form paced the hallway of Cronn's home, a humble hovel with no decorations except for a single silver-plated, three-pronged flame sculpture, hanging from a nail in the wall. Staring at the holy symbol of The Author, Alina wondered how long it would take for Cronn's partner to show up.

Seriously, did they not live together?

Oh, wait. Taru had said something about Cronn having been "assigned" to Kellfyute. Like an arranged marriage maybe?

Alina sighed, which of course was silent since her lungs were several hundred feet away—with her body, guarded by Mezami.

One thing was for sure: Cronn was *boring*. Since returning home, all he had done was shower, walk around shirtless, and meditate for a while before bed.

Given the choice between watching a four-hour, director's cut, making-of documentary about staplers and Cronn's nighttime routine, Alina would pick the staplers every time.

She stood over his sleeping form and felt the dull, throbbing panic of knowing she was in for a very long and tedious night.

Kellfyute never showed up.

Alina whiled away the nighttime hours by walking circles around Cronn's living room, dancing on the walls and ceiling, wandering into his bedroom, and jumping around while waving her hands in front of his sleeping face. But that all got old *fast*.

Periodically, she'd check in telepathically with Mezami. He'd been occupying himself by hunting up and down the alleyway where Alina had left her physical body. By morning, he'd stalked and slain five rats, a spined eel, and one garbage-sifting, long-fingered *iurket*.

Glad one *of us is having fun,* Alina thought at him.

At last, Cronn woke up, relieved himself in his chamberpot (while, in the other room, Alina covered her ears and loudly hummed), and poured himself a bowl of oatmeal and hot water. The kettle heating over the wood stove, he said a prayer to The Author and, interestingly, nodded and asked followup questions. As if he were responding to a voice in his head.

Slurping the oatmeal down, he set the bowl in the sink, prayed again, and walked toward the door. On his way out, he passed right through Alina, who followed.

Go to Kellfyute, Alina willed, wiggling her spirit fingers at him.

She confirmed the direction he was headed, and then tugged on the cord tethering her to her physical body, pulling herself back into it.

With a jolt, she opened her eyes to find Mezami on a pile of rat bones, belching contentedly.

"Well, thanks for that. You've solved the problem of my hunger. Come on, bud. Tracking round two: engage."

For half an hour, Cronn led her and Mezami on a merry little jaunt through the Sixth Stack, stopping to greet and gossip with several clusters of Sanctumite street-side shouters. They really were everywhere, and in greater numbers than Alina had ever seen before. They hailed Cronn with passion and respect.

Eventually, he found his way to a stone stair carved into a sheer wall. At its top lay a plateau on which had been built a longhouse whose triangular roof split a waterfall. The water ran down both sides of the structure, forming a moat around it, the excess draining to the plateaus and other buildings below.

Gray-clothed guards had been posted at the front door, so Alina had decided against physically sneaking inside. She ghosted herself up into the rafters.

Through spirit-eyes, gazing down upon the meeting being held below, she counted ten men and women, arranged in a circle. One of the women, bald like the others, with tiger-stripe scars on every inch of her exposed skin except for her face, clearly led the conversation. The others immediately shut up every time she spoke and bowed in deference at her every word.

Kellfyute, I presume? Alina's shadow grinned.

While Alina contemplated how to best approach her target, Kellfyute said something that drowned the conversation in a well of silence. In shock, the Sanctumites began to look around frantically as she said, "Cronn, you idiot. How could you not know?"

Alina's projection crept closer, straining to hear.

Cronn knelt before Kellfyute, gaze glued to the floor, sputtering, "I'm sorry. I'm so sorry."

"Ten lashes while reciting the First Tenet," she commanded for all to hear.

He nodded quickly, wringing his hands. "Thank you."

Then she looked up. Right at Alina's hiding spot. Directly *at* Alina.

Nope. There was no *way* anyone could've noticed her astral form.

The Sanctumite's eyes flashed white.

Oh, not good.

Four fingers extended, Kellfyute pointed toward the rafters—

Very bad.

—and four arrows of white light surged upward, striking Alina down.

28

CHO-ZEN

ESCAPING THE AUTHORITY WAS terrifying. Bizong, the strange
Aelf who'd rescued (and/or captured?) Cho and Kinneas, drove his motorcycle like it belonged to an ex and he was trying his darnedest to trash
it.

Fingers interlaced around his trunk, Cho buried her face in his flapping shirt.

Forget about the zapper drones—little electrically charged cubes designed to
crash into and stun fugitives—and the spiked roadblocks. The worst part was
the ride itself. Bumpy. Full of hairpin turns. Rocketing down the streets and alleys on a rusty metal tube, nothing between the asphalt and Cho's bones except
a layer of thin rubber.

Then there was all the shooting. Bizong alternated accelerating and steering
between his four prehensile limbs, using whichever two weren't operating the
vehicle to grab a weapon from one of his bike's many satchels. At one point, he
handed Cho a belt of six pulse grenades. She held it for him while he plucked
the explosives like apples, lobbing them at the formation of Tranq hovercycles
in hot pursuit.

Filtered through his gas mask, his roar of defiance rang tinny. His eyes were
burning kerosene. Death had a hand on his shoulder, guiding his arm.

Other than all the, you know... *skin*... he reminded her of Eilars.

Even after they'd left their pursuers behind in a cloud of dust, shrapnel, and burnt rubber fumes, he tore across the plateaus of the Sixth Stack, away from downtown, over an old stone bridge that should not have been able to bear the weight.

A steep, rocky hill ahead, Bizong shifted into low gear, and the engine growled the entire way up the spiraling trail. Only when they neared the mouth of a cave did he slow.

Parking the bike, he grabbed Kinneas by the scruff, threw him over one shoulder, switched on a flashlight to carry in his free hand, and walked back out of the cave.

Cho watched his loping, bowlegged gait. "How much farther?"

Brow furrowing, Bizong fiddled with a dial on the apparatus attached to the gas tank on his back. "But, we are already here. Did you not know?" He turned, head cocked. "Can you not feel it?"

"Feel what?"

"The Abyss. It surrounds us." He closed his eyes a moment. "Curiously, it is inside you—a *depix*." Adding, as if thinking out loud: "They will want to know."

Against her better judgment, she followed him into the cave, saying, "Who's they? What're you talking about? *Where* are we?"

"You carry a piece of it with you." His breath hissed from his mask. "What do you know of The Abyss?"

"The what?"

"Asked and answered." He chuckled. "Lower your sights, *Krukkel*."

She looked down, expecting to see your basic damp cave floor. Instead, she found herself standing on a flat, patterned sandstone surface. The pattern took the shape of interlocking hexagons. Each corner bore repeating sets of six symbols written in a language she had never seen before. Each line was inlaid with seams of smooth green stone that shimmered against the flashlight's beam.

"Chrononite?" she said.

"A low and limiting name, but, yes." Bizong rotated his arm; the beam of light went round and round. "Touch it."

Cho looked at him.

"Do you wish your friend to live? Then I must witness your leap of faith."

"You'll save him if I do what you say?"

"I won't if you don't."

Her eyes shifted from Kinneas's slack-jawed face to Bizong's scaly gray forehead.

She shook out her wrist and pressed her palm to the floor.

It was warm.

She woke in a cell.

Four walls. No windows.

No doors.

"Kinneas," she shouted until hoarse.

Hours went by.

There was a cot in the corner. A hole to pee down.

Somehow, eventually, she slept.

Metallic hiss, like an old radiator kicking on. The tinkle of water drops against hollow steel.

Cho opened her eyes to the darkness. Bizong was standing over her.

"So, I'm your prisoner. Now what?"

"The others will decide what to do with you."

They must have body-searched her while she was out; the reassuring weight of the blade she'd kept in her hip pocket was gone. Still, she had some weapons they couldn't take.

"Where's my friend?" she said, but didn't wait long for an answer. As Bizong cleared his throat, she lunged for the Aelf. The plates in her left arm slid apart, the limb stretching like a spiny tongue; the digits of her hand split into eight segmented pieces, sharp as a set of chef's knives.

He barked in surprise, hopping aside. Falling onto his elbows, his long, oddly shaped legs shot up, hooking around her arm, dragging it down.

Her shoulder joint popped, and she cried out, dropping to the floor.

Foot planted, his finger-like toes clenching her forearm, he actually laughed. "Well. I already knew there is more to you than my eyes can tell, but—clearly— I underestimated just how much." He stared down at her. "That was very, very stupid, do you agree? If I let you up—if—will you behave?"

Sweating from the pain in her arm, the frustration, and the repeated blows to her pride, she nodded.

He let her go. Arm retracting, she slid backward until she hit the farthest corner, still only six feet from him.

He sat, scratching his chin with one of his feet.

For a few minutes, silence.

"You have to let me see him," she said finally.

"You're no good to him now anyway."

Lump in her throat. "He's not dead." He couldn't be. She would not let that be true.

She watched the orange gas inside Bizong's tank fold and churn. The yellow-and-gray-scaled Aelf grumbled, a distorted warble through the ventilator in his mask. His inhuman eyes and half-hidden face made his expression very hard to read. But there was something about the particular way that his wrinkles deepened that suggested consideration if not concern. "Not yet."

She sagged into her corner, deflating, settling into its murky shadow.

"That *Jovarkanist* is tougher than he looks." His voice was quiet now, but grating—a nail file raked across flakes of glass. "What is your name?"

Except for Mezami, she had never met an Aelf before. What sort of powers might this one possess?

"Very well," Bizong said, rubbing his eye with the back of his hand. "I shall still call you '*Krukkel*,' then. Fitting: it means 'little fool.'" The scaly flesh around his orange eyes crinkled. A half-hidden smile?

"You don't know me."

"Ah, but I do know you are a child who, with her child friend, infiltrated an *eshfin* of the enemy. I know that, having disrupted our long-planned attack on that *eshfin*, you only live by the grace of my and my compatriots' intervention."

Gritting her teeth, she looked away. She had no counterargument. "What is this dump? Where've you taken us?"

"Ah-ah. You first, *Krukkel*. Tell me something I don't know. Who are you, and why have you come to Ozar?"

"How d'you know we're *not* from here?"

His words had all the energy of a deep-sea creature nestling languidly on the ocean floor until, suddenly, its stinger extended to skewer its prey. "Because I am not a child. I use my eyes, my ears. You are as much an Ozari as I am a cuttlefish." He crossed his lean arms, revealing the bony spikes protruding from his elbows. "The truth will serve you better than a worthless lie, and it may yet be the difference between gaining a useful friend or a vengeful enemy."

She noticed the brand on his forearm: a hexagon, its design and symbols miniature versions of the Chrononite-inlaid pattern in the cave.

She gasped. "The Chrononite, where'd you put it?" Alina might not want it, but she would *need* it.

"That Abyssal sliver never belonged to you, girl. As so many other beautiful and wondrous things, it was stolen from the earth by your people." A few breaths later, he added, "However, it may yet be returned to you."

"If…?"

"Good question. You have come to a place of faith, the true currency."

She remembered what he'd said in the cave before she'd touched the symbol and—what? Passed out? Been hypnotized? Before, anyway, she'd ended up imprisoned by him. Once more, he was asking her to take a leap of faith.

This wasn't how she'd imagined finding Anarkey would turn out. Bizong and his people were one big, annoying question mark. Yeah, she'd wanted to contact the anti-Authority resistance in Ozar. But now that it had actually worked, all she could think about was the cost. To herself. To Kin.

Ancient riddles and magic stones… She was a simple girl with simple wants, and she grew tired of mysteries.

On the other hand, if she didn't play along, she felt certain these would be the last four walls she'd ever see.

Bizong didn't blink, seeming to watch for even the tiniest shift in Cho's expression. To her, being on the receiving end of that kind of scrutiny—for once—felt intensely uncomfortable.

"I see you looking, questioning." Flexing his arm, glancing down, he pointed to the brand. "It is a declaration of intent. There are yet those, in Ozar and all parts of the world, who'd sooner assume a funeral shroud than a slave's chains, gilded though they may be. What are your intentions, then, *depix*? Again, sincerity is advised."

In one of the thousands of books Cho had sped-read, someone had once written "the enemy of an enemy is a friend." Seemed short-sighted. Personal experience taught her, given enough time, even enemies' enemies become your enemies. The real value of the quote lay in its justification of using people to accomplish your goals.

So, sick of second-guessing herself, she simplified the problem: Bizong and Anarkey were the immediate threat, and The Authority was the larger, more long-term one. There really wasn't any choice to be made here.

Live now. Deal with later *later*.

Deep breath. "My name is Choraelia Rodanthemaru Dreintruadan Shazura-Torvir. I'm technically Matriarch of the Torvir Family and governor of Torviri Province and all its Assets. My family was murdered in front of me, and I came to Ozar to get justice for their deaths. I am going to kill Kaspuri Walazzin. And then I'll find his father and his brothers and sisters and cousins, and kill them, too."

Bizong sucked in a long, unsteady breath, wheezing. "That is fascinating." The gas in his back-tank hissed and swirled. "I don't believe you're lying. You may yet be as crazy as I." He bowed his head. "I now formally introduce myself as Bizong, which in your tongue means 'mud-stirrer.' I am of the *Razenzu*, among the last of that proud people. A survivor of the genocides of the *depix*, your people."

"If by *depix* you mean the Elementals, they're not my people. I hate 'em as much as you do."

"I doubt that," he said, eyes crinkling again. "But your hate, plain on your face, is a most appreciated sight."

As if drawn in sand by a stick, a door manifested in the wall behind him. He rolled his shoulders, bones cracking, and stood.

"Just like that?" she asked.

Nudging the door, he waited, holding it for her.

She took a tentative step, then exited the cell.

Her feet found stone floors smoothed by time and tens of thousands of footsteps. The walls were rough-hewn sedimentary rock. There was only one way forward, and the passageway led her to a large, open cavern awash in soft light emanating from bluish floating orbs. Clusters of people occupied the space, eating from pewter bowls, whispering to each other, sharpening long, straight blades. Many of them were human, some with dark, steely appendages. Many more were Aelf—though Cho couldn't tell much more than that. Pale skin and watery eyes, pointy ears, speaking in strange languages, walking on two legs, or four, or more. A couple of them looked like hulking, rippling-muscled dogs as tall as Cho—heads swiveling to follow her.

She hurried along.

As Bizong led her between stacks of crates and chairs, she noticed the same hexagonal design again and again. Humans and Aelf alike wore it in the form of necklaces or tattoos. They'd had it emblazoned on their bracers, sewn into the banners hanging from the cave ceiling.

A tall creature—reaching several heads above both Cho and Bizong—barred their path. It crossed all four of its arms, flexed muscles bulging. Bending at the hip, it lowered its flat, frog-like face to Cho's. Papery lips stretched into a grimace, and then it croaked a few high-pitched notes, followed by a gurgling sound. One of its four hands drifted toward the knife at its belt.

Bizong said something Cho couldn't understand, but the creature understood all too well. It spat between her feet, glared at her, and walked away.

Sticking close to Bizong, just in case—better the devil she knew than the one she didn't—she glanced back the way they'd come, wary.

Without turning, Bizong said, "Your very nature discourages trust. And whether you leave—alive—depends entirely upon your reversing that flow."

The next tunnel had many doors on either side. "More prisoners?" she asked.

He pointed. "Sparring room. Medical and quarantine facilities. Alchemical lab. Computer lab."

"Computers?"

"Just as your race took from us, we took from you. You assumed only humans could master electronics?"

"Sorry." She rubbed her nose. "I'm just not used to dealing with Aelf."

He shook his head. "Scour that word from your lips. Such ignorance marks you a *depix*."

"I'm sorry. I'm willing to learn."

"Which is why I haven't bothered to kill you since plucking you from the enemy's clutches."

"Great, yeah. You can quit threatening me whenever. I get the picture." She crossed her arms. "Where're you taking me?"

Ushering her down one flight of stairs, then another, he said, "To the *Fyarda*. They are a deep-seer, a moon-magus. And they will tell if you are lying."

"I thought you believed me now."

"I do, but mine are the kill-skills—blade and bone. The *Fyarda*, though, will see through the deep lies, if in such wrappings you have enshrouded yourself. And that is no threat. It is barest fact." He opened a door, held it for her. "We must be careful, you understand. We cannot risk sabotage. Of which you seem particularly capable."

"Fair enough."

"As one of many forward operating bases serving at the Hextarchs' pleasure, our mission is larger than ourselves."

"So, just curious, but how would someone—hypothetically—join your merry band of rebels for a night on the town?"

"Rebels?" he said, and he let her flop around in her confusion for a moment. "We are much more than that. We are the hammers, swords, and fists of the Hextarchy, who are the great and Noble enemies of the *depix*. The war has raged eternal; I am but one weapon, one arrow in the bundle. Will you yet become another addition to our quiver? I may one day have a use for your strong heart, but we must first do something about that thick skull of yours. As long as we don't execute you for a spy first."

"You're asking for a lot of faith from me, but you're sure not giving me much in return."

"That is because I have all the leverage."

"Ouch. Guess I appreciate the blunt honesty. For what it's worth, I hope you don't decide to kill me. 'Cause I'm ready. Seen a few big scraps already, and I'm still kickin'."

"Yes, barely, and by the grace of nameless gods. Girl, your fury I respect, but, if you ever hope to amount to anything worthy, your violence must serve a greater cause. Your childish pursuits are worthless, for every *depix* will surrender or die in the end. Your familial squabbles do not concern the Hextarchy."

Jaw bone popping at his dismissal of her family's brutal end, she said, "What are the Hextarchy?"

His eyes widened. "Have you not heard of the living gods, they who have walked the earth since its beginning? How is this possible?"

"The people you call '*depix*' prefer a dumb population. Easier to control."

"They've taught you nothing of us, then? We don't merit even a mention in your histories?" He kicked his balled foot against the wall.

With a shrug, she said, "Look, I got no interest in the business of running a government or the history of ancient wars. I just want what's fair: the Walazzins took everything from me. Just last week, they had another of my friends murdered. I know it was that toad Wodjaego who signed off on the order. I can feel it, like a snail on the back of my neck. But he used The Sanctum to do it. They're his tools. He didn't even dirty his own hands. So, that's why I'm here—to drag them into the dirt with the rest of us. Now, I'll say it one more time: I'm nothing like them, so you keep my name and your word *'depix'* far away from each other. Yeah?"

Bizong seemed stuck on her ignorance. "That you have not heard of the Hextarchy is… disgusting."

"I mean, we, like, know there's a war going on here, but the reasons and specifics aren't really advertised. Basically, ninety percent of what we get are Watchbox sound bites and Aetherthread memes. It's all like 'for the glory of the empire *this*' and 'protecting ELCORP's interests *that.*' So, forgive me for not knowing the ins and outs of this geopolitical conflict. You gonna keep making me feel dumb, or you gonna be straight with me?"

"My rage is justified, girl. It is for the memories of my people that I fight. My people, and all others enslaved or massacred by the *depix* invaders and their pawns. That they do not teach their children even of our existence confirms their desire not only to conquer but to erase. The *depix* will not rest until we are exterminated." Closing his eyes, he held up both hands at ear level, knuckles facing Cho. A peace offering? "There is much we might learn from one another. The ripples of today's events are felt in my mind even now. For good or ill, I see the hands of the Hextarchy at work in our meeting."

"Uh. Sure."

"Come along, now, *Krukkel.*"

"I want to see Kinneas."

"Impossible. The doctor operates on him even now." Bizong clonked his gas tank. "Dzu is a talented healer. If the *Jova*'s life may be saved, he will save it."

If. If his life may be saved. Cho shook the thought from her mind.

She wished suddenly for a distraction. Just about anything would do.

"Fine. Let's go see your moon-magus and take your stupid lie detector test. Just stop calling me 'crew-kill.'"

"The day you cease acting like one shall be the day you earn a new name. *Krukkel.*"

Here, the hallways were built on a grid system. Cho busied herself logging every turn they took into her memory banks. Just in case she had to make a quick getaway.

Leaving the narrower passages, she entered a wide, high-arched common area. There, she saw dozens of men and women, human and Aelf, sitting with one another, playing card games, drinking, reading. No two of them wore the same outfit; there wasn't an ounce of military decorum to be found among them. Yet, you could tell by the way they spoke to one another, laughed together, and sang songs, that they were family. And the mark of their family was that hexagonal sign Bizong loved so fiercely he'd had it seared into his flesh.

Curious, Cho tried to catch snippets of their conversations, but what they spoke of was mundane: dinners, plans for the future, recent marriages, broken friendships. What stuck out to her were snatches of song—spirited tunes, their fast-paced rhythms carried through the hall by fleet-footed feet.

Then began a slow, mournful song. And all conversation ceased, every voice rising to join.

White tower, lonely by the sea
White tower, by three stars a-crowned
O tower, dark wings 'gainst the clouds
Light tower, come a-tumbling down

Now, boy'o, call the men to arms
Now, boy'o, ring the bell and shout
O boy'o, none hear your alarms
Poor boy'o, there's no clean way out

Woe, wyrm king, now let catch your spark
Woe, wyrm king, flames and tail a-lash
O wyrm king, have you found your mark?
Fright, wyrm king, burn the boy to ash

Lo, people, the foolish boy'o's dead
Lo, people, now the moorings shake
O people, we rise as the waves
Now, people, in the dragon's wake

White ruin, burning by the sea
White ruin, stars like eyes a-close
O ruin, dragon slain afield
Night ruin, shadows 'pon the stones

A few seconds of silence.

Then someone yipped and stamped their feet; others clapped their hands. Quickly, quickly now, a new rhythm was taken up.

They say the Ivoir heir is dead
Oh well, oh woe, oh why gods why
They say the Ivoir heir is dead
However did the fair lad die?

Turns out, my friends, the Ivoir heir

For all his toys and mercs and wealth
Amounts to nothing more than air
A toast, now, to his Family's health!

Laughter. The clinking of mugs and chugging of beer.

Cho imagined Ivion's pale lips twisted in disgust at the content of those last two songs.

Moving beyond the most raucous singers, Bizong grunted.

"You're not a fan?" said Cho.

"Merriment distracts." He paused mid-stride, turned, and stared pointedly at her. "The shark either swims forward or dies."

At the bottom of yet another stone stairwell lay a beach of black sand lapped by midnight waters. An underground lake, whose waves were caused by the constant flux of various hot springs, pushing the current in opposing directions.

At the far end of the beach was a cluster of trees, their pale yellow bark like decades-old, crumbling newspaper. Within the grove, there sat a lone figure wearing a headdress of leaves and a suit of lichen and tree bark. It turned its head at the crunching sound of Bizong's footfalls (Cho doubted her own steps could be heard).

The figure had hair like willow strands, shaved to the scalp on one side, long and reedy on the other. Its bark skin had been intricately scarred in spiraling patterns. It stood up, considering them with its tennis-ball-sized, dark green eyes. Each had three black pupils, arranged in a tight triangle, spinning like wheel spokes before landing on Cho.

The creature—another Aelf—waited, expectant. It smelled of herbs and mud.

High, high up, what Cho had believed to be stalactites hanging from the cave ceiling shriveled suddenly and retracted into the rock.

The creature followed her gaze. "Deep roots."

"Huh," said Cho, completely failing to understand.

Bizong coughed. "Crabgrass, I need you to do that thing you do."

"Crabgrass?" said Cho, thinking it some kind of curse word.

"That's what they call me," said the bark-skinned being. It lifted its arm, palm toward Cho, a sheepish smile on its face. "Your hand please."

"What are you—"

"Just do it," said Bizong. "Their bark is worse than their bite."

Their eyes downcast, Crabgrass curled her willowy fingers around Cho's wrist, squeezing a little. Cho felt a slight tingle, the blood pulsing against those sandpaper fingertips.

Crabgrass's six pupils rotated as they looked Cho up and down.

"So." Cho popped her lips. "You're the living lie detector?"

"If it helps you to think of me that way, close enough. More accurately, I can sense even the minutest Niimantic impulses coursing through the blood, the lymph nodes, the pores. My freedom-fighter comrades have put my talents to use many times in sussing out the claims of suspicious individuals."

Squeezing her wrist, Crabgrass hummed under their breath.

Cho said, "You don't have any questions for me or anything?"

"Words may be twisted. Niima may not."

Bizong went *tch*.

One of Crabgrass's sets of pupils rotated towards him. "Scoff if you like. I've yet to be wrong." To Cho: "Never fear. If you have no pall of the arcane over you, the process will be painless and swift, and we will probably let you live."

"And if I do?"

Crabgrass smiled unsettlingly. Finally, they said, "Ah, you have no magic." Craning their neck, chin over Cho's head, they listened for something soundless. "And no spells of deception or illusion have been woven upon you. You are human. Biologically female. But, there's something else—"

The knife flashed free of Bizong's belt. Cho tensed, but he did not attack. Yet.

"No." Crabgrass shoved Bizong's chest. "No need for that, you oaf. The girl has Authority-designed tech, but she's no spy of theirs. No, no. What I'm sensing in her is…" They closed their eyes, again listening to the silence. "You come carrying a great burden, don't you? All that data rammed into your brain, it's a marvel you haven't lost your mind."

"Had you seen her behavior back in town," Bizong said, "you might change your assessment."

"Put that blade away before you hurt someone."

Bizong complied.

Crabgrass turned to Cho. "You're more enhanced than anyone I've seen or heard of. Hardly an inch of you wholly organic. When was your first surgery?"

"Don't remember," Cho mumbled. "What's all this, huh? I thought we were cool, Bizong, and ya pull a knife on me?"

"It's called caution. You attacked me earlier."

"That was a whole twenty minutes ago, man. And you're the one who threw me in a box."

Crabgrass cleared their throat. "Do I need to be here, or…?"

"Okay," said Cho, taking a step back, watching for any abrupt movements or shifts in mood. "You trust me, finally?"

"Bizong hasn't killed you," said Crabgrass, grinning faintly.

He clapped his feet. Then he pressed his fists to his temples, knuckles forward, in that same odd gesture as before. "Introductions are in order. Crabgrass, this is *Krukkel*."

"How does this help me? You call everyone *Krukkel*."

"That may be, but this one's special. I couldn't believe my ears at first, but with you vouching for her... Hex us, but I think our fortunes have taken a sharp turn for the better. This *Krukkel* here—she's one of the Twelve."

"Ah. *Really?*" Crabgrass adjusted their crown of leaves. "Why *haven't* you gutted her, then?"

Cho made a noise like *chuh*.

"Because I foresee," said Bizong, his scaly brow knitting, orange eyes narrowing, "a much better use for her."

"There's no way I'm agreeing to any of that," said Cho, crossing her arms. "I'll steal, fight, blow stuff up, but what you're asking—"

"Your life's in our hands," said Bizong. "Back at the *eshfin*, we went in hot—early—to pull you from the fire. Though our people incurred minimal casualties and gave far worse than they got, you owe us a great debt."

Cho looked to Crabgrass, who shrugged apologetically.

"I appreciate your free-spiritedness, *Krukkel*. But you will do as I've so politely instructed."

Leaning her weight on the balls of her feet, Cho considered activating her speed and reflex boosters.

Bizong chuckled. "Try it. Unshackled as you are, you might get away. But do you suppose you'll be able to escape with your unconscious boyfriend? Could you reach him? Find him, even?"

Cho growled under her breath. Yeah, she'd never break her way out of this place. Having arrived unconscious, she had no idea where she even was. And she wasn't prepared to leave Kinneas behind.

"Sunk in yet? No?" said Bizong. "Talk some sense into the girl, Crabgrass. We hit the station tomorrow."

He walked away, prehensile feet crunching in the black sands, leaving Cho with the lanky, bark-skinned, alien Aelf.

"Now that he's gone, can we start over, maybe? My name is Cbarassan."

"Um. Cho."

"I would like to show you something, Cho." Crabgrass—Cbarassan—led her along the arc of the beach, warm waves caressing their toes. Steps hidden in the rocks ahead took them uphill to a glass dome. Inside the small building, bolted to the stone, were rows of shelves. These were laden with glass bowls containing pale plants—miniature trees that wriggled, bristling at the sound of footsteps.

Cbarassan turned a valve in the wall. Water trickled from a series of hoses running along the shelves, the liquid dripping into the bowls.

"Hydroponics," said Cho, noticing the lack of dirt, the way the roots squirmed inside their tinfoil wrappings, causing tiny ripples in the pools of water.

"They're particular. It's the only way I can keep them healthy."

"What are they?"

"Prenatal *Fyarda*." At Cho's blank expression, Cbarassan explained, "An imperfect analogy would be the human embryo. We have here the unborn children of my species."

Despite her captivity, Cho allowed herself to be impressed. "How long till they're born?"

"I don't know. It's been a decade. I've pored over tales of *Fyarda* births, but one can't learn everything from stories and books, it seems. Growing the stem and branches is difficult enough. Regression—shriveling—is all too common. As for instilling consciousness?" They shook their head.

"There's no one to ask? Another, um, *Fyarda*?"

"You're looking at them." Cbarassan spread their arms. "If I don't care for these unborn, there's no hope. No future." They said something in a strange language, a half-muttered mantra. "Ah, well." They grabbed a chair, sat leaning their elbows on its high back. "Have a seat, Cho. Let's talk. I'm sure you have questions, and we might as well pass the time while we wait for your companion to convalesce."

Sighing, Cho accepted the invitation, taking the chair between the steel sink and a pair of leaning shears. "Bizong's a real piece of work."

"There's more truth in that than you know, but try to refrain from hating him. I won't say 'he means well.' He's simply been through so much. Such grief." Cbarassan's willowy hair draped over their eyes. "That man's among the very last of his people, the Razenzu native to the Suur-al-Swalpan (the 'Sea of Dreams,' which you would probably know as the Gulf of Caelus). They largely kept to themselves, a deep-sea-dwelling race, content to subsist off the fish and other sea creatures that populate those sulfur-rich, volcanically heated waters. But they were to the Nation of El a nuisance. I don't know the particulars, and it hardly matters. The Elementals wanted something from the domain of the Razenzu, and so the Razenzu were devastated by the Elemental war machine. The continuous growth of El has come at the cost of everyone else's homes, families, freedoms…" Cbarassan fixed their strange eyes on Cho's. "That's why we need you to help us. Given what you are, a word from you may well be worth more than any hail of arrows and slings from us. You could be our voice, a voice ringing out in the name of freedom."

For some several minutes, Cho hugged her knees, watched the dark waves, and chewed on Cbarassan's words.

Cbarassan said, "The tragedy of the Razenzu is far from unique, Cho. The Elementals fear what to them is 'Other.' Look at me." Cho did. "I am what you humans call 'Aelf.' That word binds all manner of creatures, from beasts to those like me to beings far more venerable. Humans have reduced us all to a single label in order to justify their genocides. To use another human term, the subcategory of Aelf I belong to is Uardini—a Monraïnian word, meaning 'protector sprite.' Though a few human scholars may remember the origin of that name, this is small consolation to the innumerable dead of my people." They fell still a moment, the memory of a smile tracing their lips. "A conclave of human druids once named my ancestral home the Forest of the Moon and my people 'moon dryads.' They saw beauty in our peace—" The echo of contentment was drowned out by the drumming of their heart—"but fled the fires all the same. They weren't there for us when—Ah, that's all in the past now. My home is no more, so I transplanted. You can, too, you know."

Cho looked at them.

They said, "You could be one of us. Have a family. Isn't that what you—what we all—want?" They nodded toward the hole in the glass ceiling; the shadows and stalactites shifted strangely. No, not stalactites—roots. "When the Aelfravers drove us from our lands, some of us took with us seeds of the old forests. I carried with me enough for a small grove which, over centuries, has grown into a beautiful, dank, tangled mess."

"That sure is something." Cho found herself beginning to like this Cbarassan character. "You should be proud."

"Oh, I am. And not solely because those roots run deep, the trunks wide. I love each one of them for being a limb of home. Resilient, dark, *defiant*. But I'm especially proud of these surrogate children of mine for the reason that they are a terrible headache for The Authority: each night, I agitate the roots and apply my essence to the swelling of the trees' numbers; each morning, The Authority pawns move in with their flamethrowers and incendiary grenades, but it's never enough. The forest grows. The roots run deep."

Remembering Ivion's lecture about the dangers of the Fourth Stack's Ineffable Forest, Cho said, "You're the one causing all that trouble? Just you?"

Cbarassan shrugged. "The *Fyarda* remain with me in spirit."

Cho nodded, thinking. "Why do they call you Crabgrass? It's not your name?"

"People are lazy. I've had to learn to live with, in more ways than one, the concept of 'good enough.' All I want in these final years (or months) of my life is to see some measure of progress toward the peace I've worked so hard to encourage. If the simpleminded must call me 'Crabgrass' because they can't pronounce my actual name—because I look, to them, like a houseplant—fine. I've dealt with far worse."

When the quiet grew uncomfortable, Cho blurted, "The rebels up there." She pointed in the direction of the staircase via which she'd come to this secluded lakeside. "Human and Aelf, working together. I wasn't expecting that."

"That's because you're an Elemental," said Cbarassan, grinning.

"I'm not anything, and definitely not that."

"Prove it." Their smile held. "Aid us."

"Listen, I feel for ya. I do. Horrible things've been done to you." She trailed off.

"Do something, then. Are you not as brave a fool as the rest of us? Weren't you the one caving in Authority heads mere hours ago? News travels quickly down here. It was quite a show you put on, you and the *Jovarkana* boy. Our friends were amazed you weren't dead by the time they intervened. They pegged you for a little lioness."

Cho squirmed at the comparison. The lion's head was the central component of the Walazzin's heraldry.

"If you didn't come to Ozar to bend ears or break necks in the name of freedom," said Cbarassan, batting their three-pupiled eyes, "to what *do* we owe the honor of your visit?"

"It's like I told Bizong, right? I'm just here for the Walazzins. Wodjaego, if you got him. But I'll settle for Kaspuri."

"Well, what are you waiting for, then? The men you speak of lead the charge against the Hextarchy. Harming The Authority as a whole, therefore, harms them greatly, too. It's basic logic."

"Your war's too big for me. I just want the Walazzins dead."

"Why though?"

"The world'll be a better place with them gone."

"Oh, Cho, *Krukkel* indeed you are. Can't you see? The Walazzin lion is but one head of a many-headed beast. Sever it, and another eleven remain poised to bury their fangs in you. If there is to be any hope for the future, we must poison the beast's heart." Cbarassan snapped their fingers. "The cancerous old Walazzin may lead El today, but do you suppose a Malach, a Reautz, or an Ivoir would be any better? For anyone?"

Cho gritted her teeth at the name "Ivoir."

Who were these people, Cbarassan and Bizong, telling her what to think and how to act? She could see what they were doing, playing on her sympathies. She'd been through a lot, too, but they didn't seem to care about that. They had their plans, and she was just another of their tools.

Then she thought about Rooster's tooth, all the viruses and bombs she'd planted to get it, the information it contained, and what that information could do for her. She was so close, so very close to succeeding. However, if her recent fight had proven anything, it was that she sure could use some more allies. Think of the damage she could do, if only she had the right kind of friends.

In her mind, she saw Kinneas take that bullet to the face—again, again, again. His pain, it had to mean something.

She'd come too far. No stopping now. She'd be betraying Kinneas and Eilars if she did.

So close. Her fingers itched for her knife.

Slowly, she said, "If I do you this one solid, will you help me?"

All six of Crabgrass's pupils remained fixed on Cho as they said, "By the Heart-trees and the Alders Past, I give you my word. I will deliver the Walazzin commander to you myself if I must, but you shall have your blade at his throat if such is your wish."

Agreeing to Bizong's plan was a terrible idea. The highest of risks. Alina would be beyond furious if she ever found out. But it seemed a straight line from this insanity to Cho's deepest desire. So…

"You got a deal. It might feel good, besides," she said, "to rub The Authority's noses in it. Let *them* feel confused and powerless for once."

"Yes. Think of the morale-shifting effect that—"

"Cbarassan, I said I'd do it. Now, can I please see Kinneas already?"

"Afraid not. You'll see your friend once you've done as we've asked."

"Ya kidding me?"

"The boy is our insurance. As blustering as Bizong may appear, he's no dolt. Young Kinneas is all that binds you to our cause as of now; we all know it." They stood, dragging the chair away. They paused. "Thank you, by the way."

"For what?"

"For saying my name—my real name. No human has uttered it in… Hmm, I don't suppose any ever has." Ushering Cho out of the dome, Cbarassan turned out the lights, closed the door, and said, "I do hope neither of us dies tomorrow night. Welcome to Anarkey."

Stuck killing time, Cho remained with Cbarassan. Both closed their eyes, breathing in tandem, keeping time by the lapping of the lake's waves.

Time. So deep underground, with only electrical and magical light to go by, Cho had no sense of it. And she'd never been any good at meditation. Her thoughts ran free, and she gave chase until she bumped into one that gave her pause. "There may be a slight issue."

"Yes?"

"I have this friend."

"Another one? Someone's popular."

"I kind of snuck out on her, and, if I'm not back soon, she'll probably come looking for me."

"It's a big Stack. She's welcome to try."

"She's more… of a pain than you're used to, I think. She's a, uh, an Aelfraver."

Cbarassan sucked in a hissing breath.

240 J.R. Traas

"She's not like the others," Cho said quickly. "She's nonviolent. Never kills anyone, I swear. I'm only bringing it up because she has… this annoying habit of always finding what she's looking for."

"And what do you propose we do about this 'friend'?"

"Go see her."

"Hah. Good one."

"I'm serious! Escort me if that's what it takes. I've already agreed to your ridiculous plan. Let me talk to her, show my face, have her bug me about how irresponsible I am for fifteen minutes, then we can head right back here." Cho bit her lip. "Trust me, you don't want her on your case. You think I'm stubborn? Wait till you get a load of *her*."

"Congratulations, Cho. You've irritated me. See, I really don't want to believe you, but, as the resident trap-spotter, I'm agonizingly aware of how honest you're being."

"So?"

Sighing, Cbarassan opened their eyes. They stood up, dusted the sand from their pants, and began to walk back to the stone steps leading up into the heart of Anarkey stronghold.

"Ooh, one more thing," said Cho, nervously tapping her thumb and fingers against her leg.

Cbarassan turned.

Cho removed from an inner pocket in her bag the microchip she'd received from Eilars. His final gift to her.

She held it up to the glow emanating from lanterns flanking the stairs. "Happen to know anybody who can install cybernetic implants?"

Cbarassan swiveled on their heels, and continued toward the stairs.

Cho followed.

The chair could've been pulled off a curb after being abandoned. The surgeon, a bleary-eyed, slouching man in his forties or fifties, seemed like he was experiencing a severe allergic reaction. Wiping away his snot on a stained rag, he strapped Cho into the chair.

He took a swig from a bottle of clear liquid, and offered it to Cho. She refused, at first. After the first needles went in—a local numbing agent to desensitize her skin, then a blood clotter—she told him to give her some of the booze.

"Too late," said the 'doctor' as he doused his hands in the strong, sticky liquid. He wheeled in a hospital tray laden with scratched stainless steel surgical equipment.

Hand tools. Oh no.

"What d'you mean, 'too late'?" she said.

Gulping down what was left in the bottle, he said, "All gone."

"You're really gonna do this drunk?"

"What are you," he slurred, "my mother?"

"Cbarassan," Cho shouted toward the door. "I've changed my mind." She tried to tear free from her restraints but couldn't. They'd been built for bodies much larger and stronger than hers.

Years ago, her mods had been implanted by a team of medical drones. They'd cut her open and patched her up with a level of precision only achievable by machines supervised by the foremost specialist in the field of cybernetics. And, well… her parents had been there for her, too.

This time, she was alone with a man half-drowning in grain alcohol.

Hand tools.

Her head swam. Fear setting into her, she was a spinning top of terror trapped in flesh, strapped to a torn up, rank-smelling chair.

"This one's not optional," said the surgeon, and he squeezed Cho's cheeks, levering open her jaw and dumping a glossy violet liquid down her throat.

She choked and said, "What is that stuff?"

"Diluted essence of *Vlindra* spores. One banger of a sedative. Know anything about Augmentative Elixirs? Well, some of them buff the mind and body. Good for utility or combat, depending on the type. This one's different: too much, you end up in a coma; just enough, it dulls the senses. You'll be awake, but the sting'll be… less."

"Wait, that was an Auggie? You gave me a Raver potion? Don't you have any, like, actual anesthetic?"

He flung his arm out to indicate the dusty basement lab around them. "It look like we're flush with cash down here? Were it up to me, you'd have chugged *only* half that bottle, sat back, and shut your flapper. But Crabgrass vouched for you, and they make the rules because they also make the Urggss—erhm—Auggies. So." Taking a scalpel in hand, he pricked the inside of her forearm, below the elbow. "Feel that?"

"No." A haze fell over her.

"Try to breathe." He hiccuped. "This will take a while."

The process was way more terrifying and painful than she remembered. By the power of her enhanced nervous system, she remained alert throughout most of the event. She pinched her eyes shut and distracted herself by praying to Buthmertha. Although, Alina's goddess hadn't done her any favors lately.

Thankfully, as the mind-haze thickened, her thoughts grew sluggish.

Despite being conscious the operation, she'd remember very little of it. The major reminder, the scar running from her left middle knuckle to her elbow, curling around her wrist.

After the operation, her cognitive software had to reboot, so she passed out on a sofa in the lab. She became coherent and aware again, she was informed, about two hours later.

Her backpack containing all her things, including the Chrononite chunk, had been set beside the sofa. She slung the bag over her shoulder just as Cbarassan entered the room. "How do you feel?"

"Normal," said Cho, surprised. She hopped onto her feet. "Time to see what this thing does."

It was the Aelf's turn to be surprised. "You mean you didn't know beforehand?"

"Nope. But I trust the man who gave this to me. He sacrificed himself to save me and my friend."

"The one you want to visit, I presume."

Cho nodded. "Anyway, Eilars really was kind. To me, at least. Whatever the chip does, I'm sure it'll be useful."

"Oh, I'm certain it will."

Something about the way Cbarassan said that, and the curl of their smirk, bugged Cho. "Hang on. Do *you* know what it's for?"

"Absolutely. I had our mutual friend Doctor Dzu analyze it before I approved your operation."

"Invasive much?"

"Caution is a virtue."

"Tell that to your doc. Coulda warned me dude's an alcoholic. Not my first choice."

"Dzu's demons are no fewer in number or lesser in strength than yours or mine. He's a good man. Capable, persistent, fair. Those like him give me hope."

"Yeah? How's that?"

"He's former Authority, a combat medic. Knows the ins and outs of cybernetic enhancements and magical Augmentatives, having patched up dozens of humans who made use of them."

"The doc—Dzu—mentioned you cooked up the Auggie he gave me. Where did you learn how to do that?"

"From whom do you suppose *your* people learned?"

"You taught that skill?"

"Not personally, no. And the word 'taught' implies a contract willingly entered by two parties. Humans stole much alchemical knowledge from the *Fyarda*. But that's a long, maddening tale, and one I don't wish to tell you now. Broken though he is, Dzu proved to me your kind is capable of better. He saved your race for me. He's special. And, I suspect, so are you."

Cho opened her mouth to speak, but she didn't get the opportunity. Before she could even shout in alarm, Cbarassan snatched the bloody scalpel from the medical tray and slashed at her throat.

There was no time to think. She leapt backwards, spinning, placing the chair between them.

The Aelf flung the scalpel at her face. The blade should have pierced her eye, but she arched the small of her back, bending just far enough for the stainless steel blade to sail over the tip of her nose.

A sensation she hadn't felt before: total control coupled with total awareness. Every item in the room, from the cabinets filled with bandages and other supplies to the low-basin metal sinks, became instantly known to her. She could tell exactly how far and how fast she'd have to move to get to each one, and which tools would give her an advantage over her opponent. Her mind scanned Cbarassan as well, instantly identifying the weakest points in their bark and skeletal structure, which muscles provided their organs the greatest and the least protection—against unarmed strikes or attacks using any of the improvised weapons available.

Basically, she suddenly, effortlessly became mindful of every useful detail in the room.

The Aelf raised their hands. All hostile intent had disappeared, Cho knew. She didn't know *how* she knew, but she did. She relaxed.

"Do you understand?" said Cbarassan.

"I've never moved like that before. I didn't have to even *try*. Everything just kinda... happened." Something puzzled her. "I don't think my processing power's been increased, though. Doesn't feel like I'm thinking any faster."

"Correct. You aren't. I'm no expert by any means, but Dzu informs me that a data processor would have required brain surgery."

Cho nodded. Yeah, that tracked.

Cbarassan said, "That device he installed in your arm, it's a nervous system auxiliary of sorts. Its design mimics the decentralized nerve-endings and neural receivers found in the *Ziv rodoji*, an Aelf that can essentially 'think' without relying on one big brain. It manages this trick because each of its organs respond to environmental stimuli independently. The left limb doesn't know what the right is doing because it doesn't need to."

"So, I've got, like, a second brain in my arm now?"

"More accurately, your hands and feet don't need to ask your brain for permission to act anymore."

"Woah."

"I'm sure you can already imagine the combat applications, but that chip in your arm should, in theory, activate during any moment of heightened stress."

"That's awesome. Still, could ya have just *told* me that, rather than trying to slice me like a loaf of bread?"

"Probably." Cbarassan nudged the door open. "But that would have been far less exciting." They stepped into the tunnel. "Shall we go see this Aelfraver friend of yours?"

"Really? Now that I'm way harder to kill, you suddenly trust me?"

"You're far from earning my trust. But, yes, *really*. We need you strong as can be for the mission, and now you've got your upgrade, but—" the Aelf's willow-branch hair stirred, ruffled by some unseen force—"don't think you've yet seen everything I can do."

"Noted."

"Before we head out, let's make one thing explicit. Please don't take this the wrong way, alright? I like you, but—if you betray us—your friend dies."

"Yeah, yeah. And now I say, 'You kill him, I kill you.' Or, here's an idea: we could just stay pals and not back-stab each other."

"No objections."

"Let's just get this social call over with. Ew. Gods, I've gone all clammy just thinking about it. I'd rather solo a Tranquilizer squad then face Disappointed Alina."

Cbarassan sniffed. "You're being honest. Wow."

Headed up the stairwell and into the mess hall, Cho added, "You're gonna like her, though. She's weird, too."

"Is she as brash and impetuous as you?"

"Hells, no. She's way worse."

29

ALINA

PITCHED BACKWARD, ALINA PLUMMETED. But gravity held a weaker sway over astral bodies, and *Rego* unfurled beneath her, the cloak flapping like wings, catching her. She hovered in place a moment—and dashed aside as another light spear burned past, bursting into sparks behind her.

Alina's translucent dream form touched down, *Rego*'s folds relaxing again.

Pretty handy, owning interdimensional clothing items. Not only had her cloak automatically reacted to break her fall, but it had swatted away two of the four magical bolts. The other two, though, had char-grilled a couple of her ribs. She grunted.

Gray tunic hugging her muscular figure, her bare, scar-crossed arms tensing, Kellfyute—Exorcist of The Sanctum—approached with quick, deliberate steps. Fortunately for Alina, outnumbered as she thought she'd been, only Kellfyute seemed able to see her. The other Sanctumites regarded their leader intently, their surprise giving way to confidence. None of them asked her why she'd attacked something they clearly couldn't see.

It didn't make any sense. Alina's hiding in the rafters should have been an unnecessary precaution: astral projection required magic; only a Maggo could've discovered her.

Only a Maggo... So, Kellfyute was casting spells. (Whatever happened to magic being a sin?)

Cursing her own carelessness, Alina pulled up her hood and threw on *Ida*, sizing up her opponent. Her hot, shallow breaths bounced off the mask, dampening her face.

"Demon." From thin air, Kellfyute drew a slender, hooked sword. "Sanctumites, a sorcerer spy stands before us. This specter's body must be nearby. Find and destroy it." Leveling the tip of her blade with Alina's throat, Kellfyute closed the distance, declaring, "I shall lay to rest the foul spirit."

Mezami, Alina fired off a warning-thought in the direction of her body. *You're about to get pinched. Get us out of there.*

A brief pause—thought-lag—then, his reply: *Excitement: finally, we.*

The other Sanctumites rushed from the building, calling for reinforcements. Alina didn't want to think about the repercussions of losing her body while caught between the material world and the Revoscape. (Hint: that's one way ghosts were made.) If anyone could save her corporeal self, though, it'd be Mezami.

She'd have to trust him. The opponent before her required all her focus.

In her current state, Alina wouldn't be able to physically affect the other woman, but the reverse was true as well. Magic was their only effective weapon now. Not a wonderfully comforting realization in this context, Alina thought as she pressed her hand to her ribcage, feeling the echoes of the stinging, burning, crackling energy that had slammed into her moments before.

"Submit, demon—" the ritual, root-like scars tracing the length of Kellfyute's neck bulged—"and I'll end you quickly."

Alina had to assume Kellfyute had seen her face before she'd remembered to put on her mask. So, there really were no options here. She was going to have to fight—and win.

A horizontal scythe of light arced toward Alina. On all fours, she darted forward. Kellfyute responded with an uppercut; Alina flapped *Rego*, pushing backward, avoiding the gleaming blade-point by a fraction of an inch. The heat emanating from that sword burned Alina's spirit, and that's when she understood. Kellfyute was a Deïmancer, a disciple of the art that channeled divine, demonic, or generally spirit-based magic. She hadn't been afraid to use her abilities in plain sight of her fellow Sanctumites, and none of them had been surprised.

Clearly, The Sanctum had a more complicated relationship with magic than advertised. Were there others like her? Could all Exorcists do as she did?

A wave of bright white energy exploded from her then, hammering Alina and hurling her backward. Being intangible, she flew clean through the wall of the longhouse. (Willpower was required to manipulate or stand on physical objects or surfaces while astral-projecting, and that was hard to keep up while being blasted to bits). Standing among some bushes, steadying herself, Alina glanced up and dodged just in time; Kellfyute had dived from the window above, spearing downward, a blinding flash preceding her. Her hooked sword sliced the ground; sparks flew, flash-cooking every plant within a five-foot radius.

Within one second, Kellfyute would be on Alina again. This second chipped away as the Sanctumite spun for another cut. Alina twisted aside, the hook raking her cloak.

Kellfyute was tireless, her "I'm going to burn your house down" expression unchanged.

How fantastic it would be if Alina's brain would feed her some useful information—or, y'know, just *work*.

Then, in front of her eyes, as if she were holding the dusty old tome in her hands even now, she saw the charts and diagrams of the eight magical Disciplines, and she remembered that Deïmancy and Revomancy were thaumaturgic inverses. Within the arcane spectrum, they balanced each other in the same way that fire and water, earth and air did. Because their skill sets were polar opposites, Alina and Kellfyute could very easily blow each other up by circumventing each other's defenses—even by accident.

There was no dominant art; all were equal. It all came down to how well you used what you had. Knowledge was key. Alina was again grateful for the untold number of hours she'd been forced by Dimas to study Aelf and Niimantic lore; she remembered an exploitable weakness of Deïmancy. The connection between the caster and her spiritual or divine patron was the source of her powers. A Deïmancer was nothing without that link.

By contrast, Revomancy came entirely from within—the subconscious of the caster.

There, on cue, was the Crow—hunch-backed, writhing, a tightly wound tangle of rope-limbed darkness. Behind her mask, Alina grinned.

So far, she'd been losing because muscle memory had kept her mentally stuck. As if she were still drilling with her grandfather or sparring with the other students of The School. Until now, she'd been fighting like a Geomancer, dodging and blocking. But she wasn't just a Geomancer anymore.

Kellfyute brandished her glimmering weapon and lunged, but the Crow seized her by the elbow and throat. The Sanctumite gasped, her eyes searching for the cause of her paralysis, but *it* she could not see.

Niima rising from her lungs like a song, Alina told the Crow, "Hold her there."

Its grip tightened. Kellfyute yelped.

"Cool light show. Seven out of ten." Alina's shadow grew long and wide, and it lifted from the ground like the crooked neck of a carrion bird. "My turn."

Kellfyute touched the flat of her blade to her nose as if in salute, a wave of light flashing from her core, but she'd been too slow.

The tendrils of Alina's shadow wrapped themselves around her opponent, bent her neck back, pried apart her mouth and eyelids. Alina strangled the Sanctumite's scream, and—as if a welcome mat had been laid out and the front door had glided open—stepped inside her mind.

Sorry in advance, Kelli. I'm sure you're a lovely, ah, fanatic. But I need some things from you. Your face. And your memories.

The first time is always awkward.

Alina fumbled around in the dark, groping for the mental knobs and levers in Kellfyute's unconscious. She was trying to reverse-engineer Ydeleh's Somnambulic Stride, the dream-walker spell Ruqastra had used on her just about every other day. It was complicated and terrible, and Alina had only been taught the theory; they'd been working up to the practical portion. But with her test subject captive for now, she could experiment. It had to work, or Kellfyute would escape knowing what Alina looked like, and this whole Ozari field trip would've been for nothing.

In the black expanse of dream, she conjured a visual aid—a representation of Kellfyute, floating, head lolled, eyes blank. Like a cup of water scooped from a lake, this representation was part of the whole. Though separated, the cup and lake water remained the same, connected. In this case, bound to Alina's will. Now that she had an access point, she flipped a switch, and her Kellfyute-image opened its eyes.

The image, channeling Kellfyute's emotions, tensed and screamed into the darkness.

Unseen, in her best customer service voice, Alina said, *Your patience is appreciated.*

The Crow lurched forward, gawking at Kellfyute. Guided by its yellow eyes, she lunged at it and slashed; the Crow weaved. Then it closed its eyes, rasping laughter, and disappeared.

Alina could hardly focus. She told the Crow, *Gimme some room to breathe.*

"Show yourself." Kellfyute spun in circles. She swung her sword this way and that, the darkness of this mind-cell swallowing the glow of her holy weapon. "The Author protects me. I am swaddled in His Light. His Whisper dispels darkness. His Word, my salvation from the wicked."

Well, he's gonna have a hard time removing me without permanently damaging you. That's not a threat or anything. Just sayin'. You're kinda in a delicate state here. And I need your mind to not break into a million pieces.

"My Lord guides me." Kellfyute's voice cracked. "Though I am beset by demons, His Holy Fire burns away the unclean."

Do me a favor and keep it together, 'kay? Niima flaring, Alina sifted through the miscellaneous feelings and thoughts pouring from Kellfyute like sweat on a humid day.

The trouble with the human mind was that it was always thinking, and most of what it worried over was pointless, unrealistic, or petty. To get to a specific idea inside this practically infinite web felt like performing brain surgery blindfolded. With buttered fingers.

By Buthmertha, where is the center—Ah-ha. There. Now I can hear everything.

Author, save me, Kellfyute thought. She could see only the length of her blade and the dimmest outline of her hands, arms, and feet. Protect your most faithful servant. Please.

"Get out of my head!" she shrieked, throat raw.

Gladly. When I have what I came here for.

Kellfyute hacked at nothing until her sword grew heavy and her arms fell limp. Tears welling, she said, "Damn you, creature." Faintly: "Damn you."

First the light of her sword, then the weapon itself, faded into mist.

She found she knelt in a field of yellow wildflowers, her fingers rifling through them like the pages of a book. Someday, she'd find a blue-petaled one. Her brother Gralen reminded her the odds of that were one in one thousand, but she searched anyway. One day, she'd find just the right flower, lay it on auntie's grave, and—

"No!" She wailed into the darkness. "Not that."

No, yeah, I see what I did there. That wasn't fear, was it? Sadness, loneliness. But not fear. Frustrating. Alina latched onto another strand of memory. *Give this one a go.*

Kellfyute lay in bed, eyes pinched shut. Strange sounds came from the hall. Face dark, outlined by blueish electric light, her mother poked her head into the bedroom. "Kelli? You awake?" Mother's voice didn't sound... natural. It dripped out all slow and foul—globs of honey on rotten meat.

"Mommy," said Kellfyute, trembling under her covers.

"Go back to sleep," sang Mother. Then, sharply: "Don't make me come down here again."

"Sorry. I'm sorry."

"Will you finally be good?"

Kellfyute nodded.

"You know what happens when little girls can't be good."

Quick nod.

The door drifted farther open, and the light behind Mother went out. As Kellfyute's eyes adjusted, Mother's hair stood on end, wriggling like worms, like tentacles.

"Please, don't hurt me again. Please."

The bedroom and bed vanished, and Kellfyute fell three feet, striking the invisible floor of darkness. Grunting, drenched in sweat, she said, "I'm strong now. You won't touch me, or Gralen, again. I won't let you." She tried to summon her Soulblade—the holy weapon granted her by The Author's grace.

It wouldn't come.

Better luck the third time around, I guess? Ma'am, I'd just like to apologize, one more time, for putting you through so much. For what it's worth, I'm not enjoying this either. I know that doesn't take away from what you're feeling, but—Know what? I'm gonna stop talking.

No Soulblade. Kellfyute's divine instrument, lost. What surer sign that The Author had abandoned her?

Ooh, that's good, actually.

Her unworthy, worthless—

Yes. Hold that thought.

The ground pulled out from under her, and Kellfyute fell into the colorless nothingness of hell. The Author had abandoned her. Undeserving, she should feel nothing because she was nothing. Yet, she felt sorrow, regret, fear.

She didn't want to wallow in non-existence forever, couldn't face becoming a shade. Had she not served Him well? Sacrificed everything?

Her fall ended abruptly as she slammed onto a glowing surface, the palm of a giant's hand, extended to catch her. Winded, she took a moment to recover, gasping, and came face-to-face with the awe-striking visage of her God. His beard, a brewing thunderstorm, swirled around her. His eyes were twin stars, and gazing upon Him was agony, for He was more beautiful than she'd ever dared imagine.

"Lord, You have not forsaken me. Thank You! Praise You!"

Her euphoria was short-lived, however. When He spoke, His words knocked her to her knees. "Kellfyute Erestes." He uttered her name as the filthiest two words in any language, living or dead, on any world. "Your failure sickens me."

"Please, Lord." She prostrated herself before Him, clasping her hands. "Don't abandon me. Grant me the strength to slay this demon! My life is yours."

"Indeed, it is," said the One True God. "And so I dispose of it."

His mighty hand clenched into a fist, swung back, and lobbed her into eternal darkness.

She faded into shadow.

Even she could not hear herself scream as she spun like a seed adrift in a gale, never to find purchase.

There was nothing left to her now, save fear.

The return to the material plane jarred Alina.

Exhaling, her shoulders sagged. She felt absolutely terrible in so many exciting ways, familiar and new. There was the usual nausea that followed spending a lot of Niima very quickly, and then there was this novel sensation of guilt at having broken the will of a fellow living creature as if she were a vending machine toy.

Alina looked down at the scarred arms of the body she now occupied—Kellfyute's body—and felt the phantom pain of every cut.

Raised voices just outside. Sanctumites approaching. Oh no.

Barely in control of a strange new form and exhausted, she was hardly in fighting shape. Her improvised combo of Ydeleh's Somnambulic Stride and Nirazlo's Perfect Suggestion had drained her almost to empty.

The longhouse doors burst open and the Sanctumites surrounded her.

She waited for them to notice something was wrong with their leader, to somehow intuit that Kellfyute wasn't feeling herself. But they seemed only concerned.

"We scoured the grounds, sister," one of them said, bowing his head. "The spies are nowhere to be found."

Play it cool, Alina. "No matter," she said, eyelids drooping, stomach churning, "for the demon is slain. Without its spirit, its body will wither." Knees shaking, she took an unsteady step.

"You're unwell," said Cronn. He took her hand.

Resisting the urge to jerk away from his touch, Alina said, "The battle was grueling. I will be fine, but I need rest."

"Should we not send for a healer?"

"No, I'll recover soon enough on my own. Just need to sleep it off." She remembered to add, "Praise The Author for our victory over the darkness this day."

She patted Cronn's wrist, which seemed to surprise and confuse him. Oops.

Then she took off. Like ducklings, the Sanctumites followed their mama outside. They walked the path that led under the waterfall spilling into one of the Sixth Stack's many lakes.

"I had full faith the Lord would watch over you." Cronn paused mid-stride, calling after her, "But?"

"What?" She spun around, glowering at him.

He winced, saying, "Our home. It's that way." He pointed in the opposite direction.

"Ah. Yeah. Yes. Got a bit turned around, there, didn't I?"

The other Sanctumites eyed her, still too fearful to stare. But she could feel their suspicions taking root like weeds in a brick wall. She'd have to channel more of Kellfyute. Drawing from the deep well of memories inside, she barked, "Don't you all have places to be?"

That snapped them out of it.

"Off to it then. Don't let me catch any one of you standing idle, not while there's the Lord's work to be done."

They all scurried off, all but Cronn. Straightening, curling his muscled, tat-tooed arms behind his back, he was waiting for something. Alina almost felt bad for the guy. He seemed to be trying so hard. But she had a part to play, and she planned to stick to it.

"Well?"

He cleared his throat. "Just wanted to wish you luck. It's three days from now, isn't it?"

"Yes," she slowly said. "It is."

"Are you nervous? I would be, in your shoes. Not that you'd be, though." He grimaced.

"Cronn." She took a long stride forward, locking eyes with his. "We are nothing alike."

"Of course. I'm sorry." A smile broke across his face like glass on pavement. "Will I see you tonight?"

"No. I have, uh—" she covered her stumble with a cough —"urgent matters. Elsewhere." She hurried away.

The longer the conversation carried on, the higher the risk. And piloting Kellfyute was becoming far too much of a strain. Not to mention, holding the line between their consciousnesses. If she dropped concentration on any of these tasks for even a moment, she'd be booted from her Sanctumite puppet.

Growing stronger by the moment, Kellfyute's will thrashed against Alina's. No time for anything but getting back to the Safehouse. She could only hope that Mezami had successfully dragged or air-lifted her own body away. The alternatives were to live as a ghost forever or permanently steal Kellfyute's life. Which would've been gross on both practical and philosophical levels.

Dashing through the cave under the waterfall, she spasmed and stumbled down the steps leading downtown. There, she drew concerned or amused looks from pedestrians and drivers all around her. Smoke rose from several intersections away, the area having been cordoned off by Authority tanks and soldiers. The flashing purple emergency lights reinvigorated her nausea. She focused her attention on her feet.

So dizzy.

There were way too many blocks between her and safety. She thought of calling Ivion or Cho, but her phone was with her *other* body. Doncha just hate it when that happens?

The Sanctumites she passed in the streets shouted greetings, but she ignored them. If she opened her mouth, she'd be sick. If they got too close a look at her flushed, clammy skin, they might stop her and ask too many questions.

Barely cognizant of where she was going, she vaguely registered the sensation of climbing stairs as her field of vision narrowed, like looking through the wrong end of a pair of binoculars. When she could see almost nothing, her fingers wrapped around the rusty rungs of a ladder.

The ladder to the Safehouse. "Thank Buthmertha for that," she breathed.

Like a death metal drummer at concert, pain struck up and down her verte-brae.

She began to climb.

30

BARAAM

H E HADN'T DREAMED OF Ruqastra in years. Not since those first lonely months at The Gild, in the wake of his decision to leave behind Dimas's School.

She'd walked in his dreams then, a novice Revomancer, begging him to return. "Little brother, little brother."

The stronger he became, the weaker her voice. She'd tried, off and on, to find him. Fed him images.

The goat and the coyote, drinking from a mountain creek.

An eagle circling overhead. Danger.

Return to the creek and the mountain, young goat.

With time, the coyote stopped coming; the creek ran dry. The mountain fell away from the horizon. The goat grew older. There were ever more eagles in the sky.

He hadn't dreamed of her in so long. Not since his sixteenth year, when she'd given up on him.

The mountain sprang into his dreams tonight. The creek overflowed—viscous, red. Screaming, an eagle swooped, tearing the bleating goat from the creek bed.

Baraam awoke and reflexively grabbed the lightning rod embedded in the floor of his room. He poured into it all his fear, his confusion. Thousands of volts, draining from him until only he remained. Sweat-drenched. Cold in the night.

Alone.

In the shaded garden terrace, the Sahamans of the Saludbabni hummed, eyes closed. The vibration ran through Baraam's entire body, his own voice indistinguishable from the others'. They were, in this moment, one.

The stillness of the afternoon's meditations, the embrace of their mothering Kadician desert, was interrupted, however, by the roar of engines. The sound preceded, by several minutes, the first glint of sunlight reflected off an approaching aircraft.

The Sahamans gathered outside, muttering to one another. Was it to pass them by? No, it slowed as it neared, making clear that whoever piloted the craft meant to land.

It touched down beyond the low garden wall encircling the compound, crushing several cacti and scattering a colony of desert mice. The roar ebbed to a highpitch, low-volume squeal. Then, silence; the dust settled.

Standing beside Baraam, Jija asked quietly, "Friends of yours?"

Baraam walked in front of the semicircle of Sahamans, the hem of his ragged robes dragging. He noted the decal on the aircraft's rear hatch. A white vase on a turquoise diamond. The emblem of The Gild.

The hatch slid up with a hiss, and eight figures quickly disembarked, all but one of them clothed in Gild turquoise and black. Six of the seven Gildsmen wore the tunics of Masters. The robes of the seventh—a thin-faced, silver-maned man of aquiline nose and jutting jaw—were much more lavish and ceremonial in nature; he was literally and figuratively a cut above the rest. The eighth and odd one out wore a sharp gray suit jacket in contemporary Elemental style, the neckline of his undershirt reaching almost to his hairless chin, the pins in his sleeves studded with jewels. His skin was rubbery, glistening, and blue-black spider veins interwove around his eyes.

The six masters, Baraam did not recognize; they must have been more recently promoted. The seventh he'd know anywhere as the most politically powerful Mage in the Nation of El.

"Gildmaster," Baraam said, dropping to one knee.

"Master bol-Talanai," said Pontifex Ridect. "Rise, lad. There is no need for such formality among old friends."

"To what do we owe the honor, sir?"

"Our voyage has been a long one. Uncovering your whereabouts took some doing. We are road-weary." His gaze swept across the Sahamans, and he smiled politely. "Perhaps we might discuss our business over afternoon tea?"

"Of course. Come out of the sun. Make yourselves at home."

Bearing their concern with practiced stoicism, the Sahamans set to the task of entertaining their surprise guests: speedily sweeping the courtyard stones, arranging their few cushions (they owned no chairs or divans), fetching pitchers of well water, setting out bowls of sun-dried tomatoes and dates and pecans.

In the common area, Ridect seated himself on the dusty pillows, cradling his sweating plastic water cup. Two of the Masters joined him on the floor, as did the man in the gray suit. Watchful, the others remained standing behind the curious Sahamans.

The Gildmaster thoughtfully chewed on a tomato or two, his eyes never leaving Baraam. Spitting the food onto his handkerchief, which he neatly folded, he said, "It is good to see you well, my boy. I feel no shame in admitting that, in the wake of your sudden retirement and disappearance, I'd feared the worst."

"I never meant to cause a stir."

"But that you did. I want you to know that you were never far from my thoughts, from all our thoughts. Some of our best men spent months searching. You were the greatest Aelfraver in El, one of our Nation's most invaluable Assets. How could we not see your suffering and grow concerned?" Ridect sipped at his water. "What possessed you to abandon us?"

Baraam had no answer to that question. None that he felt comfortable giving, anyway.

Ridect said, "I did not come here to needle you with guilt, lad. Please understand that, after all we've been through together, I think of you as one of my own children. Am I not deserving of the same respect and love you might show a mentor—a father?"

Baraam couldn't meet the man's eye. He thrust off the supportive hand Jija had placed on his shoulder.

The Gildmaster continued, "Alas, this isn't only a social call. Now, as always, but more than ever before, your country needs you. It commands your loyalty and summons your power to battle. I doubt you get much news living, as you do, among rocks and sand in this quaint, isolated province. So, I must inform you that the political and military quagmire in Ozar reaches its dramatic conclusion. The Aelf that have long run amok in that foul land festering with dark sorceries and demonic dealings—we have them cornered at last. They languish behind their final fortifications. Do you hear what I'm telling you, son? Centuries of strife, coming to a close."

"If it is a foregone conclusion, as you suggest, what need have you of me?"

"You were born and trained for a singular purpose, Baraam. You are an Aelfraver of unparalleled strength of will. And Ozar's final defenders are *Aelf*. Is it not obvious what I—what *El*—asks of you? Side with the right. Fulfill your purpose."

So. The Gild called on Baraam to kill again. It was always the same command: destroy. But, this time, he could only think of Alina.

Alina, whom he'd sworn to protect. A girl who, in some ways, felt more like his sister than Ruqastra did. A girl who was the progeny of Aelf.

The truth about Alina—and Dimas, his Master—had complicated everything. No, it had *ruined* everything for him. His life, his career, his purpose, swept from under him, and now he was falling. He'd already been thrown from the highest peaks of achievement, and still he fell, and there was no end in sight.

Yet, in the falling he had begun to learn to surrender. To lose himself to a will infinitely larger, a voice speaking through the cactus flower, the rattlesnake, the summer storm. This voice had, sometimes, in those rarest moments of peace, even spoken through Baraam. And, when it did, he found the strength to step outside himself, to remember something he'd never before learned: that he was nothing and everything all at once. That he could be whatever he wanted, if he only so chose.

But here returned The Gild. An abyss opened beneath him, and it now seemed to call him back to his old self. He grew confused: if the voice of creation spoke through all things, it must speak through the nothingness that awaited him.

He feared what he saw before him, down this road Ridect had offered.

All he wanted was peace, to spend his days contemplating abstractions, the health of the vegetable plants he nurtured, the warbling song of cicadas. And, still, he felt obligated to the Gildmaster, to whom he owed his life, his status and wealth, and the many glories of his Aelfraving past.

These conflicting desires paralyzed Baraam. He could not choose.

"Told you this was a waste of time," said the man in the gray suit, sneering.

"Should I desire to hear your opinion, Jejune," said the Gildmaster, "I shall ask you for it."

"Let's remember that, without my assistance, you would still be scouring the northern reaches of Xaveyr Province, checking every ditch in search of this pathetic excuse for a man. *I'm* the one who pointed you to Kadic and, specifically, this sandy armpit."

"Ignore him, son," said Ridect. "Uncouth though he is, Jejune has been of great service to The Gild and the Empire."

Something that had been bothering Baraam, a thought he'd been chewing on, soured in his mind. He spit it out: "Since when does our Gild involve itself in the Plutocracy's wars?"

Ridect raised his hand, eager to interrupt. "Is not the creed of the Aelfraver to slay Aelf? In this matter, the Plutocracy shares our goals of safety and prosperity for all humankind."

"Aelfravers are protectors, not soldiers," said Baraam. "Throwing Gildsmen into battle like pawns… They'll be killing humans in Ozar alongside Aelf."

"Those who choose to align with the Aelf can no longer be considered human."

An electric charge, the scents of petrichor, of ozone, filled the room. The hairs on Baraam's head and chin, as well as those of the Sahamans behind him, stood on end.

The Gildmaster sniffed. "Your time in hermitage has changed you, my son. This hesitation, it isn't like you. Where is the proud warrior, the flying avenger, he who annihilated Aelf scum beyond count?"

Through the window could be seen a line of dark gray clouds, like a formation of battleships, gliding over the horizon towards the Saludbabni. The weather service hadn't predicted rain.

"Baraam," Jija whispered. "You can say 'no.'"

His voice a whirlwind compared to his friend's soothing breeze, Baraam said, "He's still here, Gildmaster. The man you seek still lives."

Ridect smiled, setting down his water cup and popping a date into his mouth. Chewing, he said, "It enlivens me to hear it. If your spirit truly is not cowed by your extended absence from civilization, then you will recognize the needs of country and empire as greater than yours or mine. You have a gift, son, and you have frittered away too many months atrophying in this purgatorial retreat."

The clouds rolled forward. Flashes of lightning, the distant booming of thunder.

"You misunderstand me, sir. I am not agreeing with you, nor to anything you've said. For, you see, I am what I was—" Rising winds blasted open the shutters, which rattled and clacked against the walls—"but I am also someone else now. Between these two selves, a new man exists. Here, at the Saludbabni, I seek him. Myself."

"How poetic," said Ridect, unfazed by the gusts flinging cups and plates and chimes off their shelves and tables. "Even so, your self-serving quest will have to wait. As I have intimated, when tangled in the very fabric of history, it matters little what you or I or any one man may desire. Stop your childish flight from your responsibilities, and return to what made you who you are."

Jija said, "He's manipulating you, brother."

"But he's not wrong," said Baraam, sweat dampening his brow and his trembling hands. "I did swear to serve The Gild and humanity. If I break my word, it is worthless, and so I must be worthless."

"No oath binds you to this or any place. It is your choice. You are our brother, Baraam. We offer you a home without judgment. *We* will never tell you who you are. We trust you to discover it for yourself."

The wind howled now. Ridect shouted over it, "Do all those years of training mean nothing to you, son? Was I not a good master? Did I ever ask more of you than I knew you were capable of?"

"No," Baraam cried. Behind the Saludbabni and the parked aircraft, the sky darkened, and a tornado touched down.

Robes and hair buffeted by the gale, Ridect cupped his hands around his lips and yelled, "Everyone abandoned you, Baraam. Your parents, Dimas K'vich, everyone. Except me."

That was true. Dimas K'vich had used and betrayed him. Everything that disgusting creature had tried to teach him of virtue and wisdom—all lies. Leaving The School for The Gild had been Baraam's best decision: Pontifex Ridect had been a stern—often cruel—teacher, but his lessons had shaped Baraam into an invincible fighter, the greatest in the world.

His destiny. He'd forgotten himself, forgotten his oath to The Gild and the people of his country.

Still, some part of him resisted. It asked if the strength in his body and spirit needed to be turned to hunting and war. Could his hands not be those of a farmer, a potter?

He answered himself: duty, honor, oaths, and sacrifices; these were the only true constants in his life. Dimas, Alina, even Ruqastra—all people—were untrustworthy. Only his ideals, instilled in him by years of training and hardship, could be relied on. Fourteen-year-old Baraam had known this as he'd donned the blindfold and weathered the cane-strikes of his Master Ridect, losing his balance, getting up, falling again. And thirty-two-year-old Baraam knew it, too.

The black column of air above the Saludbabni retracted, swallowed by the clouds. The winds abated, humming rather than howling. Thunder crackled in the distance as Baraam rubbed a dirty hand across his face.

He looked to Jija, who said, "Always your choice." Then to Ridect, who smiled.

Baraam said, "As ever, I will serve."

The abrupt disappearance of the storm shaking their paralysis from them, Jija and the other Sahamans' expressions took on discordant shades of relief and grief as they collected the cups and half-empty bowls of food, tidying up.

Knees and elbows popping as he stood, helped up by one of the Masters, Ridect beamed at Baraam, saying, "I knew you would see reason." Gripping the back of Baraam's neck with surprising strength: "You're a tad thinner than before, but we have a tailor aboard who can make any needed adjustments to your uniform. And we certainly will have to get rid of that stringy mess on your head."

Without another word, without even a backward glance, Baraam allowed himself to be led outside and aboard the Gild aircraft. He was barely aware of the Sahamans standing by the wall to see him off.

There was some comfort in the total absence of emotion.

The aircraft was a luxury vehicle, equipped with the finest digital entertainment, top-shelf liquor selection, and other five-star amenities. Three flight attendants took care of his every want before he could even voice it, plying him with alcohol, smoothing the knots in his muscles, deafening him with hits from Sanzynna's latest album.

Though the flight lasted the better part of ten hours, for Baraam time moved neither quickly nor slowly. He felt locked in a constant state of *now*, where each moment was at once an eternity and a flicker of fire on a candlewick. Ridect's voice cocooned Baraam, deadened him to suffering and its estranged cousin, contentment. His thoughts drifted, often lingering on the Saludbabni—a dream, no more real to him than shadow puppets imitating life—before returning, always circling back, to his battles with the Aelf.

Ridect was right. Baraam was a man of war; the Saludbabni, a shrine to peace. He must never return.

31

CHO-ZEN

BACK AT IVION'S BUNKER, Cho entered the code and, when the electric locks released, she and Cbarassan slipped inside and shut the door behind them.

Scratching their tough forehead with a curled finger, the Aelf said, "It really isn't much, is it?"

"Yeah, it's a dump." Cho leaned in and whispered. "Also, I don't trust the dame who owns the place."

Cbarassan whispered back, "Then what are we doing here?"

Alina was nowhere to be found.

"Really thought she'd be back by now." Cho sat down, crossing her legs. "Or, like, left a passive-aggressive note. Something. Lemme try her phone."

It rang. And rang.

Then someone picked up; there was a lot of scuffling, thudding, and scratching as something bashed against the mic. Finally, she heard, "Greet: Cho, I."

"Mezami? Great to hear from ya, buddy, but why you got Alina's phone? She with you?"

"Yes: no, yes-and-no."

"Uh. What?"

"Bunker: almost, I. Ready: be, you."

After a rhythmic series of clacks, during which Cho imagined Mezami kicking the phone's screen as he tried to strike the "hang up" button, the call ended.

Turning to Cbarassan, Cho said, "So, not totally sure, but I'm thinking this is probably going to be one of those good-news-bad-news situations."

In awkward silence, they waited by the reinforced front door.

Sure enough, about twenty minutes later, there came a knock. Cho punched in the code yet again and flung the door wide to reveal Mezami. He gripped, by her collar, a wide-eyed, unblinking, blue-lipped Alina.

Cho screamed. "Is she—"

"Dead: not, she." With Cho's help, Mezami laid Alina's body down on one of the cots. "Fought: Sanctum, she."

"Aw, hells. She's, what, unconscious?"

"Elsewhere: spirit, hers. Body: save, I."

"So, just to be clear, we have *no* idea where she—where her soul is? Or, when—*if* she'll be coming back?"

Mezami scrunched his mousy face.

"Cool." Cho picked at her cuticles. "Awesome."

Felt like days. Was only two hours. Cho knew because of her perfect internal clock, but she still kept checking the time on Alina's phone anyway. Every three minutes on average.

This was her nightmare: stuck in a room, Kinneas imprisoned, Alina lost.

"It wasn't supposed to be this way," she said.

With her fingers, she'd closed Alina's eyes. Staring at the ceiling like that, they'd been seriously creeping her out.

After a while, from the corner, Cbarassan said, "Curious." Fixing their gaze on Alina's still form, they approached, kneeling. Their palms held an inch above the lifeless body, they traced an invisible outline, and their brow furrowed. They broke focus with some urgency, telling Cho, "You really ought to have mentioned."

"Mentioned *what?*" said Cho.

"Your friend—your Aelfraver friend—is an Aelf."

"Yeah… hah. I probably should have told you that. But it's kind of a life-or-death secret in her case, you know? I wasn't sure if I should go around putting up flyers about her being a hybrid. Where we're from, that's a pretty big deal."

"It is here as well, though we don't execute them like your barbaric Authority does. But, to be clear, she's not a 'hybrid,' as you called her."

"Well, but she said—"

Cbarassan interrupted. "For her to be a *hybrid*, there'd have to be some part of her that is human."

The gears in Cho's head spun at triple speed until what she'd just been told *clicked.* "Wait, so, she's—You're sure?"

"By the core of the Heart-tree and the roots of Malais, I am."

"Alina's not…? Like, not even a little?" Cho considered her friend's unmoving form. "Not at all?"

What was there to say to that? She couldn't process the information, so she set it aside, and she continued to check the time until the phone's battery gave out.

Not too long after, frantic banging on the front door of the bunker startled Cho into alertness.

Peeping through the hole, she did not recognize the thirty-ish-year-old woman standing just outside. Bald, scarred, and dressed in Sanctum grays, the stranger said, "Cho? Kinneas? Don't be weirded out, okay? It's me. I just, uh, look a little different. But it *is* me, um, Alina. Be chill, I'm coming in."

Whatever the word was for when anger, guilt, frustration, dread, confusion, and relief were all impossibly balanced inside a single human mind—that particular cocktail of emotions infused Cho's thoughts. And because she was Cho, she chased it with a poor and poorly timed joke: "Y'know, most people'd be happy enough with just the one body."

"Cho, I can't hold this spell much longer. She's pushing back."

"It's gonna be twice as hard to pick an outfit in the morning. Just sayin'."

"Cho! Outta my way."

"Okay, okay." Cho stepped aside, hearing the booping on the keypad. The door swung open a third time in as many hours, and other-Alina entered, turned to Cbarassan, and said, "Uh, hey?" To Cho: "Who the hells is this? How did they get in here?"

"Nice to meet you as well," Cbarassan muttered.

Other-Alina glared at Cho. "You *left* the bunker? And, you brought in some rando? You—I can't believe—What did you *do?*" Her whole body spasmed, and, catching herself, she said, "Never mind. There's no time. I'm gonna need you all to do something for me."

"But how do we know you're the *reeeal* Ali—"

"By Buthmertha, if you don't start taking this seriously, I'll—"

Cho nodded thoughtfully, telling Mezami, "Yup, it's her, alright."

"Great," said Alina. "Now, I need you to—and this is important, okay? I need you to tie me up. And, no matter what I say or do over the next two or three minutes, don't listen to me. Got it?"

"But should we listen to you *now*, or—"

"Tie me up, Cho!"

"Yeesh." Cho turned to Cbarassan. "So, looks like I hafta ask you to help me restrain my best friend, who seems to have body-snatched a total stranger."

The Aelf said, "Accessory to abduction. Joy. Do you do this sort of thing often?"

"Not, like, all the time, but enough to make it a recurring theme."

Mezami tossed a bag into the center of the room, tearing a length of extension cord from it. "Found: rope, I."

"I'll do you one better," said Cbarassan. From their arms and legs sprouted gnarled vines, which they tore off. "Use these. They're spell-made."

Cho blinked.

"Unbreakable, except by counter-charm," they explained.

Everyone else spent a minute or two binding the Alina-possessed woman's wrists and ankles using the magically grown vines. For good measure, they bound her arms to her sides as well.

As soon as she was tied up, other-Alina let out a long, shaky sigh. A change swept over the captive's face, sudden and jarring as winter wind sneaking under the hem of your shirt. The woman began to shriek and thrash, her struggle growing more and more violent as the seconds scraped by.

"In the Name of The Author, I'll unmake you all!"

Then, from the cot in the other corner of the room, a sputtering fit of coughing caused Cho to turn and rush to Alina—back in her own body—as she sat bolt upright.

"I'm beyond upset with you," she told Cho.

"Good to see you, too."

"She needs to shut up," Alina said, rolling to her feet and stumbling over to their prisoner. "Agh, my foot's asleep. Hate that." She shoved a sock in the hostage's mouth. To Cho: "We can't let her talk. She's a Maggo."

"I thought you said she's Sanctum."

"She is. And I'm tellin' ya she's *also* a Maggo. Powerful. Don't let her say a word."

"Li. Hey, hi. So, it's literally been only two days. What in the Seventy-Seven hells happened out there?"

Eyelids low, Alina released a tired chuckle. "Things may have gotten a teensy bit outta control, but once again my improvisational skills saved the day." She pointed a black-gloved hand at Cbarassan. "What's with the *Fyarda?*"

"Things may have gotten a *teensy* bit out of hand," Cho said, imitating her friend's flippant tone. "This is Cbarassan. They're kinda my warden? Caretaker? Representative rebel? Anyway, they're alright."

"First you run off when I told you not to. Then you bring back some stranger to our secret base? We're wanted women."

"Yeah, but now I'm internationally notorious, so guess I win."

Alina dragged her hands down her cheeks. "You drive me crazy with how irresponsible and—"

"Oh, sure. Because you've clearly made all the right choices." Cho stomped her foot near the squirming captive.

"Where is Kinneas?" Alina snapped.

"Where's Ivion?"

"Here," came a voice from the other room in the back of the bunker.

In an all-white, fur-collared jacket, Ivion sauntered into frame, forehead misty, eyes narrowed. She must have entered via the super secret trapdoor.

Her focus lingered on Cbarassan, who hissed under their breath while circling Cho. Opening a clear lane of attack.

Crossing her arms, leaning against the wall, Ivion put on full display the plasma pistol clutched in her right hand. "Would anyone care to explain what I've just walked into, or shall I start guessing?"

32

ALINA

STEADY HAND ON THE ivory-inlaid grip of her long-nosed pistol, Ivion said, "Who do you work for, Aelf?"

"The children of Ozar, born and unborn," said Cbarassan the *Fyarda,* "who are owed freedom."

"Anarkey, then." The staring contest intensified. The gun resting at her hip twitched. "A spy."

"I invited her here," said Cho.

"That was unwise. You don't know of what this creature is capable."

Cbarassan took a step. "If I desired your death, Elemental, we wouldn't be having this conversation."

Even though her limbs felt rubbery and all the blood rushed to her head, Alina dragged herself between them. "Yeah, you're both tough and scary." She stared Ivion down, saying, "Cho, d'you trust your new friend?"

"They could've had me killed a whole buncha times by now, and I'm still here."

"And where, exactly, is Kinneas?"

"The boy is with my comrades," said Cbarassan. "Safe. Recuperating."

"You'll have to do better than that," Alina said. Then, her fingers found Ivion's elbow. "Come on. Let's just talk this out." Turning to Cho and the Aelf again: "Tell me everything."

Tense, Ivion set down the takeout bag she'd brought. Mezami tore it, opening cardboard containers stuffed with spiced veggie burgers and kale chips.

Ivion's fingernails clicked against the wall, rapid-fire. For now, she refrained from any other kind of firing. She hung back, listening as Alina and Cho took turns recounting the events of the past thirty-something hours. They argued over which of them had set the new all-time record for Most Number of Near-Deaths in a Single Day.

Cho went first: scraps with Tranquilizers, following a gun-toting stranger to a second location, Kinneas's coma. The dam of Alina's silence threatened to burst.

Then it was her turn. Before she started, though, she knelt beside Kellfyute, waved her hand, and sent the Sanctumite off to sleep. Despite the presence of the *Fyarda*—from whom flowed a steady, raw Terramantic energy—Alina decided to spare no details. Keeping the group ignorant wouldn't make them any safer.

Once both stories had concluded, Ivion finally set her pistol down beside her as she sank to the floor. "Plutonia preserve me. What have you two done?"

The question lingered, Cho and Alina's eyes downcast. There was no answer, no defense. Sure, it seemed they'd each achieved what they'd wanted to some degree. But the cost had been high already, and they almost certainly weren't done paying.

The *Fyarda* spoke up. "*Krukkel.*" (Cho snapped to attention.) "You've spoken highly of your friend, and now I see why. Many are your secrets, each one more baffling than the last." They inclined their head toward Alina. "The Niima that flows from you... With so few Revomancers left to this world, your identity is obvious. You're Morphea, the Dream Queen."

Cho said, "Close, but not quite. This here's Alina."

"I'm—I was Morphea's student."

"Was?" said Cbarassan. Their expression, searching. "I see." They combed a rough hand through their reedy hair. "Well, her passing is disheartening news. I never met her, but her work was known to Anarkey and Ozar at large, wherever free peoples fight the Elemental fires."

Ivion scoffed.

"And if even half the stories of her ring true, then nothing she did in life lacked purpose and wisdom. If you are here, she had a hand in it. Any friend of Morphea's shall be mine also. Although, I must say I find peculiar the bedfellows you keep."

The *Fyarda* glared at Ivion, who said, "Not all Elementals are evil, *Aelf.*"

Swiftly as a tree swaying with the wind, the *Fyarda* ignored the jab and faced Alina. "Your friend has told me something of your history. The Aelfraver who doesn't kill. Instigator. Friend to Pyct—" They nodded toward Mezami, then Cho and Ivion—"and Plutocrat. You are a walking Contradiction." They bowed their head, covering their eyes with willowy fingers.

Something about the way Cbarassan emphasized the word "contradiction" didn't sit well with Alina.

The Aelf said, "Disciple of dream, I feel fate has extended a branch to shade our meeting."

Cho's upper lip wrinkled. "'Ey, what gives? Quit fawning over her, will ya? You came here with me."

"And I am delighted I did. Why, Cho, I speak of you as well. Don't you see? Bizong finding you when and where he did. Your leading me here. Our encounter, at the end of centuries of war. These moments transcend coincidence. We pull on the threads woven by the Hextarchs, unknowing of where they may lead, yet in full faith. I believe that, united, we will drive out the invaders."

Ivion snorted.

"I don't know about all that," said Alina.

"I came here to still Cho's heart on the eve of a pivotal battle." The *Fyarda* was taking care to be vague. They didn't trust everyone present. "But our meeting changes things. A debt demands Morphea's apprentice request of me a boon."

"You owed her a favor? Why?"

Cbarassan turned thoughtful. "Even in death, your teacher is owed her mysteries. She should rest secure in her power. But I can tell you that, for years, she served as spy and interrogator for both Anarkey and The Coven. Hundreds owe their lives to her intelligence. Therefore, one gift I offer. Anything within my power. And may it prove my sincerity beyond doubt. Or—" the Aelf's lips pulled away from their fangs in a lopsided grin—"you could look into my mind and see for yourself. Couldn't you?"

This didn't feel like a trap. Yet.

"Do I have your permission?" Alina asked.

Cbarassan nodded.

Closing her eyes, Alina took deep breaths, feeling herself stabilize. Her heart rate slowing, headache receding, she stepped inside the *Fyarda*'s mind.

She had expected to find the usual tangled web of random images and feelings. Instead, there were only a neutral emptiness and, at its center, a pool of fog.

Far more than Alina could manage, such stillness must have taken years of patient practice to achieve. How unusual.

Cbarassan's thoughts echoed through their mind-space. *Meditation. I do not control. I invite in, and allow to depart.* A pause. *Your questions?*

Is Kinneas Amming alive? Alina asked.

The fog assumed the form of Kinneas, unconscious in an old hospital bed, yellowed sheets draped over him. Though he looked rough, he was breathing.

Alina's relief gave way to curiosity. *Show me what you know about Morphea.*

Shifting again, the fog solidified into a figure cloaked in midnight, wearing silver gloves and a coyote mask. Her single golden eye flashed as she exchanged hushed words with a room full of Aelf and humans. They differed wildly in shape and size, their only common feature the yellow uniforms and blindfolds covering their eyes. Through the *Fyarda*'s memories, Alina knew these warriors—tall and muscled, or thin and feathered, or multi-headed and scaly. At least, she knew *what* they were, if not *who*.

"The Coven," she said, returning to herself.

What the Aelf had claimed was true. Ruqastra had been involved with Anarkey. Why? Did her purpose have something to do with Mateus? Had Dimas sent her here on a mission?

Cbarassan's memories made clear they didn't know the full story. To them, "Morphea" was just a war hero—focused, effective, one-dimensional.

Alina remembered her teacher as something else. Human. Replaying in her mind the bursting of Ruqastra's body into a thousand flecks of light, she wished they'd had more time.

She met Cbarassan's eyes, which rotated, the triple pupils oddly hypnotic. Their stare bypassed the physical world, triangulating on a fixed point inside Alina's soul. Faced with those questioning eyes, she felt renewed senses of urgency and guilt.

Now, she looked to Cho, who blinked.

Alina should never have let the kids come along. She had no means of protecting them.

Through Cho, Alina had learned the terror of loving someone—a sibling, a best friend—she'd inevitably lose. By bullet, imprisonment, or random accident, she saw Cho's end around every corner. How stupid of her to think hiding the girl in a *safe*house would keep her from harm.

Cho was so much like Alina in some ways, and so much tougher in others. But was Alina ready to let her fight—to become whoever she chose to be?

No, Alina decided. But she'd try. She had to try.

The reality was they both needed all the help they could scrape together, and, since Cbarassan was offering favors…

Would Alina regret trusting this Aelf? Maybe.

Indicating the unconscious, tied-up Kellfyute, Alina said, "I came here to settle some business with The Savior. A hard man to pin down. I got the body I needed to get started, but things didn't go the way I'd hoped. And I'd rather not break into her mind by force."

"Why?" said Ivion. "It would be the simplest way."

"Going in with permission, like I just did with Cbarassan, is one thing. But Kellfyute's put up thick walls. Even if I could break through, there's a chance I'd do permanent damage. I won't take that risk. Still, if I can't figure out where the Sanctumites have their get-togethers soon, it won't be long before someone— her husband or a friend—gets suspicious about her, uh, *my* weird behavior earlier today. Can't have The Savior getting spooked." Alina sighed. "Long-shot, but I'll ask: can you get me an audience with him?"

Cbarassan said, "Regretfully, I cannot. However, though the crow may fly straightly toward the light, it is the endarkened and indirect path that shall best serve her. The Coven holds the key to your entry into the heart of The Sanctum."

Ivion said, "Dark sorcerers. Demonic pact-keepers."

"Maggos. Are they like The Gild back home?" said Alina.

"Farthest from it. The Gild, though it certainly has its flaws, is an establishment founded on order, hierarchy, propriety. The Coven, by contrast, is a den of undisciplined fanatics."

"She speaks so surely," said Cbarassan, "for one who knows so very little. The Coven pursues power, but not for its own sake. And, indeed, the old ways and the dark ways are often one and the same. But is darkness evil? Are they who peer into it?"

"How could they help me find The Savior?" said Alina.

"As the closest servants of The Hextarchy—venerable guardians of lore and legend—to them the dust and gloom of forgotten time yields all secrets."

Cho cracked open a can of soda. "Those certainly were all words."

"So, they know stuff. What's in it for them?" said Alina.

"I know of many who would gladly meet a Terrestrial rebel, who flew from the paw of the wolf straight into its fangs. Yours is a story seldom heard in Ozar, a tale whose outcome is uncertain and, therefore, rife with hope. To honor Morphea's name, I will vouch for you."

"Are the Coven like you? Aelf, I mean?"

"Some. Only some, and fewer each season."

Ivion laughed bitterly. "Alina, don't fall prey to this sympathy act. They're a millenarian cult. Human sacrifice, blood drinking, doom-saying—such are their calling cards. They hate all things El. Their ruling cabal of six would tear the world apart if it meant killing us."

"Think what you will, Elemental." Cbarassan uttered that final word as if it were a curse. "That you are here, at this pivotal moment, can only mean one thing: the Hextarchs have a plan even for you. Though, what that plan entails..."

"I have had my fill of this." Ivion got up. Whipping out her tablet, her fingers skittered across the holographic keyboard. "I'm itching to be productive. Alina, please do what you need to in order to emulate that Sanctumite's identity."

Nodding, Alina placed *Rego* on Kellfyute's face. The mask vibrated and pulsated, multi-hued veins of crimson, auburn, and rust coursing from the brow to the beak. It changed, then, becoming a perfect replica of Kellfyute's peacefully sleeping face.

Alina backed away. "Done."

Ivion unzipped her travel bag, and a melon-sized metal ball drifted upward, hovering over Kellfyute. A ripple traveled across its surface, and from it sprang eight segmented limbs, latching onto the Sanctumite, wrapping around her tightly, and hoisting her.

"What're you doing?"

"Think. We can't leave any possibility for her escape. She could undo all our plans."

"Right, but where are you taking her?"

"For your own safety, and that of my contacts, I shouldn't tell you. Trust me, though. She will be treated humanely."

"You'll let her go then, once it's over."

Ivion winked.

Out of the corner of her eye, Alina caught Cho gagging.

"Be safe out there." Alina hugged Ivion.

"Take your own advice," said Ivion, pulling her in close enough to whisper. "Please. For my sake, watch your back around that Aelf."

They all watched the drone carry out and half-set, half-roll Kellfyute onto the back seat of Ivion's APC. Revving the engine, sliding the vehicle's gearshift into reverse, Ivion waved. Then, she peeled down the corridor to join the main flow of traffic a few hundred yards away.

The hours of stakeouts and chases caught up with Alina again. She could feel her body shutting down. Exhausted, she closed the bunker door. Looking from Cbarassan to Cho, she said, "In my place, would you meet with The Coven?"

"Eh." Cho wiggled her hand in front of her chin. "Sure...?"

The *Fyarda* remained impassive, their steady smirk revealing little.

Cho added, "Anyway, we both know there's no way you'd pass on the chance to tangle with a buncha—" in falsetto—"dangerous Ozari witches. Oooh!"

"A compelling point. Alright, Cbarassan, I'm game to head out basically whenever. When's good for you?"

"*Krukkel* and I have business to attend to tonight, and there are some preparations yet to be made. We ought to be on our way. Our social visit here took a little longer than expected."

"What've you gotten yourself mixed up with, Cho?" said Alina.

"I honestly don't know. But it'll hurt the Walazzins and make Anarkey our chums. That can only be good for us."

"Can it?" Alina thought a moment, yawning. "Obviously, you're not gonna listen to a word I say, and I can't stop you. Can I at least help with whatever you're planning?"

Cbarassan opened their mouth to speak, but Cho preempted them: "Nope. Got it covered. More than covered. We're great. How 'bout *you* kick it in the bunker a while? See how you like it."

"Sorry I asked." Alina yawned again, jaw cracking. Ironically, her dream magic hadn't allowed her any opportunities to rest. Feeling completely drained, she slouched across the room. As she slid into one of the cots, she told the *Fyarda*, "Keep my friend outta trouble. If I'm still dozing when you get back, just gimme a shake." She tugged the blanket over her head, and her eyes immediately closed. "Mezami, go with them just in case. You're the only one of us that's reliable."

Then she thought she'd heard Cbarassan say, "I'll swing by tomorrow. Provided I'm not dead." But she must have misheard.

"Same," she murmured, already asleep.

She dreamed Kellfyute's dreams.

Knees raw on concrete. Eighth consecutive hour of prayer. A saint died tonight. Repent, repent…

Cat o' nine tails. Strike his back first, then he does mine. So, we purify ourselves. I love him, I think. I wish he were with me. The barbs dig deep. Thus: Gone, all desire. Cleansed. Made clean again….

Our column of pilgrims marches through the jungle. The village lies that way. One of our number falls to a snake bite. His will be Nehalennia, to kneel forever in the glow of the Lord. I can only pray that, one day, such light finds me…

The Author calls the faithful to the final battle. Judgment falls upon Ozar. It is as the saints foretold. To have been blessed with a life in this time—at the end of all worlds—

Her face awash in tears of ecstasy, Alina woke. She felt dry as an old sponge.

She lumbered toward the fridge, heavy-limbed, and snapped the cap off a bottle of water.

Two bottles later, she collapsed back into her cot.

The dreams resumed.

33

CHO-ZEN

A BARRAGE OF GUNFIRE weakened the ground-floor windows of Revelation Studios on the Sixth Stack. Hammers did the rest. The two guards in the lobby had died before realizing they were under attack. Through the building's shattered facade, Anarkey entered.

Revelation Studios was an Authority-backed operation putting out a constant stream of pro-Elemental and pro-Sanctum propaganda. As the rebels poured into the lobby, wall-mounted Watchboxes broadcast the hateful rants of "cultural experts," "political commentators," and "economic insiders." They all conveniently shared a single opinion about Ozar: it was a haven for evil that must be cleansed. Furthermore, The Author had appointed The Authority and The Savior as His destined, divine instruments of justice in this "righteous war."

There it was, Cho thought. That word again. Justice. That was her word, but people kept stealing it from her, watering it down until it drowned in meaninglessness.

Cbarassan took Cho by the hand, dragging her onward. Bizong bellowed commands to his twenty fighters, who fanned out and sprayed bullets at anything that moved. Clerks, messengers, interns, and other employees of Revelation fled before the shrieking rebels, dashing into corners and hallways. From ceiling-mounted speakers tinkled the blandly soothing tones of Sanzynna's latest hit—

His Radiance (Lay Me Down): the crew upstairs kept playing the scheduled programming. Even once the killing started.

Cho reeled at the sight of so much blood, the screams of the wounded echoing in her perfect ears. Shock was all she felt.

She hadn't known what to expect. Any resistance movement capable of giving The Authority even the least bit of trouble, she'd figured, had to be serious.
Still. How had she come to this point?

So far, she had lived three separate lives: her warm, comfortable earliest days,
barely more than a memory; the middle years, bouncing between being
Wodjaego Walazzin's bride-to-be and a sticky-fingered thief; and, the most recent stretch, hanging with non-violent, vegan Alina. Death had stalked Cho since
before she'd lost her first milk tooth. However, for all her talk, she didn't know
if she could go through with it—stick her knife in someone with intent to end
them.

Clearly, she was the only one here with that problem.

Led by Bizong and his sawed-off shotgun, Anarkey shot their way through
the office, blasting anyone who stood between them and the top floor. Cbarassan
and Cho stuck to the rear. The *Fyarda* proved they didn't need protection when
a security officer rushed them, and their fingers hardened and extended instantly,
spearing the man's chest.

The remaining guard teams attempted to surround the intruders, but were
cut down by blade, bullet, and grenade.

The smoke cleared. Just like that, the first wave had been shredded like wheat
in a grist mill.

Finally, the recording of Sanzynna and her mediocre acoustic guitar-playing
cut out. Mere minutes after busting in, Anarkey took the main stairwell, pushing
past fleeing sound engineers, camera crews, and pretty, teary-eyed Watchbox
personalities.

The rebels broke into the now vacant main studio and got to work.

Cbarassan and some others barricaded the doors and posted up by the windows overlooking the street. Bizong hauled the cameras into position, angling
them for a full view of the desk at the center of the crescent-shaped stage. A trio
led by Ilai (one of the humans, who made up fifty percent of the party) tore open
the computers in the control room. Without being told, Cho recognized that
they were rerouting—or reversing—the direction the airwaves would travel.

Revelation existed to funnel El's news and entertainment directly into local
home and office Watchboxes. A one-way arrangement. Anarkey, however, intended to unshackle the transmission, sending it to everyone in Ozar and the rest
of the world. To do that, they had to trick the computers into thinking this station was located in New El (where all approved programming originated). The
phony signal would then be sent along a vertical shaft drilled through miles of
solid rock, up to a relay station on the surface, which would broadcast it across
the planet—from The Capital to the colonies and beyond.

Cho stared at the desk. The three sheets of paper crunched in her tightening fist.

"Nerves?" said Cbarassan.

Grip slack, Cho's arms numbed. "*Chuh.*"

The *Fyarda*'s hand found her shoulder. "Show me the overly confident girl who infiltrated a military communications tower by herself." They leaned in, whispered, "The Plutocrats tried to silence you, but couldn't. You are free. You are here. And your face will become a weapon more powerful than ten thousand bombs." They patted her back.

For the benefit of everyone present, Bizong barked, "This is our chance to arrest the whole world's attention." To Cho, "Make them eat your anger."

"So many dead," Cho murmured. She could still see the shredded paper, the sprays of blood, the sparks of electricity as light bulbs burst.

"This is war, and it demands sacrifice. Did you suppose those who worked here innocent? Here? The invaders' lie factory? These people may not have been soldiers, but neither were they schoolchildren, blind to the evils of their cause."

Cho said nothing.

"They fight for gain; we, for freedom. Simple. There is no comparison. We are in the right, so we fight, and we die. For justice."

Justice. Everyone laid claim to it, but to whom did it belong? Chasing it had nearly cost Cho and Kinneas's lives, and dozens more had died on the way to this moment. But Bizong was right, wasn't he? This was war. And Cho hadn't been the one to start it. The Walazzins had, that night they'd butchered her family. Surrendering to her doubts would be a betrayal of the Torvirs' memory.

Propping open the control room door, Ilai gave the thumbs up. "We're good."

Bizong patrolled the area, checking the windows, the doors, watching the ceiling. "I give it five minutes," he told Cbarassan.

"More than enough." They clasped his shoulder. "For the Hextarchy and the *Razenzu.*"

He growled through his gas mask. "For the *Fyarda.* For Ozar and all the races culled by murderous imperials. *Krukkel,* it's time."

Cho nodded, swallowing. Her mouth was suddenly filled with cobwebs, her limbs leaden, but she somehow made it to the desk, seating herself in the rolling chair behind it. She uncrumpled the papers on which had been written her speech as Ilai counted her down. "Five, four, three..."

He held up two fingers, then one.

A little green light flicked on above each of the cameras facing Cho. The stage lights were blinding. Sweat ran down her temples. She thought of Eilars.

Staring at the green light, she dragged her voice from her throat like a two-ton stone slab: "A-Assets of El, Terrestrial and Elemental; citizens of the world, human, Noble, and Other. You don't know me because my survival has been kept from you. My existence is a secret protected by murderers and thieves. To-night, I break their silence. Tonight, I tell you the truth about the men you call your masters. I am Choraelia Rodanthemaru Dreintruadan Shazura-Torvir, daughter of Faundasim and Levanil Torvir and heir to Torvir Province. My birth-right was stolen from me by Wodjaego Walazzin, the man who governs you as Consul. Like him, I was born to a life of privilege, safety, and complete material excess. Like him, I lived easily where so many across our world suffer for the luxuries of the few at the top." These were not her words. Cbarassan and others had written them. But, deep down, they felt right. "Unlike Mr. Walazzin, how-ever, I have changed. *He* changed me that night, in the year 3497, seven years ago, when he ordered my parents' assassination, when he took for himself eve-rything that was mine by right." Where, when she'd started, her voice had wa-vered, now she spoke boldly. "I owe him so much—including a dagger in the gut—" She saw Cbarassan waving frantically, silently demanding she stay on-script. "He, he—I've learned, since his betrayal, that the world is more compli-cated than it seemed to me as a child. Now, my eyes are opened to the truth, which I share with you all."

The window beside Bizong shattered, and he spun around, shouting, "Con-tact!" Pulse and ballistic rounds scythed through the air. The rebels rushed to the windows, returning fire. "The door!" one of them cried. "They're ramming the door!"

Heart pounding, Cho continued. "Wodjaego Walazzin is only part of a larger problem. He's only one tumor in a cluster, a whole cancerous web spreading across, beneath, and *above* the surface of our world. The Authority pollutes the skies, the land, and the underworld with its venom."

Raised voices—Tranquilizers—could be heard all around. They hadn't bro-ken inside just yet, but the rattle of their gunfire and the whine of their emerald pulse rounds tore through the recording studio. The tinkle of falling glass, flames blooming on the curtains.

Recoiling, Bizong cried out. Orange gas leaked from the tank on his back. Cbarassan rushed over to him, plugging the crack with a rag.

"Keep going," Ilai told Cho. His expression was stoic, his eyes unblinking.

"The war in Ozar," Cho said, voice faltering again. She shouted over the din of battle, "This invasion of Ozar is only the most recent act of aggression. The Elemental Empire has spent every century of its existence breaking its neighbors and other nations across the globe. Now, only Ozar remains."

The pounding on the door grew in volume and intensity, the desks and chairs piled in front of it rattling. Grunting and shouted orders accompanied the rhyth-mic thump-thump-thump of a battering ram.

Still, Cho continued. "The Elementals, my former people, are corrupt, selfish. And you have this chance, this one chance to rise up. Join Anarkey. Fight with us. Wherever in the world you call home, whatever your race, species, religion— stand with us. Because if Ozar falls—if we fall—the Elementals will own the world, and there will be none left to stop them. I am the heir of the Torvir Family—" Gritting her teeth, she went off-script one last time—"and, if you're hearing this, you are the resistance."

There'd been more paragraphs to follow, but several explosions rained pieces of ceiling on the news anchor desk, concluding her speech. She fell backward as the lights cut out. The barricade and door behind it burst open. Flashlight beams intersected in the dark, followed by muzzle flares.

A mass of white-and-black-uniformed Ivoirs, green-and-blue D'Hydromels, and other Tranqs piled into the studio, and what started as a firefight quickly devolved into a melee. Cbarassan swung her arms back and forth, stabbing, wrapping her enemies in vines, pulling them up toward the ceiling, skewering them. Bizong fired two shells, then drew a hatchet from his belt. Ilai and the others threw themselves at the Tranqs from the sides. Cho thought better of pulling her knife. She jumped forward, bounding off the back of one of the downed Tranqs, driving her knee into the next one's helmet.

She heard a click behind her. Without knowing why or even what she did, she rolled to the side—missing a bullet by an inch. Unthinking, she swept the legs from under her assailant, kicking him while he was down.

More than once, Eilars's chip saved her from bullets, bayonets, flying elbows, and fists.

Her perception of the brawl was flawless, she anticipated every strike and shot, and positioned herself ideally. It wasn't so much that time slowed down. Rather, every second was now long enough for her to accomplish what she needed to, dodging, striking, shoving aside. Because of her heightened awareness, however, she also saw and heard—too clearly—the death rattles and cries of terror, every single casualty. By boot, blade, or bullet, the Tranqs were each finished off as they fell. Anarkey was dying too. People Cho had talked to on the way over. People whose names she knew.

A nauseating weight pressed on her stomach. Only her spiking adrenaline kept her from being messily sick.

The chaos seemed as though it would never end—until, suddenly, the fight was over.

On shaky legs, Cho stood, surrounded by the bloodied dead. Now, the Tranquilizers were all, well, tranquil. Except one, who wheezed in the corner, under a table. Bizong put him out of his misery.

Then he turned to the rebels. "To their great misfortune, the enemy has underestimated us once again. But there will come more of them. Time to move."

Even as her heightened awareness faded, Cho noticed the slouch of his shoulders, the flushed, reddening color of the scales on his face and neck. "Bizong, you're hurt."

"My sulfur tank's pierced."

She grabbed his elbow, catching him as he slumped. "Let's get you back to base, patch you up." She glanced at Cbarassan, who shook their head.

"*Krukkel*," the *Razenzu* grunted, straightening. "My gear's materials are so rare they may as well be… irreplaceable." He drew a shallow breath, voice cracking. "The art once used to craft them, all but forgotten. My end will come in minutes."

"No," Cho breathed. "Just slap some tape on the glass or something. Come on, man!"

Grabbing her by the shoulder, Cbarassan dug their claws in enough to startle, saying, "To the *Razenzu*, oxygen is poison. Lethal. Already, his cells are beginning to rupture." She thumped her fist against Bizong's chest. "Let him pass with pride."

The rebels gathered round, heads bowed. Haltingly, Bizong told them, "Make for the service tunnel. Follow it to the same cistern as before, but take a right this time. Go the long way."

Anarkey's survivors, including Cho, each put a hand on Bizong's shoulder, head, back. He closed his eyes.

A moment later, the huddle broke.

As one, they raced down the stairs, through the lobby, and out of Revelation Studios.

The streets blazed with violet emergency lights. Sirens screeching, three armored personnel carriers tore onto the sidewalk, lurching to a stop, their rear doors swinging open.

Because of her new chip, Cho counted instantly that there were dozens of Tranquilizers incoming. The rebels wouldn't stand a chance. They'd be trapped and shot to pieces.

However, one of the APC doors slammed shut, then, trapping a few of the Tranqs inside. The rebels hunkered down, searching for the cause.

Cho blinked, spotting a tiny, blue, mouse-shaped bullet with wings just as he caved the side of a second truck inward. His fists warped the steel as easily as tinfoil.

Mezami had been tasked with covering Anarkey's retreat. As always, his timing and style were flawless.

The rebels used the distraction to rush into the street and away from The Authority reinforcements.

Mezami paused upon seeing Bizong limp toward the enemy, alone. The Razenzu swatted at him, roaring, "Go!" shooting in the general direction of the second wave of Tranqs as they leapt from their vehicles. No great precision required. There were so many.

The Pyct hesitated another second, until Cho shouted, "Mezzy, this way!"

Fingers like thorn bush branches wrapped around her wrist, Cho was yanked away by Cbarassan.

The rebels emptied their clips and magazines in the direction of yet more advancing Authority transports. They lobbed entire belts of grenades, retreating under cover of flying shrapnel.

Bizong charged the Tranqs, firing wildly before tossing his shotgun aside. Empty-handed, he charged.

Over the rattle of machine gunfire and the screams of onlookers and the rush of her own unsteady breaths, Cho heard his last words—a defiant scream: "With joy."

The Authority brought him down with a final volley of bullets, several of which struck the gas tank on his back. The tank burst, and the explosion tore through the amassed soldiers' ranks, their wails drowned out by the groan and crunch of metal as several APCs were thrown through the air onto their sides.

Glancing over her shoulder, Cho saw only a flower of flame, spewing sprigs of sickly, yellowish smoke.

34

JEJUNE

THE PRIVATE JET ROARED across the sky at three times the speed of sound. Its only passenger, Mr. Jejune, held a holopad in one hand, charting the latest dips and climbs of the stock market index. In the other, he gripped the dainty stem of a crystal glass, ferrying sips of sparkling white wine to his bleeding lips.

He had concluded his business with Gildmaster Ridect and ex-Number One Raver Baraam bol-Talanai, placing another deliciously volatile game piece onto the board. Now, he tapped the semi-transparent blue display projected from the holopad, initiating a call.

"Captain?" said Mr. Jejune. "Captain, can you hear me? I think we have ourselves a spotty connection. Hold on, I'll face northeast, see if that helps."

Captain Tiberaira's response was hardly more than a whisper over the rustle of static. Even Jejune had to strain to hear her say, "Shut. Up."

"It's just that, I've been looking over your stats, and I spotted a bit of a trend that gave me pause. Thought I might bring it up with you to clear the air."

"Not. A. Good. Time."

"Yes, now I can hear you a bit better. Anyway, I'd like to discuss your weekly Pray-to-Plutonia hours. The past few days, your unit's seen a collective drop of twenty-two percent of Penance Points accumulated, with you, personally, slipping by a startling twenty-*seven* percent. Collectively, that means the Cutcords are underperforming by roughly eleven percent this week. I do hope you're not trying to make me look bad."

"Quiet." Tiberaira's voice was a low growl. "I have her."

"What's that now?" His eyes widened with glee. "The girl? Choraelia? She's dead?"

"Not. Yet." Pause. Shuffling, as if Tiberaira were crawling. "Have her in my sights. Report later. Cutting connection."

"Captain! Hang on! Where is she? Where have—"

The line crackled. The call ended.

"She hung up on me." He swirled his drink around in his glass before hurling it across the cabin. The crystal shattered, a shower of shards and sparkling wine.

Rubbing his temples, he told himself, once again, that all was well as long as the good captain got the job done. How it happened didn't matter.

Even now, nooses slipped over the heads of rebels and upstarts the world over, and soon the weary throat of the last threats to the Empire's prosperity would be choked into eternal silence. And, especially with that irksome Torvir stray put down, the wolf packs would battle one another, the victor culling the herd of sheep—a bloodletting in accordance with the Master's grand design, solidifying His all but supreme control.

Upon the conclusion of his part in this grand drama, Jejune promised himself, he would seek out Tiberaira and pry out her insolent tongue. Perhaps he'd devour her soul himself; perhaps he'd leave its refuse for his lessers. He'd just have to see how the moment struck him.

Through the oval window to his right, he watched a trident of lightning spear the clouds. The supersonic jet sped him to Ozar, where one era would end, and another begin.

Imagining Choraelia's sad blubbering as she bled out in a gutter, he smiled.

35

CHO-ZEN

BIZONG. GONE.

Although they'd hardly known each other, Cho felt his loss, but there was no time to mourn him and the others now.

Authority aircraft beamed spotlights down at the fleeing rebels. Search-drones weaved through the alleys like rats through a maze. Soldiers on hovercycles and APCs stuffed with strike teams sewed up the streets. All these, Anarkey could handle. They knew the Sixth District better than anyone else alive, and quickly shook off The Authority.

With one exception. A lone Tranquilizer, chasing the rebels. Gaining on them.

Cho wondered if she and Cbarassan would ever stop running.

"Just shoot them already," shouted one of the human members of Anarkey.

"No. We're being baited," said another.

"Split up. They can't catch us all."

How comforting.

The rebels paired off and fanned out, Cho sticking with Cbarassan. Mezami flew ahead to scout their shortest course back to the sewers.

A backward glance showed the Tranq chasing them hadn't slowed for even a second, ignoring every pair except for Cho and Cbarassan's.

"Friend of yours?" said the *Fyarda*.

"Could be after you."

"If they were after me, a non-human, I'd be dead. They're not shooting, so they must want you." Cbarassan flashed their habitual grin, the rush of air whipping tears from their eyes. "My, you have been making waves lately."

Focusing, Cho scanned her stalker, analyzing their body type, the weight of their footfalls, any and all details that might reveal who they were. Her face hidden behind a gleaming metal helmet, the Tranq was a woman, muscular, with several cybernetic prosthetics—arm, jaw—and artificial organs. The prolonged chase hadn't winded her in the least.

Cho thought of herself as being in pretty good shape, having done combat training and eaten mostly homegrown, nutrient-rich foods every day for two years. Even so, she was starting to tire. The scary woman, however, was not.

Mezami returned, offering to take the Tranq out. Cho told him to hold off. There was something about this soldier she couldn't place. In her experience, mystery usually meant hidden danger. Mezami might get hurt. Besides, because of his speed, he could flit ahead and back every thirty seconds to warn Cho and Cbarassan of oncoming obstacles like Authority patrols, roadblocks, and crowded side streets. That should give them enough of an edge to lose their pursuer.

Cho tried every trick she could think of—leap-frogging stacks of boxes, sliding under small gaps in fences, cutting through shops, jumping over rooftops two stories up. Nothing worked. The Tranq only gained, popping out of sidestreets, rolling under awnings and fizzing power lines, and hopping walls on her long, springy legs.

"Leave me," Cho said. "If it's me she's after, leave me."

"I refuse."

The Tranq was so close now that Cho could hear her powerful, steady breaths, which kept time with the slapping of her boots against the pavement only half a dozen feet behind.

"Just go," Cho yelled. "I can't have you dying for me."

"Likewise," said the *Fyarda*.

"You stubborn, dumb—"

She had an idea. Time for a gamble.

The Tranq shouted, "Choraelia Torvir! Wait!"

Then Cho Zero-Oned herself—splitting her awareness into two pieces. The first controlled her body, continuing to propel her forward. The second soared toward the Tranq, sweeping over her like a whisper of frost at the onset of winter.

Seeking accessible data nodes, Cho found one in the woman's artificial lung. It, like all smart organs, had an internal chip to regulate its functions—in this case, temperature and oxygen flow.

Cho disabled that chip.

The Tranq gasped and buckled against a nearby wall. Though the upper half of the woman's face was covered by a visor, Cho imagined her wide-eyed shock with satisfaction.

The Tranq was out of commission.

A few quick and confusing turns later, Cbarassan, Cho, and Mezami came to a heavy iron grate. The Pyct pried it open, replacing it behind them as they entered the sewer tunnels. He then perched on Cho's head.

They waited in darkness, listening.

When almost twenty minutes had passed without incident, confident they were no longer being followed, they trekked through the tunnels toward the floodgate nearest the rocky, spiraling road that would return them to Anarkey headquarters.

A magical orb hovering over Cbarassan's palm lit the way. "Most impressive, how you managed to incapacitate our tail."

Cho followed the glow. "Wrong day, wrong girl."

36

ALINA

DREAMS WERE THE PUTTY—the building materials—of Revomancers. One of the first skills every student of Revomancy learned was lucidity—full awareness and control of the unconscious self.

It had taken Alina a long time to get the hang of this trick, and it'd been even harder to extend that awareness and control to *other* unconsciousnesses. Now, asleep, she did her best to learn as she went, organizing the jumbled mess of Kellfyute's thoughts, emotions, and fears she'd scooped into one big mental bag and run off with like a cartoon bandit.

To act the part of Exorcist, Alina needed more info.

Having taken the Sanctumite's face and inhabited her body, even briefly, a sliver-thin stamp of her consciousness had been imprinted in Alina's own mind. Alina combed through it for any leads regarding The Savior and his plans for Ozar. However, the downside of tapping into the unconscious was the mixed signals: whatever was foremost on the mind of the spell's victim would be the most strongly transferred. Alina's internal vision, therefore, was clouded by a constant stream of images and feelings conveying doubt, terror, guilt, and rage—the emotions of a Sanctumite higher-up, laid bare.

The pointlessness of her attempts to sort through that mess became obvious after a few hours. It would've been easier to hand-glue a giant glass sculpture dropped from a tower onto concrete.

The Crow stepped out of the smoky visions, dispersing them. Alina gave up for now.

As she knocked out another set of handstand push-ups, the Crow stood over her, silently counting her reps with its long, clawed, curling digits. Eight, nine, ten...

Kellfyute. Alina's dumb mistake. She'd let her guard down. There shouldn't have been any Maggos among the Sanctumites—let alone ones who could see astral projections—but she should've been more cautious. Magic, by its very nature, defied the reasonable, logical, and possible. Any sensible Revomancer remembered that the more power one had, the likelier it would attract attention.

Right side up again, Alina rolled her shoulders and cracked her neck, falling into a push up. The Crow sat cross-legged on the small of her back. One, two, three...

At least now Kellfyute was Ivion's problem, which was partly a relief, partly another source of guilt. Stealing an identity, a life—it didn't matter who it belonged to—that regret wriggled around Alina's gut like indigestion.

Twenty-nine, thirty, thirty-one...

Off somewhere with that Cbarassan character, Cho didn't come back that night. Alina struggled to drive the big-sister angst from her brain, but couldn't.

There was more to the *Fyarda* than they let on. They could be centuries old for all anyone knew. And they were so far from their home in the Four Isles. What had brought them to Ozar, and what did they want with Cho?

Making partners of Anarkey could be greatly beneficial. There was, after all, truth to the adage, *the enemy of my enemy is my friend*. But, equally true, *the enemy of my friend is my enemy*. How many enemies would Cho make for herself in joining her cause to Anarkey's?

On the other hand, Alina distrusted almost everyone and had very little to show for it.

Cbarassan had offered her a branch, and, despite her better judgment, she wanted to take it. There was something about the *Fyarda*. A feeling. A sort of calling...

She could almost hear Ruqastra's voice, exasperatedly reminding her that Revomancers had to trust the little pings of their unconscious—signals from their deeper selves. Dream-walkers guided their own steps.

One-hundred and fifty-seven, one-hundred and fifty-eight...

The Sanctumites hated and longed for the eradication of all Aelf, and therefore any Aelf should be inclined to help Alina make trouble for The Sanctum. She and Cbarassan didn't have to be friends to be useful to one another. That would have to be enough for now.

The Crow lost count of her reps.

Sweating, she grabbed a family size bag of chips, popped it open (scattering pieces everywhere of course), and began to simultaneously snack and "meditate," which was code for "enter a mini junk food trance." *Snackitating.*

She was just killing time until Cbarrassan showed up to escort her to The Coven, where supposedly she'd find help in locating her uncle.

Mateus. What was he after?

Alina sealed the bunker door behind her and stepped into the street.

Cbarassan sported fresh cuts, glittering green blood oozing from under bandages on their shoulder and cheek.

"Do I want to know?" Alina asked.

"That depends."

"Just tell me Cho's alive."

"She is."

Unable to resist, Alina pierced Cbarassan with her gaze, and saw *flashes of explosions, gunfire, a pitched battle. Running, being chased, peeling off in different directions, diving into the safety of the shadows as the searchlights cut across the streets. The fearful stillness, the hum of their pulses, as they waited for the drones to pass by.* The images were grainy and shaky, as if captured by a sprinter's handheld camera; Alina wasn't as proficient at thought-snatching as Ruqastra had been. Even so, she'd just gotten a pretty strong taste of last night's events involving Cho and her new Ozari rebel friends.

In the alley, around Alina, the shadows intensified. "You brought her into danger," she said. Above her, a row of light bulbs exploded. "Was it worth it?" A manhole cover popped up, rolling into traffic. "Whatever you all did?"

The *Fyarda* hardly flinched. "Worth it?" If they knew their mind had just been read, they didn't show it. "My last friend is dead. So, no, of course none of this has been worth the cost. Not by a mile. But, was it necessary? Will it make a difference? Absolutely. Last night, a bell tolled for the Empire. They don't yet know it, but their end is nigh. Your friend Cho is a remarkable young woman. You are lucky to know each other."

Alina deflated, and the shadows retreated, returning to their natural shapes.

"You love her," Cbarassan said. "Though I have not felt it in a lifetime, I too have known this kind of love. Take it from me, you must water it with trust, or it will wither."

"I'm only trying to protect her."

"Are you? Of what value is a life lived without conviction? And how could she hope to discover hers if you steer her every move?"

"What would you call what you're doing with her?"

"She came to us by following her passions."

"'Passions' that'll get her killed."

"Possibly. However, death may come at any time and by any way."

"You're only defending her behavior because it's useful to you. Stop pretending you know her better than I do."

"*You* act as if you know her better than she herself could."

Words crowded the tip of Alina's tongue, shoving each other aside. The struggle for a strong answer left her speechless.

"Go on then. Be cross with me if it will ease your conscience. Your anger won't sway the truth, nor will it change what you do next. You will follow me because you desire my help. Isn't that so?"

Alina fumed, but then she took a breath.

The *Fyarda* allowed the silence to grow and flower. "Your friend will find her way. In the meantime, she has done extraordinary things. If only you could see that. Ah, well. Perhaps, with your assistance, Aelfraver Alina, we'll deal another blow to the Elementals—a slow-burning but ultimately fatal one."

She grunted. "Just take me to The Coven. We'll see from there."

They began to walk.

"You do not trust me," said Cbarassan, revealing their fangs with their narrow-eyed smile.

"Am I that bad at hiding it?"

"On the contrary. You are not easy to read. A product of what you are, it may be."

"And what am I, in your eyes?"

"A mage. A rebel. Like me." They shrugged. There seemed to be more, but it went unspoken. "Pity that the current of sympathy between us flows only one way."

"Sorry. It's not you. Not totally, anyway. I—let's just say I haven't had a lot of healthy relationships. For some reason, Cho trusts you. I will try to."

"That will be necessary soon enough." They turned away, walked off at a brisk pace. "I've let Hexhall know you're coming. As it happens, there's someone inside who's quite anxious to see you."

"Who?" Alina jogged to catch up.

Cbarassan chose not to answer.

"Who?"

Oh, no, they weren't getting away with this bogus cryptic garbage. She flexed her mind-reading muscle—the process easier and smoother every time—hooking her mental talons into the *Fyarda*.

After a moment, they said, "Find what you're looking for?"

"No," she grumbled. Once again, she saw only what Cbarassan wanted her to—this time, a towering light, humanoid in shape, but filling the full breadth of even her imagination. Pressed against this titan—forehead to forehead—was a being of equal scale. They struggled forever, perfectly balanced in power and influence. And between them—minuscule, a mote of dust beside these forces—stood a man. In the vision, he drifted closer and closer, hands outstretched. The dark in one, the light in the other; he wielded both.

He was the sword and the scabbard, the drawing and the sheathing. He was the breath of the dying caressing the cheek of the newborn.

Alina blinked the sweat from her eyes. "What is the Achemir?"

Now Cbarassan did pause. "I rather hope that *you* might be."

The *Fyarda* dashed across the street, finding a locked door leading into a maintenance tunnel. Their practiced finger grew into the keyhole, expanding, branching like a miniature tree, busting the lock.

The door squeaked open.

Cbarassan said, "If you'd kindly follow me, a near-perfect stranger, into the dark?"

Snorting, Alina glanced sidelong at the Crow.

It went inside. So did she.

Since The Authority had a bounty on both their heads, Aelf and Aelfraver traveled the Sixth Stack via ventilation shafts carved into the earth. Alina could have passed on the streets. The talking, fanged, tree-being? Not so much.

As they walked through the hundred-foot-tall passageways, advancing against the rush of air, Cbarassan said, "Awe-inspiring, isn't it?"

"Sure."

"The story behind these vents' creation is dramatic. It happened long before I immigrated: the Hextarchs ordered their *Erdarkanists* to completely bury the city."

"*Erdarkanists?*"

"Terramancers, you would call them. They created a complex series of interconnected light-funnels that—as recently as a thousand years ago—allowed sunlight to reach even the Seventh Stack."

"What changed? Why the total darkness now?"

"Light brings scrutiny. And drone bombings. Darkness and earth did shield Ozar from the worst of El's treacheries—for a time. However, the sealing of the city in the earth presented new challenges: how to circulate clean air, how to maintain the food supply, etc. Much hardship ensued, but Ozar survived as it always has. Then, as the invaders conquered, they assumed responsibility over these ancient systems—including the shafts, and the constant need to clear away the debris and vermin that dirty the fans and clog the airways. The *depix* have always been far more proficient at destroying than creating; through their mismanagement, for example, Authority engineers have spread a series of respiratory illnesses among the populations of the Stacks." Cbarassan sighed. "When Anarkey finally drives out the sky-dwellers, we will restore harmony."

Wishful thinking. Alina hadn't yet seen anything on the Ozari side that could compete with the tens of thousands of pinkojacks pouring in. Led by the Walazzins, The Authority coiled around the city, poised to strike.

As much as Cbarassan seemed to be fooling themselves, Alina thought she might still be able to use them and their Coven contacts before Ozar was inevitably crushed under the Elemental boot.

It didn't make her happy to think that way. She was only being practical.

In the dingy tunnel, wads of paper and animal fur blasting past, she stopped in front of a mural. Pictured was a man in white with angel's wings. Brows knitted, he glowered.

Finding Alina's side, Cbarassan sneered at the spray paint. "The Savior." Then the *Fyarda* laughed, pointing to a swirl of black paint above him.

"What am I looking at?" said Alina.

"A reminder."

"Of?"

"Hope. The Sanctum's preachers spit venomous words: 'Burn away the dark,' 'kneel in light.' Well. However quickly light may travel, upon its arrival, it will always find shadows in wait." Cbarassan kissed their palm and pressed it to the concrete wall. Softly, to themselves: "Every day, the grace of The Abyss ebbs. It's just a trickle now. Soon, it will be gone."

"Cbarassan."

Pinching the bridge of their nose, they said, "You asked about the Achemir. Truly, I don't know what they are supposed to be. No one does. But I do know that they are coming, a guardian summoned forth in the final hour, a product of the collective wills of all free peoples. The word itself underscores the truth: '*Ache*,' meaning 'reflection of the self'; '*Mir*,' as in 'the un-self, inner opposition.' No direct translation from ancient Iorian to our modern tongues—*Fyardan* or Ellish—is possible. But the term means something like 'that which compels the consuming inward gaze to catalyze the rebirth and re-death of the self.'"

Alina blinked.

The *Fyarda* continued, "It's a legend older than Ozar. A promise. As the world breathes what might yet be its dying breath, more than ever, we need— we deserve—a miracle."

"And you think *I'm* that miracle?" Alina shook her head. "You're much more desperate than I thought."

"Faith and desperation are not the same." Cbarassan spoke as if kindly explaining to a six-year-old why it was time to leave the theme park. "Faith is the preservation of hope. Desperation is action in its absence."

Alina grew tired of all the philosophizing. "The Sanctumites have faith."

"They have delusions."

"What's the difference?" Alina scratched the back of her neck. "I believe in Buthmertha, you believe in your gods." She shrugged.

The *Fyarda*'s six pupils gyrated until they found Alina's two. Again, that infuriating grin. "Buthmertha, patron goddess of home, hearth… and orphans."

Bored, Alina smacked her lips and walked away.

"The Achemir, according to legend, will be an orphan."

"Plenty of 'em out there." She gestured back the way they'd come. "Go bother one of them."

"How many street urchins, do you suppose, are also masters of Revomancy?"

"The Achemir's gonna be a Revomancer? Please. How gullible do you think I am?"

"No, but it is said they will be a bridge between realities." The *Fyarda* smirked. "The Revoscape and our material world, perhaps?"

"Sure, and, lemme guess, she'll wear sneakers just like mine and also be addicted to caffeine patches."

"Not quite. They will, however, be born to a great destiny, and aspire to one even greater."

"Oops, y'see? Can't be me. I'm the laziest person I know."

The *Fyarda* held up a hand. "There's one more detail I should mention."

"Does it have anything to do with my very real, not-made-up desire to meet with The Coven? Or is it more pointless prophecy?"

"I'll let you be the judge. Though, I think, after what lies ahead, you may shed your thorns. If I'm being honest, I'd be shocked if the Hextarchs had chosen you."

"Ey, what's that supposed to—"

"However, it is not my place to judge but to act. The Achemir, it is written, will be a master of the Eight Disciplines of Magic." Cbarassan stared pointedly at her, talking over her attempted interruption. "I suggest you tread more carefully in the future. Not everyone will make as great an effort to be your friend as I. When you read my mind earlier, you left some memories of yours behind." They tore aside a rusty chainlink fence and crawled through the opening. As Alina followed, they said, "I saw some of what you did in New El. Trapping a demon in your cellular device, becoming lighter than air, altering the chemical makeup of water, manipulating fire. Based on these visions, and my not insignificant understanding of the arcane arts, you have proven skills in—as you would call them—Deïmancy, Caelomancy, Aquamancy, and Igniomancy. By my count, that's four out of eight."

Clambering over oil-stained pipes, Alina kept her lips sealed.

Without turning, the *Fyarda* said, "I already know you're an accomplished Terramancer and Revomancer, bringing the total to six."

"Cut it out, already."

"I will not. I have lived some three hundred years, and I can't think of a single person—human, Noble, or Other—who has possessed as wide a power set as yours. I dare you to claim it coincidence."

Alina kicked a bucket across the corridor. It crunched like a beer can against the far wall. The Crow bent double, wracked with silent laughter.

Everyone always seemed to have these epic plans for her, grand ideas of who she was supposed to be. It worked out so conveniently for them—every time—that she just happened to be there. The answer to their problems. Ready, according to them, to do what *they* needed done.

"I'm not your jack, Cbarassan. Not yours, not anybody's."

They left the giant vents behind, entering a long, narrow passage abandoned by time. Alina, at least, lost all sense of it during the remainder of their silent adventure. They winded between hanging pipes, skirted built-up garbage clogs, and hopped over cracks until, finally, Cbarassan had them stop.

"Nice." In the slightly moldy stillness, Alina's laugh grated. "A dead end."

Exhaust valves emitted puffs of steam as Cbarassan indicated the solid cement wall some forty feet ahead. "The Abyssal Shell. Or, *Peregar's Grief,* as the Elementals have named it. We have come to its underbelly."

Remembering Ivion's mention that Peregar's Grief was enchanted in some way to repel any kind of direct approach, Alina squinted at the obstacle. No doors, windows, or other points of entry. "How do we get through?" She tried taking a step forward. As expected, an oppressive Niimantic aura quelled the very idea.

"You won't be able to. This is the first barrier, the outermost defensive layer of Hexhall, where dwell The Coven and our deific lords. The Abyssal Shell saps the will, confusing and strongly discouraging entry."

"Is this a test? I hate tests."

The *Fyarda* brushed off a nearby crate with the back of their hand, sitting. "We shall see."

Sure felt like an awful lot of hoops to jump through for basically a quick, informal meeting. She muttered under her breath, "Your Coven creeps better be worth it."

Well, if Cbarassan wanted to see what she was made of, Alina would show them.

She held out her hand, fingers splayed. Her thoughts grew sluggish, then still. In the inviting emptiness of her mind, there was now more than enough space for new perceptions.

Even from two or three dozen feet off, she felt heat on the pads of her fingers, her palm.

"Igniomancy," she said, closing her eyes. "But not like anything I've ever learned about. It's... drinking heat. It's self-sustaining by absorbing the heat of

the city around it, and it doesn't burn flames—not, like, actual flames, but…"
She strained, beads of sweat forming on her forehead and upper lip as she focused on the aura's sensations. This defensive spell, it was somehow connected
to a living energy. The whole tunnel was soaked in the stuff.

… The Abyss? Whatever that was?

"It's an anti-fire wall. If I tried to force my way through, even if I somehow
got past the energy-sapping effect, it would KO me?"

Alina turned to Cbarassan, who said, "Impressive, to have intuited the effects
of the Inner-Fire Wall so quickly. Well, how to pass it, do you think?"

"Not offering any hints, yeah?"

"I'm sure if you only *thought* about it…"

Grumbling, she returned to the invisible barrier before her. She did a bit of
quick math, mentally retracing her way back to the Sixth Stack.

There was no reason for the foundations of Peregar's Grief to reach this low:
Alina wasn't a military strategist by any means, but getting to the Seventh Stack
from here, where two people could barely walk comfortably side by side, would
be a logistical nightmare. Solid rock surrounded the Stack. Hundreds of feet of
it, in every direction. And any openings in Hexhall would be guarded. So…

The 'Inner-Fire Wall' spell probably was the real obstacle, and the dead-end
ahead an illusion.

Alina smirked in *Revomancer*.

Illusions, mind-tricks, and dream-walking were quite familiar to her now.
Even so, she doubted that she could shadow-step past this problem. The Abyssal
Shell, whatever it was, would almost certainly be warded to prevent teleportation
(and possibly even astral projection).

Cbarassan's "hint" began to irritate her all the more: "I'm sure if you only
thought about it."

Then she heard what they'd really been saying: "If you *only* thought about it."

Thinking. Revomantic theory held that *thoughts* traveled through a different
plane of existence. They were, after all, a form of waking dream. The best Revomancers could control and command their opponents by the power of their
minds alone, locking them in a sort of "daymare," unable to think anything other
than what the Revomancer allowed them to.

Advanced Igniomancers could raise or lower the intensity of their emotions
as one might stoke or smother a flame. In that way, it was similar to Revomancy.
Dreams, thoughts, emotions—all of these could be manipulated in oneself and
others if one had enough awareness and self-discipline.

Alina felt her way along the invisible threads of The Abyss that fed the Inner-
Fire Wall. Unlike Revomancy, this barrier didn't control the emotions and the
will; it *consciously* diffused them.

"The Abyss, I can feel it. It and the wall, they're alive." Even as she said it,
she knew it was true. "The Inner-Fire's connected to the Maggo who cast the
spell. It's a part of them, their emotions— protective, fiery desire made real by

magic. Which means…" She stepped forward, proceeding until she should have bashed her nose against the wall—but met no resistance.

The concrete barrier disappeared because it hadn't ever really been there.

Cbarassan got up. "You—how did—"

Alina smacked her lips, suddenly very thirsty. "I felt what the wall—or the caster of the wall—was feeling. The emotion that went into casting the Igniomantic spell. Then I convinced myself that I *didn't* want to get to the other side, and stepped forward."

"You *tricked* it? You deceived *magic*?"

"Was I not supposed to?"

"I don't know." Cbarassan laughed. "It's as valid a method as any, I think?"

Her mood made considerably lighter by this success, and for having thrown the *Fyarda* off their game for once, her chest swelled with pride. She walked a little taller through several tunnels that eventually fed her into a cavern so large she couldn't make out the sides, ceiling, or floor.

Halting before a sudden drop into damp darkness, she gaped at the sight of a tornado ahead—crackling lightning, swirling stones, and dark sheets of hail and rain. To her right, a two-foot-wide rock bridge cut across the chasm, leading into the heart of the vortex.

"Right. You're joking." Alina glanced at Cbarassan whose expression could not have been more deadpan. "Hilarious. I'm completely tickled."

"The warded wall was no match for you. What of this challenge?"

Alina looked from the *Fyarda* to the storm and back again. "Time out. Serious question: how is watching me die going to benefit either of us?"

The *Fyarda* snarled, then, a jarring change in mannerism. "You seek an audience with the servants of living *gods*, Aelfraver. Gods your kind has attempted to dethrone for over a thousand years. You descend from a long line of fools and ill-minded conquerors. That you must prove your worth is not up for debate. But, if it is fear that quenches your determination—"

"I'm not afraid."

"Across this canyon, you'll find a powerful ally in The Coven." Cbarassan stood at the precipice. With their big toe, they nudged a stone into the chasm. "Perish, fall, or otherwise fail, and you may return to your own devices."

"Good deal," Alina said absentmindedly as she watched the rocks circle round and round. Ranging from fist-to car-sized, they were held together by storm clouds shedding lightning and gouts of rain. She waved her arms at the circulating insanity. "How?"

"That depends on you." Cbarassan crossed their arms, watching, expectant.

She glared at the Aelf. She didn't need this. Buthmertha smite her for even considering joining these Coven people. Her time would've been more wisely spent banging heads with Sanctumites until one of them talked.

She huffed, pacing.

The *Fyarda* said, "You're a woman of faith. I know it. That's all I ask for now. Have faith in my intentions."

"Why the hells would I do that?"

"Because I have faith in your ability to cross. Read my thoughts if you must."

Alina didn't have to, though. The *Fyarda* was practically bleeding sincerity.

"We all have questions," they said. "How far are you willing to go for answers?"

Two Alinas competed for control of her next move.

Pre-New-El Alina wanted to flip Cbarassan a rude gesture before returning to the Safehouse to drown in self-pity and loneliness. This was the same Alina who'd locked herself in a moldy, leaky apartment with no one to turn to. However, her problems—seeming so insurmountable at the time—were nothing compared to Post-New-El Alina's. This new-edition Alina, having been called out, would not back down.

The second Alina won out, and she quieted her mind.

She analyzed the revolving storm, picking out four distinct magical signatures: Terramancy, Caelomancy, Aquamancy, and Deïmancy.

The first she could work with—the earth was literally her element, her comfort zone since childhood.

The second was its exact inverse: sky magic, Baraam's expertise. According to all the studies and philosophies centered on the Arcane Disciplines, a Terramancer could never be any good at Caelomancy, and vice versa, because the two skill sets were complete opposites.

The third Niimantic thread in the storm, Aquamancy, was at least closer to Terramancy—both being tangible, surface elements. However, although she'd taught Kinneas to develop his own Aquamantic talents, Alina herself had only ever been able to do basic telekinesis with, like, a jug's worth of water. And she had converted split water molecules once, when she'd nursed Mezami back to health. That'd been beginners luck, though. She'd had time, safety, and spell components on her side then. None of which she had now.

The fourth signature, Deïmancy, was of the same category as Kellfyute's magic had been—but with one key distinction. Niima derived from the spirit and emotions of the caster, and the spell protecting this stone bridge seemed stretched and sorrowful. A complete contrast with the Exorcist's piercing rage.

Alina assessed her odds. Sure, she could protect herself against the flying rocks, but all that other junk?

Then she noticed the Crow calmly striding forward, its shadowed form soundlessly passing over the narrow stone bridge. Though her semi-imaginary friend had no facial features to speak of, it seemed almost content. Happy, even.

It disappeared in the fog.

"Thanks a bunch," she hissed, voice drowned out by the storm.

Well, she wasn't about to let a figment outshine her.

Over her shoulder, for Cbarassan's benefit, she said, "If I die, I'm gonna be pissed," and she followed in the Crow's footsteps.

Inching closer and closer to the magical vortex, she tasted metal on her tongue, and felt the static pull on her hair. A boulder whooshed past—a blast of freezing air against her cheeks—and she lost her balance.

With nothing between her and the long way down, she swung her arms, digging in her heels, drops of her sweat falling into the chasm. Three heartbeats later, she leaned back and recovered.

Steady. Steady.

She could do this.

She took a breath...

...And telekinetically snatched one of the body-pillow-shaped rocks from the air. With her left arm, she held it in place as she grabbed a second boulder, positioning it to her right. A shield on either side of her, she proceeded.

Forks of lightning struck glancing blows, piercing the thin Niimantic film she'd cast upon herself, charring her extremities. Gouts of hail shattered against her shields; some razor shards raked her flesh anyway. With chunks embedded in her shoulder, she discovered it wasn't hail at all but glass. What kind of sadist conjures a glass tornado? Then she was pelted by thick, viscous globs of rain, which — it turned out — were not made of water at all. The acid scalded and bubbled flecks of her skin, singing her clothes. If not for her rock shields, she'd already be a goopy puddle, trickling down into the chasm below.

Not too much farther. The calm eye of the storm, and a hexagonal archway, lay just ahead.

Before she could choreograph her victory jig, though, all the air was sucked from her lungs. Her disintegrating rock shields fell away, tumbling into the dark. She landed on hands and knees, blinded and deafened, all physical pain subsiding.

Sightlessly, she looked up and there was her Tahtoh, Dimas. Beside him, her parents, Zatalena and Yurgeius. Then, Ruqastra, Eilars, Ugarda Pankrish, Ordin Ivoir and other faces, shaded faces. So many of them. They did nothing, remained silent. They only stared. But it was enough; it was too much.

She curled up, unaware of the burning of the acid rain and glass hail ripping at her.

The faces gazed down on the pathetic pile she'd become, wishing she could've been more than she was now, judging her for her every failure and shortcoming. And she knew she deserved it. They were right.

"You all think I don't condemn myself for my mistakes every day?" she said.

The ghost of her mother drifted forward. *Our sacrifices mean nothing because you do nothing.*

Alina felt hands on her cheek, at her throat. Smothering, throttling.

She wanted to go home, but she remembered she had no home to return to. The School, Truct, even Mount Morbin had been taken from her.

Why can't you find the rage within yourself? It is your power, said the shade of Ruqastra. *Fear is* your *weapon. It cannot be turned against you unless you let it.*

The good continue to die while you cry for home, said Ugarda Pankrish. *You're a child.*

To think the destiny of the Sevensin ends with the whimper of an unmotivated, talentless ingrate. Dimas shook his head. *It should have been Ruqastra born in your place.*

It should have been me, she said.

Rest, surrender. Stooping, Zatalena combed her fingers through Alina's hair. *It's alright. No one expected you to come this far.*

Alina slipped into the warmth of her mother's embrace.

But the Crow had other plans.

Burying its claws in her arm, it hoisted Alina upright so violently it almost dislocated her shoulder. Drawing blood, it pried open her pinched eyelids. It bit her hand, a flash of white pain driving away the haze, forcing her to *see.* These weren't the souls of the dead at all; they were shades. Deïmantic shades, summoned by an offensive spell—not quite an illusion but not much more either. Such magic held only as much power as it could siphon from its victim. Alina had been feeding it her guilt and fear; the Crow had burned these emotions away with its rage and pride.

Blood dripped from the twin semi circles of teeth marks on her hand.

Now that she'd seen through the workings of the spell, she found it possible to walk forward, shouting back at the specters' increasingly furious but futile droning, until she'd left them behind.

Just like the dead they'd imitated, they were only what she let them be.

Shredded and seared by acid, scarred by lightning and jagged flying rocks, nearly every part of her ached and burned. She lived, though, and now faced the final obstacle between her and the archway.

It took her a moment to process what she saw, and she had to blink a few times to be sure this wasn't some trippy afterimage spit up by her own exhausted, battered mind.

No, her eyes weren't deceiving her. She looked at the skeletal constructs of various sizes and shapes, roughly one hundred automatons of black bone—all humanoid. Forged through Corpromancy by a Necromantic specialist, these constructs weren't identical to those that had swarmed Eilars and Ruqastra, but the similarity was undeniable.

Two important differences: the killer bone-creatures accompanying Tolomond, though reinforced by magic, had been entirely human in shape; they also had worn wrappings, some sort of funeral shrouds. These naked skeletons on the bridge were humanoid, but not human. The skulls were too long, the eye

sockets too large. Too many teeth. Still, the common features were too convenient to be coincidence.

The Niimantic signature she felt now reminded her of the one from that night
on Morbin. Not the same, but related. Had the Hextarchs, or someone working
for them, been involved in the attack?

Not for the first time, Alina wondered if she blundered into a trap set by her
enemies. The ones Dimas had warned her about.

Again, she wished he'd just given her a name, location—something. How
terrifically unhelpful to be like, *Hey, watch out for a nameless danger that I will tell you
nothing else about.* Thanks a zillion, Tahtoh. She'd had nothing to go on. So, after
their... reunion at the top of City Hall in New El, she'd found it easier to believe
her grandfather had simply been sick in the head.

With the events of recent weeks, she began to doubt that conclusion. Maybe,
he hadn't been completely disconnected from reality at all. Maybe the old Revomantic master, who was both Aelfraver and Aelf, had known more about the
secret workings of the world than he'd ever let on during his masquerade as a
human being.

Maybe Alina had been wrong about him.

Oh, if Ruqastra were here to read her mind now...

Anyway, trap or not, turning back now wasn't an option. She wasn't about to
face the storm again.

The appearance of these skeletal constructs injected adrenaline into her
bloodstream. She wanted nothing more than to grab whoever lay on the other
side of that archway by the throat, give them a good, hard shake, and scream her
questions in their face.

One way or another, she'd claim the truth Dimas and Ruqastra had promised
but failed to deliver.

"I'm coming through," she told the dusty automatons.

No reaction.

She kept her distance, squinting.

Must not get much action down here. Few uninvited guests likely made it
past the multi-layered spinning deathtrap. The things were therefore stiff-limbed,
creaky. And they had no organs, no minds to influence with Revomancy.

But she had other skill sets to pull from.

With a final Geomantic lurch, she drew forth all the boulders and stones
behind her, tearing them from the spiraling storm, and sent these crashing into
the rows of skeleton sentinels. She lobbed boulder after boulder until she ran
out.

The constructs were thrown from the bridge.

Stepping over the twitching limbs of the crushed skeletons, she kicked aside
a few grasping hands and champing skulls. Then she came to the hexagonal archway.

It had no doors. No more barriers lay between her and the chamber Cbarassan had challenged her to reach.

"I did it," she shouted. "What else ya got?"

Turning, she entered a six-sided, high-ceilinged hall, imposingly large but entirely empty except for one central stone pedestal. About four-feet tall, the pedestal held a display case, illuminated by a magic glowing orb drifting just above it. Inside the case, a phone with a lightly smudged touch screen. All the smudges were concentrated near the bottom.

Alina shook her head. She waited a moment, trying to calm herself, but her cuts and bruises and acid-bubbled skin and the psychological torment she'd had to undergo just to get to this *empty damn room* nearly drove her over the literal edge.

A flash caught her attention.

She turned toward the display case again and jumped. Someone was standing there now: bubblegum-pink hair, straight bangs, fluffier around the ears; tattoos of sky-blue stars and emerald crescent moons on her chest, throat, and the back of her neck, and scorpions marked her wrists and hands (the left one blue, right one green), their tails coiling around her palms; between her eyes had been painted mirrored emerald crescents; a bandolier of gold, purple, and orange Auggie bottles wrapped around her black tank top; dangling from her right hip, a chain whip ending in a needle-thin blade, a strip of yellow cloth tied to its handle.

Physically, she'd changed quite a bit since their last encounter, but her quiet confidence and leather bracelets were the same.

"Vessa?" said Alina. She forgot to stay angry. "Vessa Tardrop?"

"VMG, it really is you." Vessa sized her up. "Been taking care of yourself, I see. What happened to you?"

"I have your friend Cbarassan to thank for all this." Alina indicated her torn clothes and skin. "Beginning to think they might hate me."

"Nah, that's not it. They just have this pet theory you're some kinda chosen one or something. Wasn't really paying attention when they were talking about it if I'm being honest." Vessa chewed her gum thoughtfully. "So, are you?"

"Am I what?"

"The chosen one."

"I mean, like, probably not? How should I know? And chosen for what? 'Most likely to get tricked into running head-first through a death-tornado'? If so, then, yeah, sure."

Vessa laughed. "VMG, you haven't changed a bit."

"Why do you keep calling me that?"

"Vending Machine Girl. Remember?"

Alina did. "*Cherry Punch!* Of course. That's right."

"Still my favorite flavor."

Cheeks burning, Alina said, "It's, uh, good to see you. Gotta say, you're one of the last people I'd expected to find way down here. At what really feels like the end of the world."

"Well, I've got the day free. Let's do lunch. Catch up. Give me the opportunity to thank you for saving my life."

"Oh." It felt like someone had pumped Alina's stomach full of helium. "Yeah. Sure. Sounds, uh, great. And you're welcome by the way. Really glad you made it out okay. I was scared I hadn't caught you in time."

"It was a close call. I'm grateful."

"Don't mention it." Alina cleared her throat. "It's just, uh—Hate to be all business and stuff, but I'm here for some kinda—I dunno what you'd call it—informational interview? Supposed to be meeting with a Covenant."

"You're lookin' at her." Vessa grinned and pointed to a black hexagon tattooed near her belly button. "I'm sure you've got a ton of questions. I know I did when I first got here. But let's save the chat for when we get inside. This big empty room full of nothing always creeps me out."

"Get inside?"

"Yeah, you didn't think you were standing in Hexhall proper, did you?" Vessa smiled and opened the display case. "You got this far on your own. Why don't you tell me what you feel?"

Inside the case, the little orb of light framed the perfectly ordinary-looking phone. A fairly recent model, it was obviously and completely out of place in this chamber of carved stone. But there was something else, something almost familiar about the device…

No, on second thought, it wasn't the phone, but rather what emanated from it—a Niimantic signature Alina had felt a hundred, a thousand times.

"My grandfather wove this spell."

Vessa leaned in, her round face lit from below by the magical orb. "No kidding?"

"I'm sure of it." Alina frowned. "How is he tied up in this war?"

"I really have no idea."

More questions, and still no answers. Alina scanned her face and decided to believe her. "Now I'm really gonna need ya to pencil me in for an ASAP-convo with the Hextarchs."

"It'll be tricky. We'll get to that. You're not gonna stand me up on the date we agreed to a minute ago, though, are you? I've kinda called dibs on you for the day."

"Guess so." Play nice with Vessa, and Alina would get the information she was after.

"So?" Vessa crossed her arms. "Have you figured it out yet?"

"What, this?" Alina pointed at the phone. "It's basic."

Vessa laughed. "Basic? The absolute, ultimate, and *last* guard against an invading army, and you call it 'basic.'"

"Fine. 'Simple.' 'Elegant.' Feel better?"

"A bit."

"It's a dreamway. Fundamental Revomancy. It's how we get around the Revoscape."

"We? Then, you are a Revomancer. I didn't realize anyone still taught that stuff."

"Not many do. The Gild tries, but... My grandfather was one of the last true teachers. It's part of what made his School so famous back in the day."

"Sure, that and the fact that he Raved the *Talaganbubāk* when he'd barely graduated The Gild. But I heard he'd kicked the bucket a few years back, and I owe my life to you being a Terramancer, specifically. The timeline doesn't add up. Who trained you in Revomancy?"

"Does it matter? I apprenticed under Ruqastra bol-Talanai. Baraam's sister."

"Good one. Fine, don't tell me, then." Vessa stuck out her tongue.

Flustered, Alina returned to the phone. Accessing her mental stores of magic theory calmed her. "This enchantment is a modification of Rimu's Transpiritual Locus, which shouldn't let you literally teleport somewhere. Standard theory claims you can't use dreams to move through physical space. Like, I couldn't hop into one person's dream and then leave through someone else's. Not with my physical body, anyway. To do that, I'd need an anchor of some kind." She tapped her forehead, grinning. "So, that's gotta mean that where we're going..."

"Yeah?"

"It's *physically* in the Revoscape? You've found a way to tether a chunk of our reality to a shared dream?"

Clapping her hands, Vessa said, "Clever. You definitely get a cookie." She licked her lip. "And *I* didn't do that, no. But the concept has been painstakingly explained to me more times than I can appreciate. Anyway. I'm not ashamed to admit, you've impressed me. You've changed." She gave Alina another once-over, perhaps looking for more surprises. Perhaps looking for something else. "Now that you've figured all that out, care to do the honors?"

"Why not?" Alina touched the button, at the same time weaving a web of shadow and dream around herself and Covenant Vessa.

Were anyone there to witness this moment, they would have seen two young women fade in a dark haze of static, and when the reality-distorting fuzziness disappeared, the chamber would be empty again. The display case would snap shut. And the roiling violence of the storm outside would be the only sound to punctuate the stillness of this hidden fissure in the earth.

A few hours of Vessa Tardrop's company wasn't the worst way to spend an afternoon. The Covenant gave Alina the tour of Hexhall's outer perimeter, which was comprised of (naturally) six towers. Connected by ethereal bridges, the towers held floor after floor of shared apartments. Families ate their lunches on balconies overlooking azure and cerulean clouds that flowed across an infinite bed of twinkling mango and pomegranate stars. Pink and blue ghosts phased in and out of sight between groups of children racing across ephemeral, shifting pathways. Directed by riders who carried bell-covered rods, balloon-shaped, suckermouthed creatures ferried from the astral sea nets overflowing with writhing, winged worms.

Vessa showed her guest the common areas, such as the terrace where residents relaxed after a long day's work. Across from where Alina sat, a *Gighifnol* stood for a portrait painted by a young human girl. The artist continuously complimented the way the light of the thousand suns gleamed against the *Gighifnol's* chalk shell; the creature's mandibles clicked with (what was probably) delight, their dozens of tiny arms rustling against their orange exoskeleton.

Next, Vessa and Alina grabbed a bite at an open-air restaurant run by an aging Xyloph. Despite his milky eyes and slow hands, the graying, eight-foot-tall cat man made a mean noodle soup. Cracked an egg to fry in the broth and everything.

With a bit of Ivion's spending money still in her pocket, Alina offered to pay, but Vessa held up her hand. All provisions and necessities were provided by the grace of the Hextarchs. And, even if they weren't, gelders were no good here. Currency of the invaders.

After lunch, they settled at an overlook in the center of the six towers, where they could watch the collisions of stars, the celestial dance of galaxies ever in motion, ever drifting apart.

Here, the ground beneath their feet was one solid piece of stone—hard as steel, smooth as glass, slightly green and shining. An upside-down pyramid, suspended over the infinite void into which all universes fed: the face of The Abyss.

Into this pyramid had been built many, many more homes. In the centuries since Ozar began to lose ground in the war against El, Hexhall had expanded from military stronghold to mass refuge. Every Aelf that had escaped the swords and spells of the Aelfravers and Authority had been offered a home here. Even the non-sentient ones had their place: herds of *marlok* grazed distant, floating fields, tended to by winged guardians; some families walked leashed *hrilliuk* (though, the toxic spines had been removed); and in some apartment windows sat proud *utch-Aharan* (Kadician war dogs).

A city where Aelf and humans lived together. In El, this would be unthinkable. The schools, the news, the government—every story, every mention of anything the Aelf ever did was designed to cause fear, to justify their extermination.

As far back as she could remember, Alina hadn't bought into the idea that Aelf should be butchered simply because they were, well, Aelf. Still, her pacifism had centered on her own distaste for violence. Even she hadn't let herself believe that true peace between humans and the hundreds of species of Aelf was possible.

Seeing Hexhall with her own eyes changed her forever.

She leaned over the edge, a foot away from Vessa.

Each of them held in her hand an ice-cold can of *Cherry Punch!* soda.

"This, right here," said Vessa, sighing contentedly, "is the best thing to come out of El." She slurped the rest of her can before chucking it into the star-spattered expanse. Crossing her arms and leaning on the waist-high ledge, she glanced at Alina from under her pink bangs. "Two years. That's how long you said it's been."

"Yeah. A while and a half."

"It's been longer for me."

The Crow, apparently bored by the conversation, took wing, circling high, drifting lazily on astral winds.

"I mean that literally." Vessa cracked her knuckles. "We have this dedicated Abyssal shard here, not much more than a splinter. The Coven uses it to store time. Everyone gives a little, and some take a lot. Others, like me... we *get* it even if we didn't ask for it."

Storing time? It sounded like she was talking about Chrononite. Alina inferred that the temporal mineral and The Abyss were somehow connected— maybe even the same thing. She resisted the urge to sink her claws into Vessa's thoughts.

Sometimes the best way to get at what was really bothering someone was to ask a roundabout question, giving them the space to breathe before returning to the heart of the issue. So Alina asked, "How'd you get here, after that day in The Capital?"

"Lost a lotta blood from that arrow I took. Came to and just kinda panicked. Went numb. I don't remember where or how far I ran, but I was one of the lucky ones. With those pinkojacked-up Enforcers swatting Ravers like flies, throwing the survivors into trucks and hauling them gods-know-where, I escaped being arrested. Instead, I got kidnapped."

"You were *lucky* to be kidnapped?"

"Didn't think so at first, but, after a stint of solitary confinement and interrogations, my keepers figured I wasn't a threat. They brought me here, to Hexhall, and introduced me to The Coven. I got a choice: stay and fight for Ozar, or die so I couldn't reveal Hexhall's location."

"They twisted your arm."

"It's not like that. After the scrap at Pluto Plaza, I was looking for a fight, but I didn't know with who. The Coven showed me the real enemy." She coughed. "Can I ask, why were *you* chasing the Bane of New El?"

No sense in lying (about everything). "I was flat broke, and I had something to prove to everyone. I didn't want to lose The School, my home."

"I've heard this story before. It's the same with so many of us Terrie Aelf-ravers who ran to the big Rave like we were summoned by a dog whistle, drool-ing at the idea of all that money that was gonna solve all our problems. But, ya know, even if one of us had taken home the bounty, it would've only helped one family, one community. All the rest would've just kept on suffering, like they'd always done." She pointed a finger gun at one of the stars and fired. "My own story's nothing special, either. Good family, loving parents. Nothing to complain about there. Not until Ma lost her fingers to a bonesaw at the meat processing plant. And the factory shut down before we could get any of her medical bills paid. Ma and Pa, both unemployed, did the best they could, and we were still fine, mostly. I started making more money with a little Rave here and there. It wasn't enough, after a while, and the parental unit found jobs somewhere else. Kept worrying about my dad's back, you know? Thought to myself, if I could just make more money, I could set them up for retirement."

For almost a minute, there was silence. Alina gave the conversation and Vessa all the space they needed to reorganize for the final push.

"There was a flood. A city's worth of people, wiped out. Just like that. A handful of survivors were found, but my parents… The official report claimed it boiled down to 'overzealous fiscal prudence.' 'Understandable human error,' they said. We all know that's just legal nonsense meaning 'we didn't care to spend enough money to properly fix what was broken, so it broke worse than before, and, well, *oops.*'"

"Vessa." Alina reached for the other woman, hand hovering over her back. Hesitated. Pulled away. "I'm so sorry for your loss."

"Why? Did *you* ignore the recommended structural repairs to a dam that sup-plied power to an entire city full of human beings? Did *you* sign and stamp the inspection papers? Stop it, Alina. Don't take credit for the sick, self-serving greed of the Elemental elite." She fiddled with one of the Auggie bottles strapped to her chest, twisting it round and round. "Returning from a job, that's when I heard the news. A few months of drinking later, I woke up and saw the Plutocrats had put out that whopper of a reward for this 'Bane of New El.' Didn't even care about the money by then. Just wanted to—like you said—prove something. To myself. Probably to the Elementals, too. If I could be the one to bag the Bane, me, a Terrie…" She waved her hand as if taking an eraser to a whiteboard in front of her face, wiping away her words. "Joining The Coven gave me a new purpose. A better purpose. Doesn't hurt that it gave me power, too. But every-thing's got a cost." Meeting Alina's stare: "For you it's been two years. For me, more."

Finally, an opening to ask, "The Abyssal shard, it's Chrononite, right?"

"Yeah. Sorry. I've been here long enough I forget the lingo's not always the same." Vessa tasted the word as if it were a favorite meal from childhood, "Chro-nonite. That word takes me back to final exams at The Gild. Five hundred mul-tiple choice questions. Damn. Raving was easy after that hell." She shook her head. "Anyway, I swore my Covenant to the Hextarchs, declared them my living gods. But I was still fresh meat, needed toughening up. I wasn't good enough, coming in wounded and shy and basically too Ellish. Initiation day was scary but also awesome. A kind of toll was taken. The Abyssal shard was passed around like a collection plate, and people donated their time to me. A huge honor, so I was told. Often." Alina watched the scorpions on Vessa's hands wriggle as she became more animated. "In my old life, I used to think Gild training was rough, but it's nothing compared to the pace at The Coven."

"What's it like being a Coven-er? Coven-ee?"

"Covenant," said Vessa, smiling. "Most days, I'm just me. Others…" Her eyes flitted to the armband tied around her bicep. It, too, bore the hexagonal mark of the Hextarchy. "I am sworn to serve my living gods, to defend them against all enemies, even at the cost of life and soul."

"That doesn't sound too bad in exchange for cool powers."

"Right?" Her smile widened. "Might give you a demo sometime. You seem like a fun partner—" she let the word linger—"to spar with."

Unsure of how to answer, or if she even should, Alina twiddled her thumbs.

Thankfully, Vessa filled the silence with another question. "Anyway, what's your deal? What took you from dorky amateur vending machine tech to rebel without a cause? You're Darkthread-famous, ya know."

"Heard about all that, huh?"

"Hard not to. I'm in the same boat, besides. Half the world's hunting us. That why you wanted to meet the Hextarchs? Protection? Smart play, honestly. This is the last place in the world the Plutocrats can't get ya. And that's probably because it's not even *in the world*, technically."

"I didn't come here to hide. The opposite, actually. I'm looking for info on The Savior."

Vessa stiffened, leaning back and crossing her arms. Suddenly defensive. "Why's that?"

Alina had rehearsed this conversation during the truck ride through Kadic, during the stakeout of Cronn's apartment. Her rehearsals, however, hadn't included Vessa, who definitely muddied the puddle. She couldn't think clearly right now. This easy familiarity was way too distracting.

In response to Vessa's question, the truth seemed the right call for two reasons: Alina would eventually have to be straight with someone, or the lies would twist her till she snapped; and, Vessa's appearance here and now felt just the teeniest bit like—dare she admit it—fate. After the day, week, and year she'd had, she knew this fleeting pleasantness would be gone soon enough. Maybe, rather than shy away, she could afford to lean into it for once.

The truth, then:

"The Savior's my uncle." Alina felt a small tickle of satisfaction as Vessa's eyes bulged. "I've got some strong words and a long list of questions about my family for him."

"One sec. Still processing." With her thumbnail, Vessa scratched her chin. "Your uncle? Yeah, I'll *bet* you got questions. What kind, huh?"

"The kind I'd rather keep to myself." How much was too much to tell Vessa? Alina settled on more half-truth. "I think he's got inside info on the Bane of New El."

"The Bane's down for the count, though. Taken out of commission, at the Plaza. I remember the Elementals tripping over themselves, they were so relieved they didn't have to dig any more nobles' graves."

"Hey, so, you don't need to tell *me* what did or didn't happen on that tower. I was at City Hall. At the top."

"Well." Vessa dragged the word. "My apologies."

"I'm just saying, it's not a done deal. Believe me. 'Kay?"

"Okay." The Covenant held up her hands. The twin coiled scorpion tails, blue and green, did little to soothe Alina's racing heart. "Okay. You want the goss. How can I help?"

"I want more than 'the goss.' Cbarassan told my friend, who told me, that you've got a spy watching the Savior?"

For the third time today, Vessa's gaze drank Alina in like a can of her favorite carbonated purple garbage. "Maybe they were right about you. Cbarassan, I mean. You've more than proved yourself today. To have gotten past the Wall and the maelstrom, you're something else, alright."

"Thanks. Appreciate the compliment, but are you gonna help me or not?"

"That depends."

"On?"

"How far you're willing to take that encounter with The Savior. If it could be set up. If."

"What're you getting at?"

"You seem like you want to talk to him. If we weren't at war right now, I'd say, 'go for it,' and I'd give you a little pat on the back on your way out the door. There's just one problem: we *are* at war, and The Savior's our number one person of interest. It's all hands on deck because he's one bad dude. Old man Walazzin could waltz into a room with The Savior, and every Covenant would know to shoot the holy man down first. Not playin'." Her shuddering inhale gave way to a long, halting exhale. "You being his kin and all, we could use you. Get you in close. You fire off some of your questions, get your answers, and then—"

"I'm not helping you *assassinate* him."

"Family or not, Alina, the man's trash. He's nothing like you."

"It's about principles."

Vessa snorted. "Oh, you're one of those."

Fists against her cocked hips, Alina said, "Um. What's that supposed to mean?"

"You think we can all just *get along* with the Elementals? They live in the sky and have all the money. They *literally* look down on the rest of us."

"So, what? Should I just be cool with killing all of them?"

"Not all, no. I got no beef with civilians. But soldiers—I've fought plenty, and lived to talk about it. No tears, either. My pillow's dry as dust. A dead pinkojack can't lie, rob, or kill. That's the truth. Evil doesn't go away when asked politely."

"Listen, I'm no friend of The Authority's."

"But you're not willing to do anything to stop 'em either."

Alina flinched at the sight of the Crow, perched on the ledge to her right. Its hollow, shadowed eyes were fixed on Vessa. Asking permission.

"No," Alina told it. To Vessa: "No, that's true. You can't stop bad people with happy thoughts. But I'm not gonna kill the only family I have left just because you want me to. I don't care how big a turd bundle he turns out to be. I've made up my mind. I know what I'm ready to do, and what I'm not. If you Covenant types in your weird triangle house aren't gonna help, that's no big. Been handling my own problems since I was in diapers anyway."

"Alina." Vessa's voice went soft. "I know what it's like to lose everyone." Her hand pressed against Alina's, a touch that burned like scorpion venom. "There's a place for you here. If you want it."

Maybe she did want it.

No.

She jerked her hand free, clutching it to her chest as if she'd just been stung. "This was a waste of time." She hadn't meant that. "I mean, dammit, not the seeing you part—you're really cool. Crap, I mean, the rest of this sucks. I came in here really hopeful, you know? And that's just been like…"

"A bummer?"

"I was gonna say 'like diving headfirst into a *Paoph* nest,' but sure. Yeah, it's a bummer too."

The edge returned to the Covenant's voice. "I'm sorry The Coven can't be of more help to you, Alina K'vich, but we have our own to care for."

"I understand," Alina grumbled. "That's the worst part. I get it. You've got a lot on your back. Honestly, can't believe I'm talking to a Raver who fights *for* Aelf."

"Right. Almost as unusual as a Raver who refuses to kill 'em?" Vessa winked.

"Last time I saw you, you were…" Alina couldn't find the words.

After a long exhale through the nose, Vessa said, "Different? Thirteen years will do that to a gal."

"Thirteen? You got that much extra time? You—ya look good."

"That's Chrononite for ya. It also pays to work for actual wizard gods." Vessa pushed off the ledge, scuffing the ground with her heel. "I really am sorry, but it has been good to see you, too. I didn't…" Suddenly, she choked up a little. "I guess I didn't realize how much I'd wanted to see a face from back home till you showed up." Wiping away a tear with her knuckle, she chuckled. "Nninithin blast me, I'm being ridiculous."

"No, hey. I busted into your place, acting a fool." Before Alina knew it, they were hugging. She was locked in a Vessa-press.

Strong arms. For a heartbeat, she relaxed.

Then she pulled away. "I should go. Need to clear my head and, uh, figure out next steps."

"Yeah, yeah." Vessa sniffed. "Cool."

"I'll see myself out," said Alina, backing away.

"Uh, hey. So you know, by making it here, the spells'll recognize you. In case ya wanna come back. For any reason."

"Nice. Um."

"Just, don't tell anyone I told ya. Secret dream fortress and all that. Kinda messes with the program if we start letting guests come and go as they please."

With a smirk and a curtsy, Alina said, "I solemnly swear that I shan't abuse your trust in me."

She snapped her fingers, returning to the material world.

As they woke from their shared dream, Vessa shouted after her, "Stay away from The Savior."

When she opened her eyes, and stood up from her curtsy, she wondered if she'd been honest there, at the end of their conversation.

It was getting hard to tell.

Alone again in the chamber with the pedestal and phone, Alina stared at her reflection and found the Crow staring back.

Its face was hers, a furious mask.

What a colossal waste of time this day trip had been. The only relevant piece of information she'd gleaned was that The Coven had put a hit out on The Savior, which meant even more urgency. If she didn't find him soon, someone was gonna wind up dead.

Now that she'd experienced The Abyss's caress firsthand, she pinpointed tendrils of its energy gently pulling at the collar of her cloak. *Rego* responded, fluttering against this ethereal breeze.

The Abyss and Chrononite. Time and dream.

Ah, she'd have to puzzle that one out later.

For now, she'd head back to the Safehouse. Find some other way to get herself in front of Mateus K'vich.

"Fat lotta good you were," she snapped at the Crow.

It helpfully pointed out the exit.

At least crossing the bridge this second time was nothing. The skeletons had reconstituted themselves and reformed their defensive line, but, for her, they stood aside. She also passed through the maelstrom, no worse for wear than if she'd poked her head out her front door to be caressed by a morning misting of rain.

Cbarassan was nowhere to be found, which made sense: Alina and Vessa had spent hours together.

On her way back to the Safehouse, Alina agonized over her every idiotic word-choice and bone-headed question, replaying their entire conversation, over and over.

"'I shan't abuse your trust in me'? Really, Alina? Really?"

And had she actually curtsied? Why? Just—why?

It was a long walk back.

In the Safehouse, the boredom persisted. With no one to workout or argue with, Alina was hit hard by exhaustion.

The hours scraped by. There was no paint to watch dry, so she observed instead the superhumanly quick healing of her cuts and scrapes.

Later, she curled up in her sleeping bag, too nervous to sleep.

She had plenty of good reasons to be anxious. She simply couldn't tell which particular one was keeping her up and pacing, and that made her even more nervous.

At last, the door to the bunker hissed, opening, welcoming the slightly less stale street air inside.

Ivion entered.

Fresh from her encounter with Vessa, Alina couldn't help but notice the striking contrasts between the muscular, tattooed Ellish Raver-turned-Ozari-Covenant and the svelte, long-limbed, elegant Elemental now sauntering into the bunker.

Of course, Ivion was strong in her own way: sharp, assertive, fully herself. Her stare cut to the bone anyone caught in it. And she looked good in that athleisure wear—shorts and a long-sleeved sweat-wicking shirt. Really good.

She'd supported Alina from the beginning, even when no one else would.

And the Crow was somehow always calm when she was around.

Maybe it was Alina's pent-up frustration regarding the failures of the day, or the desire to think about anyone or anything else besides her hells-bound uncle for just a few minutes. Maybe she was projecting Ordin onto his sister, and, yeah that was messed up, but she didn't care anymore. Not right now.

Whatever the reason for her next decision, it would remain a mystery that night.

No, Alina couldn't rightly say what came over her, what compelled her to stand, stride over to Ivion, take her by the hip, and—without a word—kiss her.

PART FOUR

DEPRESSION

37

CHO-ZEN

AGED BARRELS OF WHISKEY and vinegary wine burst under hammer blows. Anarkey crowded around the flowing rivers of sticky alcohol, catching it with cups, mugs, saucers. Hands drenched, they were hazy outlines of people, silent silhouettes resisting the low light of candles and braziers. Anarkey was used to darkness, welcomed it, preferred it.

When the revolutionaries raised their drinking vessels no cheer accompanied the toast. Everyone present had lost someone they'd loved that night.

One of the humans gave a short blunt speech about honor, sacrifice, and destiny. She spoke of loss too, sobering, deep-cutting. "Our commitment separates us from our enemies and our pretenders both."

At the word "pretenders," Cho no longer could meet her eye.

Anarkey, she discovered that night, was a leaderless band. Each member was equal to all others, equally responsible for failures as well as successes. Tonight felt like quite a lot of both.

The speech wrapped up. The others rose in turn to praise and lament their lost friends. Cbarassan was among them, speaking of their memories of Bizong, how they'd met and fought together a century prior at Briar's Gorge. Both refugees from their respective homelands, they'd developed a kinship. "Like siblings, we were," the *Fyarda* said. "And that is precisely what you *all* are to me—family. The Lightbringers have done their utmost to deprive us of liberty and, yes, life.

But not all is gloom: tonight, we forced them to listen. Tonight, our message was cast to the corners of the world. Through The Authority's own communications network, we hijacked the attention of our entire planet, if only for two minutes." They closed their eyes, breathed deeply. "By my ancestors, I feel it is enough. Bizong and all our friends will share in our victory even in death. For, by their sacrifice, we declared our independence—staking a claim for our country, a country not of borders or laws but of conscience. Tonight, if only for tonight, we are truly free." They lifted their cup. "Bizong."

"Bizong," said the others, including Cho.

"Katja," said Cbarassan.

"Katja."

"Nestro."

"Nestro."

"Ufior."

"Ufior."

"Ilai."

"Ilai."

Done reciting, the rebels drank in silence, heads bowed.

Cbarassan finished with, "Their part in our battle is ended. May the Hextarchy usher them into heaven. Now, rest well, for tomorrow the war continues. OSO."

"OSO!"

When the rebels scattered, forming pairs or trios, Cho approached Cbarassan. "What's 'OSO'?"

"An acronym: 'Ozar shall overcome.' A phrase used to greet comrades, defy slavers, and mourn losses."

Cho watched people pat each other's backs and exchange baleful looks. "This feels like my fault."

The *Fyarda* cocked their head.

"If I hadn't told you who I was, we wouldn't have hit that tower, and Bizong and the others'd still be alive."

"Perhaps they might yet live *now*. But tomorrow would have brought with it new dangers. So, too, would the next day, and the one after that. We are rebels against The Authority in the same way that sand resists the tides. The two will clash, and the waves move the sand where they will." They picked at their fangs with a long, wooden fingernail, their strange eyes unfocused for a moment. "Bizong isn't the first to fall for our cause. Long before you arrived, Choraelia Torvir, we were dying in great numbers. That will not change, I suspect, even long after you are gone. The water washes away the sand, erodes the stone, rusts the iron. However, the shore and the rock remain; the iron is changed but survives. So, too, will we endure. And we will fight on. Your assumption of responsibility for our losses is arrogant, childish, and inaccurate. You fought alongside us, and gave Bizong the honorable end he's sought for most of his hard life."

They clasped Cho's hand between their own. "Moreover, you have proved yourself, Choraelia Torvir, Plutocrat, Child of El. You are a rebel now. One of us."

"I don't feel like I am."

"Feelings can be deceptive. Look to your actions. With fist, knee, and—more importantly—with ironclad word, you have declared yourself."

"I'm not like you, though." The words hurt worse than the recent operation on her arm. She faced them head on. "I just want the Walazzins out of the picture, but you're dying for the freedom of your whole country."

"Not just our own nation, but all nations. All peoples. None will ever be free as long as The Authority exists. You're seeing now that killing the Walazzins will only replace the figureheads."

Cho stared at the ground.

"Elemental terrorism will persist until we erase its source." The *Fyarda* released Cho's hand.

"You don't even sound like you think you can *win*."

"Sometimes I imagine ultimate victory is possible. Though, I doubt it will come in my lifetime. We stand athwart a three-thousand-year-old war machine. Since the days of the Twin Dragons, the Elementals have conquered realm upon realm. Their Authority has had hundreds of human lifetimes to perfect its warmongering and war-profiteering. Our side has been disunited, broken and scattered from the start. Only recently have we united in hope. Fools' hope, perhaps, but it binds us." They drained their cup of water, set it down on a table. "The Authority subsists off lies, the most damning of which has been that the 'Aelf' and humanity are mortal enemies."

Cho watched Mezami hop across the bar, sucking up the leftover booze from half-finished cups, one after the other. His belch knocked a pewter plate onto the floor, where it clattered. He stumbled, falling after it, landing with a thud. Even his magical metabolism couldn't keep up with that much liquor.

Chuckling, Cho shook her head.

If the Authority had their way, Mezami would've been exterminated with the rest of his hive. There wouldn't be a single Pyct left.

Cbarassan said, "The Authority seeks to divide us—to destroy all Aelf and rule all humans. Therefore, are the Aelf and the human underclass not natural allies?"

Cho remembered the *Fyarda*'s revelation about Alina. Fully Aelf. Nothing human about her.

By now, it was clear Cbarassan had had no reason to lie about that, and Alina's self-ignorance seemed equally genuine. She may have kept a lot from Cho, but her search for herself showed how lost she was. As her friend, Cho owed her a heads up.

Human rebels caught by The Authority at least stood a chance of life in prison. If they got hold of Alina, and they figured out what she was, an axe to the neck was literally the best she could hope for.

Cho would not let her friend be tortured.

Again, she considered Cbarassan—all wispy hair, tough bark, wisdom and sass—and dug out of her heart a deep well of respect for them. It'd been a mere couple days since they'd met, but she wanted them to live. And win.

"Maybe," she said, "there's a way we can both get what we want. With a hundred thousand pinkojacks marching in to crush you all, you lose this battle and you lose the war."

"True."

"But if we take out their leaders, and blow up their headquarters... maybe that'd create enough chaos to slow them down. Maybe then more people could see that it's not a hopeless cause. The Authority hasn't really been beaten in a long time, right?"

"They enjoy a certain aura of false invincibility, yes."

"What if we could take that away from them?"

"It's a lovely idea, my friend, and one I whole-heartedly support. But, what is it you're suggesting? Knowing the location of their leaders and their base of operations isn't enough. We don't have the numbers or firepower to bloody their noses where they are strongest."

"What if you did, though? Have the firepower, I mean." It was time. "I'm choosing to trust you." Cho showed Cbarassan Rooster's tooth. "This is a disguised data stick packed with troop movements, battle plans and strategy sessions, and all that good stuff. But, even better, it has access codes and passwords." She was shaking now from the excitement. "When I hacked into the relay tower the other day, I stole even more data about a place called the Lion's Den."

Blank-faced, Cbarassan listened. They tried to conceal their wonderment, but their micro-expressions gave them away.

"Between all the fights, I've been decoding big, fat piles of tasty data, cracking encryptions. This thing is the key to getting us inside, I'm sure of it." She palmed the tooth. "You wanna hurt The Authority? The Lion's Den is where you hit them. But if you charged head-on, you'd just be mowed down. That's dumb-dumb sauce. What you should *actually* do is sneak in with a small group, get to the control room, and upload a virus."

Cbarassan nodded, sucking their teeth, thinking.

Cho pressed on. "All Authority drones and even their soldiers' gear is plugged into the same network. To be fair, it's so ridiculously, thoroughly firewalled that it might as well be one of the Hells. But! If you get *me* on the inside, I can hack my way in." Rooster's gray tooth rested on her slightly trembling hand again. "I was built for it." She lifted the green locks of her wig, revealing the grooves and tiny rivets in her skull, scars of the trillion-gelder implants she'd received years ago.

"We don't have anyone in Anarkey skilled enough for this kind of job. You're sure you're ready?"

"No. But I stand a damn good chance, and I'm your best option. We both want the same thing, like you said." Nerves taut, she blew a raspberry. "I'm trying to work with you here."

"Hmm. Supposing we did as you suggest, what of this 'virus'? We have no such weapon."

"You're not hearing me I guess. I *am* the virus." Cho grinned. "As soon as I'm in, the system will shut down. It's a defense mechanism to stop any outside force from taking control of The Authority's official Aetherthread network. If we're lucky, I can do enough damage to put the system on ice for a day. Not a permanent fix, but it could give you the PR you need to rally more troops. And attack more targets."

"For a barely adolescent human, you know far too much about Elemental national defense. From whom did you learn all this?"

"My mother. After I got my implants, she uploaded tons of data into all our heads, my siblings and mine. I never knew why, and I didn't understand what any of it meant at the time. I've started to, now." Cho's pulse pounded in her ears. "My mother wanted us to be prepared."

"For this exact moment?"

"No, no. None of that destiny stuff. I don't buy it. She was just protecting us. Probably from the Walazzins."

"That may be, but you can't well deny that your mother was arming you for battle. Which battle, who can say? Nevertheless, she clearly expected you to make powerful enemies."

"She was always five moves ahead of everyone else. Maybe she knew I'd go looking for her killers one day."

"For one so forward-thinking, revenge would be an awfully small-minded motive." Cbarassan spread their arms, tilted their head. "Were I to pursue the men responsible for Bizong's death, what would that achieve? I might die in the attempt, and who then would fight for the *Fyarda*, for Ozar, and for all peoples wearied by the chains of the Elementals?" They paused, plucking at the air as if picking fruit. "Your abilities suggest your parents' desired to save you, not throw you into the fire. I believe you were meant to *matter*. I believe you came to us at the fated hour." They cut short Cho's protest with a wave. "You need not trust in Providence or the powers of the Hextarchy, but I choose to."

"We doing my idea or not?" Jittery, Cho tapped her foot. "Clock's ticking."

"I will think on it. You will have my answer in the morning." They turned to walk away but paused, and they said, "Your parents are proud of you, Cho."

She crossed her arms. "You don't know that."

"But I know *you*, and I am proud of the courage and ferocity you displayed tonight. I am proud to call you my friend. I am proud of you."

Around the arch overgrown with hemlock, the dancers formed a circle, clapping in rhythm, tapping their feet on the straw-covered ground outside the barn. Strung electric lights twinkled in imitation of the stars, which hung low over the silver fir trees.

They were all so happy, Cho thought, and her eyes lingered on her daughter, easily the bubbliest of them all. Her daughter, of striking long gray hair and sharp chin; she gripped her new husband with all the ferocity of a bird-of-prey. They had eyes only for each other.

For tonight, they could be happy.

As twilight transitioned to darkness, the wedding teetered on the edge of disaster, but Cho must not let them find that out. She must smile and clap along and back away; she must speak with the sharply dressed, four-armed man who stood just beyond the ring of light cast by the bonfire.

He was much taller than she was, and much wider too. His suit strained against his muscles, buttons threatening to pop off any second. Wire-frame, circular spectacles pinched the bridge of his nose. Crossing both sets of arms—two of flesh and two of black steel—he told her, "Don't try anything. You're surrounded."

They were out of earshot of the party. Softly spoken words only, she reminded herself. Should this conversation sour, the crystalline illusion of peace clinging to her daughter's special night would crack like so much ice. Worse, there would be inconvenient questions, and she had become invested in this new face of hers. She'd foolishly built a life upon it. She'd invested too much.

"The famed Aelfraver Ugarda Pankrish. It's a delight, meeting you," said Cho, approaching him, raising her hands lightly. "Why so on edge? This is meant to be a happy occasion. Had I known you were such a sharp dresser, I'd have convinced my Zatalena to invite you to the festivities."

Pankrish said, "I have no desire to crash your daughter's party, Mr. K'vich. I come bearing a message from my employers. And I feel obliged to inform you that, should you try anything *forward*, my colleagues would be forced to intervene."

Cho sensed them all around her—emanating strong Niimantic auras, killers lurking just out of sight.

Pankrish said, "I'm certain you could make quick work of us all, but not before that happy little gathering turned quite bloody."

He was right. When she closed her eyes, Cho could see all the assassins, their magical secretions like beacons to her ether-sight. She could have torn them all to shreds in seconds, but odds were high they'd fire into the crowd first. They'd hurt Zatalena and her dopey human husband.

Cho felt like a leashed dog, yanked violently to heel.

Unacceptable.

Pankrish shifted uncomfortably. "That's not the outcome I seek."

"Well," Cho said, "even in my old age, I'm still capable of being surprised, it seems. The great Ugarda Pankrish—supreme among Aelfravers. In my defense, who could have guessed you would be working for The Coven as well. A double agent. Here I thought *I* had a taste for dangerous games." She spoke directly into his mind, then: *Whose side are you truly on?*

He shrugged off her mental attack. "It would be challenging to decide which of us is the bigger fool, K'vich. I may walk both in shadow and light, but you're an Aelf who trains Aelfravers. Six decades spent in masquerade, waiting, refusing to act in service to anyone but yourself. Do you crave death? Is that it?"

"In trying to get a rise out of me, you waste your time. I did not survive four millennia of human folly by entangling myself with strutting mortal fools. You have my attention. Deliver your message."

"Very well." Pankrish took a bold step forward. "The Hextarchy summons you."

When no followup seemed on its way, Cho said, "Is that all?"

"The Elemental Empire will not stop until the whole world lies in ruin. The Authority strangles all nations. The Gild and Sanctum are united through the Ridect brothers, both of whom seek the total annihilation of all Aelf. If you won't act for yourself or your lords, act for your people."

"I don't have a *people* anymore, Pankrish. I have a *family*. What you call a 'masquerade' has remade me. 'Our people' is a nebulous concept—an abstraction, meaningless. 'Family,' however, anchors the soul."

"Then fight for your family, K'vich. You could be great again."

"I do not desire greatness any longer. Only freedom. Happiness."

"There can be no happiness nor freedom as long as the Elementals lash the world in chains. When they took that flying sphere as their own, soaking it in Dragon's blood, they declared war on every living creature that looked, believed, or wanted differently than they."

"You mistakenly assume I do not seek the destruction of El. I do."

Pankrish seemed taken aback. "You have a strange way of going about it."

"I wouldn't expect a human to understand. Even to the cleverest fox, the will of the forest is unknowable. While I do long for the end of the Lightbringers, my time in human form has shown me that war isn't the answer to our prayers."

"You've surrendered."

Cho swelled, shadow wafting from her like fumes from dry ice. "You accuse me of forgetting the very purpose of my existence? I have seen much in my six lifetimes, Ugarda Pankrish. Each span of my existence has lasted centuries. Nations, alliances, and the squabbles of man and Noble are nothing to me. Craving peace, I still see the Enemy with my waking and my sleeping eyes. Not a day passes without my thoughts turning toward His defeat. Like your Hextarchs—"

She laughed derisively—"I have worked toward His demise since before there *was* an Elemental Empire. Unlike them, I do not cower in a crevice at the edge of the world."

"Indeed. You hide behind a mask of humanity, instead."

Cho growled.

Pankrish spread his four arms, palms toward the heavens. A plea. "Join with us. Bring your strength to The Coven."

"My days of bowing to the whims of others are behind me. I may have been designed—a weapon forged for a singular goal—but I shall choose my own path forward." Cho looked toward the wedding party, toward Zatalena, the hem of whose dress twirled as her husband spun her around and around.

"Think of it as an alliance." Pankrish's Niima began to flow. He readied himself. "I'd prefer you come along willingly."

"Strong alliances are not built on threats."

"The threat was not my idea. I was the one who tracked you down, uncovered your identity. I wanted to meet with you peaceably." He sighed. "I grew up on stories about you, you know. The human you pretend to be. You're the reason I wanted to be an Aelfraver in the first place."

Cho shook her head. "You regret that decision."

"Yes. The things I've been forced to do... I'll never be able to atone."

Here was a man broken by self-pity, Cho thought. A feeble creature bolstering itself with anger. Fool. Anger could not rehabilitate him.

However, there was something behind his rage—a seed planted. If nurtured, it could grow.

Cho took an interest in this man, this nobody. "How did you find The Coven? Rather, how did they find you?" With her guidance, perhaps he could be something. Perhaps he, too, could be Collected.

With his small finger, the Aelfraver nudged his sliding glasses higher up his nose. "I killed one of my fellow Gildsmen. There was a child—a *Fyarda* infant. We'd just burned and torn apart the little sprite's family. Something in me... I snapped. I couldn't let the child—"

"The Aelf."

"—I couldn't watch them die."

"So you killed the man instead."

Pankrish nodded, tears in his eyes. The lenses of his spectacles fogged as his powerful shoulders shook.

Cho gazed into his soul, weighing him. "You're not a Gildsman at all, Pankrish. But you *are* an Aelfraver." Like a cup of water after a long day in the sun, she sipped at the contents of his mind. Such potential. "The truest one I've yet seen."

"I don't understand."

Cho chuckled. "Have your masters not told you the original meaning of the word? I'm not surprised." Thinking, she added, "Am I to understand that the

Hextarchy's threat against my family stands as long as I don't agree to assist them?"

Pankrish nodded.

"They want an assassin, as before."

Another nod.

"Very well, Ugarda Pankrish. I will submit and obey—for the sake of my family, and on *one* condition."

"Name it."

"You will be by my side. When I stalk our foes in the night, you will be there to witness what you have asked for."

"Why?"

"Because I have an eye for good people, and you are such a one. I have come to have faith in a small number, and I hope to add you to that list. I will teach you, Aelfraver, why it is that you saved the Aelf child and killed the man. I will help you see, in time, why the Hextarchy's plan could never work—and why mine must."

Pankrish's next words were muffled, his answer lost in the rising fog.

One of the happy dancers, a freckle-faced girl of thirteen, sauntered over. Her winter-pine-black hair haloed her dark-skinned, sweat-dampened face. She looked right at Cho and said, "You wonder why you're here."

"Yes," said Cho, suddenly realizing that she didn't feel quite like herself. "I'm confused."

"You are attuned to it now," said the girl. "The Chrononite."

"How?"

"I don't know, but apparently you no longer even need to be near it to pick up its signal."

"Because of my cybernetic plugins?"

The girl shrugged. "How should I know? This hasn't ever happened before. I'm not even real. We shouldn't be having this conversation." She bit her lip. "Actually, maybe I am real? Did you wake me?"

"No," said Cho, remembering. "That can't be right, see. 'Cause I know you, and you're dead."

"Really?" said the girl who was Ruqastra, looking at her arms. "Isn't that something." She fiercely gripped Cho's hands. "I'm curious to know what would happen if you snapped awake right now."

"You're hurting me."

Ruqastra's eyes flashed gold. "I wonder, would I reside in your mind with you? Permanently?"

Her nails drew blood from Cho's wrist.

"Let me go!" Cho wrenched free, staggering back.

When she looked up, Ruqastra had gone. The dancers had faded into the mist. She was alone.

This would have been a great time to wake up. She kept expecting to, but it didn't happen.

She waited a long time.

Finally, hugging her knees, she felt a hand on her shoulder. It was Kinneas.

"I'm awake," he said.

She squeezed his fingers.

"I'm awake."

And then, so was she.

She ran to the infirmary, skidding through the corridors of Anarkey.

Doctor Dzu met her at the door, informing her that Kinneas had stirred a few hours ago. He'd wanted to monitor the boy first, to be safe, but had been just about to summon her.

"Actually, hold on, how did you know your boy was conscious?"

Ignoring the doc, she burst into the room and half-fell onto the foot of Kinneas's bed.

His first words to her were, "Alina was right."

"If I weren't so happy to see you alive," she said, "I'd *kill* you for saying that."

Kinneas's smile stretched into a grimace of pain. His face was pale as the underbelly of a fish, his eyes set in sunken purple pits. "Cho," he coughed. "I got the Nids."

She drew in a shuddering breath. "You sure?"

He nodded, wheezing.

Niima Deficit Disorder. Alina had often lectured on that topic.

A resource generated by the body, Niima acted as both sword and shield. Using it with care, while maintaining a reserve, the body remained protected against magic's natural radioactivity. However, if a Maggo expended too much of their Niima, they left themselves open to damage. Often permanent. Sometimes fatal.

"How bad?" said Cho.

"Dunno. I must've pushed myself pretty hard in that last fight." A tear rolled down his cheek. "I feel terrible."

"You were so brave. It was, like, ridiculous." She was crying now too. "I thought you were dead there for a hot second."

"Cho. I don't regret it."

She couldn't face him like this. "If you got the Nids, bud, you better get some rest. I can check on you later."

"Wait."

"I'm here. I'm still here."

"In case I don't, y'know…" Another tear welled in his eye. "I want you to know something."

"You're gonna be fine, Kin. You're a strapping young lad. You'll bounce back in no time flat."

He was shaking. At first, Cho thought she should call for the doc, but Kinneas was trying to speak, so she waited.

"I'm glad I came with you. You're so amazing. Never met anyone like you."

"It's my fault this has happened."

"No. I *chose*." He was seized by a coughing fit. Calm again, he said, "I'm gonna work to get better as fast as I can. I don't wanna let you down."

"Kin, you could never disappoint me. I don't deserve you."

"Yes, you do. You *do*. You deserve everything. You're the best person I know."

"I'm not, though." She stared at a single, squarish stain on the bedsheet, focusing all her attention on it. "I'm not a good person."

"You don't know you like I do." He smiled, rivulets of shadow around his foggy eyes. "Any strength I have comes from you. You make me want to fight for a better world. I know it's cheesy, but you inspire me every day. You were there for me, after dad died and Calthin left. You're always there." His voice faded along with his feverish breath.

"Kin, if I really was your friend, I'd have convinced you to stay in Truct."

"I'd rather die for you than spend one more day in that ghost town." He reached for her hand, taking it, barely able to hold on. "It's you, Cho. When I met you, it was like… how I felt when I swam for the first time."

She wrapped her fingers around his wrist, lightly. Lightly. "Get some sleep. I'll be here. I'll visit you whenever you want. We'll get you back to your goofy old self."

He swiveled his head away from her. "Where're you going?"

"I need to check on Alina. Need to tell her something. I think it's pretty important."

"Yeah, sure it is."

"I'll see you soon, Kin." She didn't know who she was trying harder to convince—him or herself. "Thanks. For everything. Coming with me, fighting with me. All of it."

As she opened the door to leave, he said, "I know you don't love me. Not like I love you, anyway. But it's okay. I'd still do anything for you."

She left.

A dozen feet down the hallway, Cho leaned against the wall, sobbing quietly.

She pulled herself together at the sound of approaching footsteps.

It was Cbarassan. "Some others and I have agreed."

Cho dabbed at her eyes with her sleeves. "'Bout what, exactly?"

"You have served our aims, and now it is clear that there is much to be gained in our union of purpose. Your plan is sound. With you, we will infiltrate the Lion's Den. Tonight."

38

ALINA

FIRST TO BREAK THE kiss, Alina said, "Sorry."

Arms looped around Alina's waist, Ivion said, "For what?" and pulled her in for the sequel. Breathing into her ear: "Not that I'm complaining, but what brought this on?"

Expanding the series to a trilogy, Alina felt herself drifting higher and higher. Ivion's lips held her like a cobweb snagging a feather from the breeze.

A squeal from the bunker door cut the moment short. *"Yuuugh!"*

Thrusting herself away from Ivion, spinning toward the bunker door (which she hadn't heard open), Alina said, "Ah! Cho, Mezami, you're back." She couldn't even have this *one* nice moment, could she?

"Oh my gods, I sure wish I wasn't," said Cho. "Can't tell if I got here way too early or way too late. For once, I'm with Ivion: what *are* you doing, Li?"

"Um, how about you keep outta my business."

"Your 'business' seems just a smidgeon tangled up with pleasure. Ew, by the way. I can't believe you made me use 'pleasure' to refer to *her*." Cho covered her face with her hand. "I can't even look at you right now."

"Then don't."

Eyes rolling upward, Cho said, "Mezami." The Pyct crested her wig. "Help me out, brother. How are you hanging on to your lunch?"

"Lady Torvir," said Ivion coolly. "May I apologize for the indiscretion. Had we known you'd be arriving, we—"

"Yeah, you woulda continued to lie to me." She made a production of gagging. "Anyway, ignoring *all that*, the reason I'm here is to invite my—" She used air-quotes—"'friend' on an outing."

"The nature of this 'outing'...?" said Ivion.

"Doesn't involve you. So how's about you scram?"

Raising her voice, Alina said, "Let's not forget Ivion's a big reason we're even here right now. It's time you treated her with basic respect." She met Ivion's hazel eyes. "And, anything you can say in front of me is safe with her."

"I'm gonna baaarf."

Hands clasped at her waist, Ivion said, "Perhaps the Lady Torvir is uncomfortable with displays of affection because of her own lack of experience." She clicked her tongue behind her pearly teeth. "If only she'd had more positive role models."

"Perhaps if Lady Ivoir would keep her porcelain nose where it belongs." Cho huffed. "Fine, Li. Have it your way: me and a buncha rebels are moving on the Walazzins' HQ tonight, and we sure could use your rock-throwy, shadow-creepy powers." Leaning against the wall, hands in her pockets, she crossed one leg over the other. "There it is. So, you comin' or what?"

Stomach knotting, Alina unthinkingly steadied herself against the Crow, who like Ivion, hung back, content to observe.

Alina's Aelfraver training kicked in: assess, engage, neutralize. This impulse, which usually served her well, competed with her heart's warning: tread carefully, find the right words.

Cho had never had the chance to be a kid. A one-two punch of terror and tenaciousness had cracked the shell of her victimhood, and what had emerged was a street-smart thief, reclaiming her power through the trinkets she stole. During her days on Mount Morbin, she'd fully transitioned into a creature of crevices; the hate that sustained her she'd turned into an inky poison, striking out at any threat within reach.

In short, she'd become someone usable by Anarkey. A thief who thought herself a warrior. And a warrior's purpose was battle, to die on a field in the name of someone else's ideals.

Because their mutual hatreds were in alignment, Cbarassan and the other rebels had fed Cho their dreams, and she'd allowed herself to be consumed by them. Just another seasonal change to avoid dealing with her past. Maybe she thought the darker she became, the likelier she could turn her terror against its causes. If so, she was wrong: killing the Walazzins wouldn't erase the fear. By submitting to it, she'd only give it strength.

There'd always be the next target, another man who deserved her knife. One more step down this path, and Cho might become lost forever.

But how could Alina express all this? How could she explain these feelings grinding through her gut?

Whatever she said next, it would be the wrong response. Her imminent mistake, she knew, approached with all the certainty of an executioner's axe. It was like being back behind the coffee shop counter again and seeing that dreaded Picky Customer yank open the finger-print smeared front door.

Shaking the echoes of "I said *extra cream* you moron" from her thoughts, she looked at her friend. Really looked at her for the first time in days.

She didn't see Cho-Zen, only Cho. Fire-scarred wig. Deep circles under-eye. Fiddling with that knife in her pocket. Bruised all over. It was almost impossible to imagine that this muddy goblin, in her well-used, blood-spattered sneakers, was barely more than a child. Alina, however, managed to anyway.

You're just a kid, she wanted to shout, knowing full-well it made her the biggest hypocrite.

The truth? She had nothing meaningful to say; she simply wanted Cho to stay out of the coming fight. More than anything, she needed Cho safe.

But it was unavoidable, this moment. It'd been coming for weeks, months maybe. A train with no brakes. A scream to knock free an avalanche. Alina understood how Cho must be feeling, how everything must have seemed stacked against her.

Even though no answer would've been the right one, Alina could have done a hundred times better than what she settled on, but she couldn't help herself.

"You idiot. That's a *terrible* idea. I'm not gonna let you go charging into their home base. At least come up with a plan." She was stalling now. "Something!"

"So-rry." Cho pushed off the wall, baring her teeth, an animal imitation of a grin. "Am I not talking to the same Alina K'vich who broke into The Gild to steal a *rock*? Did you have a plan back then?"

"Yes. Well, I did. Kind of."

"Got a lot of nerve tryna stop me from doing what you'd do in my shoes, ya two-faced coward."

Alina watched the Crow slowly circle Cho.

Tail taut with alarm, Mezami zoomed between their heads. "Need: calm, we." He was roundly ignored.

From the corner, Ivion said, "Alina, stop me if I speak out of turn, but I think what you're driving at is that Lady Torvir's intended course of action is so brazen it can only end in chaos. Even if she somehow accomplishes what she sets out to do."

"Don't talk about me like I'm not here, *depix*," Cho growled. "And, stupid me, I thought we'd all agreed the Walazzins gotta go."

"We've been over this a hundred times. Killing them, or anyone else, won't fix anything," Alina shouted. Venomous words erupted like vomit. "This isn't a comic book. Grow up."

"Like your way's any better. Huh?" Cho bit back. "When does the healing drum circle start, Li? Make sure you gimme enough time to grab my bead necklace." She forced a laugh. "Who's talking about 'fixing' anything anyway? Maybe I just wanna burn it all down—the Walazzins, The Authority, and, yeah, even *you*!" She prodded Ivion's chest.

Brushing her white jacket with the back of her hand, Ivion took a step back. The aches of her acid- and glass-scarred flesh washed over Alina. Her patience expired as Cbarassan's mocking grin flashed in her mind's eye. "Cho," she barked, and the fluorescent lights went out, all at once. "Shut up." In the darkness, everyone else seemed to shrink. The searchlights of her eyes bore down on Cho, who stumbled backward.

What had she seen on Alina's face that'd made her leap away like that?

The girl tripped over a trash bag, and it was the Crow that caught her before she could fall. The Crow that no one else could see. It, not Alina, had helped her.

Rego's folds extended throughout the room, a darkness deeper than black. "Shut up," Alina repeated quietly, advancing. "Pretending you're a soldier, what good's it done you so far? What good's it done Kinneas?"

Cho said nothing.

"You barge in here making demands when you're totally unreliable. All that tech in your brain, but you can't think past the basic urge for revenge. Shut. Up."

Cho bolted for the door but skidded to a stop when Alina appeared in front of it, looming over her.

"Where do you think you're going?" Alina grabbed her wrist, claws extending. Pinpricks of blood.

Squirming and kicking, Cho cried, "You're just like her."

Alina's grip slackened. She released her friend's bruised arm.

"You and Ruqastra, you're the same."

Before Alina had time to protest, Cho laid her out with a gut punch. Knuckles like bullets.

Gods, when had she become so strong?

On the floor, head ringing, Alina recovered her senses to find the bunker door wide open. The Chrononite Lorestone lay beside her, its soft green glow washed out by the lamplight entering from the alley.

Rising, she picked up the stone—the Crow fluttering with excitement—and made to go after Cho, but Ivion blocked her, saying, "Give her space. She won't go through with it. She's a frightened child. In a ploy to get attention, she'll pretend to run away. Let her go." Her fingers interlaced with Alina's. "We have work ahead of us, besides."

Voice ragged, Alina told Mezami, "Go after her. Make sure she's safe."

"Stronger: united, we," he said. His glare fixed on the back of Ivion's head, above which he hovered. "Find: her, we. Together: you, I."

"Be off, Aelf, and see to it that Lady Torvir doesn't injure herself. Alina and I must make plans of our own."

Though the Pyct's glassy eyes delivered a deeply cutting accusation all their own, he twisted the knife anyway by reminding Alina, "Promised: you, I. Keep: in check, you."

"I know what I said," she snapped. "Just get out of here."

Tail drooping, he shook his head, but obeyed.

Ivion smelled of cinnamon, charcoal. Her soft, light arms enveloped Alina in a hug. "You did what needed doing."

"Then why do I feel so lousy?"

"The truth hurts. Your friends should treat you with more respect. You're the only one pursuing a course of action that can truly make a difference. Anarkey's terrorism can't create lasting change."

"What does?"

"Stability. Justice. Order. These ideals are worth fighting for, but they can't be won with knives and slings alone. Getting close to The Savior, determining what he's after, will enable us to unravel the Walazzins' plot. Their push with The Sanctum clearly is the linchpin of their military strategy. They seem to believe they can maneuver their zealot pawns to overthrow the Hextarchy. We simply don't know *how* yet. When we do, we'll be able to stop them."

Massaging her abs, Alina said, "The Coven was a dead end." She carefully skirted the topic of Vessa Tardrop. "They got a spy with The Savior, but aren't interested in sharing the deets."

"No surprise there." Ivion examined her silver-flecked fingernails. "The Coven serves at the pleasure of the Hextarchy. They'd never reveal anything that might compromise the security of their 'gods.' So much pointless tradition—if only they'd work with us."

"Cho's in good with the rebels. Maybe I should've—"

"Please. Anarkey is merely a minor tool of the Hextarchy. They're disposable, and useless to us."

"But Cbarassan seemed plugged in with The Coven."

"As a messenger, maybe. A go-between. Don't put your stock in creatures like them. They only want the destruction of The Authority. Such simplistic aims run counter to what we're trying to accomplish."

"And what *are* we trying to do, here, Ivion? I'm honestly all turned around. It doesn't sound pretty out loud, but I'm not trying to save Ozar or anything. Really, I just want answers about my family's past. And future." She reminded herself to breathe. "It's been two years since Dimas... died. Two years since he commanded me to find my uncle. And, now that I've found him (sorta), I'm no closer to learning anything useful. I'm only making things worse, seems like."

"Alina, babe, what are you talking about? You have all the tools at your disposal. You just need the right one for the job. Can't you see that you're so close. By Plutonia, you stole *the face* of one of The Sanctum's Exorcists. You have her *memories* in your mind. You're incredible. If anyone can make sense of these pieces, it's you."

"Last time I tried to sort through Kellfyute's memories, I got lost, and it was... painful. I'd rather not try again."

"You have no choice." Ivion walked behind Alina. "You said it yourself: to get to The Savior, you'll have to attend one of his secret gatherings. The Coven's no help whatsoever, but this Kellfyute was high enough in the chain of command to know where he might turn up. It's worth a second try."

It still felt wrong.

Massaging Alina's shoulders, Ivion said, "What if I came with you? I could help with the sorting."

"You'd do that? It'd be super weird." Alina looked up, blushed. "But not unwelcome."

"Of course. I'd do just about anything for you, Alina K'vich."

"Just about?" She smirked.

"Well." Ivion's eyelashes fluttered. "I wouldn't betray my principles or my country. But, short of that, it's you and me, through and through. I swear it. By the Seventy-Seven Gods, I swear." She straightened, withdrawing to a corner again. "Breaking this siege will destroy the Walazzins' credibility, paving the way for a new dawn in El. It's for the greater good. And I am so happy you'll be there to share in our nation's rebirth."

"Sappy, and oddly patriotic and treasonous at the same time." Alina sighed. "Like before, I'll accept your help. Gladly."

"We'll do great things together. I'm sure of it. Shall we start?"

At Alina's direction, the two of them shoved the sleeping mats, empty candy wrappers, and other junk aside. With the space cleared, they sat opposite each other, and Alina encouraged Ivion to take deep, slow breaths in time with hers. They had to be in sync, or they might become separated in the ether.

After patiently breathing in tandem with Ivion, staring into her eyes, Alina felt their consciousnesses mingle and shift from the physical to the intangible.

A breath later, and they were sitting in a long room whose wooden pillars had been wrapped with straw padding, straw mats covering most of the hardwood floorboards.

"My mind," Alina explained. "Centering myself in a calm space first should give me more control."

Gracefully twirling, Ivion took in the space. "It's so much like what Ordin told me about Machinamancy. Whenever he ported into the Darkthreads, he always did so from his staging ground. What did he call it? The Air-some-thing…?"

"The Ordin Airy. Hadn't thought about it before, but it is pretty similar. Guess the main difference would be Revomancy connects minds, not data."

"If Ordin were here, he'd probably say something like, 'What is a mind, if not a collection of organic data?'"

"Yeah." Alina trailed off, remembering.

"Fascinating, being inside your head."

Not quite sure how to react, Alina said, "Anyway. I modeled this space after The School."

"Where your grandfather taught you Terramancy."

"Even after… everything that's happened… it's still the only home I've ever had." Alina wandered over to the window and pried it open. The hinges squeaked. "If things get rough, here's our exit."

On cue, a knock rattled the front door.

She walked over, gripping the handle, hesitating. "I'm going to let them in now. Kellfyute's memories."

The only other door in this space rattled and shook violently. From the other side, there came scratching noises, harsh breaths.

"Wait. Where does that lead?" said Ivion.

"It's just the bathroom. I use it for, um, storage mainly."

"Storage of *what*?"

Something slammed against the bathroom door.

"Wouldn't worry about it," said Alina. The last thing she needed was for Ivion to see the Crow, a murderous imaginary friend that—in this unreality—could cause very real harm.

She opened the front door.

Into The School marched three people: two men and a woman, each wearing a vacant, slightly open-mouthed expression. The woman Alina recognized by feeling rather than sight—Kellfyute's mother. One of the men was probably a bit younger than Alina herself. He had a soft face, pouting lips, and curly hair. The older man was unmistakable; Alina faced down none other than the dream-shade of The Savior himself. His bushy eyebrows, dark skin, and gray beard made those intense gold eyes pop.

"Strange," said Ivion. "Do memories always take physical form?"

"That's just how I've decided to visualize them."

"A sorting system." Ivion nodded approvingly. "Reminds me again of my brother's work." She stared at the three specters until they'd lined up in front of Alina. "Do they talk?"

"Sure. Get them going and you'll have a hard time shutting them up. But they can only say what Kellfyute remembers."

"Not terribly reliable, then."

"That's memories for ya. These three people—The Savior in particular—blab on and on about The Author and salvation and yadda-yadda. That's mainly what was on Kellfyute's mind when I trapped her."

"Can't you just ask him," Ivion said, pointing at Mateus, "to tell you where he'd be?"

Alina shook her head. "Has to be the right question, the right key-words, or the memory won't trigger. Kellfyute never would've walked up to her Savior and been like, 'Yo, man, where we hangin' tonight?'"

"Ah. So, you need a password of sorts." Humming to herself, Ivion tapped two fingers against her temple. "A key-phrase, related to a time and place The Savior would definitely show himself. Something he would have told his entourage." She stopped pacing. "Can you filter out any memories older than the past week? We don't want any outdated information."

Alina waved her hand, and the three image-people flickered and flashed, their eyes spinning. Then they resumed their vacant stares. "Done."

"And well done. May I?"

Alina bowed. "My kidnapped victim's memories are your kidnapped victim's memories."

Hands clasped behind her back, Ivion placed herself in front of The Savior's image. "My lord, what is your command?"

No response.

"I suppose that would've been too easy. Let me try again." She cleared her throat. "As your Exorcist I live to serve. I seek your divinely inspired guidance."

Nothing.

Ivion hissed under her breath, but her frustration quickly gave way to a satisfied grin. "My lord, The Author's earthly army swells with recruits. Will there be a Fire Vigil next mass?"

His expression suddenly animated and lifelike, Mateus said, "Indeed. Summon your Exorcist brothers and sisters, my child. We shall baptize our would-be initiates in the flames of light and truth."

Eyes wide, Alina muttered, "You're on a roll. Keep going."

"I am, as ever, His Instrument," said Ivion, beaming. "Shall we gather in the Cathedral of Martyrs, as before?"

"No," said The Savior. "We must press our advantage. The sway of the Hextarchy shrinks from the Sixth Stack, so we will establish yet another holy site from which to grow our ranks. Reach out to our Authority contact. Demand they demonstrate their piety and dedication to our cause through the donation of a space suitable for a new temple. One large enough to house our fervor and our Lord's presence."

"It shall be done," said Ivion.

The memory of Mateus returned to its dead-eyed default state as Ivion turned to Alina, clapping her hands and saying, "I know where they'll be. And, better yet, I even know *when*."

"What? How?"

"There's too much to tell, and too little time, but the short version is that I very illegally hacked into a few Authority servers and bribed an official or two, which is how I came across rumors of a certain high-ranking officer with the Foreign Command's Department of Tranquility. He has been securing 'temples' for The Sanctum on the Fifth and Sixth Stacks."

"Any idea who it might be?"

"Absolutely not," said Ivion cheerfully. "But, good news: we don't need to track that person down any longer because The Savior's effigy here just gave me the missing clue. Lately, there's been very little activity out of the Cathedral of Martyrs—the previous Sanctum stronghold."

"They moved on to better digs."

"Exactly. And their efforts in the Sixth have only increased as a result. Around the same time as the Sanctumites' relocation, a relatively small sum of Authority funds—a few million gelders' worth of black ops money—disappeared in the Calder Ward of the Sixth Stack. One detail the thieves couldn't hide, though, was all the scheduled demolitions. Someone's been remodeling the old Fzetsia. I'd bet anything that a quick sweep by a surveillance drone would show Sanctum patrols centered there."

"Fzetsia?"

"A hospital. Shut down when the Hextarchy forfeited control of the Stack."

Alina spared a moment to wonder if, after the closure, people in need of medical treatment had had anywhere else to go. Then, she said, "Been busy, I see. Ivion, I could kiss you."

Still grinning, Ivion said, "Don't hold back on my account."

Grabbing her by the neck, Alina delivered on her promise. Roughly a minute later, she said, "So, where's the meet? Also, please tell me this won't take another stakeout. Even though my last one went amazingly well and created zero fallout, I don't think I could handle round two."

"No need. I know the appointed time, and we're in luck. The Savior will almost certainly be at the Mass of Saint Ponduza. Tonight."

"How do you know?"

"The last such event happened two weeks ago, and the memory you accessed was no more than one week old. So, it stands to reason that the mass The Savior mentioned to Kellfyute must be the next upcoming—Ponduza's."

"Makes sense. Oh, *man*. I'm going to have to pretend to be Kellfyute. Tonight." Here came the nausea. "But can we be sure Ma—The Savior will be there?"

"During special gatherings, the Sanctumites hold Fire Vigils, baptisms that make spectacles of initiates. Our great Savior always personally attends these."

"Crap. Then there's no time to get ready."

"You've never been one to prepare much anyway." Ivion winked.

"Valid."

Every nerve in her body tingling, Alina inhaled deeply. She closed the window and shooed the dream-specters out.

Then she and Ivion opened their eyes to the material world once more.

After all the madness, all the running, the time had finally come for a family reunion.

39

ALINA

DURING THEIR SHARED CAB ride, Ivion gave Alina a crash course in Sanctumite ritual and hierarchy, preparing her to revisit the role of Kellfyute. The Ivoir heiress's wit and knowledge base reminded Alina of Ordin. Pensive genius must run in the family.

A pang of guilt stabbed Alina's insides. She'd liked Ordin. A lot, in fact. Making out with his sister felt like a betrayal. But, maybe things were complicated enough right now without her overthinking the spark between herself and Ivion.

Reality neatly re-prioritized her concerns, and she focused on Ivion's words—rather than the wry curve of her smile.

The Firelight Vigil was an initiation ceremony as old as The Sanctum itself. Traditionally, whenever a new prophet appeared, he would personally induct hopeful recruits into the religion. Each also put his own spin on these events. Some gave droning speeches about sobriety and piousness. Others forced their initiates to publicly reveal shameful family secrets. However, The Savior had a reputation for being the most theatrical to date, severely testing the wills of the fresh meat on the chopping block. His guidance had transformed the Vigil into a true baptism of fire, a gauntlet designed to break the unworthy. The worthy became Porters—foot soldiers of The Sanctum—the shouty street preachers and pamphleteers out pounding the pavement every day.

Sanctum hierarchy included four other ranks:

There were the Lectors, who organized the daily operations of the Porters, administering whichever type of motivation their underlings needed to get the job done. Kellfyute's husband/partner Cronn was a Lector.

In turn, the Lectors were commanded by Exorcists, holy warriors so devout their god had granted them spiritual weapons, which—Alina knew from experience—could be summoned at will. The Exorcists, as their name implied, had a second, even more critical function: to exterminate Demons (which, according to their doctrine, included *all* Aelf and even quite a few human "infidels"). Ivion confirmed that these "Soulblades" were brought forth using Niima. In other words, the Exorcists were using Deïmancy—magic—in direct violation of the foundational principle of their entire belief system. But they passed it off as "a holy reward" or "an Instrument of Justice bestowed by the Lord." Soulblades weren't magic because The Sanctum said they weren't. Pretty convenient!

Using that logic, Alina could claim she wasn't a Terramancer at all, that she simply *asked* the earth to move, and that it only did so because it liked her.

Tolomond was an Exorcist, though she hadn't seen his Soulblade. He hadn't been shy about swinging his greatsword around The Capital, but that had been a tangible weapon, made of real metal. On Morbin, when he'd struck Ruqastra down, his sword had been enchanted with Deïmancy but still solid. Kellfyute's Soulblade saber, on the other hand, cut more wickedly than serrated steel but was purely spectral. (Scary, imagining the Soulblade of the man who'd killed Ugarda Pankrish, the demon Osesoc-ex'calea, and the mechanical dragon H'ranajaan. With all he'd put on display, what could he be hiding?)

Next in the organization, overseeing the big-picture doings of the lower ranks, were the Acolytes. They formed the senior council of the Hierophant—the biggest of cheeses, the highest-ranking member of The Sanctum.

Men like The Savior were special cases. Every decade or two over the past three hundred years, a prophet would appear and shake the faithful into wakefulness. The organization's recruitment efforts would surge, and more bodies meant more tithes. (Initiates were expected to donate their worldly possessions, shedding all "attachments"—anchors that dragged otherwise decent men and women into the depths of materialism and, ultimately, their spiritual doom).

By the way, Ivion imparted one more little factoid: the leader of the Sanctum—the Living Voice of The Author of Creation, the Hierophant himself—currently lived in a thirty-room mansion in The Capital. You know, like you do when you're a man of the cloth, humbly preaching minimalism.

With Ivion's run-down out of the way, Alina spent the remainder of the car ride practicing the call-response statements a Sanctumite was expected to know for the ceremony. Ivion patiently quizzed her, correcting when she messed up, applauding (with tiny, two-fingered palm-taps) when she got an answer right.

Five minutes from their destination, Ivion pinched a wrinkle of Alina's black cloak between her long pale fingers, rubbing the lightweight but dense fabric. "Sanctumites, above all, hate variety."

"Oh, right. Gotta go gray."

"Hustle. We're nearly there."

"I'll change now."

"A private show?" said Ivion, grinning impishly.

Alina surprised herself with a giggle. "Hey!" She willed her cloak to become as boringly gray and woolly as possible, and it did.

Ivion crossed her arms and pouted peevishly. "Never imagined I could be so irritated by magical cloth."

Alina smiled.

Ivion had the cab driver pull over. "Good luck, beautiful." She kissed Alina's cheek.

Getting out, Alina waved the cab off, watched it disappear from sight.

A row of Plasticks whistled and whooped at her. Groaning, she walked away.

So, Ivion had gone off to "take care of some important business." For the best, really. If she'd tagged along, someone might have recognized her. She was, after all, one of the richest people in the world. And one of the most striking.

Several minutes later, as Alina neared her destination, a little blue blur startled her out of her daydream, dragging her into an alley.

"Mezami?" she whispered. "Are you crazy?"

The Pyct crawled into the folds of her cloak to hide.

The image of a furious Cho wriggled its way to the front of Alina's thoughts. "Why aren't you with her?"

"Lost: I, her. Quick: very, she. Scent: hidden, hers. Magic: use, someone."

"Damn," Alina breathed. And the full force of her mistake punched her in the gut even harder than Cho had.

Now Cho was in the wind.

"I messed up. I really, really messed up." Leaning against a wall, she quickly tapped out a message on her phone:

Cho im sorry

i didnt mean any of it

just come back to the safehouse and lets talk

ill help
well figure this out
just please please come back
i got something to take care of but ill be there in a couple hours
wait for me

Picking at her gray getup, Alina said, "What am I even doing here, man?" She raked her fingernails across the wall, leaving deep, wide gashes in the bricks.

"Shutting Cho down. Totally losing track of Kinneas. Mentally torturing Kellfyute... I can't even say it's for the greater good because, truth is, it's all been for me." She saw herself, then—every bit as self-important as Baraam, Ruqastra, and Dimas. Gone, the illusion that she was (or could be) better than they'd been. "I just need so badly to know. Know what I'm doing here. What the point of all this has been." She rubbed her knuckles against her forehead. "Ruqastra said, 'Use fear, fear, the Revomancers' weapon,' but it seems so wrong. Kellfyute and her people are bad news, yeah, but I *still* don't want to hurt them. Does that make me weak? A bad person?"

Mezami landed on her shoulder and patted her neck. "Bad: not, you." Thumping his chest, he added, "Fear: no, me. Fear: no, you."

"But I'm not afraid, not anymore. Not for my life, anyway. I'm so much stronger than I'd ever dreamed I could be. I think I hate even the memory of fear. And breaking Kellfyute down like that, it made me ask myself: why am I doing this, any of it?" She sighed. "I used to think of myself as morally superior because I never took a life, but am I? After what I've done, *am* I really any better than the Sanctumites or The Authority? Is murder any more terrible than turning someone's darkest, most shameful moments against them?"

Mezami scrunched up his mousy face. "Difference: big, yes. Important: you, they? Better: you, they? Yes: yes."

"Care to clarify?"

"Battle: Tolomond, mine. Taught: lessons, me." He thought for a moment. "Pain: him, I. Pain: me, he. Suffer: both, we. Fight: suffer, all." Flicking her earlobe with his tail: "Become him: not, I. But brothers: he, I."

"Brothers? You're nothing alike."

He shook his head fiercely. "Connected: all, we. Affect: choices, all. Necessary: sometimes fight, we. Examples: give, I. Disease: fight, we. Protect family: fight, we. Fight: sometimes, must. But difference: outcome, make. And difference: intention, make."

She kept quiet, keying into how carefully he considered his choice of words. Her arm extended like she was preparing to receive a hunting bird. The Pyct marched up and down it a few times. Then he said, "Battle: fists, some. Battle: knives, others." He punched her shoulder. "Battle: hearts, we." And he took wing. "Teacher: owe, not. Grandfather: owe, not. Me: owe, not. *Yourself*: owe, you."

Seemingly satisfied, he burrowed into her sleeve. Tickled.

The Fzetsia lay three or four blocks ahead.

Cracking her neck, Alina backed into the shadows. She slipped *Ida* over her face and willed it to assume Kellfyute's features. Once more, the mask and her own skin became indistinguishable, a transformation transcending simple illusion.

Face and memories—her tools. Regardless of how she'd come by them, the greater sin would have been to set them aside now that she was so close to her goal.

A tired coat of blue paint chipped off the classical stone columns and walls of the old Fzetsia. Blotches of dark plaster sloppily covered up a faded green circle—the international symbol for medical treatment. The doors and windows had been boarded shut, the walls decked with flyers warning of falling debris, rusty nails, and other hazards. Coming from inside, rowdy shouts and snippets of excited conversation.

Before Alina got to the front door, a bald, gray-robed man with hairy forearms stepped from behind one of the columns.

Half the trick of any disguise was faking confidence: she kept moving forward.

The guard nodded. "Sister Kellfyute."

"Any trouble?" she asked, assuming a scowl.

"None. The Lord's light shines brightly, even in this dark and odious scab of a city."

"Praise The Author." She continued past the man, pulling open the doors.

In case anyone needed reminding that the Sanctumites worshiped a light god, firelight assaulted her eyes as soon as she stepped into the refurbished lobby area. Sconces lined the walls. Tallow candles had been stuffed into every cubbyhole, covering every shelf. Roaring fires framed the hall, all that fizzing and popping wood choking the space with heat, smoke, and glare.

She hid her discomfort just as several dozen heads swiveled to clock her entrance.

Packed with gray-clothed men and women, to match the exterior, the interior's open hall hinted at the building's past. Surrounding a wide central staircase were many doors leading from the lobby into former doctor's offices and patients' rooms. Two out-of-service elevators were taped off and covered in warning signs.

Above all this, smeared across the walls and ceiling, were Author and Savior iconography. Done in three colors—white, black, and red—the images portrayed the familiar tableau of little bright figures kneeling before a giant bright deity. Painted fires consumed shrinking, fleeing shadow-creatures, whom The Author's chosen chased off with sword and spear.

There must have been between two and three hundred Sanctumites inside the Fzetsia already. With each passing minute, that number grew.

Alina patted the lump in her baggy sleeve, a gesture of reassurance for Mezami's benefit—and her own.

She worked her way toward the middle of the crowd. Pressed between hundreds of eager, sweaty bodies, she retreated inside herself, her senses numbed, battered by waves of excited murmurs. The cacophony gripped her by the throat, robbing her of breath.

She noted the recently installed light fixtures in the walls and ceiling and the spotlights shining down on a central stage. In a nearby corner, a production crew fiddled with wires, speaker connections, and a bunch of complicated electrical equipment. The logos on their vests and gear marked them as employees of several major multimedia and news networks—Triple-I, El Vision, Patriot's Watch, E-dify, and more. Gleaming in the firelight, apple-sized camera drones glided in circles, filming the crowd.

Second only to their hatred of magic, the Sanctumites famously despised technology. The fact that they tolerated all these modern lights, sound systems, and recording devices really said something. What exactly that something was, Alina wasn't sure yet. Clearly, though, tonight was big news.

Perhaps to build suspense, no one took the stage for quite a while. So, she was cursed with more time to think.

Apparently, the secret, behind-closed-doors affairs of The Sanctum weren't so "secret" after all. The exact location had been kept hush-hush, but the presence of the news crews demonstrated The Savior wanted an audience of millions for whatever was about to happen.

Overconfidence and pride, she thought. Exploitable weaknesses.

What could the Elementals possibly have promised Mateus—child of a Demidivine Sevensin, creatures of legend—that would lead him to side with them? They couldn't have known his true nature—a Hybrid, a direct relative of the Bane of New El. If they had, they'd have shredded him.

That, too, Alina could use if she were absolutely desperate. She'd prefer to keep that tidbit in her back pocket: revealing his identity would lead The Authority straight to her.

She wondered what she would even say to him when her window opened. It's not like she could lead with, *Hey, it's me, the niece you stopped coming to visit after your sister and brother-in-law were buried under a million pounds of rubble. Just had a few Q's about our cursed lineage. Got a minute? Cool, thanks.*

If nothing else, she was confident her uncle could not be trusted: after more than a year of peace and quiet on Morbin, all it took was one accidental astral outreach to Mateus, and—*bam!*—a joint task force of Sanctum and Authority hitmen drop in for a midnight murder spree.

Alina didn't put any stock in fate, but neither did she believe in coincidence. To her, everything and everyone had its pattern. If enough about their motivations were known, people became predictable. For instance, she could always expect them to disappoint. It was also a fair bet that they'd want her dead. Most did, and her uncle was no exception.

With fifty questions and no answers, she clenched her fists. She could smell the halitosis wafting from the man behind her, the stench of excitement drifting from an armpit to her right. Too many witnesses here to make a big play. She'd have to wait at least until the ritual was concluded. If The Savior found out who she was, he'd throw his horde of Sanctumites at her, and that would be that.

So, she'd cling to her disguise and her plan. Exorcist Kellfyute was an important figure in The Sanctum pecking order. Using her face, Alina might be able to pluck a few kernels of valuable information—about Mateus's plans for the Hextarchy, about how Alina herself fit into them.

At last, an infectious silence stole away even the sounds of breathing and the rustling of robes as The Savior entered the hall. His bodyguards, a man and a woman, followed him to the stage steps. There they stayed as he ascended alone.

The crowd twitched with anticipation. No applause. Except for Alina's, awe spattered every face. Eyes bulged and drool dribbled, but The Savior's climbing onto the stage was greeted with reverent stillness.

The bodyguards stood out to Alina. The woman wore Sanctumite grays, tunic and pants, but done up in a silkier, more angular cut. She was also the only one wearing sunglasses. The bangs of her bowlcut partially covered her bald eyebrows. Her lips were sealed, expression neutral. Alina felt nothing from her. No Niima. Minimal life force, even.

Before she could wonder too long at how strange that was, Alina did a double-take: she'd caught sight of the man. Tall, broad-shouldered, he wore a Gildsman's uniform, black with turquoise trim. The tan lines on his face revealed that he'd come from a place of strong sunlight and had recently shaved his curly hair and beard to black stubble. She'd recognize that condescending scowl anywhere.

What was *he* doing here?

Hardly believing the evidence of her own eyes, she closed them and reached out with her other senses. Detecting his Niimantic aura—a brooding, crackling thunderhead of energy rolling outward—she confirmed that he was, undoubtedly, the one and only Baraam bol-Talanai.

He hadn't sent so much as one text since they'd fought their way off the streets of New El together, but, now, here he was, stiff as a lightning rod. Another complication. Though she'd rather not admit it, Baraam knew her well. That human hurricane could easily lay waste to her scheme. She was going to have to be *very* careful not to give herself away now.

Breaking the silence with his clear, powerful voice, The Savior said, "Brothers and Sisters in Light, my apologies for having kept you waiting. The dealings of our Lord have lately stretched me thin. He has blessedly prevented my hands from being idle for even a moment. Thank you for your patience with me." He spent several minutes running through a series of calls and responses, in which he invoked the favor of The Author, asking that this congregation be endowed with wisdom and strength, etc., etc.

Alina mumbled along, all the while mentally contrasting this experience with her own worship of Buthmertha, a goddess who prioritized protecting orphans and growing families. No mentions of fire and infidels. Buthmertha's first commandment was to take care of your neighbors and friends; the second, to be kind and honest even if it hurt (that last part she *swore* she'd get to, one day soon). Buthmerthan church events involved stuff like handholding and singing, a shared meal on special occasions, and community volunteer work.

With her background, Alina was deeply troubled by what she experienced that night at the Fzetsia.

Under different circumstances, it could've been cool that all these people had found such firm common ground. But these were the same folks cheering on beatings, killings, assassinations, proclaiming all other gods false, declaring magic a sin and all Maggos worthy of death. And they somehow followed this agenda in the name of their *kind* and *loving* Author. They basically made up an army of glaring, wide-grinning, identically dressed bigots who recited, in perfect time, long verses in response to their charismatic cult leader.

Yep, this was fine.

The worst was yet to come, though.

Once the required divine "how-do-you-dos" were dealt with, The Savior extended an arm. "Bring forth the crucibles."

Torches in hand, four Porters marched onto the stage, each taking up one of its four corners to light the braziers.

"Hopefuls, arise and come forward," said The Savior, reaching out to the audience as if to embrace them.

From the front row, a group of twelve climbed onto the platform. They'd also been shaved only recently, the scabs on their scalps and their shabby street clothes speaking of a rougher arrival than Baraam's.

Alina had never seen fresh Sanctumite recruits before.

As they lined up by the lit braziers in groups of three, The Savior said, "Our Lord is righteous and just, but He is also strong. He abhors weakness."

"Let the weak be judged and cast out," the crowd said as one.

"This night, we shall test the resolve of those who would name themselves our brothers and sisters."

"They shall be tested."

"Any found lacking in mettle shall be removed from His sight."

"They shall be banished."

"Hopefuls. Your trial by fire begins now."

Four of those on stage stepped up to their respective braziers and folded the sleeves of their shirts up to their elbows. Then they held their arms above the flames.

Fire licked their flesh, the seconds burning away as the audience watched in silence.

Rigid, Alina forgot how to blink.

The "hopefuls" held out for far too long, gritting their teeth, trembling, shrieking in agony.

Alina covered her mouth, almost gagging at the whiff of cooking human.

Finally, one of the new recruits broke, screaming, tearing his arm away from the scalding heat.

"Cast him out," said Mateus calmly. Two Sanctumites dragged the failed, whimpering candidate from the building. The Savior told the remaining three, "Cleansed by the light of truth, we witness your transformations, sisters and brother." To the room at large: "Bathe and clothe them as your own."

"Praise The Author!"

Those who'd passed the test descended the stage steps to be surrounded by their new spiritual siblings.

Afterward, the process was repeated twice more. Each time, the first of the four contestants to come to his senses and *stop burning himself* was tossed outside, while the three traumatized "winners" were cheered by the congregation.

When the selection process was over, Mateus walked up to one of the braziers. "By the power of The Author, all things are possible." He plunged his arm directly into the white-hot coals.

Biting her tongue, Alina was shocked that no one else seemed, well, *shocked* by this.

His robe caught fire, the flames quickly fluttering up his arm, then enshrouding his entire body.

Her nerve almost broke; she almost leapt onto the stage to stop this insanity unfolding before her. She couldn't watch another K'vich die.

But then she felt it—a pulsing undercurrent of Corpromancy—the magic of flesh and blood. Even as he burned, he was casting a spell.

Transfixed by silent horror, she waited.

The flames dissipated.

Smoke and steam rose from him. Standing naked now, his flesh and even his hair were untouched, as was the necklace he wore—a simple strip of leather from which hung a shard of faintly glowing green rock.

Chrononite. He had a sliver of Chrononite around his neck! And, unless Alina was fooling herself, it looked to be just about the right shape to have been chipped off the Lorestone she'd permanently borrowed from The Gild.

"Praise The Author!" screamed someone in the congregation, slightly ahead of everyone else. The crowd echoed the cry until, finally, Mateus raised his hands.

One of the Sanctumites ran up to offer him a fresh robe, which he accepted. As he covered himself, he said, "You have seen this miracle before."

Miracle? Alina glared at him. He was using magic—that thing Sanctumites supposedly hated above all. Yet, she saw only the hearth-fire glow of adoration on all those faithful faces. How could none of them *know*?

She answered her own question: he had them all in the palm of his hand. He could make them repeat his every word, burn themselves, torture and maim, and they'd only love him more for his lies. They were in awe of him, of the deity he supposedly represented. Now *that* was power—the power of fear, the weapon Ruqastra had tried so many times to thrust into Alina's own hands.

"I am protected," Mateus said, "by the Lord's grace. I am His Instrument and His Voice. Is there such a one here as would doubt me?"

Absolute silence. By comparison, a crypt would've seemed like a high school rager.

"None would step forward? But, I am confused by this, for I have heard whisperings of doubt. Reports from my Acolytes of murmurings. There *are* those—perhaps in this very chamber—who remain unconvinced of my divine mandate."

The congregation skipped right past booing and hissing, diving directly into muted fury. Each pair of eyes searched the room as if combing for ticks.

"However," said Mateus, smiling again. "After tonight, the doubters shall be stricken dumb forevermore." He pointed stage right, and four Sanctumites carrying a stretcher marched forward. "After tonight, none will dare argue I was not chosen by the Lord."

On the stretcher sprawled a man, still, open-eyed. Dead.

The Porters laid the body at Mateus's feet. Rolling up his sleeves, The Savior dismissed them and knelt near the corpse's head. Closing its eyes with thumb and forefinger, he muttered a few words, and his hands and arms began to glow whitish blue.

That was Corpromancy, too, but of a type Alina hadn't studied. And there was another essence mingling with it, one she couldn't identify.

Collectively, the congregation held its breath. Even Alina joined in now.

Mateus said, "Faithful servant, loving husband, our brother Icthid was taken from this world before his time."

Magical light flowed from his arms to the dead man's, which swung suddenly upward, swatting limply at the air. Revived, he opened his mouth, releasing a shuddering gurgle.

Alina's gasp was drowned out by the uproar—applause and shouts of "Miracle! The miracle of life!"

"Arise, Icthid." The Savior helped the un-dead man to his feet, and two of the Sanctumites rushed over to steady him. "Behold! Our Lord has willed Icthid's resurrection! Our Firelight Vigil has received the ultimate blessing. Praise Him!"

"Praise The Author! Hail The Savior!"

At a loss for words as the Sanctumites' fervor rose to a frenzy, Alina drowned inside her own thoughts.

Resurrection wasn't possible.

Corpromancy and its sub-disciplines could do a lot. Zoiimancy could heal wounds and cure disease. Necromancy could reanimate a body and call forth lost souls. But one fact was undeniable, immutable, and beyond question: what was dead *stayed* dead.

Yet, by all appearances, Mateus, Savior of The Sanctum, had just restored a man to life.

If he had *actually* just pulled off what he'd claimed to, then he really might be—

No. She refused to believe it. There had to be a trick. Had to be. It wasn't possible. She'd missed some sleight of hand, the key to explaining what she'd seen, but she mustn't allow her lack of knowledge to lead to unthinkable conclusions.

Scrutinizing the stumbling, shaky Icthid as he was hurried off stage, she wracked her brain. It didn't make sense.

There'd be time to unpack what she'd just seen later. Right now, she had to stay focused.

The Sevensin. The Author. Dimas. Tolomond. The Hextarchs. The Authority. The Sanctum. Mateus and his Chrononite necklace. The connection between all these stories and her own, that's why she'd come out tonight.

Alina listened as The Savior performed a few encores of his greatest hits. She waited impatiently for the Firelight Vigil to end.

Finally, the stage lights dimmed. The cameras returned to their charging docks near the news crews. The Savior collected his two patsies—Baraam and the strange woman—and left through a side exit.

Heart pounding, Alina gave chase.

If things go sideways, she telepathically told Mezami, *I want you to bug out. Find Cho. Keep her safe. Got me?*

Shoo: not, me. For you: here, I.

I'm not worried about me.

Should be: maybe, you.

4⊙

BARAAM

BARAAM WAS A STORM trapped in a bottle. He could see beyond the walls of his prison, yet there was no escape.

Not for the first time did he silently wish for an earthquake to collapse the ceiling on The Savior's head, for a colossal *Dan'yn'daup* to tear through these tunnels of Ozar, instantly and specifically pulverizing everyone in this room with its bony, saw-like protrusions.

Baraam smiled to himself, imagining the "prophet" melted by a spontaneously erupting jet of molten rock; a rogue spark of wild magic combusting him in his sleep; a pretzel lodging in his throat.

This crowded space had all the trappings of a performer's dressing room. A vanity stuffed with makeup and haircare products, topped by a tall, oval mirror. Patterned burgundy curtains. And gifts, so many gifts. Offerings from hundreds of destitute young fools who worshiped their prophet almost as intensely as they did their God.

The Savior slouched in his chair, his sigh fogging the mirror. "Have you carted off the invalid?"

Ah, yes. Icthid, the victim of the charlatan preacher's phony healing ritual. Although The Savior was a (highly) powerful mage, his abilities fell far short of the "resurrection" he claimed to be capable of. What had supposedly brought Icthid back to life was nothing more than Necromancy, the spell reducing him to a puppet without strings—lumbering remains thrown into the back of a windowless van. Destined for an unmarked grave.

Spectacle. Illusions. Lies. Such were the pillars of The Sanctum.

Now, as always, a ring of sycophants surrounded their Savior, singing his praises, inhaling the exhaust of every whiff of hot air blowing from him. These Acolytes, if any knew the truth about their master, would not dare speak it.

One of them said, "Yes, Your Eminence. The gibbering husk has been taken to the slaughterhouse for preparation, as you instructed."

A slaughterhouse? Surely, they weren't planning to eat the wretched creature? Even The Sanctum wouldn't stoop to cannibalism. Ignoring the immorality of the act, the Niima-infused meat would be fatally toxic.

Fingers interlaced in mockery of prayer, The Savior stared at his own reflection. "Leave me, all of you. Except you, bol-Talanai."

Baraam, standing behind The Savior, tensed at the sound of his own name. He felt again the urge to strangle The Savior where he sat. But the thought of the repercussions to the Saludbabni, to Jija and the other shamans, stayed him.

The gray-robed yes-men, buzzards crowding a single corpse, bumbled out of the room. When they were gone, Baraam waited quietly for the upcoming order.

Although she hadn't been singled out by The Savior, Eva Schoroto—the other bodyguard—did not abandon her corner either. Since Baraam's arrival at least, she'd been a constant presence, to the point that he'd begun to question whether she were here to protect or monitor. Curved of spine, hands in her pockets, elbows splayed, she had short brown hair that curled behind her ears like the wings of a bird-of-prey poised to dive-bomb. Her face was timeless. Any guess as to her age could have reasonably fallen between a weathered thirty and a burnished sixty years. Her eyes, hidden behind opaque sunglasses, remained focused on a single point in space (as far as Baraam could tell, directly between and slightly above his and The Savior's heads). In the days since they'd met, she hadn't said one word.

Eva, within whose hunched body flowed a boiling river of raw Niima.

She hid it well, her power, but Baraam's training allowed him to cut through her deception. In all his years of Raving, of probing the depths of his own soul, touching on sources of arcane energy from all over the world—human and Aelf—he'd never sensed anything that could hold a candle to her magical reserves. Unmoving, unspeaking, she terrified him. Her oppressive Niimantic essence siphoned his breath. It felt like being sucked into the vacuum of a tornado. She was awe-inspiring. By Éétion, what leverage could The Sanctum hold over her that she would stoop to working for such inferior men?

The Savior let him stew in his angst a few moments before saying, "I know you were brought here under duress, bol-Talanai."

Baraam felt his whole body clench.

"I understand your resentment, though I'll not apologize. Your coming here wasn't my idea, yet we must all play our parts—however large or small—in this grand theater. My role, for example? Wave my hands and spout fiction, until I finally find my way into Hexhall to claim my divine birthright. Your lot is to brood in that corner, a weapon waiting to be aimed. And, I must say, you're doing a terrific job so far."

Clinging to the mental image of clear skies, the infinite blue above white dunes, Baraam nevertheless could not escape. The Savior's harsh chortle dragged him back to grim, musty-smelling reality.

Baraam said, "I was told I'd be joining the war effort, not watching haggard fools gasp in awe at the parlor tricks of a second-rate magician."

"Quite the sharp retort from so blunt a tool. You must have been saving that one, huh? Mulling it over, perfecting it? And here I was thinking you a brick-brained flesh golem."

In a tone like hail chipping away a cliff-face, Baraam said, "I am the highest-ranked Aelfraver in the world."

"You *were*, yes. I did hear about that." The Savior combed his fingers through his thick, graying beard. "But, the higher the climb, the longer the fall. You only think you've hit the bottom, bol-Talanai, but you've landed on my plateau. Endeavor to stay in my good graces, for, if you displease me, you'll find it's quite a long way down yet."

Tamping down the tempest in his chest, Baraam reminded himself of the futility of resistance. He must surrender, accept, move on.

"Oh, be at ease, boy. We're only talking." The Savior laughed at him. "You speak of the battlefront. Is it glory you're after? At my back, you're worth a thousand spell-slinging grunts on the front lines, for I am the Elementals' best chance at unseating the Hextarchs and conquering Ozar once and for all. I am the only one who can hand your people the victory they've sought for centuries. So, if it appeases your over-inflated ego, console yourself with the certainty that you are doing more than any front-line grunt to tear down this decadent, corrupt society."

Duty, Baraam reminded himself. Honor. Sacrifice. Loyalty to The Gild, to El.

As he'd sworn to, he would protect this arrogant, self-important buffoon. So help him, he would. He was, after all, only as good as his word.

His thoughts scattered like wisps of cloud as the door opened.

It was the monied bureaucrat, Jejune, who bounded inside, saying, "I told her to buzz off, *my Lord Savior.*" His voice dripped with all the nectar of a carnivorous plant. "But she insisted you hear her out."

A Sanctumite woman in her mid-twenties shoved Jejune aside (an act of which Baraam heartily approved). Like the other faithful, she was bald. However, she bore a distinct pattern of scars—rings like those of a tiger—marking the flesh of her arms, neck, and scalp.

"Kneel, child," said The Savior, rising from his seat.

The Sanctumite knelt, a little awkwardly, bowing her head. A droplet of sweat tumbled from the tip of her nose onto the stone floor. "Your Eminence, I am your servant, the Exorcist Kellfyute." Her voice was hoarse, as if she'd been screaming for hours. Still, there was something about it—some indescribable quality—that tickled the back of Baraam's brain.

Because she stood still for such long stretches of time, whenever Eva *did* move the effect was eerie—a hawk sighting a field mouse. She circled this Kellfyute now, gaze fixed, head swiveling as her feet silently traced circles around the room.

"Arise," said The Savior.

Kellfyute obeyed. "Shun the darkness."

"Embrace the light." His warm smile crept from behind his beard. "What troubles you, child?"

"Eminence," said Kellfyute, eyes wide with awe. "I am here to serve you. And our faith. Praise The Author."

Baraam rolled his eyes.

She continued, "I need your advice. Our Lord came to me in a dream, showing me the way. I have done as I was told. Now, I have come to you—as Our Lord directed—to tell you of my success."

"Strange that the Lord did not relay this message to me directly." The Savior flung his robe out behind him, the cloth settling like a dusty gray wing. "Yet, He may Write His Will through anyone. What news do you bring?"

"An answer to the problem of The Coven."

"You have my attention."

Still, Eva circled.

Baraam scoffed at all this dream-vision nonsense. If Kellfyute spoke truly, at least the war would soon end, and he'd be free to return to the desert where he belonged. *However*, very little would make him happier than to witness firsthand The Savior's ultimate failure. (Yes, yes, duty, loyalty, and all that. He could wish for his employer's death while still working to prevent it.)

Hair hanging, obscuring his eyes, The Savior stood over his Exorcist. "What have you found out?" His voice was quiet as the flutter of moths' wings. "And how?"

"I've met one of them, a Covenant. Talked with her," said Kellfyute, quickly, quavering slightly. "Befriended her."

He gripped her shoulders, pressing. "For what reason?"

"The Author gave me the words to disarm her. She's fond of me, for some reason. She can be used."

"Explain." Hunger in The Savior's eyes, a glow like embers, drawing him in. "Quickly." He practically salivated.

"The Coven watches over Hexhall—where the false gods live. They have many shields of, uh… foul magic protecting them. But, a Covenant can pass through these… without issue."

"We have never captured a single Covenant." The Savior scoffed, robe flapping behind him, as he stamped away from her, growling, "You waste my invaluable time."

"But, Your Eminence, The Covenant I spoke with wishes to recruit me."

"What?" He turned toward the Exorcist again. "Impossible. Their prejudice against our religion—"

"She's not like the others, the one I, uh, speak of. She's kind—and, and gullible. I could pretend to join her, keep pretending to be sympathetic to their cause, and find some way to open a passage, a back door for your—for the faithful and The Authority to come through. The siege could end in days instead of months or years."

"And what would you, Exorcist Kellfyute, desire in return for such risk and sacrifice?"

"Faith is its own reward." Kellfyute bowed her bald head. "But."

The Savior's bushy brows knitted. "Well?"

She stammered a moment before saying, "I do ask for one blessing: that you reward my faith with your trust."

"Did you, by chance, have in mind some particular demonstration of that trust?"

"Yes, Eminence. Forgive me if I ask too much. I only—I desire only to better *serve* The Author. And you." She cleared her throat. "I have witnessed you perform miracles. Your faith's granted you powers so far beyond the heretic mages'."

"Do not needle me with the vice of flattery, Exorcist Kellfyute. Speak plainly, or begone from my sight."

She clasped her hands, thumbnails pinching her forehead. Her self-humbling appeased her master, but Baraam caught something wild in her eye, just beforehand. Hesitation? Thoughtfulness? Insincerity?

"I want to be closer to Him, to Our Lord," she said. "I want to know where your miraculous powers come from. To be more like you. I want nothing more than to be your Instrument, to annihilate our enemies with sacred flames."

"But you are an Exorcist already. Your Soulblade is proof of your compact with the Lord, yet you desire more?"

"Yeah—yes. For that, and the truth behind the mysteries of our faith, I will do anything." Her lip trembled.

The Savior thought a moment. "This I can understand. But what you ask is the purview only of myself, the Hierophant, and the Acolytes. Were you an Acolyte, you would be initiated into the deeper 'mysteries' as you call them. What you seek, therefore, is promotion."

"Are Acolytes granted visions of the Lord?"

"Not visions, no. They are, however, visited by the blessings of angels, our most divine messengers."

An enigmatic grin slithered across Jejune's face. No decent man had ever smiled like that. Baraam should have driven a spear of lightning through that snake's chest and have done with it. Should have, but didn't.

"It's power you seek, is it?" The Savior smirked. "You pretend to love wisdom, but I see your mind. Humility lies outside your virtues."

Kellfyute didn't take the bait. She closed her eyes, saying, "May I serve you as I have asked, sir?"

Fingers curled strands of his coarse beard, The Savior said, "Exorcist Kellfyute, I tell you truly, I see no reason not to chance it. Whether you succeed or fail, the only difference in outcome is the length of time it will take to raze this Godforsaken hole of a country. Short or long, the end is coming." He waved a hand dismissively, seating himself again. "Go, then. You have my blessing."

"And, if I do—"

"If you prevail," he interrupted, "you will be an Acolyte. Once The Authority's flag and the Silver Flame of Our Lord hang over Hexhall, I will *personally* teach you all I know."

A mask of awe, Kellfyute's face almost cracked under the pressure of her sudden smile. She repressed it, bowing low. "Thank you. Thank you."

"Off with you, child. The Lord's work has taken its toll. I must rest."

After bowing far more times than necessary, she made for the door. She paused, turning. "Your Eminence, what *are* the Hextarchs?"

The Savior ground his teeth. "Demons. The progenitors of demons. The wicked parents of all that is evil in this world. When they are gone, a new era of light will begin. As was foretold, our Lord will reign supreme. The Sanctum will become the only extant religion, as God intended."

Although the briefest flash of a grimace suggested she was unsatisfied, with a final curtsy, Kellfyute said, "Praise The Author," and exited.

Jejune slammed the door. "Yuck. Thought she'd never leave."

Immediately, The Savior slumped. "My gods, these simpletons. It's so incredibly tiresome to deal with them day in, day out. You really have no idea, bol-Talanai."

"It's not too difficult to imagine," said Baraam.

"And you're fine, *my lord*, letting one of your own run off to basically guaranteed death?" said Jejune in far too cheerful a tone.

Massaging his forehead, The Savior said, "However improbably, it's possible she will succeed. Either way, there are thousands more, exactly like her, eagerly awaiting the chance to take her place."

Sickened, Baraam said, "Excuse me" and made to leave.

"Where are you going?"

"To relieve myself. Do I require a chaperone?"

"Really, you ought to be nicer to me, Aelfraver; I'll soon be the most powerful being in this world."

Shrugging, Baraam said, "They'll give that title to anyone these days."

"A wounded ego encourages insolence." The Savior tut-tutted. "There is no comparison between us. You summon rainclouds, whereas I, in a matter of days, will become a god."

With that, Baraam left the prophet to his delusions.

On his way out, he saw Eva's mouth slacken, her lips parting as if she struggled to say something. He paused for a breath, but then her jaw clamped shut again. The moment had passed.

He hastened after Kellfyute.

"Hey, you. Wait." Catching up with Kellfyute just before she left the Fzetsia, Baraam said, "You willingly throw yourself into the fire, and for what? Why do you follow him?"

Kellfyute was visibly surprised to see him. "Isn't that kind of question dangerous?"

"What have I left to fear? I'm robbed already of my liberty."

"Sounds like you got plenty of problems of your own, but here you are, getting on my back about my choices. Typical."

This woman seemed so familiar to him, but why?

"What I don't understand," he said, "is why you Sanctumites serve masters who are so obviously using you for their own ends? Do you truly believe the Hierophant and Savior care for you?"

She scoffed. "How's about you acquaint yourself with a mirror, Baraam. I'm not stupid. I know The Savior's after power. Well, so am I. A different kind, but power all the same. I happen to be looking for answers to important questions, and I don't need a washed up celebrity has-been stepping on my toes." She bit her lip, looking like she'd just triggered a land mine.

That expression! He'd recognize it anywhere. But, it couldn't be...

Quickly, she added, "Why are we even having this conversation, uh, *infidel.* We don't know each other. Leave me alone." She cleared her throat. "Praise The Author. Bye."

She hurried off.

Momentarily stunned, he watched her go. In the whole world, there were only two people who could so thoroughly infuriate him with so few words: his sister Ruqastra and—

He hardly dared utter the name aloud. "Alina?"

Turning on her heels, she stuttered, "Um, no. Who's that? Who're you—" Suddenly, she dropped all pretense. "Alright, guess ya got me."

"What in the hells are you doing here?"

"Could ask you the same question."

It was disturbing, to knowingly watch this person before him display Alina's mannerisms while looking nothing like her.

Thrown off, he leaned his forearm and elbow against the door. "You want to know? I'll tell you. The Gildmaster gave me an ultimatum. He was going to… hurt people I care for."

"Why didn't you just kill him? That's what you're good at, isn't it?"

"Kill the Gildmaster? Are you hearing yourself?"

"So, don't, then," she hissed. "See if I care. But you still don't gotta do what he says."

"I'd forgotten how simple life is through your eyes, blind to all complexity."

"My eyes are wide open. That's how I avoid blindly obeying bad people."

A bulge near her collarbone revealed that she'd brought along her little blue Pyct companion. She'd brought an *Aelf* to a Sanctum Firelight Vigil. Marveling at her boundless stupidity, he said, "You're still the same infantile fool you've been all your life. Ruqastra may have taught you some new tricks, but, obviously, you've kept up your knack for throwing yourself into the nearest fire."

"At least I make my own choices."

"Yes, terrible ones." Why did he always fall into the trap of locking horns with her? Nothing good ever came of it.

"A sheep, that's all you are," she snapped. "You're just being herded from field to barn and back. And, one day, they'll slaughter you, too—snap your thick neck, and you'll thank 'em just before they do."

"Careful," he said, sparks arcing from his fingertips.

"*There* it is." She crossed her scarred arms. "Anytime you hear something you don't like, you take a fighting stance. Well, your snorts and foot-stamps won't cut it anymore. Whatever you might think, I'm *not* the same as before. Used to be, you were much, much stronger than I was. But that's changed. I could probably tear you in half now—so, do us both a favor and *don't* try me."

Baraam snorted, shaking his head, and he felt an ache (he'd grown used to the way his long locks had brushed the notch of his spine and tops of his shoulders). "How have you become even more arrogant?"

As she had often done before, she completely ignored him, instead continuing with her rant. "A while ago, I finally realized the truth about you: your spirit is weak. You're afraid of all these terrible things that are supposedly going to happen. To you. To me. And being afraid of the future has become part of who you are now, so you don't work to change anything. You'll always be stuck, grounded, claiming you have all the answers, offering unwelcome advice to the people you care about. But, in the end, you're just paranoid. Even becoming the greatest Aelfraver in the world only gave you more to lose. You built your own cage."

Utterly exhausted, he sighed and retreated. "I don't care."

"Tell me I'm wrong." Her greatest gift was how easily she could get a rise out of him.

"Few are those fortunate enough to be free of all obligations and responsibilities. Enjoy it. Your leisure is paid for by those like me."

"Bootlickers?"

"Those who do what is necessary, ensuring the stability of civilization, providing for the future, so that troublemakers like you can dance your way through life. I might be the one who summons storms, Alina, but you're the true whirlwind: you'd pick over the corpse of El if you could make a game of it."

"Poor choice of words. I'm looking at the king of the corpse makers."

"I've only ever taken lives in service to my nation."

"Yeah, yeah, keep telling yourself that, lightning rod."

Their argument had gotten heated enough that a Sanctumite approached them, asking, "Sister Kellfyute, is everything alright?"

"Of course. I was just telling bol-Talanai that he needed to brush up on his theology. Why don't you recite a few of your favorite edicts, brother?"

The Sanctumite smiled graciously.

"Get out of my face," Baraam barked, shoving the Sanctumite aside and following Alina as she flung open the doors and left the building.

"Leave me alone," she said.

"What are you after?"

"I told you, answers."

"Stop bickering with me. There's something you should know. The Savior thinks defeating the Hextarchy will grant him the powers of a god. You're wrapped up in events you couldn't possibly understand."

"You chump." Alina chuckled. "You don't have any idea who The Savior really is, do you, you smug jerk?"

He glared at her.

She leaned in to whisper, "Mateus *K'vich*." She tapped her nose. "Tell me again how this isn't any of my business." Grappling with the news he'd just received, he failed to reply before she chided him again: "Honestly, I know it's been a long time, but you're slipping if you didn't recognize him. The past couple years must've done a number on you."

Still, he didn't answer.

"Yowza. Is Baraam bol-Talanai, supreme pontificator, finally at a loss for words?"

How had he been so blinded to the truth? How had he not felt the Niimantic signatures of Mateus K'vich, his old master's only son? How had he not remembered the man by sight?

Memories of Dimas's betrayals rained down upon him, soaking him in his own fury. And here was Alina, Dimas's granddaughter, niece of Mateus. The K'vich family plagued Baraam like ticks, infesting his soul, bleeding it dry, riddling it with disease.

Yet, he could do nothing. He bowed to the will of Gildmaster Ridect, and so must serve the son of the man he had come to hate with all his passion.

No, Dimas had never been a man. The aged Aelf had only pretended to be. As did the creature standing before him now—the one he'd once thought of as a sister, who wore a stranger's face in more ways than one. Still, he could not quite hate her.

"Just promise me." He took a deep breath, inner rainstorm dissipating. A fog of war crept over his heart, shrouding it. "Do your best to be careful."

Her exhale had an edge to it. "I managed fine last time. Ancient super Aelf, gods—what's the difference?" She cracked her knuckles. "You're the one who needs to take care. There was a demon in that room with us. One of The Savior's little helpers is more than they seem."

He nodded, hiding his anger at having missed yet another vital detail.

When had Alina become so capable?

As their eyes met, hers flashed gold.

"Before you go," said Baraam, trailing off. "How is my—how is Ruqastra?"

Alina tugged at the sleeves of her gray tunic. "She's... been better."

"Take care of her for me. And of yourself."

"I'll, uh, do what I can."

"And..."

"Yeah, what?"

"Once you've got what you're after, whatever else you do, get clear of Hexhall. When The Authority marches in, there will be chaos. Surrender to the Tranquilizers if you must. Just stay alive."

"It won't come to that." Alina laughed just like Ruqastra now—a single, sharp *Pah*. "See, you think The Savior's using me, but I'm the one who's using *him*."

"How can you be so sure?"

"Because I know his secret identity, but he doesn't know mine. Knowledge is power, and all the liar's dice are in my cup. So, I'm going to take what he knows, and then I'll decide what to do with him. Until then, zip your lips about my involvement in all this, yeah? If you really care about me living past tomorrow, you'll keep a tight lid on this convo. Cool?"

His nod seemed to satisfy her, and he watched her head off, into the cold, ancient streets of the Sixth Stack of Ozar, toward Peregar's Grief. Behind that wall lay the world's last anti-Elemental holdout, soon to be the site of the greatest battle in generations.

The potential for glory meant nothing to Baraam now, but honor was everything to him. His code demanded he serve his masters to the end of ends. Yet, one of his masters had betrayed him.

Dimas, his teacher, who'd been most like a father to him, had turned traitor. This caused Baraam to wonder when his other mentor, the Gildmaster Ridect, would do the same.

When would Ridect's treachery make itself known? Why could Baraam only wait for it?

He desired the desert, and the quiet company of Jija and the other Sahamans. Instead, he wallowed. In a hole. At the damp end of civilization.

The Sanctumites broke through his stupor, then, retrieving him, herding him back to The Savior's side. The Savior, who was Mateus K'vich, the son of an Aelf—and an Aelf himself—one of the very creatures Baraam had once sworn an oath to exterminate. But Gildmaster Ridect had Baraam protecting him instead. Had Ridect been aware of The Savior's true nature before assigning Baraam this task?

He should have confronted the Gildmaster, should have demanded the truth. Should have, but wouldn't. He didn't really want to know.

Perhaps Alina was right about him.

He clenched his fists.

Unable to decide.

Unable to act.

Waiting.

Weak.

He followed his Sanctumite handlers back inside the walls of his prison.

41

ALINA

RETURNED FROM THE FZETSIA, back at the Safehouse, Alina shoved *Ida* and *Rego* into the corner with the rest of her belongings.

Right away, she felt off. Even from fifteen feet, she could feel the phantom caress of the cloak, the face-hugging rigidness of the mask, as though she'd set aside a pair of limbs. She drove the unsettling idea from her thoughts, slipping into her routine breathing exercises.

With Mezami out hunting, she addressed her own hunger, stuffing artificial chocolates, baby carrots, and two-day-old rice donuts into her mouth.

Good news: she was still alive after her semi-private meeting with Mateus.

Bad news: he would tell her nothing until she delivered him a back door into the Hextarch's fortress.

Worse news: she didn't know how she could possibly deliver on that promise.

Worst news: no matter what, now she'd have to pick a side in this war.

She could either gain her uncle's trust by sacrificing Hexhall—handing The Authority a big fat win—or she could go back to Vessa and give him up. The Coven really wanted him dead. Alina wouldn't even have to be the trigger woman, they'd say; she could simply help them get close, be a distraction or something.

Of two things, she was certain: one, staying neutral in the upcoming epic showdown would be impossible; two, the bag of chocolates was now empty.

Dunking the last of the baby carrots in cocktail sauce (eh, why not?), she mentally retraced the night's events, from the madness of the Firelight Vigil to Baraam's appearance.

She wasn't a fatalist, but sometimes it sure did seem like her thread was being tugged in all directions by forces she couldn't sense, powerful as they were cruel. Ruqastra had once told her, "The Sevensin are creatures of prehistory. A chord of destiny chimes within the discordant noise of your soul." Of course, directly afterward, she'd muttered, "Though you are deaf to it."

Maybe the teacher had been right about her student, but it hardly mattered. It was easy to claim destiny in hindsight—applying all manner of meaning to events, related or not. Humans, after all, were pattern-spotting machines while fate and destiny were resealable plastic bags: people could cram more leftovers into them than they might think.

Meanwhile, from the destiny-burdened person's point of view, what seemed like fate *after the fact* still required agonized decision-making *now*. Whatever Alina decided to do, right now, would snag on the fabric of creation like a barb in thick hair. "Fate" would work around her ruinous insertion, reweaving the threads, but the shape and color of the tapestry would be forever altered.

She, alone, didn't have the power to decide the contest between The Authority and the Hextarchs, but her choice would help one over the other, and sometimes a nudge was all it took to throw a man from a cliff. Except, the balance of this battle put millions of people—whole races and species—on top of that cliff.

She found herself silently praying for a third option. So, she did what she did best. She procrastinated, making it Future-Alina's problem.

She lifted the Lorestone from her bag, and thought again of Cho. Cradling the Chrononite in her palms, she let its gentle warmth seep into her.

Deep breaths.

She confirmed her suspicions from earlier: the chunk missing from the Lorestone in her hands matched the sliver of Chrononite on Mateus's necklace. The stone had already been damaged when she'd claimed it. So, how and when had he come by his piece?

According to the Librarian—the strange blue-skinned, flame-haired Aelf living in The Gild's Crystallarium—Dimas had magically modified the object decades ago, back when he'd been a Gildsman-in-training. Had he given the missing piece to his estranged son, or had Mateus taken it by force?

Alina stared at the thing. She knew of one way to find out. Still, though she'd been successful last time, the process had been unpleasant. As a mineral, Chrononite was unique in that it existed both inside and outside of time. The visions it granted were potent and confusing because they drew from the mind of the user as well as from any number of *possible* pasts, presents, and futures. For these reasons, dream-walkers knew it by a different name: Revonite.

"Time is but another dream," she could hear Ruqastra saying.

Thanks to this very Lorestone, Alina had first learned of the Bane of New El's true nature—that Dimas had been alive for centuries, wandering the world as the *Talaganbubăk*, "the Old Man of Long-Candles." This ancient rock was connected to the K'vich family in ways she couldn't yet dream of.

Couldn't yet. However, it was again time to *try*.

Her sugar high burned out, the resultant sugar low dropping her to the floor, where she decided to make the best of her drowsiness by meditating.

Cross-legged, she closed her eyes. Almost immediately, reality tore away from her like a sheet, the bars of her mental cage bending, parting for her, as she stepped into the Revoscape.

The dreamworld could take an infinite number of forms, the mere presence of the traveler changing it intentionally and unintentionally. Because the mind connected to the Revoscape via the unconscious, the generated worlds usually shaped themselves in particularly symbolic ways. Symbols were the only permanent residents of dreams, and their currency was emotion.

To Alina, this time, her entrance into the Revoscape became the refuge atop Mount Morbin, where she'd felt—not exactly safe, but productive. Ruqastra's training had been a waking (and dreaming) nightmare. However, her strict, often dangerous, teachings had pushed Alina to excel. She hadn't been so intensely challenged since her days training with Dimas.

Tolomond and his bony horrors had stolen that productivity from her.

She decided not to wonder why her unconscious had brought her here of all places. The meanings of dreams were easiest to unveil when allowed to drift through the mind at their leisure. In trying to capture a bird, you changed its course. So, she let the bird-like thoughts and anxieties fly freely as she wandered the woods for a while.

She passed by Eilars's hut, each tool hung from its proper hook on the walls. No one inside, though.

She kept walking, and time strode beside her, at ease. Neither she nor this microcosm seemed in much of a hurry.

Moving in a spiraling pattern, she drew closer and closer to the pond with the white and orange fish. The wind offered her a cranberry blossom, which she tucked behind her ear. Her reflection showed her a green-eyed, red-haired, tired young woman she halfway recognized. Scratching her chin, she grimaced at the hard, gray flesh of her elbows and forearms and the black blade-feathers they bore.

As they had in the material world, worn smooth by storms and the slow passing of time, the seven statues' featureless faces seemed to follow her.

She spotted an animal, ahead on the trail, on her seventh circuit through the trees. A dark-furred coyote. It heard her approach, and it pattered in place, turning to her.

The Crow went to it, but Alina held back, wary.

After receiving a single tentative pat from the Crow (who then stepped aside), the coyote rested on its haunches. One of its eyes flashed gold, and it said, "You have been disturbingly sloppy."

Alina shoved her hands into her pockets. "Well, 'hey' to you too, puppy." She blew a raspberry. "Rude."

The animal said, "You do not wear your mask."

"Um, I don't need to take fashion tips—or abuse—from some weird dog, so—"

"And you still have not learned to think before you speak."

The coyote melted into a puddle of oozy darkness. Stretching like elastic slime, it grew to human height, forming legs, arms, a torso, and a head. Though it hid its face behind a black mask, Alina recognized the figure before her by the gold eye, dark cloak, and silver glove.

"But," Alina whispered, "you're dead."

"I had figured that much out on my own, thank you." Ruqastra head bobbed awkwardly on her craning neck, as if she were unused to having either. "How did it happen? I can't seem to recall."

Dazed, Alina said, "Using his sword as a focus, Tolomond Stayd hit you with some kind of Deïmantic charge."

"The Sanctum's mutt? Are you sure?" She pulled off her mask, revealing her freckled nose and confused expression. She looked around as if for the first time. "Ah. I remember now. He was not himself."

With so many questions swirling, waiting to be plucked from the ether, Alina resisted the urge to shout them all, rapid-fire. Ruqastra was clearly working through a tricky patch, like walking to the bathroom through an unfamiliar house in total darkness.

"I was useless against him. Not because he was blocking my powers. No." Her nose scrunched in thought, the expression making her look years younger. "It's like he wasn't *in there* at all. In effect, I was battling Tolomond's body but not his will. Each time I attacked him, I was met by a resistance beyond anything I have ever faced. A force not of the mundane or dream planes." Seeming to remember herself, she snapped, "Why have you not yet consumed Mateus?"

"It's not that simple."

"But it is. You are enemies. He will tear you apart if he finds you out."

"So, I have to kill my uncle before he kills me?"

Ruqastra sighed like a preschool teacher talking a particularly stubborn child out of a tree. "There is no other way."

"We don't know that."

"You won't *accept* that."

Alina gritted her teeth. "Buthmertha damn you, even *dead* you're giving me the hardest time."

"I was—and am—your Master."

"Is cruelty in the job description?"

"My only concern is saving you."

"By pushing me along the path Dimas blazed for me?" Alina wobbled her head from side to side, cracking her neck. "How are you even here right now?"

"Uncertain. Something Choraelia did. Theoretically, her proximity to the Lorestone may have interacted with her cognitive enhancements in unforeseen ways, allowing her to transcend this dimension and—possibly—pull an echo of me from the ether." She shook out her coarse curls. "I believe it was an accident."

Well, that made no sense. One more thing to ask Cho about later.

Ruqastra's frown suggested she really was at a loss, so Alina opened a new line of questioning: "Do you know what Mateus's plans for the Hextarchy are?"

Dark eyelids fluttering, Ruqastra smiled and pointed to the Crow. "Why not ask him?"

"You can see it?"

"How could I not? He is right there."

The Crow's shadow flickered like static from a bad Watchbox signal. It lumbered toward her, one step, then two.

The Master Revomancer's head swiveled. She fixed her stare on Alina. Stone grating, the seven statues behind her did the same. "You'll have to let him in. One day."

"But not today." Alina willed herself to wake.

She sank through the ground into a dark, vacant space. The familiar feeling of weightlessness preceding wakefulness came over her. However, instead of opening her eyes to Ivion's Safehouse, she saw the cobwebbed guts of the bell tower atop New El's City Hall, the very place where the story of her childhood had ended. Here, she'd seen her grandfather for what he'd truly been all along—a scheming, monstrous ghoul.

Appearing behind, Ruqastra said, "You claim to seek answers, yet you brush them off at every turn." As mist and shadow, she wafted around Alina. A flash, gold eye in the gloom. "Own that you are a creature of contradictions. Just as I am. Just as *he* was."

By the biggest bell, where Alina had once tangled with the *Talaganbubăk,* there waited the Crow, biding its time.

"He lied to me."

"So?"

"Used me."

"Yes?"

"Threw me into a war."

"Oh, do make an effort to grow up, Alina. If we all felt entitled to an exhaustive explanation each time we were challenged, nothing would ever get done."

Alina puffed, throwing her hands above her head. "You sound just like Baraam now."

"Then Baraam, for once in his life, spoke sensibly? I must truly be dead, and the Seventy-Seven Hells turned inside out and emptied." Ruqastra's shadow swelled, eating up the others in this dark and dusty room. "I gave you clear instructions. Wear your mask and cloak. Meditate. Accept that you no longer have a grandfather, that you are no longer anyone's granddaughter. You and Dimas are now *one*. You have frittered away too much precious time denying the truth. Embody it." The teacher's gold eye spotlit the student. "Become whole."

"No," Alina shouted. "You don't get to tell me how to grieve, Morphea." Her words were strangled by a sudden and unstoppable sob. "I miss him, okay?" It was true, she realized in the moment. Even after all the lies, and his abandonment of her, she did miss him. "If I accept that he's gone, he really will be."

"Hmm." The glow of Ruqastra's eye dimmed. She shrank until both women were the same height. "He is a part of you, and you him. He can't ever leave you."

"Usually," Alina choked, tears welling, "when someone dies, you can think they've moved on, that they're at peace. But I *know* he's not at peace. I can feel him kicking around in here." She stabbed her finger into her chest. "You have no idea what that's like. How could you?"

Her hand on her student's shoulder, she asked, "What are you afraid of, really?"

"No longer being myself. If his soul completely joins mine, won't I become someone totally different? I've only just been getting to know myself, and I don't want to lose me." She curled her arms around her head, and cried into the crooks of her elbow, dampening her sleeve. "Like I lost him. And you."

"Alina." Ruqastra shook her head, not unkindly. She cast about the belfry, searching for the words. "To live is to die a thousand deaths: the first time your mother screams at you; being rejected by your first great love; bringing your first child into the world. None of us emerge from these moments as we were before we endured them. We die with each change, for that's all death really is—change. The death of the body is no exception." The smile on her face was warm, open, giving. It wrapped around Alina and clung to her. "Even the death of the individual soul is merely rebirth into the infinite. We are all bound to one another through memory, dream, suffering, and every other part of us that defines who we are as sentient beings. Do not fear death. I can tell you from experience that it is no evil."

Finally, it set in, the strangeness of the opportunity Alina had been given: a second chance to tell someone she'd lost how she really felt. Wiping away a bubble of snot with the back of her hand, she said, "We were terrible to each other, but I should've done better. I was a bad student. If I'd done more—"

"I'll not stand here and listen to you blame yourself for my end. *The enemy* killed me. You had nothing to do with that, and you know it. So, stop this."

The space of that second or two had Alina wondering if they were about to hug.

Instead, Ruqastra's eyes widened as if she'd just recalled she'd left the stove on. "Have you been taking your fortifier?"

"Huh. About that." Alina blinked away her tears. "The vial kinda… broke. When you portalled me, Cho, and Mezami off the mountain."

"So, you have not been drinking the concoction. How long?"

"Not sure. Few days maybe?"

"And how do you feel?"

"Terrible. I feel shaky, moody, and like I gotta barf all the time."

"Withdrawal symptoms. They will fade, and you should feel much better soon. As with the passing of any other poison."

"Poison?"

"Yes, I was drugging you."

"What?"

"*Vlindra* spores do not amplify Revomantic powers. Rather, they inhibit them."

"Hold on. *Vlindra?* I've been drinking *Vlindra* juice?"

"I held a ceiling over you. With good reason. I could not risk you drawing attention to us. You had no control over your abilities, and your spells were a thousand times more powerful than a novice's ought to have been. You should know this already. Did you not once think to check that silly application on your cellular phone?"

Alina remembered very well the malfunctioning Niima-measuring app and the "!xXError#%" message it'd kept feeding her.

"And." Ruqastra clicked her tongue. "What are the properties of *Vlindra* spores?"

"They're soporific."

"Meaning?"

"They put stuff to sleep."

"But that's not all."

Throwing her head back, Alina said, "I know that even a small amount can kill, but I just thought it had some kinda special alchemical effect on Ravers. Besides, you were diluting it." She waited. Her teacher said nothing, but looked smug. "You *were* diluting this toxic ingredient, weren't you?"

Slowly, Ruqastra shook her head.

"You gave me a lethal dose? Every day?"

Nod. "I told you why. You can thank me later."

"You were weakening me?" The bell tower burned away, black ash swept aside by Alina's outburst. "You kept telling me I was a failure!"

They were back on the mountain again. The fish in the pond went *blub*.

"I was *lying*. Judge me all you like for my teaching style, but did it work? Look at you. There has never lived a Revomancer with more potential, and my goading you only ever *increased* that potential. Yet, during your training, every flare of your spells could have acted like a beacon, drawing the enemy to us. I therefore did what I had to; I poisoned you, to lessen the intensity of your Niimantic signature. A signature which, by the way, is a perfect match for Dimas's now. The very instant you were united, you became The Authority and Sanctum's primary target."

"Why? Because I'm a Hybrid? A Sevensin?"

"Indeed. You are also the only one who can end the tyranny of the Elementals." Before Alina could ask how, Ruqastra added, "All my efforts to shelter you were in vain."

Alina winced. "I left the mountain to meet with Ivion."

"They would have found us sooner or later. From the start, we were simply playing the odds."

Squatting, Alina batted the water-color surface of the pond with her fingers. "I so wish you were still with us."

Standing over her, Ruqastra said, "As do I. There was much I'd wished to accomplish with you."

The erratic patterns of the swimming fish blurring the dark reflection of her teacher, Alina said, "When I wake up, will you be gone?"

"Almost certainly. My presence here is... tenuous. I'm bound to the Lorestone, but holding the strands of my consciousness together while the currents of the after-life endeavor to sweep me away, it's taxing."

"Can I ask you one last question, then, before you go?"

"You *can*."

"Who is this 'enemy' you and Dimas were always talking about?" Alina stood, facing her former Master. "Why won't you just give me a name, a physical description, his favorite movie—something?"

"It wouldn't be my place to say. However—" Ruqastra waved at the Crow— "you know what to do. You only have to decide that you're ready."

"Damn you, Morphea."

"Fortunately for me, you don't have that power." Ruqastra grinned, and she donned her mask. Even as it slipped over her dark face, she blinked her gold eye shut, and the mask morphed from a coyote's head into a jackal's. "I would say 'take your time,' but Ozar might not outlast your teenage identity crisis." Before Alina could form her next question into words, Ruqastra read her mind and said, "I spied for Anarkey because Dimas K'vich asked me to. Because he was my father of choice. For him, I braved many dangers, gladly. I loved him—" Her voice was the hushed rustle of an animal prowling in the bushes just out of sight— "as I must now love you."

The shadows wrapped around her like tentacles, pulling her up and into the trees. The branches and leaves swallowed her like an inky black pill.

Alina called after her, "Why does it matter if Ozar falls? What do the Hextarchs have to do with anything?"

"I don't know, Alina," the echo of her teacher said quietly, "but you do."

42

CHO-ZEN

WATER DROPLETS SLITHERED DOWN stone walls. Wads of paper moldered in the corners. A one-eyed rat scurried off a stack of ration crates. From the darkness, a sudden squeal as the jaws of a steel trap snapped shut on its head.

Cho entered the armory, in the bowels of Anarkey. There, she, Cbarassan, and a small group of the meanest rebels in the country armed themselves for their mission. She got herself a fancy tactical belt and throwing knives. The *Fyarda* preferred magic, so they kept their loadout light. The others grabbed flashbangs, frag grenades, shotguns, rifles, and boxes of ammunition.

Meanwhile, seven texts from Alina. Seven.

Cho shook her head and switched her phone off. "Tell me to 'shut up,' and now you wanna play nice?"

Too little too late. See how Alina liked it when information was kept from *her* for a change. Cho had planned to give fair warning about all her weird dreams of Ugarda Pankrish and the K'vich family, but Alina apparently was too busy to listen. Well, she could keep twirling around if she chose, making out with her porcelain-faced mannequin.

After all her blabbing about needing more time to dig for the truth, what did she have to show for her investigation, anyway? A couple dates with Ivion and the kidnapping of some Sanctumite chick? Yawn.

As usual, Cho was pulling all the weight. In just a couple days, she'd already befriended a small army, helping them to sow chaos in The Authority's ranks. And the Walazzins' were about to eat a huge loss tonight. All thanks to her.

While Alina designed invitations for her pity party, Cho had setup the biggest play against the scum that had ended Eilars and Ruqastra's lives. Unlike some others, Cho wouldn't allow her pain to stop her from seeking justice for the dead.

There were people still alive counting on her, too. She thought of Rooster and the Truct team. Like wild animals grown too used to their cages, they'd forgotten what it meant to be free. They needed to see that there was still hope, that The Authority could bleed. She would prove it to them.

Firelight caught the flat of her knife as she honed it. Reflected in the metal was a green-bruised face under a fire-brushed wig. A damaged face, but one she happily recognized: the girl who'd taken to The Capital's streets instead of becoming Wodjaego's collared pet; the girl who would choose death over anything less than total self-determination.

Alina couldn't understand that kind of choice. Few could. Of all the people in Cho's life, Kinneas had been the only one to *almost* see where she was coming from. But he was, unfortunately, still too sweet and too kind. It made him weak.

To change anything at all, you had to be the right mix of caring and ruthless. Lean too far in either direction, and you'd end up either a kitten or a man-eater. Cho knew how to prowl the line between pacifist and killer; clawless Alina lacked the will to act because she refused to hurt anyone, even the worst of the worst.

Once, Cho had thought that way, too. Eilars had shown her how wrong she'd been. Much more than self-defense, he'd taught her the true nature of her enemies, the Plutocrats and their Authority. Because of him, she understood why the men who'd terrorized and murdered her family had allowed her to live.

Sure, the Walazzins benefited from having a doll to dress up and play the part of Wodjaego's wife. Her existence made things neat and tidy, but they didn't need her. If all they were after was control of Torvir Province, they had her cousin Silisir for a willing puppet.

So, why let Cho live? Eilars had shown her the answer: her suffering was the point. To the Plutocrats, cruelty was its own reward. The Walazzins reveled in her loneliness, her despair. And, happily accepting their neighbors' extermination, Elemental high society had only cared about preventing the story from becoming public knowledge. Now, enough years had passed that the truth had lost its bite, and the Elementals didn't care at all.

Even though politics had very real consequences for the ninety-nine percent, to the one-percent it was a game. A game the Torvirs hadn't taken seriously enough. A game the Walazzins played better than anyone else.

To reset the board, then, Cho would have to start removing players. Not for her sake alone, nor even her parents' and siblings'. No, it fell to her to eviscerate the Walazzins because, as long as they lived, they'd never stop cheating—consuming families in the process.

That's right. The game would continue, unless…

With her pinky nail, Cho picked her teeth. She holstered a stun gun and, on impulse, packed two smoke grenades.

Phone in hand, she stared at the seven notifications.

The Authority might be able to track her using this device.

She crushed it under the heel of her boot.

The stolen Authority armored personnel carrier exited the highway, cruising through the streets of the Sixth Stack. Inside were Cho, Cbarassan, and six other fighters—chosen for their long track record of successfully completed guerrilla operations and their even longer rap sheets.

Thanks to Rooster's tooth that contained tera*bytes* worth of intel, Cho was able to guide the driver between drone patrol routes and security checkpoints on the way to the Walazzins' forward base. A wireless VR headset covering the top half of her head, blinding her to the physical world, she traced indigo and green light-lines on a digital map, indicating the enemy's paths.

One nice downside about The Authority's ruthless efficiency: it made them predictable.

Still, the journey was harrowing. At every intersection, even in their commandeered hovercraft, they were in the crosshairs of machine gun nests, crowd control microwave cannons, and squads of riflemen scanning traffic.

Anarkey's small squad of eight was split unevenly, the four Aelf and Cho hiding in the back of the vehicle while the three human party members occupied the front, smiling and waving at any Enforcers who glanced their way.

One of the Aelf, a pink, reed-thin creature named Liott with purple spines all over their body, sharpened a bone dagger. "Agony," they said.

"What is?" asked Cho.

"Every second I spend outside the Seventh. Hexhall calls to me."

"How long've you been away?"

"This is my seventh tour breathing in the invaders' stink." They blinked their beady maroon eyes. "Never do get used to it."

A smooth-furred, heavyset feline Aelf blew hot air onto their hands. "Right about now, we'll be passing by the waffle joint where I proposed to my partner. Heard it's become some richy shoe store."

Eyes closed, legs crossed, Cbarassan breathed.

After a nerve-wracking hour and a half, they ditched the vehicle in a vacant lot, smashing the last few working street lights with rocks. Hopping a median barrier, they found the narrow stone stairway leading to a system of caverns. On its opposite end would be the overlook near the Walazzin's headquarters—the

Lion's Den. The rebels had used this little-known passage on several previous occasions, but they'd never before dreamed of infiltrating the triple-electric-fenced, drone-surveilled, land mine-covered fortress beyond.

Navigating by the pink glow of bioluminescent fungus, their progress was slow but steady. Cho had never been especially claustrophobic, but the tight, moisture-slick corridors through which she walked and sometimes crawled were beginning to awaken in her that stifling fear of getting stuck—of being abandoned—in this pink-highlighted darkness.

They did eventually make it through, reaching the overlook, a defiant, angular jaw of jutting rock.

From its edge, Cho squinted down, her enhanced eyes acting like binoculars as she scanned the compound hundreds of yards ahead.

Alternating layers of barbed wire and trenches protected the perimeter of the Lion's Den. Hugging the outer fence were the soldiers' barracks, prefabricated plastic structures. Storage warehouses, bright lights, and El's national anthem blaring—the cookie-cutter Authority camp reminded Cho of home.

Something felt different about this place, though.

Her gaze shifted toward the center, where three looming towers surrounded the main building. With its face of marble and gilded dome, it looked every bit a palace. From its buttresses and arches hung shiny red and gold drapes bearing the rampant lions of the Walazzins. In its shadow rested dozens of launch pads, most occupied by combat hovercraft.

"It's a bit much," said Cho quietly, counting the reddish-orange blobs that represented human heat signatures. "Five or six hundred by the palace. Definitely want to avoid that spot. Another thousand-ish in and around the barracks."

Beside her, Cbarassan said, "You're looking at a key strategic location and staging ground. From this plateau, half the Stack can be monitored."

"Those towers look way old."

"Once a *gahool* fortress, it lay vacant for thousands of years, until the Hextarchy claimed it. But, as you can see, our lords, too, were driven from this place. Two or three centuries ago, I think that was. I've lost count, but no matter. This place has developed a reputation."

"Oh, yeah?"

"It's said the towers are cursed, inhabited by vengeful spirits—the final raging echoes of a forgotten people."

"Hope the Walazzins soaked in all those bad vibes."

"Indeed."

Recalling the digital blueprints she'd memorized, Cho pointed at the eastern tower. "There. That's where we'll find a network access point. Underground, basement level two. Keeps it safe from air strikes."

"Don't get many of those around here," said the pink-and-purple Aelf, indicating the cavern ceiling hundreds of feet above.

"Standard Authority procedure." Cho shrugged. "Habits are hard to break."

While she compared the patrols around the fortress with the data from Rooster's tooth (only minor differences), the seven rebels lashed cables to the rocks and slipped into harnesses.

Ensuring all the anchors and knots were secure, Cbarassan gathered the others. "Listen in, and remember. We are family. Where one goes, all go. We live and die together. Bizong and the many others who fell before us, their sacrifice has led us here, to our destiny, one that lies within the very jaws of the lion. Our actions this night shall shape the future of this war: a victory here will shake Ozar—and the whole world—and show beyond disputation that even the Elementals are merely men." The *Fyarda*'s three-pupiled eyes glowed in the hazy darkness of the cave mouth. "Were Bizong here, he'd tell you 'to die in service of our worthy cause is the greatest honor.' He believed that vengeance was the ultimate end for any warrior. I honor him, yet I must disagree. It is not vengeance but peace in victory that we must strive for. If we do not fight for a better world, we doom ourselves to eternal strife and attrition. That cycle has to end, I tell you. More than anything, I want freedom for our children, for those who will struggle when we are gone. That dream cannot be realized if, in our fury, we scorch the earth we call home. Yes, Bizong and the vengeful dead, our siblings, delivered to us this one chance to pierce the very heart of The Authority. But we are the ones who, through our actions tonight, must give meaning to their sacrifice. So, seize your legacies, Anarkey. Your true glory as warriors will be the world you leave behind. For the Hextarchy."

"For the Hextarchy," the others murmured.

"For Ozar."

"OSO."

"And for the family we've lost. What is remembered lives eternal. Tonight, we become immortal." Cbarassan fastened Cho's harness to one of the cables, and patted her arm. "The descent awaits. After you, Cho-Zen."

43

ALINA

THERE WAS NOTHING ALINA could do to be rid of the flowers. They'd sprouted from every nook and cranny of the Safehouse, even the kitchen sink. Yellow petals, everywhere. She could see them even when she closed her eyes.

She'd tried pouring salt down the shower drain, lighting candles (well, *candle*, singular—old, dusty, found in a drawer), and burning herbs (sprinkled from the half-empty shakers in the pantry). She even peppered the front threshold and trapdoor with paprika. Ghosts hated paprika—probably? She was pretty sure she'd read that somewhere.

Still, the flowers continued to haunt her.

Heart-leaved zolcas, said no one. *That's what they're called.*

"Yes," she said. "One day I'll find a blue one, and prove the legend true."

Both she and no one, the noise of absence, sounded a lot like Kellfyute.

"I'm losing it, finally," Alina said, and she replied, "'Losing,' present tense? That's optimistic." She retorted, "Nobody asked you," and gasped, "Who's there?"

Then she saw herself in the mirror, gold-eyed ghoul, prowling in a dark, paprika-crusted sub-basement.

What she needed was a little fresh air. Oh, and one other thing.

When she'd been rooting around for spices to sprinkle and burn, she'd found an opened bottle of booze—something smelly and strong.

It tasted like vinegar but did the job.

No more voices now. Hah.

Blissfully empty of flowers, the alley mouth yawned against the forever-night of Ozar, sidewalk ahead lit by harsh purple-white fluorescent lamps.

Cho still hadn't come back.

Making a fist, Alina held her gray arm up to the mist-laced light.

Okay, so she'd had a little rice wine. So?

She worked up the nerve to check her phone yet again, still finding no notifications awaited her.

Growling, she slapped her palm against the wall, cracking it, claws scarring the concrete.

Enough was enough.

Claws retracting, her thumbnails clicked across the touch-screen keyboard, autocorrect helping her to type.

I know about the weird dreams youve been havin theyre my fault 2

So much is

I love you cho please talk 2 me

Fiiii-nuh. Maybe Alina was *wrong* about *everything.* Maybe her ideas, which required no one to die, weren't worth trying. True, this city-wide battlefield had proved that some people would never change. The Walazzins, for example. Hells, the whole Authority and the rebels—they'd all fight on until the end of time or until the other side was extinct. The Elementals deserved to be defeated, yeah, but did they deserve death? Were The Coven and the Hextarchs any better? Both sides used terror, both armies mowed down the people living in the middle. So, even if Alina stood beside the Ozari defenders against the Elemental aggressors, which seemed great on paper, she'd still be signing off on dirty bombs, toxic gas, suicide missions, and all the collateral death that came with "fighting for freedom."

Why couldn't Cho see that? Why didn't she care anymore?

The little girl who'd once been the conscience on Alina's shoulder was gone. That kid who'd once saved the last thing Alina still loved about herself had vanished. This new Cho probably would've cheered on Alina's attempt to kill Ordin, on that rain-washed, empty highway.

Steam rose from the sewer grate nearby. Alina lifted her gaze to the cavern ceiling, made invisible by all the neon signs and advertisements and searchlights and blinking dirigibles—the Elementals' all-smothering light pollution.

Damn. It was unfair of her to have put all that on Cho, wasn't it?

She stared at the unanswered message thread.

Read 1:34 PM.

Under each arm, Mezami hauled a fat rat, each large as a lapdog. For once Alina didn't comment. Her rice-wine headache had broken her will, and all she could do was stay on her cot where she'd collapsed some hours ago. Feeling like a leaden puppet, she told him he'd have to eat on the go: she demanded he put his frighteningly good tracking abilities to test once more.

"Find Cho," she groaned through barely parted lips.

He made to protest that his senses couldn't compete with the sewers of the Sixth Stack, that someone or something magically obscured Cho's position, but Alina barked at him to go anyway. Do it. Try again. "I need her."

The next time she opened her eyes, Mezami was gone.

She called Ivion, and started to cry as she asked, "How bad am I on a scale of 1 to Worst Friend in the History of Friends?"

Ivion said, "Seven-and-a-half? That was a joke!" The speaker crackled as she took a breath. "You did the right thing." She shut down Alina's attempts to disagree. "She's a teenager. Like it or not, you're the closest thing to a mother she's had. A little rebelliousness is natural. She'll cool off. Give her her space. Trust her to realize how lucky she is to have you."

Alina should have felt relieved, but the pressure in her chest would not subside. She moaned, feeling sicker by the second. "Where are you?"

"Business. But I'm on my way back. Lie on your side, drink water if you can."

With a slurred thank-you-see-you-soon, Alina dropped the phone.

Lying under papery covers, on the thinnest of air mattresses, Alina could feel the gruffness of the concrete floor through the deflated plastic. She thought for a minute she'd awoken to The School. For long months, she'd grown used to sleeping on basically cardboard, having pawned her bed for grocery and gas money.

She sat up. Along with the little flecks of yellow eye crud, she rubbed away the after-confusion of her dreams.

Returned to the Safehouse, Ivion had gently jostled her awake before sitting behind her, stroking her hair, massaging her scalp.

"That's nice," said Alina. She checked that her sleeves covered her inhuman arms. They did.

"Tell me what's bothering you, babe."

Babe. Alina burped against the back of her hand. "Maybe it's better if I never learn what my uncle's after."

"You've already put together so many pieces." Ivion's fingers dug in a little more sharply. (Alina winced.) "I'm not trying to add to the pressure, but the fate of nations is at stake."

"Exactly. What am I even doing? I'm nobody. A rookie combo Revo-Ter-ramancer with a side of self-doubt and a tall glass of family baggage." Make that an *extra*-tall glass of family baggage, with whipped cream and a cherry on top.

"Your name's plastered on practically every wall in Truct and all over the country."

"For stuff I didn't do."

"We've been over this." Ivion lightly tapped Alina's nose once, twice. She stared into space, thinking. "At a certain point, the difference between how you're perceived and who you 'really' are doesn't matter. We're social creatures. Our worlds define us. Some things will be true regardless of our opinions of ourselves."

"And what's true about me?"

"You're powerful. Strong-willed. Kind-hearted." Ivion chuckled. "A bit na-ive, but in a cute way. You also have good taste in romantic partners."

Alina's heart sank. "About that."

The twin arches of Ivion's ivory eyebrows sank. "Something you want to tell me?"

"It's complicated. I've had to lie to someone that I really, really don't want to hurt. Someone I met once. Before, at The Capital."

Between Ivion's arches, an iron chasm of a wrinkle set in.

"It's not like that," Alina said quickly, although there was no spine to her words. "We're not *really* a thing. I'm just using her to access Hexhall. It's all part of my too-complicated plan to get in good with The Savior. And, well, abusing her trust, I just feel scummy."

"How are you 'abusing her trust,' exactly?"

"Pretending to like her." Pretending? "Getting some drinks. Ugh. Sounds so icky out loud."

Ivion's wry smile had a note or two of bitterness to it. "Wonderful that the per diem I gave you is being put toward wining and dining my competition."

"She's not competition, Ivion. She's…" Alina thought carefully. "Necessary. And you're… just so…" The Crow appeared behind Ivion, slouching, gawking at Alina, who said, "No, not again."

"What?" Ivion got up. "What's the matter?"

The Crow shuffled toward them.

"Excuse me a sec." Alina untangled herself from the sheets and dashed to the bathroom.

Door slammed, she filled the sink, plunging her head into the cold water, holding her breath as long as she could. When she looked up, the face she saw in the mirror was not her own.

Wild wings of gray hair. Hooked nose. Gray skin. Dimas, his stare expectant, locked eyes with her.

"Stop," she hissed at him, but he wouldn't leave. Without words, he claimed he'd finally cornered her, and now she'd at last have to deal with him. There was a Heart-leaved zolca tucked behind his ear.

Her punch shattered the mirror. She yanked the sink stopper free, and the drain gurgled.

All the thoughts and memories she struggled to hold separate—they were blending. Merging.

Face dripping, she stepped out of the hidden bathroom compartment to catch Ivion hunched over her jacket on the floor, rifling through its pockets.

"Hey," said Alina.

Glancing over her shoulder, Ivion flushed.

"What're you hoping to find?" Alina stuck out her tongue. "Wait, you're not jealous, are you?"

Straightening her form-fitting shirt, Ivion stood. "Well." Lifting her chin: "You can't just saunter in here, boasting about some new girlfriend and not expect me to be curious. I'm sorry. You shook me more than I thought."

"Alright." Alina crossed her arms. "I'll forgive you, but you need to trust me. You don't have anything to worry about. Vessa and I couldn't work even if I wanted us to." Did she want that? "You and me, we're on the same team. And, once this is all over, if we can figure out a way to, like, expunge my criminal record or whatever, well—it could just be you and me on a longer-term basis."

"Oh?" said Ivion, smiling again.

"Like, semi-permanent. Subject to annual review."

"I'll have my lawyers draw up a contract." Ivion became more serious again. "I promise you this, whatever happens in the coming days, I will devote every resource at my disposal to clearing your name. My people are already on it. When you return to El, you'll be greeted as a hero."

"Not sure about all that. I just would rather not be considered a criminal."

"My parents' influence will unravel that knot. Perk of being a trust fund kid." Ivion winked. "It just takes time. The machinery of El encompasses everything, and is therefore slow-moving."

"Having that weight lifted would be amazing." Though, Alina hardly believed a fresh start possible. "Honestly, I hadn't thought to ask you for that favor before. Didn't want to assume."

"You should start asking for help when you need it." Ivion took her hand. "I'll always be here for you, Alina. If you let me."

Letting out a shuddering sigh, Alina said, "There is one thing you could do for me."

"I'm all yours."

Alina explained what she was about to attempt.

Ivion nodded. "And you'd rather I not join you in the dream?"

"This is something I have to do on my own. Just you being near me will help keep me calm, and I could use all the calm I can get."

Sitting on the cot, Alina rested her arms, palms up, on her knees. She ran through the breathing exercises, stilling her racing thoughts, letting them pass through her mind and fly away, freed.

Ivion knelt across from her, breathing in time with her, eyes half-lidded.

Fastening one end of a cord of energy around her physical body and the other around her spiritual self, she strode into the Revoscape.

Inside her dream replica of The School, the mirror image of the place where she and her Tahtoh had built a life together, her back braced against one of the wooden pillars, she waited.

Sham of a life.

Giving herself a few minutes to change her mind, she eventually inched past the kitchen toward the bathroom door. The thing inside battered the portal with all its might, rattling the hinges.

She flicked the lock, and the door squeaked, opening slowly inward. Long, black, clawed fingers curled around the wood.

"I hate violence," she said, "but since you're a figment, if I kick the crap outta you, I'm not really hurting anyone but myself."

The claws carefully slid back into the bathroom.

"No, no. You're coming out. Been in there long enough."

Somewhat hesitantly, the Crow emerged, a sketchy thing, as if it had been scribbled into existence by a toddler's pencil. The orbs of its pale white-gold eyes were the only definite feature on its rough figure.

"Ruqastra says you got answers." She wrapped boxing tape around her knuckles. "I'm here to collect."

Cocking its head, the Crow lifted one of its arms, lurching forward.

"This isn't a negotiation." Flinging off her cloak and jacket: "You've been following me around for way too long. Time to finally make yourself useful." She kicked off her boots. Her own clawed hands went up, bladed feathers on her arms bristling. Sinking into a fighting stance, knees bent, right foot forward, weight on her left, she said, "Who is the 'enemy'? What am I?"

A hiss, coming from the Crow, or its general direction, at least. "My little Cabbage."

"So, you can speak."

The voice skipped like a bad recording. "Good of you to finally reach out." It almost sounded like Dimas.

She stepped toward it. "I'll beat the info from you, and then I'll throw you out—for good." She punched at the Crow, which knocked her arm aside, but she followed up with an elbow, catching its forehead with her feathers. It flailed, stumbling backward, hissing like radio static.

In those same halting, buffering, poorly filtered tones, it said, "We are bound. You'll sooner pry your shadow from your heels than be rid of me."

"You're a hitchhiker, and the free ride's over." She delivered a combo meal: elbow appetizer, double-decker knuckle sandwich, and front kick for dessert. The shadowy creature crashed through the kitchen.

Colliding with and crushing the stove, in a blur of scything claws that shredded the cabinets above, the Crow unraveled to its feet.

It seemed unfazed by the beatings.

Fine. She would hit harder.

She pummeled it around the space, shattering tables and chairs, cracking its head against windowpanes. It teetered, fell, got back up. Every time.

"Fight!" she shouted in between shallow breaths.

Rolling its head, it said, "Someday, you'll forgive me."

"Wanna bet?" Leaping punch, punch-punch, flying knee, grapple the neck, knee, knee, knee.

The Crow crumpled.

Rising from her fighting stance, she flicked the sweat from her brow.

The straw mats bunched up under it, from the floor, the Crow said, "We've become so strong, but still nowhere near enough to fight *him*."

"Him." She grabbed the Crow's head, yanked it back, and readied her fist. "He got a name?"

Static pulses—ebbing, flowing, rhythmic. "The old master." Its lidless, pupilless eyes glowed, betraying curiosity, apprehension, even fear. "Many are the names he's worn. Once, we called him *Elwoch*."

"Elwoch."

The radiator attached to the brick wall exploded, steam hissing from the ruptured metal.

"What the—" She turned on the Crow again. "Okay, sure. But why the thousand-year-plan? Why didn't Dimas just kill him?"

The utility closet's door caught fire. The Crow chuckled, a jarring, record-scratch of a noise.

"Well? He had no problem butchering people, and stealing children from their parents' arms. But he didn't feel like giving his 'enemy' the same treatment?"

Nails fired through the walls like bullets.

"There is no simple way to explain what Elwoch is." The Crow swatted at her hand and got to its feet. "Think of the Nation of El, its banks, its bureaucracies. Think of The Gild, The Sanctum. Think of the Plutocracy itself. Realize that Elwoch is *all of these* and more."

"Oh, really, is that all? Wow. Why didn't you say so sooner? Let me just roll up my sleeves and hop to it. Now that I know that I'm supposed to defeat *everything in the world*, I can probably have this wrapped up in a weekend or two."

The flames quickly spread to the rest of The School, engulfing the walls, the ceiling.

As it began to burn, the Crow said, "He can't yet pinpoint your location. Thank the dying remnants of Ruqastra's protective spell for that. But soon he will find and kill you." Its entire body caught fire. Although the heat had become almost unbearable to Alina, it continued to speak softly: "Your only chance is Mateus. Consume him, gain his powers. Then, confront the Hextarchs. Take them all into yourself, and you might just be strong enough to guard against the firestorm that comes for you."

"Might?" shouted Alina as the ceiling beams cracked and the roof sagged. She coughed in the smoke. "Why the Hextarchs?"

Through the window, a fierce, white light, brighter than the sun in summer, tore apart the shadows, framing her entire world with radiance.

The same voice that had rumbled through her mind before—when she'd been sifting through the information in Rooster's fake tooth—it returned. Like the grinding roar of shifting tectonic plates, it said, simply, *Vrana.*

Unlike last time, she now could guess who was calling.

"Elwoch," she said, flames consuming everything around her. "So, not a butt-dial situation after all."

The voice did not respond. It seemed like, maybe, it couldn't hear her. A result of Ruqastra's protective spells, hanging on with everything they had?

The Crow had gone. It would be back, of course—as long as she survived.

I am He who Authored Creation, Authority's cradle and crypt. I am the stars and blinding death. Kneel before your master eternal, and be saved.

Smoke swallowed the dreamscape, the flames slithering closer. Alina cried out as she began to burn.

And the voice called out, *Vrana*—

"Alina!" said Ivion, shaking her awake.

Still coughing, Alina rolled onto her hands and knees.

"You were burning up," said Ivion.

As the terror subsided, and Alina's physical mind caught up with the fact that she wasn't currently on fire, her pulse slowed. "Accurate."

"Are you sure you're alright?"

"Absolutely not." She gestured for a water bottle. Ivion tossed one over. She chugged, half the contents spilling down her shirt (and she choked up most of the other half). "Doesn't matter." She wiped her mouth on her sleeve. "I got what I needed. Even though it hurt, and it makes no sense, I know what I gotta do."

"Care to share?" said Ivion, still kneeling.

Her thoughts flying wild and free, Alina hardly registered the other woman now. "You come into my house and burn it down? My house? My School? Oh, you picked the wrong—dunno who he thinks he is, but now it's personal."

Ivion grabbed her by the arm and hip. "Alina?"

"The name *Vrana* mean anything to you?"

Ivion shook her head.

"Me neither, but there's some creeper arsonist out there who seems to have me confused for whoever that is." Alina dashed toward the pile of her stuff. "And, it's gonna stop. Tonight." She flung *Rego* over one shoulder and her bag over the other. *Ida* nestled in the crook of her arm, she made for the door.

"Where are you going?"

"To pay the Hextarchs a visit."

"They're unreachable."

"It'll be messy, but I got a way."

"Something to do with—"

"My contact, yeah. Like I said, you're gonna have to trust me."

"But I do." Ivion cradled her chin in her palm. "Alina."

She stopped. "What?"

"Be careful." Ivion spread her hands—a gesture to calm, an attempt to embrace? When Alina didn't respond, Ivion looked away. "The Hextarchs, The Coven, they're not to be trusted."

"I don't care. All I want is to be normal again, and that can't happen while everyone keeps throwing jobs at me like I'm some kind of freelance government-toppler. But if that's what I gotta be to make it all *stop*, then, well." She gave an exaggerated shrug. "Whatever. I guess I'm gonna go spit in the eye of some thousand-year-old gods and whatnot."

"Hold on."

Alina hammered the access code into the keypad. "Time to pull the K'vich Special."

"What does that mean?" Ivion watched the door swing open. "What's your plan?"

Fastening *Ida*'s straps, Alina heard her own breaths as the drawn-out hisses of a vulture readied for a fight.

Closing the gap between them, Ivion reached for Alina's hand.

Rego ruffled like a mass of black feathers behind her, Alina said, "I'm gonna wing it," and bolted out of the bunker.

44

CHO-ZEN

EMBEDDED IN HER WRIST. Part of her now. Eilars's implant didn't only improve Cho's combat instincts. It also freed up a lot of processing power she could now use for her ZOs, allowing her to more easily hack into multiple drone sentries at once.

The little, floating, tennis-ball sized camera drones were sent bumping into corners, allowing her and the band of sneak thieves to slip past the perimeter of the Lion's Den.

Rappelling from the overlook down to the canyon floor had taken the better part of an hour, but that'd been time well spent. Their cave-side approach gave Cho and the rebels plenty of cover along the way, and there were fewer search-lights angled toward this side.

Crossing the shelves of rock and dry ravines, they passed under a guard tower. Carrying very big guns, patrols of exo-armored Tranquilizers cut across the plateau with their flashlight beams. Whenever the lights would glide their way, the rebels hit the dirt. Meanwhile, the chip in Cho's arm fed her a stream of impulses focused on the optimal way to ambush the squads. Some of these muscle spasms were quite difficult to resist, but she kept her head down.

The perpetual darkness of Ozar was Anarkey's best friend. Spotlights scythed across their path, but they timed their halting dashes well, remaining unseen. First, they went at a half-crouch, then a crawl.

There'd been one tense moment when a Tranq wandered over to the ditch through which they crawled, relieving himself on Rem (one of the human rebels). But Crabgrass had magicked a layer of dirt over all of them, a trick just good enough to avoid detection. Scowling, the now-soaked man wrung out his stringy hair, but stayed silent like the rest.

The first fence lay just ahead.

From afar, Cho deactivated a set of stationary, automatic gun turrets, hoping the soldiers would fail to notice this gap in their defenses until she was well on her way home again.

Cbarassan set themselves up to tear the fence apart with vines, but Cho stopped them. "It's electrified," she whispered, slinking up the sizzling, humming metal. "Generator's under our feet."

The *Fyarda* inclined their head as if to say, *All yours.*

Tugging the glove from her hand with her teeth, she pressed her palm to the ground. It took a moment, but then: "Gotcha." She sent a piece of her consciousness after the weak signal.

The beauty of Authority engineering—everything was online. Even power supplies were wrapped up in the Aetherthreads. Meaning, they were exploitable.

She flipped the switch, and the fence fell silent.

Cbarassan flashed a bright-fanged smile and proceeded to cut a hole in the barrier. The eight rebels crawled through, dragging themselves along another slimy ditch, past more complaining guards and whirring drones, and up to the next fence. There, Cho repeated her process, again without issue.

Going well, so far. She kept a level head, staying focused, watchful, but began to think her ludicrous plan might actually succeed.

The third fence in sight, she ZO'd herself again, controlling her physical body even as her mind flitted from drone to camera drone, ordering them aside or shutting them down, whichever method met less resistance.

Finally, they cut a section near the edge of the third fence, lifted it, and rolled to the other side.

A hundred feet away lay the eastern tower. From there, to basement level 2.

They were so close now. All they had to do was cross one more open stretch of asphalt, using the parked APCs and aircraft for cover.

For several minutes, as the rebels crouched behind a tank, Cho analyzed the routes of the patrolling pairs of Tranqs, timing them carefully.

Her thoughts blurred as she computed reams of data. Conclusion: if she led Cbarassan and the others at a sprint, starting in seven seconds, it would take them about ten seconds to clear the gap and duck behind those crates on the left. That would leave about three seconds for those two riflemen to skip by, and then… Yeah, that could work.

"Come on," she breathed to Cbarassan, "now!"

Like fish fleeing through murky waters upon sighting a prowling crocodile, the eight intruders darted from hiding spot to hiding spot, zigzagging across the drill yard and past the barracks until they hit the tower.

Cho panted, heart thudding in her ears.

They'd done it. They'd actually done—

Then came a piercing screech, like a steam whistle. Wincing, she scratched her pinky around her ear canal.

Strange. The lightbulb above the main tower door wasn't on. Why wouldn't it be—

Suddenly, a bright white spotlight blinded her. She reflexively shielded her face with her hands.

There was no time to speak. She heard the *thud-thud-thud* of rifle rounds striking the stone wall beside her head. She ducked, the crackle of the sniper rifles finally reaching her ears. And she screamed.

Back-to-back now, the rebels were shouting, firing toward the lights.

The impeccable senses granted Cho by Eilars's implant alerted her to the shotgun-wielding Tranq behind. Without thinking, she flung one of her throwing knives at him, the blade burying itself in the meat of his thigh. He fell backward as she grimaced.

Another knife handle found its way into her palm, but something was different this time. She felt the problem only as it happened—her superhuman speed glitching—and was too slow to react. Her arms and legs twisted, kinetic energy coursing from her heels to her fingertips and through to the tip of the knife. But the blade didn't land where she'd intended. Instead, it pierced Cbarassan's gut.

Cho began to shake, a wave of horror purging her adrenaline as she realized how automatically—thoughtlessly—she'd hurled the knife.

The *Fyarda* clutched their stomach, bright green blood soaking their sleeves. The look on their face—shock, rage. Fear.

"It wasn't me," Cho tried to tell them. "I can't control myself." The words, however, were glued to her tongue, pressed against her palate. Her jaw locked, her every joint grinding as she tried to do anything except what she was forced to do—stand there and watch.

She watched dozens of Tranqs approach, forming firing lines. Watched as, with a storm of rubber bullets, they knocked the seven Anarkey rebels down. Watched as clubs were pulled, the rebels beaten bloody before being cuffed or tied up. And, finally, watched as Cbarassan burst free, growing tremendously in size.

Chunks of stone and concrete broke off the walls of the tower and the ground underfoot as the *Fyarda* floated in the air, emerald eyes flaring, competing with the intensity of the spotlights. The slabs of stone created a shield around their body, a giant suit of improvised armor.

One of the soldiers shouted, "*Uardini*!"

"Flamethrower!" came the reply.

Although Cho couldn't so much as turn her head to see the source of the hissing, popping, and whooshing, she had a front-row seat to witness Cbarassan—their stone armor only half formed—burst into flames.

Through gritted teeth she wailed, eyes bulging, neck muscles spasming as she willed herself to break free. She pushed and pushed, her unending, tight-lipped scream drowned out by Cbarassan's shrieking.

Her internal temperature regulator short-circuited. She blacked out.

PART FIVE

ACCEPTANCE

45

ALINA

CROSSING A BRIDGE OVER an eight-lane highway, Alina lost herself in the monotonous droning of the cars below.

The glow of the Sixth Stack's mixed skyline of ancient spires and newer megamalls embraced the constant dark of Ozar. As much as The Authority had attempted to modernize it, this underground realm resisted. Sinkholes swallowed churches devoted to the Seventy-Seven Gods of El, leaving the rest of the neighborhood untouched. Elemental executives with no history of sleepwalking would wake in the middle of the night to find themselves standing in a parking lot, surrounded by strangers who'd had the same thing happen to them. Despite the bounty on the *Onshoru*—a thousand gelders per ear brought in to an Authority control center—the saber-toothed, camouflaging beast bats continued to colonize the stalactites of the Second, Fourth, and Fifth Stacks.

It was as if Ozar itself had a message for the invaders: *you Elementals are beings of light and air, and there is no way yet to shine the sun upon my house.*

Was this the will of The Abyss? When Alina quieted her mind, she could feel a mysterious static-like energy all around her. In the air, in the water and the food, in the Ozari natives. Or, maybe these strange happenings were the Hextarchs' doing. Maybe "The Abyss" was just another fairytale told to the hopeless to keep them trudging forward to their doom. When the Hextarchs and their magic were gone, would their people stand?

Alina listened to the national anthem of El, booming from downtown, reverberating against the buildings, shaking the bridge under her feet. *Dragon's blood, dragon's blood…*

Faced with all this noise and light, old Ozar resisted. And in swooped Alina, ready to pull the thousand-year-old rug out from under it. Did she have it in her to cost this entire city its war—its freedom?

Finally, she heard the sweet, melodious chime she'd been waiting for. There it was, a text from Cho, which read:

srry phone died but im fine. was pretty peeved with u for a hot minite but I get were ur comin from. Just need some space b back 2moro.

Alina had never been happier to see Cho's grumpy, little, cross-eyed cat avatar pop up. Shaking from relief, she leaned against the bridge railing, and immediately replied.

U didnt end up doing The Thing??

Nah like u said… too risky. Well figure someting else out
also Kin sez hey

OK tell him I say hey. b good miss u. Lets hang, just like chill a while, when u get back.

"I have to be better," Alina said, tucking her phone in her back pocket. "For you." But first, she had work to do.

And along came the Crow, walking toward her, slowly, from a good sixty feet off.

"Right on time, killjoy," she shouted.

No answer.

She waited for it to catch up. "Can't talk outside my dreams? Or just got nothing left to say?"

The Crow held back five feet.

"Shoulda known." She sighed. "Let's go, then."

It cocked its head, curious, but did not yet move.

"No, I don't mind you tagging along anymore. Pretty soon, things are gonna get bad. Then worse." Alina's smile made it flinch. "Coming with me, I think, will be punishment enough."

Through the service tunnels and maintenance chutes, Alina retraced the steps she'd taken with Cbarassan, making her way back to the bridge and Hexhall's secret entrance.

On the way, she again passed the pro-Savior graffiti, which the Crow defaced with a slash of its claws.

Alina shook her head. "Easy for you to say."

Some time later, she rediscovered the wall of fire and passed through it easily. She crossed the stone bridge without issue as well, a bubble of force surrounding and protecting her from the flying stones and glass and other elements. Even the black-boned skeleton guards parted, welcoming her.

She opened the clear display case, her finger suspended above the smudged phone screen.

To comply with her uncle's orders, she'd have to open a way inside Hexhall for The Sanctum before The Authority somehow broke through Peregrar's Grief and conquered the Seventh Stack on their own. And to accomplish *that*, she'd have to use Vessa.

Begging Buthmertha's forgiveness in advance, she touched the device and was transported to that pocket of the Revoscape containing the hidden fortress of Ozar's illusive living gods. Hidden for now.

She drifted down toward the roof of the inverted pyramid floating among slowly cartwheeling galaxies and infinite blackness. The Abyss, here, was a tangible presence. She was a tea leaf sinking into boiling water, steeped in the power animating this sub-world. As her feet touched the stone of Hexhall, the drumline of stars and comets played above.

She waited.

Waiting led to thinking, and thinking was always a gamble for her. Now, she began to *think* about how much she could relate to Vessa, who'd had it so hard, losing her family to the petty cruelties of life made crueler by the negligence of society. Right or wrong, for years, Vessa had worked toward a new life. Then, out of nowhere, came Alina to strike the match that would burn it down. All so she could pluck the secrets from Mateus's mind like a vulture picking over a fresh corpse.

She could tell herself all she wanted that Ozar's fight was hopeless. She could keep fixating on the idea that thousands were going to die no matter what she did. She could even imagine that the answers she searched for might serve the Greater Good. After all, her family history tangled with the doings of gods, and creepy voices stalked her waking dreams. Ruqastra had believed the fate of the world at stake, had urged her onward. The Dream Queen couldn't have sacrificed herself for nothing. Unearthing the truth might at least give meaning to her brutal end.

None of these justifications, however, changed the reality: what Alina did, she did for herself. She knew this and could not hide from it.

Sickened by her desires, she almost turned and fled—but then a hulking, white-furred, ape-like beast, with silvery blue stripes on its back announced itself with a bellow. Its boulder-sized fists pounded the ground as it lumbered toward her.

"A *Mil'iggini.*" Recognizing the species of Aelf, she raised her hands, shouting, "Wait! Wait! I'm Alina K'vich, here to see Covenant Vessa Tardrop."

She staggered as a second, four-armed Aelf, leapt ten feet high and landed in front of her. Its quartet of hands twirled a bo staff, and it licked its fleshy, sticky tongue across its pale eyes.

Alina had read about *Jallantopes* before. Toad-like, with rubbery skin, wide noses, and slit nostrils. Twitchy, elastic-limbed creatures; one well-placed crack of this one's staff could have shattered her bones, and then the *Mil'iggini* could pummel what was left of her into a spreadable paste.

Both Aelf wore the color of The Coven: the *Jallantope* had an open yellow vest that showed off its ropy muscles; the *Mil'iggini* wore a jaunty yellow cap on its dome, held in place by a string tied under its chin. They both also had a strip of cloth looped around their arms.

Alina reached for the sky. "I didn't come here to fight. I—"

"Skwagzaa, relax. She's with me." Vessa had popped out of an opening, a stairwell leading into the pyramid.

The *Jallantope* rose from its low fighting stance, swinging its bo staff to rest under its armpit. The *Mil'iggini* bowed its head to Vessa, and she paused to scritch behind its bulbous ears. Behind her, the stairwell disappeared.

"Ms. K'vich," she said.

"Ms. Tardrop." Flustered, Alina forced a smile. "Can we talk?"

Vessa tapped the *Mil'iggini's* chin, saying, "Go on, get. I'll be fine, ya big softie."

The *Jallantope* Skwagzaa said something Alina didn't understand, but the bite to the syllables conveyed the gist: "Careful now" or "watching you."

The Aelf guardians leaving them alone, Vessa said, "Surprised to see you back, honestly. So, what's up?"

"This isn't easy for me to say." Alina paused. "I came here to tell you that I'm sorry. And that you were right."

"About?"

"Since our chat, I can't stop thinking about The Authority. El. The Savior. I've made up my mind. This is bigger than what I want, and I'm ready to do what I can to help."

"Still not sure what you're getting at."

"You told me The Savior was a threat that needed to be taken out of the picture. Now that I've had a tour of the messes on the Sixth and Seventh, I can see your point. Clearly. I'm sorry for how I acted. I was wrong. The Savior's gotta go."

"And you're suddenly fine with nixing your uncle, your own flesh and blood?"

"No, I'm not 'fine,' and I'm not 'suddenly' anything," said Alina, temper flaring. "I don't even know the guy. I only wanted to figure out what he knows about some, uh, personal stuff related to the rest of my family." That much, at least, was true. "But he's stoking the flames here, and I'm not okay with letting him burn a whole city down, even if he is the last K'vich other than me. So, my perspective has changed." Half a lie. "If there's a plan to cut him down, I want in. And I'll just have to gather what I can from his remains."

"Wow. Ice-cold," said Vessa, scratching her star-tattooed elbow. "But you must've seen how bad things were out there before we met up. Why the change of heart? For real."

Alina glanced away. "Maybe what you said got to me."

"Oh."

"I can't call El home anymore." Busting out the hard truths now, Alina's voice quavered. "I'm wanted Dead or Even More Dead just about everywhere. Without help, best I can hope for is to starve in some black ops torture basement. I could use friends, a little mutual protection. Guess I'm being a little selfish, but I need *someone* to have my back. And, if I'm honest, I wouldn't mind at all if that someone were you."

"Well." Vessa clasped her hands behind her. She closed one eye, squinting hard at Alina for an uncomfortably long time. "Fine, then. You're in."

"I don't hafta, like, audition or anything?"

"Why are you fighting me on this?" Vessa laughed. "You want the gig or not?"

"Yeah!"

"I dig it." She seized Alina's hand, shaking it vigorously, stopping to say, "I have faith you belong." She let the silence drag its feet. Then, from under her pink bangs, she grinned. "But, first, think fast." She shoved Alina backward, her fingers unclipping one of the buckles on her belt, her whip flying free. With a fluid flick, the chain unfurled, the stiletto blade at its end driving toward Alina's eye.

Her first instinct was to spin her front leg backward, a minimal movement to put just enough distance between her and the flying knife point. But she sensed a Niimantic aura emanating from the weapon, and knew that dodging would be a bad move.

Like Baraam, Vessa was a Caelomancer. However, unlike him, she didn't specialize in the flashy Luxomantic branch. Her powers were Umbramantic, so the real threat wasn't her steel whip but its *shadow*.

In the quarter-second she had to react, Alina closed her eyes, visualizing the unfurling shadow, standing perfectly still.

An inch from her face, the blade caught in mid air, whip taut.

Vessa gave the chain a tug, but the weapon was stuck. She laughed. "Alina, I'm blown away."

Alina opened her eyes. Arms at her sides, she stood straight as a pillar. Her *shadow*, on the other hand, still held a firm grip on that of the Covenant's weapon. "Did I pass?" Her voice was rigid as the chain.

"No doubt. You can let go now."

"You're not gonna try to whip me again, are you?"

"Not without your permission." Vessa winked. Alina's shadow released the chain. "So, how'd you pull off that trick?"

Relaxing a little, Alina wiggled her fingers dramatically. "A Revomancer never reveals her secrets. They're kind of our whole thing."

"Sure, sure. Gotta say, though, waiting to be speared through the eyeball was bold." She hit the "d" in bold extra hard.

"Actually, you had the riskier play."

"Oh, yeah?"

Alina's hand swept across the starry sky. "This might be your home turf, but it's *my* element. In the Revoscape, my illusions become real."

"I'll have to remember that."

"Nice job with the shadow, though. Never seen that play before."

"I'm flattered." Hands in her pockets, Vessa tapped the ground with her heel. "So."

"You look like you could use a drink and a dance floor."

"I was actually hoping we'd chat with your Covenant buddies about—"

Vessa booed her. "Later. Let's get outta here, have round two of our date, yeah?"

"Uh." Alina completely lost her train of thought. Time slipped between her fingers, minute by minute, but she couldn't press her luck. Not just yet. She had to play it cool. "I'd be lying if I told you throwing down for The Coven was the only reason I came here tonight." (Okay, maybe she'd press her luck a *little*.)

"Sweet." Vessa fidgeted with her ear gage. "I know just the place."

Via the northeast staircase that hugged one of the six massive, central pillars supporting the pyramidal structure, Alina followed Vessa down several floors. They descended to one of the outer platforms (built into the same pillar) and were rewarded with a panoramic view of the galactic dreamscape.

When she was pulled into an out-of-order public bathroom, Alina's heart nearly burst from her chest, but Vessa was only showing her another secret portal in and out of Hexhall.

Logging the exact procedure for future use, Alina memorized the way the Covenant turned on all the faucets (hot first, then cold) and climbed through the mirror.

From the other side of the glass, Vessa waved, and Alina clambered after her.

They'd emerged into what seemed to be the same unused bathroom. In fact, down to the messages scribbled on the tiles, it was identical, but Alina could feel that she'd been returned to the material plane.

They exited the bathroom onto a street running parallel to a canal. This district had been designed around a petrified forest, and between the branches glided thousands of moth-sized sprites, shimmering silver and green.

Although she didn't recognize the area, it was definitely somewhere in Ozar. Vessa moved on.

Receiving no response to her question, "Where are we going?" Alina took in the sights as they walked.

The still waters of the canals glistened in the lamp-glow. Clearly, these were the off hours for this part of town. Very few people were out and about, and most of them were closing their shops or hauling carts of goods, cleaning supplies, or trash. The air of solitude set her at ease, and there was even the slightest of skips to her step.

Nearby, a group of friends tossed stones into the canal. Two were human; the other two, something unfamiliar. With a pale blue tinge to their skin and big, solid black eyes, they must have been Hybrids, with Mythidim blood in them. The sight of those four laughing together, shoulder to shoulder, ensnared her— a spell broken by Vessa's call. She left them to their small happinesses.

Nestled in a cardboard box, a kitten had curled up on top of the huge, wrinkly head of an *utch-Aharan*. The silver-and-black-furred, purebred war dog's ponderous snores rumbled the little shelter. The perfectly average, perfectly tiny kitten purred.

The sight of sentient Aelf and humans living together, and tamed animals mingling with lesser Aelf, implied Alina and Vessa were somewhere on the Seventh Stack, which remained (for now) under Hextarchy law. To Alina, lifelong inhabitant of El, it was jarring to see this sharing of worlds. Moreover, she now found herself in the heart of the peace she must break.

Under a low-hanging sign that read "Cafe Linozerpa," Vessa knocked on a well-worn yellow door. The place had been locked up, its windows showing a completely dark interior. A minute later, however, the owner appeared. She owed Covenant Tardrop a favor, so she unfurled one of the patio umbrellas and set the young women up at a small iron table for two.

The bear claws she brought out were stale, day-old, and tough. The coffee, not even lukewarm. But Alina barely tasted the midnight snack and watery black sludge. She watched Vessa tear one of the pastries apart with thumb and curled forefinger.

"You're different than I remember." Vessa swallowed a lump of chewy bear claw and licked her fingers. "Hope you don't mind me saying so."

"The feeling's mutual." Alina leaned back, sipping. "For one thing, you're not totally ignoring me like you did back at that crappy motel." So many of the finer details of that one fateful week had become blurred. "What was that shack called again?"

"*The Preening Peacock*. What. A. Dive. Can't believe we didn't get fleas."

"You, uh, didn't get fleas, huh?"

They laughed.

"Yeah." Vessa sighed. "Sorry about back then, if I bugged you or whatever. I just—well, this is kinda embarrassing to admit, but I thought you were hot. And I used to be mad awkward about that stuff."

Alina felt a jolt in the pit of her stomach that could not be explained by the strong, rank coffee or the cloyingly sweet pastry. "'Were'? Past tense?"

"Alright." Vessa smirked over the lip of her mug. She set it down and leaned in. "Are."

A giggle fit overtook Alina. So annoying, but she couldn't catch herself before it swept her away. She began to feel like she'd swallowed a fistful of the sprites drifting above them. Warm. Buoyant.

"So," said Vessa.

"So?"

Running her hand through her curly hair, Alina snorted. She could feel an opportunity opening to her. This was it, her "in" with Mateus, ripening for the plucking. She had no idea what she was doing, but it seemed to be working. All she had to do was keep the charm levels steady, and she'd get what she needed.

It was at once a terrible and wonderful sensation. The wonder was easy to understand: Vessa was sharp, calming, cool, collected, and, well, really, really attractive. The terror, though? Alina wasn't quite sure if it grew from guilt or something else, something unnameable, something that she was realizing—frighteningly quickly—she'd never felt before this moment.

She was falling into her own trap.

Double-bladed delight and panic pierced her chest like a pincer, like a venom-dripping scorpion tail. So, when Vessa pressed, "Is it mutual, would you say?" she didn't need to put a label on what "it" was.

And the only natural response was the one Alina gave: "Yes."

The cafe's owner stepped outside just then, her voice like the alarm of one of her walk-in ovens. She was quite polite, considering how late it was, but the gist of what she hinted at was "get out."

Vessa slapped down some coins for the stale food and coffee, tipping generously while Alina complained about wanting to pay her fair share.

They got up to leave. Looping her arm through Alina's, Vessa said, "Buy me a drink?"

46

CHO-ZEN

CHAINED TO A METAL-PLATED wall, Cho pulled against her restraints. Subtle, rhythmic pulses reverberated through the chain links and into her skin, down to her reinforced bones. This minor electrical current running through her body was just strong enough to dizzy her, throw her off-balance. Each time she tried to Zero-One, her mind filled with static, and a piercing, steam-whistle of a screech tore through her skull.

Three of the walls of her cell had been built of that same, constantly vibrating metal. The fourth was transparent, a bullet-proof window to a white-painted viewing room beyond. There, on a metal stool, a guard in full riot gear leaned his shoulder against the wall. Trying to talk to this man had been, as expected, a total waste of time. He clearly hadn't been hired for his conversational skills.

No clocks on the walls. The only way to tell that time was passing at all were those moments when the guard opened the door to the hallway behind him and stepped out. He usually returned within thirty seconds. Well hydrated, small bladder.

It was hard to think. Something kept scrambling Cho's thoughts. Every now and then, she'd remember the constant stream of electricity, that it must be the reason she felt so dazed and unfocused, but the realization would be jolted from her mind as quickly as it had come.

Eventually, the man-guard was relieved, replaced by a woman-guard. She wore the same armored uniform. The colors—abstract symbols of prestige and affiliation… Cho thought about them, what they meant. The colors showed sides. Which sides, though? Hadn't she had colors, once? What were they, again? She looked down at herself but couldn't make sense of what she wore—gray sweatpants and shirt. Why was she gray, and what should that tell her about herself?

What did this guard's red-and-gold armor *mean*? And why a lion's head?

The reason Cho had come here remained frustratingly out of reach. Every time she turned her mind's eye toward it, it slipped away. However, she did understand that this was a cage. She'd been scooped up in a net and was about to be dropped into the fryer. Crispy Cho-calamari.

Trying to make sense of time, she began to count. "One, two, three…"

Doing so allowed her to notice that, at regular intervals, screams tore through the sterile, cold air. Arriving to her ears from the hallway or through the vents.

She heard the screams clearly when the guard opened the door to the hall, and that's when she remembered—

She called out, "Cbaras—" choking on the name, throat dry as dust.

The pulse increased to a sharp zap, a spinning wave of pain cutting through her nervous system.

Everything went blurry.

Then dark.

Her eyes opened.

The familiar scene came into focus, with one key difference.

Behind the glass wall stood a room full of observers now. All wore red and gold attire; some sported carbon fiber armor plates, others were done up in fancy, shoulder-padded suits. One of them, the one in the smartest suit, slinked to the fore, smoothing down his greased, wavy hair (the sides of which had been shaved to a quarter-inch). Cho followed the quirk of his bone-white lips to his wide nose to the pair of reptilian, underbelly-white eyes.

She should have recognized this man, but couldn't.

Wiping his hand on the lapel of his suit jacket, his voice oozing from his tongue, he told one of his subordinates, "Cut the power. I want her alert for our tête-à-tête."

The sickening vibrations ceased. Cho's body had grown accustomed to this constant discomfort, so its absence felt like a new form of pain. It took a few moments for her teeth to stop chattering.

The man clicked his pointy fingernails against the glass. "Can you hear me?" His voice was throaty and erratic, as if he'd been screaming for days and it hadn't yet recovered.

Hanging limply, arms restrained overhead, Cho glared up at him.

"Good," he said. "Do you know who I am? You should."

Her thoughts were dandelion seeds, carried away from her grasping fingers. But she caught one, and so regained a little piece of herself.

This man before her, he was someone she hated.

He said, "I certainly know you. Although, I will confess, until I had the chance to personally read your colorful little file, I would never have guessed that our own sweet Choraelia Torvir had been operating under a criminal alias, engaging in insurrection against the very government she was born to uphold." He laughed at her, foamy white spittle collecting at the corners of his wide-smiling mouth. "To think I have here before me the heir to the Torvir Family *and* the saboteur of Truct, 'Cho-Zen'—and, Plutonia pinch me, they happen to be one and the same weedy tramp! I do so appreciate life's scrumptious little surprises."

Cho wanted to scream, but knew she'd barf if she tried.

Where had she seen his face before, this guy? She *knew* him. If only sheer willpower could restore order to her thoughts.

"Your infiltration of our Den was a decent attempt, I will say. Were it not for our spy's timely intervention, you and your merry band of miscreants might have affected a far greater level of harm. Make of this admission what you will." Nostrils flaring, he sneered down his long, wide nose at her. "But, only a *child* like you could earnestly believe—even for one second—that a gaggle of mongrels and race-traitors could hinder The Authority of the Plutocrats of El. We are le—" He halted, glowering at her. Turning to one of the soldiers on his left, he asked, "Why is she ogling us like that? Is she stupid? The inhibitor was switched off, wasn't it? Then, why—" Grumbling, he faced Cho again, singing, "Cho-Zen. Oh, *Cho*-Zen." Loudly: "Do you understand anything I say?" He raked his sharp fingernails across his arm, then growled. "Look! You broke her. She was too fragile. Your containment measures boiled her brains."

"Lord Walazzin, I assure you—"

For Cho, their voices faded into the background. Her entire world filled with a dull buzzing. Then there came a noise like an explosion at the base of her skull, followed by a *whir*.

Her operating system booted up, harmonizing with her brain once more, and she said, "*Walazzin*. You're Kaspuri Walazzin."

The Walazzin heir, son of the current Consul, and commander-in-chief of El's assault on Ozar, flashed his silver-plated teeth, filed down to points. "Ah, she speaks at last."

Straining against her chains, the anchors in the wall squeaking, Cho said, "She'll do more than that. When she gets out of here."

"'When,' eh? And how do you propose to escape? Hmm." He sat back in his chair, resting his right leg on his left knee, lifting his chin. "You're funny, and I do enjoy your spirit. I can understand why my father kept you around. Although, he's a better man than I, I fear. I'd have had you throttled in your sleep and replaced with a stand-in years ago."

"I'm gonna kill you."

The red-and-gold clothed yes-men around Kaspuri snickered. He held up his hand, silencing them. "If only spirit were enough. Still, we'll never get anywhere if we're not on the same page. Lieutenant, the monitor."

One of the nobodies near Kaspuri tapped a small remote control. A ceiling-mounted projector beamed images of the seven captured Anarkey rebels onto the glass wall of the cell. Cbarassan, Liott, Rem, and the others. Each picture displayed Cho's companions in varying states of bloodied ruin—cut, bludgeoned, contorted.

"I want you to see, Choraelia. Each one of these faces belongs to either a traitor to humanity or a degenerate Aelf. Cowards who harass my men, the defenders of order, of civilization itself. And now, at last, they're being punished for their crimes." Closeups of their broken fingers, twisted limbs, snarling faces, bloodshot eyes. "Anyone who sides with the Aelf is no better than the Aelf—a subhuman, fit only for backbreaking labor or the firing squad. Your rebel friends would burn the world to cinders, so long as they could rule the wastes. Yet, they have the audacity to call my father 'tyrant.'"

Then came a special slide show of just Cbarassan, bark-skin charred to ashy flakes, bruised eyelids running green with their blood.

"Don't you understand, Choraelia, that The Authority has *saved* our planet from the chaos and corruption that the Aelf represent? Think of all the progress that would be undone if those animals were given even one inch. They would multiply, swarm humanity, consume us."

Shot after shot of Cbarassan's suffering played for Cho's benefit, and, whenever she pinched her eyes shut, a fifty-volt jolt wracked her body until she opened them again.

"Stop," said Kaspuri. "We need her lucid." Half-lidded, his white eyes smiled in concert with his pale white lips. "You're a race traitor, Choraelia, but it's not yet too late for you to redeem yourself. You'll be pleased to learn you still have one way out of this. *One* chance to escape the unmarked grave already prepared for you."

Wailing, Cho shook her head, drooling on the floor.

"The Authority will erase the Hextarchy from existence, but there will never be peace until *all* dissent in the Stacks is quelled. Help me bring justice to Ozar, Choraelia."

Justice? What right did Kaspuri Walazzin have to utter that word?

"Give me the location of the rebel base, and you can go home. To Father."

Home? Visions of The School back in Truct swam in the tears that clouded her eyes.

"You'll be restored to your former status, a ward of our noble house, all your needs provided for. We'll forget that the regrettable events of these past two years ever happened. All you have to do is identify the hole in which your rebel friends have interred themselves. Give me Anarkey."

A gurgle—the confused mingling of laughter and sob—escaped Cho's throat. "Well? How do you answer?"

She hawked a glob of bloody spit, spattering one of the white floor tiles pink.

"Unfortunate. I'd hoped to have this wrapped up before tomorrow's press conference. But I suppose it can't be helped." Standing, he lifted his chin again, as if inspecting the ceiling for mold. "My associate was hoping you'd resist. He'll relish the chance to better get to know you."

A man with short brown hair, neutral features, and slouching shoulders set down his briefcase and cleared his throat.

Kaspuri gestured toward the window. "She's all yours, Mr. Jejune. Do hurry it up, if you could. Above all else, I abhor delays." Then he, followed by every one of his lackeys, exited.

That left only the man, Jejune. He fiddled with the cuffs of his sharp coal-gray suit jacket. "It's not often I get to work with celebrities. Not directly, anyway." His breath fogged the glass. "But please don't mistake my giddiness for nerves."

He stepped through the glass wall as if it were air, taking a deep, shuddering breath of the perfume of acerbic sweat and tears inside the cell. Without warning, he pounced, the tips of his fingers pressing into the flesh of Cho's naked head. Nails digging, he wrenched her neck upward until her eyes locked with his, and his pupils swirled and spun like gimlets, drilling.

All She could see—all she could focus on—were his eyes, and the jagged, horizontal "C" of his mouth, split lips parting to reveal triangular fangs.

She probably screamed, but she could hear, see, and feel nothing other than the piercing squeal—the same one that had stupefied her before. So, *he* had been the one to take her out of the fight when the rebels were being picked off, while Cbarassan burned alive. He'd been the one to force her to hurt Cbarassan, her friend.

She was a tightly wound ball of rage, but, chained and gripped, her will to resist drained from her.

Jejune's eyes cut through her mind like scissors shearing paper, snipping the sheafs of her thoughts into neat rectangles, stacking and collating them as he went. The physical sensation of his grip was nothing compared to the nerve-searing, clenching pain he caused her as he cut and cut and cut.

Then he released her. "Wow." He straightened his collar and spit-smoothed his hair. "Now *that* was what I'd call synergy. We work well together, Choraelia. Thank you for being so forthcoming." He phased through the glass wall again, collecting his briefcase beyond. Over his shoulder, he told her, "And don't you worry your shiny little head: I'll be sure to pass your warmest regards along to Kinneas Amming and the others." He paused. "That goes doubly for Alina. She's a crafty one, isn't she? Wriggling her way into The Sanctum, that's—dare I say—inspired. Almost a shame that I have to sic Tolomond Stayd on her."

Pressing up through her toes, Cho lunged forward but rose no more than an inch or two. The chains held firm. Her fury, pointless.

Jejune closed his eyes, smiling blissfully. "Yes. I can taste it, your zesty anger. But it's always so much more satisfying when seasoned with *loss*. If only I could stay with you a little longer, Ms. Torvir—wait for you to finish, mmm, marinating. Alas, I'm needed elsewhere to file my detailed report on Anarkey." He pursed his lips mockingly. "Aww, why so glum? All your friends will be joining you soon! In this world or the next, depending on their resilience—and your attitude. But, either way, you'll be reunited. Won't that be nice?"

He left her alone.

She slumped.

So thirsty. No more tears to shed for the lives hanging in the balance.

Thoughts scrambled. But. No. Couldn't give up. Had to stay awake. Keep thinking.

Some way to escape.

Alina. Mezami. They'd be out, searching.

She had to believe that they'd find her.

47

ALINA

THE BAR WAS MUCH livelier than the cafe had been, but that was a low hurdle to clear.

Afterward, Alina would remember almost nothing about the place. Name, location, general vibe—nothing. What she did remember was sharing "a few drinks" with Vessa. The music blasting from the speakers. Seventy bodies packed onto a hardwood floor in a building meant for, at most, thirty people. And everyone bouncing and jumping all over each other to the punk alternative classic "Cry Wolf" by Howling Mad Billie & the Werewolf, her favorite band since she'd turned fourteen.

"I love this song!" Alina said, and Vessa grabbed her hand, spinning her around and around until the track faded into the next—a slow song, still with grungy overtones, a rawer brand of electric bass and guitar.

Vessa cupped the back of Alina's sweaty head, drawing her in, and they just swayed awhile.

Time simultaneously fled past and stood still.

"Party like the world's ending," Vessa said as she handed Alina yet another drink. "Because it might just be."

They downed shots of cinnamon-flavored whiskey and pineapple rum until they both smelled like spicy tropical fruit. Then they half-fell out of the bar into the cool night air, landing on a park bench.

A stretch of pleasant silence followed, Alina's eardrums recovering from the musical battering rams they'd just endured.

"Wanna go someplace a little more quiet?" Vessa asked.

Alina, who could feel her heartbeat in her toes, nodded.

The walk cleared Alina's head a little. She felt taller, lighter. Along the way, she leapt onto ledges and fence posts and skipped around poles. She was venting energy, a seemingly infinite amount generated from her core. Rolling around her gut was a super-heated iron ball that, somehow, both held her down and caused her to levitate an inch off the ground.

It was a short walk she wished could have taken all night, and each second of it felt like an hour. Her thoughts tangled in braided chords, fraying and reweaving themselves at Vessa's every word.

The water park, their destination, was closed when they arrived. Sewage line maintenance, the sign warned. However, the iron gate was protected by only a rudimentary padlock, which Alina picked using a shim fashioned from a sliver of soda can.

She nudged the gate open.

"Scoundrel," said Vessa.

"Flatterer."

In many places, the pavement had been pulverized, the cracked pipes beneath exposed to the open air. The smell was atrocious, but the young women found a spot away from it, high up on the tallest water slide. Climbing the faded pink plastic was difficult, slippery, but the view was worth it: ahead twinkled all the lights of the Seventh Stack—windows, street lamps, and the glow of house-sized mushroom caps poking out of cavern walls.

"This place is so much different than El." Alina looped her arms around a metal bar, stretching her legs. "Huge, but also stifling somehow."

"Takes some getting used to." Vessa sat down, dangling her feet over the edge. "I'm not ashamed to say I cried like a baby the whole first month I was here."

"You had a lot going on." Alina plopped down beside her. "Did you ever want to go back? To El, I mean."

"Honestly, no. There's nothing for me there." She rubbed her jaw. "I hate the government. The way it runs people down. The Elementals on top, always. And we're just 'Assets' to them, right? Landsiders like us, we're just *things* to them. Dirt-scratching animals. To the hells with all of 'em. At least here, I'm valued for my skills."

"I don't get it. You're a soldier here, too. All you did was trade seventy-seven gods for six."

"Maybe. But the gods I serve now command me to fight for a world where the Aelf and humanity can live in peace. What've the Seventy-Seven done for anyone lately? The Elementals don't really care about most of them anyway. The only one they really buy into is Plutonia, Goddess of Wealth. The almighty gelder, that's the true altar of The Authority, the only thing that'll bring the Plutocrats to their knees."

Alina didn't have a comeback. She found herself agreeing with Vessa, and, worse still, wanting to agree even where she didn't quite.

"Everything's more complex than it seems," she said, finally.

"Truth."

Silence enveloped their tower of plastic and metal. Here, it felt like they could almost run their fingertips along the ceiling of the cave that housed the entire Seventh Stack.

It seemed as good a moment as any.

"There's something I should tell you," said Alina.

"Oh, damn. You're not *straight,* are you?"

"What? No. I mean, I'm not anything, really."

"Kidding! I'm kidding. Ninithin save you, you're so serious. This—" She indicated the whisper of space between them—"is a judgment-free zone. You can tell me anything."

"I'm not so sure. Once I say what I'm about to say, you'll never see me the same way again. You might even hate me."

"A little dramatic, doncha think?" With her thumb she pulled her eyelid down and stuck out her studded tongue. "I'm a trained Aelfraver who defected from her birth country to serve its enemies, and I'm now a bodyguard for a buncha gods. I don't think you could tell me anything so shocking that I'd totally change my mind about you."

I come from a family of liars, and I'm going to betray you, Alina wanted to say. *Get away from me before I trick you into giving up everything you've worked so hard to build.* But that was the central truth, and she must not say it. Instead, she must provide a related but peripheral truth, dancing along the edges of her motivations, feeding with facts the lie of omission she needed Vessa to believe.

"My grandfather was an Aelf."

Vessa started to chuckle, then stopped. "Wait, for real?"

Alina tugged on *Rego's* sleeve, which slithered away from her now bare right forearm. It took constant effort to hold the spiky feathers *inside,* so it was—physically, at least—a relief to let her guard down. From her finger tips to her elbow, her skin began to gray immediately, black feathers sprouting, her fingernails extending into claws the length of a lipstick.

"Hex on us," said Vessa. She held up six fingers, three on each hand.

"Soak it in. I'm a Hybrid freak. For a while, I thought maybe I could hide, or find a way to blend. But I understand now that The Authority, The Gild, they'll never stop hunting me."

"Alina, you are *not* a freak. These?" Vessa caressed the feathers, gently, avoiding their prickly tips. "They're part of what make you who you are. And you are amazing."

"You—" Alina swallowed—"don't think less of me?"

"Not gonna lie, my answer would've been a whole lot different a few years ago. But I've changed too. Ozar and The Coven have remade me." She tapped her temple with two fingers. "I work for Aelf, and some of my best friends are Aelf. I trust them with my life. The prejudices I carried through my past, the labels—they don't matter anymore. All I see is the *person* in front of me."

"You're not afraid?"

"What, of you? Of course I'm afraid. But, not in a bad way."

"I don't get what you mean." Alina's laugh was forced, clipped. She looked away.

"You don't? How?" Vessa stood, stretching. "How many hints do I gotta drop, here?" She walked to the other side of the little platform.

Before Alina could reply, Vessa disappeared into the tube of the slide. "Hey!" Vessa's shrieking laughter made her deaf to Alina's cry.

Counting three long seconds (to avoid potential collisions), Alina got on her back, crossed her arms, and scooted forward until she, too, torpedoed down the slide.

She landed in a filthy, brackish pool. Green algae clung to her skin as she spat and sprung to her feet.

Vessa was there, waiting. Her eyes were red. From the traces of chlorine, or...? Through the undulating swirls of greenish goop, she took a step, then another, until there was nowhere for Alina to run.

Noting how wretched she felt, how elated, Alina couldn't deny the tugging of the thread fastened to each of their hearts. The urge to remove every inch of that physical distance, to never let it open again—

"Vessa," she said, shaking her head. She met the other woman's eyes. *You don't deserve to become the latest casualty of the K'viches' ambitions.*

The fingers of Vessa's dominant hand fidgeted with her whip. "What?"

"I—I'm—" Alina lifted her face, letting out a quick, gruff exhale. Balling her fists, she resisted, holding out. She could not say it. It wouldn't be fair, or right, or—It flew free anyway, a bird escaping its cage: "I like you, damn it."

"That's ridiculous." Vessa pretended to be outraged, but she broke into a smile so warm that Alina couldn't imagine how the water around them hadn't yet turned to steam. "How could you?"

Alina sigh-growled again. "Gods, this is *so* embarrassing."

Vessa lost it, laughing, gasping. "Can't breathe."

"I mean, here we are, covered in slime, and you barely even know who I am, and I just told you I'm not even, like, totally human and junk, and then I drop a big, fat bomb in your lap and I'm, all like, 'Hey, handle this for me.' Where do I get off? And now I can't stop talking, can I? Oh my gods, the words just won't stop flowing out of my mouth. I'm like one of the sewer pipes out there, just spilling this never-ending stream of—"

"Alina. Would it be alright if I kissed you right now?"

"No," said Alina slowly. "It would not be 'alright.' 'Alright' is not at all the word I'd use to answer that question." She swiped sludgy water and tears from her cheek. "It'd be a freakin' delight, okay? So, yeah, I *require* that you kiss me."

She expected Vessa to close in, but Vessa always surprised. Her shadow drew its whip from its belt, cracked it, and caught Alina's own shadow by its waist. One shadow dragged the other; pulled, Alina lurched forward. Vessa's arms enclosed her, fingers latching onto her neck and chin, digging in.

For a second, they stayed this way, the length of an eyelash separating their faces. Then Vessa drew her in for a kiss which—although it tasted vaguely of chemicals and pool scum—was its own kind of poison. Vessa's lips delivered a scorpion's sting, numbing, intoxicating, paralyzing. Alina dissolved into it.

And all else faded.

48

CHO-ZEN

S NOT CRUSTING HER LIP, mouth dry, eyes stinging. Everything a blotted blur.

Lab coats entered the observation area outside Cho's cell, flipped a switch. The current raced through her veins, and she went rigid, tightening like a screw until she snapped and saw no more.

When she returned to consciousness, someone was inside the cell with her, strapped to a metal folding chair just out of reach. She noticed his features in isolation, almost randomly. Wavy brown hair. Soft, round cheeks. Slightly crooked nose. She recognized this boy.

"Kinneas," she rasped.

His bruised eyelids stayed closed, his swollen face down-turned. Neck limp. Hands purple from the tightness of the cuffs binding his wrists. Hoodie and shorts spattered with blood.

She looked to the guard beyond the glass, squinting against the glare of the heat lamps, and begged him to at least position Kinneas more comfortably, loosen those manacles—something.

The guard ignored her.

Back against the wall, hanging by her numb arms, Cho wept.

Emptying herself of tears and plans and all desire to ever move again, she became as a deep sea creature swept up by the current, dashed against the rocks, baking in the sun. The tide was receding, and with it all hope of release.

After a time, she was too exhausted to cry any longer. Her guilt at Kinneas's suffering was a thing she felt in the abstract, too complicated to understand or analyze.

Eventually, even the question of when—if—Alina would come for her faded, too.

Heavy head rolling onto her shoulder, Cho slept.

49

ALINA

THE INVERTED PYRAMID OF Hexhall cut through the infinite astral seascape like a glimmering, obsidian masthead. Gently, it revolved, passing through an asteroid field—the celestial rocks incinerating upon contact with its force barrier. Flares of crimson, bright against the light-drinking, velvety, violet dark.

Near Hexhall's lowest level, the downward-facing point, lay The Coven's triangular fortress within a fortress. Row after row of interlocking apartment blocks housed the soldiers of the Hextarchs, one Covenant per cell, every cell forming the whole.

Inside a particular single-room apartment, Alina forgot about everything she ought to have been doing.

When Vessa brushed her fingers along the quills of her bared blade feathers—tenderly, curiously, no sign of fear or hate in her eyes—

That's when Alina knew.

All Alina wanted was to stay in bed and cling to Vessa, to arrange her own limbs so as to perfectly fit the arch of the other's back. The hardest part was lifting her heavy arm off, breaking away from her warmth.

Kissing the spot where Vessa's shoulder met her neck, Alina murmured, "I'm sorry." And she pinched her fingers together in front of Vessa's closed eyelids, weaving a spell to send the Covenant into a sleep so deep a horse could have galloped across the bed, and she'd have been none the wiser.

Well, Vessa would be out for a couple hours. Alina resisted the urge to snatch a glimpse of her dreams, unsure of whether she wanted to see herself there.

Rolling onto the floor, standing, she scanned the room. It was sparse, a warrior's chamber. Lining the walls in the cramped space were only the double size bed, ice box, chest of personal belongings, small wooden table, and one straight-backed chair. A yellow cloak hung from its peg by the single entrance. Beside it, a circular window, like a porthole, offered a view of The Abyss. Nebulae as pink as Vessa's hair winked at Alina as she tiptoed over to the foot of the bed, where *Ida, Rego,* and her other items of clothing had tangled with Vessa's yellow Covenant vest.

Getting dressed, she gripped the mask tightly, then crept toward the door, sliding one foot after the other, slowly adjusting her weight to prevent any inopportune floorboard creaks. (Overkill, sure. But she was trying to play things safe for once, a completely new approach for any K'vich.)

She slid the chain lock free, and slowly pulled the door open.

This far down into the bowels of Hexhall, the apartments had been built into the outer walls, connected by stone balconies and pathways that bordered a massive, central, triangular pit. Gazing into it, she could see a long, long way down. Only the stars cast any light. The rest of the triangular expanse was brushed by a wispy mist, which thickened toward the bottom of the pit—her destination.

Hood up, checking for other midnight strollers but seeing none, she followed the paths to a nearby stair and descended.

She continuously kicked herself for not having paid more attention to her surroundings on the way in last night (to be fair, she'd been somewhat distracted). At the end of the stairwell, she exited.

Orienting herself in this next hallway accelerated the worsening of her headache. By now, she had a fair amount of experience navigating the strangeness of dreamscapes, but Hexhall challenged her every attempt to make sense of it. Much of its organization laughed in the face of conventional physics. There were doors in the ceiling and floor; doors of brass and marble, wicker and animal hide, shifting positions each time she blinked. Glowing runes, millions upon millions of them, had been etched into the smooth walls, spiraling up pillars and disappearing into corners, shrinking and expanding with her every breath. And she couldn't fully brush away the feeling that the stars were watching her through the windows.

She recalled Ruqastra's earliest teachings: no matter how similar they might seem, the Revoscape didn't behave at all like the physical world. Attempting to move through dreams systematically was pointless. They had a habit of taking you where you needed (but not necessarily wanted) to go. Hexhall had been born of that same unruliness, dialed to the max—a dream shared by *thousands* of humans and Aelf. With all these competing imaginations giving it life, its twistiness was naturally unnatural.

So, instead of trying to comprehend the nonsense runes and signposts around her (or, worse, pulling out pen and paper to draw a map), Alina simply took a steadying breath and chose a direction that felt right, holding in her mind her intended destination.

She opened a wicker sliding door.

Great. Another hallway, this one made of oak rather than stone. But, hang on... There it was again. The thread of magical energy that would lead her to the heart of the maze: thin, distant, but growing stronger—Dimas's Niimantic signature.

Her plan was simple. It had come to her in a dream, and she was confident it would work.

Though not a master yet, she knew enough about the spell her grandfather had cast on this place—Rimu's Transpiritual Locus—to root out the "anchor" he had created: the symbolic object that tethered Hexhall to its original location in the material world. If she could get her hands on that anchor, she could dispel the Transpiritual Locus. Then she, along with the entire fortress, would be returned to Ozar—fulfilling her end of the bargain with Mateus. And his knowledge would become hers.

She crossed the hall, noting the amber sunlight filtering through the paper walls, the wind rippling them like sails, distorting the black hexagons painted on them. These hallways, transition points, were like pockets inside pockets. Here, time, light, sound—so much was purely decorative.

She closed her mind to distractions. There was only forward, only her goal.

Through the next door, she entered a great, dark emptiness, thousands of feet tall and thousands of feet wide at the least. No boundaries that she could see. Standing on a four-by-four white platform in the middle of this nothingness, she turned to find the door she'd just used had disappeared. Vertigo almost knocked her from her tiny perch, but her balance held.

Other platforms, identical to hers, dotted this vast emptied pocket, some connected by double-helix-shaped staircases. Hers drifted without anchor, but that was something she could fix. She took comfort in the energy that flowed all around her, this force beyond thought that connected the platforms to each other, to the blackness, even to her mind. This, she felt somehow, was another aspect of The Abyss—a connective cord that bound objects, hearts, and even abstracted ideas.

Flaring her Niima, harmonizing with the frequency of these soundless waves around her, she began to understand that the Abyssal power she'd felt throughout the Sixth and Seventh Stacks was similar to—no, the *same* as—Dimas's. And its signal grew stronger the deeper into Hexhall she delved.

The Crow alighted on her shoulders. It weighed nothing, said nothing, was nothing. It simply pointed to the platform straight ahead.

She imitated it, partly to mock, partly to experiment. She willed her desires to take shape in this unreality. And then, just like that, an egg of gray energy appeared between her and her target, splitting open. A fresh double-helix stairway sprouted from this fissure in space, connecting her platform with the other.

Leap-frogging her, the Crow jogged up the stairs.

Blowing on and holstering her finger gun, she fidgeted with *Ida,* nestled underarm. She was stalling.

Her phone vibrated against her thigh, then, startling her.

Whenever she astral-projected, her phone and other tangible objects stayed behind with her body, dormant on the physical plane. Hexhall, however, followed a different set of rules. Built on a dislocated parcel of land shunted into the Revoscape, it brought the traveler to itself in a more complete sense—body, soul, *and* cellphone, apparently. She ought to have expected such strange occurrences like the transportation of her belongings. But receiving a phone call—having a signal in the first place—was harder to explain. Shouldn't have been possible... but there were no radio frequency or para-physics experts handy to answer her burning questions.

Were Ruqastra here, she'd scoff and say, "Sometimes things happen in dreams simply because they must."

Thrown off by her ringtone, Alina's awe quickly soured to irritation. She fished the device out of her pocket and sucked in a breath.

INCOMING CALL FROM
CALTHIN AMMING

It felt like the platform had been yanked out from under her, like she was falling into that deep, dark nothing.

The device buzzed in her hand, but her fingers wouldn't obey, wouldn't swipe the little "answer" icon.

She knew why he was calling. She'd taken his kid brother on a wild, potentially deadly adventure to a foreign country. And why? Because he'd asked to come along. She could almost hear Calthin screaming at her already, and there was no defense she could offer that made her look like anything other than what she was—irresponsible, selfish.

Oh, no. Here came the self-loathing death spiral:

She should have told Kinneas "no"; for once, she should have been the adult, but she had no talent for taking responsibility; her knack was for using people to get what she wanted; having tried to reconnect with the world, that was her mistake; all those years alone, with no one but Dimas (and sometimes Baraam) to talk to had taught her how to cope with misery and loneliness; only able to hurt, she was better off alone; she should've stayed in The School until the money ran out and then faced the music; instead, she struggled and dragged everyone into her problems because that's all she ever did.

Ahead, on the double-helix stair, the Crow—upside down—crossed its blade-feathered arms.

Habits. Hard to establish, terrifying to break. For the longest time, Calthin had always been there, Alina's habit. And then his dad got sick, and Calthin had enlisted with the National Guard. A trainee, marching up and down the market square in Truct, wearing the Torvir blue-and-orange. It was only the National Guard, he'd explained; he'd probably never see a day of fighting. But all Alina could feel when she thought of him now was his allegiance to The Authority. At first, she'd tried to convince him to turn deserter. Yet, even though his pay hadn't trickled in quickly enough to save his father, even though the Tranqs were after his friends' heads, he'd stayed.

To be fair, desertion would have earned him a mock military trial followed by the death penalty. To be *fair*, she'd trusted him since their days digging in a sandbox together. And, when he'd needed her, she had made a habit of "forgetting about" his texts and screening his calls.

Her phone buzzed again.

She couldn't hide from him forever. It was past time to face his outrage. Least she could do.

She held up a finger to the Crow, saying, "Just a sec," and picked up the call. She could hear heavy breathing on the other end of the line. "Hey? Calthin?"

More harsh breaths, then: "Alina." He was running, she realized. "I'm in trouble." His voice was strained.

Phone pressed to her left ear, she covered her right. "Where are you?"

"I'm hurt, gotta keep moving. I need you to hear me right now, okay? I'm in Ozar, on the front."

No, that wasn't possible. He was National Guard, stationed in Truct. "Hurt?" she repeated numbly.

"Compliance Officers. They're after me."

"My gods, Cal. What do you mean, you're in Ozar?"

"Alina, please. I tried reaching Kin. He's not answering. Neither is Cho."

Alina shouldn't have been surprised that she was his last resort in the call chain, but it pained her anyway.

Through the phone speaker, a crash and hissing noises, like rushing sand. Calthin said, "You check in with them yet today?"

"Cal. Why are you being chased?"

"Conspiracy to commit treason." He was crying, so she started to cry too. "Before I escaped, they told me Kinneas was involved. They mentioned something about a girl, too. Figured it was Cho." He groaned into the mic. "I didn't do anything, I didn't. But I think the kids are in danger. You gotta get them out."

Stuttering, she said, "I haven't heard from them since—" Since Cho had texted her that everything was fine. About a day ago.

Cho had lied.

His voice husky, his words halting, he said, "Kinneas has to be alright. He has to be. I've never asked you for anything. You have to take care of him for me. If I don't—"

"You will, though. You're gonna be okay. Where are you right now? I'll come find you."

"Aren't you listening? I'm in Ozar, thousands of miles away from—"

"I know," she interrupted. "That's where I am, too."

Static. Shallow, laborious breathing. He said, "No. They're not with you. You had better tell me my brother's not in a war zone with you, Alina K'vich."

It felt like her skeleton was sinking through her skin. "Cal. I'm gonna fix this, Cal." He started to bark something at her, probably unable to scream for fear of being overheard, but she talked over him, her voice dropping into The Abyss like oil in water. "Hey, I swear to Buthmertha on my soul that I *will* keep them from harm. You just focus on getting somewhere out of sight." She gave him the address of the Safehouse. "Hide there. There's medical supplies, food, water. I'm on my way, and we'll figure this out together."

He didn't answer, and for a moment she was afraid something had happened to him. Then, quietly: "How could you do this?"

So many excuses came to mind: *I sent Mezami after them again, even though that didn't work the first time; I thought they were fine because they told me they were, and I'm an idiot who doesn't fact-check rebellious teens; I needed them out of my hair for a while, so I lost my cool and yelled at my best friend; she was the one who took Kinneas, not me; and he does whatever she asks because he's in love with her.*

She could've said all this and more, but anything she might tell him now would be worth less than nothing. So, instead, she said, "I'm so, so sorry." Her voice broke. "Damn it, I'm sorry." She stared into The Abyss and, again, felt the stars and the dark spaces between them watching, weighing, and measuring her. "I'm sorry for everything I've done. But I'm going to make it right." Tight-fisted, she felt a tongue of warm blood lick between her fingers, down her wrist. "I promise."

While Kinneas may have been the Aquamancer in the family, and particularly fond of ice spells, Calthin's voice was far colder than any of his little brother's magic as he said, "I'll meet you at the Safehouse."

"Calthin, it's going to be okay." But he'd already hung up.

Silence settling on its scratchy, shifting substance, the Crow gestured for Alina to follow it up the stairs.

Breaking into a sweat, she spun in place. The door behind her, gone. The way ahead, open. She was so curious—desperate—to know, and she'd worked so hard to get to this point. Of course, she didn't want to abandon her plans when she was possibly minutes away from bringing them to fruition, but there simply was no choice to be made here. She had to find Cho and Kinneas. And, if they really were in trouble—

As she'd done last time she'd been in Hexhall, Alina snapped her fingers.

Nothing happened.

She tried again.

Same result. No spark, no *poof.*

There was some kind of Niimantic knot around her, keeping her here.

She looked up at the Crow and growled, "You. Why?"

Its back to her, the shadowy thing dashed up the steps in long strides.

She went after it.

Puffing, eyes wide against the rush of dead air, she ascended. She rode the wave of nausea as she reached the point on the staircase that flipped her upside-down. Drawing a mental bead on the Crow, she leapt, *Rego* unfurling like a raven's wings, and steadied herself as her world spun, her center of gravity shifting again and again—right side up, upside-down, right side up. She landed and rolled, springing to her feet, peeling off after her prey.

At the peak of the stair, a portal appeared and swallowed the Crow. She jumped in after.

She was now in a corridor whose walls, floors, and ceiling were covered in gray, white, black, and yellow wiring. There were no windows, the only light coming from the occasional electric spark off a wall panel or exposed strip of copper. She took care not to touch any metal surfaces, balancing as she walked along an uneven, tight-rope-like tangle of wires—searching for the Crow.

It was a long straight stretch to the far end, where she dropped through a hatch into a grand, open, multi-tiered chamber built almost entirely of granite, each corner and pillar sharp and rectangular. At every level, sections of the balconies were separated by iron-barred gates. There were yellow-robed Covenants everywhere: six patrolling the paths at the highest level, from which they could easily see down to the lowest; two posted at the base of each of the six pillars; three in front of a ten-foot-tall pair of solid, reinforced metal doors. A wide, stone stair led down to those doors, on whose right a glassy blue orb had been built into the wall.

Standing there, unseen by the guards, was the Crow.

A yellow-robed human Covenant rounded the corner, five feet in front of Alina. She ducked behind a pillar, melding with its stone, holding her breath.

He cleared his throat and walked past.

She exhaled, closing her eyes, noting that the residue of Dimas's energy emanated most strongly from beyond those sealed metal doors, which bore the familiar hexagonal sigil of the Hextarchy. Had the Crow been leading her here on purpose?

Either way, she had to reach it, force it to let her leave the Revoscape.

As Dimas had taught her, she analyzed the threats and obstacles in her path. There were several barred and locked gates between her and the steps leading to the lowest level. And there were many watchful eyes, besides—too many Covenants to take on by herself even if she'd wanted to.

She had to admit that Hexhall, final bastion of the Seventh Stack, impressed. In addition to its existence inside a Revomantic pocket dimension, whose access points in the material world were all well hidden and shielded by powerful enchantments, the fortress's interior was protected by Covenants. Each one radiated a calm, resonant strength—still as snow-capped mountain peaks, ready to drop an avalanche at the first provocation.

The architects of Hexhall's defenses had made one fatal mistake, however: they had failed to account for the arrival of someone like Alina. Revomancy and desperation were a volatile mix. By inviting her in, Cbarassan and Vessa Tardrop had unknowingly created the biggest gap in the Hextarchs' armor.

Rego embracing her warmly, she became a shadow moving among shadows, slipping between patrols, gliding like mist through iron keyholes. She blended in with the darkness behind another of the huge pillars, calculating how she could get past the three guards unseen and unheard—by them and the others watching above.

Then the Crow walked right through the metal doors, out of sight. Beyond her reach.

She could have screamed, but didn't. Instead, she ran through a breathing exercise.

An idea came to her: the Crow may have cut off her normal means of returning to the physical world, but there was another way.

She could feel the Revomantic anchor nearby, calling to her from the other side of those tempting metal doors. With it in hand, she could undo her grandfather's magic, freeing herself of this place, allowing her to fly to Cho—and dooming everyone living inside.

The Aelf refugees.

Their human compatriots.

Tens of thousands of people.

And Vessa.

Alina's guilt and fear competed with her curiosity. There were two (totally unequal) reasons to proceed through the doors: first and foremost, finding Cho; second, she needed to know why—in the name of Holy Buthmertha—her grandfather's energy had seeped into the very stone of this sub-world. What had brought him to this place? What was drawing her and Mateus here?

She grappled with herself, unable to move.

Cause and effect.

Once she busted the anchor, Hexhall would likely reappear near the cavern with the phone display case and the barrier storm. (Even a Maggo as powerful as Dimas had been couldn't have shunted an entire mega-structure across a huge *physical* distance.) The Authority would quickly find the fortress, and the slaughter would begin…

Consequences.

It would be her fault. It would be as if she'd killed all those people.

But it was the fastest way she knew to get back to Cho—the only way she could think of.

And what if something truly incredible waited for her, deeper in? What if whatever secrets the Hextarchs were keeping could change everything (as she, in her darkest dreams, hoped they could)? Every part of her vibrated with the aching need to discover what lay beyond those metal doors.

She was so close, yet she was paralyzed by the puzzle, by the potential consequences, by her hunger.

Stop hesitating.

The Savior had promised answers, and even more could be hers for the taking.

Make a decision.

Pawing at her face, she began to hyperventilate.

If you don't go through with it, Cho will die.

But, if she did, many *more* would die.

Hexhall will fall, with or without your intervention.

She didn't have to contribute to its destruction, though. The unselfish choice would be to fail her friend.

Is it less selfish to sacrifice her in the name of your morality?

In one hand, she held the life of the first person she'd ever loved by choice. In the other, the Seventh Stack. But the scales were perfectly balanced—there was no deciding—the burden threatened to crush her. Here, at last, she'd come to the edge of her values, her sanity, her very sense of self.

Everything she'd fought for—needed—lay on the other side of those doors, but opening them would destroy her.

Cho's fierce scowl was plastered like wallpaper across her mind.

Push.

And then she decided: no.

No, she couldn't do it. Here, at the precipice, she couldn't save her friend. Not like this.

Hexhall wasn't just a temple to Ozar's living gods; it was more than a barracks for the holy warriors they called Covenants. People lived here. Throwing away thousands upon thousands of *people* who wanted nothing more than peace—

even to save Cho—was a weight too great to bear. Besides, if she did take it on, Cho would hate her forever anyway.

Alina had reached the end of a long road, one that had started with a stack of utility bills and a simple desire to become more than a survivor. Fully feeling how tired she was, how much her feet and back ached, she thought about all she'd given up to arrive at this point.

None of that mattered to her now.

She saw herself reflected in the dark glass of her phone screen, a selfish creature wearing the mask and golden eyes of her grandfather, who'd lied and killed and sacrificed so much to further his own plans.

She could no longer be this thing she saw. Not anymore and never again.

She surrendered to this sudden and complete flash of self-awareness, the full appreciation of how petty she'd become. Always been. Ruled by desires, a craving for the acceptance of self and others, she'd dragged Cho, Kinneas, and Mezami into her personal quest to pad out her own backstory. Had she been thinking straight, she'd have—

No. Irrelevant. All that mattered was this: set against the price the people of Hexhall would have to pay, her wish—to save her best friend—had become unthinkable.

The anchor would remain whole and undisturbed.

"Cho, I'm sorry," she murmured, "There has to be another way out."

And, in fact, there was. Before she could discover what it might be, however, an ever-present background force came to the fore, exerting itself. Though more often subtle by nature, now its touch became direct, dynamic—almost conscious.

It did have a will, this power that mortals long ago had named The Abyss. And after centuries of restless slumber, acting on inspiration beyond the grasp of human minds, it made that will *known*.

Alina heard its call…

50

CHO-ZEN

... AND CHO HEARD IT, too.

Knowing beyond sense, she felt a tickle at the back of her brain. A tickle and *scratch*. Talons scraped away at her mental defenses—bypassing billion-gelder technological failsafes and basic biology—and burrowed into her thoughts.

For a moment, it seemed as if she held in her palms the glowing, green mass of Chrononite—Alina's Lorestone...

Then she was a wraith, claws glinting like silverplate in the moonlight. Like an arrow loosed from heaven, she soared across a barren peninsula toward a lonely tower, spearing through its highest window.

Landing on a plush carpet, she was surrounded by high-collared, lacy-sleeved noblemen. Some gasped at her entry, and there was a moment's hesitation, in which they looked to one another for guidance. The quickest ones drew ceremonial daggers and long rapiers with fanciful, gilded guards.

All fell to her claws as she slashed in a series of spinning arcs, tearing these pathetic men apart. Their blood spattered her red crow mask and dappled her wide-brimmed hat and long black cape.

One of them she kept barely alive, so that she could relish in his squeals for mercy, and so that she could growl at him, "Where are the children?"

The man blubbered, "I—I know you! You're the Talagaba—the Talgabanbaba—"

"*Talaganbubăk*," she said.

He struggled through several complicated hand signs for banishing evil. (Quaint superstitions, empty comforts.)

Amused, she staggered back, grasping at her chest, pretending to panic. Then she strode over to him, grabbed him by the heel, and—one-handed—clobbered him against the wall.

Now that no life-signs remained in the room with her, she moved on.

She'd chosen this tower because of the precious commodity it held: children, little more than lab rats to the Plutocrats and their servants; subjected to magical experiments; mangled through teleportation; devoured by extra-dimensional beasts.

Enough. She could think of far better uses for them.

Descending the stairs, she listened for heartbeats. There were nineteen of them in all. Each was elevated, but twelve of them quickened with a flood of adrenaline. The other seven beat almost in time, a cacophony of clustered tiny drums.

She must restrain herself. Exerting her full strength would obliterate the tower and the children with it. So, she worked her way steadily down, clearing room after room of armed guards. Some managed to land a club-blow or pierce her with a spear. She shrugged each of these feeble attackers off, shredding them to ribbons.

With twelve life-threads cut, flicking blood from her claws, she listened again. The remaining seven heartbeats, they were just below her now.

She flung aside the large table (ornately carved and inlaid with pearls), hearing a satisfying splintering as it collided with the wall. Kicking aside the rug, she tore the trapdoor clean off its hinges and, ignoring the ladder, crossed her blade-feathered arms and hopped into the darkness.

There they were, resembling a seven-headed beast, their smudged faces, shriveling limbs, and mops of hair clinging together.

The final obstacle, the metal bars of the children's cell, she bent aside as if they were made of tin foil.

"Don't be afraid," said Cho, stepping back. She remembered to remove her mask, the face beneath still causing the prisoners to gasp in fright. The light from above touching her hat, deepening the shadows enshrouding her, she smiled. "You may call me Dimas."

"Lord Dimas," said the oldest of the children, perhaps thirteen. "Please help."

"I am not your 'lord,' boy."

"Haven't you come to save us?"

"No. Unlike your prior captors, I shall be honest with you, children: even as I free you from one prison, I bind you to another. Though, this charge I place upon your shoulders will be the lighter of the two by far."

"What would you have us do?"

"Become soldiers for my cause. Spend your days in resistance against the slow-burning madness of human society."

"We—They're only children," said the boy of thirteen, thinking himself a man.

"You will grow. In time."

"Where would we live?"

"Wherever you like. Though I will provide for you, your destinies will be your own."

"But you said we were your prisoners."

"Clever human." Cho grinned. "You must forgive me my riddles." She walked up and down that ragged line, watching for the tiniest shifts in expression. "It is in my nature to confuse, and nature can be difficult to subdue." With a snap of her fingers, she shattered the chains binding them. "There is no true freedom to be had, in this world or any other. All choices come with prices and penalties. You'll not find a better deal than mine, a kinder guardian than me, for the only condition I set upon my saving you is that you offer yourselves to the service of the lost, the weary, the orphans of your world. Others like you. Help them, and let them join you."

"I don't understand, Lor—Dimas."

"I will be among you, to guide and teach, until such a time that you no longer need me. Now, your first lesson." The children, from their seats on the dirty floor, watched with wide eyes. "Listen carefully. There is a certain truth in Contradiction. As a Noble who often walks in the skin of a man, I am all, and I am nothing. If I am your savior, so too am I your destroyer. Even as I add you to my collection of souls, you shall be collected and Collector. Submit yourselves to the knowledge that you are living and dead—that your lives mean nothing and everything—and free yourselves of petty human morals. Understand?"

The children gaped at her. None dared speak.

"Perhaps you shall, one day yet. This first lesson will cost you nothing, except the lifetime it will take you to learn it. All subsequent lessons you will buy with your labor, anguish, and ferocity. Now, I offer you the choice: do you accept my gift, or will you die—some days from now—alone in this tower prison?"

They rose, fists clenched, lips trembling, but they rose. Buried beneath the surface of these muddy, knobby-jointed, sickly goblins before her, there was the iron of warriors waiting to be unearthed.

"Very well." She touched the tops of each of their heads in turn. "To my service, unto the seventh generation, I bind you all."

She nudged them forward, out of their cell, and led them from the tower.

Though her first foray into the rescue of dispossessed and abused children, this night would be far from her last. For five centuries, in fact, she traveled the Provinces of El—most frequently Torvir and its neighbors—and, over the course of a generation or two, her "Collectors" began to act of their own accord, without her direction, widening the search net, increasing the numbers of the rescued. From the ranks of the abducted, the diseased, the abandoned, gangs began to form. From these networks, an irregular army took shape. As the decades built up, brick after brick, eventually there were thousands of them, and most of Cho's days were spent touring the country, visiting their meeting places, providing words of support and encouragement, and only the occasional command.

She had stopped her tours for a generation or two, when the grandchildren of the original rescues began demanding what this was all *for*, what their purpose was.

Summoned to that dank cellar, one of many secret meeting places, she smiled proudly at these descendants of her first disciples. They had begun to think for themselves.

A man named N'dalte spoke for the group: "Why save anyone?" Cho remembered liking him; he'd also never been satisfied with anything that came too easily.

Mockingly, she asked, "Is it no longer enough to lend a hand to those in need?" Though grown by the standards of their young race, like schoolchildren they needed to be led to each answer.

"There's no greater design, then? Our numbers are many, and always growing. We could enact lasting change. Once and for all, we could destroy the Order and all others who prey upon the weak, even as you once destroyed those who preyed upon our sires."

"To destroy is easy, to build... You will always be my chosen children. I ask you, be patient. The hour of need will not come in your lifetimes. It may not come even in the days of your grandchildren. But it will come. Oh, yes, it will."

"How will we know that moment when it arrives? Who shall be the messenger?"

"*I* shall return, though with a new face. For now, have faith in yourselves and each other, and instruct your descendants to watch for my sign. When I reveal myself, I shall cut a path to the very heart of The Capital, and—together—we shall drive The Authority and the Plutocrats before us." And, on that day, the Old Master would know to fear her—at last, but too late.

She left them then, N'dalte and her other Collectors, to their labors. She had her own tasks ahead of her, her own plans to make.

The work kept her quite busy for some time.

For every knight or scholar she beheaded, another ten lined up. The process was a treat all its own, of course, so she shouldn't complain too much.

Then there were the hunters dogging her trail. Especially delightful were the Aelfravers who'd pop into her swamp on occasion; they always seemed so shocked when she gutted them.

With each spent year, she sensed her death draw ever closer. However, its approach filled her with increasing joy: her downfall would begin the end of the world.

Sometimes, she'd walk among the humans, peer into their little minds.
When she dreamed, she dreamed of ruin.

ALINA

A vibration, starting in her jaw, humming its way up her skull, burrowing into her brain.

Then, she heard it. A voice, a hiss.

As below, so above, Vrana.

Her vision went funny—too bright, too colorful. The Covenants guarding the chamber melted into puddles of yellow soup.

She became vaguely aware that she no longer crouched in her dark alcove but stood openly before the metal doors, gazing at the black-and-yellow hexagon emblazoned upon them. The Crow had returned to her. Its long, rough fingers held up her chin.

The glassy blue eye embedded in the wall flashed, bathing her in a ray of light that passed from head to toe. A soft, melodious voice chimed, "Unique Niimantic Signature recognized: *Vranakvius-rhin'erlin*. Access granted."

The doors scraped open, revealing darkness so thick and gelatinous she could have spread it on a slice of bread. She stepped forward, and then it was too late; the doors shut behind her.

The Crow merged with the blackness.

A pinprick of calming green light flickered far, far ahead, and she moved toward it, feeling her way along the wall.

"As below," she panted, "so above." She didn't know what she said anymore, and it didn't matter. The word *Vrana*, familiar and alien, was the only guide she needed. Tugged forward, her feet trailed the whispers. Invisible threads cradled her head like a twiggy nest would an egg. Gravity shifted continuously: her red curls hung in her eyes, then away from her forehead. Light on her heels, airy-headed, she bounced from floor to wall to ceiling, and back again, down dark, twisting corridors.

And there, ahead of her, went Dimas. She endeavored to take the opposite path: he'd turn left, she right; he right, she left; he straight, she backward.

Then he was gone, replaced by Ruqastra, who beckoned her. As they progressed through the maze of corridors, the paths rising and falling like the chest of a sleeping stone giant, Ruqastra became Mezami—and that was odd because hadn't Alina sent him to go find Cho?

Hmm. There was something important she needed to remember about Cho. But the green light pulsed like a heartbeat, thrumming along the walls, unraveling her focus.

Vrana.

The corridor fell away, and the green light lured her up flights of stairs and across a narrow stone bridge overlooking a pitch-dark chasm (the Hextarchs were big fans of chasms, apparently). Through canyons and over hills, the ever-changing stonescape of Hexhall drew her more and more deeply into itself.

She needed to leave.

Vrana.

But her parents—yes, there they were, right there—were calling her onward. She had to follow them. She didn't want to be late for her first day of school. Strange that her school was so far underground, but Alina was only five years old, so she didn't know what school was supposed to be like anyway.

And—so strong here, stronger than anywhere else she'd been—the ever-present Abyssal energy flowed over her, scouring her mind like a pumice stone scours the body. The Abyss bathed her, passed through the molecules of her—like air, an updraft lifting her hollow bones.

When she stepped out of the tunnel and into the ring of dim green light, she found herself in a hexagonal stone chamber. Six podiums, carved of living rock, surrounded a floating, gyrating, translucent sphere—the source of the light *and* Dimas's ghostly energy. Despite the fog settling over her thoughts, she realized this sphere must be the anchor she'd been searching for. But she devoted what little unclouded brainpower she had left to processing the sense of imminent danger compressing her chest.

She looked up.

On each of the podiums stood a long figure, hooded by a yellow cloak, veiled by a mask: toad, mongoose, fly, centipede, hornet, cat.

Each wore several gold accessories—rings, chokers, studs, bangles—and rich gold thread was woven through their clothing. Each also had gold eyes.

As one, the six revealed their faces, their features humanoid but stretched, flattened, twisted—as if sketched by a representational artist who preferred abstract lines.

The figure nearest Alina inclined its pale, spike-ridged head, blinking its milky eyes. It waved its sinewy arms, webbed fingers trailing tendrils of light.

Though Alina couldn't understand how, she knew its name. "Haba."

The second figure sniffed with its bright pink nose as it scratched its flaking, mottled white and gray skin. Fangs poked from between its leathery lips. Six tufts of flame floated behind its head.

"Gurm." Alina's eyes widened.

The third had a large head and a translucent cape resembling insect wings; its opalescent skin glittered in the illusory light as it jittered, a necklace of icicles tinkling against its chitinous chest.

A headache coming on, Alina breathed, "Etia."

The fourth was swaddled in a black robe to complement its black skin and hair, causing its bright orange-yellow nose and eyes to stand out starkly. Its six sinewy arms crossed its chest, a spike protruding from each elbow.

"Stonoz."

The fifth had wispy blond hair and mirror-like eyes. Draped over its shoulder, a fur-lined cape. It clutched a curved, nail-thin dagger. As it moved, raw electricity sparked from its limbs.

"Nasres."

The sixth and final figure held one gold eye open, the other closed. Black tattoos striped its graying skin, its tail looping around its wrist as it grinned. Pointed ears flicked curiously. Around its neck hung a purse, which Alina felt certain was filled with grave dirt.

"Aam." She pressed her fingers to her temples. "I know you. How do I know you all?"

"It has been a lifetime, Vrana. We hardly recognize you now that you've shed the disguise of that old human male," said Gurm. "We had expected you to arrive in the guise of another."

"Although," said Stonoz, "this flesh-suit is less unsightly."

"Yet, the fact that you continue to wear the face of a human at all is... disturbing," Nasres said.

"Come now, friends. Certainly, Vrana must have a sound reason for their... willful rebelliousness. Hmm?"

"You're the Hextarchs?" said Alina. Her headache was unreal. Like she'd swallowed a beehive. "How did I get here? How do I know you?" She had to hold herself together.

"Bizarre. Why feign ignorance? Do they play a game with us?"

"No," Etia twitched its head, membranous eyes glistening. "They truly *have* forgotten."

"If they remember nothing, why have they come to us? Why now?"

"Perhaps we should ask them."

"Recall, Vrana has been untrustworthy in the past."

"More than once. Yet, we are siblings still, we seven. We cannot deny this chance to parley, now, when the hour of our doom draws inexorably near."

"Indeed. Our Old Master comes to finish what we so long ago began."

"Yes, this is the end. We may as well come to terms with that fact—"

"—and each other—"

"—before we rejoin the stars at last."

"As dust."

The illusory green light winked out, leaving the seven of them in total darkness for an instant. However, as Alina's vision adjusted, she became aware that what she'd thought to have been a floor of obsidian actually was glass. Under it, clearly distinguishable in the absence of the magical light source, swirled the constellations and galaxies of The Abyss. As Hexhall glided through infinite space, comets streaked past, suns blinked in and out of existence, and black holes devoured all matter and light within reach.

Stonoz hummed before saying, Have you come to betray us to the forces of our Old Master?"

"I, uh," Alina said, mouth dry, "don't know what you're talking about."

"Oh, but there are no secrets between us," said Aam, their single, shining gold eye the only visible part of their body. "Eons past, we were forged in the same crucible, made of the same stuff. We see your mind, deceiver that you are."

"Very well," croaked Haba. "Let us commune."

"On this ultimate night."

"One last time."

"Uh," said Alina, and the brain-fog lifted a little more. *Cho!* she remembered. *Kinneas!* What was she still doing here? Fear for her friends' lives, as well as her own, dampened her burning curiosity. "I really need to go." She took a step back, bonking her heel and head against stone.

The passageway behind her had sealed itself, stone scabbed over, smooth. As if it had always been that way.

She pounded the barrier with her fist. Solid.

"Now, now." Etia tut-tutted.

The six Hextarchs loomed over her, and she shriveled before them like dry skin peeling from a corpse.

And that was when the fear *really* set in.

"I feel sick," said Alina, hugging her stomach. "Have to—" she coughed— "find my—"

"The seasons you've wasted among the humans have addled your mind. Have you forgotten the blade overhead, its point poised to strike?"

"Understand, Vrana."

"It is fate."

"Now that we are together once more—"

"—as below, so above—"

"None of us shall leave Hexhall alive."

CHO-ZEN

Cho blinked awake to knuckles grinding against her skull.

Still in his coal-gray suit, Jejune rapped her forehead. "Oh, you're awake. I take it you've reconnected with your cute little friend over there?" He jerked a thumb toward Kinneas. " No? Guess he's still tuckered out from his big day in the interrogation room. Nasty case of NDS, that one. Someone really ought to get him some medical treatment, pronto." He turned to leave the cell, side-stepping the chair that held Kinneas. Then he halted, lifting a finger. "Before I forget." He regarded her again. "Full disclosure: good Kinneas's older brother, Calthin, has also been detained for *thorough* questioning. We aren't sure if he's involved in your little insurrectionist plot, but it doesn't hurt to, heh, ask nicely."

Cho heard a pop that felt like it originated from the point where the notch of her spine connected to her skull.

Something inside her cracked. She began to laugh.

"Have fun while you can, little girl," he said, though he couldn't quite hide his discomfort at her response. "Anarkey is broken. We hold all the pieces."

"Nergali-irra'cuthirgal," she said quietly.

"What did you jus—" He closed in, pawing her face, reigniting her aches and pains, but she didn't care. As she continued to laugh, he barked, "That name, where did you hear it?"

She sucked in a breath. "It is yours, isn't it?

Turning on his heels, he dashed off, phased through the glass wall, and snatched the remote from the dozing guard's desk. Returning, an ember of fury in his eye, he clicked the button repeatedly, and she screamed as jolt after jolt hammered her nervous system.

Twitching from the aftershock, unable to look at him, she muttered, "Doesn't matter what you do to me, Nergali-irra'cuthirgal." Her tongue was numb, the words hard to form. "I know what you are."

"You know nothing."

"Demon." She chuckled, dangling from her chains. "Pretty soon it'll be open season on the likes of you."

He growled, preparing to slap the button on that horrible little controller again. First, however, he jerked the dial as high as it could go.

"Sweet dreams, Choraelia." His jaw unhinged, his off-kilter grin too wide and too sharp to be human. "For me, anyway." The sweet smell of rotting meat wafted from his lolling tongue. "Your deliciously futile wrath will feed me for *days.*"

She roared all her hatred at him, her voice breaking, until her lungs were empty. Then she slumped, and he smiled as he grew in height.

She had just *fed* him, she realized, as he pressed the button again.

Electricity knifing her nerves, her operating system initiated yet another emergency shut down.

During its last conscious nanosecond, her mind seized up, receiving a series of flashes—three fevered visions:

First, she saw the three great chains of New El snap, the floating Capital itself crashing toward the surface, its eight million souls screaming as they plunged toward certain death.

Next, she found herself shaking hands with… Tolomond? Shaking *hands* with him? Calmly? The man's arms, up to the shoulders, had been burned black; his touch was charcoal. He fell to his knees before her, and she placed a hand atop his bowed head.

Lastly, she cowered beneath a searing sun—locked in a static heaven of infinite, unchanging whiteness.

"*I am The Author of Creation,*" said the great ball of fire and light. "*I am Worldmaker. I am Elwoch.*"

Lost, disoriented, seemingly at the sun's mercy, Cho floated in this place beyond gravity and time. However, digging through her confusion, she found strength enough to blearily shout, "Oh, yeah?" After everything that had happened to her the past few weeks, she'd had enough. Hallucination or not, like it or not, this voice was going to get a piece of her mind. "And I'm... not impressed."

"*Prostrate yourself. Kiss the earth in reverence and gratitude. Crawl before Me as did all your ancestors, back to the beginnings of your House.*"

She gave it two big thumbs down. "Pass."

"*Since the dawning of your race, your people have submitted to Me. As will you.*"

"If you're so badass, why doncha, I dunno, *make me.*"

"*I have worked miracles, child. You are less than nothing. Do not seek to bend My will toward your utter obliteration. Admit to your awe. Devote yourself.*"

"Eat me."

There fell upon her a silence, one imbued with blazing heat and a sort of indescribably titanic, far-reaching, stewing fury. To call it an "awkward silence" would be an understatement of mythic proportions.

Flares erupted from that false sun, streaking through the heavens. Cho's flesh began to crisp.

"*As you wish.*"

The blinding whiteness blazed all the brighter, overtaking, charring, incinerating everything.

Cho rolled upright, baring her teeth, her chained arms crossing her face.

She had not, in fact, been burned. The sensation of dying, and the voice that had taunted her, had been just another nightmare. And, frankly, one not too much worse than what she'd woken up to.

After zapping her into another mini coma, at least Jejune had gone away.

Kinneas still hadn't moved. Depending on how long she'd been knocked out for, that was either really worrisome or terribly worrisome. But all she could do was say his name, desperately attempting to call him back to consciousness.

Later, from beyond her cell and its observation room, there came muffled rattling and booming noises, rapidly growing louder. She strained to listen, to make sense of the sounds. The rattling was gunfire, she realized; the booming, explosives.

Screams. One, two—five. Judging by the noise, people were dying in that hallway, lots of them and quickly. Casualties of a fight that was creeping nearer and nearer.

Cho's first impulse was grim satisfaction: good; she hoped her captors suffered as much as possible before they popped like water balloons. But the screams dragged her back to that night that, for years, she'd desperately sought to erase from her memory.

That hour she'd spent under her bed, hands over her ears, praying for an end to the shrieking and the fireworks and the thunder. Even at six years old, she'd known, when her bedroom door swung open, the men who entered had not come to help her.

The copper reek of blood dappled their hands and their knives. Muddy footprints seeped into the plush carpet.

In their black body armor, masked and hooded, they'd swept aside her barricade of pillows, blankets, and stuffed animals. They'd torn her from her den. She'd cried and kicked them, bitten their fingers, clawed at their eyes.

Her father sprawled on the ground, she'd called out to him, but he wouldn't get up. She'd called to every one of her siblings, her mother, the servants, but no one came. No one would come. Eventually, she'd learn why: she'd been the only Torvir to leave that house outside of a body bag.

The masked men had left her alive because she'd been the smallest. The least threatening. The easiest to control.

As the memory receded, she shrank against the wall of her cell, shaking. "Kinneas," she muttered, her voice failing. "Kinneas, please, please wake up."

The gunfire and death-gurgles were close now. Just beyond the door.

She reached for her friend, straining against her chains.

The guard on the other side of the glass wall aimed his sidearm squarely at the door. She stifled a shriek as it burst from its hinges, and crushed him against the wall.

Pop-pop-pop. A trio of flashes accompanied more gunshots, and a soldier fell into the observation room, dying on the tiled floor.

Stepping over the soon-to-be-corpse, a woman entered and turned toward the glass wall. Through the smoke, Cho observed her. She had shoulder-length black hair on one side of her head, a metal plate covering the other. Most of the left half of her body had been replaced with iron-colored prosthetic limbs, as had her lower jaw. With her suntan, she couldn't have been in Ozar long. In one hand, she gripped an automatic pistol; the other telekinetically cradled a fireball.

Ducking behind the guard's desk, she lobbed the projectile at the glass wall. Fiery force exploded against the barrier, cracking it from the center outward, corner to corner. Standing, the woman tossed back her coat and drew a long-barreled shotgun, blasting the cracked glass, damaging it enough to turn it opaque. A steady, repeating thud shook the wall until it finally gave way, shattering and falling down.

The stranger used the legs of a metal chair to brush aside any hanging jagged shards. She dropped the chair, considering Kinneas a moment, then fixed her gaze on Cho.

Cho recognized her, then: the modded soldier who'd pursued her and Cbarassan after the fight at Revelation Studios.

Chained. Cornered. This time, there was no hope of escape.

Between the woman's fingers, threads of flame ignited.

51

ALINA

PERCHED UPON THEIR STONE pedestals, the Hextarchs watched her, unmoving. The only exception was Aam, the dark one whose face was stuck in a permanent wink, whose playful eye Alina could feel grazing the back of her head. Aam had put themselves between her and the only way out.

A silence settled with the dust. The living gods of Ozar waited for her to say something; their curiosity picked at her like fingernails at a scab.

She heard a murmuring, then, felt its pull. Her feet shuffled closer to the center of the chamber and the floating green orb. Such was the call of The Abyss, which here was inseparable from Dimas's Niimantic signature. His Revomancy and the power that bled from this place both prodded her forward, onward to some kind of conclusion. Yes, it was close now.

But Alina was quite practiced in resisting the tug of destiny. "I have so many questions," she said at last, "but I gotta go."

"You haven't changed much, not truly," said Gurm, bright pink nostrils flaring. "As always, your love of futile strife twists you this way and that. Stay with us instead. Our end is nigh."

"That a threat?" Alina's claws came out. She widened her stance, tensing. Letting loose felt good.

The Crow mimicked her.

"We have no reason to raise our voices against you, little echo." Haba blinked their milky eyes. "We shall all scream our last soon enough, when the Master's pawns break through those doors." They pointed behind her, toward where the corridor leading out had been.

Under Alina's glare, Aam's angular ears twitched.

"Let me go," she said. Aam ignored her. "Last warning."

They smirked, showing their curved fangs.

From opposite sides, Alina and the Crow lunged, slashing with their claws. The mirrored attack failed halfway to its target. An incredible weight landed on Alina's shoulders, her knees immediately giving way. Her heart fired like a jamming machine gun. She couldn't breathe.

"You're just an echo," said Aam, standing over her, giving an apologetic shrug. "Unless you're restored, made full again, there's nothing you can do to us."

On her hands and knees, Alina certainly had a hard time denying their claim.

Etia's laugh was all bitterness and brine.

Stonoz flexed their six sinewy arms, veins bulging, saying, "Now do you feel it?" They closed their eyes, inhaling. Their sharp exhale buffeted their thin black hair. "Finality."

"Yeah," she grunted, sweating. "Sure, I get it. The Authority's coming." On the ground, she turned away from Aam and toward the other five, using every trick Ruqastra had taught her to seal away her thoughts, to hide why she'd come.

If they weren't going to let her leave, she might just have to break their Revomantic anchor after all. The green orb twinkled ahead, so close and yet so far. How to get to it, though, when she could barely move?

For now, she'd keep the Hextarchs talking. "Things look bad. But you seem pretty tough, and isn't there, like, a whole army ready to fight for you? All those soldiers and cult-y Covenants?"

"Fight, indeed," said Stonoz.

"And perish," said Etia. "It is the natural order."

"A sad inevitability," said Haba.

"There was valiance to our struggle," said Stonoz.

"Yet, our doom was writ in primordial rock," said Nasres.

Although they spoke in such close agreement with each other, passing their thoughts as if playing a languid game of catch, they weren't of one mind. As their attentions shifted from speaker to speaker, Alina noted subtle glimmers of frustration, annoyance, respect, and affection in their golden eyes depending on what was said—and who had said it. These were not entities connected by a hive mind; no, they were siblings, well-versed in the others' opinions, strengths, and mannerisms. They loved and irritated each other like any family would.

Whatever Alina had expected the Hextarchs to be like, the reality surprised her.

"So, am I hearing you right? You've already given up?" She felt so weak, nauseous. Could feel her heartbeat in her nostril, and behind her eyeball. "I thought you were supposed to be gods."

Aam laughed, blinking their open gold eye, pale fleshy tail quivering. "What is a 'god'?"

"To the warrior, a blade. To the sun-parched man, water or shade."

"We fed the hungry, clothed the naked, housed the homeless. Thus, to the Ozari masses, our arrival seemed an act of providence."

"A misconception we did not discourage."

"For their bodies fueled the war."

"And our own survival."

Fuel. The word returned Alina's attention to her feelings of sickness, a sapping of her will she had only vaguely registered until just now. The peculiar detail about it was its sense of direction—a outward flow. Her life-force was unraveling, drawn from her like spider silk, floating invisibly through the air, spooling around the Hextarchs.

"You're feeding on me," she said. "You're *Thaal*." But that couldn't be true. Ancient Aelf parasites, the *Thaal* had supposedly gone extinct centuries ago.

"Behold. Live too long among dull mortal fools, Vrana, and risk forgetting the lore that birthed you," said Gurm. "You call us *Thaal*—but what we are, *so are you*."

Alina had gone shaky at the wrists and elbows. Head hanging, she shouted, "Whatever. I might be a quarter Aelf on my grandad's side, but I think I'd know if I were a leech."

"Do our abilities define us?" said Aam, winking playfully again. "Consider the murderer and the soldier. Both do kill, but only one is revered for the act."

"Choice," Haba croaked.

"Choice is the prime determinant. Will births action, and therefrom springs character."

"You call us 'leeches.' '*Thaal*.' Such words are meaningless. The concept of the 'parasite' rules out the truth, that all energy in all worlds is spun and trussed from the selfsame source."

Etia stroked their translucent wings with long, double-jointed fingers. "Thaal. Demon. Iorian." They cackled. *"Sevensin."*

"Many are the titles heaped upon us over the thousands of years we have inhabited this earth. Names die with the sons of the men who wrought them. All pass eventually; endings are the only constant."

"The appellations granted us by mortals are of no significance."

"We are what we are."

"What *you* are."

Woozy, Alina shook her head. "Nope. What I'm feeling now, it's a side-effect of the feeding." She crawled to the nearest pedestal, leaning against it. "You're scrambling my brain."

"No, Vrana." Gurm cracked their long neck, wrinkling their pink nose. "You are simply remembering."

"After so much struggle—and such fervent desire to stay away—why did you return to us now, of all times?" said Aam.

"To join us in death?"

"That *is* fitting."

"We should help them," said Nasres thoughtfully. "It is unseemly that we should surrender to oblivion, we seven, while one of our minds remains so fractured."

"Nothing can be done about that. Their ruin is of their own make. Indeed, where there were once four, then three, there yet remain *two* of Vrana."

"You're talking about Mateus?" Alina groaned, hugging her stomach. "The Savior?"

"Indeed. Though the only name truly of import is the one you share with him—*Vrana*."

"Killing me," she gasped. "You're killing me."

"We are not," said Haba. "Rather, the human mask you wear withers as your true self bursts forth."

"Like a pupa from its cocoon," said Etia, nodding.

"I grow weary of their piteous cries," said Stonoz. "Let us help them escape their prison of mortal flesh and self-deceit."

"Four?" said Alina, her sluggish thoughts finally catching up with the Hextarchs' bad math. There weren't *four* of her. She didn't understand.

"Look down," said Aam.

She did, and where she'd expected to find the deep, full, writhing blackness of The Abyss, clouded with constellations and supernovae, instead *seven figures in gold cloaks knelt before a tall man wearing a knee-length, flowing white beard.*

"*Elwoch,*" she said without thinking.

"Yes. However!" Aam flitted over, walking their fingers up her back. "Even this vision is part lie. As I recall, he was a short man, and red of beard—not white. But, today, his will infects the very fabric of reality; The Abyss is a perfect mirror, and therefore must reflect truths and deceptions alike. Even in this sacrum, we see some of what *he* wishes us to. Ah, but what is life if not a merry-go-round of lies?" They clutched Alina's chin, forcing her gaze downward again.

The dots and eddies of astral rivers and streaking comets bypassed her eyes and banged against her brain. The churning colors filled her vision with sight beyond sight.

On blood-washed marble stood a cadre of soldiers in strange, smooth armor like liquid metal. Their weapons were hooked, right-angled. From each off-hand dangled a gold, chained pocketwatch. However, these were not normal time-keepers: the devices had four hands and multiple concentric circles of unsettling symbols. When, in unison, the pocketwatches stopped ticking, a green portal appeared before the soldiers, and they stepped through it into a world of lush rainforests.

"Not another world, Vrana, but another *time,*" said Aam.

Haba cut in, "Could they truly have forgotten the Order? Absurd!"

"*We* wrote its charter," said Nasres. "We founded it."

"Hush now," said Aam, redirecting Alina's attention to The Abyss. More for her benefit than Haba's, they added, "Patience."

A short, gray-haired old man stood before a murky pond flanked by seven stone pillars.

The sun and moon wheeled overhead as he spent days, weeks, chiseling the living rock into exquisitely detailed statues, whose models must have been beautiful indeed. Each sculpture represented a sharp-eared, narrow-faced, androgynous figure trapped in an imperious pose.

Finished, snow beginning to fall, the old man laid down his sculptor's tools and stretched out in the snow.

He didn't get up.

At the end of the season, the snows began to melt. The statues began to move. *Rather, specters pried themselves from the stone—things long dead but* returned *through the grace and sacrifice of the snow-preserved old man, the Bearer of the Iron Seal.*

They came down, these phantasms, down from their pedestals, separating completely from their stone likenesses. And they pressed their translucent hands to the cold body. By their will, the leaves and earth shifted.

Though he had been the one to kill them, they buried him with honor, singing songs of his valor and virtue.

They lingered then a while, unsure of what to do next.

Eventually, one of them looked up. Under ghostly hair that licked the air like flames, its eyes were puddles of spilled ink, its expression frighteningly alien and hauntingly familiar.

Across time and space, it looked directly at Alina.

And Alina recognized Mount Morbin and the pond where she'd meditated with Ruqastra and—

"Me?" she said, a tear falling from her chin to the ground. "That's me?" The moisture sizzled when it struck the clear window on which she stood.

"Us, yes. And the Iorian who was called Iron," said Aam quietly. "Though our foe, we buried him upon our awakening, for he fought well."

Wistfully, Stonoz said, "His greatest weapon was peace."

"And he wielded it with a vengeance." Etia inhaled, wings fluttering. "Our battle was legend. We love and curse him to this day."

"He made you?" said Alina, head thumping. "Us?"

"By the iron of his blood," said Gurm, "he sealed our great doom. Blissfully, his hex nears its conclusion at last."

"Look. The Abyss," said Aam. "It shows another memory."

Entranced, Alina saw *through the eyes of a flying creature. Forking through the stormy air like lightning, she sighted a perfect sphere topped by a pyramidal temple—the cherry to a scoop of chocolate ice cream. The sphere had been tethered to the earth by three massive chains, ones Alina knew well. Consortio, Libra, and Concordia they were called; "Fellowship," "Balance," and "Harmony." They were the Chains of El, and the sphere was New El. Although, it was naked, conspicuously missing the shining glass and steel towers and glowing neon lights of the modern Capital.*

Dropping down, her point of view revealed a battle burning across the city's heaven-facing side. The fiercest fighting centered on a temple, a ziggurat that crowned the sphere. Upon this structure stood two towering figures; from them poured waves and jets of flame. Around the temple, human men, women, and children fought with improvised, functional weapons—clubs, picks, nets, fishing spears, wood axes. The two flame-wielding giants were surrounded by bodyguards, richly adorned in fine but impractical leathers and furs, their ceremonial armor no match for the ferocity of the nearly naked hordes attacking them, bludgeoning them with wood and stone, fist and elbow.

Then, facing the two fire-breathers, Seven shadows appeared.

They sprang forward, into the fray, even as Alina was pulled from the vision by Aam's voice: "We had convinced ourselves that liberating the human race would steal away Elwoch's primary resource, robbing him of sustenance, of life itself."

"We were mistaken," said Nasres, reflective eyes glistening.

"We taught the humans how to resist, arming them with the one tool capable of winning them their liberty."

"Magic," said Alina. "You taught them magic."

"Fools," croaked Haba, and Alina couldn't be sure if they were talking about themselves or humanity.

She was swept into another vision of that same battle:

Flame and water, earth and lightning—blasts of Niimantic energy coursed through and from one dozen human champions. They fought their way up the temple steps and toward the two figures crowned by teeth of light, whose limbs glowed with unquenchable radiance.

It was a terrifying struggle, but—with the Seven channeling their full might into their human paragons—the mortals prevailed. The light-haloed twin kings were cast down upon the altar of their temple, that monument to their arrogance and greed.

However, as the Seven approached to congratulate their twelve champions, they recoiled in horror: for among the mortal mages had appeared a globe of light.

It was the Old Master, whose fury tore apart the Seven as easily as a tidal wave would destroy man-shaped paper cutouts.

Dwindling into death, the Seven could only watch as the globe of light—avatar of Elwoch, their enemy—bent the minds of their twelve champions to his service.

"He made them many promises, gave them the strength to rule their people forever," said Aam. "In exchange for undying devotion, unflinching fervor, to him." Their tail flicked behind their head. "The Old Master has always been skilled at transmuting weakness into strength."

"Twelve champions." Although Alina had never much cared for history lessons, the connection was obvious even to her. "The ancestors of the Plutocrats."

Aam's mischievous smirk faded.

"Our war against the Twin Dragons cost us everything," said Etia. "We fled."

"We rebuilt," Stonoz corrected. "From nothing."

Her knees locked, her jaw set, nevertheless, Alina could feel herself growing stronger. Depression and determination welled within her in equal measure, as did melancholy and happiness, serenity and terror. Internal Contradiction set into her heart, vibrating in her blood, stirring her cells to dance.

Without prompting, she returned her focus to The Abyss.

And there—with a full head of charcoal hair and a coarse, round beard—was Dimas, significantly younger than how she remembered him.

Standing over the familiar pool on Mount Morbin, he drew forth its waters, lifting them into the air, shaping them into an oval roughly the size of a loaf of bread or a doll. The water crystallized. Without moving, he sculpted the ice into something that looked remarkably like a human infant.

The ice-baby drifted toward him. He blew upon its brow a gout of flame, and the ice melted away, revealing skin, hair, eyes. Pressing his ear to the flesh-and-blood baby's chest, he gasped at the whisper of a heartbeat.

"Fire and ice." He brushed his index finger over the child's scalp, painting a thin line with his own blood. "Mateus. My first. My progeny."

He set the babe down in a basket of wicker, upon a pile of handkerchiefs and towels. Over the silent boy, he draped a woolly blanket of faded red before turning away.

For a long time, he cupped and rubbed his chin, wandering about the forest (though he never strayed too far from his "son").

"I overthink it," he mused aloud. "Pure earth and air, drawn from this sacred place; these will suffice."

On his shins, he reached into the pond until his beard and nose, chest and arms up to the shoulders, were drenched, scooping forth handful after handful of mud. "With my own two hands." He molded the muck into a shape resembling a mud baby, bulbous head and fat body. Standing, he looked to the sky and called a bolt of lightning, catching it in the webs of his fingers. He pressed his palms to the mud, and glowing gold and white heat—pure energy— baked the earth, hardening it.

He got up, stepped back.

Where he'd left his black hand prints, the earth cracked like ancient pottery, thin layers like birch bark peeling away, swept off by rising winds.

The cocoon shed, what remained was a baby girl. "My second, superior progeny." said Dimas. She was almost human and, to him, "Perfect," which was the very word he used to congratulate himself.

Taking the baby to meet her brother, laying her in the basket beside him, Dimas said, "Earth and air. Zatalena."

Breaking free of the tendrils of The Abyss, Alina shoved Aam away from her, shouting, "It didn't happen that way. That's a lie."

"You seek answers?" Aam's gold eye flicked downward. "Be still. *See* this."

The sun and moon wheeled across the sky, chasing one another, speeding through the seasons.

A tall, youthful, graying-haired Zatalena wept over the failing breaths of her newborn child. "Do something," she demanded of Dimas, her "father."

But he knew there was nothing that could be done for this thing before him, this hybrid creature he cradled in his arms. The baby—whom her foolish parents had named Alina—had been doomed from the start: the Sevensin's curse had predictably reached the crib. None of their natural-born children, including Zatalena's, could survive. Thusly was it inscribed upon the Iron Seal, more binding than chains, more lasting than stone.

"Take this poor thing and bury it," said Dimas, offering up the child. "There's nothing to be done."

"You're a monster," cried Zatalena, snatching the weakening baby from his arms. "Heartless. Hopelessly cruel. If I could trade your life for hers—" Her rage broke away from her, as the clay had done from her un-living body long ago. It was replaced by grief, a shameless sorrow. "I'll do anything. Anything you ask. Use me to save her."

"What we are, Lena—you ask the impossible. Ailments I can heal, but it is death that has her now. That thing you hold is nothing more than a decaying husk. It is tragic, yet I can't—"

"Coward!" screamed Zatalena. "All the secrets at your fingertips, all the power in the world, and you can't revive one girl? Or, is it that you won't? What's the point of being what we are, if we can't save those we love?"

"My little Cabbage, to be what we are is to watch those we love perish. We must die a thousand deaths before finally reaching our own end."

"You made me," she said, "to torment me."

In that moment, inside him, something changed.

Confronting her complete agony broke him, for it was his own brokenness, reflected. Though their bodies, their voices, their thoughts were separated by thin shells of matter, they were the same being after all.

Her fear shattered his resolve.

"Give her here," he told his daughter. "Give me the child."

Shocked by his change of heart, she hesitated, thoughts strafing her mind, before giving him her baby. Sobbing, she asked, "What will you do?"

"What I can."

The child in his arms, Dimas scaled the mountain. One last time.

Against the rising storms, the sheets of hail and blasting winds, the torrent of leaves—he climbed. And so he reached the sacred pool that was still flanked by seven weathered statues, the font from which his soul had been restored to this world after each of his deaths. The selfsame place where he, in his arrogance, had created a parody of life—as Iron had done, so, so long ago for him. Here, he'd birthed his "children," Mateus and Zatalena. He'd sought to understand himself through this disembodiment—to see into his own soul through six eyes, not two.

This act had been his truest folly.

His children had been born into a world that hated them, where they were neither human nor Iorian, neither living nor dead. He'd raised them to be free of the pathetic constraints and strictures of mortals, but in their hearts—from the beginning—had grown a Contradiction of self. One that they were not equipped to contain.

At this pool, he'd performed his greatest sin. Twice.

And, there, he would sin again. One last, third time.

The baby's breath gave out. The infant girl—Zatalena's biological daughter, the failed offspring of an Iorian echo and a human man—died in Dimas's arms.

The old man, who was neither truly old nor man, knelt before the pool and lowered the baby into its wind-churned waters.

Of ice and fire, he'd made Mateus.

Of earth and air had been born Zatalena.

Alina, hybrid child, was gone… but from her body, another *Alina would be born.*

The human form—essence of the tangible, what mortals called 'the real'—this cold flesh would provide one of the elements needed for the spell of creation. It would serve Dimas's purpose. However, he also required a counterpart, a thing equal and opposite.

If he was to fracture his soul a third time, forging an effigy of life from a human body, he would need something unreal *to counterbalance the realness of the baby's lost life.*

Vitality, creation, matter, energy—the spark animating all living beings held true weight, an undeniable realness. By contrast, death and dream were products of the unconscious, the otherworldly. Unbound from flesh, they were fluid…

"Yes," he thought. "It might just work."

Once upon a time, death had begun as an idea only, but was granted power through collective belief. Fearing it, sentient life had given it teeth: a sudden end, a veil of total blackness, or any number of a million conceptions of eternal planes of reward or punishment… Mortal dreams had reshaped death without affecting its purpose: it remained the transitional stage between different expressions of life, a reshuffling of matter and energy into ever-changing forms. A step in a dance, a rung on a stair. In the end, death was the ultimate dream, from which all life eventually awakened, again and again, only to drift off once more. (Dimas and his six siblings—only they would truly 'end' when they died, for they had never been *alive. They were merely shades of real things, echoes of echoes.)*

Sighing, he had found his answer, his final ingredient.

He'd always held an especial love for the Revomantic art, the weaving of subconscious strata to give substance to the substance-less. It would serve as his perfect tool now.

Still, he shuddered at the audacity of what he was about to attempt: to bind the reality of *life to the* illusion *of death. To carve* consciousness *from the hollow between something and nothing.*

Even as he raged at himself for what he did, he did it. He cast the spell.

The torrential downpour continued to beat against the mountain, a storm dwarfed by the one in his heart.

In the vortex of the pool floated the lifeless baby—a still thing, cold and dark.

He waited, partly hoping he'd failed.

And then the baby's eyes opened. Bright gold eyes, fading to light green as she began to cry. He retrieved her, weeping as he did. "I'm sorry," he said. "I'm so sorry."

Then he brought her down from the mountain, placing her in Zatalena's arms.

Zatalena returned to her husband.

They raised the girl as if she were their own.

Alina closed her eyes to the visions.

When she opened them again, she saw only stars and galaxies and blazing comets. Gone were the layered symbols that had played her mind like an instrument. The Abyss's job was done: she had been shown what it had wanted her to see, what she now wished she could forget.

He'd made her. *Dimas. Her grandfather.* Had *made* her.

Mateus. Her uncle.

An experiment.

Zatalena. Her mother.

A product.

Alina. Her… self?

A mistake.

The faces of her family became entangled in her every thought, spinning before her waking eyes—eyes she felt she hadn't ever fully opened before now.

Dimas. Mateus. Zatalena. Alina.

Personalities, memories, emotions. She was none of these; she was all of these.

The Contradiction within her swelled, threatening to burst from her chest, squeeze like jelly from between her eyes, pour like magma from her parted lips.

It was true. Somehow, though it shouldn't have been, it was all true. She felt the distinctive honesty of this revelation of self from the ends of her hair to the darkest recesses of her soul.

"The real Alina died before her first birthday," she said, knowing it was no lie.

"I am Vrana."

52

CHO-ZEN

T HE SMELL OF BURNING oil hung thick in the air as the modded woman knelt beside Cho, her fingertips spouting blue spears of flame like five mini blowtorches. She slashed with her flame-claws.

Cho winced, cried out. Her arms went limp, knuckles striking the ground.

Breathing hard, it took her a moment to realize what had happened. As blood began to flow through her limbs again, she opened her eyes and saw she'd been cut free.

"Lady Choraelia," said the stranger, her metal lower jaw hardly moving, her voice surprisingly mellow but muffled like music pouring through a blown-out speaker system. "Years ago, I served your father. I was his close protection officer. I've come to take you home."

Dehydrated, recovering from the disorienting effects of the electric current, Cho said, "My father?" She tried to get up but fell, rolling onto her ribs. Stinging prickles at her shoulders and elbows, behind her knees. She whimpered, unable to see, hardly able to draw breath.

"Hold still." The woman produced a syringe, jabbing the needle into the meat of Cho's thigh.

Energy shot through her body. Her vision focused.

"I was his bodyguard. When you were a child." The woman lifted her to a seated position, locking eyes with her. "Do you remember me?"

Rubbing her wrists, her racing heart rate slowing, Cho shook her head.

"No time now to explain everything." The woman's organic ear twitched at the not-too-distant clamor and screams. "On nights when you couldn't sleep, you'd come down to the kitchen, and someone would make you an 'ice cream bar sundae'—a microwaved, chocolate syrup-coated, after-midnight sugar rush. Remember?" She offered Cho a water bottle.

Cho's eyes went wide. Cracking off the bottle's cap, mouth aching as she guzzled the water, she reconsidered the hard, angular features of this soldier's face, imagining the dark metal jawbone and plate in her head were flesh and blood. Behind the added years and brutally repaired damage, she could see a person she once knew. She shook the last drops of liquid from the clear plastic, throwing it at her feet. Tears fell on her grimy, bruised wrists as she wiped her face. "Hael?"

A corner of the soldier's mouth quirked upward, briefly.

Lifting shaky fingers, Cho wanted to touch her but couldn't find a spot on her body that hadn't been severely scarred, riveted, or stitched together. "What's happened to you?"

Before her time on the streets of New El, before her captivity in Wodjaego Walazzin's Capital manor, Cho's favorite fixture of her old family home had been Hael. Whenever Cho had been lonely, confused, or scared, she'd run to Hael, frequently found hanging around Father's study or the atrium, with one hand hanging at her side, ready to draw and fire, always. The only breaks Hael ever took were to pull funny faces at Cho over Lord Torvir's shoulder. And, yes, in those days, Cho had asked for ice cream bar sundaes quite a lot.

"I've been trying to get to you for days now," said Hael.

It seemed impossible, but—in this moment—Cho was more than ready to believe. She threw her arms around the woman. "How did you find me?"

Hand on Cho's frizzy-wigged head, Hael said, "First, we need to get you out of here." She stood. "Can you walk?"

"Pssh. You kiddin'? All this wall yoga and shock therapy's got me totally relaxed and limber."

Appraising her, Hael said, "Somehow, you're a far sight more *Cho* even than that wild little thing I used to drag out of the kennels." Quietly: "It's good I've found you." Turning away, she ducked into the hole she'd shot through the glass fourth wall of the cell. Sticking her head back in: "Come on. What are you doing?"

Cho had grabbed Kinneas by the shoulders, snapping her fingers in front of his nose, tapping his cheek. "I'm not leaving him behind."

"Very well." Hael came over, drew a knife, and sliced through the cords binding the unconscious boy's wrists and ankles. She slung him over her shoulder. "Any other requests?"

"Actually, yeah. Two."

"I was joking. An army bears down upon us as we speak."

Legs spasming, Cho braced herself on the chair. She grunted through the pain. "If Cbarassan and the others are still locked up, we're busting 'em out."

"As you command. And the other task that simply cannot wait?"

Cho pushed off the chair, striding forward, unsteadily at first but with growing confidence and balance. "Get me to the computer mainframe." She swallowed as another pang of nausea stirred her insides, squatting to steal a knife from one of the dead guards' belts.

"What are you planning to do?"

Rising, Cho said, "What I came here for."

Bawling alarms pummeled Cho's eardrums.

As they crossed the cell block, she asked Hael to avoid, if possible, killing any *more* Lion's Den personnel. Yes, including Enforcers and Tranquilizers. The request didn't seem to bother the soldier, who proceeded to expertly dismantle her opponents in hand-to-hand combat, using her metal elbow and knee to break and maim—but stopping just short of incurring additional fatalities. The efficiency with which Hael fought was unlike anything Cho'd seen from her in the past. Cho remembered often sneaking out of Torvir Manor to watch Hael grapple with the hand-to-hand combat drones on the training grounds. Young Hael had been skilled, but she was nothing compared to the veteran version. With techniques clearly honed on many battlefields, her brutality was jarring—punctuated by sickening pops of joints and snaps of bone. Even more impressive, she managed these feats without ever setting Kinneas down.

For the most part, Cho focused on moving forward, staying low. At one point, though, she got ahead of herself: she ran to check what she thought was an empty cell. One toe in the observation room, however, and she was surprised by a pair of lurking Tranquilizers, their bullets biting the door as she leaped behind it.

Hael strode forward, emptying her pistol's magazine into the desk the Tranqs were using for cover. They shrank from her. When the firing stopped, they popped their heads up, and she was ready. She looped her arm around one of their necks, providing her the leverage to deliver two swift knees to the man's gut. He went down. The metal plate in her head went *thunk* against the other one's nose, and he slumped against the wall. Neither got up again.

She told Cho, "Stay behind me, and check your corners."

Clearing every cell they passed, they uncovered the same sickening result each time. Individual Anarkey members, Aelf and human—stretched out, seated, hanging from chains—every one of them dead. Though Hael rushed their progress, Cho checked each body, identifying the rebels who, with her, had entered the Lion's Den. She found many other Anarkeys as well, captured from their home base during her imprisonment.

How long had she been trapped here? Days? Weeks?

Some of the cells had been crammed with dozens of people, left to rot. Seeing the tangle of bodies—faces frozen in gaping-mouthed terror—Cho retched in the corner before moving on.

With each horrifying discovery, fear clawed its way up her spine.

Please. Let Cbarassan live. Please.

At the end of the hall, Cho and Hael came to the last room.

Through the reinforced glass slit, they could see a small, steel-barred holding cell containing a figure hunched over the back of a chair.

Hael tried the door, which opened inward.

The previously hidden Walazzin guard shrank into the corner of the viewing area, an accident darkening his red pants. Hael laid him out with a kick to the head. Cho flinched at the crackle of cartilage, the shattering of his nose.

"That them?" said Hael, rapping the steel bars with her knuckles. On the other side, the prisoner had been lashed to the chair. Fiercely bright lamps beamed blinding whiteness at them, washing out their features.

Cho crept up to the bars. From only a few feet away, even through welling tears, she recognized her friend. "Cbarassan. Cbarassan, wake up."

Forced to sit on their bound hands, legs and arms hyper-extended, the *Fyarda* looked up weakly. The lights overhead deepened the lines of their agonized expression. "... Cho-Zen?"

Hael hissed through her teeth. "An Aelf?"

"A *person*," Cho snapped. "Now, go on, do your angry-smashy thing."

"Against solid steel? There's an easier way." Hael took a knee beside the unconscious guard. "Your enclosure was special, Cho. This one isn't. Which means..." She rolled the man over, searched his belt and pockets. Then she walked up to the panel beside the bars, swiping a card across it. It made a little *ding* noise, and the cell door slid open. "Master keys," she grunted. "I keep saying they're a security risk."

Cho limped up to Cbarassan and, with her knife, began to carefully saw the white plastic zip cuffs around their wrists. "Got any more of those adrenaline pokies, Hael?"

"Sorry."

"Great. Guess you're carrying them too."

Hael sighed, a noise that, soft as it was, nearly overpowered the rasp of Cbarassan's voice: "The mission. Leave me. I don't matter." The Aelf had been disfigured; one eye burnt away, not a patch of their bark skin on their right side unscarred by flames. Strangely, Cbarassan and Hael mirrored one another—Aelf and human, each with half of their bodies ravaged by war.

Sucking on her swollen lip, Cho continued to saw, telling Cbarassan, "Y'know, you and Bizong aren't so different after all. You both have messed up senses of self-worth." She cut through the zip ties and threw the Aelf's arm around her neck. "Why's it always—" She grunted, lifting from her legs—"gotta be complete the mission *or* save a friend?"

Hael's frown made clear her opinion of the current odds, but her tone was all-business. "The elevators are locked. I cut the power to the whole building, which shorted most of the doors. Backup generators will be keeping the essential operations running, so we should be able to make it out the way I came. We'll take the stairs to Maintenance and, from there, cut through to the depot."

"Computer room first," Cho insisted as she tried again to lever her friend off the chair.

Flopping back, Cbarassan coughed. "Basement level two. But taking me with you makes it suicide."

Hael glared at them. "I'd have left you in here, but Choraelia has made her decision. You're coming with us. Now get over yourself, and get up."

"You." Cbarassan bared their fangs. "What is your game, human?"

Cho said, "Hael, Cbarassan. Cbarassan, Hael. Look, I trust you both, and if you trust *me* at all, that'll just have to be good enough for right now."

The look the Aelf and human exchanged made clear that they trusted each other about as much as a rotten, old rope bridge suspended over a thousand-foot chasm. But they nodded.

In addition to her bulletproof vest and multiple weapons, Hael still wore Kinneas like a hundred-and-twenty-pound scarf. Even so, she grabbed Cbarassan's other arm and steadied them as they got to their feet.

"That's more like it," said Cho.

"Once, I swore to protect you with my life, and now I see you're bent on making me a woman of my word." A growl rattled around Hael's throat. "Promise me you'll run if things turn ugly."

Crossing her fingers behind her back, Cho said, "Sure thing."

Back in the hall, red and amber warning lights flashing overhead, emergency LEDs guiding their path, the group hobbled around a corner. Ahead, the stairwell was in sight, but the corridor leading to it was clogged with dead—these guards having received, several minutes earlier, the full brunt of Hael's wrath.

Gods, she'd done a number on this place.

The Authority, apparently, needed more time to scramble reinforcements. No additional soldiers poured down the stairs.

Finally, Cho thought, *some good luck.*

Her relief was cut short by a throaty cackle.

Cho glanced backward, shuddering as she saw Jejune.

His eyes bulged, jaw distending like a snake's, triangular fangs rotating within his maw like sluggish drill bits. "Captain Tiberaira. Now, this *is* a surprise. I must admit, being what I am, my pride suffers for having been deceived by the likes of you."

Hael cursed. Passing Cbarassan's full weight to Cho and setting Kinneas on the floor, she muttered, "You'll have to drag him."

"What are you gonna do?" said Cho.

Hael's mechanical arm snapped up, parallel with the floor, fingertips pointed toward the ceiling. A squeal like a teakettle left too long on the stove was the only warning before a missile jetted from her prosthetic, spiraling across the corridor. The resultant explosion shredded Jejune.

Or, it *should* have.

As the smoke cleared, he remained standing, no longer *whole* but very much not as super-duper-dead as he should have been. Parts of his chest, shoulder, and head were missing, revealing oozing, pink pulp—and the fact that he had no *bones* inside his body.

"Okay…" said Cho. "Um."

"Go." Hael tore off her cracked and smoking prosthetic arm at the elbow, tossing it aside. "I'm right behind you."

Locking her fingers around Kinneas's thin wrist, and curling her other arm around Cbarassan's, Cho growled and *heaved.* The boy was still unconscious; the *Fyarda,* awake and upright but sluggish. Cho tapped into every ounce of energy she could steal from her own failing muscles.

Jejune's body inflated like a super-accelerated tumor, bulging out in all directions until he'd grown into a rippling, pink-green-brown, fleshy, puffer-fish-like mass.

Hael stepped forward. "I am hearth-heat, star-heart, Dragon-scream." Blade-like, white-blue flames engulfed her remaining arm, air-frying the oxygen around her until the hall reeked of ozone. *"Godspark."* The uniforms of the nearest dead Tranquilizers ignited.

"Adorable," said Jejune, with a two-foot-long sneer, "how you humans delude yourselves into thinking you can beat us with weapons we invented." His eyes, stretched like elastics, rolled under the skin folds of the pustule-pocked, singular blob he'd become.

Fang-lined tentacles whipped out at Hael. She ducked under one and then pounced forward, flying like a torpedo between the rest. She drove her flame-bladed arm into the center of Jejune's cancerous mass, and he shrieked as she carved into him, the sheer heat cauterizing the wounds on contact. Each of her strikes dug deeper—hissing, milky blood spattering the floor, walls, and ceiling as her flames flashed again and again.

A second, smaller head wriggled wetly out of Jejune's maw. It curled around Hael's leg and up her midriff, biting into her flesh. She screamed, her fire dimming.

"Hael!" cried Cho.

"Go!" she roared, and her words turned to literal fire, a stream of it erupting from her mouth.

A wave of flames and smoke flooded the corridor, and Cho lost sight of the action as she helped Cbarassan and dragged Kinneas down the stairs. Her skin began to blister. Every inch of her epidermis stung, partly from the dramatically rising temperature and partly from the fact that she was too dehydrated even to sweat.

She yelped as a Tranquilizer fell down the center of the stairwell, landing with a *thunk* far below. Then a second one soared past her, crashing onto the steps, colliding with a wall (out cold).

From a floor or two above, a third Tranq was shouting, "—our reinforcements? Aelf have infiltrated the Den. Repeat, we are overrun with—" A grunt punctuated her clipped sentence.

Doors slammed, and Cho looked up to see the Tranq slump over the stairwell railing (also unconscious).

Her ears picked up the flutter of tiny wings.

"Is: Cho, you?"

"Mezami?" she said as the beefy blue mouse-man buzzed toward her. "Boy oh boy, bud, am I glad to see you. How…?"

The Pyct fluttered around her head before hoisting Cbarassan up by their collar. Their legs dangling, the *Fyarda* said, "Excuse me."

Tail flicking with embarrassment, Mezami set them down but continued to support their weight. To Cho: "Search: hours, I."

"Well, I won't say you couldn't have come at a better time, but I'm insanely grateful." She paused. "Alina's not with you?"

Grabbing Kinneas from her with his free arm (she'd never cease to be amazed by his absurd strength), he cleared his throat. "Hextarchy: face, she."

"Such an idiot," Cho muttered, though she might as well have been talking to herself. If only she'd answered Alina's texts, maybe none of this would've happened. Her anger hadn't felt wrong at the time, but it seemed so pointless now, after everything. "Gotta get to basement two. Fill me in on the way."

With Mezami literally carrying the team, the trip became far less difficult.

He told Cho about having tried to find her the previous night, and failing. Because of his particular speaking style and her stress at navigating the hallways, it took her a few minutes and several followup questions to piece together the details of his story:

Though he'd picked up traces of her scent, they were too scattered and marred with the exhaust fumes of Authority vehicles and other types of pollution. He kept getting confused, finding himself flying toward an empty cave, too far away from all the roads. (She figured he must be referring to the same cave that Bizong had taken her and Kinneas to.) Frustrated by what he'd thought was a dead end, Mezami had returned to the lake district. There, he'd crossed paths with a warrior who'd recently been in close contact with Cho—someone who carried a fresher touch of her scent. A woman with a metal arm and mouth.

"Hael Tiberaira."

The Pyct nodded. "Follow: you, she. Was: unhappy, she." Hael had been staking out Anarkey's base, but had missed Cho's leaving by a few hours. Then she'd witnessed the Walazzin-led raid, but Cho hadn't been among the captives. She'd decided to follow the prison convoy (headed for the Lion's Den) when a stroke of luck had put her in Mezami's path. "Appreciated not: me, she. Skirmished: briefly, we. Explained then: myself, I. Made: short-term alliance, we."

"And how was she able to track me to Anarkey when you couldn't?"

"Skilled: hunter, she." He shrugged. "Are: weird, Maggos."

"Or, she snagged some inside information. Someone coulda talked."

Next, Mezami told her about Alina.

"Lemme recap, see if I got it straight: her *plan* was to sandwich herself between Ivion and this Vessa chick, play the Hextarchs and The Authority against each other, and then hope The Savior would lower his guard long enough to dish about the K'vich family's destiny? How does *any* part of that make sense?"

Mezami shrugged again. "Alina," was all he said.

"My Gods. If there was a tournament for Baddest Dumb Decisions, she'd be the reigning champ." Her vision blurred for a second as she scanned the area. "And I'd be the runner-up. That's it." She pointed ahead, at reinforced steel double doors slapped with a big fat label:

RESTRICTED AREA
AUTHORIZED MACHINAMANCERS ONLY

"Another chance to do what I do best." She cracked her knuckles. "Ignore warnings."

She walked up to the panel beside the door, and a holographic keypad flashed into existence. Her hand passed straight through the 3D projection to press against the panel. Nine-digit strings of numbers clicked onto the small screen. Each series was replaced faster than she could blink as she ran through all possible combinations, seeking the access code.

Twenty seconds later, the doors swished open.

"Peh." She dusted her hands.

She, the two Aelf, and knocked-out Kinneas entered a perfectly rectangular, sprawling space filled with rows upon rows of eight-foot-tall interconnected computers.

Cbarassan said, "These machines must hold all The Authority's secrets. Shutting them down will cripple them."

"Give them a headache, at least," Cho said.

"Pass that here." Cbarassan indicated a loaded pistol, discarded on the floor near freshly spattered blood.

Handing it over, grip first, Cho said, "Why isn't there anyone else down here? Don't get me wrong, I'm not itching for another scrap. But still. Something feels off."

"Evacuated base: Authority, most. Separated then: Hael-Tiberaira, me. Fight: defenders, I."

"Honestly, Mezzy, I'm not sure which is scarier, her or you." Cho hurried farther into the room, following the slimmer wires as they connected with fatter ones like rubbery black tributaries feeding into an electric river. "Guess the Walazzins figured their defenses were enough to stop anything trying to bust in. With you and Hael splitting the difference, though, they didn't stand a chance."

The thick wires, like pulsing synapses, led her straight to the brain—a spherical, undulating supercomputer. Parts of it see-through as it phased in and out of sight, this marvel of modern technology and magical theory was known by several names. The technical term, "Multidimensional Inter-System Coordinator," was the least popular. Mechanical lore nerds had lovingly dubbed this type of device a "Simultaneity Engine." Darkthread hackers like Cho, however, had a much simpler and more colorful word for it.

"Well, soak me in hot sauce because that's a wrap." She whistled. "It's a *Stutterframe*. No one in the chat threads is gonna believe this."

"Can you work with it, whatever it is?" said Cbarassan.

"Does the Hierophant poop in the woods? *Yuh*, it's not impossible. Just—impossibly complicated." Her fingers hovered over the computer's curves, feeling an almost magnetic pull. "The dang thing doesn't even fully exist in our dimension. Part of it's, uh, somewhere else."

"*Somewhere* else?"

"I'm not a planar scholar, *okay*? A Machinamancer could tell ya specifics, but me? I don't got magic or a fancy certificate to wave around. What I can tell ya is most ThreddHedds think the existence of Stutterframes is a hoax. Everyone else agrees they're legendary—and uncrackable." Deep breath. "But I can hack this thing. It's just gonna take everything my CPU can throw at it."

"Can we help in any way?"

She bit her lip. "Cover me, I guess?"

Cbarassan braced themselves against a nearby computer tower. Gripped tightly, the pistol rested at their hip. Mezami propped Kinneas against the computer opposite the *Fyarda*. The two Aelf locked eyes, and some private, non-verbal communication passed between them.

Cho focused on the job ahead of her.

To pull this off, she'd have to throw nearly all her available mental resources into the unknown. She'd be leaving in her physical brain only the absolute minimum brainpower needed for its survival: three quarters of a percent (0.77%, if you're picky).

That, by itself, would be more than enough of a risk. However, even if she succeeded in getting into the Stutterframe, she'd be up against a state-of-the-art *ViiCter*—The Authority's military-grade Virtual Intelligence. A watchdog for when flesh and blood failed. A guardian that never slept, that could calculate and react a billion times faster than even the most amped-up cybernetic mind. But she, of course, had a workaround.

"Maybe Alina's right about me," she muttered, calculating how to exist not just in two *places* at once, but two *dimensions*—kind of. It was complicated. And boring. There were just too many opinions.

Okay, so Cho hadn't read *all* the multiverse-theory and quantum books in her files quite yet. And applying abstract concepts to hacking a computer came with a slew of unique problems. But most of humanity's achievements had resulted from a combination of guts and luck, hadn't they?

Anyway, the main idea she'd absorbed from the stuffy armchair-dads' latest pet theories about "infinite digital sub-worlds" and "applied recursive self/other-ization" was this: *perception equals reality*. So, theoretically, if she went in with—like—the right attitude, she *could, theoretically*, beat a supercomputer's V.I. at a high-stakes game of blitz chess. And she *could* be a little ball of humanity stretched across a canvas of multiverses—physical, digital, and beyond.

As Ruqastra had been fond of saying, *What is reality, after all, but another dream?*

Cho braced herself, counting the frequency of the Stutterframe's jumps, calculating the duration of nanoseconds it existed in this reality—Blinkpoint 1.

Where, oh where, would Blinkpoint 2 be?

One nanosecond off, and—best case—she'd be jettisoned into the void. She chose not to think about the worst case.

"Here goes."

With one last look thrown her friends' way, in the ZO to outdo all others, she split her consciousness, her virtual mind burrowing into the semi-intangible guts of The Authority's supercomputer hub.

The majority of the person that was "Cho" became a string of code, syncing with the Stutterframe's rhythm. Vanishing into the Hackerdox state, she slipped into the liminal space between prayer and madness.

At the end of her year-long string of operations, after months of recovery, Little-Kid-Cho had asked her parents, "Why did you hurt me?" She couldn't remember their answers now.

When Lord and Lady Torvir weren't around to ask anymore, Slightly-Older-Cho began to wonder, "Why me?"

Post-New-El-Cho, however, no longer questioned. She no longer cared to learn the reasoning behind the metal-reinforcement of her skeleton; the cognitive and reflex implants in her spine and brain; the splicing of her genes with the snakes and fishes of the jungle, and the cephalopods and crustaceans of the deep blue sea. It didn't matter *why* her parents had put her through all those surgeries, *why* she'd become what she was. What mattered was that her brain was decades ahead of its time.

She rivaled anything The Authority could build.

Now, in the void between Blinkpoints—a soundless, nameless, moment-less place beyond place and time—her metaphorical grip slid along the boiled-noodle of her mind, which stretched and flopped. It threatened to tear. But she would not let go, could not give up.

She felt something pulling on the other end of her psyche. An anchor point, almost magnetically drawing her in. The pull was a summer storm, the scent of drying earth, the kiss of static on her scalp. It was the grinding of rusted chains, cold and gritty, and the shallow breaths of a deep sleeper on the verge of waking.

The 99.23% of her consciousness she'd sent forth chiseled its way into the Stutterframe's registry, disguised as a duplicate subroutine. A glitch.

And that's how she'd seen herself for so long—bad code, an accidental copy of the person she was supposed to become. No use in feeling that way, though. The past was unchangeable; the future, an illusion. Only *now* was within reach, and, right now, her friends were counting on her. More than for them, though, she moved forward for her own sake.

The battle ahead was one she had chosen for herself.

She could accept that she'd probably never know why her parents had spent a hundred fortunes weaponizing her. At some point, she had abandoned the search for meaning to her suffering. But, if there were any to be found, let it be found here.

Among the streams of data, the glitch that was Cho-Zen sped toward her goal. The mainframe.

Then she heard it—a ping in the silence. The Authority's data hub was calling to her. Or calling her out.

It was a challenge she must accept, for no one else could accomplish what she hoped to now. To her alone had been given the key to this particular digital lock.

Since turning five, she'd been able to plug herself into outlets, see through walls, hear heartbeats. Back then, she used to cry every time she saw her own reflection. All she'd wanted was to be a normal kid again.

Now, though, as she answered the Stutterframe's summons, she could finally see the benefit of being something else. Something other than human.

Only a machine could beat a machine.

The strain almost broke her mind, but she'd successfully hacked an *interdimensional computer*.

Arrived at Blinkpoint B alive (though not in one piece), she got her bearings.

She recognized the coding. She was somewhere in the Aetherthreads, The Authority-monitored web of virtual sub-realities where users could do just about anything, like post news stories or pictures of their breakfasts, host remote watch parties for the Latest Hit Shows, and generally interact with anyone—anywhere, all the time. Of course, very few people bothered to read the fine print: every piece of personal information and every photo shared instantly became the property of the government. The food they ate, the clothes they wore, the deodorant they used, the private messages they sent, how they felt about themselves and any problematic thoughts they'd been having, their biological family's predisposition for disease or anti-government action... Any and all of it could legally be used by The Authority to incriminate anyone—from anywhere.

Cho much preferred the Darkthreads, where at least the locals made no attempts to cover up how weird and awful they really were. The Darkthreads were chaotic but free. The Aetherthreads, though, were too neat, too ordered. Every terrible thing that could happen to you here was perfectly legal.

She could feel a watchful presence, raking through archived folders, trawling the data streams, hoping to uproot her from her hiding spot. Somewhere out there, *ViiCter* was scanning for her. An anomaly, a bit of errant code, she had been noticed, but not yet found.

At most, only minutes remained before her violent purging.

So, she moved quickly, having given herself every possible micro-advantage: she'd suspended the applications responsible for various day-to-day tasks—regulation of her digestive, adrenal, lymphatic, and sensory systems. All that extra processing power went straight to her brain's computational abilities. She'd also switched off all her major personality components. Likes and dislikes, opinions, beliefs, and values. The apps that supplied hopes and doubts and sanity she'd chucked in the trash bin, too.

She'd even flushed her memories for now. Tea with Mother (which, for Cho, had mostly been an excuse to stuff her face with dainty biscuits). Chasing her older sister around the fountain. Singing in front of the mirror, all her stuffed animals arranged behind. Her earliest days at Torvir Manor faded, as did the jumps between New El's cold streets and the perfumed prison of the Walazzin estate. And the two years with Alina. All set aside.

Unshackled from her limited meat-brain, having compartmentalized everything that a doctor, philosopher, or priest could have used to identify her as human, she became a thing of pure calculation, a loosely connected series of numerical expressions—a Cho-shaped reflex machine crawling along a limitless seabed of information. Data clouds stirred like sediment at her touch. Each speck of muck, a constellation of compressed files.

With speed and precision, she searched. There was only stimulus and response as she devoted every ounce of her input and output to the singular task of finding the Stutterframe's hub and shutting it down.

She wriggled her way through fissures stuffed with intelligence, personnel dossiers, and encrypted chatter. These entangled her mind like fronds of seaweed might snare her legs, complicating her progress through this virtual ocean.

Just as she'd suspected, The Authority's forces had centralized all their communications. Everything was here, stored in the Stutterframe, ready for her grubby little fingers to tear apart: drone pilot signals, Tranquilizer shift schedules, medical records, morale-boosting strategies in progress... But until she reached a terminal of some kind, she could only see, not change.

She cut through rushing undercurrents of information, her thoughts sifting through the unimportant, probing for the useful. In many ways, this process of data mining felt like exploring an underwater cave, with its treacherous, unlit pathways and the constant danger of injury and infection. Yet, after all the gunfights and hovercycle chases, she felt... not at ease, no. Maybe "familiar" was a better word for it.

In Truct, she'd been a big fish in a little pond. Here, even way out of her depth, she was still the same sleek carnivore. If she wasn't ready to out-swim the whales of the Aetherthreads by now, she'd never be.

Propelling herself out of a narrow, algae-slick corridor—a back door into a startup application—she found her way forward, but it was guarded. In the shape of glowing globules, antivirus programs criss-crossed the gloomy path ahead, beaming searchlights to and fro.

Any uninvited strips of code that fell into those lights would be quarantined and destroyed.

Basic. It was hardly any bother for her to take cover behind some boulders of archived files, analyze the glowing orbs, and instantly emulate their passcodes. Figuring that shutting them off would draw too much attention, she instead forced them to recognize her as friendly software.

Frog-style, she swam between the orbs, and all seemed fine until one of them got a little too friendly and started trailing her. She couldn't stop now, though. There was light ahead, brine-green, bright and flickering at high speed.

Not too much farther now.

Hoisting herself from the water, she clambered onto some rocks (made up of system recovery points), hoping to lose her tail.

With a splash, the orb also left the pool.

"What the—" She kept walking, and it continued to follow.

Several seconds later, she stopped in her tracks, spinning to catch it by surprise.

As she inspected it, it went dark.

Resisting the urge to shout, "What d'you want, huh?" she watched the orb fill with molten gold, a sliver of a black pupil forming at its center.

She stared at this thing that looked like a crow's eye. It greeted her with a text bubble pop-up.

Even as she read the words, more sneaked between the lines, burrowing into her mind before she could stop them:

/IF YOU ARE READING THIS/

(... answer ...)

//YOU ARE THE RESISTANCE//

(... the call ...)

///CHZN///

Those were *her* words. A spot-on imitation of the cheeky digital signature she'd left behind on each of The Authority servers she'd hacked.

Someone was playing games, and she wasn't in the mood.

"How do you know my name?" she whispered at the eye. "Wait, lemme guess, you're conveniently 'here to help'?"

Another text bubble appeared.

//WE COLLECT//

(... were summoned ...)

//WE SAVE//

That hardly seemed a reasonable answer.

She eyed the flickering light source ahead. The Stutterframe had to be close. Its defenses were oblivious to her, but only for now.

"Yo, I don't know who ya think you are, but you're gonna blow my cover."

Unbothered, the crow's eye popped out another text bubble, displaying a gently rippling "..." icon.

Then:

//THE OLD MAN FORETOLD YOUR COMING//

(... not all is as he said it would be ...)

/THE SIGNS

ARE UNDENIABLE/

Wiggling her fingers at it, saying, "No thanks to whatever this is," she tried to put some distance between her and the eye.

Urgently, it bonked her shoulder.

WIELDED BY A MASTER

MACHINAMANCER/

EMPOWERED BY

(... young/corruptible intentions...)

THE 3NL1GHT3N3D ONE/

(... enemy ...)

A PRODIGIOUS FORCE OF ENGENIOMANCY

(... weapon ...)

ACCUMULATES

//IN HEXHALL//

She gave up on running. The ball easily kept pace with her, anyway.

"Okay? So?"

YOUR FRIEND/

(... unique niimantic signature ...)

//SHE IS THERE//

THE ONE

(... the answer ...)

WHO WILL

(... must ...

... could ...)

LEAD US

"Alright." She grabbed the eyeball, pressing her fingers against its glassy, warm-to-the-touch surface. "Now, see, you *couldn't* be talking about my friend Alina, could ya?"

//YES//

(... perhaps ...)

"How d'you know her? What's your deal? Does she need help? She hurt?" She shook the thing, rattling its birdlike pupil.

HEXHALL

(... hideaway ...)

IS A SPLINTER

OF DREAM-STONE IN THE INFINITE

Had she not unplugged herself from her emotions—anger, for example— she would have been feeling quite frustrated by now.

"Ya got the wrong girl. That mystical stuff's not my forte."

//WRONG//

(... a child ...)

YOU ARE AWARE OF MORE

THAN YOU KNOW/

"If ya want something, say it simple, or shut up."

AS BELOW, SO ABOVE

(... the abyss/chrononite...

... talaganbubăk/crow ...)

//UNDERSTAND//

REVOSCAPE AND DARKTHREADS ARE ONE

AND THE SAME//

(... enemy/ally ...)

UNION OF NATURAL AND ARTIFICIAL/

ABSTRACT AND CONCRETE/

(... contradiction ...)

RIPE

TO BURSTING

(... rotting on the vine ...)

"This is making no sense to me, pal."

It occurred to her that this strange messenger might have been setting her up, distracting her with nonsense just long enough to drop a cage. But, in the off chance it wasn't a trick, she had to know.

"What're you trying to say about Alina?"

//HE IS COMING//

(... hand of the enemy ...

... wielding a splinter of the dawn ...)

WAKE THE SLEEPER

(... end her endless dream ...)

"Again, if you're taking notes, I got one for ya. Want someone to do you a solid? Drop the riddles and be straight with 'em."
The crow's eye bobbed up and down.

NOW / NOW / NOW

THERE WOULD BE NO FUN

IN THAT

//CHZN//

"Wow. You seem great. I loved this. Anyway."

HEXHALL

(... readied for war / loss ...)

IS POISED TO FALL//

//SO BEGINS THE TRUE TEST//

She gave the crow's eye two big thumbs down.
Its pupil winked out of existence. The gold sphere bubbled like molten rock.

//WE COLLECT//

(... were collected ...)

//WE SAVE//

"Said that already."

NOW WILL YOU STAND/

(... suffer / grow ...)

OR KNEEL

Before she could reply, the crow's eye dissolved into an inky cloud of black, sinking into the muddy ground.

"Thanks for nothing," she said, eyes peeled for an ambush.

She decided the encounter had been too weird to be an Authority trick. The pinkojacks had no creativity; if they'd wanted to grab her, they would have rushed her head-on. No, that bizarre eyeball had been sent by someone else. Someone with enough know-how to crack a Stutterframe.

Later, Cho could dissect what'd just happened. For now, she had to keep going.

The farther she wandered, the denser the data packets became, until they formed a wall of total darkness. She hesitated only briefly.

Forging ahead, she groped around until she found a slack length of chain lying on the sand. It gleamed silver in the blackness, so she followed it.

The chain's links thickened with each of her steps until she stubbed her toe on a half-buried anchor, which began to shine with emerald runes at her touch. It rose from the sand, bathing her in its glow, pulling the chain upward and out of the mud. Out of reach. As she swatted at the air, her fingers brushed against yet another link—this one the height and thickness of a lumberjack on steroids.

Her guiding line well out of reach, and with nothing else to grab on to, she had no choice. Blindly, she continued.

A long, snaking line of sentinel orbs appeared, lighting her path.

She could now see the big chain again. It hung over a wide, dark, nearly empty field. Scattered like a young man's first chin hairs, ore anchors glinted far off. They were tethered to a central point—the beacon of green light—the terminal, her destination.

The orbs—like murderous fireflies—suddenly sped toward her, and no amount of code-weaving could trick them into leaving her alone this time. From all sides, they swarmed her like flies crashing into a piece of rotting meat. She ate a few hits before she was able to escape; facing the flickering green beacon, she rushed across the field, dodging defenders left and right.

Unfortunately, she didn't get far. The goalie was not so easily sidestepped.

The Virtual Intelligence, *ViiCter*, materialized ahead, and Cho skidded to a stop.

Featureless face locked onto the intruder, the V.I. raised its shining hand. The orbs broke away from her, orbiting the V.I. for a few seconds before streaking into the distance.

ViiCter stared down the digitized girl, and she gawked right back at it.

A thing of distinctly human-like outline, even though its features were in the right place, its perfect smoothness was beyond unsettling. It cocked its blank "head," analyzing. Its voice emanated from everywhere except where its mouth should've been: "Critical Error 23896732320991."

Face to face with it, Cho could hardly imagine this derpy effigy controlling currency values and food supplies, guiding missiles, commanding armies… But, in a very real way, it really was the Nation of El's brain.

She couldn't let the surrealism of the moment overtake her; one unhappy thought, and she'd be tracelessly erased.

Faking calmness, she walked forward, leaving *ViiCter* behind.

It jumped, cutting her off again. "Running diagnostics… Conclusion: corrupt registry file."

She pushed past it. The beacon lay just ahead; the Stutterframe's hub was near.

With swinging, mechanical strides, the V.I. kept ahead of her. "Error. Registry file not found." Its neck craned. "Program, what is your purpose?"

"Uh. Defrag?"

"Accessing defragmentation schedule… Error. Registry file not found. Program's unauthorized access attempts have been logged and flagged for user review."

She ran.

"Solution 1: Quarantining malicious software." *ViiCter* gave chase. "Failure: Corrupt registry file. Solution 2: uninstall." A blade of light longer than Cho's entire body materialized in its fist, and the V.I. speared toward her. Dropping, she narrowly dodged the whining, humming arc of energy. She was a particularly slippery olive sliding out from under a toothpick, rolling left then right, as the V.I. attempted to stick her.

The day Kinneas had gotten hurt, Cho had stolen an epic number of Authority passwords and login credentials. Furiously, she cycled through them. There had to be something in there she could use to slow *ViiCter* down.

Within nanoseconds, she'd given it hundreds of thousands of tries. No hits yet.

Sliding behind a boulder, she flung stones at the V.I., stalling, stalling. They bounced off its chest.

Still nothing.

ViiCter lunged toward her, slashing. She hopped onto the boulder, flipping over the V.I.'s wrinkle-free head.

Another million attempts. C'mon, c'mon…

There, that one. *Yes!*

A well-placed kick from a soap-smooth foot knocked her down. She rolled over some rocks and groaned.

The V.I. was on her, raising its light-spear.

"Command: software update," she yelled.

"All systems are up-to-date," it politely informed her, blade thrusting toward her chest.

"Override!" She tucked and rolled, sprang up. It sprinted after her, and she shouted over her shoulder, "Chief Technician Deglaseus, P. Authorization code XF0-90."

She tripped, face-planting, flipping onto her back in time to watch *ViiCter* charge her.

Breathlessly, soundlessly, the V.I. came—each step taken with care but also incredible speed—knees kicking up to its chest, arms akimbo, long neck locked. No failed experiment of nature could have competed with it. Only the imaginations of men could have birthed such an awkwardly dexterous monstrosity.

She scrabbled backward, but *ViiCter* was on her now. It loomed over her, light-spear held high.

Then, mid-strike, it froze.

Where it had been shining brightly seconds earlier, its body had now gone dark, covered in red exclamation points, overlapping, flashing angrily. In clipped tones, it said, "Error. Authorization conflict. Contacting Administrator."

"Woah." Swiping mud from her nose, Cho wheezed. "It actually worked."

Figuring she'd bought herself maybe sixty seconds, she dashed toward the pillar of green light.

Around her, she could make out shapes in the dark. More silvery chains, rising from the mud. She ran parallel to these toward the beacon. Once her eyes adjusted to its light, she saw the Stutterframe's "terminal" for what it really was: a tall, floating... creature?

Humanoid in shape but at least thirteen feet tall, suspended vertically, it dangled from three more floating anchors. There were little glimmers of silver where a dozen chains had been embedded in its body. A chandelier of blood and bone, a dessicated cocoon, it had been tightly wound from head-to-toe in waxy wrappings. Its arms were cinched to its chest in an X, its bound feet brushing the ground. Nearly every inch of it had been mummified; only its mouth—and fangs—could be seen. Although Cho did not understand why, the sickly, mucus-green color of that little oval of papery flesh reminded her of the Lorestone.

"Hang on." This wasn't her first encounter with the comatose creature. They'd met once before, the other day, when she'd hacked into the relay station's mainframe.

The shrieking prisoner. Only, now its sleep seemed less troubled. Or, maybe it'd become too exhausted to cry out.

Whispers of sand sliding from metal filled her ears. The being's breaths were slow but strained, each one vibrating the air and ground around it.

"*You're* the Stutterframe's hub," she told the Sleeper, hoping it couldn't reply.

She was sure of it. Somehow, The Authority had set up an organic supercomputer *inside* an interdimensional one. Scanning the lines of code laced through the chains and scratched onto the creature's wrappings, she tried to understand them, but they'd been written in a programming language she'd never seen before. There was no denying it, though: the Sleeper tethered the Den's servers to all other Authority bases in Ozar.

Cutting that connection would blind and deafen the Elementals. (But would doing so kill or free the creature?)

Not possible, she realized. Unsure of where the insight had come from, she nonetheless understood that, just like the Stutterframe itself, the Sleeper existed in multiple places at once. She was only seeing a fraction of the larger entity; she wouldn't be able to deactivate it from this terminal. Permanent disconnection would require traveling to its physical location—somewhere in New El, apparently.

Still, even if she couldn't destroy the whole network from here, hobbling the Authority's grand army right before its big bad assault on the Seventh Stack would be a swell consolation prize.

Although the Sleeper's true nature remained a mystery, it was the Stutterframe's power source, and the chains were the keys.

"Well. I only got one idea." She dusted her hands, grabbed onto the Sleeper's dangling feet, and began to climb.

The waxy wrappings were flaky like river-birch bark. She slipped and nearly fell a few times, but managed to scale the creature's trunk and latch onto the chains.

Running her fingers along one of them, she felt that same magnetic pull as before.

"You want me to...?" Her skin tingled. She was being attracted to a particular spot. Guided.

Clambering in circles around the Sleeper's torso, she tested each chain, feeling for the right one. Until—

There.

Hanging off its right shoulder, she clutched the specific chain that drew her to it most strongly. The one through which the Sleeper interfaced with the Stutterframe's Blinkpoint A in the Lion's Den.

Then *VüCter*'s voice cut through the emptiness. "Administrative override accepted. Manual operation engaged."

Crap.

The V.I. shone brightly again as its shape began to shift. She squinted at it, its body violently popping, snapping, and twisting into an outline she unfortunately recognized. Ridged scars covering neck, arms, back, and legs. Broad shoulders. Buzzed scalp. Eyes and mouth sewn shut with red threads. Greatsword scraping the ground as he advanced.

Utterly quiet, the digitized specter of Tolomond raced toward her.

Quick, quick, quick. She planted her feet. Her fingertips vibrating against the metal, she gripped the base of the chain embedded in the Sleeper's skin.

Everyday-Cho would have apologized, but computational, bare-minimum-humanity-Cho simply threw all her digital weight into tearing this anchor free from its fleshy, waxy port. (There was just enough Everyday-Cho left in her to shout, "Yuck.")

As Tolomond closed the distance between them in bounds, the thuds of his footfalls booming in her ears, he beamed like a shooting star.

She heaved again, screaming out of frustration and strain. And, finally, the wax paper and skin tore. With a disgusting *squelch*, the chain swung loose. Tumbling backward, she clung to it, spinning through the air.

The Sleeper only grumbled, gnashing its fangs, and then resumed its slumbering, pained breaths, although a bit more shallowly.

The environment itself reacted with much greater violence: flashing red and white emergency lights beat down and subdued the darkness, the stillness shredded by sirens. Frantic messages spilled into the void from all sides—shouting about a security breach, inert drones plummeting from the air, hundreds of unresponsive units on the ground—before cutting out.

Cho slid down the chain and hit the ground.

Her plan must have worked: she'd just overheard a real-time excerpt of Authority technicians noticing their communications network in Ozar was falling apart. Their sudden silence spoke volumes. They were cooked.

But the celebration would have to wait. Over her shoulder, she saw Tolomond coming. She ran, randomly, ran to buy herself even a second longer to think.

She felt a prickle in her palm. Lifting her hand, she found jammed in her skin a thumbnail-sized silver hook—the little bit of metal that had tethered the chain to the Sleeper. It must have snapped off and come with her during her stunt-swing. Still running, with a gasp, she yanked the barb out and clutched it between thumb and forefinger.

Tolomond was gaining, and she willed herself to sprint faster.

The Sleeper had other plans.

Wracked by another nightmare, perhaps, it shrieked as it had that day at the relay station. However, maybe because Cho was much closer to it this time, the effect was amplified. The noise jackhammered her heart, and an avalanche of terror, anguish, and fury crashed over her body, burying her rational self. The Sleeper smothered her with its pain, and she couldn't move.

The echo of its cry faded. A hush prevailed as Tolomond came within fifteen feet.

Paralyzed and panicking, Cho could only listen as something whispered to her, each syllable like the tearing of a sheet of tracing paper:

request to interface.

does the User accept?

"Uh."
An internal notification chimed in her mind.

INCOMING PACKET > UNKNOWN LICENSE

DOWNLOAD > Y/N?

Behind, Tolomond didn't speak or breathe, but the tip of his sword said plenty—a keening scrape against stone.
Another chime.

DOWNLOAD > Y/N?

No better options presenting themselves, through frozen lips, she mumbled, "Yes."
A third chime—

PATCHING

—quickly followed by a fourth and final one.

SOFTWARE PATCH COMPLETE

The whisper rustled in her skull again:

find me.

Suddenly freed, she stumbled, barely catching herself.

A backward glance showed Tolomond closing in and the green glow of the Sleeper fading out. The creature's jaw creaking open, it wailed one more time before disappearing completely, chains and all.

That's when Tolomond struck, his blade sparking off the ground between Cho's feet as she leapt back.

And the chase resumed.

To make the Sanctumite killer's job just a bit harder, she generated three mirror images of herself, which flanked her. The Cho-quadruplets charged into the unpopulated gray field ahead.

He caught one of the copies with a swing, cleaving it in half in a burst of light, rectangular fragments of code ricocheting through the Aetherthreads.

"What's your end-game, here?" Cho yelled at herself.

She remembered the silver hook still in her possession. She had to lose it, or the Stutterframe's maintenance programs would retrieve it, plug it back in, and undo all her hard work.

Her enhanced mind severely overclocked, she calculated the best move available to her. This took all of .03 seconds, which was fortunate. Any longer and Tolomond's next strike would have taken out all three remaining Chos in one go. Instead, he only lopped off one head.

Nodding to each other, the twin Chos divided the labor. One raised a glitching, flickering wall of junk data between them and Tolomond. The other swiped two fingers upward, creating a portal in the wall, Cho-side. The Chos stepped through. However, as they touched down on gray sand, before either of them could seal the portal, Tolomond cut Cho number three diagonally in half.

The final (real!) Cho sprinted along the beach, each step shifting the sands, stirring whispered voice mails and wisps of text:

"Yeah I could eat"

"U here, bro?"

"no joke im done with drama."

The static hiss of foamy spray beside her churned—black water on black, star-speckled sky—trillions of unsent, lost, corrupted, archived, or otherwise neglected messages; condolences, admissions of guilt or love, school essays... all this homeless data forming the Sea of Deleted Comments.

Winding her arm, Cho lobbed the gold hook into the water that was not water, and a satisfying cacophony of clipped voices crashed into her eardrums. Text bubbles and digimail drafts rippled outward from the splash. The silver hook sank, and was forgotten.

Human Cho might have sacrificed one second of initiative to gloat, but ninety-nine percent-digital Cho wasted no time in logging out. As if sucked through a vacuum tube, her essence shot out of the Aetherthreads. With the murderer clinging to her heel.

Her quick thinking hadn't been quick enough.

Oops.

Muscles heavy. She had to move. Had to.

Cho's physical eyes blinked open. Eilars's super chip whirred into overdrive. In the span of a microsecond, it supplied her with thousands of details about the situation and the optimal course of action.

Cbarassan and Kinneas were still where she had left them, the boy unconscious and the *Fyarda* pointing a smoking barrel at a bullet-scarred computer twenty-two feet away.

She couldn't see Mezami (and infrared would be useless in a room that generated so much heat), but she sensed he was close; there were three unconscious Enforcers lying nearby. The Aelf had been busy in the half-minute that Cho had spent out-of-body.

Even as she thought through the problem of how to stop Tolomond, her head-start shrank to nothing. The killer materialized behind her.

Since his deathly transformation, he'd only become scarier. The sewn-shut eyes and mouth, the purple-black veins curling under bloodless skin. This man—thing—had killed Eilars and Morphea. And now he was in a room full of Cho's wounded, cornered friends.

A warning cry wouldn't cut it: the others wouldn't react in time to protect themselves.

She had to help them, yes, but if she didn't also knock Tolomond off-balance at the same time, they'd all be dead.

For such a heavy-footed, clumsy-looking beast, Tolomond was terrifyingly fast. Springing forward, the Sanctumite raised his greatsword in an overhead swing aimed at Cbarassan, who only now had begun to turn, a grimace of shock cracking their burned face. But the blade missed its target, slashing through some extremely expensive pieces of hardware a foot to Cbarassan's right: Cho's shoulder-shove against the hulking man had stopped one fatality, but a more permanent solution was needed.

"Mezzy!"

A blue, mouse-shaped bullet, the Pyct slammed into Tolomond's gut. Though thrown backward, the man hardly reacted, and showed no signs of recognizing his tiny attacker. This was odd because, in their last encounter, Mezami had killed him. Even so, Tolomond's brow didn't so much as wrinkle.

Alina was right about him: something unnatural slammed the gas pedal of his rotting brain. This Extra Special Secret Pal must also have been the one to transport him between Blinkpoints. Hacking required knowledge and cybernetic enhancements. As someone who hated magic and technology *religiously*, he couldn't have digitized himself on his own.

Squirreling that line of questioning away for future "what the hells," Cho squared off with the bruised, scarred, sandpaper-skinned hulk.

She grimaced at the stitches crisscrossing his stomach and chest. He came at her with a front kick and a diagonal cut. Before she could counter, he swung again. She back-stepped right into his backfist, and bounced off a computer cage with a clang.

He fought as if bored, but each strike crumpled solid metal sheets and sprayed shattered bits of plastic everywhere.

She knew she couldn't beat him. Throwing every pound of her weight into every jab and hook, she accomplished nothing because he felt nothing. He shrugged off the couple spearhands and roundhouses she landed. It was like punching a slab of frozen meat. She could've thrown a flying knee against his eyeball, and he'd probably block it with a blink.

The battle was lost, but she meant to keep her promise: leave no one behind. Whatever happened would happen to *all* of them.

"Hey, Patches," she said, out of breath, "the Stutterframe's busted. *You're* busted. Just let us go."

No reaction. Whatever controlled Tolomond either ignored or couldn't understand her.

He lunged, the business end of his sword driving toward her throat.

The crackle of Mezami's lightning-quick fist preceded the thunder of shattered bone, and Tolomond crashed into one of the computers to his right, flipping it. A few behind it fell like dominoes.

He got up immediately, a welt on his ribs indicating where the Pyct had scored the hit. The brute was unfazed. He went for a horizontal cut, aimed at Cbarassan, who was closest. Just in time, they fell backward, firing two wide shots that sparked off the ceiling and burst a light fixture.

In a shower of broken glass and beads of mercury, Mezami attacked. Tolomond swatted him away with the flat of his blade. The Pyct went *plong* against something metallic.

"Damn it." Cho raised her bloodied, shaking fists.

What were they supposed to do? The guy didn't get angry or tired, seemed immune to pain, and wasn't going to stop until everyone else in here was fully piece-ified.

She lowered her center of gravity. "Round three, let's go."

Even bruisers have weak spots—joints, pressure points. Maybe she'd get lucky. Several times in a row. Enough to make a difference, enough to slow him down for even a minute. Then they'd escape. With Kinneas... who was still out cold. Dead weight. Yeah, solid plan.

"Mezami, Cbarassan!" Their only *real* chance was to go all out, all at once. Take Tolomond out for good.

Charging, Cho slid at the last possible instant, sliding under his wild swing, spinning, trying to sweep his legs. Predictably, unable to retreat with a computer at his back, he jumped over her hook kick. This left him wide open for Cbarassan's next shot, which slapped into his chest, flinging a wad of viscous blood. He squared up with the *Fyarda* as Mezami delivered a double-fisted slam to the top of his skull.

Tolomond crumpled.

Before Cho could say, "Keep hitting him," a silvery flash blinded and staggered her.

When the garbled screen of pink and blue fuzzies fell from Cho's vision, Cbarassan was on the ground, a shiny chain constricting their throat. Viscous blood dribbled from the gash in Tolomond's wrist where the chain ended. He jerked the bloody length of gleaming metal, fused to his forearm bones, pulling it tighter. His other hand had traded his greatsword for Mezami, who squirmed in his crushing grip.

The *Fyarda* gritted their teeth. The Pyct growled. Neither could do anything.

Spittle flying, Cbarassan's eyes rolled back.

Mezami's thrashing began to slow.

"Let them go!"

As he strangled Cho's friends, the expression on Tolomond's face was strangely peaceful. That he could be so numb...

"You can have me," she said, voice failing her. "Please. You can have me."

A glimmer—a gossamer trail unraveling from his closed eyelid. A tear.

The chain loosened. Just a little. Just slightly.

"Let them go," she begged.

The chain slackened a bit more.

Despite the threads binding his lips, he bared his teeth. Blood ran down his chin, his jaw clenched, and she was surprised to recognize his expression, the first emotion he'd shown her. She knew it well; that particular ink cloud had smothered her for weeks, months, years.

"Please," she said again.

And he turned his blind gaze toward her.

"Get down," shouted someone behind Cho, who dropped to her belly.

A drumbeat of shotgun blasts—*dum, dum, dum, dum*—launched Tolomond backward, pinning him against a now cracked and dented computer tower. Cbarassan uncoiled the hook-bladed chain from their neck and scrabbled upright. Mezami zipped away.

Hael leapt over Cho's prone form, discarding the spent shotgun and jabbing two fingers toward Tolomond. A cone of fire enveloped him.

"That won't hold him for long," said Hael. "Back door. South side of the room. Everybody move."

Mezami swung Kinneas up and shot forward, Cho kick-flipped to her feet, and Hael supported Cbarassan.

They proceeded at an agonizingly slow pace, row after row of identical, tall, black computers humming all around them. The monotony of it, the fear that

Tolomond would catch up any second, nearly drove Cho nuts. Finally, though, they reached the exit. Cho ZO'd the electronic lock, and the door swished open. Once they were all through, she sealed it, Cbarassan shooting the keypad for good measure.

The dim, floor-lit corridor connected with several identical, perpendicular paths.

Mezami said, "Go: straight, we."

"The Aelf's right," said Hael. "There's an emergency hatch just up ahead." She cursed. "My spell just broke."

They kept going.

Mere seconds later, Cho heard ferocious banging against the door they'd just come through. There was a ladder ahead, though. They could make it.

Mezami went up first, hauling Kinneas through the hatch. Then Cbarassan, pushed by Hael. Lastly, Cho. Her head poked into a small cavern supported by wooden beams. A secret entrance, probably leading to a postern gate (like in one of her trash adventure books). She was pulled through the hatch by Mezami.

"Back," he told her.

As soon as she was clear, he ricocheted around the space, cracking the support beams. They groaned ominously.

The escapees backed away, then turned and continued to run.

A rumble and resounding crash behind them sang the praises of Mezami's sabotage.

"Nice!" said Cho. "But even a cave-in won't hold a monster like him forever." She sneezed at the rush of dust.

"Keep up," said Hael. "The depot. I've got a ride waiting."

The metal depot doors rattled upward.

Searchlights crossed like swords, highlighting the vapor trails of drones circling above the Lion's Den. Then, the drones began to free-fall. First one after another, and then in droves. Crashing into the barracks, the side of the central tower, and the caverns and canyons beyond, their hydrogen cores exploded in spears of blue fire. A beautiful contrast with the orange glow of the slithering lava rivers on the camp's south side.

Transfixed for a moment, Cho watched Tranquilizers rush around the base. They searched above and all around for signs of attack. The comms built into their helmets malfunctioning, they tossed their protective gear aside, frantically hollering questions and orders at each other.

Cho looked at her own hands, which were shaking. She'd done this. In less than an hour, she'd cut off their ears and gouged out their eyes.

True, some drones remained airborne—older, manually controlled models that hadn't been connected to the wireless network. And officers began to take charge of their subordinates, ordering them into columns. All digital communications disabled, the technicians would eventually get the bright idea to dig through storage and start handing out analog radios to all the squad commanders. However, the roar of blue fire and the cacophony of competing shouts proved what Cho had often suspected: take away their shiny toys, and The Authority were just bullies with pop guns in tin suits.

"Cho!" Hael called.

A hovercycle patrol team zipped past Cho as she dashed back into the depot.

In the driver's seat of an unmarked van, Hael hit the ignition button. (Kinneas, Cbarassan, and Mezami had piled up in the back.) The hydrogen-powered engine purred as the hovercraft lifted a couple feet off the ground. Cho hopped into the front passenger's seat, curving her spine, making herself small, as the vehicle swung out of the building.

Hael played chicken with a formation of Tranqs, who rolled out of her way at the last possible second. She then set a course for the front gate, barreling toward it.

Cho expected a spray of bullets to slap the van any second, but it didn't come.

Chaos camouflaged the escapees' vehicle, just one more flailing limb attached to a seizing body. Most of the Tranqs didn't give it a second glance. The few who did could only shout as Hael, flooring it, zoomed by.

She did, however, hit the breaks for the two guards at the closed gate.

Lowering her window, she said, "Emergency orders from the Consul's son. It's about the spies responsible for tonight's cyber attack."

One of the soldiers stepped forward. "We're locked down. No one in, no one out."

Hael extended her hand, fingers flexed. She reached out the driver's side window, slashing at the damp cave air. Immediately, the hiss of boiling moisture. The guards shrank away, but too late.

They screamed as their flesh bubbled inside their armor.

"Non-lethal," Hael assured Cho. Crushing the accelerator with her heel, she added, "I love how cheap The Authority is, you know."

"What?"

"That gate might well be reinforced enough to stop a truck traveling at top speed, but..." She crashed the vehicle through the electrified perimeter fence.

Quickly shrinking to little blips in the rearview mirror, a squad of soldiers rallied and fired uselessly in the van's general direction.

A minute passed. Cho remembered to breathe. Her adrenaline regulators could keep up no longer; the pain of all the beatings and electrocutions—her sprained ankle and bruised bones—all caught up with her.

At last, she broke down, hyperventilating.

"It's alright," said Hael.

Even though right next to her, Cho could hardly hear her voice.

Muffled as if underwater. "It's alright now."

Cho stared out the window. Streetlights flitted past. In the tinted glass, she saw her reflection. Broken-nosed, swollen-faced. Her head grew heavy, lolling to the side.

Sliding open and crawling through the slot in the wall that separated the cab from the back, Mezami nestled in the crook of her neck and shoulder. His little breaths rumbled in his chest, tickling her throat.

"Dangerous little guy. Glad he's on our side." Hael swiveled in her seat. "Everybody good back there?"

"The boy needs medical attention," said Cbarassan.

"Can't take him to a hospital."

"And Anarkey has been compromised." The *Fyarda* groaned.

"The Safehouse," Cho murmured. "There's first aid stuff there."

"None of us can treat Niima deficiency."

"It's our only option," said Hael. "We're all dead if we stay in the open."

"I'll tell you how to get there," said Cho. Tears fell from her cheeks, spattering Mezami like rain. "It's my fault. All of it. Kinneas is gonna die because of me."

Maybe, selfishly, she'd hoped someone would correct her.

No one did.

53

BARAAM

BARAAM HAD BECOME HIGHLY skilled in ignoring painful realities when they conflicted with his duty. To him, The Savior remained The Savior. The name "Mateus K'vich," he buried.

Alina had always been one for exaggeration and half-truths.

Thinking further on the matter would only prevent him from fulfilling his function.

Yet...

The aromas of fresh coffee grounds and flaky baked goods wafted from the open windows of the third-story shop. Flowing-robed servants sped along the late-night refreshment service. The employees welcomed the extra hands, for the entire building had been rented out for a special meeting between the scions of two Plutocratic Families—and The Savior himself.

Silent sentries, Baraam and Eva flanked The Savior, who leaned against the third-floor balcony overlooking the assembled cohorts of Tranquilizers.

For the coming strike on Hexhall, The Authority had amassed the grandest army seen in centuries. Organized in blocks of ten by ten, dozens upon dozens of units moved into formation, shadowed by the looming Wall the Elementals had dubbed Peregar's Grief.

Tonight, it seemed that Grief would be turned upon the Hextarchs and their Coven.

Baraam's heart told him that, somewhere down there, Alina was causing trouble. Again, his restlessness returned. An itch in the toes, the soles of the feet. A desire to fly.

The Savior's eyes bulged in anticipation. Otherwise, he clung to his habitual aloofness.

The dry-skinned, reptile-eyed Kaspuri Walazzin, however, was anything but cool. He spasmed with barely contained delight, licking his papery lips and obsessively running a small bone comb through his oily black hair.

Several patio tables had been pushed together, lined with trays of confections, teas, soft drinks, coffees. He had his feet up, the heels of his polished boots crushing a cluster of mini-muffins.

On several official occasions over the years that Baraam had been a member of the Top Ten Ravers, he had met the Walazzin heir, and he'd always been utterly unimpressed by Kaspuri's unfounded confidence. Born with every privilege imaginable, and unused to even mild disagreement, Kaspuri would constantly boast about his achievements, the exotic locales he'd been to, the artists he'd patronized. He'd always get key details wrong, though—naming the mountains of a region famed for its flatness, or mispronouncing all the words in one of the many languages he'd supposedly "mastered at an early age." Kaspuri Walazzin was, in a word, a narcissist. He loved only himself, and was so egotistically fragile that the merest hint of correction would break him. Like one of the mirrors he was so fond of staring into.

Opposite him sat Ivion Ivoir, whose showy perfection highlighted everyone else's mortality. Even as she tossed her head, her freshly washed and scented hair remained curled behind her ears, her white vest and pencil skirt as smooth and immaculate as she was. A flower so beautiful had to be poisonous.

The Ivoirs, long-considered the second-most powerful of the Twelve Families, kept mostly to their own affairs, doling the grunt work out to the lesser nobility. They were the Xaveyrs' pets, and monopolized key, cutting edge industries such as information technology, digital security, and space exploration to name a few.

Because of these skills, two years prior, Baraam had previously contracted Ivion's older brother Ordin to keep an eye on Alina. Baraam had intended to prevent her involvement in the Rave for the Bane of New El, but—true to her nature—she'd found a way to throw herself into the fire anyway, with expectedly disastrous results. And Ordin had been murdered in the process, supposedly by the hand of the Sanctumite Exorcist Tolomond Stayd, although The Sanctum's involvement was never proved. Fortunately for Baraam, his deal with Ordin had been under the table; he wouldn't want to have the Ivoirs—especially Ivion—for his enemy.

As if sensing his unease, Ivion watched him with ravenous eyes, delicate fingers rapping against the armrests of her chair. A platinum spider sizing up a bloated fly.

"You have performed your part well, prophet," said Kaspuri. "The feeble-minded people of this wealth-forsaken dive do not resist our final approach. At last, the fateful hour draws near, Plutonia be praised." He remembered who he was talking to. "And your Author also, of course, of course."

The Savior inclined his head. "Naturally. All has progressed as decreed by the One True God." He seemed to enjoy the discomfort that this slight against Plutonia, chief goddess of El, wreaked on the other man. "But you get ahead of yourself, Lord Walazzin: my greatest contribution is yet to come. I shall dethrone the Hextarchs."

Kaspuri waved the comment off. "Doddering relics locked in a cave? They're nothing to concern ourselves over."

"Forgive your humble servant, but my lord is mistaken. In fact, the Hextarchs pose the gravest threat to our combined forces."

"We are one hundred *thousand* strong," Kaspuri barked, rising, a strand of his greasy hair breaking free of the slick mass.

Ivion chuckled. "Could one hundred thousand men defeat a hurricane? A black hole? How clearly out of your element you are, Lord Walazzin. Sit down before you hurt yourself."

Frowning like a chided child, Kaspuri flopped back into his seat. "I don't understand what *she's* doing here."

"Lady Ivoir is taking care of a… sensitive issue, alleviating a great concern of ours," said The Savior, not meeting any of their eyes, instead appreciating from on high the assembled grand army. The frayed ends of his theatrically shabby cloak were ruffled in the wake of a passing drone.

Fiddling with his blood diamond cuff links, Kaspuri pouted. "What 'sensitive issue'?"

"This full frontal assault of yours." Ivion rolled her eyes, crossing and uncrossing her bare legs. "Did you really think it had even the minutest chance of success? If so, you're even stupider than ever I'd dreamed."

"Watch your tone with me, Ivoir. Your shield's worn historically thin these days, and the number of your supporters is ever shrinking. I am not to be trifled with!"

"Indeed, for you *are* a trifle." Ivion grinned. "To the axe, all problems seem solvable through brute force aided by gravity. Your mistake, you axe-headed lout, is thinking our Authority invincible; they are *not*. The Hextarchs are vestiges of the ancient world, an evil beyond both the comprehension and ability of blunt instruments such as yourself. Like anything else, however, they have a weakness: they've grown complacent in their 'cave,' as you called it. Strip away their shell and, like a tortoise exposed to the full power of the sun, they will shrivel and die."

"I am that sun," said The Savior. "By the light of The Author, I will tear them apart. But I cannot get to them, protected as they are. To put it bluntly, Hexhall exists in a parallel dimension, inaccessible to us. *That*, Lord Walazzin, is the obstacle to be overcome by Ivion's agent." He paused. "By the way, how *did* you enlist one of my own Exorcists to your cause? Who is Kellfyute to you?"

Kellfyute. They were talking about Alina.

Sweat sprung from Baraam's scalp. The flesh of his palms tingled. He shifted his weight to mask his discomfort.

"No one," said Ivion. "I simply discovered she had a potential connection to one of the Covenants, determining that hers was the subtlest approach to undermining Hexhall's defenses. As a true daughter of the Empire, I seek neither fame nor glory; I live only to serve." She closed her narrow eyes. "Excuse me a moment." Baraam felt quickening pulses of Niima emanate from her. Then she rose and straightened her skirt, saying, "I sense Kellfyute is nearly in position. Goodnight, gentlemen. Baraam." Baraam glowered at her passing, shifty eyes. Eva she completely ignored as she sashayed through the open balcony doors and into the warm coffee shop. "I shall prepare the spell. Be ready." With that, she left.

Baraam marveled at the scale of the mess Alina had gotten herself into.

He turned to The Savior, straightening. "Sir. Would you excuse me?"

"An odd moment to run off." The Savior raised his brows. "No, you'll stay right where you are. Witness the impending show."

Anger crackled from Baraam's gut to his fingernails, but he said nothing.

Kaspuri laughed. "I see you've got your own well-trained dog now too, eh, prophet? Good on you. And Eva will finally have some company. A shame she lacks the capacity to feel, well, anything at all." An oily grimace was plastered on his face. "Baraam, while we have you here, would you like to know how my family came by our dear Eva?"

Baraam quelled the urge to chop the Walazzin noble in half with a blade of force and air. A flick of the wrist, that's all it would take.

Kaspuri continued, "She was a child—twelve, thirteen? Oh, who cares?—a mere child, anyway, when my father's private security firm acquired her. Apparently, she'd blown up a school."

Eva's facial muscles did not so much as twitch at her master's cutting words.

"On accident, according to the reports." Kaspuri draped his leg over his armrest. "Blah, blah. The result is what counts. Dozens of kiddies died, horrifically, in what witnesses called a 'miniature supernova.' I always loved that description—'miniature supernova.' Far more poetic than practical, though. Anyway, long story short, my father had the little prodigy apprehended and spirited away. She was a dangerous little slip, and there were casualties as we looked for ways to use her powers. After much experimentation and sacrifice, however..." He let his tongue loll for a moment. "Well, allow me to demonstrate. Eva, be a dear and strike yourself. As hard as you can."

Still staring into the middle distance, Eva removed her sunglasses, hanging them from her collar. Then she lifted her arm, made a fist, and punched herself.

Limb now limp at her side, a red mark darkened around her left eye.

"Marvelous, isn't she?" Kaspuri said. "But, darling, I know you can do better than *that*."

Once more, her arm flew up, but Baraam caught her before she could hurt herself again. "Stop," he said. "Tell her to stop."

"Why ever...?" Kaspuri chuckled. "I suppose I should have expected such bestial sympathy. Even curs in a kennel will cling to one another for comfort."

"A tiresome display, Lord Walazzin," said The Savior, and he returned his attention to the army below.

Still trying to obey her master's latest order, Eva struggled against Baraam's grip. She began to glow from within, her skin growing so hot that it burned his hand, forcing him to let go. Unfettered, she drove her fist into her face a second time, staggering from the force of the blow.

"Good show, Eva. Now, go and wash yourself. Your face nauseates me."

Watching her leave, Baraam marveled again at the immense energy emanating from her. In addition to his skin, she'd scaled his very spirit. She was by far powerful enough to obliterate Kaspuri, The Savior, and probably a full cohort of Tranquilizers without much effort. So, why did she let the likes of that bottom-feeder Kaspuri Walazzin control her? How had he managed to break down such an exquisite Mage into so empty a vessel?

A question bloomed then, a ball of lightning bouncing around the crevices of his mind. Was he any different? Thoughtless commands had brought him here, made of him a beast of burden. Now, the givers of these commands threatened the life of Alina. And, still, he did nothing.

He heard Jija's voice in his mind, a desert memory: *You are lost, my brother.*

Some wars are righteous, I suppose.

But, how to tell the difference, hmm?

I'd rather stay out of them all-together. I've changed.

Now, Baraam wondered if that were really true. Had he changed, or simply traded masters?

Perhaps the only difference between him and Eva was that *he* was still conscious of his abuse. Eva had been shattered and reconstructed—a hastily glued vase crammed with black powder, ready to be tossed into the nearest fire. Baraam—a supposed virtuoso Mage, a great warrior—could see under his feet that same path. He might have years to go before he caught up, but the destination was the same.

To his memory of Jija, and himself, he said, *What I do is who I am.*

At last, against The Savior's wishes, Baraam fled the balcony, dashing through the coffee shop and down the stairs.

Not knowing what he'd do upon finding her, he chased after Ivion.

Calling out to Ivion as she'd been about to slide into the back of an olive-green APC, Baraam noted she had shed her white vest and pencil skirt for a black-and-white flack jacket over gray urban camo fatigues. The black-and-white-armored Tranquilizers on either side tensed, fingers flexed over the triggers of their rifles. She waved, and they relaxed slightly, still focused on Baraam's every step as he approached. (He caught the tail-end of a hushed conversation between Ivion and one of the bodyguards: "Comm links are down, Ma'am. Wasn't aware of any scheduled downtime"; "That's because it *wasn't* scheduled"; "What do we do?"; "Your job, commander. The Den will update me on its status soon, I'm sure.")

Having molted her social attire, in uniform Ivion's demeanor had shifted, expanded. Nakedly wearing the calculated, cocky smirk trademarked by the Ivoirs, she faced him.

For a moment, her stare stunned him, made him feel as though he'd just fallen through a trapdoor. But he was Baraam bol-Talanai, damn it; he rallied. "You'll let Kellfyute go. Find another way into Hexhall."

A smile slowly curled her lips. "What's it to you?" Her eyes widened. "Ah, you *know*."

He scowled at her, a response that was apparently answer enough.

She beckoned him closer. He hesitated before complying, leaning until in range of a kiss. He felt her warm breath on his neck, numbing him as if she'd sunk her mandibles into his flesh. "Alina is mine." Her words were injected venom, and his blood ran cold.

Never mind how Ivion had figured out who Alina was or how Alina had become ensnared by such a treacherous spinner. No time to distill bitter truth from sweet-dripping lies. Baraam said, "You are going to get her killed. I won't allow that."

"What are you going to do about it?" Ivion showed her teeth, waggling her pencil-stroke eyebrows. "Fight me? Kill me? Somehow, I doubt that."

It was Baraam's turn to smile. "You don't know me very well."

With her middle finger, she flicked his chin. "Don't misunderstand. Your capabilities aren't in question. You could destroy me without so much as dirtying those charming Sanctumite grays that have come to fit you so well. However, have you paused to consider—even for a second—what would happen if you did end my life?" She laughed. "How very Kaspurian of you, failing to imagine how quickly you yourself would be butchered by The Savior or by the Walazzins or any of the other thousands of soldiers assembled here. Soldiers loyal to me, not you. Perhaps you'd put on a good show, but even the greatest Aelfraver alive couldn't stand against the full might of the Elemental Empire. That, my dear Baraam, is why you're wearing someone else's colors, and I my own. Your impotence stays your hand. And, ever generous, I'll provide you one more compelling reason: harm me in any way, and I'll have Alina killed. I and my associates know where she is at all times. All I need do is expose her, and the Hextarchs, The Coven, The Sanctum, The Authority—they'll all queue up to take their shots. Right now, believe it or not, I am her only shield against the multitude of extremely dangerous enemies she's made. That's why you will shut your little snarling mouth and be a good boy again." Her eyelashes fluttered. "Have I convinced you?"

Clenching his jaw, Baraam's repressed instincts threatened to resurface. He held himself back, tamped down his Niima, though it ached to burst forth.

He did not wonder *if* she lied, only *how much*.

"Tell you what," she said. "While you're here, you may as well watch me work. You'll appreciate this." One of her bodyguards passed a holopad to her, and she activated it, scrolling through projected lines of code. "Remarkably quick work, if you'll permit me some well-deserved self-congratulation. Once I cloned Alina's phone, giving myself a back door inside, I scanned and probed the Revomantic shield around Hexhall for weaknesses. Not easy, considering it's Old Magic. 'Old' with a capital 'O,' Baraam. As in, not of human origin. Everyone said finding a workaround would be impossible. But, combing through The Gild's Crystallarium records, living through countless Lorestone-locked memories, I did it. *I* succeeded. You see, it all makes sense now. This 'Abyss' the locals bark about—it's their protection, their life force. And it's connected to the Chrononite somehow, flowing from the Hextarchs themselves. They are the key! After making that breakthrough, all I had to do was find a way—even for a moment—to interfere with their—" She searched for the right word—"signal. Then, in a flash of inspiration, I figured it out. Using Alina's cellular phone, which now lies inside Hexhall, I could—" She smacked her lips. "Ah. I almost gave away the game, there. But we mustn't let the excitement of this momentous occasion get ahead of us."

"Clearly—" Electricity forked from Baraam's balled fists, skittering across the asphalt beneath his feet—"a few too many microchips have been jabbed into your brain." The temptation to snap that long, pale neck—

"Now, now. Touching and pathetic as this uncharacteristic display of loyalty is, we have already decided that you *will* do nothing."

"Your tactics against the Hextarchy do not interest me. Why drag the girl into this?"

"Oh." Covering her mouth with the back of her hand, Ivion laughed. "Alina's no 'girl.' I don't know what she is, exactly, but she's certainly not human. And—" Her eyes flitted from Baraam's hair to his boots—"judging by your heart rate and micromovements, I now know you are also aware of this fact. Parsing The Crystallarium's records revealed to me much of the buried lore of our world.

Still, I couldn't find so much as a veiled reference to the type of creature she is. And *then* I learned that a particular Lorestone had gone missing. A Lorestone that, according to the records, contains accounts of Iorian antiquity. A Lorestone that was reported stolen on a date coinciding with Alina's singular week in The Capital. Curious, to say the least." She gave him a knowing grin. "You treat her like a child—no, a doll in need of perfect preservation. But you can't admit the truth about her: she is special, irreplaceable. How, I cannot yet say. But, if needed, I will devote the rest of my life to uncovering the truth."

"A minute ago, you threatened her life, and now you expect me to believe you care what happens to her?"

"Your doubt is irrelevant. Alina's presence in Hexhall and her usefulness to me, these are unintended but fortunate circumstances." Ivion's narrow eyes widened, revealing the intricate circuitry connecting them to the nerves in her skull. "I love her. More than you, I'll wager. You belittle her, unwilling to protect her in any meaningful way. Fear hamstrings you, whereas I would lay down my life for her without hesitation. If I had to."

"What are you talking about? You're insane."

"No, Baraam, I'm really not. I am simply the only one willing to do what's necessary to end this war, secure The Capital, and restore order to El. That is all I've ever wanted, and I have died for that ideal once already."

That's when it clicked in Baraam's mind: it had been strange to hear her jabbering about magic because there was only one mage in the current generation of Ivoirs. A Machinamancer. And he'd been murdered two years ago.

I have died... once already.

"Not possible," said Baraam. "It was all over the news. The body was recovered. What remained of it."

Ivion Ivoir smiled broadly. "Amazing what the world's largest supercomputer farm, trillions of gelders, and the blessings of God can accomplish."

"You're not Ivion." He looked to the bodyguards, who either hadn't heard or didn't care.

"Bravo." She took a bow. "Finally, after chewing on my words, your goat's brain extracts the truth. As it happens, the real Ivion has been made quite comfortable in a lavish bomb shelter, somewhere in the colonies. She is under heavy guard, safe as can be. However, I must advise you, one last time, against blabbing the truth to anyone. We both know what I'll do if you disobey."

"If you love Alina as you say, you will let her go. Save her from the fire."

"Do not insult me. I do love Alina, more than life itself. She and I are, however, merely two souls. The needs of the multitudes must come before our own. Our Nation of El is set to be torn apart by civil strife; don't you care? The only thing that can save us is the unifying power of victory in war. But, first, the Walazzin-led coalition must bloody itself against the Hextarchs."

"So, it's politics. All your schemes, just to harm a rival. And you'll lead thousands to slaughter to see it done."

"The circumstances are regrettable but necessary. My gambit resolves two problems at once. The Walazzins will prevail—thanks to the timely assistance of my elite personal guard—but not before incurring *crippling* losses. Songs shall be sung of their valiance in combat, as we lay wreaths upon the graves of the dead. God willing, Kaspuri will be among the fallen I must officially mourn upon being anointed the next Consul. But I'm getting ahead of myself."

Baraam scoffed. "You're a megalomaniac."

"I am a patriot."

"Why tell me all this?"

"Someone should be witness to history in the making. Now, hush, and do your part. Watch. You'll never forgive yourself if you miss what I'm about to do: Zero-One myself into the very heart of our enemy's stronghold and pry it open like a jewelry box. Peregrar's Grief, and all their arcane countermeasures and defenses will be rendered *null*. I want you to see me, the one you discounted—the ever-ignored lesser Raver, mocked and ridiculed—see me accomplish what no one else ever could."

Ivion's thumb tapped the screen of her holopad, which projected more lines of code. Her fingers skittered across these, and then she set the pad on the ground, took a step back, and waited.

"*ViiCter*," she said. "Call Alina."

"Calling Alina," said the neutral-toned voice through the speakers of the pad.

A beam of light shot up from the device, widening to the width of a door through which two adults could easily enter side-by-side. The beam struck the cave ceiling high, high above, rebounding, driving west—toward Peregar's Grief.

"There you have it, Baraam bol-Talanai," shouted Ivion over the sudden roar of rushing air. "Ordin Ivoir saves the world. At the press of a button."

54

ALINA

FEW NINETEEN-YEAR-OLDS WERE EVER cursed with knowing exactly how their lives would end.

Her self unraveled. The fraying blanket of identity thrown aside, she could no longer hide from the truth:

"I am Vrana."

Blinded to the Hextarchs, Alina faced the Crow.

"You." She stepped forward.

Placing a hand on its chest as if to say, *Who, me?* the Crow stood firm.

"You *chose*. You chose not to tell me. What I am. I thought I was—but, instead I'm—"

The Crow's shadowy outline flickered, buffeted by the force of her shout.

"You told me my parents were *junkies* and *thieves*. That all they cared about was money. That they were too *high* to know what they were doing half the time. That they were killed in a tunnel they'd dug under a bank." She swiped the tears from her cheeks, her lengthening claws nicking her skin. "But none of that was true. They were good people whose only real crime was trying to break free from the Elemental Bank and The Authority." She threw herself at the Crow, who dodged her sloppy jab. "They loved me. But you—"

The Crow cocked its shadowed, ephemeral head.

"You," she growled. "Show me your face, coward!"

It tried to back away, but she bowled it over, fingers looping around its stalk-like throat.

Color flooded into the Crow's amorphous face. A nose formed, then eyes, lips—all features she recognized, but none of which she wanted to see.

Her reflection.

When the Crow spoke, it used Dimas's voice: "No, Alina. *You*. If I am responsible, then so are you. We are, after all your denials, the same. Are you ready at last?"

She drove her fist into its mouth, then its nose, and felt the pain as if she'd struck herself.

"That is exactly what you've done," said the Crow.

"Get out of my head."

"I *am* your head," it shouted back, laughing.

Gripping its throat, she choked the creature that had ruined her life. She felt herself choking, too, but held on. She would have given anything to silence its grating laughter.

As her vision narrowed and grayed, she finally relented. Gasping, she released the Crow, who crawled out from under her and stood.

Her own face gazed down at her, impassive. *Ida* and *Rego* lay in a bundle on the ground between them.

The Crow retrieved the mask and placed it over its own head, fastening the straps.

Pulse pounding in her eyes, she willed the Crow to just *die*—until a hand settled on her shoulder. It was Aam's. They said, "You must forgive yourself."

"I didn't do anything wrong. *It* did this to us."

"We are more than we wish ourselves to be," said Aam, tail scratching their back.

To the Crow, Alina said, "Your daughter—my mother—lay dying, and you came to her, just in time to be useful. You could've done for her what you did for me. She's like us, Egogenetic. We're all Sevensin. You *should* have sacrificed yourself back then." She wept. "Why for me but not her?"

"You know," said the Crow.

"The answer lies within you," Aam agreed.

Closing her eyes, Alina remembered a moment she hadn't lived. At least, this body she now inhabited *hadn't* experience it firsthand. But Dimas had. And, therefore, she could see it as clearly as one of her own memories. Because it *was* one of her own memories.

On that day, fourteen years ago, in Clerica Viridim, Zatalena and Yurgeius and so many other peaceful protesters had been gunned down by Enforcers.

Dimas had arrived, determining that his daughter would die from the wounds she'd sustained. *She'd never been strong enough to endure. Alina, however…*

Yes, he could have let Zatalena feed on him, and so revived her. But that would have made her *the dominant personality, and all that power and potential would have been wasted on Zatalena—always weak—who'd fled from conflict and denied her nature at every turn. She was, in many ways, the inverse of Mateus (too prideful, too narrow-minded).*

The choice to watch her die was agony. Dimas stayed strong by reminding himself there was a war to be fought—a bitter war, one that would end within a human lifetime, maybe two. The world needed soldiers, and Zatalena lacked the heart to become one. If she limped through time long enough to witness that dreaded day when Elwoch's dominion became absolute, at that point, she'd certainly succumb to despair. Because she was weak. And what kind of father would Dimas be if he let his little girl suffer such a final chapter?

She was nothing like her own daughter. Rather, nothing like the fourth piece of Dimas, the fraction of himself that inhabited the human body named 'Alina.' That child must be nurtured. Even if Zatalena must die for it. Even if he, Dimas, must follow her into darkness someday.

Yes. Alina was the hope, the one. She who would fulfill the Sevensins' contract—iron, unbreakable. She would raze El, and end the age of men in ruin. It must be her. She was their last chance.

"I had plans for me," Alina murmured. Her thoughts were all twisted; she hardly knew what she said. "I mean, *you*," she barked at the Crow, correcting herself, "you had your schemes. You made us to suffer."

"Maybe," said the Crow, speaking in Dimas's voice, smiling with Alina's lips. "Maybe at first. But I changed. I came to love you. Because the truth of it is, Cabbage—"

"Don't call me that. Don't you ever—"

"The truth," it spoke over her objections, "is that you are more than the sum of your parts. More than my 'schemes,' as you call them. More than the soul of Vrana, which we share. Certainly more than the human form you inhabit. You are all these elements, but you are also a dream given life, the union between opposites. You *are* and *are not*. I could not see this, not fully, until we were united, that day in New El. When our minds fused, I understood, at long last, why I favored you above Zatalena and all others."

"Why? Why then?"

"Neither human nor Aelf, you may be whatever you choose to be. You are a warrior who abhors fighting; a child who's lived forever; you intuitively tap into all eight of the magical disciplines. Most importantly, your empathy—"

"What do you know about empathy?"

"Precious little, until you taught me. When you, this six-year-old brat, came to live with me, I admit that I reviled you at first. You were, to me, an abomination born of my sorrow for Zatalena. But then I saw the terrible intensity with which you were able to love everything, no matter how profoundly you yourself had been hurt. The loss of your parents, the coldness of my own old heart… The suffering of all living things cut deeper into you than anyone else. And that's

when I knew—by the essential, ineffable qualities that make you what you are—
you would be the one to finish what we—" the Crow pointed to each of the
Hextarchs—"began millennia ago. I don't honestly know how you'll do it, but I
am supremely confident that you, of anyone, will find a way." The Crow was also
crying now. "I thought I'd made you out of spite for this world, Alina. But it
wasn't anger that I poured into you that night, at the Well of Sistren; it was hope.
This cold lump of flesh in my arms—as I breathed life into it, giving of myself,
I inadvertently imbued it with my secret wish for a better world. That wish led
to you: human and Aelf, together, in one body."

To Alina's shock, she'd been speaking in unison with the Crow toward the
end of its monologue, its words pouring from her own mouth. And, when she
spoke, her anger hissed from between both its teeth and hers. "I should've
known sooner."

In perfect synchrony, they rattled off the rest of their conversation:

"I'm a ghost in a dead girl's body."

"Death is only a doorway leading to new life."

"I'm not even real."

"Reality is but one mode of existence."

"I've let everyone down."

"I am loved."

The force of those words knocked her to her knees.

I am loved. I have failed so many times, but I am loved.

The Crow's voice—Dimas's voice—faded, becoming her own. "This world
is worth saving. And so am I."

Hearing a thunk, wood on stone, she opened her eyes. *Ida*, her mask, lay on
the ground.

The Crow had gone.

She called out to it, but could no longer sense its presence anywhere in that
chamber or in her mind. And she never would again.

The door in her mental replica of The School, the one that locked away her
memories of Dimas, was wide open. The bathroom was empty. The mirror and
the sink and the misty reflection of pale gold eyes—all gone. She and Dimas—
her *Tahtoh*—had truly become one, which is how she knew, wordlessly, doubt-
lessly, that Uncle Mateus had long-since learned the truths now clear in her own
mind. But he had gone down a different path from hers: she'd chosen to deflect,
deny, but ultimately accept; he had begun and ended in a place of never-ending
hate for his creator.

To despise Dimas, she now understood, was to despise herself. Therefore, to
fear Mateus was to fear herself.

At her side, Aam smiled. The other Hextarchs descended from their stately
podiums. Surrounding her, they weren't as tall as she'd first thought. In fact, they
seemed old, bent. Tired.

"I know what I have to do," she told them. "And you gotta let me leave to see it through."

"The Authority's forces amass before the Wall," said Haba.

"To leave now would be folly," said Gurm.

"Expose us all to danger," said Stonoz.

"You're waiting for oblivion anyway," said Alina. "Why stop me?"

"It is right that we face our ending together."

She opened her mouth to reply, but stopped when Aam winked at her and turned to their siblings. "But we are not 'together,' not truly. Didn't you witness the same scene as I, just now? Have you all forgotten that Vrana's soul remains fractured? What once lay in four pieces is now made two, but one more union must yet occur. The 'Alina' and 'Savior' fragments must be rejoined, and only then may we—the Seven—bow our heads and depart this world with our honor intact."

"Hrrmm," croaked Haba, blinking.

Stonoz grumbled. "It is Vrana's own doing."

"That matters not. Aam speaks wisdom," said Etia. "What harm is there in a broken mirror's wish for restoration?"

"Let me go," said Alina, "and either Mateus or I will return. Whoever wins will be *all* of Vrana. And then we'll see what happens to us."

The six of them quivered. "The Avatar of Elwoch—"

"Tolomond Stayd," said Alina.

"We sense him. He is close."

"I've dealt with him before. But he won't recognize me now."

Stonoz adjusted one of their bangles. "We shan't bid you 'good luck,' O splinter of Vrana."

Muscular arms crossed behind their back, Haba said, "It matters not to us which part of you dominates the others."

"It should," said Alina. "Mateus will destroy you."

"One way or another," said Gurm, pointy ears twitching, "our lives will be forfeit. What care we who delivers the mortal blow?"

They chattered among themselves, spouting gloom and doom and honor. Aam hung apart from the others.

Alina shrugged. "You're frightened. I understand."

That shut them up.

Lightly, Aam's tail coiled around her arm. "Well, *I* shall say 'good luck,' Vrana-Alina." They smiled.

"Thanks." She offered her hand. "For sticking up for me."

Aam inclined their head, shook her hand, then swept dramatically backward. With a feline leap, they returned to their podium.

The passageway through which Alina had entered the Hextarchs' sanctuary reappeared.

Stooping to recover *Ida* and *Rego*, she left. They did not try to stop her. As she'd suspected, they'd all but given up the fight.

It was up to her now to show them surrender wasn't an option.

The nausea and fogginess melted from her, replaced with a sense of clarity unlike any she'd ever felt before. She had come to Hexhall a lost, desperate child, but she left it having finally understood a fundamental truth about herself.

Her mind held everything her *Tahtoh* had known. Her mother lived on, inside her. And, if she listened really carefully, she could hear dozens—hundreds—of other voices, too. Yet, stitched together from these countless pieces was a persona all her own. She was more than her desires or the desires of others hanging over her, more than her anger and her drive, her skills or her knowledge. She was more than the sum of her parts. Her genetic and spiritual destinies meant only as much as she wanted them to; she would decide what—and who—she wanted to become.

Contrary to what the Hextarchs might think, the battle was far from finished.

As soon as she stepped out of the chamber, a metal blast door sealed behind her. She strode down the corridor, her movements easy, her path sure. She might as well have been walking in slow motion, with a soaring orchestral rendition of some string-heavy soundtrack rising to greet this portentous moment.

Then her phone rang, and she was thrown off by her Brass Key Makers' *Live At Blackrock '74* banshee-shriek ringtone.

On the screen:

BLOCKED NUMBER

She answered. "Um. Hello?"

All she could hear on the other end was a sort of rising whine.

For a second, she felt a Niimantic signature. Hauntingly familiar.

Then her phone exploded.

55

CHO-ZEN

A BLUR ON THE pockmarked highway, a dark van weaved between lanes, exiting toward the Sixth Stack's lake district. It drifted dangerously close to the guardrail of the crescent-shaped ramp. Under normal circumstances, a traffic monitoring drone would already have photographed and digitally tagged the vehicle with a ticket. The circumstances, however, were far from normal.

While the engines of non-military cars still hummed, and many city lights still gleamed in the spires and towers of downtown, the conspicuous absence of police and military units on the roads filled the perimeter tunnels that surrounded the Sixth Stack with a hush, a tingling anticipation. A damp blanket of disquiet had smothered the usual car horns and blasting radios.

The van entered a tunnel. Same as everywhere else, the checkpoint there was disabled, its gate locked in open position. Its guards were powerless to challenge the vehicle barreling through. The only evidence of the illegal crossing was the snapped-off side view mirror that smashed onto the asphalt.

There had been a break in the flow of electricity, so the tunnel was lit only by gas-powered emergency lights. Many commuters had pulled over, poking their heads out of their cars, gazing about in slack-jawed wonder.

Dug thousands of years ago by colossal worms, these tunnels had once been pilgrimage routes lined by kneeling faithful and babbling mystics. Generations of the Hextarchy's servants had called this place holy. In the still, glassy pools, the people had once washed themselves clean of sin. Upon living walls of rock, they'd carved their names or those of loved ones lost to the perils of the dark— a darkness, dire as it was, that nonetheless embraced all as equal. Through faith and cooperation, for an age, human and Aelf had survived—together—in this hard, lonely place, protected from the tempestuous elements of the surface world. Ozar had always been a realm of mystery and loss, but, to these hardy millions, it was home. Steadily, over a thousand years or more, The Authority had taken from them so much of what made their land uniquely theirs. Cho had seen the crystal caves, the rivers of lava, the roots of sentient trees... Ozar was not her place, and the Ozari were not her people; she knew very little about the many cultures that shared this country. But she could understand sacrifice and theft, having been on the receiving and giving ends of both. The Ozaris' loss was her own. It bound her to them.

Like so many pieces of Ozar, the pilgrimage routes had been irreparably scarred by the coming of The Authority, who had repurposed them into modern highways complete with harsh, electric lighting. The glare of street lights and headlights—the heat of burning fuel and expanding metal—on a daily basis, these assaulted the senses.

Today, though, the curving highway, and the side-tunnel roads that fed into it, lay darker than they had in centuries. Today, no Authority cameras surveyed the byways. Anything with an autopilot function—trucks, hovercycles, tanks— sat on the sides of the streets, inert.

Lights out.

Arriving downtown, Hael finally was forced to pump the brakes. Rush hour traf- fic had been made infinitely worse by the hundreds of dead vehicles lining the streets. Navigating these obstacles took forever, which gave Cho plenty of time to catch snippets of unsettling scenes from the front passenger seat of the stolen van. Her thoughts shuffled, cut by constant pain signals. Her overworked scan- ners automatically interpreted dozens of facial expressions, one after another: fury, fear, excitement, exhilaration. An increasingly complex cocktail of emotions that, like the blasts of fire hoses, doused the Ozari. What would come of it, she couldn't tell. But, just like all those people out there, she felt the ripple in the waters. Something big was coming.

What unfolded across the Sixth Stack imitated the mayhem at the Lion's Den, but on a much larger scale. Authority squads, used to moving in concert, guided by the voices of their commanders which fed directly into their helmets—scat- tered in almost random directions. Without the usual oversight, they barked at one another like schoolyard bullies, hopelessly outnumbered by agitated citizens but attempting to retain control.

The change in atmosphere was not lost on the Ozari. Many had gathered in the streets to watch the novelty of El's armies struggling to mobilize. The wings of the rank and file kept bumping into each other. Arguments broke out, followed by scuffles. Then, fights. As The Authority's storied discipline broke down, some of the Ozari laughed, some panicked, and others simply stared as if watching a looped montage of people falling down flights of stairs.

Although detested by many, The Authority was a symbol of stability. Now that they behaved no better than unruly students before the teacher walked into the classroom, they were suddenly humanized. Pulling off their helmets, they showed their faces and were revealed to be mere mortals, after all. And the Ozaris' agitation—that pre-lightning-storm, tangy taste to the air—brought masses of their people outside to watch. And wait.

Then, it happened, but in stages.

A driver stuck his head out to gripe about the immobile tank blocking half the street.

On the sidewalk nearby, a burly man in a tracksuit flailed his arms in front of a slender Tranquilizer. He put his cigarette out on the soldier's uniform, which earned him a shove.

The tracksuit guy fell backward into a group of teenage onlookers, wearing baggy school uniforms. They picked him up and charged forward to wrestle the Tranq's pistol from her.

Farther down, a child threw a stone, striking a helmet.

There came a wall of hard plastic shields, a line of black batons. At first, the Authority advanced, and the Ozari retreated. Then, amid the rising jungle birdsong of jeers and shouts, glass bottles and bricks began to fly.

More people spilled into the street. Cho flinched as hands and bodies banged into the van. The Ozari were herded out of the intersection by baton-blows and rubber bullets. Flashbangs went off somewhere behind.

So it began. And, though Cho did not know it at the time, the flood that rushed forth here, today, would not recede for years to come. It would not pass until it had drowned half the Empire and the world.

Fingernails shredding the fake leather arm wrests, she looked to Hael, who said, "The doors are locked, and the glass is bullet-proof."

"What's happening out there?"

Hael changed gears with her one good hand, allowing the vehicle to coast at two miles per hour. Tapping the brakes, she said, "What'd you think would happen?"

Dumpsters were overturned, glass shattered. Shop displays and ground-floor lobbies were rushed, their contents smashed to pieces and scattered. Fires rose from unseen sources.

With The Authority's attentions divided between conquering Hexhall and containing this flare up of Ozari anger, the disorganized Tranq patrols waved Hael's unmarked vehicle right through the next checkpoint.

Cho noticed with a mixture of awe and dread that chaos seemed to be overtaking not just the lake district but the entire Stack. Wherever she looked, she found Tranqs pushing back against an ever-growing tide of human bodies, but the Tranqs were having to spread themselves more and more thinly.

"I thought there were thousands of these guys," said Cho.

"They'll be at the Wall," came Cbarassan's voice from the back.

On Cho's knee, Mezami said, "Make: war, Elementals. Unconcerned: people, for."

Hael grunted. "The rodent is right. Kaspuri Walazzin—Seventy-Seven curses on his name—will stop for nothing. The Elementals are punching through Peregar's Grief tonight, even if it costs them every soul on the Sixth."

Cho slid down her seat. "I missed my only shot."

"Is: chance, still." Mezami patted her forehead, his tail tickling her nose. "Find: him, we. Punish: him, you."

"I'm a failure."

"Left or right ahead?" said Hael.

And the ride continued.

Eventually, the captain's driving and Cho's directions brought the escapees within walking distance of the Safehouse in one piece. Well, in fewer pieces than they might have been without Hael's timely intervention.

They abandoned the vehicle several blocks away, hiding it under a tarp and assorted bags of trash. Hael threw a hooded rain coat over herself, collecting Kinneas and the others, urging Cho out of the car. Unfocused, Cho followed, favoring her mostly undamaged leg. At the Safehouse door, she punched the code into the keypad.

Inside the bunker, they were alone. Ivion was, as usual, somewhere else.

A few deft flicks of her knife and Hael cut away the torn left leg of Cho's pants up to the knee. Cho had been more badly hurt than she'd realized: a nasty gash in the shape of a question mark spanned her shin.

"You," said Hael to Cbarassan. "Antiseptic. Booze. Something. Now."

Slouching against the wall, the *Fyarda* was barely conscious.

The one-armed woman chewed her cheek. "Little Aelf," she grunted at Mezami. "Be more useful than your friend, here."

The Pyct grumbled at her tone but did as asked, returning a minute later with a bottle of rubbing alcohol.

She snatched it from him, then handed it back. "On second thought, you do it." With her right hand, she gestured at the metallic elbow joint where her other arm now ended. "I'm a lefty."

Cho wadded the hood of her jacket in her mouth and bit down hard as Mezami doused her wound, sterilizing it.

"Amazing it isn't worse. Obviously, those bones of yours were well worth the investment," said Hael casually. "That madman's sword should have hacked you clean in two."

"Almost did."

"Are you able to shut off your pain receptors?"

Cho shook her head. "Well. Some of them, I think."

"Do that now." Hael clicked her tongue. "No point in asking, I'm sure, but do we have any anesthesia handy? Injectors? Hells, even strong spirits will do."

Shaking a pill bottle as big as he was, Mezami tossed his find over to Hael, who nodded. She snapped the cap off and produced three capsules, feeding them to her patient. "Down the gullet, Cho-Cho bird."

The pain pills clouded Cho's thoughts within seconds, and so she laughed giddily at the nickname she'd forgotten half a lifetime ago. She imagined her head popped off her shoulders, sprouted little legs, and started kick-dancing back and forth across the room.

"Ya used to tell me stories," she slurred, sniffling. "Puppet shows. No, what'm I sayin'? It was shadow puppets. Shady pup—puppies?" She began to giggle, soundlessly, sweat pouring from her like foam from a shaken soda can.

Hael cracked a smile. "Your brothers and sisters were all too old for that trick. Only you were able to appreciate my storytelling genius." Stern again, she added, "Hold still."

"Why didn't ya come for me?" Cho couldn't see for the tears filling her eyes.

"I did. By the Seventy-Seven Gods, I swear I did." Fire blazed from Hael's fingertips, then the flames retreated inward, causing the pads of her fingers to glow red- then white-hot.

Mezami passed Cho a plastic spork he'd scrounged from somewhere. "This: bite, you."

Hardly aware of what she did, she clamped the bit between her teeth. Hael proceeded to drag her blazing fingertips along the curving tail of Cho's sanitized wound.

Cho could only imagine how much more terrible the pain would have been were she fully feeling it. Turning down her internal pain dial was risky because there was always a chance she wouldn't be able to turn it up again. But, in this moment, she was once more grateful for her inhuman body.

With even greater gratitude, as the intensity of her agony rose and she smelled her own flesh cooking, she fainted.

There, the pattern of small hexagons within a giant one, all glowing green. The symbol Bizong had shown her in the cave. His trap.

She felt its ridges with her bare feet. She was in the cave again, but its walls were an infinite distance away, and yet she could reach out and touch them with her fingertips.

This was a dream, she knew.

"Yes," someone said.

A sandy-furred coyote padded onto the symbol. It looked a lot like the one she'd seen in the desert, on the way to Ozar. Could have been the same one.

"That was just a coyote," said the coyote. "You know who I am."

"Morphea," said Cho. She instinctively balled her fists, raised them.

"You've become distrustful. Good."

"How are you here? Where *is* here?"

The coyote shook out its fur as if shedding water. "The one you called 'Sleeper.' You weren't careful enough, and now it's imprinted on you."

"Huh?"

"Your new connection is accelerating your—whatever is happening to you."

"How do I know you're not a nightmare?"

"But I am." The coyote showed its fangs, narrowing its eyes (one brown, the other gold). "I want to thank you for having me along for the ride."

"I don't remember okaying that."

"Nevertheless, we are bound."

"Permanently?"

"For now. Until other accommodations may be arranged. I wish to be free."

"You don't have a body."

"The body is a prison."

"Grah. Fine, then. How do I get you out?"

"Alina." The coyote seemed to have nothing more to say on the subject.

Cho slapped herself across the face.

"What are you doing?" said the coyote.

"Trying to wake up."

"Don't you want the information I've dug up for you?"

"Why bother? It's just gonna be a big pile of symbolic crap."

The coyote smiled. "You are going to pay attention to it anyway."

"Oh, am I?"

"If not for your sake, for hers."

Huffing, Cho crossed her arms and legs and fell onto her backside. "Well?"

"Listen."

A tape recorder appeared in the animal's mouth. It placed the device on the ground, tapping the "play" button with its paw.

... In the depths of the floating temple
—built to honor Gods slain by its builders—
there lies an inverted tower

Its floors number Seventy-and-Seven
the final of which holds Seven Doors

The Eighth will open only
for the Uniter of the Keys,
the Chosen Reject,
Eighth of Seven Children,

THE ACHEMIR—
Sealed in Iron
breaker of the Wheel
marked by The Abyss…

"Hell yeah," Cho said. "Love me some cryptic poetry. Where'd you collect that garbage?"

"Your connection with the Sleeper isn't a river but a road. Information may travel both ways. What you just heard is a snippet of Pre-El, Ciirimaic legend. Recorded originally in Chrononite, re-recorded digitally, and, finally, corrupted beyond repair. Most of the salient details, of course, are lost."

"Sounds about right. The part we heard, what's it mean?"

"War is coming."

"It's already here. Wow, that was an easy riddle to solve. Next."

The coyote sighed. "I speak of a war not for land nor resources but the very nature of reality."

"Against who?"

"God."

Cho rolled her eyes. "Which one?"

"That's not the right question. If you don't already know, you couldn't possibly understand."

"Try me."

"No. Never mind. There's something else. More immediate."

"Fantastic."

"A source of interference. Ancient Machinamancy designed to dampen—to inhibit Alina somehow."

"Okay, Morphea. So, what's causing it?"

"Not what, but who." The coyote paused theatrically.

"Are ya gonna tell me?"

"Where would be the fun in that?"

"Like, can I go then?"

"Let me show you instead."

… A shadow circles overhead. A bird, it seems, but no—
A Dragon. Circling, vulture-like.

And like a vulture it swoops down, scooping up the ruined remains of a... giant spider?

The hairs on the arachnid's torn up legs and abdomen begin to glow, flashing the color of lightning during a summer storm. Its wounds bleed blue.

The spider is carried far, far away and deposited on a shoreline. Little ants recover it, drag it to their underground lair. There, they drop it in a pool of clear water.

It shrivels. Lies there a long, long time.

Then its many, many eyes pop open, one by one.

And it crawls out, renewed. Pure white.

"Is any of this supposed to mean something to me?"

Pacing along the edge of the grand hexagon, the coyote said, "I'm sorry, are you unimpressed by portents and prophecy?"

"I am when they're low-quality, grocery-store-novel junk like that, yeah."

"You truly do not see the sense of it? What it means?"

"Dunno what to tell ya."

The coyote backed into the shadows beyond the glowing hexagon. Briefly, it assumed the rough outline of a woman, cloaked. Before disappearing completely, it said, "We're doomed."

Cho fell through the floor—

—and woke, smelling something pleasant. Floral.

Water bubbled in an antique cast iron kettle on the stove as Mezami shook tea bags over it. He treated the bags like dusty sheets in need of a thrashing; dried, flaky leaves spilled everywhere. Some even landed in the kettle. The boiling water was allowed to settle, beaten-up tea bags steeping for two minutes. Cbarassan poured.

Gathered on the floor, soon they all had mugs in their hands. All except Kinneas, who still did not wake. And Mezami, who treated his mug like a hot tub, sinking to his chin with a sigh.

"I'm worried about him," said Cho, resting a hand on Kinneas's blanket-wrapped legs.

Hael sipped. "He's alive. That's about all that can be said. Seen his condition more than enough on the front lines. He's pushed himself too hard."

"It's my fault. He only came here 'cause of me. He's got the Nids 'cause of me." Cho looked around at them all, all silent. "Will he make it?"

"He might. I've seen worse. Though, he'll need treatment. From a real doctor. Myself, I'm not even a field medic. Just picked up a few useful things here and there." Hael finished the rest of her still scalding tea, setting the mug on the floor. "There's nothing more we can do for him."

Cho hid her face in her hands. If only she could sleep now, and wake up with Eilars and Alina, and Kinneas as goofy and alive as ever. All the badness, just a nightmare…

Hael's question called her back. "How did you ever end up in this living graveyard of a town, of all places?"

Cho cradled her warm mug, steam condensing on her chin. "I came here to kill Walazzins."

Hael nodded. She didn't need to be told why. A tear appeared, sizzled, and evaporated from her cheek. "I never got the chance to tell you how immensely sorry I am for your loss."

Staring at the hairline crack in the concrete between her shoes, Cho had yet to partake of her tea. Instead, she let its warmth seep into her palms, its scent returning her to Mount Morbin. If only for a second.

Perhaps sympathetically, Hael's own gaze seemed to shove its way past her physical surroundings, to a far-off place, long ago. "I've replayed the events of that night in my mind a thousand times over. What were the signs? Was there anything at all I could have done?"

Cho did not answer. How should she know?

"Your father was wrong to take a chance on me."

Grabbing Hael's fingers, Cho squeezed.

The soldier stared at their knuckles a moment. "Lady Torvir was already dead when I found her. I pulled Showennu out from under her body. She passed in my arms. After that, I grabbed a gun and ran out, firing at anyone that wasn't one of ours. Thought I'd lose my voice forever, thought I'd shatter the mansion's foundations, I screamed so loud." She paused. "The incendiary grenade came out of nowhere. Funny, what sticks with you. I remember the *plink* of the pin dropping. Or, maybe that's only my imagination. But, either way, the results speak for themselves." She pointed to her mechanical jaw, eye, the stump of her arm, her leg.

Voice light as the swish of jellyfish tentacles through deep waters, Cho said, "Every Walazzin needs to die."

Tears steamed from Hael's cheek like summer rain from a tin roof. "What would it solve?"

"Does it matter?"

Hael searched the bottom of her mug as if she'd find the meaning behind all her suffering hidden among the tepid tea leaves, under the soggy bag. Cho knew that look, the very same one she now cast upon Hael's half-metal face.

When Hael spoke, she addressed the ceiling with a whisper. "The Walazzins are just one cog in a twelve-toothed wheel that's been turning since the beginning of human civilization."

"My family were victims. They were betrayed."

"Not all of them. Your cousin's still alive." Hael fixed her good eye on Cho's. "And you can't believe the Walazzins acted on their own."

Having no answer to that, Cho switched gears. "Something's been bugging me. Who taught ya to play with fire? Never knew you were a Maggo."

"I wasn't. Until that night."

"I thought you're either born magical or not."

"Yeah. That's true, but there are, apparently, some people who can't tap into their Gods-given potential without... help. There're different ways to awaken it, depending on the person. For me, it was trauma." She cleared her throat. "Something in me broke that night, burned away, but there was a trade off. For that part of my soul I'd lost with your parents and siblings, I'd gained a fire within me—roaring inside. The grenade should have killed me, but I lived. It was anger, I think. Anger saved me. When I came to, in some army hospital, I was informed that every last Torvir had 'tragically perished in a cowardly attack committed by foreign agents.' The incident was blamed on Ozari assassins attempting to destabilize the Plutocracy." A glint caught in her organic eye, a spark. "Even though my handlers never said it out loud, I *knew*, if I disagreed, the only way I'd be leaving that hospital bed was in a body bag. After all the skin grafts and secondhand prosthetics and wiring to patch me up, soon as I could, I joined The Authority division created for dispossessed Torvir soldiers like me: the 31st Forward, Department of Tranquility; 'Coneys' became our callsign. We were masterless soldiers, loyal first and always to each other. With the 31st, I trained under specialist Mages. My commanding officer found me the best Igniomancer drill sergeant government money could buy. I learned a lot: my pain threshold, how long I can hold my breath in toxic gas, the easiest way to break an armored man's bones... Found some peace in connecting with the lost grunts who'd served in your parents' good name. Our new Walazzin COs had ordered us to slice through our cords, the symbols of our old oaths of service. 'Cutcords,' the title was meant to shame us, but we all still wore our honor. Low as we were, we were proud of our ties to the past. Between us, there grew a bond—one that can't be severed." She drew a ragged breath. "Spent years finding myself again. I got even better at killing. Even with this patchwork of secondhand parts they grafted onto my bones and nerves. I'm not bragging when I say my unit became one of the very best on the field. Then, one day, out of nowhere, some suit comes to Kadic, where we've been stationed, and he says he's got a job for me." Her knuckles rapped the floor. "Of all the people he could've come to, Jejune offered *me* a contract on *your* life." She laughed. "The Gods are ruthless jokesters."

"I'm a problem," Cho said.

"A loose end. Honestly, I hardly believed you'd be alive after all this time. But I had to be sure. So, I took the job immediately and got my Coneys dropped into this pit. Even as paranoid as I am, though—and that's saying a lot—I never expected Jejune was secretly a big bag of teeth and tentacles wearing human skin like a hat. That's a new one."

"You got him, though? Back at the Lion's Den?"

"Can't kill something like him. Not for real. Death just slows them down. Death is what they're *made* of." Hael purposely left something unsaid, something important. (Cho could tell by the scent of her sweat, the droop of her eyelids.) "He'll be back. One day. And there's *lots* more where he came from." A long silence followed. Then, "You still got your sights on the Walazzins?"

Cho watched Kinneas take hissing, shallow breaths. Her answer surprised her: "I don't know anymore."

"Running's the smart option. You could come with me. Go to ground. Burrow deep."

"While the world burns, yeah? That's your idea?"

"What do you care about the world? What's it ever done for you? I thought you wanted to punish your family's killers, that's all."

"I want justice. I want bad things to happen to bad people."

"Life doesn't work that way."

Cho flung her mug across the room. Like overripe fruit, it burst against the wall, shards of ceramic falling away from a dark splotch of cold, dripping liquid. Kinneas murmured, his facial muscles squeezing into a frown.

"Are you finished?" said Hael. "I was about to say, 'Life doesn't work that way—without a little encouragement.' Sitting around, waiting for divine judgment to lay low your enemies—well, you'll be waiting forever. On the other hand… You listening?"

Cho nodded.

"There's no horror in this or any world too terrible for the Walazzins, but nothing'll be solved if you just knock Wodjaego and Kaspuri's heads off. Next week, there'll be a new Consul. Business as usual. But we have a chance here to do much more than that, and get justice for the Torvir Family in the process. Interested?"

Leaning in, Cho held her breath.

"Figured you'd feel that way." Hael's metal joints squeaked as she shifted positions. "So, you're not interested in doing the smart thing—hiding to fight another day. Well, there's a second path. Bearing in mind my former job on your family's security team, I can't in good conscience recommend it, but my days of 'doing the right thing' are long behind me. I'm goal-oriented now. And, I have a hunch, so are you. So. When the Walazzins assumed control of Torvir Province and all its wealth and Assets, they also absorbed its military. Authority is Authority, after all. That's what they say." She smiled devilishly. "That's what they *think*."

"What d'you mean?"

"Upwards of seventy percent of the Torvir Enforcers and Tranquilizers were deployed here, in Ozar, by the Walazzins. To be used for cannon fodder. With the Torvir Family wiped out, their fighting units are more than expendable. Torvir soldiers are a liability. Better off dead, as far as old man Walazzin and his trollish son are concerned. That's why there's a vanguard of twenty thousand

Torvir soldiers out there, getting ready to charge Peregar's Grief." Her fingers brushed the severed length of orange thread pinned to her jacket. "Twenty thousand veterans. Cutcords, Cho, like me."

"You mean—"

Hael cut her off excitedly. "We swore oaths of service to Lord and Lady Torvir, who were slaughtered by the Walazzins. It's an open secret. We all know it. We get by, day to day, because we're working a job like anyone else. Serving the Consul and the Plutocracy pays the bills. How it's always been. But the Walazzins don't own us. They never had our loyalty. With the Torvir dead, that didn't matter. But the Torvir aren't dead now, are they? Not all of them."

"My cousin." Cho's heart punched her sternum. "And—"

"Your cousin is a tool. No one loves or respects him. There's only *one* person left alive who can command authority over the Cutcords."

It was a rare thing, to be completely aware of the full, life-changing power of a single decision even as it's put in front of you.

"Me," she said, and threads of fate wove into a braid around her, falling heavily upon her shoulders, coiling around her neck. She felt them tugging her in two directions—up to the surface and the light, and down into ever greater depths. Which way led to safety and success, she had no hope of telling. Nevertheless, she must choose: run and hide, or answer her calling.

It seemed she'd been moving toward this choice ever since she'd followed the Walazzins' trail to Ozar. There was a pressure in the air here, a force she'd sensed as she'd run from The Authority, tied herself to Anarkey, and escaped the Lion's Den. This presence she felt all around her, was this the touch of magic? Was she being guided, or did it only seem that way? And, if fate were tugging at her, pushing her along her path, did it loop around her throat a shawl—or a garrote?

The sensation reminded her now so strongly of the cave. When Bizong had shown her the hexagon carved into living, glowing green rock—Chrononite—he'd given an answer to her wordless question: The Abyss.

Though she couldn't understand how, the ideas were so clear in her mind, if only for a second or two. The Abyss was like a great, mindless beast, she thought, reaching, reaching, its tentacles wrapped around every living creature. Directing, nudging, influencing.

"Can you feel it, too?" she whispered to Hael.

Having either not heard or ignored the question, the dutiful, resolute soldier plodded onward, completely unaware of the threads connecting her to Cho, to Cbarassan, to Mezami and Kinneas and every creature on—or under—the earth.

The moment of absolute clarity passed, and Cho's mind shrank down to its usual size of One Standard Cho. She shook off the last waves of giddiness.

The pain medication. Those three little pills must have scrambled her brain. Yeah, that's what'd happened. That's all.

Hael said, "Discounting the handful of cowards who won't heed the call, the only thing standing between Choraelia Torvir and the command of *twenty thousand* battle-hardened soldiers is a *word*. Give the order, and we will fight and die for you. We'll throw ourselves into the lowest hells. For you." Hael took a knee before her. "I've spent eight years waiting for this moment, with shame for my constant companion. Let me redeem myself. Lady Choraelia Torvir, accept me into your service, as I once served your father and mother."

Cho stared at the top of Hael's fire-scarred head.

Twenty thousand soldiers.

Twenty.

Thousand.

Weighed down by the gravity of the decision, she felt fully her age—only fourteen. And, inside her, there was also an eleven-year-old, part-time runaway demanding to know what the hells she'd been thinking, getting wrapped up in an international war?

Well, Cho was done being a victim. Having outgrown the role of Alina's rescued stray, she'd become a fighter, resistor, hacker, Aelf-friend. But would she add 'commander' to that list? 'Killer'?

With a *word*, Hael had said. A *word*.

It's not like she hadn't dreamed of this moment, but only her wildest fantasies had included her at the head of an avenging army. Here, now, she'd been given a chance to reclaim her honor, to take back everything she was owed. To be—unironically—Lady Choraelia Torvir again, a resurgent shadow of her parents' power and prestige. Was that what she wanted?

The threads pulled, and she began to tear.

Hael said, "We could rewrite the destiny of El. Here and now. You and me."

If she turned down this opportunity, she'd be the biggest fool in the long and storied history of fools.

"The Authority stands ready to deliver a final victory to the Empire, and the Walazzins will get the credit. Stop them here, in Ozar—keep them from taking the Seventh Stack—and, win or lose, your name will live forever."

"I don't want to live forever. I want my family back."

"We can't raise the dead, but *you* can make it so no one else has to suffer like you have. That's within your power, Cho. Your power."

"You said yourself that none of it matters. Take out the Walazzins, they'll just be replaced by someone the same or worse."

"If you just kill the Walazzins, yes, sure. But let yourself think bigger." Hael snatched Cho's hand and squeezed. "The Authority isn't real. It's made up of real people who've been trained to obey. Soldiers like me, we just want to serve our country, so we fight. But our leaders' battles aren't bettering the world. Dropping bombs doesn't make anyone freer. It only makes them afraid. Fighting is my purpose, but people like you can *give* people like me something real, something meaningful to fight for."

"I don't know who you think I am, but you're wrong."

"No, Cho. You're the one who doesn't know who she is. You could give hope to Landsiders everywhere. So many of us are starved of it. We need you. You might've been born in The Capital, but when the Elementals betrayed you, they made you one of us."

Taken aback, Cho wondered at the honorary title she'd just been given. "Landsider." Surface-dweller. Someone the Elementals sneered at, a human being not defined by her status and wealth. Freed of the stigma she now realized she'd been trying to offload ever since she could remember.

The Elementals were devouring the whole world, all its resources and peoples included. To be one of them was to be cursed. She'd trade anything to rid herself of that connection, and Hael had just given her permission. A way out.

"After years of searching, I found myself on the battlefield. In a pool of blood, I saw the empty vessel I'd become. I need someone to fill my mind with vision. When I learned you were alive, I hoped—I prayed to the Gods that you would be your parents' daughter—that you'd be more than théy'd dared imagine when they put you under the knife. And my prayers have been answered, Cho. You could be the spark that burns away the old rot to make way for fresh growth. You could be anything you want to be. And, if you'll have me, I will devote every waking second to serving you." Hael bowed her head. "Think of all the good you could do."

How? Cho wanted to scream: How?

Again, she could understand sacrifice and theft, having been on the receiving and giving end of both. She'd seen, even in Bizong's sharp, alien glare, a spark of familiarity. His hate had been her own. And Cbarassan, for all their attempts to stay noble and forward-thinking—hopeful even—bore on their bark-like hide the deep gashes of misery beyond any words' ability to express.

Both Aelf had endured the extinctions of their species. One had found the death he'd chased for so long; the other had stayed behind to tend to the still-living, the still-struggling. They'd each lost so much.

She could understand why they'd chosen as they had, even though their choices had led them down vastly different paths. Now, she found herself similarly challenged. It was her turn to decide who she wanted to become.

Unlike Cbarassan and Bizong, Cho's own species survived. Her tribe, however, was gone. Her family was nothing more than memory. But maybe it didn't have to stay that way forever. If she became Choraelia Torvir again, she could resurrect Torvir Province and its people. She could become the woman her parents had hoped she'd be.

But Hael's mixed signals confused her: The Authority is full of good soldiers, decent people, but led by wicked men; The Authority, not just the Walazzins, must be defeated; Choraelia Torvir must be reborn... but Choraelia Torvir, legitimized and restored to her family's house, would become part of The Authority. How could her name act as a rallying cry for Landsider resistance when that same name had helped build the Elemental Empire?

It shouldn't work. And, even if it did, what then? Should she burn the old world to clear space for the new, or plant the seeds of hope she'd never see flower?

Slapping the heel of her palm against her forehead, she ignored the giant philosophical problems and focused on the facts.

Her family was gone. *She* had been offered the means to settle the score. The choice lay before her. It was hers to make. No one else's.

The threads pulled and guided, though to *where* she could not yet see. She sank deeper into the depths of herself, and held her breath.

At last, she said, "Hael Tiberaira, I accept your oath of service." All the military history books and trash paperbacks she'd read jostled in her mind, feeding her the words and confidence she needed. "Consider yourself promoted to general. (I can do that, can't I? Oh, phew. Awesome.) On one condition."

Hael bowed her head.

"I'm callin' ya 'Tibby,' like I used to."

"Fine," said Tibby, bowing lower to hide her slight smile. "But only in private."

"Granted. Now stand up. You're weirding me out."

On her feet, Tibby said, "What are your orders, my lady?"

"Huh." She hadn't thought about specifics yet. The gears in her mind turned at turbo speed. "How long'll it take for you to get a message out to all the Cutcords?"

"Since your act of sabotage, the normal modes of communication are off the table. However, I've got an idea." Her smile was unsettling.

56

ALINA

SHE WAS HAVING A dream. Not her own.

... its many, many eyes pop. Open. One-by-one. And it crawls out. Renewed, pure. White.

What did it mean?

Her body woke slowly. Ears ringing.

Cheek pressed against cold, foot-worn rock, she opened her eyes. She rolled over. Everything was blurry.

Her thoughts were dew on a stone tower; they clung to but could not penetrate the battered and blasted fortifications of her mind. She was a duchess trapped in her own castle, locked away in one of the forgotten broom closets.

Then, between the hammer-blows of her pulse against her skull, she remembered.

Her phone. The explosion.

The quills of her arm-feathers stood on end. She was still inside Hexhall, yes, but something was wrong.

As her vision cleared, she realized several figures had surrounded her and were closing in. One bent over down, backhanding her face. Felt like touching her arm after she'd slept on it funny.

The dull pain refocused her vision enough for her to cough, shake her head, and push herself to a seated position.

"You look familiar," she said to the one who'd smacked her.

The tattooed, jacked sailor retracted, crossing her bare arms over her bullet-proof vest.

"You're Rancisca Cuenzi, the new Number One Aelfraver." Alina stood up, the other woman's eyeline stopping at her collarbone.

Rancisca spun her fingers in front of her forehead in a foppish little salute. "Always nice to meet a fan. So, you're our contact?"

"Contact?" said Alina, drinking in Rancisca's rippling muscles and the sharp-edged, no-nonsense faces of the others. Most carried several weapons; a couple were unarmed. From all of them emanated strong, distinct Niimantic signatures. "Hang on. You're *all* Ravers, all… ten of you."

The Top Ten Aelfravers of El, pride of The Gild, nodded, flexed, or stretched their rotator cuffs.

In peak physical condition, they'd adorned themselves with platinum time pieces, gem-dusted headphones, and diamond studs. The cost of their collective haircuts could've bought Alina a nice used car (from the back of the lot, but still). Each of their body-hugging, teal-and-black uniforms was shiny, new, and de-signer brand. Their cybernetic enhancements had been installed so cleanly that only the small tattooed serial numbers on their necks, knuckles, and calves gave them away.

"Oh, wow," said Alina, who'd never been in the presence of so much celeb-rity before. (She didn't count her friends and family. Baraam was a big deal to many, but, to her, he'd lost much of his mystique years ago, when she'd helped nurse him through a bad stomach flu. Then there was Ugarda Pankrish, who'd been just so darn approachable that it was easy to forget his status. And Tahtoh had been, well, her Tahtoh. Still, it was kind of cool that she'd personally met or known three out of three of the most recent Number One Aelfravers.)

"Not the brightest, are ya?" Rancisca snorted in her face. "Somehow the De-partment of Tranquility always lands a total moron on the inside."

"The smart ones would not betray their own people," said Xali Sontil, Num-ber Three. "Most rats know to run from trouble." He was taller than Alina, slightly darker-eyed and darker-skinned, with ashen runes sketched onto his face, neck, collar, arms, and any other body parts not covered by his uniform and white velvet shoulder cape.

"A dumb rat's better than no rat at all." Rancisca turned to Alina. "So, rat, you lettin' us in, or you planning to shake us down for autographs first?"

Some of the Ten chuckled, some kicked their heels. All of them were flaring their Niima now.

Feeling the signatures, Alina noted their specialties. *Geomancy, Igniomancy, Divinumancy...*

"You're here for the Hextarchs," she said.

"Got it in one. Good for you." Rancisca clapped her hands. "Kaluu's fiddle, girl!" She rattled off a litany of swearwords. "Get outta the way, or open the door. But, either way, let's finish this. Some of us got places to be."

"Your book tour won't launch itself, eh?" said one of the others, shaking out his shaggy, golden hair. (Must have taken a lot of effort to get that practiced *I don't care what you think of me* style just right.)

"'War hero' will nicely round out my resume. What's it to ya?"

Blondie backed down.

The metal blast doors Rancisca had referred to—the Hextarchy's last barricade—lay sixty or seventy feet down the hall, behind Alina. The worst of her shell-shock worn off by now, it dawned on her that these Aelfravers couldn't be standing here unless the Revomantic bubble protecting Hexhall had been pierced. Which she assumed meant the whole fortress had been returned to the physical world.

She glanced down at what remained of her phone: a twisted, blackened, smoking piece of scrap.

"Which one of you did it?" she said. "Which one of you busted the Revomantic anchor?"

"This supposed to make sense?" asked the one who couldn't stop fiddling with his silvery earring, a tiny holographic blue dragon orbiting it.

"The Locus?" Alina said. "Rimu's Transpiritual L—"

"Girl," said Number Eight, whose name Alina half-remembered from all the Watchbox sandwich commercials. Something like Girga or Gyga. (Or was it sneaker endorsements?) "No more patience. Do as promised. Any problems, ask boss. Not us." The fierce strawberry hue of his sunburn told of vacations in the tropics. He looked fresh off the plane, as if mere hours ago he'd been sipping a tangy alcoholic drink. Something with coconut or maybe star fruit. And a little green paper umbrella.

Confused, Alina stared.

Rancisca threw her arms up and sighed dramatically.

The Top Ten marched past.

Judging by their total lack of understanding what she'd been getting at, Alina assumed none of them had been the one to destroy Hexhall's anchor. So, how...?

Her phone had been the key. Somehow, someone had traced its position and turned it into a bomb. No Revomantic spell she knew of could've managed that. Maybe The Savior had grown impatient, or he'd planned to use her this way from the beginning. But, no, he was a Corpromancer. Tapping her phone was one thing, but focusing a teleportation spell through it? That had to have been some upper-level Divinumancy, or...

Had she confronted Mateus sooner, maybe Hexhall could've been spared its fate. Then again, had she rushed in, she wouldn't have been armed with all the knowledge and understanding now roosting in her mind.

The part of her that once was Dimas clucked, *There's no way to win without someone getting hurt. Drop the speculation. Focus on the present.*

In front of her was living proof The Gild, The Sanctum, and The Authority were working together to annihilate the last enemies of El. Unlike all past wars, which she'd been able to ignore, this time she felt personally responsible.

Her phone. Her presence in Hexhall. The timing was too convenient.

She focused on the present. Being used angered her.

Dashing to bar the Aelfravers' path, she spread her arms. "Who do you work for?"

Xali Sontil said, "The human species." He moved to shove her aside, but a jet of pulverized rock struck his hand.

Niima flaring, Alina said, "Who sent you?"

"We're Gildsmen," said Rancisca, as if that were answer enough. She must have caught something in Alina's eye. It gave her pause. Over her shoulder: "Brolm."

"Yah," said Brolm, a swarthy man with scars on almost every inch of his arms.

Surgery could've given him perfect, baby-smooth skin. With his money, he could have laughed off the cost. Those scars were a statement.

"Brolm, boy," said Rancisca. "Looks like we're goin' it the hard way."

Long-nosed and narrow-eyed, he was every bit a wolf as he snarled. "Ooh, that's my favorite of the ways." From his pocket, he pulled a vial and chugged its gold-flecked, purple contents.

Alina sniffed the air. She knew that scent. *Chymaeric fortissimio.* Street name, "Bull's Blood." An Augmentative Elixir that released all the body's stored adrenaline, allowing for tremendous feats of physical strength. She'd tried it once. The hangover just wasn't worth it.

The fact that Brolm had downed an Auggie was proof these Ravers had come itching for a fight, and having to tear through Alina to get to their targets didn't seem to give them pause.

Nevertheless, she remained in Brolm's way.

The big man laughed. "Hilarious, but now it's time to wake up and realize what you're asking for. I didn't travel thousands of miles to humiliate a little girl."

"Neither did I," said Alina. "But here you are anyway."

His eyelids scrunched until nearly sealed. With each breath, ghostly crimson flames burst from his nose and mouth.

Bull's Blood did make you stronger, but all that borrowed adrenaline came at a cost: it was very hard to think rationally as the Auggie cooked your insides and the fight-or-flight instinct ate up every inch of your brain space.

Alina had known exactly how to get under Brolm's skin. As expected, he immediately did something stupid.

His fingers wrapped around her arm, which he locked in a crushing grip. "Warned her," he told the other members of the Ten. "You all saw it." He breathed in her ear, "This's gonna hurt you *a lot* more than me."

Winding back, he threw a haymaker that definitely would have knocked Alina out—and quite likely would have snapped her neck—had she been human.

She took the punch on the chin. She barely flinched, only blinking at the burst of air.

As Brolm pulled his fist from her face, she grinned at him. She twisted to her right, catching him off-guard, and he lost hold of her. Her claws dug into the meat of his shoulder, applying pressure, her other hand snapping around his wrist. She held him in an armlock.

Brolm groaning, Rancisca stepped forward, a bubble of frost surrounding her.

Alina warded her off with a look, keeping her hostage between them. She clicked her tongue at Rancisca. "Figured you must be something special to have replaced Baraam. The way you let those crusty old dudes at The Gild have it, made them sweat, I liked that. But I see you now. The real you, under the glitz. You're a weapon, like all the other Gild dress-up dolls. All your charm? It's just makeup, stage lights, and good editing." She shoved Brolm forward, and he sprawled on the ground.

Hurriedly, he picked himself up while his friends snickered.

Rancisca crossed her arms. "Who d'you think you are, kid?"

"I'm an Aelfraver."

"Nice. And *I'm* the Consul of New El."

"A traitor's what she is," said Number Five, her blue hair wafting upward, animated by an invisible force. "A double agent. Probably took out our mole. Cut her down, Ranny."

"You're right, Cress. I'll make quick work of this one." Rancisca's neck twitched, tendons popping. "You really stepped in it. Neat trick, taking Brolm's punch. But you'll have to do better than stage magic to beat the best."

"The best? You really think you've earned that title?"

"I am the strongest Raver in the Empire."

"Yeah, *now*. Because everyone better either quit or died. You couldn't measure up to Ugarda Pankrish's knee."

The Number One Aelfraver tried to play the comment off, but it was obvious Alina had hit a sore spot. Whether about her height or hunter's pride, Rancisca fumed. "Don't go comparing me to some fossil who got himself offed by a whack job pavement-padder. I was the youngest Master Aquamancer in the east."

"You're a swabbie in a leotard."

Rancisca actually shrieked. The moisture in the corridor crystallized, and a shower of icicles shot toward Alina from all directions. As soon as she'd finished casting her spell, Rancisca leapt forward, ready to follow through with a front kick.

Ice shards flying toward her, Alina contemplated her next move.

During her bout with Kellfyute, she'd discovered just how far she'd transcended her old teenage Geomancer self, and her exchange with Brolm two minutes ago had reminded her of how physically strong she'd become. Even still, that couldn't be the extent of her new powers. All of Dimas's skills should now be hers. Because she *was* Dimas. For nineteen years, they'd stayed separate, but now they were one being again.

Full acceptance of her new self had unearthed in her untold reserves of power, but how deep did the well go? How high soared those clouds? *All of Dimas's skills...*

The icicles suddenly veered off course, splintering against the ground and walls around Alina. A few whizzed toward the Ten, who hopped out of the way, but not one touched her.

Skin coated in armor of greenish ice, Rancisca, meanwhile, occupied herself screaming and kicking at thin air.

"Ranny," said Number Five, the one called Cress. "Get hold of yourself! Ranny!"

"'Ranny' is busy," said Alina. "Can I take a message?"

"Caution, fellows. This one's a Revomancer," said Xali Sontil.

"Technically accurate. But that's only one small part of a big picture."

And Dimas had taught Ruqastra everything she knew, which meant that Alina should also be able to...

A wave of bubbling, hissing black energy swept outward from her, creating a sphere of force that locked all eleven of them inside the cramped corridor, cutting off all possibility of retreat.

Alina tugged *Rego* her cloak tighter, and it hugged her, protecting her as any Sister would. Then she pulled *Ida* over her face.

She must have been quite a sight to behold—a lithe, black-shrouded, red-beaked ghoul, mistress of the eternal dark beneath the world of men. Luckily for the Top Ten, they wouldn't have to *see* her for long.

Inside her orb of hissing gray-black energy, her little pocket of nightmare, she could control her enemies' senses; she removed their sight and watched them scramble and bump into each other. Great warriors, reduced to children falling out of bed, fumbling blindly on the floor.

"I don't think anyone could've been more surprised than I was." Alina took a step forward, hand-chopping the back of Rancisca's neck. The Number One

Aelfraver's head smacked against the wall, and she fell to the ground. Breathing still, but unconscious, she wore a grimace of pain.

Claws lengthening, blade-feathers slicing through the undulating folds of her cloak, Alina paused, remembering. "Yeah, it's fair to say I know a thing or two about Revomancy. I helped invent it."

None of the Aelfravers seemed quite so keen to challenge her now.

Taking a step forward, she asked, "What happened to all your cute little jokes?"

They stepped back.

She laughed.

The semitransparent membrane of crackling, black energy grew denser, thicker. It coated the skin, seeping into the pores. The ancient strength of the Sevensin—Alina tasted it like fat on her tongue, felt it like beach glass between her fingers.

Did it have a ceiling, this power? Now was as fine a time as any to find out.

57

CHO-ZEN

KINNEAS FINALLY OPENED HIS eyes.

Cho had spent the past hour or two fretting over him, rinsing and replacing the damp cloth on his forehead, dribbling water onto his parched lips.

From his sweat-soaked bedroll, he smiled at her. "You're okay." He coughed.

"Hey, Kin," she said, her tears pattering on his shirt. "Good to have ya back."

"Anarkey. They're…"

She shook her head, her gaze falling.

"Oh. So, that's it, then. If only I coulda—"

"Not your fault."

"The Tranqs busted in, so damn many of them. People dying all around me. Then, next thing I know, I'm in a cell with you. I tried waking you, but you wouldn't answer. I was so scared you were… Merciful Buthmertha, how'd we ever get out?"

"A friend." She looked up at Tibby, whom she'd ordered to treat Cbarassan's wounds.

Kinneas groaned. "They're all gone. All the non-humans, dead. They didn't stand a chance. But the Tranqs, they didn't kill me. They dragged me outta bed—" He gasped, choking.

Cho shushed him, softly. "You're safe now. I'm gonna take care of you."

"I'm alive." He seemed uncertain.

"You are. And I swear I'll punish everyone who came after you. They'll all pay."

"I'm not asking you to do that."

"Ya don't gotta. They hurt my friend. Now I'll hurt them."

"Cho, please, don't—you'll be—"

"Hey, now. Easy does it, bud. Close your eyes."

"But, it'll never end." His head lolled to the side. Feverishly, his eyes runny and purple rimmed like toxic swamp flowers, he murmured, "Please. You don't have to do this. Just stop. Everything's a choice. Even hate." He closed his eyes. "I can't die worrying about you."

That remark. How dare he make this about him?

But, wait. That's what she was doing, too.

Who was she angry at? Who *for*?

"I'll be alright," she told him. "You just take care of yourself, just this once, okay?" She kissed his forehead.

Eyelids fluttering, soon, he slept again.

His words caught like bits of gristle in her mind as she chewed on them. *It'll never end,* he'd said. *Everything's a choice.*

Everything, huh?

She couldn't accept that. Neither she nor any of the Walazzins' victims had *chosen* their fates.

One thing was for damn sure: the end of her story wasn't going to be "forgive and forget." Her journey couldn't be condensed to a one-liner on the back of a grocery store greeting card.

Why should *she* always have to be the better person? Did Kaspuri Walazzin not deserve even one millionth of the suffering he'd caused? Seemed like the powerful constantly managed to wriggle their way out of all consequences. Well, if she had anything to say about it, their lucky streak was about to end. Fate would always spring its final trap on even the most cunning and elusive of creatures, and Cho would be its instrument tonight. She was well suited for the job, a being of shadow, an animal nestled in the sand, camouflaged. For eight long years, she'd patiently waited for the chance to ensnare and strangle her prey.

She could almost smell Kaspuri's inky blood.

Murmuring in his sleep, Kinneas tried to turn over, but couldn't.

With each passing hour, he grew weaker. He should be more furious than anyone else, but *Everything is a choice,* he'd said.

Cho swept onto her palm the shards of the tea mug she'd smashed earlier. A piece nicked her finger. She tossed the bits into the trash bin, and watched a glob of blood spread out and creep beneath her fingernail.

Sure. Fine. Her choice, yeah? Then she'd choose fairness: a just end for an unjust man and his hideous family. With Tibby on her side, she could at last bloody the tyrants. Doing anything less would be immoral.

Cho hadn't been born with any magical abilities, and she certainly was no Aelfraver. But she could still slay monsters.

58

ALINA

BLANKETED IN BLACK, THE corridor was consumed by stillness. For a moment, only the faint fizzles and pops of Alina's oozing bubble of darkness could be heard. Then, her excited breaths filled the air. In response, the Top Ten called out, their confused shouts muffled by her viscous fog of dream.

Rego shielded her body from the spell's numbing effects. *Ida* protected her face, allowing her to see clearly, where her opponents stumbled and fell. Through whispers, she force-fed them the unease and anxiety that had been her companions for most of her life. They tried to appear unimpressed, but it was obvious their nerve had been dampened along with their senses. The smart approach would have been spreading out to surround her. Instead, they groped sightlessly. Finding each other, they huddled, back-to-back.

Their fear empowered Alina, just as Ruqastra had claimed it would. The rush was intoxicating. Never before had she been so confident, so in control. That sweetness, however, had a bitter aftertaste. She didn't have time to dwell on her growing disgust, though, because the remaining nine Ravers rallied.

They put on as good a show as they could, flinging spells of all types at her—fireballs, thorny vines, shrapnel from their pockets, a lightning bolt or two. She calmly weaved between the attacks so that the casters either missed entirely or harmed one another. Blind, infuriated, they screamed as they were cut, burnt, and knocked down by their own comrades.

Good old Brolm managed to guess her location and kick at her solar plexus, but he was too slow. His foot struck the wall instead, his yowl indicating he'd broken several small bones.

"And that's why we don't kick with our toes," she said.

Distracted by her own giddiness, she failed to notice what Number Nine was doing before it was too late. Straining, sweat soaking his shirt, he plucked at invisible threads crisscrossing the air.

Alina had forgotten that, rare as they were, not all Revomancers were on her friends' list.

With a ten-fingered twist, Number Nine dispelled the black bubble.

The Ravers blinked away their blindness, picking themselves up, and they turned on Alina (with the exception of Brolm, who had crawled away, unable to stand).

Her advantage gone, she faced her panting, bloodied adversaries. Sure, she'd taken two of them out of the fight, but that left eight upright. Eight elite hunters. Professional killers.

Reading their surface-level thoughts, she could tell they were seconds away from frenzy. Their Niima burn-off, fueled by fury and years of conditioning, was immense. You could've spread it on toast, it was so thick and cloying.

Well, she'd poked the lion's nose with a stick. Now what? Despite her new weapons and self-assurance, she still was Alina at heart: her arrogance had kept her from running when she should have; her inexperience, from efficiently defeating her opponents.

Orders, ideas, and instructions tangled in her mind, each cord a separate cry demanding her attention. The noise of her soul was a chorus of jumbled voices. She couldn't understand a single phrase or word. Though they were her own thoughts, they were alien in language and meaning, and the more she struggled to make sense of them, the more of a senseless murmuring they became.

With great effort, she hushed the voices, and tried to think her way out of her current deadly problem.

Mostly stalling for time, but also curious, she focused on the Gildsman Revomancer. His face, unlike hers, was uncovered. He wore no cloak of dream. She said, "Not bad, your counterspell. But, I gotta ask, where are your Sisters?"

"What?" He swept his sweaty locks from his brow.

"Your Sisters. The basic tools of Revomancy? *Ida, Rego*?"

His blank stare answered for him.

"You seriously don't know what I'm talking about, do you? Yowza. That's a pretty ridiculous gap in your education. Who even trained you?"

The scrawniest of the Ten, he stuck out his bony chest. "I'm self-taught. I pored over the ancient tomes and Lorestones of The Crystallarium. I revived the lost art. I am Azuta, the only Master of Revomancy since…" He trailed off, understanding dawning on his face as he saw Alina in a new light.

She forced her way into his thoughts. *Since Dimas K'vich? Good guess.* Her mental punch rocked him, but she wasn't done. She gave him a glimpse of what she truly was—*dark wings, hunter of hunters, shaper of nightmares*—and he gulped. Actually gulped.

You're of his blood? he thought at her.

She nodded. *I'm a real Revomancer.* Out loud, she added, "'Self-taught,' huh? So, to be clear, you shelled out all those tuition fees just so that the Gild instructors could shove you into the dustiest corner of the library and tell you to 'figure it out'? You basically majored in 'Light Reading.' Is it too late to get a refund?"

In a real fight, there was no such thing as cheating—just different means of winning. Azuta had much less control over his powers than Alina did, and she used this against him. Revomancy grows from the imagination, and his was running wild. His emotions spilled like water over the rim of his mind, soaking his colleagues. What he felt, they felt—magnified.

Thus, Alina's shot at The Gild ended the brief intermission. To defend their honor, bellowing and braying, the eight Aelfravers swarmed her again.

She felt she really ought to be panicking, but she didn't. Perhaps this was because she'd glimpsed into Azuta's mind and found a young man just as off-balance as she was. Or, maybe it was the shift in tone of her thought-chorus, still garbled but approving. The voices were trying to tell her something.

Uninvited but welcome, memories sprang forth:

There she was, in front of the wall-wide row of mirrors at The School, her grandfather running drills with her and the other students. Pacing the line of practitioners, critiquing all, but focusing especially on her. Her minor mistakes. Constantly adjusting the alignment of her shoulders, the angle of her knee. "Widen your stance." "Raise your hands." "Lower your stance." "Tuck in your backside." "Switch your front foot." "Don't stand on your toes! The balls of your feet, now. This isn't the ballet!"

It was strange to think that these memories were of her teaching *herself*. Stranger still was her growing awareness of countless additional memories, spanning dozens of centuries. Visions of places and times that had been implanted in her mind but that, nevertheless, nestled naturally in the cracks, as if they'd always been there. She heard two distinct voices—Dimas's and hers, separating from the hundreds of others—gradually harmonizing. *You are more than you were before* became *I am more than I was before.*

She didn't dwell on the paradox of being and not-being herself. It threatened her with a headache she didn't have time for. All she needed was the intuitive understanding that—beyond her expanding magical abilities—she could now *also* drag out of herself the full expertise and literally thousands of years of Dimas's experience in the martial arts:

Clearly, then, she saw herself as her Tahtoh. Depending on how you counted it, they— she—would have been about forty centuries old at the time but appeared to be no more than thirteen. The newest arrival among the first years, she wore the teal training uniform of a Gild novice. There were a hundred others like her in the Iron Wheel training yard. The drill master had stepped away, and two larger novices thought they'd amuse themselves by throwing the new boy to the ground. Unfortunately for them, the new boy was Dimas/Alina, who broke their hip bones with a back kick each.

Years later, with her mint-condition Raver X License tucked in her wallet, she slogged through sewer tunnels. She peered into the dark through the slits in Ida, her red crow mask, and enshrouded in the folds of Rego, her midnight cloak. Ahead, coiled around the ancient machinery of the cistern—the Lamia she'd been tracking. Without warning, the stinger on their tail whipped toward her face. She ducked under the swipe, wrapped her scarf around the creature's tail, and redirected their momentum so that they stabbed themselves instead.

Later still, old and gray, she strolled along a narrow, cobblestone street at sunset. To drink in the gathering serenity of the dark, she had left behind her cloak and mask. A mugger fell upon her at moonrise, knife aglow. She smacked the man's chest with the flat of her palm, and he went flying, crashing into some crates. His fellows, hiding in the shadows, thought better of trying their luck. Wise of them. Treachery and darkness, these were hers and hers alone. She adjusted her wide-brimmed hat and moved on.

The flashes of memory came faster and faster, and, with them, understanding and muscle memory. With them, the realization that she had stopped thinking of what *he'd* done versus what *she'd* done. His skills were now hers, completely her own. *I am more than I was before.*

She was more than just a decent student of self-defense. More than the girl who'd almost died at the Battle of City Hall.

She could win.

A flame-wreathed fist flew at her face. A mesh of hook-thorned vines. A line of stone needle darts. She dodged them all, bouncing like a tumbleweed freed from the earth. With ease and grace, she sidestepped a flying kick, shoulder-bashing her attacker, who was pitched backward against the wall. The stone cracked with the force of the collision; his body slapped onto the ground like a slab of meat onto a cutting board.

The Ravers paused to regroup and reassess.

With each charge, they became ever more frustrated. As they grew sloppier, she became increasingly agile, precise. Their spells and strikes she blocked with shields of stone or knocked aside with her rock-sheathed arms. Their Revomancer's attempts to invade her thoughts skidded off the ridges of her scowling mask. She redirected one of his illusions back at him, spiking it into his mind, and he fell, screaming, pawing at his eyes and throat. Pink buds burst from the ground, flowering and spewing glistering pollen into the air. She swirled her cloak in a figure-eight, knuckles cracking as she bent and hooked her fingers. With a gasp, she separated her hands, and a gust of wind plastered the walls with the poisonous pollen, withered the flowers, and knocked down the Top Ten.

Posting on her elbows, blue-haired Cress coughed. "Xali, you said she's a dream-walker. But the little brat's lobbing stones and making wind tunnels!"

"Geomancy. Luxomancy," said Azuta. "Earth and air. Purely opposite elements…"

"What are we fighting?"

"… not human."

The Geomancer, who'd been shooting pebbles like bullets at Alina's head, tapped his watch, and a fuzzy blue image and paragraph of text projected from its face. "I knew I recognized you from somewhere. You're her, aren't you? The rebel from Truct."

Exhausted, Alina sighed. "Could we move this along?"

"Good old Truct. Fungal infection of a town."

"You *are* her. K'vich, right?" said Cress. Her eyes snapped to Alina's. "Any relation to…? Never mind, don't really care. Your wanted posters make you out to be some nobody *misckie* thrill-junkie. A basic boulder-tosser."

"Inbred Terrie trash," said the Geomancer.

"Foolish to underestimate. She is Aelf, obviously," said Giga (or Gyrga), pumping up his designer sneakers. Blood matted his sideburns.

"A hybrid," said the Igniomancer, spitting sparks.

"Quiet. Cease your clucking." Xali Sontil arose. "We came here to exterminate the Hextarchy, but we are—first and always—Aelfravers. What the fates have sown, we must reap. Thus, we will slay this thing. This masquerading creature—" he pointed a bloody, split-nailed finger at Alina—"has boldly been living among us, our people, in the Empire, for quite too long. We will not let it escape. Uphold your oaths, Gildsmen." He reached behind his back, grimacing, and withdrew twin blades of bone from the flesh of his shoulders. Jagged, dull killing tools. "I'd say you are a Draaken-class, given your strength. But your emulation of human magical abilities, and your humanlike appearance, suggest you are a Legionari of some kind, a Hideling perhaps. Well. What, in fact, are you?"

Alina made a rude gesture.

The other Aelfravers came to Xali Sontil's side.

Thwacking his bone blades against the ground, he said, "Understand, I ask mainly so that I may properly catalog your remains for future scientific inquiry. Nothing to say? No matter. Let the autopsy discover your secrets." He lunged, both weapons extending.

Alina leapt over him and directly into the path of a front kick, three punches, and a fireball. She ducked the last and blocked the rest with her arms, stumbling. The Ravers encircled her, unleashing blow after blow. She sidestepped, deflected, and counterattacked with certainty, without any wasted movement. Muscle memory guided her. Self-confidence swelled in her chest.

But it wasn't enough.

Too many of their strikes landed—a roundhouse kick to her leg, a knee to her gut. All her effort went into reacting, faster and faster, dodging the fatal cuts of bone blades and the lashings of thorn whips. Then a chop to the back of her neck pitched her forward. Dizzy, she heard Cress shout, "That one was for Rancisca, freak!"

Alina caught herself and charged Xali Sontil, using him as a battering ram against the others. Discovering too late that he knew how to grapple better than she did, she couldn't keep him from wriggling free, planting his feet, and leaping upward, launching her into the air.

She made an "X" with her arms, protecting her body, as she took a barrage of magical projectiles (sickles of blue energy, lightning bolts, jets of flame) that slammed her against the ceiling. Her skin and clothes smoking, reddening with her blood, she surrendered to gravity's pull and landed on the ground back-first. Winded.

When her sight returned, she rolled over, lifted her crow mask, and hawked a glob of bloody phlegm.

"Fine," she said, struggling to get up. "I can see—hoo, am I outta breath. I *see* now why you're the cream of the crop. Pretty tough, gotta hand it to ya. Oof."

Xali Sontil swished his blades through the air. "You have fought fiercely, treacherous beast. I ask you one last question: might you be a Hybrid? Does a drop of humanity flow through your veins?"

She spat. "Who cares?"

"I do. If even one one-hundredth human you be, you own a soul, a soul that I am duty-bound to pray for."

"And if I'm one hundred percent Aelf?"

"Then none shall mourn your loss, aberration that you are."

Clenching her jaw, pressing her lips tight, Alina held back. She felt completely certain that the world would be better, kinder, fuller without this man, but she must not kill him.

Even though she could hardly stand, even though they would probably have killed her a minute later, and even though she had no idea how far she could push herself before reaching the point of no return, she still believed she could win. Incredibly, she'd been holding her own against the Ten. Her wounds were regenerating; her list of abilities, growing; and her memories, organizing. If she just held out a little longer...

Then she thought of Cho, and her shame choked her pride.

Cho was in danger. Kinneas and Mezami, too. Nothing should have mattered more. Yet, when every minute counted, Alina had wasted far too many of them locked in Hexhall, pursuing the answers entombed in her own soul. Answers she'd had access to since before she'd dreamed of coming to Ozar, before she'd even climbed Mount Morbin. The truth about her "family" had been hers to claim all along, but until today she'd lacked the courage to face it. Now, there simply wasn't time.

It didn't take the mirror of The Abyss to show her how selfishly she'd behaved. What in the Seventy-Seven hells was wrong with her? Her friends needed her, and she'd let herself become distracted. Again. Friendship demanded self-sacrifice, but she'd been unyielding, unwilling to give, unable to listen. Her choices—her secrets—had isolated her. It was her fault their circle of trust had shattered. And it was her determination to do everything her own way, always, that had led them down their lonely paths of violence, of self-destruction.

"Maybe I've always been a monster," she said.

Steady breaths burned through the fog of her wrath. Her welling disgust with Xali Sontil and his cocky colleagues ebbed like the tide. Like sand, her desire to know herself, at last, sifted through mental crevices, falling away from the crystalline knowledge that Cho, Mezami, and Kinneas needed her.

Victory was irrelevant. What good was power, if she couldn't save those she loved?

Lifting her head, she opened her mouth, not to dignify Xali Sontil's bigoted comments with a response, but to end the fight and move on. She emitted a noise heard by humans only once this century: the grating, piercing, jet-engine scream that had torn through the skies of New El on the last morning of Dimas's life. That same inhuman cry burst from her lungs now.

The entire corridor shaking, pebbles and dust falling, she emptied everything she had into it, every ounce of indignation, and she forced the Aelfravers to their knees, to their bellies. They could do nothing as she passed between them, still screaming.

If her exploded phone and the ensuing fight hadn't yet woken all of Hexhall, her shriek certainly would have.

Burying their heads in their arms, the Top Ten wailed. Alina read the pain on their faces, but could not hear what they said, nor did she care.

She left them behind, still screaming. At this point, she kept up the noise mainly to see how long she could. She only stopped, half a minute later, when she'd put a few hundred feet between her and the stunned Ravers.

Filling her lungs again, she saw a cluster of Covenants round the bend in the corridor. Of all different shapes and sizes, ranging in number of limbs from two to twelve, the line of yellow-robed warriors sprinted past. Alina only caught flashes of detail as they went. One had flaming red hair and pale blue skin (inheritance of an Iorian bloodline); another, about two feet tall and beaked (a *Quixii?*), swung from the purple-black horns of a night-furred lioness (a *Xyloph*). As one, they each dragged from their pockets and belts a length of yellow cloth and blindfolded themselves. The loss of their sight somehow only increased their speed. Scythes, darts, daggers, chain-swords, and other weapons came free. With synchronized footfalls and breaths, the Covenants went as one.

Alina counted twenty Covenants rushing the invaders, but she detected only six Niimantic signatures—ones she now easily recognized as the Hextarchs'. (So, when the Covenants blindfolded themselves, they became vessels for their Sevensin masters' power. She squirreled that trick away for future use.)

Her ears pricked as the Top Ten yelled at each other. She didn't envy them the mess headed their way, but it wasn't her problem.

Turning her back on the fight, she began to run.

Sure-footed, Alina jogged through the darkness as if she'd come this way a thousand times. Maybe she had. The air in her lungs, the crunch of rock through the soles of her sneakers—familiarly alien.

The ambient, lulling hum of the fantastical had dissipated, replaced by the echoes of her breaths and the metronome of her heartbeat. Much of her earlier stroll into the Hextarchs' inner sanctum was a blur to her now, a jumble of misty color and mental record-scratching, but she could have sworn the stone corridor and chasm-crossing bridge had taken longer to traverse on the way in. The likely explanation was that Hexhall had been shunted back onto the physical plane, the removal of the anchor having stripped its pathways and chambers of their dream logic.

Maybe three minutes after she'd left the Top Ten, Alina came to the big metal doors with the blue eye beside them. The doors were ajar, the eye lidded with steel. There were no guards, which made sense. They'd probably been the ones who'd called for backup and then rushed to their gods' defense.

Nevertheless, the quiet was off-putting. Worse, however, was the distant but unmistakable noise of gathering, agitated people.

Hexhall was waking up.

Trusting her feet to lead her, she left the terraced guard room/entrance chamber, eventually coming to the colossal, open common area with its six spires of stone reaching up dozens and dozens of levels. These spires still held all the same apartments and shops, but the fortress city no longer boasted its view of interdimensional space. Gone, too, were its ethereal bridges. Above, below, and all around, there was only the primordial rock of Ozar. No sun, no moon—only earth.

The Ozari could feel the ending of their shared dream, a dream passed from parent to child for generations, which had been obliterated in a mere moment. They stuck their heads out of windows and stood in doorways. Throngs of them piled on the platforms and clogged the courtyards.

A small Aelf crossed Alina's path. They were bulbous-headed, pale, with webbed fingers and toes—a child.

She crouched, hands resting on her knees. "Lose your parents?"

The Aelf did not answer her, at least not verbally. They instead wiggled their long digits, elbows perpendicular with the ground. Their knees bobbed up and down. Once, twice.

This Aelf was a *Crûb*, a natural cave-dweller, preferring damp burrows. A very rare sight in El. Most Ravers believed them extinct.

Alina gestured over the *Crûb* child's shoulder, indicating a pair of larger *Crûb*. The parents.

They came over, wrapped their arms around their child before signing to Alina, who had never learned their language... but Dimas apparently had.

Through shared memory, she understood what they were communicating: *What has happened?*

Another frayed strand of knowledge stitched itself to Alina's conscious mind as she intuitively replied to the parents' question. *There has been an attack*, she signed.

What will happen to us?

It isn't safe to be around panicking people. Get inside for now. Wait for orders from the Covenants.

The *Crûb* parents side-eyed each other but put on brave faces when their child glanced up at them.

The child signed to their parents, *She looks like one of them.* To Alina, questioningly: *Lightbringer human?*

No, corrected one of the parents. *One of us.* They gave a flat-toothed smile.

Buthmertha be with you. Alina bowed her head.

She pressed onward into the crowd of citizens of the Seventh—and final— Stack.

The Covenants were out in force, holding increasingly nervous people in check with metal riot shields. Non-Covenant soldiers, uniformed in simple gray and green fatigues, raised barricades and activated missile launchers and gun turret installations. The guns' mechanisms squealed like antique train wheels as the weapons were rotated into position. Facing the front gates.

Alina could have broken through the defenses, but worried that would put her in their crosshairs (and cause a lot of collateral damage). She shouted at the Covenants to let her through, but her voice was only one among the many fearful.

Only the soldiers moved freely, directed into single-file columns by megaphone-amplified sergeants-at-arms.

At the end of her patience, she looked around. None of the citizens paid her any attention as they loudly demanded answers and recommendations from their defenders, so she ducked low. Standing again, she'd changed *Rego's* color to Covenant yellow and rendered a six-sided Hextarchy tattoo on the back of her hand. She showed both to the line of soldiers ahead and was let through (ignoring the uproarious protests of the people behind).

She fell in step with a column of green and yellow hoods armed with guns, staves, and spears, and followed them down a long hallway and into a gatehouse. Torchlight danced in the eyes of hundreds of Ozari warriors representing three dozen or more species. Their captains—a couple human, the rest Aelf—gathered them into platoons, then squads. Searching for a way out, Alina heard only snatches of what they were saying: "shield's down"; "Hextarchy under assault"; "last defense"; "invaders by the thousands"; "outer Wall has fallen"; "eternal reward"; "valor"; "for our way of life."

The *Jallantope* Covenant to Alina's right said, "The Wall's breached. It was supposed to have been impregnable. So, this is the doom the Hextarchy foretold long ago: the Enlightened One has come for our souls. His Lightbringers shall sweep away our safe shadows and sear with fiery gaze our wretched, naked husks."

"Sounds… intense," Alina muttered. *The Enlightened One.* She'd heard that title before.

Three rows ahead, a hood fell back from short, ruby pink hair.

She shoved her way forward to where Vessa hastily tightened the straps on her body armor, whip dangling at her hip, and said, "Hey."

"Alina." Vessa pulled her into a hug. "What are you doing out here? Got the call fifteen minutes ago: The Authority's cracked our Revomantic shield, and they've breached the Wall. Our outer defenses are overrun. They're pouring in from all sides. Us fighters inside Hexhall, we're all that's left." She took in Alina's yellow cloak but didn't comment. "By the way, was a bit worried to find an empty bed when I woke up. Decided I'd blame it on cold feet."

"That does sound like me."

"But now you're here."

"Now I'm here."

"Well? Care to fill me in?"

"Look. There's so much I want to tell you. It's killing me not to. I get that there's stuff going on that's way bigger than both of us. The Sanctum. The Authority. The Top Ten coming after the Hextarchs."

"Wait. The Gild is here? Now?"

"A crew of your pals went after them."

Vessa took a breath. "I trust my comrades."

"Against the Ten?"

"Against the world and every Demon of the Seventy-Seven Hells."

Alina listened to Vessa's heartbeat. Steady. "I wish I had your faith. I wish…" Vessa's heartbeat quickened. Fingernails digging into her palms, Alina said, "There's something else. I owe it to you, I think, and I'm just not gonna get another chance to—" A siren went off, and it seemed like it wouldn't be stopping any time soon, so she shouted over it, "There's no way to say it without you hating me, and you'll be right to. Which really sucks because—" She rubbed her nose with her clawed, inhuman hand. "Because—you know, that bar we were dancing in? When the DJ built up to the drop on that remixed version of *Cucumber Scythe* by Fl4Ptr4p? Like, when you looked at me, and we both were shouting the chorus at each other?"

Visibly straining to hear and focus over the siren, Vessa yelled, "What're you saying?"

"I'm trying to say it's just awful timing, falling in love with you." She added, "Or whatever," in an attempt to recover a handful of Cool Points. But the damage had been done.

Little tendrils of black makeup slalomed down Vessa's cheek as her eyes watered. She didn't say anything. What was there to say? What could she have possibly said?

"I love you." Alina lingered on the words. "But I'm poisonous to everyone I love. So, yeah. Um. Goodbye."

Squirming between the ranks of soldiers, she stormed off—or, she tried to. A sting, like a wreath of nettles around her elbow, stopped her in her tracks. She followed the length of Vessa's whip to Vessa's eyes.

"That's it? Just like that?" said the Covenant. "You drop a bomb like that and *just walk away?*"

"The kind of baggage I'm dragging... trust me when I say you don't want any part of it."

"I will decide what I can handle. Now, what were you doing, sneaking around Hexhall?" Two types of venom coursed through her tone—warning and something else. Something rawer.

Drunk off that mixture, Alina still protested, "There's no time."

"Give me the abridged version." Vessa pulled, further restricting her captive's blood circulation. "What did you do?"

"You've got your battle to fight, and I've got mine. Let me go!"

"Who're you really running from?"

Arm bowing, blood trickling from her gray skin, Alina growled. She could have overpowered the Covenant, punted her through the ceiling. Physically, it would've been easy to do—but Vessa had snared more than her arm.

"Fine. You want the truth?" Unable to meet Vessa's eyes, Alina focused on the mirrored crescent moons tattooed on her forehead. "I seduced you to get close to your gods. (Wow, it sounds so much worse out loud.) They were gatekeeping information I needed, secrets kept from me my entire life. Now that I know, part of me wishes I didn't. But *all* of me would take it back rather than hurt you again."

"'Seduced' me, huh?"

"Somewhere along the line, it got heavier than that. I dunno."

"Alina."

"I, uh, I've never felt this way before, so."

Vessa cracked up. She slackened her grip, and the whip uncoiled.

Alina flexed her freed arm.

Vessa burst out laughing. "Here I was—Oh, I can't breathe," she wheezed. "Here I was, thinking I was the predator, when actually I've been the prey. I feel like such an idiot now, for lying awake, guilty at the thought of having seduced *you.*"

Alina blinked. *"What."*

"There were three of us involved in the conspiracy: Cbarassan, me, and my Lord Aam. It's not normal that a group of Covenants are summoned for a private audience with just *one* of the Hextarchs. Normally, they deliver their edicts to us unanimously. But then they heard about you. Something about Cbarassan's intel had gotten them all worked up and at each others' throats. Right off, I was intrigued. We all were. Then I heard your name, and I knew it should be me they send to meet the Vending Machine Girl. I did owe you one for saving my life at City Hall. Once I volunteered, Lord Aam gave me the job of assessing your intentions and, if you were a potential ally, bringing you in."

"If it turned out I wasn't? A friend, I mean?"

Vessa patted her whip. "This right here's the best you could've hoped for. And Lord Aam would've treated you less tenderly. Again, can't stress enough how weird it was that the Hextarchs had their eye on you, a Raver from the boonies. They've been cagey about the details, but ever since The Savior came to town a few years back, our Lords have been watching for signs of special arrivals. You were one, Aam was sure of it. You were a sign."

"Of?"

"The end. Or a beginning. It depends on who you ask. Some of the Covenants started a rumor about you, you know. That you're the Achemir. God and god-killer."

There was that name again, the one Cbarassan had used. *Achemir.* Alina logged that tidbit away for future anxious pondering. "I'm just an orphan of Truct. And you were supposed to bring *me* in? Turn *me*?"

"Like you said, it got 'heavier.' Can't say exactly when. But it did."

"You tricked me. You tricked *me.*" Alina shook her head, grinning—probably like an idiot.

"Might say we both screwed up. Hard."

"We are *excellent* spies, clearly. But what happens now? With this." She pointed at herself, then Vessa. "Us."

"Starting as an accident still counts as starting."

Alina held up her gray arms, black blade-feathers glinting in the torch light. "I'm a monster."

"Promise?"

"This is serious. I don't know how it all works. It's still jumbled in my head. All these voices—and I literally just found out that I'm, like, five or six *thousand* years old."

"Really?" Vessa's eyes widened. "You're joking." She squinted at Alina. "You *aren't* joking. Eh. I've always had a thing for older women anyway."

Sirens still screaming, soldiers and Covenants leaned in to listen to their officers bellowing commands. More and more fighters piled into the gatehouse. The press of bodies drove Vessa and Alina into each other's arms, forehead to forehead.

Her lips to Vessa's ear, Alina said, "For you, I wish I could be human."

Vessa cupped her chin, kissed her. "'Human' is a state of mind. There's nothing between you and me." Their fingers interlaced.

In Alina's mind, they were at the club again. The stink of beer puddles, and the sweat, and bouncing to music blasted through a blown-out speaker. "I wish I could stay."

"We have to fight. Probably die, most of us."

"I know." Alina cried. "I still wanna be here with you, but I have to go."

Joined at the waist, they stared at each other. The world around them became a gently turning vortex of smoke, a waking dream.

"It's about your uncle," said Vessa.

"I have to stop him."

"He's like you?"

"A problem."

"I was gonna say 'powerful.'"

"He's also *me*. Sorta. It'd be impossible to explain. Short version: we share a soul."

Vessa rubbed her eyes. This was, no doubt, a lot to process. Taking Alina's hand: "When we make it through this, whether it's tomorrow, next week, next month, or next *year*..." She searched for the words. Becoming frustrated, she settled on one more kiss, which Alina didn't mind (preferred). "*When*, you hear me?"

Alina nodded.

"Good."

The moment was over. The roar and heat of the real world flooded her senses again.

"Now, go take down your uncle, or whatever he is. Do what you gotta do to make it. Then we'll talk."

Rushing through a confusing series of directions, Vessa instructed her on how to reach the nearest postern, a secret exit from Hexhall that would give her a straight shot to the Wall the Elementals called Peregar's Grief.

Then Vessa cracked her whip overhead and shouted for the warriors to make way. "Hey, remember," she said. "*When, Alina*."

Alina gave her the most awkward thumbs up imaginable. Then she broke off, speed-walking out of the gatehouse the same way she'd entered it—even as the front stone barrier grated upward with a gum-itching series of squeals.

The sirens were silenced as the drawbridge fell with a boom. One of the captains leapt to the fore, raising her rifle in one hand, her sword in the other.

A lone voice among the soldiers yelled, "Snuff the light!" The call was ech-oed; the soldiers marched out of the gatehouse. "Death to the Lightbringers!"

Fording against the tide of Ozari defenders—a slow parade headed through the opening gate, up to the battlements to face twenty-to-one odds—Alina did not meet any of their eyes. However, she heard some of them whisper to her, "The Seventh Lord."

Others: "You've come," and "It is written."

One, bowing his head: "Achemir."

As she fled the gatehouse, bending away from the civilians shepherded to shelters, picking her way through snaking, unlit corridors, she heard a voice. It was one she knew well. Beyond anyone else Alina had known, its owner had developed the subtle art of cutting words.

She heard the voice of Ruqastra, and could imagine the sneer on her face as she spoke. *"Like dreams, their story is a symbol behind which waits the truth."*

Alina undid a rusty latch, slamming the door, entering a long, straight tunnel. Distant booming shook free dust and grit from the ceiling. She coughed.

"Fate is a tailor. Already, you wear the mantle of myth."

"I never wanted that responsibility," Alina panted into the dark as she ran.

"Too late for that. The symbols have been stitched into your soul. However, what they represent? Well, now, that shall be entirely of your choosing."

She came to another door. The postern. Flinging it open, she gasped at the blinding brilliance of thousands of spotlights, exploding shells, and arcing mis-siles.

Her gaze traced the length of the narrow stone bridge at her feet. It led to the main road, which ended with the great, glinting, green gates of the Wall. The defenses were choked with fighters firing down at the enemy. Still more invaders swarmed the battlements, driving bayonets and sabers into Ozari flesh.

Somewhere on the other side of all that death, Cho, Mezami, and Kinneas waited.

Blood cooling, Alina dragged *Ida* over her face, put one foot forward, and stepped from darkness into the fiery light of war.

59

CHO-ZEN

SETTING OUT FROM THE Safehouse with Tibby, Cho left the wounded Cbarassan and Kinneas in the tiny but highly capable hands of Mezami.

The Pyct had requested to come with Cho, to act as bodyguard, but she insisted he stay. "I'd worry about the others, and you should stick around in case Li gets back. Someone she trusts should be here to tell her what's gone down."

Barely able to move, Cbarassan's protests were minimal. Same for Kinneas, paralyzed and half-conscious.

Cho and Tibby didn't make it thirty feet beyond the vault door before a Tranquilizer fell upon them. Tibby's knife sang through the air.

"Wait!" Cho shouted. "Stop! I know him."

Tibby backed off, but did not sheathe her blade.

The Tranq, a young man, staggered forward. Blood ran from his close-shaved hairline, cutting a jagged lightning bolt between his green eyes. He looked a lot like Kinneas, though older, leaner, harder. In fact, not so long ago, he'd even more closely resembled Kinneas—soft-eyed and soft-hearted, always ready with a sheepish grin.

"Calthin?"

"Cho?"

"What're you doing here? I thought the Walazzins got you, that you were in jail or—"

"Close call, but I made it out." A drop of pink blood-sweat tumbled from his chin. "Where's my brother, Cho? Huh? Put a tracker app on his phone. I check it every once in a while, make sure he's safe. Last time I looked, it said he was in Ozar. Right here, on the Sixth Stack." By the way he hunched, leaning his weight on his right leg, it was clear he'd been hurt. Bad. "How could you bring him *here*? Reckless, insane—"

"Woah, there, pal. Jam a wedge in it for a sec, 'k? How'd you even find this place? The bunker," she jerked her thumb behind her, "shoulda prevented you from tracking him this far."

"That's right. I only got close, within a few blocks. Found a poorly hidden APC, though, scratched up and beaten halfway down the hells, so I figured you couldn't be far. Then, I met your... partner, I guess? Ivion? She told me how to find this place. Hardly believed her, but when I got here, that's right around when you came out. At least *she* was straight with me."

"Where'd you see Ivion? Where'd she go?"

"Buthmertha damn you, who cares? I'm bleeding out, and I want my brother. *Now.*"

Tibby looked to Cho for confirmation. Cho nodded.

"You'd better come inside."

"Gods," Calthin breathed. He fell to his knees beside his prone, pale, bruised brother. "What have you done?"

"Everything we could," said Tibby.

"More than enough." Calthin's red-rimmed eyes scorched the room, taking in Mezami and Cbarassan. "I see you've added to your monster collection."

"You don't mean that. You're hurt, I get it, but—"

"Don't you tell me what I mean. Everything was fine with my family and Alina until she went off to New El and brought *you* back. You and that winged rodent. Now you've got yourself a walking tree friend, too. Good on you." He looped his arms under Kinneas's back.

"What're you doin'?"

"What I should have, months ago: getting him away from you and your, your carnival freakshow."

Tibby moved to intervene, but Cho said, "He's right. Kin shouldn't be here."

"Either way," said Tibby, "this private wears the navy and orange of the Torvir. As his superior, I say he owes you an apology."

Calthin rose to her level. Their staring contest cooked the air between them. "Who're you, then? You look like you lost a fight with a meat grinder."

"Watch it," said Tibby. "You must've missed the stripes on my lapel, son."

"Shove your rank down your metal throat, ma'am. After my whole squad turned snitch, consider me a deserter."

Cho remembered Kaspuri's boast, that Calthin Amming had been apprehended for questioning.

"You escaped," she said.

"Barely. Got clipped with a knife for my trouble." He smiled. Blood on his teeth. "My first real scrap, and it wasn't against the enemy but one of our own. Someone I came up with. Boot camp bonds mean less than nothing, apparently."

Kinneas's sleeping bag crinkled as he shifted. "Cal?" he said, posting himself on his elbows.

Rushing over to him, Calthin had a rapid-fire, heated conversation with his little brother. Out of respect, Cho hummed to herself to drown out what was said (because she definitely would have heard every word, otherwise). The end of it was impossible to ignore, however, Calthin shouting, "She'll never be your girlfriend, Kin. When're you planning to come to terms with that?"

The Amming brothers stared at each other in silence.

Cho's phone buzzed in her pocket, and she was glad for the distraction.

The screen displayed,

BLOCKED NUMBER

For all she knew, it could be Alina calling from a different device, so she answered. "Uh, yeah?"

The voice on the other end unmistakably belonged to Ivion, but her tone was less lilting and musical than usual. The synthesizer medley of her voice became discordant, jarring. "It never needed end this way. None of this is right. But I have sacrificed too much—I *owe* too much. Can't go back. My hands are tied, my fate sealed. Can't take it back, not now."

"Ivion? You're not making any s—"

"I have no choice." A pause. Slight static.

"What's going on? Ivion?"

"You should have stayed in your cell and cooperated, Lady Choraelia. For all that it's worth, I passionately wish events had unfolded much differently than they have. You're a wretched, obstinate child, but I have come to respect you, and—A shame you were so persistent a nuisance to exactly the wrong people, too many times."

Cho's stare effectively communicated to the others her growing sense of horror. Each of them correctly guess that something very, very bad was about to happen.

Ivion cleared her throat. "My deepest sorrow lies with Alina, however, who must today lose her closest friend. I am grateful to you for standing by her for so long. In the end, you faltered. Indecision, that is your sin. Perhaps take solace in knowing that, after you are gone, I will be there to protect her." Her voice cracked. "At least, I'm told, to die at the hands of the Martyrs is quick. Terrifying and hideously painful, but lasting only the very briefest of moments."

"Martyrs? What are you—"

"You'll see for yourself soon enough."

The phone began to hum like a starved mosquito, like a dying plane engine before the final plunge.

"Gods' speed, my lady," said Ivion.

Eyes wide, Cho sprinted for the escape hatch, flinging it open. She chucked the phone down into the tubular depths, slamming shut the hatch just as the device flashed and a wave of flame jetted back up toward her. She rolled aside as fire burst from the hatch, tearing it from its hinges, launching it into the ceiling, where it remained embedded in the concrete. Springing up, she bolted past all the concerned faces in the room and pressed her eye against the peephole at the front door.

Marching toward the bunker, in rows of three, their charcoal-dark forms drinking in the light of the street lamps, were a few dozen animated skeletons. The same type as those that had overpowered Ruqastra—the Dream Queen—and torn Eilars—an assassin android—to bits.

"Martyrs... Gotta go," said Cho. "Now."

The others were stunned; they weren't moving fast enough.

She yelled, "C'mon, people, we've got company. Of the bad type. Let's go, let's go, let's go!"

Tibby said, "Whatever it is, we're better off in here than out there. This place is secure."

"I've seen these things in action before. Doesn't matter how thick or steely the door is, it's not gonna hold. Also, the reason we're trapped in this murder hole is the *owner* of said murder hole. To the surprise of everyone except me, she finally betrayed us. Staying is not an option." She pointed to the open hatch. "Down there. That's our only out."

"Where does it lead?" Tibby squinted through the vault door's peephole. She pulled away, pale.

"Seventh Stack." Cho gazed down the escape hatch. The explosion had blasted its walls, destroying the nice sturdy rungs of the ladder.

"To the middle of a battlefield, eh," said Tibby, checking the magazine in her pistol. "Yes, we'll be much safer there."

"So, *you* were my inappropriately sarcastic role model. It all makes sense." Cho wrapped pillow cases around her hands. "We're gonna have to slide part of the way, get past where the bomb did the most damage."

"What about the brothers?" said Cbarassan, using an unloaded rifle as a crutch.

Calthin said, "If we make it out of this, Cho, I'll kill you."

Before he could blink twice, Tibby had pressed the muzzle of her gun to his temple. "Try."

Cho looped her arms around Tibby's midriff and shoved her away. "Get it together, you two. We've got *minutes*."

There came a furious banging at the door. Magically powered bodies relentlessly battering themselves against cold metal. And they were already making a dent.

Jabbing Calthin's chest, Cho said, "First things first. You can take your swing later if you gotta, but you'll have to get in line." At the blackened hatch now, she looked down. "I'll go first. Follow my lead."

"The blue mouse and I will hold them off," said Tibby. "We'll be the fastest, so we can wait till last."

"Thank you," said Cho. Then, considering Tibby's pistol: "That peashooter's not gonna hack it."

"Fair," said Tibby, tucking the weapon under Cbarassan's belt. She kicked her shotgun into her right (and only) hand and pumped it. Sunrise red, an expended cartridge clacked onto the floor.

Lugging Kinneas down that shaft would be no easy feat. Luckily, Calthin's time in the army had given him more than a curt attitude. His biceps bulged as he hoisted his brother onto his shoulder and fireman-carried him over to the hatch.

Bracing herself with her feet spread, wedged against opposite sides of the hole, Cho said, "Mezzy, promise me you'll both get out as soon as you can."

"Fear: no, I."

Cho slid down the slick, slimy stone, using her pillow-case covered hands to slow and steady her descent. Even through the fabric, her skin burned from the friction, but she was able to quickly reach the part of the vertical tunnel that had been most severely cracked by the blast. Here, about halfway down, the chute widened to the point where she couldn't reach both ends with her legs, even in a full split.

She calculated the distance. About seven feet.

She tucked in her limbs and dropped, and—after a pulse-pounding moment of free-fall—spread them again to catch herself. At this point, the ladder rungs buried in the circular wall had survived the explosion.

She waited a couple of interminable minutes for the others. Finally, Cbarassan and the Amming brothers caught up (or, in this case, down).

"Hey," she said, "one at a time. I gotcha."

Cbarassan slipped down without complaint, and she caught them, helped them grab the rungs. Calthin protested; he wasn't worried about himself but his brother. Kinneas yelled at him to "Just go."

Cho grunted as she caught him by the waist, hooking her arms under his. Cbarassan had been able to carry most of their own weight; Kin, much less. Straining, face reddening—her ankles, shoulder joints, and elbows popping—she managed to lower him to the *Fyarda*. They and Cho held him in place until Calthin, spurning all offers of help, slid down too. He nearly failed to stop in time, and almost kicked Cbarassan and his brother down the tube, which would have sent all three plummeting to their premature deaths. But he caught himself, and, leading the pack now, took charge of Kinneas again.

Fast as honey crawling down a jar, they continued their descent.

Cho could hear gunfire and shouts from above. And a cacophony of clicking bones—the only sound the Martyrs made.

She hissed through her teeth, "Faster. Hurry."

There was light at the bottom of the tunnel.

Tibby's voice thundered: "Look out below!"

With barely enough time to register the words, and far from enough to act on them, Cho was struck by a hard, blunt object. A puppet of metal-coated bone. The black skull snapped its teeth at her fingers, her throat. Then, the sudden sensation of weightlessness. Her organs a-jumble, heart skipping, she and the skeleton fell. They slammed into Cbarassan, who collided with the Amming brothers, and the five of them tumbled down the rest of the tube, a tangle of limbs and screams.

60

ALINA

BELOW HER, DARKNESS. A long, silent drop. Above, the shadows of the high cave ceiling. All around, stone stairs led to the ramparts of Hexhall's keep. Hundreds of green-armored soldiers fired projectiles—bullets, shells, arrows, fireballs, stones—down at enemies whom Alina couldn't see from her position on the slim stone bridge. They also shot upward at swooping things she at first mistook for bats or giant butterflies. When the flying objects started dropping satchels filled with grenades, she realized what they were: Authority shock troops; four-winged, power-armored chaos makers.

Clusters of defenders were scattered, slammed against walls or into the chasm Alina now crossed. Artillery shells whistled on their downward arc, exploding archways and parapets. She raised her hands, scraps of brick bouncing off her energy shield.

"They're inside!" someone screamed.

"Enemy contact!"

One of the flying shock troops noticed Alina, and dived. She pointed two fingers his way, and he went limp, his power armor carrying off his unconscious form.

Reaching the end of the bridge, she took a moment to appreciate Hexhall's messy return to the material world. During its time in the Revoscape, it had clearly outgrown its original boundaries. Like fish bones caught in teeth, the six triangular pillars jutted between titanic, cracked slabs—the remnants of the crumbling cave structure.

She ran up a flight of stairs to the nearest watch tower, finding a locked, reinforced door barring her entry. She glanced at her hands.

To the swish of launching missiles, she buried her claws knuckle-deep in mortar and scaled the tower's side. Bullets pinged against the stone around her as she prayed to Buthmertha that her friends had found some place to hunker down far from the warzone.

She flipped over the lip of the tower's tiled roof, thinking that Mezami must have found the kids by this point. Hopefully, they'd all taken refuge with Ivion— yet another victim of Alina's carelessness. Now that Mezami and Alina occupied the same dimension again, telepathic communication should be possible. Only one way to tell. From this height, above much of the fray and mental interference and Niimantic discharge polluting the ether, she reached out to him.

Finally, he got the call. *Alina?*

Mezami, thank the gods you're alive. Where are you?

Are: Safehouse, we.

All of you?

Are: endangered, we. Come: quick—

Mezami? Mezami! She faced the direction in which the Safehouse lay.

A quake shook the tower, roof tiles sliding from underfoot. She staggered, caught herself, and looked down. "Buthmertha save us," she breathed, her words lost among tens of thousands of battle cries and the cracking of as many rifles. As the artillery ceased fire, a sea of bodies advanced toward the blasted walls. Every inch of ground seemed to hold an Authority soldier. She looked left; they were raising siege ladders. Right; flinging up grappling hooks. How could she possibly make it through all *that*?

It was the kind of pitched battle you'd expect to find described in an ancient history book. However, Ozar's unique geography made the analog, tried and true strategy of overwhelming force necessary: one sloppy air strike could take down the whole cave system and the Elementals' army with it.

Alina's gaze passed over what was left of Free Ozar, her monstrous vision absorbing every gory detail. The Seventh Stack was burning, its buildings bull-dozed by El's war machines. Columns of multicolored Tranquilizers and merce-naries marched through the streets, gunning down any Ozari citizens they en-countered outdoors. A line of battle mechas—two-legged and twenty feet tall— lurched forward. Steel beams bent under their weight. Glass melted in the wake of napalm flame. The machines had been painted in imitation of sharks, yellow jackets, vipers. Their pilots stopped for nothing and no one, using beam weapons and gatling guns to shred abandoned hovercraft and fleeing civilians.

Fifty mechas made for the gate just below Alina's position, their combustion engines belching smoke and fire. She couldn't imagine anything that might stop or even slow them.

Then the Covenants arrived.

Some climbing, some flying, and some teleporting, they touched down on the tower's roof beside her. One—a small, wide pig-snouted dude—looked up at her. He was blindfolded, as were they all.

"You're her, aincha?" He gave a gruff laugh, flexing hairy arms. "You up fer some fireworks, Achemir?"

The others drew chakrams and knives, or ethereal sparks appeared around them.

"Why'd you call me that? What's it mean?" said Alina.

The pig-snouted man chuckled happily. "Mam always said I'd live to see the day, rest her soul. And, sure as sure, here you are."

"Enough fan-boying, Kosteros." A tall, crimson-skinned, muscular woman grimaced, tongue flicking through the gap between her flat teeth. "She'll do as she wills. It's her way."

A slender human with long, fine, black hair stepped to the edge. "We are soldiers. It is not our lot to question the Lords."

The other Covenants joined them, each with a foot on the parapet.

Kosteros shot Alina one last blind look.

She shouted, "Wait!" as they leapt off. And she watched them go, finally getting a hint at the true meaning of the word "Covenant."

The teleporters reached the advancing mechas first, of course, the smaller of them appearing *inside* the cockpits. The cramped knife fights were short.

Next, the jumpers caught up. Powerful legs propelled them across The Authority's battle lines as they hopped over and on top of heads and shoulders. They landed on the mechas, and—like rapiers biting the unprotected, fleshy spots between armored plates—they got to work tearing apart the wires and hydraulic coils holding the machines together. The mechas collapsed into piles of scrap.

Lastly came the runners, but they made the biggest impression on the way. Every Tranq that tried to trip, stab, grab, or shoot them met with lethal force. The Covenants barreled straight through. Their blades flicked like stingers, downing soldier after soldier; the glinting, ethereal sparks surrounding them shot outward in front-facing cones, carving a path through the rows of bodies.

The Ozari soldiers on the ramparts roared their approval.

Several of the mechas crumpled amid waves of oily smoke that, along with hissing clouds of steam, obscured the rest of the Covenants' struggle. From her perch, Alina could hear the thrum of the war machines' energy blades, the rattle of guns, and the thuds of child-sized bullet casings.

Steam, smoke, and a flashy distraction. She cracked her knuckles. It was now or never.

Problem: already the gaps in The Authority's lines were being filled. She'd never make it, unless—

"Unless I can fly," she said, numbly looking down again. Fire, death, bullets—vertigo nearly sent her tumbling, but she steadied herself.

She'd flown before, of course. When astral-projecting into the Revoscape, without the drag of her body, it was easy. However, carrying herself through the heavy air of the physical plane would be a much different story. There was only one spell in her repertoire that could manage it (she'd used it the night she'd first met Ivion). If she misted herself now, though, the choppy air would absolutely destroy her. With all the projectiles and bursts of magic going off, she wouldn't last six seconds.

Yet, in spite of her misgivings, she knew she could fly without the use of spells. Because Dimas had. "I can fly," she argued with herself. "I can."

A stray bullet glanced off her energy shield. Her knees buckled. She buried her claws in the roof tiles. And, sprawled, she thought again of Cho.

"It's all because of me." Arms shaking, she pushed up. "Me." The Seventh Stack burned; Hexhall teetered. The Covenants' screams— "I'm responsible."

Buthmertha help her, she had to do something. If she could just do this *one thing* right.

She spread her arms, fists taut, and stepped off the edge—

And fell straight down, landing like a brick through glass on top of a pair of Tranqs, who cried out.

From the ground, she wheezed, "Figures."

Spears and bayonets plunged toward her. Shaking off her daze, she rolled into a crouch—felt a rush of air—and leapt upward. Her corkscrew ascent took her *through* one of the mechas, which pitched backward and exploded.

She patted her body, hardly believing she'd escaped unscathed. "Holy crap, I *can* fly."

Rising above the smoke, clinging to the antennae of another war machine, Kosteros the Covenant saluted her as she passed.

An ear-popping, wet squeal came from the chasm Alina had crossed mere minutes ago. She turned to witness a worm, long as a road and plated in gray chitin, rise from the deep. Its head—top?—bristled with bright pink, squelching feelers, dribbling acidic spittle. It gracefully curled over the inner wall and slammed into The Authority's ranks, thrashing its gargantuan body. The serrated, saw-like protrusions on its back minced those unlucky soldiers closest to it. Hundreds more were crushed and broken.

Bullets bounced off the hide of this Colossi-type Aelf Alina at last recognized from dusty old Raver manuals. *Dan'yn'daup.* A greatworm. The Hextarchy must have been controlling it, somehow, for it continued to ignore the Ozari defenders as it thrashed through the invading army.

Alina gagged at the carnage, soaring away.

There were so many soldiers.

Continuous volleys of rocket-propelled grenades, missiles, gauss rounds, and all manner of military-grade projectiles were launched at the keep of Hexhall. Tanks leveled their cannons at its walls and barricades, blasting it to pieces, one house-sized crater at a time.

As Alina sailed through the air between the stone towers of the Seventh Stack, Authority planes and hovercraft, and news network drone carriers, she asked herself if she could've done more to help The Coven.

Flying high above the amassed forces of the Elemental Empire—which continued to pour onto the plateau in front of Hexhall, covering the lots and streets beyond—she could only gasp at the sheer difference in strength between the opposing armies. One hundred thousand marched for El. Hexhall boasted about half that number, but warriors made up less than one tenth of its occupants. And The Coven totaled only seven hundred, give or take a few dozen.

The only hope for all those people—including Vessa—was to surrender. But that wouldn't save the Aelf, whom the Assets of El considered abominations.

Alina had entertained the notion of collapsing part of the stone bridge or some buildings to at least slow the invaders' unstoppable assault, but she'd never manage that without taking a whole lot of lives. So, instead, she'd disable a different threat to Hexhall's crumbling keep: the artillery cannons shelling it from afar.

Swooping down, shrieking to stun the crews operating the cannons, she wove a net of Geomantic force. She hurtled toward the ground, a pillar of earth rising to meet her. Landing lightly upon it, she clenched her fists and thrust them toward the ceiling of the Stack's colossal cavern. The artillery guns around her were pierced by jagged fins of rock, jutting from the ground like sails above a roiling sea.

She took off once more, removing from the board any other siege weapons along her flight path, and she hoped to Buthmertha and all the Seventy-Seven Gods that her actions had bought Vessa, the Covenants, and their Hextarchs just a little more time. That's all they seemingly could hope for—a delay of the end.

Cold, damp air blasted back her wild red hair as she laughed into her mask. It was a laugh of equal parts exhilaration and bitterness; the freedom she'd gained in learning to fly was overtaken by its pointlessness. All her power and knowledge, and still she was nothing more than an arrow of shadow fired from a bow of fear, plunging toward Cho, Mezami, and Kinneas. If the gods were good, she'd find them. And, then what? Die either with them or with Vessa?

Yet, she could hear a voice in her head which tiresomely demanded she not give in to despair. *You've overcome opponents larger, more powerful, more able than yourself before. It's true, raw determination alone cannot move mountains, Cabbage.* Her grandfather's words, in her voice. *Even so, one's home, friends, people—these may give us strength beyond strength. Remember, the protector will always fight harder than the conqueror. Always.*

Shouts from below. She soared beyond the reach of the snipers and riflemen shooting at her.

It's good to be whole again, she admitted to herself. *It's good to have you—me—back. Even if it's only for one sunless day.* Reaching out to Mezami telepathically, knowing her message probably wouldn't arrive, she implored him, *Hang on! I'm almost there.*

Ahead lay the outer Wall—to the Elementals, "Peregar's Grief"; to her, now, "the Abyssal Shell." Broken, cracked open, fire-bleached. There'd be no flying over it; the barrier reached from the cave's floor to its ceiling.

Spread in front of the breach in the wall was The Authority's rearguard—a couple thousand.

So many.

Her cloak unfurling into a great black wing, Alina landed where there were the fewest Tranqs (a patch of only *several* hundred). Behind them lay the gates, still sealed and intact. Embedded in those colossal slabs of stone, which had been scarred with a pattern of interlocking hexagons, were strips of pure Chrononite. Again, she felt the draw—a beckoning—of The Abyss, but she focused on the Tranqs blocking her way forward.

The more alert among them wisely took her for an Aelf, leveled their rifles at her, and fired. Thrusting her hands forward and apart, she telekinetically shoved most of them to either side.

They were stunned. This was her chance.

Weaving a Geomantic spell, she bulleted through the air, pulled toward the Chrononite plate as if by the world's strongest magnet. She belly-flopped against it, and melded with the stone like a drop of ink in a full water bottle. The stone warbled around her, trembling at her touch, her breath—and there was a second of perfect quiet—before she rocketed out the other side, blinked, and kept running.

She entered the Sixth Stack. Unlike her first visit to this place, today there were no Sanctumites preaching The Author's Word. Taking to the air once more, she saw heaps of dead Ozari soldiers. They must have fallen during the initial defense of the Abyssal Shell.

The Hextarchs had not been ready for the Revomantic bubble to burst, but the Elementals had.

"Me," Alina reminded herself. "My doing."

Thousands upon thousands more Tranqs marched through the streets, headed for Hexhall. The Authority's initial strike forces were only a small taste of what was coming.

Too many.

They were going to win. All the world would fall into the hands of the Elementals. And there'd be nowhere on, above, or under the earth that would be safe for Alina's family.

My home, my friends, my people.

Her doing.

Strength beyond strength.

Her responsibility.

She realized, then, that she had no right to despair. The Ozari died by the thousands rather than give up their culture, their world, or their hope. The people laid down their lives for their gods.

It was time their gods did the same for them.

The protector is greater than the conqueror.

Family is the anchor of the soul.

Family...

Alina remembered, one time, Mezami punching an owl in the face (it had mistaken him for a field mouse).

Kinneas, casting his first ice spell—so he and Cho could skate in late spring.

Cho, covered in the pillows she'd duct-taped to her body, charging Alina; both of them, tumbling to the floor, giggling.

Whatever I become, whatever the cost...

Those soldiers of El that chanced to look up as her shadow passed over them did not see a flying woman. Rather, they saw a thing for which they had no other name but "fear." A shade, the sort of bog phantasm or cave-ghast to lurk just beyond the outskirts of human settlement. These soldiers' earliest ancestors would have told their children tales of warning—"Stay out of the marshes"; "Dare not enter the circle of pines." They would have had their medicine women ring salt around their homes and burn incense to invoke the protection of the spirits. And because such deep-dwelling fear cannot be erased, not within one thousand generations, these invaders of the Seventh Stack knew a demon of the ancient world when they saw one. They felt, down to their marrow, that to name themselves its enemy—or, gods forbid, get in its way—was death.

Soaring toward the Safehouse, Alina dug her claws into hope, and she became so entangled with it that the end of either one would destroy both.

... I will protect our family.

61

CHO-ZEN

BY THE CRASHING OF mortar shells and the marching of tens of thousands of feet, the homes and businesses of the Seventh Stack trembled. Most of these buildings had stood for centuries, but now they groaned and leaned, threatening collapse. Ancient stones, scraped away by lumbering mechas and the bullets of Authority firing squads executing Ozari nationals.

The locals certainly had more than enough problems to preoccupy them. Were any to look up, however, they would have seen—tumbling from a hole in the cave ceiling—a few dozen humanoid shapes: Cbarassan, Cho, Calthin, Kinneas, and a cluster of clattering Martyrs.

They had, all of them, fallen, unable to find purchase on the circular walls of the vertical tunnel. Now, the ground rose to receive them.

Cbarassan dive-bombed toward the ground, body glowing.

Cho shouted after them.

Then, from all directions—the walls of buildings, the cave floor, the ceiling—erupted roots and vines, intertwining, homing in on the *Fyarda's* shining form. A latticework of biomass wove itself beneath them, catching first Cbarassan, then Cho and the others. They bounced a couple of times upon impact, but would get away with only bruises when they should otherwise have *ker-splatted*.

They all hung barely ten feet off the ground. Cho gulped.

No time to celebrate, though. The Martyrs were upon them, and one grabbed hold of Cho's shoulder, quietly but ferociously gnashing its teeth at her. She squirmed and thrashed. Her enhanced eyes scanned its body for weak points, but found none. None of the apps regulating her brain, nor Eilars's chip, could help her understand the golden, gossamer weave of magic that bound those bones instead of muscle and ligament. Her analysis of the bones themselves proved they'd been mystically reinforced—opal-black coloration, impossible density and toughness—but offered no insight on how to break them. Gilded, glinting runes and flowing, vein-like symbols had been daintily etched into them as if with a fountain pen. Unfortunately, unlike Alina, Cho was no Maggo; at this point, she could rely only on brute force.

And it wasn't enough.

Striking the Martyr's skull only bruised her own knuckles. Kneeing it in the ribs sent a jolt through her entire body, followed by hot waves of pain.

More of the things fell through the hole, down onto Cbarassan's vine-and-root net. Under all that weight, the earth to which the vines were tethered loosened. The *Fyarda* cried out as the net's anchor points gave way, and mortals and skeletons alike dropped the final ten feet down to the Seventh Stack.

Rolling to break her fall, jumping, tripping over the lumpy carpet of vines, Cho wriggled free of the Martyr's grip. Her ears pricked, picking up a storm of gun- and cannon-fire, the hiss and whine of missiles, the screams of the dying, the thudding of bullets against stone and body armor. The cacophony came from several blocks north. So, the Elementals had begun their last battle.

Cho had more immediate concerns, shouting, "I got nothing for these freaks."

With a grunt, Cbarassan speared their hands forward, and two root nets burst from the earth to dash the Martyrs against wall and street. Their bones clacked and crunched as they struck the ground, but they quickly rose again. Their eyeless skulls creaking on naked spines, zeroing in on their targets, they sprinted forward.

Calthin emptied his service rifle, clip after clip. The rounds ricocheted off the Martyrs' empowered, gold-threaded bones. The skeletons' unbroken, humorless grins held. "I'm empty," he said, fastening his combat knife to the barrel of his rifle, his expression showing exactly how useful he thought his bayonet would be.

Yelling in a strange language, Cbarassan raised a rock wall between Cho and most of the charging Martyrs, blocking the alley's mouth. The thin barricade wouldn't last long; it rumbled as the Martyrs crashed into it.

"Help me with him," Cho said, throwing Kinneas's arm around her neck, lifting him, pushing from her heels. "Come on!"

Calthin took a swing at the nearest Martyr, his bayonet catching between its ribs. He lost hold of his rifle, cursing, and ducked under the creature's lunging grab. A kick to its back knocked it down.

The rock wall crumbled. Martyrs spilled forth.

The look on Cbarassan's face mirrored how Cho felt. She knew she'd never outrun those things while lugging Kinneas, but she tried anyway.

"Fight until you can no longer," Cbarassan said. Vines whipped at the Martyrs, dragging them down. "Give them nothing." Another Martyr rammed the *Fyarda*, and they fell, grappling with the skeleton. More piled on top.

Not like this. Cho would not watch another friend be torn apart. Not while she had a single liquid ounce of strength left in her veins.

She laid Kinneas down and, growling, snatched the nearest blunt object she could find. As if her blood had boiled over, steaming through her teeth and nostrils, her vision went red. No, on second thought, it wasn't her eyesight that had changed; the crimson light came from above.

Shooting from the Safehouse tunnel, a mini comet blazed with otherworldly flame as it hurtled toward them.

"What is that?" said Calthin, backing away.

It was alive, and it was coming right for them.

"Get down!" Cho threw herself over Kinneas.

Through glazed eyes, he stared at the burning, descending star. Delirious, he chuckled, the crackle of cooking air quickly dissipating the weak trills of his voice.

Cho covered her ears and cried out.

Crimson flames sparking off him, Mezami arced low to the ground, smashing *through* the Martyrs that had dog-piled atop Cbarassan. The sheer force of his dive scattered them. Cracking, splintering—there followed the sounds of lost ships pulverized by storm and rock. The Pyct punched plum-sized holes in the Martyrs' skulls, and ruptured rib-cages.

One of their legs dislocated, Cbarassan crawled away.

Mezami bounced between Martyrs like a crimson-lit pinball, shattering their shins, their pelvises, their jaws. He grabbed hold of one and swung it like a club, the crunching punctuated by his tiny baritone war cries. Where no one else had made a dent against the Sanctum's secret weapons, he pulverized them. Yet, still they advanced—the legless dragging or throwing themselves at him, the armless charging head-first.

Wings ablur, mousy face scrunched in concentration, beady black eyes narrowed, more predatory than Cho had ever seen him before—Mezami summoned all his impossible strength. As he whittled the Martyrs' numbers down, he gave Cho the chance to pull Cbarassan out of the fray, and Calthin found Kinneas's side. The four of them huddled as shards of bone rained down.

In spite of Mezami's ferocity and speed, though, there were too many Martyrs for him to contain. A group of them broke off and barreled toward Cho and the others.

Time seemed to slow as her processing speed ticked up.

Several hundred feet away, Tibby landed on the ground, disentangling herself from what looked like an improvised bed-sheet parachute. She gestured from Cho to Mezami, shouting a warning Cho couldn't quite hear.

Calthin sprang up to meet the Martyrs head on.

Unable to stand, Cbarassan and Kinneas watched death approach.

There really wasn't anything Cho could do to stop what was coming. All the same, she thrust out her leg to trip one of the Martyrs.

Her maneuver did not succeed, however, because the Martyrs never made it. Arriving just in time, Mezami had grasped their skulls, one in each of his paws, and slammed them together with such force that they crumpled like aluminum cans. He threw aside what remained of their bodies.

Cho spat out a bone shard, smiled up at him, and said, "Mezami, you beautiful bas—" But that briefest taste of sweet relief spoiled on her tongue.

A pair of obsidian jaws closed around the Pyct, snapping shut with a sickening crunch.

Teeth.

The Martyr had leapt through the air and bitten down on Mezami, whose back had been turned, who hadn't been ready. Locked inside its bony maw, he disappeared in a gout of blood.

Bile bubbled up Cho's throat. No words could contain the scream that clawed its way out of her. She lunged at the Martyr, gripping its jaw, cutting her fingers on its blood-slick teeth.

Then, the shrieking of five thousand winged night beasts, a hundred steam whistles, and as many tornado warning sirens swept over the street. For a moment, she thought that sudden wail had been her own, but she was wrong. She looked up to behold a torpedo of shadow—with two gleaming golden eyes.

As the shadow echoed her scream, a pall of darkness fell upon her and the others and the Martyrs.

She could no longer see, nor hear, nor taste even the bitterness of her own tears as they drenched her lips. Still, the wailing continued, filling the impenetrable black cloud.

When, moments later, the darkness dropped like a heavy curtain on a flimsy rod, the Martyrs had been reduced to piles of gray bone chips, disintegrating to ash even as Cho blinked at them.

And there, in profile, stood a figure garbed in a black cloak of night and dream. Its strange, shifting, red crow mask turned toward Cho.

In shock, Cho said, "Morphea?" That wasn't possible; the Dream Queen was dead. The mask was the wrong color, besides. But who else could this master Maggo be, who'd swooped in and wiped out the Martyrs in a second?

Then Cho remembered that the real Morphea hadn't been able to beat the Martyrs. This person, this creature, was something else.

And, finally, her sight focused, cutting through the dream-haze and confusion, and she recognized the woman standing on top of the bone pile.

Alina yanked the mask from her tear-soaked face, her irises of molten gold cooling to patina green.

62

ALINA

THERE WERE OTHER PEOPLE around. A young man, hunched over a boy. A half-metal woman. But Alina hardly noticed them as she and Cho sifted through the carpet of broken bones, searching.

Soon, they found him.

Gingerly, Alina's fingers hooked under the fallen Pyct's back. She lifted him up, cradling him in her palm.

"I'm sorry," she whispered. "I don't know any spells strong enough."

He gazed up at her, snout tight, fangs clenched. His black eyes were clear, focused. He gripped her thumb so fiercely that he broke it. But she hardly felt it happen.

Cho was beside her now, sobbing onto Alina's hands and the hideous gashes in Mezami's fur. The Martyr's teeth had snapped his spine.

"I'm sorry." Alina lost count of how many times she said it. "I'm so sorry." She wasn't only apologizing to him but to Cho, to the gods, to herself, to anyone who would listen and—and stop this terrible, inevitable thing from happening.

Mezami coughed blood onto her palm and released her fractured thumb. He leveled his sharp stare first at Cho then Alina.

His final words were, "Fear: you, no."

Alina felt his weight in her hand. Soft and rubbery. Limp. Light. A strange thing, to see him this way. She'd only ever known him as a living arrow, a grasshopper on steroids. Now... no motion. Only mass, emptying of substance.

He was still in there. Barely. Holding on.

Cho flung her arms around Alina's waist, burying her face in *Rego*, howling a long, unbroken howl. Alina let her empty her lungs.

When Cho had finished, Alina—the Sevensin—told the Pyct'Tsi warrior, "There's only one thing I can do for you, my friend." Directly into his mind, she sent her intention. Then, aloud: "It's gotta be now, though. And you gotta agree."

His eyes began to close, his head lowering, but he met her stare.

Slowly, he nodded.

No time to lose. She could feel him slipping away. "Let go of me, Cho. And stand back."

Crying soundlessly now, Cho backed off, falling to the ground.

Alina breathed through the pain, her mind clear.

She enclosed Mezami in her hands. Golden light flashed from between her fingers.

"What are you doing?" Cho shouted.

The light absorbed into Alina's skin, drifting up her arms, across her shoulders, into her heart—then fading.

She opened her hands, which were empty.

"What did you do?" said Cho.

"Pycts," Alina said, voice breaking, "are Egogenetic creatures. And so am I."

PART SIX

CATHARSIS

63

ALINA

SOMETHING IN ALINA WAS changing.

So many bones. Like an earthquake had vomited up a catacomb's worth of corpses.

Even severed, the bones hummed in dozens of disparate voices the song of their weaving. Alina could hear their story as if uttered aloud.

Once, they had belonged to faithful servants of The Sanctum, believers in the promise of everlasting life. By time or violence, however, all eventually were taken to the Undercroft of the Mountain of the Mendicant in New El. There, flesh and bone were ritualistically separated by skilled hands, and Mages of tremendous talent and inferior morals cast the spells—Zoiimancy, Necromancy, Daemoniomancy—to bind an echo of each soul to its dessicated, armored corpse. In complex, subtle patterns of gold filigree, the runes were magically etched into the remains. Alina could almost hear the screams of the victims' spirits, cruelly torn from the ether, returned to the physical world as single-minded ghouls. Servants of The Sanctum, still, but without any will of their own. Sacrifices to the cause.

Martyrs.

Alina spasmed at the disgusting reality of this tabooed twisting of death. It was Cho's voice—always Cho—that called her back.

Wigless, red-eyed, she hunched. A small thing, worthy of all love. She was crying. "You ate him? You *ate* our friend?"

"No, I…" For the second time in her life, Alina felt warmth envelop her core and bleed from her very pores as she swallowed into herself a separate being. With this addition, she became a new whole. Still "Alina," yes, but also *other*. She heard within her soul the rattle of Pyct war chants and the flutter of wings in marriage dances; within her, the voices of elders were raised in song, and young men sewed patterns of colorful beads onto their armor. She remembered Mezami telling her that he'd recovered the souls of his clan—the Tsi—after Tolomond destroyed them. So, when she'd absorbed Mezami, she'd become their caretaker, too. All the Pycts that had made up his family, his life, were part of her now.

She told Cho, "We're the same being."

He'd been dying; this way, he'd endure. In some form. She could see now, even more clearly, why and how Dimas had made the choices he had for Zatalena, for Mateus, and for her. Acts of love, not loathing. Misguided, but not entirely wrong.

Gripping the broken brick wall, Cbarassan clambered upright. They bore severe burns on their scalp and chest, along with several broken bones. How they remained standing, Alina couldn't guess.

As the echoes of Mezami and the rest of the Pyct'Tsi clan harmonized within her, Alina blinked away the euphoria of union, and finally saw those around her with clear eyes. "What happened to all of you?"

The *Fyarda* barreled over the question. "And, thus, the rebel of Truct returns. Yet, my senses must deceive me, for you couldn't have done what I've just seen you do. The dark art of Egogenesis should only be possible between members of the same species." They lifted their green-bleeding chin, inhaling. "Unless, indeed, you are the Achemir, who does not concede to the laws of our reality."

Before Alina could respond, Cho said, "It's always about you, isn't it? *You!*" She took a wild, weak swing. Her fist, and whole body, passed right through Alina, who hadn't moved.

"Hex on me, I was right," said Cbarassan.

Alina ignored their awed stare, offering Cho her hand. "You're right to be angry with me."

Swatting it aside, Cho got up. "Don't touch me. This is all your girlfriend's fault."

Alina imagined white spiders, spinning webs before her waking, widening eyes. "Ivion?"

"Who else? It's been her the whole time. She's the one who sicced those *things* on us. How could you? How could you kiss her? She's the reason Mezzy—" Cho choked on the words. "At least well-mannered Ms. Ivion had the decency to call me before she tried to have us all killed. Before she—before it all—"

"Ivion," Alina said, hearing her own voice shift an octave down, "did this?" Her tunnel vision finally widened into a panoramic view of everything that had happened the past few days. She remembered Ivion rummaging through her bag...

Ah. It all made sense now.

Anger quieting her spirit, Cho stopped crying. She stared into space. Actually, she stared at a fixed point in space, at something that wasn't really there.

"You see it, too?" said Alina.

"White spider. Why is that familiar?" She gasped. "The dream. When I was passed out, with Tibby stitching me up. Morphea was there, doing her usual pretending-to-know-everything-forever routine."

"You weren't the only one she's visited lately."

"She a ghost? Or am I going topsy?"

"What'd she tell you?"

Cho thought about it. "Nothing useful. Except—wait. There was one thing. What was it again? '...*its many, many eyes pop open, one by one.*'"

Alina caught herself saying, "'*And it crawls out, renewed. Pure white.*' How'd you know that?"

"The same way I know there's Chrononite hidden in your creepy cloak. The Lorestone's been... talking to me, pretty sure."

"'Pretty sure?'"

"Eighty-five, ninety percent."

Cho no longer seemed to want to bludgeon Alina, which was a step in the right direction, but then the half-metal woman approached and said, "That's more than enough. Back away from the girl, demon. Nice and slow."

Without turning, Alina raised her hands and read the woman's thoughts and feelings as if they'd been written on cue cards. *Fiery Niima. Metal prosthetics, personally fine-tuned. Phantom pains every night. Guilt, her primary motivator. Wounded warrior. Mercenary turned believer.*

Cbarassan said, "Best stay your hand, human. You're out of your depth." Vines wriggled from the earth, inching toward the woman.

"I won't allow a demon to manipulate her."

Rubbing her face with her filthy hands, Cho said flatly, "Cut it out, Tiberaira. It's fine. She won't hurt us."

"What do you know of this creature? Really?" said the woman, who loved Cho more than a rabbit does her kittens. "If Ozar teaches us anything, it's that nothing is as it seems. I swore to keep you safe. I've already fought one demon for you, and I'll gladly square off against a second."

Now Alina did turn around to scowl at Tiberaira, hissing into her mind, *Play nice, Igniomancer. Authority captain.*

Tiberaira flinched, shielding Cho.

I'm a friend.

Not breaking eye contact, Tiberaira asked, "How can I be sure you haven't bewitched her?"

You can't, I guess. But what could you do to me if I had?

"Use your words, Li. Nobody likes the head-speak."

Exaggerating the movements of her mouth, Alina said, "Sorry."

"Big invasion of privacy, y'know."

"I've stopped, alright? I've stopped."

Tiberaira was calmer now that she could feel Cho and Alina's bond: the squabbles of sisterhood. Such childish antics reminded her of softer years, of toddler Cho drawing mustaches on priceless marble statues, of afternoon picnics near the fountain. That calmness was a thread Alina gently pulled on until a knot somewhere deep inside Tiberaira untangled.

Cbarassan relaxed, dispelling the vines they'd summoned.

Surveying the mess of bones and debris, Tiberaira said, "So. The blue one, he's dead, then?"

Cho and Alina both looked down, away.

"Yeah, dead," barked the man kneeling beside Kinneas.

A man Alina finally recognized. "Calthin?"

"Good of you to notice me, but did you ever spot what was happening to Kin, Alina? Did you? Do you see this? All this?" His hand swept through the air, open-palmed, offering her a view of the bones, the fire, the rubble of the Seventh Stack. Not so far away, cannons sounded and metal screeched as it was blown apart. "This is what you do. You drag people into your, your insanity, and you watch them get crushed and torn to pieces. My family, we wanted to help you, care for you, even love you. And, for our trouble, you tried your hardest to kill us all."

"Whoa there, bud."

"No, you're not shutting me up, Cho. You two've got problems. Bloody, ugly ones. But I don't care anymore, got me? I just don't. All I want is to get my brother out of here."

Alina saw, reflected in his heart, the worst of herself. Petty, selfish, cruel. She didn't want to be those things, didn't want him to see her that way. Part of her wished he could remember they'd known each other since they were six, chased the same stray dog through the streets of Truct, eaten at the same table. But it wasn't her place, telling him how to feel. He'd been wounded. Yes, there was the physical damage—knife-cuts and nightstick bruises—but there were deeper gashes still.

Lost father. Brother dying in his arms.

She could have made excuses, like: *Kinneas would've come no matter what 'cause he's in love with Cho.* She could have tried to cleanse herself of sin by rationalizing her choices. She might even have apologized just to make herself feel better. Instead, she reached for his hand. "Cal. There's nothing I can say."

He flinched at the sight of her claws. "Don't say anything. Please." He lifted Kinneas, holding him like an overly large baby, grunting, "Just get out of my way."

Kinneas looked deathly ill. Had Alina any more tears to shed today, she would have.

She stepped aside as Calthin came forward.

Tiberaira called after him, "You'll never make it out of Ozar. They'll catch you."

"I'll take my chances," he shouted back. "We're guaranteed goners if we hang around here, that's for sure."

"No, clod, listen. I'm offering you an out. A real one."

Calthin hesitated, turned.

"Head up to the Sixth, at the checkpoint, this side. Ask for Yvec. Tell him the Coneys sent you. Tell him, 'Two for the burrow.' Got that?"

"Yeah, I got it." Beneath the sweat-streaked soot on his face and his buzz-cut hair, his body armor and his beefed up chest, shoulders, and arms—for a moment, Calthin seemed himself again. "Thank you. For giving us a chance."

Tiberaira nodded. Then, the older carrying the younger, the Amming brothers departed.

Alina watched them go. "Will they…" she trailed off.

"Get out alright?" Tiberaira shrugged. "Yvec's their best bet."

The brothers rounded a corner and were gone.

Facing the opposite direction, Cbarassan said, "Smoke. Hexhall burns. As our Lords long foretold, our people line the precipice of oblivion. The end is come."

"The Coven hasn't given up. Why should you?" Alina said.

Still staring in the direction Kinneas had been taken, Cho said, "You didn't come, Li. You didn't come, and now Mezami's dead."

"I will never forgive myself for not getting here sooner. Believe it. But he's not gone. We're one."

"You keep saying that like it means anything at all." Cho turned her back on everyone.

"Cho-Zen," said Alina. "Take my hand."

Glancing over her shoulder, Cho vibrated with fear.

"Mezami has something to show you. Take my hand."

Cho reached out, closing nine tenths of the gap between them. Alina crossed the remaining inch. The moment their fingers touched, they shared a vision of hundreds of Pycts of blue and gold fur, fluttering around a cool, serene lake.

"They're all in there with him," said Alina. "When Tolomond wiped out the Tsi, their life forces fed into Mezami like streams into a river. Now, they're all part of me."

"They're happy?"

"What's 'happy' anyway?"

"Are they free?"

"No one is free. But they're beyond all pain."

This set Cho's mind at ease for a moment, but she quickly found her anger again. Many years of practice made it easy. "Why weren't you here when we needed you?"

"We both know why. I couldn't see until it was too late."

"The freaky-floaty eyeball tried to warn me. And there was the white spider from the dream… I had so many chances to put it together, but Morphea *knew*. She shoulda told me it was Ivion. If I'd had a heads-up, I coulda done something."

"We weren't betrayed by Ivion."

"Of course we were! What're you saying?"

"Think about it."

"You're just like her now, y'know, like Morphea. Can't ever get a straight answer outta you anymore."

"I can't teach you something you already know. Here are the facts: I met Ivion the night Ruqastra and Eilars were killed; and, when we went looking for help, who was it that just happened to be all set to take us exactly where we needed to go?"

"Since we got here, she's been disappearing on us left and right."

"And, the last piece of the puzzle, she turned both our phones into bombs. I didn't figure it out till a few minutes ago, but the magic that blew up Hexhall's bubble was her handiwork. Machinamancy."

"She's not a Maggo, though."

"That's right."

"Unless she lied about that, too."

Alina shook her head. "Ivion Ivoir has no magical abilities."

Cho ground her teeth, arriving at the truth. "But Ordin did."

"Does."

"No. No, I don't believe it. You mean that Ivion's been—she's—*he's*—"

"Who knows what happened to the *real* Ivion, but *we* have never met her."

"The whole time," Cho whispered. "Seventy-Seven Gods damn her—him." She closed one nostril with her thumb, jettisoning a rope of bloody snot from the other. "I'm gonna need a minute."

Alina gave it to her.

Spinning on her heels, Cho said, "Sure do know how to pick 'em, doncha? The whole time… Course, why listen to me? I only distrusted her from minute one."

Spiky feathers popped out of the gray flesh on Alina's arms, her gaze gliding along her lengthening beak, sinking like fangs into Cho, who shut her mouth.

The shadow passed. Alina's anger slipped through her claws. She crouched in front of her friend. "I'd do everything differently if I could. This week. Two years ago. All of it." She bowed her head. "I'd change it all, except finding you and Mezami. Cho, you gotta believe me when I tell you I didn't know. But it is my fault. Calthin's right about me. You're right about me. I wasn't careful enough. And I'll never be able to show you just how hopelessly sorry I am for failing you—and Mezami."

"All that weird magic, and you couldn't tell we were being played by Ordin?"

"I was hiding from myself. I tried to be the corpse and the scavenger."

"Li, you're not making any sense."

"Only now have I started to see." The pain was all the worse, for there now beat within Alina so many breaking hearts. "Worse than any way I've hurt myself, I've hurt you. I'm rotting from the inside out. A liar. Selfish. That's how I've acted. That's what I am."

She felt hands on her shoulders. Cho's hands.

"Stop. We both know that's crap. You're not perfect, but you're always looking out for others. Even if you screw up, you always try. You saved me from the Walazzins before, remember? And you're the one who found Mezami when he was sick. You're the one who healed him. You're so softhearted sometimes it makes me wanna hurl. And, truth is—" She sighed—"I coulda done more for you, too, Li."

Alina looked up.

"You've been through a lot. With your family. With your body. And all the terrible fashion choices. I mean, masks and flappy capes? Really?" Cho cupped her friend's face in her palms. "You're a mess."

A laugh slipped from Alina's lips. Sharp, painful, but a relief. Like a surgical incision to reduce swelling from excess blood buildup.

"I got no idea what's going on in this head." Cho rapped her knuckles against Alina's skull. "How could anybody? You're obviously going through some stuff. But I shoulda tried to see. Shoulda tried to help you more." Her face sagged. "Me being obsessed with the Walazzins, I let you down. All I feel is hate."

"And all I did was tell you how to feel. I tried to control you."

"Maybe you thought you were protecting me. Maybe you were right. Because if I hadn't been so—Mezami might've—"

Alina drew her in. "Don't."

Their embrace was a root cracking concrete, patient and enduring. Stiffness slid from them like raindrops down bark. When they separated, Alina didn't need telepathy to feel the electric thread binding their hearts.

She said, "I've been stuck on myself—"

"Same."

"—My selves. My many lives. All these things expected of me. Whatever. It's complicated, but you get it."

"Not really. But yeah."

"All this death. And, still, something inside me is banging on the backs of my eyeballs, shouting that we can still do some good."

"What's any of it matter?" Cho pointed toward The Authority craft circling high above in a display of total air superiority. "Even though we blew up their comms hub, they still managed to get a ton of their bolt-buckets airborne again."

"Hang on. You did what now?"

Cbarassan said, "We conducted a stealth operation into the Lion's Den to sabotage the invaders' machinery. Though all but myself and Cho-Zen were killed, through her valiant efforts—and the timely interventions of Mezami and Captain Tiberaira—we disabled The Authority's digital communications. For the most part."

Hands behind her back, Cho looked sheepish. "Hey, before ya go crawlin' up my nose about it, I—"

Alina said, "That's insane, but also incredible."

"You're not mad?"

"I could implode, I'm so *beyond* mad. But not at you. What you pulled off, it's objectively amazing."

"Yeah, and it didn't do squat. Nothing's ever gonna change. The Authority've got this in the bag."

"We don't know that."

"It's like Cbarassan said. Hexhall's on fire. Anarkey's been wiped out. The Walazzins have won."

"Not yet. Hear that?" Artillery, explosions, gunfire. "The battle's not over. And we're still here."

"Great, yeah. We got a busted-up vet, a burnt vine-whipper, a shadow-creeping crow lady (that's you), and a dumb kid. I forget someone?"

Alina rolled her eyes. "Come on. You're not fooling anybody."

"What?"

"This little helpless 'woe is me' thing you've got going on? You're a terrible actor." Alina tapped her forehead. "I can read minds, remember?"

"Ugh." Underneath her phony annoyance, like an octopus ensnaring its prey in a deathly hug, Cho clung to a small but growing hope.

"Together, we stand a chance, you and me. While we were separated, Ivion—excuse me—Ordin tried to pick us off. Him, The Sanctum, The Authority, they all ganged up, but they failed to take us out of the game. We've found each other again." Alina took a breath. "I, for one, am done playing by their rules. How 'bout you?"

"Alina K'vich, an optimist? What happened to you?"

"A whole lot. But, don't worry, I'm not all sugar and butterflies suddenly. Still the same grouchy punk, here. I've just come to a decision is all."

"Oh, yeah?"

"Yeah." Alina picked up one of the Martyrs' bones. A femur. She flung it, and it spun through the air, crashing through a solid brick wall. "The Authority have been on top too damn long. It's time for a switch-up."

"Finally."

"You're the key, Cho. The Plutocrats are terrified of you. They've tried as-sassins, demons, magic bombs—"

"They're right to fear the Torvir name," Tiberaira interjected.

"Not the Torvir," Alina said, placing a hand on Cho's shoulder. "You."

Cbarassan smirked. "And what's brought you to our side at last, rebel? Per-haps it was your conference with the Hextarchs? Praise be."

Alina shot them a withering look.

"Or, should we credit the wiles of our charming, young Ms. Tardrop?"

The *Fyarda*'s wispy laugh was the only reason Alina didn't counter-jab. In-stead, she said, "I've never been much for politics or ancient history. So, I'm not stuck on The Authority because of any particular crime they committed against anyone before I was alive. Maybe it's self-centered, but I honestly don't care about what they did before. I care that they're a cancer *now*. It's obvious to any-one with eyes that everything The Authority touches burns. Them and their bosses, the Plutocrats, they won't be satisfied until they've remade the whole planet in their image—a bland, perfect corpse-world, freed of disagreement and chaos and life. And, will it stop there, or will Elemental Machinamancers dig their greedy fingers into other worlds? They've already tried to tame a corner of the Revoscape, with the Aetherthreads and all its regulations and monitoring." From somewhere inside her own head, Alina was laughing at herself, but she couldn't stop; the words bubbled from her like sap from a wounded tree, like half-eaten entrails from a choking vulture. "So many people—Aelf and human beings—have been sacrificed to build their vision. We've given the Plutocrats more than three thousand years, and all they've done is loot and pillage our world. When do we say enough?"

"Now," said Cbarassan. "Now."

"Now," Cho murmured.

"Whatever the Empire's done in the past, it doesn't matter. Far as I'm con-cerned, there is no 'then.' The past is just the echo of a dream. All we got is 'now.' And, right now, we have to use our eyes and ears and hearts. When you think about it, it's obvious what's *wrong*. We know about the killings, the disap-pearances. Remember all the people locked up in Truct, and that's just one prison. How many more 'Tructs' could there be, out there? The Empire seems to create as much suffering as possible, for as many people as possible, and today I finally understood why. Since its birth, El's been at war with the world. Its laws force us to slaughter each other—Aelf and human, human and human—for nothing, absolutely nothing, except *pain*. The Plutocracy system is a closed loop; it's designed to be cruel. And it was built by the real enemy, who is out there, laughing it up, gorging himself on our misery."

"Li, what are you saying?"

"I've seen our world for what it is, but I don't accept it. I won't accept that it can't change. But, whatever I do next, it won't be for four-thousand-year-old Aelf or the prophecies of dying gods. It's simple, really: the Elementals hurt my friends. That's all I need to know." She sighed. "I've figured something out during my time here. Until today, I was so damn scared of my own anger that I locked it in a room inside my mind, but that only gave it more control. Well, I was wrong to be afraid. Raging against the actions of terrible people is a good thing. It's given me perspective. Kept me grounded. Human." She faced Cbarassan. "As usual, I'm gonna disappoint everyone but surprise no one: I'm not on anybody's side. I just have a job to do—for my own reasons. You can be on *my* side, if that suits ya, but I don't need the baggage of your Achemir, whatever that is. We cool?"

"Certainly." Sitting, Cbarassan extended their leg until the dislocated bone popped back into its knee socket. "You are in control. I'll just be along for the ride, if you'll have me."

In *Fyardan*, Alina said, *"May the Heart-Tree's roots overgrow our graves."*

Cbarassan smiled.

Tiberaira said, "A touching speech, but were you working up to a suggestion of some kind?"

"Yeah, actually: move forward with the plan you told Cho about. Call in your favors. Get your army ready."

Tiberaira blinked. Cho told her, "I'm not gonna lie. You never really get used to it.'"

"So?" said Alina.

"Before I reveal my most intimate hopes to a stranger—" Tiberaira began (and Alina grinned) "—what's your aim?"

"Removing The Authority from existence." In response to Cho's shocked expression, Alina added, "Yeah, I still consider myself a pacifist. What of it? Being a pacifist doesn't mean rolling over. I'm not talking about killing all the soldiers fighting for El."

"Then what?" said Cho.

Alina waggled her eyebrows.

"You're weirding me out."

More waggling.

"Stop it."

"You busted up an Authority fort. Sick. Tens out of ten for everybody." She gave two thumbs up, then turned to Tiberaira. "But we need a more permanent and damaging solution. So, what are the Coneys prepared to do?"

Thumping like a hare's hind leg, Tiberaira's heart warned of danger. "Why don't we show you?" She held out her hand.

Alina took it, and felt the rush of sightless vision.

The future (that great lie that mortals felt compelled to believe in) presented itself. In fact, many futures uncurled like the legs of a resurrected spider. She could not yet understand all the pieces and how they fit, but she thrilled at the nearly infinite permutations of chance. So many opportunities to remake the world, for worse or for better.

She let go of Tiberaira's hand and took a long drag of Ozar's stale air. She said, "That's crazy. And I'm totally in."

An hour ago, panicking that she might lose everyone she cared about, she'd nearly fallen apart. Now, with Mezami gone and the odds of her own death climbing by the second, a strange serenity overtook her.

Something in her was changing.

There were no remains of Mezami's to bury. They all gathered round anyway, and Alina and Cho said whatever came to heart. Nothing too grand, sweeping, or particularly applicable to the battles ahead. They simply told a few anecdotes of their time with him.

"On clear mornings, he'd bench-press my moped, just as the sun was rising," said Cho.

"He wrote snippets of free verse poetry on the walls of his dirt-and-moss hut. Never got to read them, though, because he'd always erase them with his paw before I could see," said Alina.

"He'd always be done eating before anyone else sat down at the fire. Dude had five stomachs, I swear."

"Remember how he claimed his favorite food was rat jerky?"

"Which he cured himself, in the woods."

"Did that just to gross us out. Anyway, I know for a fact his favorite was actually the creampuff I snuck him once."

"He fessed up? That's not like him."

"No. I read his mind. By accident. It was my first time. He was... good about it. Helped me not be scared when I couldn't turn it off for a while."

Cho wrapped her arm around Alina's waist. "He'd chase his tail whenever he got drunk."

They giggled quietly, helplessly for about a minute.

"Alina?"

"Yeah?"

Cho stood on her toes and whispered, "I'm afraid."

Squeezing her friend's arm, Alina allowed Mezami to rise from her like warm, honeyed waters from a deep well. He flowed from her and into Cho, who relaxed—only a little, but still.

Cho said, "I can't keep track of who I am anymore."

"You're thinking about the Sleeper."

"It said, *Find me.*"

"Someday, you will."

They bowed their heads.

Alina shut off her mind-reading, allowing Cho the moment's silent meditation.

Her own thoughts turned to Ordin Ivoir, the absurdly wealthy technocrat who'd taken her to dinner once. As they'd worked together to size up their competition for the bounty on the Bane of New El, he'd shown her three sides of himself—the suspicious sleuth, the ambitious heir, the sorrowful poet. Even after he'd betrayed her, revealing he'd only ever talked to her because Baraam had bribed him to slow her down, she'd still sensed in him those three parts. Finding out he'd been murdered by Tolomond had filled her with regret; knowing he was alive, masquerading as his own sister, drained the regret and left only pity. She pitied the man who'd spun so many webs that he'd ensnared himself, whose three conflicting parts tore at the atrophying remains of his soul. Having returned from the grave, he was only a walking corpse after all.

Alina knew all too well the power behind his revival. Long, long ago, she'd come face to face with it as well, even made a similar deal, it seemed. This was how she knew Ordin could never be free: even thousands of years later, she was still paying the price for her past self's bartering with Greed.

Despite his two betrayals—first as himself, then as "Ivion"—she couldn't wholly blame him. Forgiving him was absolutely out of the question. But Ordin was an infant playing with a gun; the real problem was the parent who'd left the weapon within reach.

She would deal with him, but later. First, there was the matter of Cho.

Tiberaira and Cbarassan had kept a respectful distance. At length, the human woman approached Cho, saying, "All set?"

Cho nodded.

"We'll have to sneak up to the mobile command center. I've got a comrade on the inside."

"No," said Alina. "Gotta make more of a splash than that."

Brow furrowing, Tiberaira shot her a questioning look.

"With the cameras on Cho-Zen, the world will listen."

Cbarassan cocked their head. Tiberaira simply stared.

"I've seen it," said Alina.

Waving her hand between everyone to get their attention, Cho said, "What d'you mean, 'seen it'? You got a direct line to the future now or something?"

"Don't believe me?" Darting forward, Alina pressed her palm to Cho's brow, long fingers wrapping around her scalp.

Cho squawked, eyes rolling back. She spasmed, muttering something in Ciirimaic, which was noteworthy because she didn't speak Ciirimaic.

Like wind-swept ash, images fluttered from Alina's mind to Cho's: *a bird, eternal, surveys a changing world—civilizations ebb and flow like the tides upon a sea of grass; there are wars, countless wars, and lands change hands like coin. Eventually, the passing ages slow to years, then days. New El is raised to the heavens, chained to the earth. Still more centuries pass, until there flies a solar-powered mechanical dragon in the skies. Perhaps ironically, H'ranajaan, the machine guardian, falls onto Ordin the Machinamancer, crushing him. The ruin of Ordin's body is recovered and brought to The Sanctum vaults, where it is scooped into an incinerator. Deeper within the compound, a vat of liquid charged with eldritch energies grows a new body in time-lapse. The baby girl is artificially matured to biological adulthood in a matter of weeks. Soon she is "born" to a circle of hooded figures, each holding a fragment of a key to a door named "time." The woman, soulless, is shown no love. Merely a vessel, she is strapped to a machine and made empty. With sharp utensils, a doctor begins his blasphemous operation. The chip he inserts and activates removes the consciousness that naturally enters all new life; what takes its place is the digital echo of Ordin Ivoir, who opens his new eyes for the first time. And, with his new voice, he screams.*

"What've you done to her?" said Tiberaira.

Fingers brushing Cho's elbow, Alina said, "She's getting a crash course in history, fired from the hip. A few of the more important details, the ones that might come in handy."

"Couldn't you have used... language?" Behind Tiberaira's words lurked accusation. *Freak*, she thought, but to her credit held the insult back.

"Trust me, it's faster this way." Seeing Tiberaira's burning glare, Alina added, "She's not in pain. It's like a trance."

Cbarassan's gasp faded into a wheeze. "You manipulate Abyssal energy... But I thought only the Hextarchs...?" They paused as Cho's babbling grew louder. "What does she say?"

Alina listened. "*... as the Ashes of our uncountable dead / suffocate the wicked—our brethren...*"

"Meaning?" said Tiberaira.

Alina shrugged. "It's probably just interdimensional interference. That's a common side-effect of thought transfer. She's picking up on someone else's vibes. Possibly even a version of herself, from a different reality."

Bristling, Tiberaira opened her mouth to object. To save time, Alina quickly read her mind and answered, "My past and her future are connected by threads I still don't understand. You'll have to forgive me, Hael Tiberaira. I can't explain the woven fabric of the multiverse to you right now, nor will I give you the *what's what* on the unrealities of time. You're just going to have to take my word for it: I'm here to help."

With a sudden yelp, Cho fell to her knees, catching herself before she slammed her face against the ground. She groped blindly for a few seconds, then looked up at Alina. "Woah." She swallowed. "First of all, that was a ride and a half. Number two, don't ever do that to me again, yeah? Merciful Buthermertha,

Li. I had no idea." She skimmed the surface of the ocean that had flooded her mind. The roiling waters settled. "So, you're, like, the sister of gods?"

Alina clicked her tongue.

"Damn, you really *are* an old bag. Called it, first day we met." She held out her fist, which Alina begrudgingly bumped.

"Technically, I'm one of the oldest bags in existence."

"Are you done?" Tiberaira spat between them. "Listen well, Aelf. Since we've met, you've done nothing but discombobulate the girl. And, in case you've forgotten, we have a very limited window open to us right now. You still haven't explained what you meant by 'make a splash,' and I'm too old and hurt for this—"

"The mysteriousness is annoying, isn't it?" said Cho. "Welcome to my world."

Hand clenching Cho's shoulder, Tiberaira barked at Alina,"You can't honestly believe that making a spectacle of her—"

"The 'spectacle' is everything." Alina turned to Cho. "You know. You've seen it, too."

Breath catching, Cho tried to speak. Tiberaira knelt by her, saying, "*We* had a plan. The Cutcords will answer your call. Don't gamble with your life."

Cho's gaze bounced between Tiberaira and Alina.

Eventually, Alina said, "It doesn't have to be 'either/or.' You know the risk. And the opportunity."

"Talk about a slim chance." Cho rubbed her eyes.

"I thought you came to Ozar for justice. Well? This is it. Now. Your chance. Aren't you ready?"

"I don't know!"

Alina wondered at Cho's hesitation. It was confusing; Alina had said all the right words, unveiled the signs and possibilities. Had she misread how things were supposed to happen? Was anything "supposed" to happen?

Free will, she remembered. With humans, it always came down to the need for free will. They had to believe what they did was their choice, and theirs alone.

In this moment, Alina felt certain she'd truly never been human. She didn't crave the dream of freedom. The threads of interconnection, sewn into the breathing fabric of every living and unliving soul in the infinite multiverse—these transcended all notions of freedom, right-doing and wrong-doing.

But she could not explain nor show this to Cho, who was *human*. When, if ever, would humanity be ready for what Alina could now see, just beyond the edges of her vision?

"It's your choice," she lied.

Then Cho surprised her by grasping the secret truth, if only partially: "I'm just the messenger. If I do it right, it won't be my choice. It'll be everyone else's."

For such a long time, Alina had dreaded this exact moment. After accepting her heritage, she was losing herself, trading it for a mystery grab bag of jumbled personalities and desires. But, even as her grip on her own false humanity loosened, she felt another death oncoming; not her own, but that of the little girl she'd met in New El. That girl suddenly was torn in half, and from the bleeding wound emerged a young woman. A new Cho. Alina read these changes in her friend like words on a page. It was as Ruqastra had said: each stage of life ends with a small death. Cho had become everything Alina had feared she might—all hard edges, bruises, and sorrow. The child was lost.

At last, Alina released a long-carried worry, losing a burden but gaining a friend. There was only one thing to say, so she said it: "Cho, you've grown up." And what a woman she might become. If she survived the day ahead.

Cbarassan leaned in. Before they could speak, Alina interrupted, "Not a word. This is a prophecy-free zone, and I'm allergic to dusty old legends."

Cho said, "What're we waiting for, huh? Saddle up, chums. No use arguing, Tibby. We're going on a social call with Kaspuri Walazzin and his oozy pals."

"You'll die," said Tiberaira.

"Could be. But at least I'll get to see the look in his eye, when he finally loses his cool—even just for one second. It's like Li said. He and the rest of 'em will be forced to see us, just once. And I'm gonna tell him off."

"Wherever Kaspuri is, my uncle will be close," said Alina. "Cbarassan, you're hurt. You should stay behind."

The *Fyarda*'s green eyes hardened. "I will be fine. Take me with you, Cho-Zen. I'll ask nothing else of you for the rest of my days. My life means nothing, set against this chance to bear witness."

"I'm not here to tell anyone how they run their business," said Cho. "They want in on the ride, they're in." As Cbarassan began to pray, invoking the names of the Hextarchs, she added, "Now there's just one more problem. We're all banged up, and we got no car, and—"

"Cars?" Scooping her up, Alina slung Cho over her shoulders.

Alina grew in all directions, expanding until her long neck brought her head fifteen feet off the ground, and her outstretched, feathered wings—each a ship's sail in size—carved through the buildings on either end of the small courtyard.

On Alina's back, suddenly ten feet off the ground, Cho shouted, "Li, you're, you're—"

Having taken the form of a gray-skinned, four-legged, beaked, clawed monster, Alina felt the patter of Cho's panic like pellets of hail. "Hideous?" Alina's voice was the bellyaching of an earthquake, the hissing of thunder showers.

"No! *Awesome!*"

And then Cho shed her fear of Alina, sloughing it like dead skin. But it was Alina who felt the lighter for it.

Her great, golden eye narrowed on Cbarassan and Tiberaira. "Last chance to tap out."

64

CHO-ZEN

WHAT KIND OF CREATURE was Choraelia Torvir?

Obviously, Alina wanted her—expected her—to be bigger than herself. But she was a night-slinking, bottom-lurking scavenger. It's how she'd survived. Small, armed only with a stinger, in an ecosystem ruled by killer sharks and krakens.

Choraelia didn't have magic or past lives or destiny to guide her. Cbarassan wasn't telling *her* she'd been born to greatness. Even her own name—Torvir—had been washed by a red tide, dissolving in acidic self-worthlessness.

She drowned, weighed down by her identity, a constricting carapace.

What was she, and could she find within herself the will to outgrow her shell?

Ozar's air had been ignited, the damp burned away and replaced by tongue-coating oil fumes, the tang of metal, the musk of gunpowder. The stalactites, bathed in red and amber light, seemed to drip blood and bile.

Ducking to protect her head from the rock ceiling, clinging to Alina's quills, Cho shouted over the rush of air, "Since when can you turn into a giant bird thingie?"

"Two years ago? Two hours ago? Hard to say." Alina's voice was both hers and *not,* amplified as if by the biggest, grungiest concert speaker ever.

By all appearances about to lose the contents of her stomach, Tibby had buried her hands in soft plumage, the baby feathers on Alina's ridged back.

Cbarassan beamed, tri-pupiled eyes twinkling. Their words whipped away like a horsefly past a cruising car.

"What?" said Cho.

"I said, 'She *is* the Achemir.' Timeless, forgotten, born of the collective unconscious to avenge our shared but stolen destiny. A legend of the *gahool,* long dead."

"Am I s'posed to know what any of that means?"

Cbarassan smiled. "I should hope not."

Alina's sudden nose dive cut short further inquiry, Cho gulping down the lump in her throat. Between stationary Authority craft, she soared downward, straight toward the battered outer wall—Peregar's Grief, its gates smashed open.

"Uh, Alina, just a reminder that you're *huge* now." The gates rushed toward them. "We won't fit." Soldiers looked up, shrieking, tripping over themselves. Cho yelled, "Alina! Gate!"

Wings tucked in, Alina's ship of a body cut through the gap. On the other side, with a flap of her unfurling wings, she sent squads of Tranquilizers spinning away. A few fired their sidearms, missing.

As Alina gained altitude again, Cho took in the sight of El's grand army. They'd occupied every inch of street, every block, from Peregar's Grief to the cracking fortress of Hexhall a mile ahead. The concrete was choked with bodies, dead and broken, and many more still marching. They headed, like a line of ants, toward the inner defenses of the Seventh Stack, toward Hexhall, last sanctuary of Ozar's Aelf and way of life. Alina closed the distance quickly, and Cho was treated to more desecration. Even from so high up, the bodies—Aelf and human—were plain to see, slung over the ramparts, sprawled in the courtyard, pinned to the walls by javelins. Any corpse-less patches of ground had been littered with blood, bullet casings, and ash.

Authority aircraft circled Hexhall, carving it like meat with their searchlights. Coiled around the courtyard was a slain greatworm, its gray chitin plates cracked and punctured by barrel-sized holes that oozed pink acid. Hundreds of Tranqs stood in its giant shadow, waiting. The keep's inner entrance remained sealed, for now. A lull in the action had prevailed, and disquiet settled over the Seventh Stack, such that the whooshing of Alina's absurdly large wings, and the miniature cyclones of air they caused, disturbed the gathering hush. No one looked up, though; they were forced to focus elsewhere.

The air full of the cloying reek of copper and melting plastic, spotlights speared clouds of gunpowder smoke. Their beams converged on a pile of rubble—all that remained of the gatehouse. A lone figure stood there, surrounded by the flags of the Nation of El and its Twelve Families. Well, *eleven* Families, actually: the Torvir banner—orange dragons, with clashing key and hammer on a field of cobalt—was absent. The Family's motto, "Ours Shall Endure," had been reduced to a bitter joke. Eight years. That's all it took to be erased from history apparently. Cho gritted her teeth.

Ahead of Alina's feather-crested, truck-sized head zoomed a shiny chrome cloud of camera drones, speeding toward the lone figure—Kaspuri Walazzin. In that courtyard, surrounding the rubble pile, stood battalion after brightly, multi-colored battalion of Authority grunts, looking up to him, listening to his speech. Cho recognized the navy-and-orange of the Torvir worn by roughly a third of the soldiers. She became antsy, bleakly wondering if she were simply whiling away the minutes until her final, spectacular failure.

Alina continued to circle.

Slapping her thick neck, Cho said, "What're we waiting for?"

"Maximum drama."

"When?"

"Not yet."

Kaspuri wrapped himself in The Capital's flag, wiping a tear on his sleeve, and Cho gagged.

The Walazzins, like many of the Plutocrats, were overly fond of flimflam and pomp. In the name of bolstering the bravado of The Authority's armies—the Landsider and Elemental Tranquilizers, Plasticks, Kadician mercenaries, Ozari turncoats, and colonial conscripts from Oronor, Zinokla, and all over—Kaspuri Walazzin's speech was projected onto Hexhall's very walls. One hundred square feet of high definition, scaly-skinned, oily-haired, reptile-eyed dictator.

He rambled about the inevitability of Elemental victory, the futility of the Hextarch's resistance. The words flowed from him like rusty waters belched from a clogged fountain, his prepared remarks captured by camera drones and news crews and broadcast throughout the world. Triple-I, DHKB, Patriot's Watch, Skye-Eye, all the major propaganda machines were represented.

Zooming in, Cho's eyes, like twin sniper rifle scopes, showed her a grotesque scene: hanging from the crenelations, over the black chasm and the courtyard, were dozens and dozens of bodies. Two-legged, four-legged, six-legged. Humans and Aelf, suspended by ropes and chains. Unmoving. Lifeless.

Descending, Alina must have noticed them, too. Her growl vibrated up Cho's legs and chest.

Cho's more-than-perfect ears captured every lubricated word as Kaspuri continued: "Brothers-in-arms, countrymen, loyal Assets of El! I stand here today, on the field of final victory, in my father's stead. While his failing health prevents him from being here with you all, to wage war for the glory of our Nation, know that I speak with the full weight of the Consulship. The Walazzin Family stands behind you, courageous warriors of the Elemental Empire. Here and now, I say unto you that your mission is all but accomplished." Popping noises from above and below made Cho jump. Crimson and gold starbursts filled the air, a staccato barrage that nearly struck Alina, but she banked left just in time. Sparkling red and yellow confetti drifted downward like autumn leaves stripped from the gaudiest trees imaginable.

Crawling up to the slit of Alina's ear, Cho said, "I can't take much more of this."

Alina answered telepathically, *As soon as the smoke clears.*

It was a weird thing to try for the first time, here and now, but Cho figured out how to think back at her, *When I get down there, what do I even say?*

You'll know.

Stomach lurching as they dropped, Cho yelped.

Ready? Alina asked.

"No!"

Flecked with glittering confetti, Alina brought them all down, down, closer to the cameras and the blades of glaring lights. (Not to mention, the tens of thousands of armed fighters standing at the ready.)

Meanwhile, Kaspuri blustered on, speaking ever more quickly, rising to the climax of his speech, "...this unnatural conjoining of Aelf and Mankind. Any who advocate—or, Gods forbid, embody—such blasphemy are scum to be scrubbed from the world. By Elemental might, all humans will submit again to this *natural* order, to the Consul and the Plutocracy. And all Aelf will be purged from existence." He gestured, and a group of hooded, wrist-bound prisoners were shepherded toward him from the sidelines. "Beginning with these nauseating specimens. May their lives' blood water the roots of humanity's golden age!"

The one positive of Kaspuri's narcissism was that it drew all eyes to him and, thus, away from the air.

Enforcers removed the prisoners' hoods. The Aelf prepared themselves for death, each in their own way—stoic grit, hysterics, numbness.

"I know her," whispered Alina, her voice like a sandstorm. "The hybrid from the Sanctumite recruitment meeting. Nephrataru. I know her."

"I know them all," said Cbarassan.

Nephrataru looked almost human; Cho could only tell she wasn't because she had at least two heartbeats. Even the less human-looking Aelf, though, displayed remarkably human expressions of despair and resignation.

Her heart breaking, Cho corrected herself: not "human"—that wasn't the right word. *Sentient* was what they were. Cbarassan, Bizong, Mezami... Whether skinned or scaled, fanged or feathered, human and Aelf wore the same faces under their masks. Small, pathetic Kaspuri would never see that. Those like him existed only to destroy what they didn't have the intelligence to understand. And *that*, more than anything he'd ever done to Cho, was why he had to go.

The Walazzin heir instructed his guards to put the prisoners on their knees. From his breast pocket, he produced a long-nosed pistol with a silver-inlaid, wooden handle.

"That about does it," said Cho. Still dozens of feet up, she leapt from Alina's back.

Alina's bark of surprise shook the damaged guard towers, whose stones groaned unsettlingly.

Cho landed with an "oof," tucking and rolling. "Wow, ouch," she said.

And she rose as Kaspuri turned toward her, leveled his pistol with her eye, and pulled the trigger.

Good news. She didn't seem to be dead. Although, admittedly, she had little experience in this area.

Patting her face and chest, checking for bloody holes, she didn't dare open her eyes at first. When she did, she saw Alina, mostly returned to her human form, gritting her fangs, her feathered arms outstretched, her back to Cho.

The hollow-point bullet had drilled an exit wound near Alina's spine. She hunched. Her blood was thick, like tar.

Cho reached for her hand.

Gun pressed to Alina's chest, Kaspuri fired again. And again.

That horrible wet sound, *nothing* like a meat tenderizer whacking a steak. Cho would never forget it.

Shaking, Alina grunted and went down.

Cho looked from her friend to Kaspuri, back, and back again.

Then Tibby was there, to Kaspuri's right, and she laid him flat with a single punch to his jaw.

His pistol soared from his limp hand, spinning. It landed five feet in front of Cho, who didn't register picking up the weapon. Before she could think, breathe, *blink*, she was standing over Kaspuri's prone form, pressing the muzzle to his temple.

He cowered beneath her, and she couldn't speak. Couldn't conjure any words. There were no words left. There was only the gun in her hand and her enemy at her feet.

You killed the only family I had left.

Hand shaking, knuckles white, she felt her finger curl around the trigger. Panic clouded Kaspuri's eyes, yet she felt nothing.

She began to squeeze.

Then she heard a cough. The sound had come from behind. She turned.

"Cho." From the ground, Alina coughed again. "I'm alright." She stood, not quite straight, but there she was. Breathing. She spun a slow three-sixty. Where there should have been three bullet holes, she was whole again. Even her weird astral cloak-thing had restitched itself.

Tiberaira took the gun from Cho's slack fingers.

The air around Alina crackled; she radiated heat.

Reptilian face twisting in terror, Kaspuri stuttered, "By all the—What are you?"

All around, some of the bolder soldiers advanced, a ring of bayonets, gleaming. Their steps were slow, however. Unsure. Alina encouraged their hesitation by shrieking in that godsawful way that only she—and the Bane of New El—could. Cho covered her ears.

The fighters, all of them, took several *large* steps back.

Alina cleared her throat and pounded her chest as if loosening a belch. She inclined her head to Cho. "The floor's yours." Telepathically, she added, *I'm good. Do your thing.*

Well.

Cho shook her head. One insane development after another. But Alina was alive. For now, that was all that mattered.

Even as the moment presented itself, Cho was fully aware of how terribly she might screw it up. Thousands of eyes stared at her, with billions more watching from all across the planet thanks to the armada of glinting drones.

Trembling, she drew in a long, laborious breath. She felt as though every human being, every Aelf, and every other creature not just in this world but every other had her in their sights. Her decisions, here and now, would latch onto her name—her being—for the rest of her days (or, maybe only the rest of her *day*.) What echo would she leave in her wake?

Kaspuri Walazzin, knelt before her. At her mercy.

Her mercy.

She'd rehearsed this speech so many times in her mind while performing banal activities like brushing her teeth, watering the plants, replacing spark plugs at Ovaris's garage, playing her VR games at her and Alina's apartment. "I've wanted only this for so long." She'd thought about what she'd say while resting in between sparring matches with Eilars; riding in Ivion's truck on the way to Ozar; sleeplessly tossing and turning, reliving Bizong's spontaneous funeral pyre; and seeing Kinneas's sunken face, purple eyelids, and bluish lips. Every such moment, and a thousand others, she'd filled with a thousand different words of condemnation for the coward who'd orchestrated her family's finale. But each and every one of these options fled her mind as she stared into the slit-pupiled, yellow, inhuman eyes of Kaspuri Walazzin.

Quietly, Cho began to speak. "Levanil Torvir." The cameras orbited her like miniature moons flecked with little pinpricks of red light, recording every detail. "She was my mother. She was thirty-three." Cho backhanded Kaspuri across the face. Blood dribbled from his lips, cut by his own sharpened teeth. Wide-eyed, he glowered at her defiantly. She continued, "Faundasim Torvir. He was my father, and he was thirty-nine." A right hook to his nose, breaking it. He straightened, growling at her, blood now running into and out of his mouth. Tibby kept him pinned by the shoulders. Cho said, "Showennu and Aotereis were my sisters. They were eight and fifteen." By two fistfuls of his oily black hair, she slammed his face against the rubble. "And my brothers Ecrugarak and Jaevermi were ten and thirteen." Planting her boot on his head: "They're all dead because of you. My name is Choraelia Rodanthemaru Dreintruadan Shazura-Torvir, and I should kill you now, to give you the chance to beg for their forgiveness. It's more than you deserve."

So easy. She'd never imagined it would be so easy. He was powerless now. She could smell fear wafting from his every pore, the bile on his breath. Her switchblade flashed into her palm. One quick cut, and it would all be over.

She knew it. He knew it.

He was so afraid. For the first time, as afraid as she was.

All she'd have to do was bury her blade in his brain. Her knife, hard as Eilars's smile. If this wasn't the will of some bright and glorious god…

It'll never end.

She closed her eyes. Who'd said that?

Cho, please don't.

There it was again. Even in her memories, Kinneas was trying to hold her back. Keeping her from doing what *had* to be done. Unable to see that there'd be no joy in the world until all the Walazzins—and The Authority they commanded—were stamped out of existence.

Her boot was on Kaspuri's hand now. She twisted its sole; he whimpered.

She would never be whole. Not until she watched him bleed out. Not until the last drop of his blood dripped from her knife.

Everything is a choice.

Shut up, Kinneas.

Even hate.

She did hate Kaspuri. He deserved it. He—

For the first time, she stepped far enough outside herself to examine her situation. *Really* examine it. Like a naturalist studying a jungle cat, she took stock of her appearance, her demeanor, her position: she snarled, lips curling away from her white teeth; she was covered in dirt and blood (not all of it hers); her brokennailed fingertips gripped the handle of her knife like a starved dog gnawing a fatty bone, and the last remnant of her wig stuck behind her ear, singed to a tiny black tuft topped by a patch of grass-blade green; again, her boot was on Kaspuri's head, crushing him into the dirt.

Her boot. She was literally stepping on a person. Killing him.

Suddenly, the urge to be sick—the absolute absurdity—threw into bleak relief all the choices that had led her to this horrific moment. "What am I doing?"

Mother, Father, Showennu, Ecrugarak, Jaevermi, and Aotereis. Like so many fragments of memory, called forth by the sight of flowers or the smell of dried ink on paper, the visions of her family had begun to fade. She'd been so young, and they'd all been gone for so long now, that they'd become nothing more than moving pictures of people—two dimensional. Grief pierced her, a thousand wounds by a thousand poisoned darts—too shallow to kill, too deep to close. A maddening, inflamed ache. She was petrified at the thought of their second death, when she'd finally forget them completely. But she couldn't let that fear guide her any longer. That chapter had to close sometime.

Before her lay the choice to join them in death or become truly alive. All the suffering, the bloodshed, she'd endured it all just to get here. She could have taken Tiberaira's offer for revenge right then; she could have called it "justice"— the word Kaspuri himself had used to describe his own savagery. Yet, what would it all have been worth, really, if she followed that path to its conclusion?

She remembered Kinneas. *It'll never end*, he'd said. The know-it-all. How frustrating. As usual, he'd fallen backwards into being *right* and *wrong* at the same time. Earlier, she had assumed he'd meant that executing the Walazzins would be morally wrong—an opinion she'd never agree with. However, now she knew he'd been warning her of another danger: if she did succeed, she'd spend the rest of her life looking over her shoulder. The cycle of reprisals and suffering could never be broken. That's what he'd meant. And that's where he'd been wrong. It *would* end because she was about to end it.

Playing the game according to the Plutocrats' rules, she had sacrificed her friends and so many others, all so that she could kill a few bad men. No more.

At last, as she made her choice, she could feel infinite other Chos snuffed from existence, all possibilities collapsing into this first step she was about to take.

She lifted her boot off Kaspuri's head. His wince faded as he noticed she'd stopped hurting him.

Kneeling, she whispered in his ear, "I want you to know that I'm not sparing your life because I've grown a conscience or I've realized that I need to be the bigger person. I'd put you down right now, with the whole world watching, if I thought it would make a difference. And, eventually, I'd sleep just fine since we'd all be better off with you dead, see? Nah, you get to live on, for now, because I got a better use for ya."

She'd failed to see it before now, but the Walazzins weren't her enemy. They were only the product of her enemy—created by it, one small part of it. While the Plutocracy and its Authority must be eliminated, even more importantly, society at large needed overhaul. The Walazzins could never have become so powerful without the system of control that had empowered them. The Torvir, too, had been elevated by that same system, a death spiral that had enslaved all people. The Twelve's capital gains were the rest of the world's capital punishment. And it was all perfectly legal because the laws on which civilization balanced had been written by the corrupt. The Empire was a worldwide prison, and there was only one way to be free of it.

"Now's your chance, Lady Choraelia," said Tibby. "The world is watching. Take his life, and rattle the very Chains of New El."

With those big, sappy green eyes of hers, Alina nodded. Her face was unhelpfully impassive.

Cho gripped the handle of her knife but kept it in its sheath. "Choraelia Torvir died with her Family. The first of the Twelve to fall." Taking a deep breath, "I am something else. Plutocrat and orphan, I'm nobody, and I'm also all of you." She pointed at the crowd of Authority soldiers. "My name is Cho-Zen."

Suddenly, she lost control. Her knees bent and her blade was freed, flying toward Kaspuri's jugular. With every ounce of her will, she locked her elbow, and with her other arm, resisted the urge to slit the man's throat.

"Cho," said Tibby, obviously confused (but not nearly as much as Cho herself was). "What are you doing?"

Good question.

Grinding her teeth, sweat coursing down her face, Cho grappled with herself. The tip of the knife inched closer and closer to Kaspuri's throat. She had resolved to spare him; where was this mindless urge coming from?

Then she heard it, a high-pitched hum, and felt the vibration in her left arm. There it was. Eilars's little implant that Doc Dzu had surgically attached to her nervous system. It had allowed her limbs to act on impulse, to distribute harm without consulting her brain. The implant had identified a threat and made its demand, but she would not concede.

With one final effort, she punched the crook of her elbow, bending it back, and she bit into the meat of her forearm. Cutting through skin and ropy muscle, her front teeth closed around something small and fragile between her ulna and radius. Clenching her jaw, she tore the object out. Blood ran down her chin. A little green light blinked between her teeth. She spat the chip onto the ground. *Crack. Fizzle.* Its lights flickered, then went out.

A stinging, great, big gash in her arm, she felt clear-headed again. *Cho* again.

The camera drones, of course, had caught the action from every conceivable angle. Hopefully, the drama—and the blood—would add a little punch to her next statement:

"Nothing like a little cybernetic sabotage. Now that that's dealt with... I figure some of you might've seen my Watchbox improv show the other night."

To her surprise, the line drew some laughs from the soldiers. One yelled, "You looked better with hair!" Another, "Even shrimpier off-camera."

Cho said, "Got some fans in the front row, I see. Maybe you remember I invited anyone watching to join me and Anarkey in taking on the Elemental war machine. Well, Anarkey's gone now, but I thought to myself last night, 'Who better to make my case for revolution to than The Authority itself? They'll never see it coming.'"

More laughter.

"Yeah, it made more sense before I crash-landed a couple minutes ago, I admit. But I must have one thing going for me. Anyone wanna guess?"

Absolute quiet. They were listening. Intent.

"I got your big boss by the scruff, and no one's bum-rushed me yet. That's gotta mean something. Could be, you're just scared of my friend." She pointed at Alina, golden-eyed, growing in height. "Or my other friend." She pointed to Tiberaira, who held the gun to Kaspuri's cheek. "But I think it's something else. Actually, I'm betting my life on it."

No one moved.

"Before I say my bit, and you all decide whether to charge this hill I'm willing to die on, I want it clear that I'm not going to order anyone to do anything."

There came a shout: "You have no Authority!"

Cho held up her finger. "I wouldn't be too sure of that, bud." Moment of truth. "Tibby?"

"Cutcords," Tiberaira roared. "Where are my Coneys?"

The most awkward, nerve-wracking silence followed. Then, stamping in reply, a distant, rhythmic, quickening *thump-thump-thump* that began in one pocket of the army, then was picked up by another and another and another.

Thump-thump-thump.

The front ranks of El's grand army looked around, none of them sure of what was happening, none wanting to be the first to make any moves.

Thump-thump-thump. The crunch of boot on brick dust.

The click of belt buckles—

Thump-thump-thump.

—the scuffing of scabbards and holsters against body armor.

Thump-thump-thump.

Dark-blue uniformed warfighters marched out of formation to stand before Cho. The bright orange cords on their lapels—symbols of their obedience to the laws of the Plutocracy—had been severed, the threads hanging limply from their shiny brass pins. Although dishonored by the deaths of their old masters, their heads remained unbowed. There were maybe ninety of them in all.

Tibby said, "The 31st Forward swears itself to Cho-Zen. We bind ourselves to you forever, and will live and die by your command."

Emboldened, other Torvir soldiers shoved their way forward by the dozens, then the hundreds. Almost every single blue-and-orange uniform pushed their way to the front, surrounding Cho's podium of wreckage, their backs to her and their weapons facing outward. A wall of heaving, armored chests and broad shoulders had materialized at Cho's call. As promised.

In awe of the fourteen-year-old half-veiled by the fog of war, the soldiers of El stared at her. (Wisely, the man who'd questioned her right to speak stayed conspicuously silent.)

Tapping her hips with her fists, she said, "'Why,' you must be asking. Why am I here? What do I want? The answer's simple: I'm going to end this war. El has no right to Ozar, no right to exterminate the free humans and Aelf who lived here. Who are the Ozari hurting back home? Huh? Isn't it about time El stuck its nose back in its own problems? Cutcords, Tranquilizers, Enforcers, mercenaries—I ask you, is this why you signed up? Is genocide what you wanted? What are you fighting for? Who are you fighting for? Is slaughtering thousands of people thousands of miles away from your homes going to solve any of the problems poisoning our nation?" She shook her head. "Everything is a choice. And, tonight, I choose to call out our real enemy—the Plutocracy, the system that threw you into this hole to die for it. Haven't you noticed, no matter where the fight takes you, you always get nothing, but they get *everything*? Tell me that's not how it goes. Every. Single. Time. Betcha none of you can. I can see it in your eyes. You're even more done with all this than I am. Well, you don't have to keep going. You can make your choice, tonight." She waited out a stretch of silence. "If you join me now, I won't make you big, shiny promises that you'll win glory or wealth. I'm not promising anything—except your freedom. Stand with me. End this fight with me. The Empire has done enough. *It* has no Authority here." She finally petered out.

Delivering a quick kick to Kaspuri's ribs, Tibby came forward. Half the cameras now floated around her head, but she ignored the spinning, buzzing, gnat-like machines. She addressed the assembled soldiers directly. "I must look like something spit up from *at least* the Sixtieth Hell, right?"

Nervous, uncertain chuckles.

"Laugh it up. I don't mind. These scars, these phantom pains, they remind me of who I am, every day. Rather, who I was. Until this morning, I was Hael Tiberaira, Captain of the 31st Forward, the Coneys. Those of you I bled with at Gen'avn, the Siege of the Quills, the Last Stand at Baenhill—you know me as 'Rookie.' In servitude to three Consuls, I have taken lives on every continent. For nothing, less than nothing. So many of my brothers- and sisters-in-arms are gone now, fallen on one or another anonymous battlefield. My only reward? Damnation." She placed a hand on Cho's shoulder. "However, I'm a different person than I was this morning. Thanks to Cho-Zen, tonight, I throw off my collar; I choose redemption. What about you?" She slid down the rubble pile, pushing her way through the Torvir Cutcords to join the other Authority soldiers. Singling them out at random, with her one arm, she thumped their chests, shoved them. "What'll it take for you to wake up? I've been to the meetings, listened to the terrors that choke your voices and soak you in cold sweat. I've heard you. I *am* you, trapped in the same nightmare. I've burned down buildings full of people. I've executed minors. I've done it all, and worse. What about you?" One of the men nearest her broke down, crying. "Wake up, then. If you clamp your eyes shut, you'll just keep firing blindly, without even giving your victims the courtesy of a final look. *You* might not be watching, but everyone else is." Tibby snatched one of the drones out of the air and flung it away. "Are you all satisfied to live out your days as *pinkojacks*, hated the world over? For what? *For what?* Wake up, and answer me."

Silence.

"That's what I thought. There is no easy answer, is there? Cho-Zen is right, though. We must, each of us, choose. The only purpose of our lives, so far, has been to serve the will of the Plutocrats. And our service has come at a steep cost." She rapped her knuckles against the artificial voice box built into her metal throat. "I, for one, am done sacrificing my body and soul for the enrichment of trash like him." She pointed to Kaspuri. Quietly, cameras spinning around her face, she asked, "Are you?" Then she shouted, "To my Landsiders, to those among you who remember too well the tragedy of the Torvir, to all you brave fools cajoled into marching here, who still dare to dream of a better life than this, now is the time. Turn your weapons on your Elemental commanders! Drive them and any who stand with them into the pits. What's it going to be, comrades?" She raised her fist and fired Kaspuri's gun. Just once. "Choose."

The Authority soldiers in their bright uniforms, the mercenaries, the colonial conscripts—they looked to one another, and they began to murmur.

Shoulder to shoulder in their gleaming, sleek armor, the Cutcords braced for a fight to the death.

Tibby said, "You were meant for better, so choose to be better. Stand with us tonight, as we liberate Ozar from the Empire. Join with us tomorrow, as we retake the Nation of El. For the Torvir! For your families! For all those starved of freedom! Let the Elementals keep their chains and their flying ball in the sky. Ours is the surface world. *Ours shall endure!* Follow me, Landsiders of all colors and creeds—"

It was as if fate took a breath.

"—and follow Cho-Zen!"

65

ALINA

I T WAS AS IF fate exhaled. In a moment of perfect clarity, Alina listened to its breath, hearing the alarming rattle in its lungs. The world was terminally ill and could only survive if the tumor choking its heart were carved out. She felt certain that Cho must be the scalpel. Soon would come the first incision.

Abyssal energy bled from every one of the thousands of bodies crowding Hexhall's courtyard. Cho's speech had created a point of convergence. Here, there were slightly fewer than infinite possibilities, and that was unusual. It was a sign that The Abyss had been active, eliminating extraneous paths—as it had done when guiding Alina to the Hextarchs and connecting her mind with Cho's.

What was The Abyss?

Once, Ruqastra had spoken of the Revomancers of old. She'd mocked them for believing that they'd mastered almost all there was to know of Chrononite lore. They'd even had their own name for the mysterious mineral, a name as arrogant as they'd been: *Revonite*. Ruqastra scoffed at them for missing the point. The tenets of Revomancy couldn't be written down. They had to be intuited, again and again, by each new generation. A Discipline whose medium is the subconscious must change depending on the practitioner.

Few of the ancient Revomantic scrolls had survived. Alina had been shown only one. Thousands of years old, it stated, *Time is the dreamer's plaything*. Now that she knew herself to be twice as old as that dusty document, she could safely claim its teachings were the scholarly equivalent of cleaning a toilet bowl with a hammer. It wasn't entirely useless, however. The subtle truth it tried to convey was the unbreakable connection between the *mind* and *everything else*. Some Revomancers spent their entire lifetimes meditating on this relationship. Only a few eventually came to understand: perception is reality, reality isn't real, and everything that *could* happen currently *is* happening. The future will never come to be; the past is an illusion of memory and emotion. There is only one moment, and it is *all* moments—occurring simultaneously.

This lesson proved reasonably difficult to contain within the human brain, which is essentially a wad of raw meat in a bone bowl. To help students of Revomancy learn it, at the start of their training, they were presented with a thought experiment:

The simplest game of chance in existence is the coin toss. Most people would agree that there are two possible outcomes to each throw: heads or tails. This is incorrect. Flip a coin enough times (let's say 100,000, just to be safe), and the results will be remarkably close to 50-50. Sure, that much is true. However, what most people have forgotten is that the coin and the toss and the players are all affected by the simple act of observing the game. If you watch the coin fall, you will change the outcome. And, if your will is strong enough, you can *control* the nature of that change. With enough effort, you could take what should be just a simple game of heads or tails and add a third option—edge.

The outcome between outcomes, that's where strange things could theoretically happen. Mid-toss, a hawk could snatch the coin from the air, or the wind knock it off course. The coin might burst into flames, or multiply into two or ten identical copies. It was on the *edge* that Revomancy hedged all its bets. On that thin line of *almosts*, a dizzying number of possibilities presented themselves.

For example, an orphaned princess might stand before thousands of her enemies and—because of the magic of chance, the oldest of spells—capture their attentions. Through the assistance of a wounded soldier and the trickery of a dream sorceress, she might even turn some of those enemies into allies. Or, she might be shot on the spot. Either way, Cho-Zen's arrival on this battlefield was a moment of tremendous significance. A betting man might have said it was anyone's game; 50-50, succeed or fail. But Alina remembered the old truths, for, once upon a time, she had been the one to discover them: *perception is reality; nothing is real.* Even the laws of the universe could be altered.

The web-like threads that bound probability and chance were clear to her, now. As she had subconsciously been doing her whole life, she could now *consciously* modify likelihood, bend the odds. Her partnership with The Abyss made this possible, for Revomancy was the art of growing and manipulating minds, and The Abyss was the force—no, the consciousness—that flowed in, from, and through every sentient lifeform (any being that could perceive the passage of time).

The living shadow. The embracing dark. Generated *by* consciousness, The Abyss also *was* consciousness and could *influence* consciousness. In a sense, it both was and wasn't *time*, just as it was and wasn't *dream*. After all, neither could exist without consciousness to give them shape. From this relationship between—no, *union of*—self and imagination, The Abyss drew its influence and its purpose. It was a terrifying, primordial thing, and Alina was profoundly relieved that its goals and hers were in harmony.

What was The Abyss, then? Words must fall short of defining it. If you truly wish to know, step outside on a moonless night, turn out all other lights, and listen.

… There. Do you hear it?

Emerging from her waking dream, reminding herself of her physical body standing on a heap of rubble in a burning city, Alina looked around. She drank in the contorted faces of The Authority soldiers. Darkness surrounded and bound every one of them to each other. So, why did they instinctively fear it? The moment of clarity faded, the final answer eluding her. The vortex of sentient, watching, amused magical energy held her back.

Not yet, The Abyss seemed to say. *Not yet. But soon.*

In the half-minute of fragile silence that followed Cho and Tibby's dramatic speeches, Alina gauged the reactions of the audience. They were on the edge, still only lukewarm, which made sense: *turn your back on your country, government, and civilization* was kind of a big ask.

Unflappable, Cbarassan beamed at Alina like they'd just been handed a check for a million gelders and the keys to a fleet of luxury cruise ships. The *Fyarda*'s thoughts were a starburst of prophecy and fulfillment, for they had glimpsed the future called Alina the Achemir. *I may depart, happy,* they thought, *if such is the hope I leave behind.*

Knowing she could live another thousand years and still never convince Cbarassan that they were wrong about her, Alina focused instead on Cho. She appeared to be a short, bald girl standing on a mound of pulverized stone, surrounded by death and its promise, but appearances often deceived. Something in Cho was changing.

Her enemies had tried to lock her away, strip her of agency, even kill her. But they'd only helped her shed her old skin. Bursting from its constricting husk, a lithe, muscled, venomous hunter emerged. Its cry from the deep would wake generations of fury—enough to drown an empire.

Reflected in the eyes of the soldiers was a relentlessness born from pure exhaustion, the same indignation Alina had felt all her life. For so long, she hadn't had a word for that raw pain, and neither had they. Soon, they would. And Cho would be the one to give it to them.

"Just a little more, Cho," Alina said under her breath. They were tired, hungry for something they couldn't even name. "Offer it to them."

Kaspuri prostrate before her, Cho waited. Gun tucked in her belt, Tibby held out her one arm in fellowship with her siblings-in-arms.

Her Revomancer's senses working overtime, Alina registered the emotions of the servants of The Authority. Mostly, agitation. Unrest. Lots of fear. Pockets of hostility. But some curiosity, too.

She started popping into their minds, one by one, in quick succession, firing off dreams. She amped up their inquisitiveness by teasing out their memories of childhood—when, to them, the world was new. (Whether they'd ever really felt that way wasn't relevant; Revomancy was the art of the possible.) Next, she tried to smother their fear, but met with fierce resistance. So, she redirected it instead. She fed the soldiers visions of a ball of fire in the sky, always watching, which transformed into the floating, glittering Capital, New El. *The enemy.*

Her efforts made barely a dent. Even with all of Dimas's power at her fingertips, she was only one inexperienced lie-weaver. She didn't have enough thread to link all of these minds. The plan was unraveling, and she could do nothing.

Then, a needle freely emerged from the haystack. Wearing the scythe and boar's head of the Denadon Family, the soldier shoved his way into the no man's land of blood spatter and smoke. "I didn't sign up to make orphans. The name's Bas Crifring of Uduus, and I have no love for the Walazzins."

Just like that, the threads began to knot. Alina dropped her spells. The rest was out of her hands.

Another soldier, a Malach, came forward. "Vilama Ika, from Nevtic. I was broke and just wanted a scholarship. Never any of this."

"I'm an indentured servant," shouted a third, in the black-and-white of the Ivoir. "My name is Rucen Or'arei. My master sold me to The Authority to settle his debts."

In a row, the three of them exchanged a long look. Bas nodded, and he and Rucen followed Vilama's lead: they unsheathed their combat knives, brought the blades to their breasts, and cleanly cut through the bright-colored cords over their hearts. They bowed their heads, and Bas said, "Hail, Cho-Zen of the Landsiders. We accept your invitation."

Rucen chimed in with, "And honor to your bodyguard," glancing at Alina, "who reveres you so fiercely she placed herself between you and death. Such a love I have never seen."

"We swear ourselves to your service," said Vilama, "my lady who stands beyond fear."

Invisible tendrils of Abyssal energy enveloped them, creeping toward full embrace, a growing shadow that could one day reach the heavens themselves. Alina smiled. *As below, so above.*

The Torvir Cutcords among the vanguard, several hundred at least, came forward next. Openly weeping, laughing, crying out—as one, they saluted.

"She's a child!" someone else protested. "A rebel, and—"

"And that's a Demon protecting her!"

Spreading her gray-fleshed, black-feathered arms, Alina grew several feet. Mist and shadow flowed from her. A simple illusion spell, but it doused the challengers' nerves. Then she slipped *Ida* over her face and said, "I am what I am, and Cho-Zen accepts me for it." She didn't know from where the confidence originated, but she welcomed it. Taking to the air, she soared above the army and shouted down at them, "The Plutocrats demand that you fight for their money. Cho asks that you fight for your lives."

More soldiers left their stations—Udutetta, Reautz, Caelus, Denadon, Ivoir, and even Walazzin. The more seconds flitted past, the more warriors crossed the invisible line Cho had drawn for them, the delineation between their bleak pasts and their uncertain prospects.

Responding to a call from their captain, an entire division of colonial draftees in their simple brown-and-gray motley uniforms punched the air. They, too, marched to Cho's side.

The more who joined, the more easily their undecided fellows were convinced. Eventually, incredibly, the sides were equal. Then the balance shifted, and the soldiers who hadn't switched teams—mostly red-and-gold Walazzins—felt increasingly lonely. They began to back up, sidling along the wall. The Plasticks—loyal only to the almighty gelder—began to falter.

Altogether, the deserters made up only a portion of the vanguard. There were still tens of thousands of fighters who hadn't heard Cho's impassioned plea. However, the courtyard of Hexhall could only hold so many bodies; a few thousand might be all Cho would need to turn the tide.

Pro-Plutocrat morale strained to the breaking point, until one of the soldiers still holding the Walazzin-set line said, "To die for a traitor's daughter isn't freedom."

"The brat's not the worst of it," yelled another. "She's clearly being manipulated by this evil, inhuman *thing* before us. This abomination in the eyes of God! The demon tries to deceive us all, brothers. Keep to your faith." He locked eyes with Alina, fingers twisting in one of The Sanctum's showy signs of evil-warding. "May The Author erase your name."

Alina landed directly in front of the Sanctumite soldier (the others backed off, giving them plenty of space). Her touch like black iron, she prodded his chest, and his bravery crumbled like charred firewood. "How do you know your Lord didn't send me here?"

Standing near the broken gate at the end of the mile-long bridge, a man said, "Because there is only one who speaks for The Author of Creation."

Alina turned as The Savior crested the hill of fractured rebar and twisted steel. He was flanked by his two bodyguards. On his right, the woman, wearing an all-white, silk power suit and designer sunglasses. On his left, in starched Gildsman's teal and black, Baraam bol-Talanai.

Flying high again, Alina—her hands blurring—cast a few dozen shield spells on herself.

The Savior said, "My voice, and mine alone, carries the Lord's will. Mine is the power that spreads His Word, commanding the temporal as readily as the divine. Thus, when I order my subordinates to kill a deceitful buzzard circling over the field of my victory, consider it edict."

When no one seemed particularly keen to fight Alina, Mateus spread his arms as if to embrace them all. "I do not begrudge you your fear, my children. This deceiver has cast her pall over you. However, evil cannot contend with true righteousness. Even she will be destroyed, for she, too, was created by the Lord. What the Lord has made, He may unmake."

Eyes darting between The Savior, his silent subordinate, and Baraam, Alina kept her distance. "Empty words, Mateus. You don't believe any of what you're saying. Quit hiding behind your lies."

"It is not I who hide behind a mask." Sleeve of his robe swishing, he flung a damning finger toward Alina. "Behold, an Aelf in need of Raving. Fortunately, I know just the Gild-dog for the job—bol-Talanai!"

The air crackled around Baraam, and Alina's ears popped. A dark cloud passed over his features as he looked up, eyes white as the core of a lightning bolt. Sparks burst from his hands and feet as he lifted off the ground.

66

BARAAM

DESPITE ALL HIS EFFORTS, here she was again. Levitating opposite him, Alina K'vich, granddaughter of Baraam's master, constant thorn in his side, his great weakness.

A warm blast of air rushed upward from the chasm at Baraam's back. "So. This is how the gods have willed I be punished for my sins."

He'd done his utmost to leave this life behind for good, but the Rave coursed through his lungs like storm winds. It bled into his every organ. He'd been called back to fulfill his duty, the purpose for which he'd been honed since before he'd lost his first milk tooth.

"We don't need to fight, Baraam." Alina's beyond-black cloak billowed as she lifted her mask, revealing her golden eyes. "We shouldn't."

The cloak. The mask. So much like Ruqastra. Yet, different. Less. More.

More than time separated this new Alina from the stringy little goblin that had crowded him, shadowing his every step.

When had she learned to fly?

"The last time you got in my way, you were a blubbering child."

Her Niima flared oppressively. The fires of the burning city, the spotlights trained on the two of them—all light dimmed. "How 'bout now?" she said.

In his career, Baraam had hunted and killed monstrously powerful Aelf from the densest jungles to the highest peaks. He'd brought down Giants in seconds, wiped out packs of *einharthrak* with a single bolt; he'd exterminated Aelf of all levels of intelligence like termites. But he'd never sensed anything remotely close to Alina's Niimantic signature. With his eyes, he saw the girl he'd known from her infancy; his refined Raver senses, however, detected not one aura but *four*. At least.

She said, "You're comparing this thing in front of you with the girl you watched grow up. It's a lot, I know. You're confused, and that's okay."

"Stay out of my head." Ruqastra used to deny his privacy in just the same way.

As if to mock his warning, behind Alina tendrils of dark energy rippled upward, unfurling like shriveled tongues, hundreds of feet high. The tendrils tethered the ground to the great cavern's ceiling, then spread outward—thinning, filling the air, forming a see-through wall. He recognized this grayish, translucent forcefield. One of Ruqastra's spells, taught her by Master Dimas.

Then—very much unlike Ruqastra or Dimas—Alina raised a *second* forcefield behind Baraam.

From the ground, the Savior chortled, arms crossed, but made no move to intervene.

Creating a narrow strip of no man's land, the magical barriers cut Alina, Baraam, and The Savior off from the gathered army. At Alina's back lay the fragile remains of Hexhall, and its final door leading to Ozar's six weakened gods, poised to fall. Behind Baraam, the blasted gatehouse and the bald girl's swelling ranks of rebels. On both sides, soldiers and recent deserters alike forgot their tense standoff for a few moments, and they approached the forcefield, testing it with curious fingers, recoiling at its ichorous, spongy bounciness.

"Why isolate us?" Baraam asked.

"To protect them." Alina pointed at the army. She licked her teeth, an unconscious habit triggered by unrest. "It's decision time, Baraam. We need to talk."

"About?"

"Oh, I dunno, maybe the state of this war, the hellish chaos all around us? No? Then how about we discuss why you're thinking about killing me."

As usual, part of him wanted to comfort her, but—as usual—he resisted the urge. "My Gildmaster reinstated me, ordered me here. I did not want to come, yet I had no choice."

"Everything is a choice."

"The holder of my contract—The Savior of Ozar—has directed me to end your life. If I do not, the Gildmaster…"

Her eyes flashed, brow crinkling. "That old stick Ridect? You're not seriously going to choose him over me." She seemed entirely, infuriatingly confident in her assumption. As always.

"Why are you here? This is not your fight."

"You're still stuck on your head-canon of me. Look at me, Baraam. Really *look* at me. What do you see?"

He saw a dangerous Aelf of inexplicable power, a hybrid beast in need of—

"Underneath," she said.

She'd been such a little scrap of a thing, always running off in odd directions, always asking questions to anyone who'd give her the time of day. That inquisitiveness got her lost and badly hurt on numerous occasions. If Baraam hadn't been watching…

When she'd been very young, not more than seven, and he'd been training, he used to have her curl up into a ball, and he would bench-press her. Every night, she'd demand an arm-wrestling rematch, though she'd never beat him.

"I warned you. Stay out of my head," he said.

"It's not me you're confused about. You know me. The problem you're working through is *you*."

"Arrogant, prideful. Bad fruit from a rotten tree. You see everything as a puzzle only you are clever enough to solve, but all you really do is blindly grope at the threads that bind society, our entire way of life. Every frayed end you see as a lever to pull, completely unconscious and uncaring of the disastrous consequences. You don't belong here. War is the province of warriors."

"War is the playground of warriors. You talk a big game about 'disastrous consequences.' Why don't you take a godsdamned look around?" The oil fires and rock slides tearing the Seventh Stack apart, these were her answers. "This is *everyone's* war. We've been caught in it for so long it might as well be forever. All because El can't stop *taking*. It takes, and it takes, and it takes. And when it can't find enough to take from others, it turns on itself. Truct, our home—"

"The Gild is my home."

"You don't believe that."

He remembered the Saludbabni and Gildmaster Ridect's coming to take him away, remembered his self-disgust and fury.

She continued to push. "The Gild used you. They took someone with incredible potential and intelligence and reduced him to a weapon. It's tragic. But it doesn't have to be your fate."

"My Gild made me an Aelfraver, a hero. I kill monsters."

"You serve monsters. I mean that more literally than you think."

He wished she would shut up but lacked the willpower to compel her.

"They've lied to you about everything, including what the Aelf are. I'm begging you, man. See things from my side for once. Truct's become a dystopic pit, a prison where anyone who doesn't goose-step to the Plutocrats' tune is dropped and forgotten by the world. And the same thing's happening everywhere. We helped make it that way, you know. By not speaking out. By letting The Authority trample all of us and the people we know and especially the ones we don't. We looked the other way—*I* looked the other way for too long." She straightened. The pride in her eyes, that was Master Dimas, through and through. She made it her own, though, somehow embodying both his old strength and her new.

By Ëétion, how she'd grown.

She said, "I came to Ozar to find answers, to discover who I am. Turns out, I'm *really* strong. Like, unbelievably, whiplash-for-everyone, *strong*. And I could use this power to take revenge. (Part of me really, really wants to.) But I'm not looking to stay stuck in this revolving door of suffering. I'm ready to free myself, and you, and everyone else who'd like to come along for this off-the-rails spinning teacup ride." She tapped the heel of her palm against her forehead. "He's in here, y'know. Dimas. He's still trying to rearrange the furniture in my head. It's taking some effort to keep it all straight. But there's one thing he's for sure been wanting to say to you."

Baraam clenched his jaw and narrowed his eyes.

She took a deep breath. "He's sorry, Baraam. Sorry he kept you in the dark. Most of all, he's sorry he never told you."

Lower lip twitching, his voice husky, he said, "Told me what?"

"That you were his son, in all the ways that mattered." She drifted toward him, hands away from her sides, palms down. "He'd have done it differently if he could've, but nature is nature, and he was what he was. Proud, arrogant, like you said. Millennia-trained habits are hard to break. Go figure." She came closer. "But he loved you, Baraam. And I love you. He and I are the same—it's weird, I know, but true. We're the same. We loved you separately when we were separate, and now we love you as one. You're his son. My brother. Family."

The tears welling in his eyes turned to steam.

She floated still closer. "He forgave you. You know that, right?"

"What?" It was as if Baraam were thirteen again, standing in Dimas's shadow. Alina even wore the same kind of mask he had. Baraam could still picture him slipping it over his sharp face, on those long winter's nights he'd gone Raving alone.

She said, "When you left The School to study under Ridect, Dimas didn't hold the grudge. He respected your decision, even if he couldn't agree. You were his pride, and he forgave you."

"You lie."

"Why would you want to believe that?" She shook her head. "He was so happy when you finally came back. Because he'd realized how much he'd needed you. Like I need you now. Can you forgive us?"

He bit his lip, hard. Pain was familiar. It steadied his nerves. "It's truly incredible, your devastation of my life, time and time again. I have done all I can to keep you out of the chaos you've doggedly sought for years, and now you've forced me into a final trap. Do you comprehend what you're demanding? That I forever cast aside my old life, my past self—to defy my sworn duty? How could I do so? Yet, my only alternative is having to beat you to death with my bare hands. My reputation, my honor, the lineage of my masters back to the founding of The Gild two thousand years ago. All of it, erased. If I fail."

"Well, I've been failing my whole life. Wanna know what I've learned?"

He said nothing.

"Failure and success are the same. You learn from both. You move on. The struggle continues. Life and death, flow and ebb—the battle for the soul of our world will never end, and whether each of us makes a lot of noise or a little, the most important thing is choice. Where did we choose to stand? On the side of hope or despair? Pick your place, brother."

"You're painting yourself the avatar of hope?"

"I'm just the messenger."

Through the desaturated graininess of the forcefield, he took stock of the soldiers who now stood beside Alina's little bald friend. That The Authority had not gunned her down was nothing short of amazing. What sort of spell had been woven over them? Or, had the seeds of the Plutocrats' centuries-long fears finally taken root? Were these the fiery blooms of rebellion?

"That's quite enough stalling." The Savior clapped his hands—once—dispelling the hypnotic silence that had filled the courtyard. The sound echoed. "I have been more than lenient enough. You two clearly have history to sort through, but that will have to wait for the next life. Honestly, all this blubbering at one another like lovesick boarding school students? What maudlin claptrap, you two."

He jumped, lifting off the ground in a burst of dust, robes flapping about him like moths' wings, gliding toward Alina and Baraam. He clapped his hands a second time. The resulting shockwave parted them, throwing them to the ground.

In a rain of sparks, Baraam landed like a bomb, blasting rubble away as he caught himself. Alina melded with the stones, sinking into them as if they were pudding, then rising calmly. Lightly, on bare feet, The Savior touched down. They formed a triangle.

Baraam glared at The Savior. "You interrupt a Raver fulfilling his gods-given duty."

"Oh, had it handled, did you? From where I was standing, it looked suspiciously like the two of you might be collaborating. Wouldn't that be a twist? An attack dog, turning on his masters." The Savior's gaze shifted to Alina. "Exorcist Kellfyute, wasn't it? But, you've changed. How curious. Your aura, now, is the same as a very old and very sick creature, one I'd thought departed from this plane of existence some years ago. And that can only mean that you must be—"

"Hey, Uncle Mateus. Finally figured it out, huh? Took ya long enough."

"*Alina.* Come a long way from the drooling brat Dimas took in, haven't you? I can't help but feel impressed that you were able to beguile me. Of course, now that I know the *how* of my being duped, all that remains—before I eviscerate you—is the *why* of it. Why risk everything, coming to me?"

"It's what she does," said Baraam.

"Hush, dog. This is a family matter. Well, girl? Why the cheap disguise and all the trickery? What are you planning?"

She shrugged, waggling her finger. "Stick around and find out."

"Answer my question, spawn of Dimas."

Baraam sighed. So, Alina was right: The Savior did not deny that he truly was Mateus K'vich, the Master's son. How had Baraam not sensed it before?

Since retiring from The Gild, he'd thought to find direction in the desert. Reconnecting with his cultural heritage, however, had only compounded his inner conflict. As a Gildsman, he had followed orders. At the Saludbabni, he'd been expected to find his own answers, even to the smallest of questions. Neither way of life had given him the sense of ease he sought.

Not knowing—pretending, denying—had been so much easier to stomach. In younger years, when he could close his eyes to everything but the Raves, he'd thought, *This must be contentment.* But the emptiness he'd experienced in the desert—becoming a vessel for the wind and sun and sand—had tasted of true freedom. And freedom offered no firm, guiding hand. For the first time, though surrounded by Jija and the others, he'd been truly alone. It had frightened him. It frightened him still.

There must be some way to find balance. Choices...

"Very well, my 'niece,'" said Mateus. "Your silence earns you nothing. Once I've cracked your mind open, I'll simply suck the truth from it."

Unsure of how he'd gotten there, Baraam found himself between Alina and her uncle.

Mateus's bushy eyebrows knitted together, white teeth flashing behind his dark beard. "You're in my way."

"Yes."

"Never the brightest bolt in the sky, eh, lad?"

"We met, once. Do you remember?"

"You were very young. Another of Dimas's foundlings."

"The Master's faults were many, but he, at least, never crowned himself a messiah."

"Oh, you poor thing. You have no idea. The truths this mind contains—" Mateus touched his temple. "Forget it. Even with keen instincts and proper tutelage, you'd never amount to anything more than human."

The growl that tore from Alina's throat was unsettling to say the least. In it, there was still the girl who had compulsively sucked her teeth whenever she'd been caught stealing toys or staying up too late. However, there was also something else. An eldritch thrum that tickled Baraam's brain stem. "We get it, you're an arrogant wax wad." Pointedly, she flexed her clawed fingers in Mateus's direction. "This whole divine intervention song and dance you're giving us is asinine. We know you're not a believer. So, why? What's your game?"

"We do what we must to live with our circumstances, don't we? That is the commonest platitude, yes? To accept one's fate—a human derangement. Once, I let such thinking cage me, too. For decades, I struggled to find myself in Dimas's shadow. Then, one day, I glimpsed a greater truth. I have seen the light, and it shines from the well of power within myself. I am no savior, nor will I ever be. There is no salvation to be had, only doom. But I will place myself atop the ashpile anyway, and rule it as I see fit—justly—until the dying kingdoms of men fall forever. Then, in the ruin, only I will remain." Quietly, very quietly: "And the outward world will finally echo the silence of my heart." His brows knotted, deep lines in his face reflecting the hollowness within. "It's no simple thing, reinventing oneself. Why do I wear these rags? Why do I prostitute myself to phobic nonsense? You, of all, should understand. Manipulating my identity, hiding in plain sight, biding my time until the prize was within my grasp... It's what we do. It's what we are. Unshackled from hypocritical human morality, we transcend."

"Do you even know," Alina said with a sigh, "what The Author really is?"

"Absurd question," Mateus answered, too quickly. He was stalling. "Of course I do. I know that The Sanctum's creed, its celebration of ignorance, has infected all of human civilization, but I must wade through the irredeemable, teeming masses. These putrid flesh sacs aren't without their redeeming qualities, though, and numerous are the benefits of The Author's benevolence and the gullibility of His followers. Treading their path is what led me here, to this precipice of my final triumph. All that remains is the leap." A smile broke his lips, like the body of a man stretched on the rack. "The last apparition I expected, your coming is a sign. And I don't mean from the gods—if any such things exist, they'll be dead after tonight. No, creature, you herald my ascension. Once I have consumed you, I shall break down that one, last door." He pointed toward Hexhall's inner gate. "And then I'll be strong enough at last to forge what was denied me at birth. My freedom."

A flash caused Baraam to turn. He could see two figures on the opposite side of Alina's barrier, attacking it—one firing beams of bright energy, the other striking with a glimmering greatsword. After only two hits, fissures began to form in the undulating, gray wall.

Alina noticed. "We don't have to be enemies, uncle."

"That's where you are mortally wrong. It's in our nature, as specters—echoes of echoes—to abhor one another. We may represent the pinnacle of natural and magical evolution; we may be the gods last mistake. Either way, ours is the most solitary of paths. Cannibals! We were never meant to be a species."

Baraam couldn't follow any of what had been said the past few minutes. They might as well have been speaking Oronese. What he did understand: a threat to Alina was even now punching a hole through her spell, and, in a few more seconds, he'd be presented with a choice that would define him forever.

He sensed two distinct sources of Niima. The first, he recognized as Eva Schoroto, The Savior's passive, terrifying bodyguard; the second—

The greatsword scythed through the gray energy wall, and through the tear leapt a man, a silent hulk of scarred muscle and taut flesh.

"But, you should be dead," said Baraam.

"For all intents and purposes, he was," said Mateus. "However, dear, faithful Tolomond has been given a second life. He carries on only to serve his Lord. Isn't that right, Tolly?"

The pale man, half-covered in yellow-green bruises and violet spider veins, was impassive. His shriveled eyelids and lips sewn shut, he somehow took in the scene before brandishing his blade, his left hand clasping its pommel. He advanced on Alina. Slowly. Step after deliberate step.

Dimas's granddaughter, true to her training, swung her right foot back, showing her opponent her shoulder. A solid stance, Baraam had to admit.

He hardly noticed Eva calmly slip through the gap in the magical barrier, the glow surrounding her body fading. Instead, he thought about the gods of his forebears, and how they toyed with his heart and mind. His malaise must have brought them great satisfaction; they always seemed to demand more of him.

His promise to Dimas to protect the girl... His oath to the Gildmaster to uphold the Aelfraver's creed...

When his hands fell on Alina's shoulders, she didn't flinch. "Cabbage." The use of the nickname drew from her a wavering sigh. Once, he would have used that name to mock her. Somewhere along the way, however, it had grown on him. As had she. "Please. To any gods that might be listening, I pray you see reason. Stand down."

"It's far too late for that, bol-Talanai," said Mateus.

"Go home." Baraam squeezed her shoulders. "I am begging you."

"You don't get it. There's no home to go back to."

She was hiding something, but he didn't need to read her mind to know what it was.

"My sister is dead." Shaking now, he watched Alina's eyes widen. "I dreamed it."

She began to cry. "I tried." Her clawed, gray fingers curled around his arm. "I tried to save her."

He wanted to break free, but she pulled him in to an embrace that emptied him of air. Her grip was so fierce, his pulse pounded in his skull. When he thought he'd pass out, she relented.

She kissed his cheek.

For the first time, he realized how tall she was.

"D'you see now?" Her eyes, a flash of lightning at sunset. "You're standing on the wrong side."

He followed her telling glare over his shoulder, straight to Tolomond's ravaged, hideous face. The pale freak had paused mid-stride, cocking his head as if listening.

Him.

"Ruqastra. Oh." Baraam clutched his chest, head bowing. He saw her again, doing handstands on the low broken wall bordering the village of their childhood. He wanted to echo his past self's warning to her: "Be careful, you'll fall!" But then, like a fork of lightning driving heavenward, she was gone.

He turned his back on Alina, saying, "Though I stand not under sun nor moon nor desert sky, ever watchful is the eye of Eëtion, who must now weep to witness the breaking of his servants' every vow." He set his jaw.

Spotlights and flashlights dimmed, aircraft and camera drones dipped, and generators sputtered and fell silent. All electrical devices within a thousand square feet—artillery guns, computers, digital watches—funneled their energy into his body. The drones clacked onto the ground like hundreds of silvery marbles. Authority aircraft rained from the sky, dashed against the rocks. Raw power sparked from his every pore, singeing his Gild uniform. He felt the briefest of thrills as the surge short-circuited his brain and all his higher functions switched off.

Whatever it was Mateus said, Baraam could no longer hear.

In Kadic, there's a folk legend about a boy who, seeing his village burning, ran to the hilltop and began to weep. Once he'd spent all his body's water, his tears became the rain, and the village was saved. Though the boy died, he was remembered forever. Loved forever.

Baraam took a step toward Tolomond and said, "I've lost my chance to show her. I was supposed to be—" The ground cracking beneath his heels, he exploded forward, fists rising, and Tolomond followed his trajectory with sightless eyes, sword arcing upward. "—the rain."

67

ALINA

SHE'D SEEN HIM FIGHT before, of course. At The School. In the sparring ring. During a Rave, when she was ten (she wasn't supposed to have been following him). What he lacked in grace of movement, he more than made up for with raw power and speed—strike first, strike hardest. He'd taken literally The School's motto: *one technique to finish*. Always unyielding, unflappable, merciless, he truly was living lightning. The hammer of heavenly wrath. Alina held in her mind many memories of Baraam's brutality, but she'd never seen him fight like this.

She couldn't even follow his movements with her eyes; in a flash, he forked from his starting point, his double hammer-fists slamming into the dome of Tolomond's skull with such force that small stones were flung outward in all directions (and her hair was blown back). Before the pale hulk could react, Baraam's knee connected with his gut, causing a chain reaction of *snaps* and *pops*. Baraam bent over his crumpled victim to end it, but Tolomond's blade shot up with a swift cut that had the Aelfraver leaping backward. The Sanctumite Exorcist wielded his steel swiftly and nimbly as a practiced duelist; Baraam danced in a tight circle, ducking and switching feet. Looking for an opening, he found one. As Tolomond's blade sparked off the ground, Baraam controlled the swordsman's dominant arm with his palm, striking his opponent's kneecap with his heel.

Without so much as a gasp, Tolomond went down a second time. The air hissed as, grasping the other man's throat, Baraam cocked his glowing fist.

Mateus called, "Eva."

Impassive and immobile up until now, the woman in the white suit tore the sunglasses from her nose with such ferocity that the bangs of her brown bob swished against her forehead and bald brows. She opened her eyes, which were like twin white suns. Alina shielded her own face with her arms.

A Niimantic surge spread outward from Eva like an unchecked forest fire. No, it was more than that. She was pure heat, pure light. A dying star's core, primed to go supernova.

There was no warning of what came next, and Alina could only make sense of it after the fact, her perception racing to catch up. Disappearing inside a smooth arc of pure light, Eva speared into Baraam, launching him hundreds of feet into the air. She went with him, driving him ever upward. They rebounded off the gray-black wall of force and then were out of sight.

In the distance, a drum-roll of thunder claps, receding. There hadn't even been time for Alina to shout a useless "Behind you!"

Tolomond stood up, bloodied but unbothered by the most thorough of smackdowns he'd just received.

"Hold," Mateus told him. To Alina: "Shame you didn't get the chance to say farewell."

She said, "Whatever. Your girl might zip and zap with the best of 'em, but that's Baraam bol-Talanai up there. I'm not worried."

"Ah, right on cue: spasms of pride before your short and inglorious fall. However did you turn him, though? Ridect assured me he'd been broken."

"I didn't 'turn' him. He was never yours in the first place."

"You cast no spells. Again I ask, how did you manage it?"

"Loyalty isn't born from fear, Mateus. It comes from——"

"What, love?" He rolled his eyes.

"I was gonna say 'respect,' but, yeah. It's a form of love."

"Hah. Keep your secrets, then. All answers shall be mine soon enough."

"We both know you're not gonna take me out."

"Fatal confidence does run in the family."

"I'm stronger than you."

"Really." Mateus smiled, flicking his head toward Tolomond. "What of him?"

The Exorcist pounced, but Alina was ready. A sphere of bubbling, oozing, sputtering liquid energy swirled into existence around her and her uncle. Tolomond's pale skin crackled like bacon as he was thrown ten feet back.

Above the bubble, the roar of aircraft engines. Martyrs began to drop from the air like obsidian hail, cracking the courtyard's flagstones. Their tougher-than-steel bones vibrated as they absorbed the shock of their landing. They surrounded the magical sphere, but did not approach. Yet.

"And death?" said Mateus. "Are you fool enough not to fear it?"

More and more Martyrs fell, including on Cho's side of the magical wall.

"But, I've died many times by now," said Alina. "Are *you* afraid, Uncle Mat?"

He bared his teeth. "Never. Not of anyone nor anything."

She could tell he was lying, so she pushed: "The voice. You've heard it, too. It talks to you in dreams." She saw in his eyes that it was true. "Calls you 'Vrana.'"

"None of that will matter once I've consumed you and the other Sevensin. Then I will be immortal. Immutable. A law of nature. And neither man nor Aelf shall challenge my supremacy."

She slipped past his mental defenses long enough to ask, *That's it? You just want power? How lame. What're you even gonna do with it?*

He glowered at her. "Not that I owe you anything, you figment, but I plan to avenge my sister."

"What?" Caught completely off-guard, she laughed aloud. "You can't be serious right now. One second, you're dehumanizing me. The next, you're singing my *mother's* praises. How does that make any sense?"

"Because I was here first!" he screamed, eyes wide. "I was the first of Dimas's sinful offspring—off*shoots*. But Zatalena was the better. Always the better. I swore to protect her against all dangers—all evil. But I couldn't—I—" He composed himself. "You might look like her, but you're only the palest imitation. We were fashioned of the elements by choice. You were an afterthought. The spoiled product of a blasphemous union between human and Aelf. A mistake. One I will unmake."

"I see. My existence pisses you off because I got between you and the woman you put on a pedestal. I broke your little-boy fantasy."

His nostrils flared, the bristles of his mustache jittering.

Now, the Martyrs charged the oozing bubble of acid. Each time they were cast aside, bones clacking as they rebounded off stone and each other. Melting, breaking, still, they kept coming. Her concentration began to waver.

Running out of time, she said, "If you think Dimas caused all your problems, you really do know less than nothing. He's not your enemy, and neither am I. So, before one of us stupidly kills the other, allow me, a humble 'figment,' to school you on some family history. In the beginning, in another life, we were seven, and all we wanted was power, like you do now. Our endless hunger transformed us into parasites, leeches. It destroyed us. But that wasn't the end of our story. We were brought back from oblivion—as Sevensin. We thought we were being punished, but we were wrong, uncle. Our reincarnation isn't a curse. It's a second chance. We weren't reborn to suffer."

"What could you possibly know of suffering?"

She wanted to yell at him, to call him a "moss-bearded idiot" and "turd-browed dingus." Instead, she shook her head. He seemed unreachable, numb to everything beyond his own pain, but she had to try. "You're so bent on making our story a tragedy. Please, listen to me. Sure, our family's the farthest thing from *decent* and *good* in this whole universe, but you're really angling for a new low. I'm tellin' ya, it's not men or any old Aelf you should be worrying about. You want revenge for mom? How 'bout you *don't* throw your weight behind the ones responsible for her murder? You can't see it, but you've become their tool."

"I am using The Sanctum," Mateus said quietly, "to grow powerful enough to wipe out The Authority."

"Authority, Sanctum, there's no difference."

As if on cue, Tolomond returned, stamping forward on heavy feet, charging the bubble. His greatsword's point glowed white-hot as he thrust it through. Neither of the K'viches inside flinched as he twisted his blade, burning away Alina's spell, inch by inch.

She pointed at the Exorcist, "If you think *that* guy isn't going to turn on you as soon as you're done with the Hextarchs, then I can't help ya."

"He will try," whispered Mateus, "but, by then, it will be too late."

"Holy Buthmertha, I just *can't* with you. I can't believe it. You're so dead-set on leveling up or whatever that you missed the biggest clue to the whole mystery."

"Enlighten me, then, before I pull what's rightfully mine *out of you*."

"You really think you're tricking The Author?"

"I'm toying with the Sanctumites. Their 'Author,' like all the gods of this forsaken world, is a convenient fiction."

"No, he isn't. The Sanctum's god has been around a very long time, much longer than the Seventy-Seven. He's older than history. And he has a name. A forbidden one that only the Sanctum Hierophant and a few others know."

"What of it?"

"Elwoch," said Alina. (Mateus winced.) "He controls everything that happens in El. Any and every conflict is either his doing, or he has his fingers in it. If we fight each other, you and I, we'll only be *feeding* him."

Tolomond's blade had by now carved a hole big enough for his arm to fit through. With grasping fingers, he pawed at Mateus, who was closer.

"There's a reason you haven't gone for the kill yet, uncle."

Lips drawn, expression rippling like a rag in the wind, Mateus said, "Supposing any of what you say is credible, that's all the more reason for my becoming a god myself. With all the Sevensin united in me, I would outmatch all contenders to the ultimate throne."

He certainly talked a good game. However, she sensed a crack in his armor. A tear in his wing. Here's how she exploited it: "She's in me, too, Mateus."

He didn't have to ask whom she'd meant.

"She's at peace." Alina inhaled sharply as Tolomond tore—with his bare, sizzling hands—a wider and wider gap in her ooze-sphere. "We don't have to do this. Hurting each other only feeds Elwoch. We should be starving him instead." She reached out to her uncle. "Take my hand. Together, we're more than two fragments of a whole."

Mateus swallowed. They stared at each other, just for a moment. Then he backed away toward Tolomond, who, with a mighty swing, cleaved the top off the fizzling bubble.

"You must think little of me," said The Savior, "to assume I'd fall for such a transparent ploy."

She opened her mouth to retort, but Tolomond barreled into her with the momentum of a runaway truck careening down a sloping mountain road. It was all she could do to cross her arms in time. The fraction of a second she'd had to brace helped, surely, but she still went flying, flying, flying.

Just as she began to think she'd soar forever, through air and time, her back connected with something hard—carved stone. She broke through it, and she was no longer a person in a solid body but rather a liquid puddle of pain held together by sheer will alone.

No oxygen in her lungs. Barely able to open her eyes. Lying on the ground, she returned to herself. On some level, she knew this was Hexhall. Specifically, the far end of the corridor in which she'd fought the Top Ten Ravers.

Heavy footsteps, drawing nearer. Quickening. Somehow, vision swimming, she got up and skittered out of range of Tolomond's sword. Side-step, side-step, duck, and dodge. Barely, she held out a few seconds longer.

A glimmer on his cheek caught her eye. Was he… crying?

She screamed as his fifth strike, a vertical chop, cracked her collarbone in a burst of blood. He leaned on his weapon, driving her to her knees, tears flowing down his expressionless face.

Buried in her body, the iridescent blade blurred, vibrated. A wicked glimmer ran from its hilt to its tip. And it hummed, a crescendo—rising, charging. His steel seared her from the inside out.

This, she knew, was the technique that had killed Ruqastra.

Alina found her anger, a dark cloud of righteous indignation, and it blotted out everything except her purpose.

Growling, she grasped the sword's edge with her bare hands and thrust upward, removing it from her flesh and bone. Tolomond staggered back, but she still clasped the naked steel in her bleeding palms. She tensed, twisting her arms as if snapping a neck. The blade fractured, breaking in half, its light dissipating harmlessly. The top piece clattered on the ground.

Swaying, she raised her fists, but this was an empty gesture. Her strength had been sapped. Unlike the three bullets she'd absorbed earlier, the wound Tolomond had dealt her wasn't healing.

Losing a lot of blood. Unable to focus. Before she could so much as think or groan, let alone act, there came a flash of white light. A hooked blade pierced her chest, and Deïmancy—magic designed to Rave creatures like her—gnawed at her nerves, charred her at the molecular level.

The pain was incredible.

68

CHO-ZEN

THE SITUATION HAD DEVOLVED into a regular old who's who of scary-powerful bad guys. You had your phony prophet with the unibrow and long oily hair. Your quietly confident brunette with the super stylin' sunglasses. And what party would be complete without the pale, veiny zombie bodybuilder? Then there was the possibly-bad-but-definitely-dangerous Lightning Dude (a.k.a. Captain Thunderpants). Far as Cho could tell, the challengers weren't about to stop coming, and it was all of them versus Alina. So, Cho had rushed to back her friend up.

As always, Alina had other plans: dark, sizzling magic shot from her like tentacles, latching onto the ceiling and ground; these tentacles split apart, forming a lattice, which spread and thinned until they'd solidified into a solid, impenetrable barrier.

Helpless, Cho hammered the forcefield, screaming Alina's name until Tibby dragged her away, saying, "We have our own battle ahead of us."

The camera drones spun around them in quicksilver blurs, twisting this way and that to document the invisible, growing divide between the soldiers on Cho's side and those she had failed to convince. Countless Authority Tranquilizers were arrayed in front of her, staring her down. Between her and them were the several hundred Cutcords who, against all their training, had turned their backs on the Plutocrats. By how some of them hunched, shifted their weight from left foot to right, it was clear that doubt ate at them. Their hesitance was reasonable; after all, they'd just made enemies of people they'd come up with, bled with.

It was about to go *down*, and, when it did, thousands would die. Desperate, Cho tried to think of some way to avoid more bloodshed, something she could say or do, but then the hairs of her neck and forearms stood on end, and her vision blurred. Cradling her skull, hyperventilating, at first she thought she'd been hit with a panic attack, but this was something else. Her heart gave out for two beats, causing her built-in defibrillator to jolt her back to life and conscious-ness. As her systems rebooted, the clouds of static cleared from her vision.

Tibby supported her until she could stand on her own. "What happened?"

"I'm fine." Cho patted the woman's hand while scanning the area, searching for the source of the electromagnetic pulse that had just fried all the nearby elec-trical devices and energy weapons and shields. She was distracted, however, by shouts. All heads turned upward to see aircraft, spinning, pirouetting downward. Some of the crew members managed to jump before the craft plummeted into the chasm surrounding Hexhall. A few even had parachutes.

The panicked screams abruptly ended with a series of hideous, metallic crunching noises. The explosions that followed thrust spears of flame into the air.

One of the aircraft crashed onto the courtyard, and some Authority loyalists ran to the wreck. Tibby ordered a few Coneys to go help with the rescue. A minute later, two of the crew were pulled out and ushered away. Then, both the Coneys and the loyalists backed away from each other. Knives and batons were drawn. Some Cutcord Geomancers raised short walls to provide the rebels with cover. The Walazzin-led Tranqs fanned out, weapons ready.

If Cho had any hope of defusing this time bomb, she had to act now. Ap-proaching Kaspuri, who knelt with two Coney bayonets at his throat, she said, "Order them to stand down."

He grinned. "And why should I? You've already made clear you won't take my life. What leverage do you have?"

With the flick of her wrist, she whipped her knife at him. The blade stuck in the dirt between two flagstones, having narrowly missed several sensitive pieces of him along the way. She said, "You're useful to me alive, but I don't need *all* of you."

His lips slid back over his sharpened teeth, eyes watering a little. "Still. I'll call your bluff. You can't win. In minutes, I will be free."

"Or shot in the crossfire."

Nostrils quivering, he began to blubber, but he forced another grin. "I'd give my life for my nation, gladly. Glory to the Elementals. Our Authority is abso-lute."

"You..." Her hands went up, fingers bent and twitching as if she were about to strangle him. All the insults she wanted to sling at him, just to see what stuck— all the many ways she wished she could hurt this man—suddenly seemed so small. Childish. She shook her head. "You're pathetic." She walked to the front of the hundreds of fighters tentatively holding her line. "Mr. Walazzin is willing to let us all burn for his own pride. I'm not." She turned to the loyalists, shouting, "Is this where you'd hoped you'd end up? Digging your own shallow graves in Ozar? Lower your weapons."

One of The Authority commanders forced her way to the front. "Men, do not listen to this insurrectionist scum. You are defenders of the Elemental Empire, and you will hold your ground." But she must have sensed a shift in the general atmosphere because she added, "Or you will be executed alongside these traitors."

The Authority loyalists waited, but for what? A commandment from their gods, a rallying cry from their commanders? None could tell. However, after a few moments of tense near-silence, a sign did arrive: engines roared overhead. A tight formation of airships, their brake flaps extended, slowed to a stop.

In the disquiet, Kaspuri's mad cackle bounced around the courtyard. "Look up, little girl! Look up, 'Cho-Zen.' There is your death, delivered with machine efficiency."

The aircrafts' side doors slid open, and reflected amber and crimson firelight glinted off the obsidian figures within. Like bombs, by the dozens, they dropped between the armies. When the dust cleared, hundreds of animated skeletons faced the rebels.

The instinctual reaction was panic. Having cut their cords for Cho only minutes earlier, a couple dozen of the warfighters lost their nerve and left the earth-barricades the Coney's had quickly thrown together; they walked out into the open, hands up.

"Stop!" Cho yelled, too late.

The Martyrs fell upon them, and silently began ripping them to pieces.

Near Cho, a soldier retched loudly.

She'd felt this exact fear just before the Martyrs had gotten Mezami. She knew it meant more people were about to die, and that she could do nothing to save them. Or, could she?

Snatching a discarded baton, she raised it like a banner and shouted, "Line up. You can't reason with these things. They will kill all of us if we give them an inch, and they don't go down easy. So, stand together. Use shields and batons and anything blunt. Form a wall, and never let them through. Line up and fight!"

Tibby raised her voice over the turncoat soldiers' death rattles, saying, "This! This is the mercy of The Sanctum and The Authority. Your gods and kings work in concert to destroy you. The choice is clear: lay your heads on the chopping block, or fight for Cho-Zen and your own lives."

True to her Igniomancer nature, Tibby burned away all doubt. No more Cutcords dared surrender now.

"The Martyrs will tear you apart," Kaspuri screeched. "You'll be a footnote on the evening news, nothing more."

The combination of their master's voice and the arrival of reinforcements (however alien they may have been) rallied the loyalists. "Soldiers of El," said another of their captains, shoving his underlings forward. "Purge all traitors. For your lords! For the Plutocrats!" However, their new confidence was shaken when roughly half the Martyrs turned to face them.

Evenly divided, the line of silent skeletons began to advance on *both* armies—and the loyalists suddenly felt quite differently about the carnage they had just witnessed. They looked to one another, to their officers, to the Martyrs marching inexorably their way, and their ranks fractured. The rebels held firm with Cho and Tibby at their front.

At the top of her lungs, Cho yelled, "We are not your enemy! *They* are!"

The captain said, "Plutonia curse you all for your cowardice. Forward march, and fetch me that girl's head."

And that was when the time bomb Cho had been dreading went off.

Amid the clack of bones on flagstone, the mutterings of panicking fighters, and the crackle of flames, there rang out—like a firework—a single gunshot.

The captain fell forward and did not get up.

His assassin held her pistol high, shouting, "No gods! No kings!"

The uproar was immediate. Thousands of voices rose in dissonant outrage. In that whirlwind of grievances, there was a common theme: "Down with the Plutocrats!" As the grip of Authority weakened, battle cries filled the courtyard, and terrified soldiers instinctually grouped up according to city of birth—"For Wyndgaet! For Gal'lesheer!"

Ancestral homeland—"Svenn!"

And tribal connection—"Tiercel!"

What The Authority had spent centuries suppressing with commands of conformity and demands of obedience came rushing forth. All that stifled individuality became a flood, a flurry of syllable and sound. The screams were all the more freeing for having been denied to parents and grandparents and great-grandparents, the collective release of a breath held for generations.

"Sentamar!"

"Awanz-en-Tchom!"

A dark joy mingled with despair. In those moments, many of the remaining loyalists turned deserter. A small minority of them still protected their panicking officers even as mass indignation was unleashed upon the field in the forms of ballistic rounds, smoke and frag grenades, fireballs, gales and ice shards, earthquakes and tidal waves. Magically enhanced Corpromantic super soldiers crashed into lines of shiny-armored infantry. Razor-sharp rock shards pattered like rain against energy shields, around which crouching fighters fired pulse rounds. Uniforms meant nothing now; Denadon fought Denadon; Hruvic, Hruvic; and so on and on. The loyalist side cannibalized itself. And they died screaming.

"Lynca!"

"Ilicis!"

"Faehnclan! Faehnclan!"

The Elementals had all but conquered the world, strangling in its cradle every attempt at opposition. They'd done so to the uprisings in the colonies, to the resistances in Kadic and Ozar, and so many others. For 3,500 years, they took each brutal victory as further proof that the Nation of El was invincible. But that was a lie; Cho could see now that El had never truly been one nation. The Elementals had held onto the reins of power with greasy fingers, and they were slipping. There'd been rebels among them all along, just waiting for someone to snatch the leashes from their masters' hands.

If only freedom could be bought with a currency other than blood.

With a dread that went beyond the basic fear of catching a stray bullet, Cho watched the infighting among the loyalists. What she saw was the direct effect of her words. Maybe this revolution would have sparked some other way, sometime in the near or distant future, but pondering hypotheticals was pointless. *She* had been the firestarter. The burden of managing the blaze was hers now.

The Martyrs came toe to bony toe with her rebels.

Voice amplifier overloading, she said, "No gaps in the line. Give 'em everything you got." She knew conventional weapons wouldn't even scratch the things, but maybe, with enough magic, her people stood a chance. Either way, there wasn't anywhere left to run. Even if they could breach Alina's gray energy wall, behind it lay the end of the world.

The rebels resisted as long as they could, pounding their batons against indestructible frames of bone, shoving the skeletons back with their shields. The Martyrs hardly stumbled or even slowed, pushing forward with incredible strength until the soldiers faltered and fell, and the line broke.

The Martyrs fanned out, leaping onto the fallen and the standing alike. Teeth and fingers tore into rebel and loyalist without discrimination.

Lobbing fireballs, Tibby ordered the Coneys to form a perimeter around Cho. Chunks of rock soared through the air, crushing Martyrs, who got up again and again—unfazed. One sprinted at Cho; she wedged her baton between its teeth, spinning it toward the war hammer of a nearby soldier, who knocked it down. It was stunned for all of two seconds before clambering to its feet.

Nearby, Kaspuri was squealing. Its bony foot on his chest, a Martyr had him pinned. "You were meant to protect me!" he sputtered and spat. "I command you to protect me!"

Kicking up the riot shield at her feet, Cho charged. Bracing, she rammed into the skeleton, tripping it.

She scowled at Kaspuri's blubbering face, at the white foam dribbling from his lips, and said, "Oh, look. You're disposable, too."

The Martyr bowled into her, throwing her to the ground. She rolled onto her belly as Kaspuri darted off. He became just another body in the undulating push and counter-push of the killer skeletons and the more numerous but rapidly dying humans.

She covered her head as bullets pinged against the ground and half-walls around her. They made a sort of *bloop* sound as they bounced off Alina's barrier.

Then that barrier vanished, but Alina was nowhere to be seen.

The Martyr's foot came down, Cho somersaulting backward just in time. She raised her shield and baton. Her enemy dashed forward. Two Caelus soldiers intercepted, striking it with a flurry of knife and hammer blows. It grabbed one and bent his arm back, shattering the limb. The Martyr left the first man on the ground, screaming. The other, it slew with a single, skull-cracking punch.

Fewer and fewer defiant voices could be heard in the midst of the Martyr's silent assault. The divide between loyalist and rebel closed, as desperate fighters joined forces against their common, terrifying enemy.

It wasn't enough. Nevertheless, they fought. They held out hope, as Cho did. They had to believe that something was coming, something that would change the outcome of this losing battle. If only they could delay the inevitable long enough, their resistance would be rewarded. Somehow.

As they spent the last of their ammunition, and melee weapons were ripped from their bleeding, breaking fingers, hope was all they had left.

Still wounded from her torture and the battles of the past week, there was no reason behind any of Cho's efforts any longer. The entirety of her being had been reduced to a single impulse—run out the clock. She sidestepped and circled the Martyrs, slid between their legs, clonked them on the back of the head with her baton. Her shield was gone, pried from her forearm, lost in the fray.

Her adrenaline regulator busted, her oxygen supply struggling to keep up, she ran and dashed and jumped and struck—until a Martyr's backhanded swipe sent her sprawling.

69

ALINA

HER ENTIRE WORLD HAD condensed to a blank pinpoint. Her every nerve fried, she'd wrapped her fingers around the taut, glowing chain that connected her bloodied sternum to the hideous gash in Tolomond's wrist—where the metal had been fused with his bone. She thought about how much using that hook weapon must hurt him, every time.

Vaguely, she was aware of screaming and gunfire and the clash of steel and the whirl and rush of offensive spells from somewhere outside; her protective, magical walls must have broken together with her breastbone.

She spared Cho and Vessa each a fleeting thought, all she could manage.

Hardly able to think, she cooked from the inside. She could smell herself burning.

With a feeble flick of her middle and index fingers, she attempted a spell. From the ground sprang a diagonal pillar of rock that cracked into Tolomond's sword arm, crushing it against his body, most likely breaking several bones. Yet, his grip on her did not slacken. The chain remained taut.

She hit him again, a fist of stone slamming into his gut. Still, he would not let go.

She tried one more time, a roiling wave of earth rippled between them, jostling him, throwing him back. With a sickening squelch, the hooked, flame-shaped blade retracted from her wound, tearing her open as it went. She screamed, quaking, sweat bleeding into her closing eyes.

Mateus stood over her, reaching as if to take her by the arm. Instead, his fingers speared her chest, and his fist closed around something deep inside her— intangible—an orb of gelatinous, golden energy. Her essence. Her *self*. A composite of Alina, Dimas, Zatalena, and the Pyct'Tzi clan. Mateus was tearing it out of her.

"Uncle. Please. Don't."

He squeezed.

She blacked out

In the darkness, she saw a pair of crow's eyes. Like hers. The eyes of the Demidivine, granting sight beyond sight, revealing hallowed truths not meant for human minds; Ruqastra had had only one, and it had driven her mad.

The owner of the golden eyes stepped forward. Mateus, but no longer human in shape. His black beak curved down, nearly touching the crest of black razor feathers on his chest. His hard gray flesh bristled with quills. From him drifted a golden orb, the mirror image of Alina's own soul, which floated in front of her.

The two essences orbited each other, in sync.

She flexed her feathered arms, considering the mental image of her uncle. "We're in your mind?"

He nodded.

"I don't remember casting Somnambulic Stride. Guess it was a reflex. Huh. That can't be a good sign."

He took another step.

"What, you gonna fight me or something? Really, here? You're already killing me out there." She pointed upward, which was silly because space meant nothing here, inside his thoughts.

"There are only two kinds of people in this world," he said. "Those at the top, who must fall; and those at the bottom, who must rise. There is only the one pinnacle, the high throne of all power and creation, and I must reach it."

"And fall, like you said. Your revenge will destroy you. Doom the rest of us, too."

"As long as I live to see the end of The Authority, that's all that matters. Then she will be at peace. At last." He laughed quietly.

"What could possibly be so funny?"

"Your arrival. I was expecting the old man. Not you."

"Oh, he's here, though. And he's never been more disappointed."

"Good. I wouldn't want his pride anyway. He never understood me, always feared what I might become. They all did—but not nearly enough."

"Why did you run away from us?"

"... It should have been him, not you. I'll take no pleasure in it, but—"

Alina's eyes opened to a bow of golden light, stretched between her heart and Mateus's shuddering fist.

"It must be done." He was weeping now. "I promise your pain will end in an instant, Zatalena. Then there will be nothing but joy as we conquer the world. As we were always meant to, forever united."

Alina tried to speak, but spittle and blood were all she could push between her clenched teeth. Fading, on the brink, she was spared the fate of her grandfather, her mother, and Mezami by the most unexpected rescuer: Tolomond.

He loomed behind Mateus, his greatsword shining like a comet's tail. And, with all the kinetic thrust and drama of a comet barreling through the atmosphere, Tolomond impaled Mateus—the blade grinding through Alina's uncle and into her body as well. With a clipped gasp, Mateus released her essence, which jolted back into her, and she was fully reawakened to her suffering.

They were, the three of them, connected now by a coursing, expansive agony.

In her dissociative state—her mind's defense against this overriding physical torture—vibrating, burning, she watched as the wires holding shut Tolomond's eyes and mouth snapped with a quick series of *plink-plinks*. His face opened. Where there should have been irises and pupils, teeth and tongue, there instead shone spiraling white light.

The entity animating his body—the avatar of Elwoch—spoke through him: "The pieces of Vrana, rejoined at last, at the moment of their undoing. The inglorious culmination of my most illusive adversary." He took a deep, blissful breath.

Mateus's form flickered as if he were an image cast by a malfunctioning projector. As he faded in and out, his own golden orb could be seen, however fleetingly. (Alina imagined the same was happening to her.) Her uncle slumped over the brilliant white blade that had pierced him.

Whether to strangle or embrace him, she herself wasn't sure, but she reached for him, plucking the Chrononite shard pendant from his neck and clutching it in her fist.

"Cling to your un-lives but a little longer, children," said the avatar, using Tolomond's voice. "For four thousand years, you have struggled. I am a merciful master, and would not rob you of fully witnessing the anticlimax of your tale."

The blade was removed. Alina gasped for air, crawling away. Mateus fell in a heap beside her.

After sheathing his broken sword, the avatar grasped each of them by the throat and dragged them away from the scene of their defeat.

As she fought to keep her eyes open, Alina became dimly aware that they were approaching the stone doors leading to Hexhall's innermost sanctuary. The throne room. Locked away therein, the Hextarchy awaited their epilogue.

Tolomond's pilot pressed the pads of his fingers against the huge doors. "Thus was it written." The ancient stone cracked and crumbled at his touch.

Vaulting over the debris, with the last surviving K'viches in tow, the living corpse entered the hexagonal chamber of the Hextarchs.

In the middle of the six stone podiums, the avatar of Elwoch discarded his two captives, approaching the ring of waiting Demidivines.

Calmly, they watched him come.

Through the constant squeal in her ears, Alina heard Haba croak, "So." And that was apparently all that any of the Hextarchs felt the need to say.

Under the yoke of the Iron Seal, they had lived six *long* lifetimes, each of which far surpassed that of any human. Even Cbarassan, centuries old, could not possibly have comprehended the vast loneliness of such an existence. Alina could, finally. She understood their desire for oblivion. She could see why nothingness might be an appealing change of pace after being violently torn from one's grave only to be hunted and hated forever.

She understood, but she couldn't agree. Unlike her Hextarch siblings, she'd decided she wasn't willing to surrender her life. She'd sacrificed enough.

Her broken body rested unevenly. (Well, "rested" was far from the right word.) Something was digging into her ribs. Gritting her teeth through the thousand needles jabbing her muscles, she posted herself on her elbows. With a growl of anguish, she rolled onto her hip, reaching into the folds of *Rego*. From inside, she retrieved a fist-sized lump of faintly glowing green rock. The coolness, smoothness, and heaviness of the Chrononite comforted.

There was much she hadn't originally understood about this damaged Lorestone when she'd "recovered" it from The Gild Crystallarium two years ago. Until today, she'd believed it to be, basically, memory storage. Like a datastick. A rock that held moving pictures, recorded by the long-departed. Now, though, she knew better: Chrononite's functions were innumerable; the only real limit, the imagination of the user Mage.

This particular cracked Lorestone she held in her weakening fingers—as she bled out on a bed of jagged rocks—had been manipulated by Dimas while a student at The Gild. She'd known that much when she'd first found it, but had assumed he'd only tampered with its storage, filled it with hints about his life, about his dual identity as man and Aelf—Dimas and the *Talaganbubāk*. Hints for her to find once she was ready. She'd been wrong.

The cryptic messages and veiled clues of conspiracy were a smokescreen. His true purpose for the lump of Chrononite had been far simpler. He had *broken* it in a way that only a Geomancer could, chipping off a splinter without destroying the whole. In so doing, he'd imprinted his personality on the Lorestone—a programming glitch that interfered with, tweaked, and altered its stored memories.

But, that wasn't the point. What mattered was what he'd done with the pieces: he'd given the splinter of Chrononite to Mateus, and he'd left the other piece in the Crystallarium, eventually leading Alina right to it.

Now, as she held the damaged Lorestone in one hand and Mateus's splinter necklace in the other, she finally understood. Dimas had made sure his "children" would find each other again, at the end of a long and harsh road. The K'viches had always been bound for a reunion.

From within herself, she could feel Dimas chuckling. Which, given their spiritual conjoinment, felt a lot like self-congratulation. (Confusing, this *being multiple people at the same time* business.) Aloud, to herself—to her many selves—she mumbled, "Hard to catch up when you've had such a crazy head start, old man."

The Chrononite weighed down her palm. Her gaze fell upon Mateus, who was unconscious, fading in and out of existence, less and less solid by the second.

There was some peace in knowing, no matter the result, that the choice was hers and hers alone. She'd been handed a loaded gun, but no one could force her to use it.

In a two-handed grip, the avatar of Elwoch hefted his sword above his head. The weapon gleamed brighter and brighter until Alina had to squint as if looking directly at the sun. He prepared to deliver the final blow, and the amount of Niima concentrating in his impending strike was unreal, ungodly.

The Hextarchs spread their arms and lifted their chins, exposing their throats.

Alina thought back to that night on the mountain and her more recent encounter with Ruqastra. According to the Dream Queen, fighting Tolomond had been impossible for her because he'd had no mind to manipulate. But that was *then*, and this was *now*.

Then, Tolomond had been a lumbering meat puppet, simply a tool wielded by the creature inside him.

Now, fully manifesting to better gloat, Elwoch actually wore his body like a human suit. In other words, this wasn't a remote-control situation anymore. Inside Tolomond's skull was a mind—ancient, eldritch, forever starved. Ripe for the plucking.

The Chrononite, Alina realized, didn't need to be a gun. It could be a scalpel. She knew what she must do.

Born a Terramancer, a manipulator of earth and the things that grow in it, she'd specialized in Geomancy. A natural, she'd been twisting rock, stone, and sand since before she knew how. To her toddler self, it had seemed a neat trick, a fun little game. From age six onward, she'd been guided by her Tahtoh. Without bragging, she could claim to be talented.

Setting aside Ruqastra's cruel jabs about her lack of skill, Alina had also been a natural at dream-walking, learning more tricks in two years than most could in ten. And now she knew why: before being constricted by the shackles of death and rebirth, she'd been one half of the reason Revomancy existed in the first place.

Alina's original incarnation, Vrana, had been a brilliant scholar of the arcane—but all her labors had ultimately served Elwoch, the Old Master. Armed with Vrana's knowledge, Alina could at last turn the craft against him. The Chrononite was the key. A thing of reality and unreality, made of dream and time but also *earth*. It shouldn't *be*, and yet it *was*. Deriving its unique properties, its timelessness, from this internal opposition, it was—simply put—a Contradiction. Just like the Sevensin, who were neither dead nor living but also, somehow, both at once.

With the last of her physical strength, she pressed Mateus's splinter necklace into the gap in the larger Lorestone. Her consciousness drifting, the seventh and final reincarnation of the sorcerer queen Vranakvius-rhin'erlin, first of the Revomancers, wove a spell of combined Revomancy and Geomancy. Abyssal energy—anti-light, neither particle nor wave—flowed through her, through the earth, through the air and the feet of the Hextarchs, and it swirled around the avatar before embedding itself in the Chrononite. A flash of emerald light danced along the cracks, and the splinter and its parent united with a satisfying *click*. The crack in the stone fused, healed.

Now, there was but one more spell to cast. The last Ruqastra had taught her.

Being carved by the enchanted light-blade had brought Alina to the edge, edging ever closer, but she had some scraps of Niima left in her, still.

Time is but another dream, Vrana thought through her. As one, she and Alina moved her broken arms in complex patterns, bloodied fingers twitching as she lay on her back, moaning through the pain.

Vrana was telling her something else, now. *The Abyssal Shard. Use it.*

Yes. That's right. Magic required fuel. Usually, the power source was the well of Niima inside the caster. However, certain objects—foci—could be used to enhance or alter the effect of a spell. Alina's *Rego and Ida*, for example, were Revomantic foci, and Tolomond's sword empowered his Deïmancy. Chrononite could be applied in the same way. Its properties were tuned to the mind, dream, and time. With the Lorestone as her focus, Alina could put them all—the Hextarchs, Tolomond, and Mateus—exactly where she wanted them. She'd have to expend the very last of her Niima to do so, but she could force a fight on her own turf. On her own terms.

If the spell failed, she'd die. Elwoch's avatar would shatter the souls of the Sevensin, and the war would be over. If she failed, she would know nothing ever again.

If.

Tolomond held aloft a ray of purest, sharpest sunlight—its brilliance washing out all color, its hum drowning out all sound. Peacefully as their statue likenesses on Morbin, the Hextarchs awaited their fate. White-hot fire swirled around Tolomond as he slashed at them, an arc of energy cutting the air, speeding toward its six targets.

Alina clasped the Chrononite in her hands. What she'd restored, she'd now destroy.

Targeting *eight* minds at once, she cast Ruqastra's Improvised Entry. The Lorestone shattered into a million shards, ricocheting off the walls of the chamber. She cradled in her shaking palms its ghostly outline, hearing the faint but echoing scream of a young woman who sounded alarmingly like Cho.

Across the chamber, there spread a pall of darkness deeper than black, more permanent than death.

Death, too, is but a dream.

Beneath the floor opened The Abyss, a maw of asteroid belts and wheeling constellations. It devoured the physical stone, the Hextarchs and the avatar, their cries of alarm, and, finally, their bodies, too.

Then, there was nothing. If anyone had stepped inside the Hextarchs' sanctuary at this point, she would have seen only emptiness. No pillars, no blue light, no occupants. Only a perfect circle of stone, smooth as glass to the touch.

The lightless, ethereal tendrils of the Revoscape enveloping her, Alina sank into the earth, into dream, into sight beyond sight.

And she got to work.

70

CHO-ZEN

I N ONE HAND, CHO held the Lorestone. Her other was empty, open to the coyote.

The animal's tongue lolled. It cocked its head, its one golden eye glinting.

A crack formed in the Lorestone, spreading. The coyote began to whimper. It licked her hand.

"Is there anything I can do?" she said.

The coyote pattered in a small circle before settling down. Its breaths labored, it peered up at her.

The hunk of Chrononite in her hand burst like overheated glass, and she cried out, covering her eyes. The pain faded with her scream.

Looking around a moment later, she found the coyote had gone.

"Bye, Morphea," she whispered. "Hope you find better dreams."

For a second, she imagined herself free—her mind her own again. Then she heard the clinking of chains behind her. But she didn't dare turn around.

When Cho came to, her eyes were at dirt level, and she was surrounded by pounding feet. They shuffled in a pattern so intricate that it could almost be called chaos. "Dancing?" she mumbled, before remembering where she was, and why.

She rolled onto her back to find a Martyr bearing down on her, its jaws wide as if to swallow her head whole. She scrabbled away, too slowly to escape. A couple of Coney Geomancers exploded out of the earth. One pulled her up, and the other raised a rock wall, a stray volley of bullets ricocheting off it.

The first Coney emitted a shocked yelp, cut short as a Martyr pounced on him and bit his throat. The man's hand fell away from Cho's shoulder, and she shook as his blood spurted onto her cheek and scalp. The second Coney emptied her clip uselessly against the Martyr's reinforced bones before it knocked her down, her skull cracking against the ground.

Another Martyr's hand nearly closed around Cho's ankle. She sprung out of reach. Picking itself up, the skeleton lumbered after her like an enraged ape, its fingers spearing toward her head. A thorny, blackish vine lashed its arm. Attached to the other end of the vine-whip, Cbarassan teetered, straining, their expression a blend of terror and defiance.

The vine tensed against the Martyr's mindless charge. It began to tear.

Ducking the line, Cho ran to Cbarassan, the *Fyarda* wrapping their arm around her shoulder. "Well, Cho-Zen. Though brief, your rise certainly was eventful."

The battlefield contracted farther still, as more squads were herded together by waves of the undead. The fighting shifted to knives and clubs, then bare knuckles. Loyalists and rebels alike were decimated, Martyrs snapping them in half like starved men would a chicken wing. Weapons fell. Warbling screams faded. With each passing second, the courtyard became one voice quieter. It seemed the silence of the Martyrs must prevail.

Cbarassan enveloped themselves and Cho in a cocoon of densely packed roots, and as they were pressed against one another, Cho knew that everything— from her desperate demands for a better world to the *Fyarda's* intervention just now—all of it had bought them only seconds.

The Martyrs—restless, indestructible—encircled the root cocoon, and Cho clung to Cbarassan. To her credit, she didn't give up, even then. Every iota of her enhanced brain's processing power bent toward finding a way out.

Alina had taught her never to quit. More importantly, Alina had given her something to struggle for—the hope for a better world. Even in her bleakest moments, when she pretended to be a nihilist, Alina—deep down—cared about people. She made stupid choices (a lot), but always (well, usually) with good intentions. Cho, on the other hand, had been so obsessed with "righting the wrongs" that she'd hollowed herself, remade herself into the little hate robot she'd always feared to become. For years, she'd let her enemies write her script.

Only just before the end had she begun to realize what balancing the scales actually required.

Cho hoped that Alina knew just how much their time together had meant. It was for her, and because of her, that Cho could face her final chapter with determination. If nothing else, she could now die knowing that she'd *tried* to change the world—and herself—for the better. Too little, perhaps, and too late, but she'd tried anyway. And she'd do it again if asked.

As the jagged-knuckled bone-fists of the Martyrs pounded against the root cocoon, she thought that there was, ultimately, some small shred of peace even in this.

The cocoon ripped, and she was torn through its walls and hurled against the ground. A Martyr's foot crushed her chest. Head pounding, vision darkening, she saw—soaring through the air—what she thought must have been a shooting star.

That was impossible, though. She was so deep underground. There were no stars.

As if in acknowledgment, all lights went out for her, and she opened her arms to welcome the darkness.

71

BARAAM

REBOUNDING OFF THE CAVE ceiling, two bodies, gleaming white and cerulean, broke the sound barrier. The contrails of their attacks and counterattacks wove complex geometric patterns in the air before fading. The shock waves from each blow shattered stalactites, carving deep gashes into the living rock of the Seventh Stack. Their quickstep dance was deafening. Shards of stone fell like hail.

Not since he'd been fourteen or fifteen, sparring with his fellow Gildsmen, had Baraam bol-Talanai gone all out. On that last occasion, he'd put the kid in the hospital. He hadn't meant to, but his opponent had been bigger, had prodded and pushed him too far. Mocked him. Called him a "sand beetle." By the time the bully awoke from his coma, four years later, Baraam had become the Number One Aelfraver in El. Praised by millions, his picture on the front page of every newspaper, with his own brand of sportswear and *Thunderbolt* gyms dotting the country, he could've leveled mountains.

Today, fighting Eva, he was a boy again. Back in the sparring ring, with a disapproving Dimas clucking in the corner. Only, this wasn't training. She did everything in her power to kill him, and she was the faster and deadlier of the two.

As they spiraled around each other, he was always a split-second behind. Perhaps he'd grown used to eliminating opponents in one or two strikes; perhaps he'd been weakened by his hiding for two years in the desert and his complacency for years before that. Regardless, she was unbelievable, a beam of searing light, shearing the air, cooking his blood from a dozen feet away. She shouldn't have been able to dodge *lightning*—no one else ever had.

Sweating, he lost focus. The question plaguing him hit him even harder than her burning hands. *What good am I if I'm not the strongest?*

Eva. Tolomond. Even Alina. These were transcendent beings. Aberrant creatures, they defied the natural order, the hierarchy of magical and martial proficiency that had declared Baraam the greatest of all. Now, that structure seemed a cruel joke at his expense. Was everything he'd striven for truly meaningless? All Aelfravers were Mages. Therefore, the best Aelfraver ought to be the best Mage, right? How, then, had he fallen so far? There was, apparently, a whole world of power beyond the plateau he'd reached before he'd turned twenty.

He hadn't intended to fight Eva. He'd wanted Tolomond, wanted to tear that brutish lummox limb from limb. Eva was simply in Baraam's way. And he couldn't beat her. She wasn't a mind reader, wasn't predicting his movements; she simply was more agile, more focused, and more determined as she reacted to his gambits, feints, and dodges. He couldn't keep up with her, let alone get ahead. And the more obvious his inferiority became, the faster he moved, the harder he hit. Yet, it made no difference.

That someone like her could exist *and* have been kept a secret—what other monsters were The Authority hiding?

Their furious flight path sent them bulleting through several buildings, throwing clouds of brick dust, twinkling glass, and steam in their wake. Pipes burst, jets of gas and water saturating the clammy, smoky air. They crashed through a vent, warping huge steel fan blades with the heat of the magical bolts they flung. Light and lightning ricocheted from them, from the metal, glancing off rocks, fizzing and dissipating—and setting ablaze anything that would burn. Storage boxes, crates of food and goods, merchant stalls tucked into the market square, pockets of gas.

Explosions tore through the mine- and ventilation shafts as she thrust her searing palms into his chest. He grunted, his skin crackling like duck fat in a hot pan, and struck the cavern ceiling. Slamming into and through several stalactites, his vision went dark, his momentum waned, and then he—fizzing like a zapped bug—fell.

He continued to fall, thinking, *What good am I?* Denied peace, forces larger than he, greater than he, called on him to assume the warrior's mantle. Everyone wanted him to be strong, to serve their cause, but he'd been revealed as a weakling, a fraud. *How* had he fallen so far?

Why was he fighting now?

Because a storm's function is to destroy. A destroyer was all he know how to be. But there was also another reason. The ruling men of The Gild, Authority, and Plutocracy he'd served had taken Ruqastra from him. However, his own weakness denied him his desire; natural justice lay just beyond his reach. He couldn't even beat Eva—the pawn, the angelic, terrible living weapon.

She was, in many ways, just like him, only better, tougher, more perfect. Less human.

What am I?

At last, his fall ended. The impact of his collision with the ground reverberated through his Niimantically hardened bones and toughened muscles.

Eyes closing, consciousness fading, he felt emptied of all power and purpose. Hollow. Nothing. A shadow rested on his heart. Yet, its touch wasn't unwelcome. Its weight was that of a mother's tight embrace.

He hardly remembered his mother. He could call to mind only the feeling of her, her face a blur of kindness and resolve.

Mother had been the one to teach him the need to stand up for himself. Yes.

He remembered the first real fight he'd ever been in. Some older boys, jealous of Dimas's giving Ruqastra and Baraam private lessons, had cornered the siblings in the alley behind The School. There'd been four of them. Baraam been about nine at the time, Ruqastra eleven or twelve. Each of the bullies had been older. Bigger too, and much stronger. He had been outnumbered. He shouldn't have won.

How had he won that hopeless encounter? Because of Ruqastra. Their harassers had awakened the rabid animal in her heart. She'd clawed and kicked at them like a beast. One of them had drawn a knife, and when they struck her across the face, taking her eye, a jolt surged through Baraam's entire body.

Yes, they'd given him a reason to fight. Ruqastra had screamed and cried, falling back, hands bloody. And Baraam didn't remember any of what happened next. The aftermath proved that it had been a close call; they'd beaten him raw, and he'd half-dragged himself and Ruqastra back to Dimas's door when done. But the bullies hadn't been able to move at all.

After that night, Ruqastra didn't stop loving him, but mingled with that love was an emotion he'd incorrectly identified as respect. In reality, it'd been fear. She cared for him, her little brother, even as she inched away from him, unsure of what he was capable. For a long time, he'd reveled in her unease, noting with joy that others began to share it, too. The world at last regarded Baraam bol-Talanai with what resembled respect.

Any who would not bow before him, or stand aside, was a challenger. And, for years, he busied himself crushing all challengers, always convincing himself he was admired—not feared.

Now, with the mother-shadow upon him, that warm embrace of what he imagined must be death enveloping him, he realized his desire for adulation and respect wasn't the source of his drive. That first fight, he'd been motivated by one thing only, losing Ruqastra. And, hidden from the world, he'd let her die, alone.

He'd let her die.

But, he didn't have to repeat his mistakes. He could still change. Even now, as Eva sped down toward him—a comet, a winged angel of light and fire—he could arise again. He had a reason to struggle on: Alina, in danger. She'd seen his weakness in the bell tower. His shame—defeated at the hands of his old Master.

Still, she reached out to him, even as he moved away. Although she and Dimas (but not Baraam) were of the same cursed brood, she was family.

Ruqastra would have wanted her saved.

Opening his eyes, Baraam clenched his fists. *Fight.*

He searched his surroundings, realizing he was in a place full of whirring machines. Good. He'd landed on something metal, a current running through it. Strong, flowing like blood. The pads of his fingers pressed against it, and he drained it of electricity, charging himself like a battery. He pulled all that power into his body, every wire feeding him until there was nothing left.

He rose from the dented, silenced metal transformer and walked out of the power plant that had now gone dark.

Lightning bolts arced from him as he floated upward, through the hole in the roof. He zeroed in on Eva, and forked through the air. His fist caught her lip. The force of the blow, and the resultant sonic boom, popped the ears of the soldiers fighting below, shattered windows, and collapsed rooftops. Hunks of rock and concrete scattered like dandelion seeds.

A drop of blood trickling down her chin, she glared at him.

He gritted his teeth. "Again."

72

ALINA

R UQASTRA HAD ONCE SAID, "In the Revoscape, there is only one time—*now*. But that *now* is infinite, encompassing every possibility explored and unexplored; all moments real or imagined become one. In fact, concepts such as 'real' have no substance there. What *feels* real *is*. Such is the true power and glory of the Revomancer. Be your enemy warrior or lord, king or demon—in Dream, you are architect and creator. You are goddess of all you survey—inside yourself and inside them."

It began, as always, with a door.

Fingers laced around the brass handle, she opened the portal and stepped into the hedge maze. Her footfalls were light, soundless.

Whether Alina had chosen the arena or it had chosen her, there was purpose to her being here, where physical strength was meaningless and even magic must bow to the pressures of the mind. Here, she alone could decide the details worthy of focus—until someone else entered, that is. Then, she would have to relinquish some control, for dreams will change when shared.

For a time—though time also had no weight, here—she simply wandered the maze. She sought no particular end, feeling content in this stillness. The scent of red carnations. Dew dropping from twined vine and leaf.

Eventually, rounding a corner, she found a boy. He squatted, his back to her, elbows akimbo as he vigorously rubbed his eyes. She waited the span of a breath, counting the notches in the boy's spine, visible through his wet, white t-shirt.

"Hey," she said.

The boy gasped, sucking in a sob that mutated into a hiccup. Red-faced, damp-eyed, he turned. Even standing, he barely reached her bellybutton.

"My name is Alina. How'd you get so soggy?"

"I like chasing rain clouds," said the boy. "The world is more quiet when it rains."

She noted salient features: his buzzcut, the scabs on his knees and forearms, the angry blue bruise around his right eye. "You're Tolomond, aren't you?"

He sniffed. "How d'you know my name?"

Relief washed over her like summer rain, but she hid it well. She'd been right: Elwoch's hold wasn't iron-clad; the real Tolomond was buried deep inside.

"I'm a friend," she said. "I wanted to talk to you, actually."

"'Bout what?"

"Just hoping to learn more about you."

"This a trick?" He seemed wary, ready to scurry off at the first sign of attack.

She crossed her wrists at her waist, showing her hands. "Do you like where you live? Are they taking good care of you?"

His eyes narrowed. "You *are* trying to trick me."

"I want to help."

Cupping his mouth, he looked left to right before whispering, "Father will be angry with me if I say."

Squatting so that they were eye-level, she whispered back, "I can keep a secret if you can." She smiled. "Who is your father?"

"The Hierophant," he said, then clapped a hand over his lips. "I shouldn't have said that!" he mumbled through his fingers. "Why'd I say it?"

"It's okay." She winked. "I won't tell. Is your father a nice man? Is he nice to you?"

Now Tolomond couldn't meet her eye, and she could guess where the marks of abuse on his body had come from.

She wiped her tears on the hem of her cloak. Voice quavering, she said, "And your mother?"

The boy still could not look up. "She didn't come back. She told me to wait on The Sanctum steps. She said she'd be back soon. She said to wait." His cheeks became a darker hue of red, his bruised eyelids a throbbing purple. "I waited."

Alina's purpose in weaving this dreamscape had been to uncover and exploit the weaknesses of her enemies. However, this shivering child had driven that purpose from her mind. She could never forget all the misery caused by the man he'd become. But, right now, he was just a boy. Frightened, alone—desperate for, and worthy of, love.

He flinched, but her movements were careful, slow. She took him by the hand and pulled him in close, hugging him tightly, her chin digging into his shoulder.

"You don't have to wait any more, Tolomond." His burning skin cooled at her touch, his trembling fading and fading like a dying flame until he simply rested in her grasp like a lump of spent coal.

"She's not coming back," he muttered, voice cracking.

"No." Burying her nose in his wet t-shirt, she shed a few more tears which absorbed into the rain- and sweat-soaked fabric. At arm's length, she held his gaze. Those eyes, like smoking cinders. "Come on. Follow me."

His hand in hers, she led him deeper into the maze.

Four turns later, he asked, "Where are we going?"

"To find the others."

Nightshade fingers and sunflower faces twisted to witness their passing. The hedges were the deep, verdant green of storm-dappled gardens. Wild and tame, and neither.

"Who *is* that? That girl?" Tolomond pointed to the child, an Iorian, kneeling beside one of the many rain puddles. "Do you know her?"

"That's Haba," said Alina. "She's always catching slimy things like toads and worms."

"Ewww," said Tolomond, but he was grinning. "Why?"

Alina shrugged. "They're cute to her."

"Hmm. That's pretty interesting, I guess."

"Should we say 'hey'?"

"Sure."

They sat beside Haba then, who barely registered their arrival. Sturdy-boned, with a wide face, she scratched at her elbows, her indigo skin glistening with dew. Her pink, flame-like hair wafted with the gentle breeze but gave off neither heat nor light.

"You look funny," said Tolomond.

"Shh," said Haba, lifting a stubby finger.

Alina introduced them.

"Hi," Haba said. "Hang on. There's a frog under this bush I want to meet."

The three sat in silence.

Eventually, Haba gave up. "There's always tomorrow," she said cheerfully. To Alina, "How are you today, Vrana?"

"I'm good. Actually, Tolomond and I are trying to find the center of this maze. I was thinking maybe you could help us."

"What are friends for?" She wrinkled her little nose, squinting. "We're friends, aren't we?"

"Of course."

Haba took Alina's other hand.

"Gurm," Alina snapped, sprinting over to him, sliding on her shins. She pinched his indigo cheeks like one might a dog's and pried the slick, slimy, triangular lump from his mouth. "What did I tell you about biting the heads off snakes?"

"Um," said Gurm.

"Yeesh." Alina regarded Haba, then Gurm again. "Is this what happens when I leave you alone? It's only been a little while, and here you are, crawling on your belly, eating all kinds of crap you find lying around."

"But, it's not been just 'a little while.'" His beady black eyes welled with tears. "You've been gone a long time, Vrana." The flames of his fire-mohawk weakened, sagged. "We thought you weren't coming back. Well, I never lost hope. But the others…"

Alina chuckled. "You're a bad liar, my little Gurm. My wild one."

He looped his fingers behind his back, bashful. Nervous. "Have you come to take us to the Master?"

She considered it. Had she?

"Maybe…" She trailed off. After a moment, though, she shook off her uncertainty. "Huh. No. We won't be going back, I think. We're done doing what he says."

"Good." Gurm leaned in, grinning conspiratorially, little bits of black scales stuck between his sharpened milk teeth. "Never much liked him anyway." He jerked his head toward the other two. "Who's that with Haba? Another sacrifice?"

Alina shook her head. "It's not like that. Not anymore. We're free now." She led Gurm by the hand, bringing the three children together. Like an obelisk, she towered over them. "This is Tolomond. He's coming with us. This time, we're doing it my way."

"Can I still kill stuff?" said Gurm, his ears twitching. When Alina pursed her lips and glowered at him, he shrank away with a defeated little, "Aw."

She looked to the sky. The sun was setting. Soon, night would fall.

"We have to hurry to the center of the maze."

If they were caught out in the open when the sun rose again, when *his* eye fell upon them—

"What'll we find there?" Tolomond asked.

"The past. And the future." Alina strode forward.

The children followed.

"Is she always like this?" she heard Tolomond say.

"No," said Haba cheerfully. "Usually she's much bossier."

"Well, she *is* our boss," said Gurm.

"Nasres shoulda been. Or Aam."

"Pff. Aam doesn't know what they're thinkin' half the time. And Nasres is in love with his own face too much. Vrana's always been good to us."

Turning on her heels, Alina placed her hands on Gurm's shoulders. Lightly. The other two bumped into him.

Alina said, "That's not true. I royally screwed you over. All of you. But I'm here to make it right—or, at least, make it better."

Twilight sank into their bones. The shadows grew tall as they filed into the mines—yawning mouths full of iron teeth. The air within, a sulfurous belch. Alina had expected guards, but there were none. There should also have been many children, lounging in the carved out common areas, huddled in cots, curled up together in the mine shafts. Yet the corridors, clogged by sooty child-sized shirts and pants and helmets, were vacant of life.

Memories were fluid in the Revoscape; nothing would be quite as it ought.

Tolomond drifted closer to Haba. "I hate it here. It reminds me of—"

"It's alright," she said, patting the hand he'd placed on her arm. "But you have to be quiet."

"Or they'll hear," Gurm breathed.

"Who's 'they'?" whispered Tolomond.

Before anyone could answer, however, they heard grunts and the thud of bone against flesh. A scuffle.

Rounding the corner first, Alina saw a larger figure (still shorter than she but not by much) hunched over a smaller one. Their flaming hair intertwined like vines growing around the same metal grille.

As a child, barely old enough to talk, Stonoz had watched her uncle fall in a duel, held his hand as his strength waned. She'd always been a big girl with sharp fingernails good for clawing. Now she struck Etia, a much smaller girl, in the face again and again. Open-palmed, then back-handed.

"Stonoz," Alina barked. "Get off her."

The bigger girl released the littler, grimacing. "Let her fight her own battles for once."

"That's no way to teach her. We're family."

"Only when it's convenient for you." The mine walls glistered with moisture as Stonoz walked lazily toward a figure in the corner.

Gaping at his distorted reflection in a sheet of cave ice, illuminated by the green glow of a magical lantern, Nasres yawned. "You're late."

"Got held up," said Alina.

"Abandoned us more like," squeaked Etia, spitting a glob of blue blood onto the ground.

"I came back, didn't I?" She looked around, meeting each child's gaze. Their group included seven now. A good number, though eight would've been better. She still had to find Aam, then Mateus. But Mateus would have to wait until just near dawn, when it would be almost too late. Just before the waking, the dream would be at its strongest, its most surreal. Then, Alina's powers would be heightened to their maximum.

There was still a little time.

"I'm sorry," she told them all, "sorry that I didn't come for you sooner. I meant to, I really did. I just—wasn't myself for a while."

"I had a dream you were a creepy old man," said Haba.

Alina chuckled and shrugged.

Nasres turned on her, his eyes like mirrors. Alina stared at her reflection and didn't quite like what she saw. In his eyes, she looked taller, slenderer, more twisted. He said, "This was all your idea, you know."

Bowing her head, she nodded. "I know. I brought you to the Master, convinced you—"

Stonoz clenched her bloody-knuckled fists. "Convinced us to seal our souls in compact with that, that *creature*—that alien who used us."

"He sharpened us," said Nasres.

"It was the fear of him that sharpened us, bent us into curved blades."

"Never meant for it to go this far, though," Etia said. "I only wanted my freedom. Couldn't stand the thought of marrying some cloudy-minded lordling and being his tea-toting fool my whole life."

("You mean 'teetotaling,' said Nasres.

"I know what I meant!")

"Well, I wanted glory," said Stonoz crossing her scarred arms, her split lip splitting even more deeply as she grinned.

"Knowledge," said Nasres, his eyes revealing nothing of himself and everything of his surroundings.

"Communion," said Haba, her voice creaking like a wind-played reed.

"Change," said Vrana through Alina—who were one and the same. "The power to change the world. I talked you into it because I couldn't do it without you. And I'm sorry. You'll never know how sorry I am."

"And now you've come begging for our help. Again," said Nasres.

"That's right."

"Why should we follow you? Again? All you ever do is lie," said Stonoz.

"And get us in trouble," Etia chimed in.

It was true, Alina knew, all true. She felt it down to her core. All their anger. Thousands of years—forty-two lifetimes—of resentment, bitterness.

"You left us. When you didn't like the rules of the game *you started*, you left," said Stonoz.

They all chattered their agreement, even good-natured Haba.

Then a lone voice cut through theirs. It was unsteady, lacking confidence, but unwilling to give in. It rose until it overpowered the other five. Tolomond said, "But she came back!" He was standing between Alina and the flaming-haired, blue-skinned children, jabbing his finger at each of them. "She came back, didn't she? And that's something." His coal eyes filled with tears as he turned to Alina. "I hurt her. I killed her friends. I tried to kill her, too." To the other children: "But she came back for me, for all of you." He raised shaking fists. "I'll fight any one of you that says another cruel word about her. Go on." He glared at Stonoz, who weighed at least twice as much as he did.

Her bare blue feet slapping the rock, she walked up to him, prodding his chest. "I like you, kid. Didn't think one of the Master's lesser experiments could still have so much heart."

"You say you'll fight us for your new friend," said Nasres, smirking. "Will you fight *them*?" He pointed behind himself, toward the straight path and newly appeared door of light.

Several tall figures, featureless, like humanoid beams of light stepped forth, extending their hands. Reaching, blinding.

"They've come for us," said Gurm, whimpering and clinging to Alina's arm.

"They can't hurt you now," she said. "They're not as strong as you are. Don't let them make you small."

"The Irregulars," Gurm cried, his voice laden with the memories of lashings, beatings, iron-brandings, and years and years of labor in the dark.

The mineshaft began to quake, the stone groaning.

Alina shouted, "Don't be afraid. In darkness, we died and were reborn. Now, it's our haven against the light, our protection against the Master's power. We *are* the darkness, and if we hold together, he can never hurt us again."

Wrapping her cloak tightly about herself, she soared forward, crashing into the figures, sending them all—including herself—through the door of light.

The light-beings and Alina tumbled over the threshold, falling into white, flashing emptiness. Even as they spun weightlessly through the void, they clawed at her, and she imagined the terrible possibility that this was it, that she'd spend the rest of eternity forever-falling into nothing. Then a thin and glinting thread dangled before her eyes. She grabbed it, and it wrapped around her arm. It pulled her up, up, and up—as the featureless humanoids disappeared into the endless whiteness below.

As Alina glided upward, Aam's narrow-eyed smirk greeted her. "Not yet," said Aam. She took their small hand, and they repeated the declaration: "Not yet."

Alina climbed over the ledge and through the door of light, which closed behind her. She'd been returned to the maze, just outside the mines.

The silver thread slipped away from her leg and out of her hands, spooling in Aam's grip.

In dreams more than one reality may be simultaneously true. Although appearing childlike, Aam possessed all the cunning and delightedness they would bear into adulthood (and their many incarnations thereafter). But they were also literally a cat, one Alina recognized immediately.

"That day I lost my thread, when Tahtoh found me alone and crying. I was in a maze then, too." She laughed. "The cat. It was you."

Aam picked a leaf from the walls of the hedge maze, nibbling it. They handed her the spool of silver thread. "Take it back, Stitcher. Served its purpose, it has." They gestured behind her, where the other five will-be Hextarchs (and Tolomond) waited.

The cool night air settled upon them all.

Shadow-boxing, Tolomond said, "That was *awesome*. You jumped up and were totally like *bam* and *swish*, and they were all like *waaaah*, and then you were like 'see ya, idiots.' You really showed those monsters, whatever they were."

Nasres stood beside Stonoz and, speaking together as they often did, they said, "Is the fight over then?"

Alina said, "If you want it to be."

"Were we brave?" said Etia.

"Yeah, did we win? Did we? Did we win?" said Haba.

"You did *such* a great job to have come this far, but, no, the winner hasn't been decided yet."

"Then we should keep going?" said Gurm.

Aam shook their head. "Won't speak for all of you, but I sure could use a long nap."

"Vrana can't do it on her own, though," said Stonoz.

"She won't be on her own," said Aam.

"I don't get it," said Haba.

"Let's find the heart of the maze, then see," said Aam, winking at Alina. "One step at a time."

At the word "step," the world changed. The children were gone, and Alina had one hand on Aam's shoulder, the other at their hip. She was dancing with Aam, who was older now—impossibly beautiful in a jewel-studded, dark tunic, their hair a pillar of flame. When she looked down, the "dance floor" gave her quite a start: the couple swayed gently over an expanse of gray dust with the black, star-strewn blanket of outer space above.

Calmness returned with memory. Ah, that's right. Once, they'd been the two greatest sorcerers in the world, and dancing on the moon, to them, was the small-est of feats. (There'd been only one who could call himself their better—the man who'd forged freedom from slaves' chains, whose peace could shatter armies and split oceans. The man who had killed them. The first time.)

Were the moon a field, what Alina and Aam waltzed through might be called a garden of corpse-flowers. Fragments of bone shuffled and crunched under-foot, barely a whisper against the pervasive silence of eternal night. This place was where they'd sworn themselves to one another as they cut down and cut apart many a prisoner of war, many a sacrifice. Here, they'd shed blood in service to their lord—god of greed, god of power. His were all the riches in the world, and beyond, but never enough.

Taking her eyes off her partner, Alina noticed her own skin was also blue, her dark fingernails long like claws.

"I missed this."

"As did I."

They continued their waltz.

"All our fellows had their turns to confess, in the maze," said Aam, reclaiming her gaze. "Well, as for me, I did not bind my fate to Elwoch's for wealth or renown. No, I did it all for you. I wanted you. Forever."

"We had our lifetime together," said Alina dreamily, automatically, remem-bering strings of dark and heady moments as the words tumbled from her tongue.

"Not enough," Aam held her at arm's length, kissed her knuckles. "Never enough. We were good together."

"We *enjoyed* one another," Alina corrected, "but we were terrible for each other."

"We were terrible for the world."

"Same thing." Alina's skirts lifted, spinning like a slow-motion hurricane in the low gravity. Her cape drifted behind her like a distant flock of crows. "Thou-sands, dead. Because of us."

"The age in which we loved one another—"

"Is over. And I thank Buthmertha for that."

"Buthmertha." Aam spoke the name slowly, as if they couldn't make sense of its sound. "Humans are so fickle. They toss aside their gods as if even religion were subject to seasonal fashion. I remember when we ourselves were like gods."

"There's still greatness ahead of us. A different kind, sure, but still. The ques-tion is, can you be happy, shedding godhood for Demidivinity?"

Aam gave a curtsy. "In any way I can, Vrana—no, *Alina*—all I desire is to be part of you."

"Then, take my hand. It's time."

They interlaced their fingers with hers, sighing. "I'm rea—"

Carried by aromatic clouds of honeyed nightshade, she was restored to the hedge maze once more. The five Iorian children were there, as was Tolomond, who fretted with the hem of his gray tunic.

"Where is Aam? Where is—" Gurm's eyes widened.

"They folded into you," said Etia, walking circles around Alina as if Aam might simply be hiding. "Why would they do that?"

"Because." Alina's hands slipped into her pockets. "They know I'm going to beat the Master at his own game, and the only way I can win is if we all join together."

"Do me a favor and say 'aah,'" said Haba.

"Aah." Alina stuck out her tongue.

On tiptoe, Haba examined her throat and shouted, "Hey, Aam, how's the weather in there?"

In Aam's playful, raspy tones, Alina answered, "Humid, but not unpleasant."

"An artful trick," said Nasres, "but a trick only."

"You'll have no luck swaying me," said Stonoz.

"Fine, whatever." Alina gestured toward the red door that had sprung up beside them, cutting into the maze's leafy wall. "You open it, then."

Stonoz's lower jaw jutted. Her gaze gouged the door, then Alina again, but her feet remained firmly planted, her toes curling to dig the dirt.

"You know what's on the other side?" said Alina. "Are you scared?"

"I'm not."

"Well, I am. Even though I know this is a dream. Even though I'm certain the worst he could do is kill us—which he's already done, a bunch of times— the Old Master still scares me. But, you know what, I think he's way more frightened of us than we are of him. Why else would he have hunted us down every single time we reincarnated? Why else would he have conquered whole countries to capture us, if he wasn't scared out of his mind?" Alina reached for Stonoz's arm. The big girl didn't shy away this time. "Isn't there still some part of you that really wants to kick his ass?"

Stonoz suppressed a smirk, nodding.

Alina winked, gesturing toward the red door. "We'll do it together."

Stonoz placed her hand on Alina's. Alina turned and pushed the handle. The door glided inward.

And, at the threshold beside Alina, there suddenly stood the fully-grown Stonoz Titan's Bane. Black-haired, six-armed, she was half a colossus herself. The bones of mortals and Demidivines alike lined her belt, and a choker of foe-knuckles ringed her throat. Never had there lived a greater warrior—except one.

Alina remembered their last battle well. The Seven had sat, secure on their shared throne in their silent city, until along came the Iron Seal Bearer. A flash of sound, a whisper of shadow, his strike had fallen upon them like a hammer on red-hot metal, and their bodies had splintered against the ferocity of his blows.

It was a memory done in smoke; Alina and Stonoz watched the scene unfold like a puppet show. But they felt it as if it were happening to them again, now.

"This was the first time we died," said Stonoz. "You were there, beside me. You didn't run then."

"You'll always be my sister, Stonoz," said Alina. "I'm sorry for the suffering I've caused you."

"You died well with me that day. You stayed at my side, even though we never stood a chance. To think that I, who slew the Archwyrm, who wrestled Kayre-Ost Foxfriend into submission... that I could be undone by one little orphan. Four thousand years later, and I still can't understand the how of it."

"He was Iron," Alina said simply.

She remembered all too well the day Iron had come for the Seven at the city death forgot. At the height of their powers, still, they'd never had a hope against the vengeance of their Master's accidental son, who warred with the will of a trillion Demons but not one ounce of their hate.

"Even as he cut us down, he pitied us," said Stonoz.

The sky had been overcast that day, the grid of buildings white, stately, and empty. He'd come walking up the hill, perfectly confident, but Vrana had seen him for what he was—the apocalypse incarnate. A vessel for Demons, who had somehow tamed his possessors.

He'd attacked, and the Seven had resisted. Every spell at their command, every desperate treachery, none of it had been enough. He'd carved through them, one by one. And Vrana had drunk his pity like drops of crystalline water even as she cradled Stonoz in her own broken arms.

Memory blended with dream, erasing time, and Stonoz and Alina assumed that same position once more.

In Alina's arms again, just as she had been on that final day, with her final breath, Stonoz whispered, "We—"

Before the curse that had united the Seven in undeath, before even the centuries they'd spent as the killing tools of one who'd crowned himself God, Stonoz and Vrana had been the worst of rivals, the best of friends. As they lay dying, Alina pulled the silver spool from her pocket, bit off a length with her teeth, and tied their thumbs together. It was what she'd wanted to do, when this moment had really happened, so very long ago.

She did it now, in dream.

The red door disappeared on opening, leaving a hole in the living, verdant wall. Stonoz was nowhere to be seen, but there remained a loop of silver thread tied around Alina's finger. Its slight pinch, a bittersweet reminder.

"Did Stonoz go on ahead?" said Gurm.

"Kind of," said Alina, and she put a hand to her heart.

She stood at the threshold while Haba, Gurm, Etia, and Nasres peered past her into the shadows of a six-sided chamber, the marble-hooded center of the maze.

"I don't like this place," said Haba.

"Few would enjoy seeing their own graves," said Nasres.

All at once, they fell backward as a fire blazed to life.

"Enter, First Scholars. Enter, my children."

"I'll go first," Alina said, and ducked under the low archway, moving into the chamber.

There were no signs of life inside, only the walls of stone, the torch-bearing sconces, and the central brazier, in which flames twisted like grinning mouths. From them sounded a wildfire voice, consuming the silence like oxygen. *"Vrana, you have returned to me."*

Alina bowed her head in greeting. "Elwoch."

The flames hissed.

"Or, should I call you 'Author' now? What is it with you and weird little cults? Must be a lot to micromanage. Are you really *that* bored?"

"The ages, and your numerous deaths, have done little to dull your tongue." The fire flashed and crackled. *"As before, you yet lack the perspective only Eternity may yield. Permit your Master Teacher to impart one last lesson. Bring in the other children. I would gaze upon what has become of my noble Seven."*

The four remaining children filed in, timid and twitchy.

"And, the other two?"

Alina tapped her chest.

"How greedy." Elwoch cackled.

"Aam and Stonoz offered themselves. It was their choice."

"Do you suppose that matters? See, children, the lengths to which Vrana will go simply to get ahead? There is no sacrifice too great to buy her advancement in power. Unless, of course, it be self-sacrifice."

"Well, I believe her," Haba croaked. "'Cause nobody could ever make Stonoz do anything she didn't wanna do."

"And what slime-hole have you crawled from today, gutter licker? When I desire the input of a drug-addled nothing, I shall call for it."

The boy in the gray tunic took a step forward and stamped his foot. "Hey, don't talk to her like that."

Tolomond's interruption caused a stir. Disquiet. Then, laughter. *"Vrana, you clever carrion-feeder, you. How you managed to entangle my own instrument in your string of illusions... I dare say, I am... not quite impressed, no, but certainly amused."* The flames cohered, shifting into a cross-like shape—a greatsword. *"Exorcist Stayd. My champion. Undying, proud warrior. Remember yourself and your sacred charge. Take up your holy weapon in my name, and smite these creatures of darkness. Let my edict animate you to fulfill your life's purpose."* The weapon's form, wreathed in flame, glinting like steel, began to turn solid. It was still missing its tip, which Alina had snapped off earlier.

"You sound just like my father."

"I am Father to all faithful, Tolomond, my son. Take up the holy sword of your God."

Tolomond looked to Alina.

"Slay the infidel."

She nodded, slowly.

The boy swallowed, clenched his fists, and said, "I hate my father. Always telling me what to do but never why. Promising he'll give me his name when I prove myself." He was shaking, red-faced, crying. "But it'll never be enough. No matter how hard I fight for him, he'll never be proud of me because he can't love me. He just wants me to do the things he won't. And you're just like him. You're using me, too. All you do is hurt people and call it love."

The flames faltered for the briefest of moments, then rallied. *"How is it possible you are brazen enough to defy a commandment from your God, you ape? I am your Maker; you are my Instrument."*

"Hey. Eyes on me, greed-feeder," said Alina. "You and I got business, and if you think Tolomond was 'brazen' just now, best be ready because I'm about to get a whole lot *brazier*." (Nasres chuckled quietly.)

"Consider your next words with care, Vrana of the Seven. They will be your last."

She took a breath. "My name is Alina K'vich, daughter of Zatalena, niece of Mateus, granddaughter of Dimas. They are separate from me, and yet we share a soul. I was never born, but I live. I am Aelfraver and Aelf. I am the Seven, and I am the One."

Tongues of fire licked the floating greatsword, which seemed to inhale the light. *"You are a walking corpse, given false life by a false prophet, who thought himself my equal because he etched his name in metal. But I am the Enlightened One. By my grace turns the Machine. I am the author, architect, and engineer of Creation. In a word, I am God."*

"Even gods bite the dust on a fairly regular rotation. It's the natural order. But you're no god. You're just a goblin." She cracked her knuckles. "And Ul-Shibyai'olo Iron and you are so far from equal, being mentioned in the same breath as you is an insult to his memory. You keep calling yourself 'The Author' lately, but the ink of the prologue of our world dried way before you put your pen to the page, and I'll be writing the epilogue way after you're gone."

"Pride unto the end." The flames finished condensing, forming the blade, crossguard, and pommel of the sword that had struck down Ruqastra. The weapon thrummed. *"So passes from history Vranakvius-rhin'erlin."* Point-first, it shot straight at Alina, light blazing along its edge—all the crackling, seething hatred caused by millennia of chases, assassinations, and wars burned brightly within its ethereal, heavenly metal. The broken blade warbled as it flew, thirsting for Alina's blood. It came close—so close—to cutting through her like concentrated sunlight through ice.

But, an inch from her eye, it stopped.

Restored to his full height and breadth, Tolomond gripped its hilt with his meaty, adult-sized hands. He leaned back, muscular shoulders heaving, heels digging into the earth. His stony jaw set in a growl. Even as he struggled, the hungering blade dragged him forward. His bloodshot eyes threatening to burst from their sockets, he held firm as he (mostly) restrained the channeled fury of a thing as powerful as a god.

"Can't... hold him..." he said.

"I will obliterate you all," declared the sword of light and fire, the ethereal manifestation of The Author, of Elwoch.

"Your mistake," said Alina, "was fully squatting in Tolomond's mind. Before you were in there, he was a meat puppet, and I would've been powerless to stop him. Just like Ruqastra was. But you just had to come get a front-row seat for the massacre of Ozar, didn't you?" She waggled her finger at the blade. "Too close to the sun."

"I am the sun. And all the light in the world."

"And I'm the shadow you cast." She pulled the spool of silver thread from her pocket again, and saw Etia, Nasres, Haba, and Gurm press their hands against the flat of The Author's sword, two to a side.

Tolomond's face was a scrunched mess of bulging veins, sweat, and snot. Blood ran from his eyes and ears. Where he touched the crossguard and hilt, his flesh began to blacken and crack. The corruption crawled up his fingers to his wrists and elbows, slithering toward his shoulders. He didn't have long.

With a telekinetic flick of her wrist, Alina unspooled the thread and sent it racing over and under each of the Sevensins' wrists and back again, looping around the digits of her raised left hand. She lowered all her fingers, except one.

Tied to the blade, Etia, Nasres, Haba, and Gurm appeared now as their present-day selves—the Hextarchs of Ozar. Their voices filled her mind:

Break his laws.
Slay his guardians.
Raze his city.
Shatter his Machine.

Alina replied, *New laws will be written. New guardians will rise. I will uplift all peoples, even his, and so the world will forget his cruelty. His city and Machine will fall to ruin. As for Elwoch himself? I will starve him.*

By that oath, the Hextarchs bound themselves to her forever, their separateness dissolving into oneness.

And the Author roared like a wildfire tearing across forest and countryside—

Alina yanked the silver thread, pulling it taut, and the blade fell from Tolomond's hands, clattering to the ground. Lifeless, cold, and dark as the rest of the chamber had suddenly become.

Tolomond backed away, leaning against a wall. He gaped, pale-faced, at the wreckage of his fingers, which curled like candle-burnt paper. His arms, blackened to the base of his fire-kissed throat.

He and Alina were alone within the chamber. There were no Hextarchs—in any form—to be seen.

Clearly in shock, he said, "His hold on me, it is lifted." Then, looking around: "The others, where did they all go?"

"They decided to join me after all. As a 'screw you' to Elwoch? Or, maybe they liked my speech? I dunno. But they're in here. All of them. All of me." She pressed her palm to her chest, whispering, "Thank you." She glared at Tolomond.

He said, "Are you going to kill me?"

"Wouldn't be unreasonable, would it? After all the times you've tried to do the same to me."

On his shins, he looked up at her.

"I can't forget what you did," she said.

"Nor could I."

"But thanks for saving me. Why did you?" Seeing his blank-eyed stare drift ever downward, she added, "Do you even know?"

"What is there to say? I am a cursed thing." He lifted the cooling, stiffening, charred remnants of his arms. "These more closely reflect the state of my soul. A fitting punishment, lighter than I warrant. I shall bear them with self-contempt until my end."

"And that's what you want, huh? An ending?"

"Do what you will with me. My soul is worthless. My body can endure any suffering. I welcome it."

She considered him carefully, noting that he'd been healed. Rather than his week-old-corpse skin-tone, his color had returned to a regular-human kind of pale. The stitching on his body and face were gone, as were his scars. His eyes had been opened. Once more, he looked like the man who'd killed Ordin Ivoir, who'd strapped Alina to a chair and beaten her. Even so, she couldn't help but see something else in him now. A little boy, abused and discarded.

She made up her mind. "See, okay, here's the thing. Even if I was the type to torture, or have someone tortured—I couldn't do it now, could I? You just admitted it wouldn't make a difference, so what'd be the point of causing you more pain? I'm trying, but I just can't see the angle. Besides, you look like you already got dragged through half the Seventy-Seven Hells, hitting every rock on your way down. What could I even do to you that your Sanctum friends haven't already? And that Author of yours? *Oof.* Wouldn't wish him on anyone. Talk about a lot of hot air."

"You joke at a time like this?"

"It's a defense mechanism. My personality is one part energy drink, two parts bitter sarcasm. At least I have a sense of humor."

He grunted, opened his mouth, but hesitated.

"What? Let's hear it. Come on."

"You wept for me. In the labyrinth."

"So?"

"I am struggling to understand why. Weakened as I was, in that form, it would have been a simple thing to kill me. Your enemy."

"Merciful Buthmertha. I feel sorry for you, man."

"You feel sorry... for me?"

"Yeah. I'm sure this comes as a shock, but I have this weird thing I do where I empathize with others. Even if they've done awful stuff. Even if they've taken people I love from me." He couldn't meet her gaze, so she made a sound halfway between a sigh and a growl. "Look at your hands."

He did.

"Why did you save me?"

Silence.

"Why did you save me, Tolomond? Your living phony-horse-and-pony god commanded you to 'smite' me. But you didn't. Why?"

No answer.

"Why did you save my life?"

"I don't know!" he shouted, back to the wall now. His head thumped rhythmically against the stone.

"Fine. I've got a job for you then: until you figure it out, you will live on."

A pause in the head-thumping. His eyes closed, he said, "Don't you hate me?"

"I don't 'hate' anyone. Not even Elwoch, or The Author, or whatever anyone wants to call him. Hating is so *easy.* You can switch it on like *that.*" She snapped her fingers. "But switching it *off*... I don't know if there'd be any going back for me. Wouldn't be a good look. So, I can't let myself try that hat on. Not even for a second."

"I cannot understand you."

"Yeah, join the club. Baraam's the president. You'd like him. You're a real pair of sledgehammers."

A long pause.

"Why are we still here? This is a dream, is it not?"

"Yeah."

"It feels as though it should have ended by now?"

"Almost. Dawn's nearly here, and then the dream will slip away. But I'm holding onto it just a little longer."

"Why?"

"Because I'm waiting for my uncle to step out of the shadows and make his move, already."

The patch of silence behind her shifted uncomfortably.

Without turning, she said, "Fair warning, you couldn't kill me now if you tried. So, whaddya say we talk things out instead? After all—" She smiled. "—we're family."

73

BARAAM

THE DUEL OF THE flying Caelomancers concluded with the second and final fall of Baraam bol-Talanai.

He crashed through one stone tower, then a second. His body shattered a series of stone terraces before cratering in the earth. Slowly, the dust settled around him. He couldn't move his arms or legs, could hardly lift his head.

Steadying her descent with outstretched arms, Eva touched down, lightly as a parent kissing her sick child.

Where Baraam was the master of lightning—of speed and piercing, heart-stopping, raw power—Eva was as unkillable as the stars. Like the light of those celestial bodies, she was a thing already dead, yet shining on. Emotionless, inexorable, impossibly cold, yet incalculably searing. Within her flowed more power than any ten—any hundred—Caelomancers should possess. There was no comparing their respective strengths. If he was the sky, she was the cosmos.

One last time, he laughed weakly at the vanity project that was The Gild's Aelfraver rating system. A humorless joke.

Very well. Let him die now that he had been shown the truth of his own helplessness. He was afraid, but not unready. From the day he and Ruqastra, as children, had pulled the *pieces* of their parents from the flaming rubble of their family home, he had been readying himself. After all, had he not gone to market that day, against his parents' wishes, he'd have been snuffed out, too. It was true. His own end had simply been deferred. Finally, death had reached the limit of its patience, and came to collect the Kadician orphan turned Aelfraver turned monk turned traitor. Just as it had come for his sister.

He had not been there for her, but he would see her again soon.

They'd buried the remains of their father and mother in a shallow, sandy pit by a grove of cinnamon trees. In his blistered fingers, he'd clutched the only toy he'd been able to salvage. A small, wooden sailboat. Ruqastra had told him not to cry, and he hadn't. Not since that day.

Yet, now the tears were pulled from his eyes by gravity, a force as undeniable as the Mage standing over him. If Eva felt anything for the broken man beneath her, she did not show it. Those fiery eyes—real, living flame. She was a knot of blazing light trapped in human flesh. Barely contained.

Raising her wrist as if checking the time, she thumbed the holo-keyboard that popped up from the face of her digital watch. A high-definition, not-quite-to-scale projection of Gildmaster Ridect appeared.

Ridect sneered down at Baraam. "I had to see for myself." His manicured hand cupped a rounded glass. Ice cubes tinkled as he swirled the amber liquid around. It was cognac, Baraam knew. He could almost smell the reek of Ridect's breath as the old man broke him down after live-fire combat training (or worse—etiquette classes).

Baraam spat a mouthful of blood onto the ground. Leaning on his elbow, he lifted his right hand, pointing with two fingers.

The spell wouldn't come. All fizzle, no spark.

His hand flopped.

"Once, I dared imagine you could amount to noteworthiness." Ridect shook his head. "But the ties to your inferior heritage proved too tenacious even for my influence. It seems the Kadician detritus never falls far from the landfill, and Nature—again—prevails over Nurture. Subpar materials will resist even the most adept workmanship." Fingers tensing, he scrunched the cashmere of his twenty-thousand-gelder suit. "Have you nothing to say by way of apology, you failure, you abject waste of flesh and resources? Well?"

"There is… one thing I've been meaning to tell you. Dimas was a thousand times the man you are." He hawked another glob of blood. "And he wasn't even human."

"Certainly, you learned one thing from him that I could never have taught you: how to fail, spectacularly and stupidly."

Keeping his eyes open became increasingly challenging. The world twisted as if the gods were winding it up. A pipe must have burst beneath him when he'd crashed. Cool water washed his back, keeping him conscious, but he could hardly hear his former teacher and boss any longer. Instead, his thoughts turned to an old prayer. It rang so clearly in his mind that he could not help but lend it his voice.

"Blessed Eëtion, watch over my brothers and sisters in my stead, for I must now go on. I bid you take the clay and water of my body."

"What is this? An appeal to your heathen god?" The taut skin on Ridect's nose wrinkled as if he'd sniffed spoiled yogurt. "May death beat that out of you at last."

"Leave me not to rot—"

"Eva," said Ridect. "I'm done with this disappointment. Finish it." The projection disappeared.

"—but let the creatures of the world consume me and my spirit fly on eagle's wings—"

Baraam could only watch as Eva's glowing hand lowered itself onto his forehead.

"Lead my wandering feet in journey to the hidden dune. Grant me your guidance that I might rejoin my ancestors; consign my body to the beasts of the desert—"

Raw heat evaporated his sweat, crusted his blood, and blistered his skin as she readied the spell that would incinerate his body and loose his soul into the ether.

"—that I might be one with the dust and the air and the world, forever."

With any luck, he would find his way back to the desert and, there, be free of the wretchedness of humanity and war.

74

CHO-ZEN

O BSIDIAN FINGER BONES PUNCTURED Cbarassan's root-and-earth shield, tearing off its top. Cho was knocked to the ground, a Martyr at her throat. But someone shouldered the skeleton off her, picked her up, and put her back on her feet.

She lost Cbarassan in the chaos.

Alone in a torrent of panicking bodies, she was too numb to actively feel much of anything. She broke into a dash, her thoughts speeding ahead of her. She wished they could've been useful thoughts, but they were, unfortunately, totally useless ones: meandering questions that promised no closure. Still, they provided a mental shelter of sorts as people died all around her, as she dodged the Martyrs' clutches with no hope of escape. There were too many of them, and they closed in from all sides.

As her body auto-piloted itself between a growing number of dangers, her mind wandered. She'd always hated magic, but now, she decided, she loathed it. Everything about it *sucked*, especially being on its receiving end. Even worse were the people who used it. Maggos walked around like the law didn't apply to them—and, really, it didn't. What was a parking ticket to someone who could shoot fireballs from their fists? Amazing honestly, that civilization hadn't already become a giant free-for-all on a mountain of dead bodies.

So, with all these reality-bending jerks running around, how could an organization like The Gild even exist? Why did Maggos enlist with The Authority? As Cho ran between glimmering magic missiles and gouts of flame, she had an epiphany: Maggos obeyed the Plutocracy because they were too complacent to resist. And that's exactly what made them so dangerous. All that raw power, and even they let themselves be used like tools. The Landsider Maggos got ground up in the army; the Elemental ones landed cushy office jobs. But they all simply did as they were told by the Plutocrats and their middlemen. Nobody asked questions; nobody thought, even for a second, *Gee, am I being responsible with my ability to throw boulders with my mind?* And that's how you ended up with perversions like the Martyrs, forged from human bones. Running, ripping, killing by the will of their disturbed creators.

The stink of blood and bile overwhelmed her. She slipped in puddles of the stuff, tripped over bodies as she ran for her life. But there were fewer and fewer places to turn. Cbarassan was behind her somewhere, shouting her name. She turned but had to peel out again as a line of Martyrs sprinted toward her. Their fingers raked her shoulder, her ribs.

She thought about unfairness, about kings and priests, with destiny in their collective pocket. What were they, really? The killers of yesteryear, equally as violent as people today; they'd simply gotten their shares of the pie first. All their privileges had been "earned" through swords and armies of Maggos and hieroglyphs on crumbling walls—basically, loaded dice designed to attract more glory to the already glorified. According to the histories *they* had written, they owned everything. And, year after year, generation after generation, their money and junk piled higher while everyone else picked over the scraps.

Maybe the reason so few people ever stopped to consider the true face of society was that the truth was too depressing/infuriating.

She'd been too slow to dodge; a Martyr clotheslined her. Downed, winded, she stared into its vacant eye sockets and felt exactly as empty. Its sharp fingers closed around her throat and clenched. It lifted her off the ground.

As she sputtered, kicked her feet, felt Cbarassan's hands touch her but then slip away, she became angry. All the sacrifices she'd made, all the lives lost on her behalf... She choked, orange error messages cluttering her failing vision, the ports in her skin popping out like shimmering chrome-colored coral.

Why was it that luck—or fate or the Gods or whatever you wanted to call the malfunctioning machinery of the universe—allowed so much fortune and power to flow like a river toward the already fortunate and powerful?

She saw only static. The only sound, a keening, prolonged squeal.

No breath. She wheezed, numb all over. Didn't feel her own tears on her face until she snorted them up her nose.

No hope. Nothing left for her. Nothing for anyone.

But, she'd tried. Given it everything she'd had. She'd tried, just before the end, to be good—to call for good, to deny herself a baser desire for a greater. Tried.

It wasn't right. Wasn't fair. The Authority would win again, as always. The Plutocrats would cling to the skirts of their gods, cowering on their flying citadel, setting fire to mountains of cash and using up all the resources just so no one else could have any.

They claimed the gods had given them the right to rule, but that was a lie. They were tyrants hiding behind a wall of soldier- and sorcerer-pawns.

Cho didn't hate magic, she realized. Rather, she hated that it had given the powerful the monopoly on miracles.

Her sight went totally dark.

She lent her final thoughts to a question. Or a prayer, perhaps:

Couldn't there be—

Her toes hyper-extended. Kicking. Slowing.

—just this once—

Arms limp.

—a miracle for everyone else?

75

ALINA

S HE DIDN'T TURN, DIDN'T so much as shift where she sat with one knee high, one foot tucked in.

"Have a seat, Mateus."

He circled to her front, light on his feet for such a broad-shouldered man. Robes fluttering like tattered bandages, like moth wings, he tried to keep an eye on both Tolomond behind him and Alina in front. The edges of his fingernails were black, dirt-caked. The hands of a mechanic. Or a grave digger.

"Uncle. Sit."

Hesitation. Why? Could he be—

"You're—" She cocked her head, rubbing her bruised shoulder—"afraid of me." Neck craned, she smiled at him as if he were a fresh corpse in the desert, barely rotten.

His chin jerked reflexively. He was blinking a lot. Too much. Tugging at the tangles in his coarse graying beard, he glared at her with yellow-rimmed eyes.

Sick man. The battle had taken its toll on him.

"Do you understand," she said, the ground cracking at the sound of her voice, "what I've become?"

Slowly, he nodded.

"What do you think I'm going to do to you now?"

"Eat me. Like you did the others."

She shook her head, chuckled. "Still thinking like a cannibal. Still playing by the old rules." She pressed her finger onto her other palm, and he was compelled to the ground as if a ton of clay had fallen onto his back.

Once he was seated, the pressure lifted, and he could breathe again. "So? You will take what you want of me," he whispered. "My power. You pretend to be better, but we're the same, you and I. 'Cannibals,' as you put it. The spawn of Dimas."

"We *are* Dimas. But we are also free to choose for ourselves what we do with that truth."

"You say this even as you hold me hostage."

"We're just talking. If you don't like what I have to say by the end of our chat, you're free to leave. I'll see you out myself."

"Swear it."

"Which gods would you like me to swear by, huh? The Plutocrats' Plutonia and the Seventy-Seven? Or, do you prefer an older vintage—the Iorians' Asteriae? Should we go as far back as AEON and MUNDUS? Or, the prime powers that, fifteen billion years ago, shaped the universe out of raw heat and abyssal cold? Pick yer poison, buddy. I'll swear by all of 'em that, if you don't like what you're hearing, I'll set you free." She took a breath. "But I'm confident you won't want me to. By the time we're done here, we'll have found our middle ground."

At that, he cracked a smile, which broke into a laugh like a painfully clipped, hacking wheeze. His robes enveloped him like a cocoon as he said, "He really is in there, isn't he? Only Dimas could be so arrogant." Resting his chin on his fist: "Well? Let's hear your impassioned, heartrending plea, so I can dismiss it and get to work finding some way to stop you. Let's hear this monologue you've been rehearsing for my benefit."

"Monologue? Nah. I only need one word."

He leaned in, showing his teeth. Exhaustion clouded his bloodshot eyes. The weariness of decades.

The Revoscape itself shuddered as their four golden eyes locked.

Within Alina dwelled the souls of (mostly) seven Demidivines, legendary creatures reanimated by her renewed sense of purpose, but she set aside all their experience and cunning and power in favor of simple honesty.

She said, "Zatalena." And, unlike last time, she didn't give Mateus a choice: she lunged for his hand, gripping it so fiercely the bones nearly broke.

The truth, undeniable, spiked his heart. His cocoon split, and his bravado, his smirking arrogance, molted from him. What emerged was a shivering, middle-aged man, whose glare was like week-old bread softening in a bowl of water. "She's really in there? With you?"

"Of course she is. The Authority gunned her down in Clerica Viridim, almost fifteen years ago. But, through Egogenesis, Dimas—"

"Ruined her."

"Saved her. And himself. When he called her back—when she accepted that they were *one*—they were healed. If he hadn't done it, the part of *us* that we called Zatalena would have been taken away. It would have fed Elwoch." She gagged. "Can you imagine?"

"No, I don't know what that would have meant."

She leaned in. "I'll show you." She beamed into his mind images of the bright wheel of souls, ever-turning, the final destination of all the dead. She let him see that wheel for what it truly was—a conveyor belt at a buffet. And there, picking mortal morsels from that belt, was a hideous, glowing slug—a creature lit from within by the raw energy it consumed. It glutted itself on an ever-shrinking pool of life force, a well of energy that should have been self-sustaining, incapable of running dry. But because this massive, monstrous parasite ate and ate and ate forever, there was less and less *life* that could flow back into the infinite array of worlds that dotted the universe. Including their world, Alina and Mateus's home.

"Without Dimas—without *us*—Zatalena would have been devoured by that disgusting slime, Elwoch. And we would have lost her—that part of ourselves— forever." She gestured from herself to him. "This? Us fighting each other? It's insane. We're only helping him. With every second of pain, every moment we deny our connection, he grows stronger."

Mateus had been shaken by the vision. His scoff rang hollow. "Am I meant to understand *that* is the true form of The Author? Let me guess, you've discovered the means to defeat the abomination, where all others have failed?"

"No one else has ever had what we have."

"And what would that be, girl?"

"Each other."

He growled. "Where is your flower crown then? Delusional child." He made to stand.

"Hang tight, please." She snapped her fingers, rooting him to the spot. "We're almost done. But I have a question for you. What is Elwoch?" She spoke to him as if he were a particularly inattentive child disrupting the class for the umpteenth time. "Not a god, even though that's what he'd very much love for you to keep thinking."

"What does it matter? His nature is irrelevant."

She flicked her finger from left to right, sealing his lips. "You aren't playing along. Guess I'll have to carry you like a little baby through your own logic. Can't really blame you, though, because you technically weren't around, back when— Never mind." She sighed. "Elwoch, the creature that has hunted us almost to extinction, was, once upon a time, just some guy who wanted things he couldn't have. And he was willing to lie, cheat, and kill for them. Long story short, he skipped his way into the right place at the right time, and got mistaken for the messiah. Nobody bothered to correct him until it was too late, and by then he was too strong. At some point, he got his grubby little fingers on, pretty much, the controls to the universe. And the rest is dusty old history: man becomes prophet; prophet becomes king; king becomes demon; demon becomes 'god.' His song's been stuck on replay a long time, uncle. But that's where I come in."

Still silenced, he stared at her.

"I'm the shuffle button."

When she restored his voice, he chose not to speak. So, they sat awhile.

(She noted that Tolomond, leaning against the wall, had drifted off. Although shallowly, he still breathed; she could hear his heartbeat. Despite the damage to his arms, his vitals were stable, his organs healthy. Good. With Elwoch's influence dispelled, Tolomond had nearly died. Hooking and reeling his spirit in, Alina had returned him from the brink. However, this was no act of kindness, as he'd soon enough find out.)

Mateus's breath whistled through his nostrils. Sharp breaths, slowly smoothing over. Finally, he spoke: "Has she said anything about me? Zatalena?"

"It doesn't work like that. I don't talk to them. We're not separate people anymore. But I feel them." Alina tapped the place where her collarbones met. "And I know what she would say because I can feel that, too."

He inhaled, waiting.

Within herself, she listened to a voiceless speaker who painted the scene for her. Then, she said, "Do you remember when you were both teens, you and mom? You'd sit with your feet dangling over the edge of the roof of Tahtoh's crappy apartment, watching the hovercraft light trails, counting the twinkling satellites. You asked her why Dimas had bothered to have children. He didn't want to deal with kids. It seemed he'd rather you had popped into existence, fully formed—twenty-two-year-old twins with high-paying jobs. So, why, you asked, did he drag you into this world when none of you seemed particularly happy about it? You, especially, always felt so out of place. Remember what mom told you, Mateus?"

Unsteadily, throatily, he answered, "She said that he'd fathered us so that he could see himself through the eyes of another. Mirroring the genesis of the cosmos, he sought to know himself through us."

"Through you and Zatalena, he did learn so much about who he was—who *we* are. Who *I* am."

"My sister was so kind. And wise. But I barked at her, often. Called her terrible names. Accused her of being his pet, his favorite."

"You were angry."

"I've always been angry."

"You feel guilt."

"Yes. On a night much like that one, I ran away, not returning till years later. By then, you'd come along. And I'd been—"

"Forgotten? Replaced? Is that what you think?"

She granted him visions of Zatalena kneeling beside her bed, hands clasped; Zatalena, lighting little candles and placing her brother's photo on Buthmertha's shrine; Zatalena, showing baby Alina pencil sketches of Uncle Mateus.

Alina said, "My mother prayed most nights. For you. A simple prayer. All she asked for was that you somehow find your peace on this earth."

He blinked at her like a contrite boy (but with a beard and bushy eyebrows).

"You don't need to suffer. There's no debt to repay."

"But I was—"

"Let go of your grief."

"But—"

"She loves you, Mateus."

Her uncle's cry caught in his chest, locking his jaw. He sobbed dryly.

She let him feel it. Their time was almost up. Soon, the dream would end. But she could let him have this. Everyone deserves compassion.

Eh, almost everyone.

"Elwoch is a Greed Demon," she said. "He *is* Greed. The suffering of others is his favorite dish. By tearing each other down, we raise him up. He wants us to do as much damage to ourselves as possible. And, for too long, we've played by his rules. For too long, we've acted just like *that* guy." She indicated Tolomond, slumped in the corner. "We've been just as blunt and narrow-minded. Across all our many lives, we fought steel with steel, fire with fire. But I'm suggesting a different approach going forward. So far, we've all agreed to it, the six-and-three-quarters of us who have united. The only one that's missing is me—well, specifically, *you*." She stood, shaking the pins and needles from her limbs. "I'm asking you, please, give me your strength. I can't do it without you."

She offered her hand.

He looked up. In his glassy stare, she saw, reflected back at her, Dimas K'vich, the parent smiling softly down at his child. Mateus shrank away, as if fearing a backhand, but then his gaze met hers again. The echo of his long-lost sister, she bolstered him. And she knew his emotions as surely as if she felt them, too. In a way, she did; their minds tethered, their souls entwined.

"The opposite of greed is generosity, uncle. It's our ultimate weapon against *him*. In its name, the Hextarchs entrusted me with their lives, their country, and their people. They've joined me on the path. Won't you walk it with us?" Her hand hovered in front of his awed face.

He took it, and she helped him up.

Hunching, favoring one leg, he seemed to age half a lifetime in an instant. "I have grown so tired."

"Then, let me carry you a while."

"I see now what he must have seen in you." He patted her arm, eyes crinkling. "You have your mother's smile."

Tendrils of dim, golden light unraveled from Mateus's astral body, his soul coursing through these veins as they enveloped Alina's arm. Arteries joining arteries, connecting heart to heart.

Fading, his body translucent, he said, "What comes next?"

"I don't know. We'll hafta see."

He was barely more than a ghostly outline now. "I feel... calm." He took a breath and held it. And, before he'd finished exhaling, he disappeared.

The last vestiges of his essence joined with Alina's.

From the Seven, one.

Some dreams close as gently as the cover of a book, ready to open again like arms, welcoming the reader's return. Such dreams leave their dreamers with a deep breath expanding their bellies, spring's early light dappling their brows.

This one was different. Woven of stone and desperation, of blood and twilight fleeing dawn, bound by fraying sinew and the final thread of hope plucked from a stitched-together heart, this dream ended not with a sigh but a seven-gun salute. The universe-in-miniature Alina had built from the blocks and tiles of her fractured mind collapsed around her. The seams tore, revealing nothingness behind the threadbare tapestry she'd strung together. Every wall, every inch, every dimension quivered—a band pulled, and pulled, and—

Waking, Tolomond limped to her side. He didn't even look down as his heel bumped his sword, which slid across the cracking floor, spinning.

"Why do you not kill me for what I've done?" he asked, as the Revoscape groaned and shuddered.

Voice rattling from the force vibrating up her legs, she said, "Get over it. Besides, death would've been a breeze compared with what I got planned for you. There, does that help?"

"Oddly, yes. Whatever it is, I deserve it."

"Alright, enough of that. Sleep."

He crumpled, hitting the dissolving earth, and snored peacefully.

Alone at last, she took this moment for herself.

She allowed the weight of forty-nine lifetimes of defeat to fall upon her shoulders. In the same breath, she was uplifted. The ultimate end of Egogenesis—the union of cumulative thousands of souls—had been achieved. The Sevensin had become one. Within her lived the hope of all ages past, and hers was the burden of clearing a path to the future. Inside her soul, seven voices shouted at one another, each vying for attention and control. One day, she would learn to tame them, to consciously draw from their power and experience, to guide their wills in unison with her own.

For now, she would simply wake up.

Some dreams leave behind a sense of grief over things or people we never really had nor knew, yet we feel their loss anyway, wishing we could return to them. Others endow us with hope—however briefly—that our days will be just a little lighter going forward.

For the most part, dreams are of no consequence except to the dreamer. *However,* every several millennia, give or take, a dream of considerable significance comes to life as if from nothing and nowhere, connecting the consciousnesses of millions. Born of their aspirations, their yearning, and cradled in the hope that survives at the utter end of hopelessness, a power awakens. Call it the work of chance or providence—either way, the dreaming multitude summons into existence a force, a creature bursting with raw magic; the union of a multitude of opposites, her strength derived from embracing her inner Contradiction; a being that generates change as naturally as breathing; Creation's answer to ages of stagnation.

A god.

No—

A Dragon.

PART SEVEN

ASCENDANCE

76

BARAAM

EVA HAD BARAAM ON his knees, pinned to the earth. Her palm scorched his forehead, blistering his flesh. Her heat—her very aura—broiled the oxygen and compressed his chest until breathing was no longer an option for him.

All the gunfire, explosions, and ominous groans of the cavern ceiling faded from his perception. His awareness shrank to a mere hand span. Her hand. It was as if he'd been caught in the orbit of a dying star; the light radiating from her, the final warning before she went supernova.

He should have been dead already. With his broken bones and fractured mind, by rights, he should have been dead. But it wouldn't be long now. Any second, she'd spear his brain with an energy beam. He felt it coming.

Eyes dry, spit evaporating from his tongue, he glared up at her, steeling himself.

Her Niima suddenly shifted, then. She spasmed, her pale, blank-slate of a face twitching.

His ears popped, and a wave of dizziness struck him.

All at once, the heat receded; her hand pulled away. Pupils dilating, she clutched it to her chest. Though she still glowed from within, the porcelain mask of her expression had cracked and fallen away. What remained was something he—even lying on death's doorstep—recognized all too well: fear and self-loathing; disgust.

She looked down at him. Then at her bloody-knuckled hands. At him again. Lip trembling, bright brown bangs swishing across her brow, she said, "The things they made me do."

Of all the emotions racing through him, confusion won out. Something had changed, but what?

His bewilderment only intensified as he watched her begin to shine again, even more fiercely than before. Crescents of light curved outward from her heart, eyes, and mouth.

Lifting his head, neck muscles burning, he said, "What are you doing?"

She met his gaze. The crinkle of her brow, the dimple at her right cheek—undeniable humanity burst from her so forcefully that not even her unearthly, blazing eyes could hide it. When she looked at him now, tears flowed. She smiled shakily, weakly, as if those muscles had atrophied from years or decades of disuse. "I'm destroying their weapon."

Backing away, she slapped her palms against her temples and began to *push*. Inner glow flaring, she radiated energy like an overloading nuclear core. Smoke and light and the stench of charring meat pervaded the air as her skin smoldered. She did not relent, even as she screamed.

Her cries lanced his ears, his brain, his every nerve. Her misery was his own.

Drained and brittle, he could not explain how he rose to his feet, nor how he closed the distance between them. But, when he arrived, he placed his hands over hers.

"Stop," he said.

"Get back, or you'll die too."

He believed her. At first, her heat was like a sandstorm, raking his face and hands. Within seconds, though, she became so hot to the touch that he lost all sensation in his fingers.

"Let me go." She glared at him through her sweat-matted bangs. "I almost killed you."

"You are me."

His skin dark, hers pale; his hair black, hers brown; superficial differences. Beneath these, Caelomancers was what they were, trained to scorch and to fly. Deeper still was the truth: they were what Eva had called herself—weapons, forged to kill. Unthinking instruments. No less brainwashed than Tolomond. Indeed, Baraam was just as unthinking, reactionary, and pliable as any Sanctumite fanatic. The realization smothered the fire inside him at last.

"Look at me," he said.

She wouldn't, glowing ever more brightly.

The two stood at the center of a tornado of ash, boulders raining down around them. Cracks ran up the side of the surrounding buildings. The parking garage behind her collapsed on itself, level after level, starting at the top.

"We are the same. Do what you feel necessary. But if you go, I go with you."
He rested his forehead against hers. Her skin—like rubbing his face against a gas
flame. He shut his eyelids and gritted his teeth. "I forgive you."

Soon, his knees buckled, his nerves and pain receptors giving out.

The agony ended.

And he wondered if maybe he'd died. Maybe opening his eyes would snuff
the last flimsy spark of his consciousness. At first, he resisted the temptation to
behold the world, even one last time. In his heart, he feared that he'd be lost to
it forever if he tried. So, he waited—until, that is, he remembered he was not
descended from timid men.

Meeting his fate, he found himself alive and staring into Eva's eyes.

Another lengthening moment unfurled between them like a tattered flag.
When she lowered her hands to her sides, he held on. A current passed from her
to him, him to her, connecting them. Grounding him.

He wanted to say something—anything—but his iron will finally snapped,
and his body gave in to the damage it had sustained.

Surrendering to gravity, he pitched backward. Parallel with the earth, the last
things he saw were Eva lunging to catch him—and the freight truck-sized stal-
actite plunging toward them both.

The back of his skull smacked against the ground. Limp as a child's doll, he
slipped away.

77

CHO-ZEN

BONY FINGERS SLACKENING, THE Martyr released Cho's throat. She slipped from its grasp, sprawling on the ground, coughing.

Air filled her lungs. The error messages plastered across her vision disappeared one by one, each with a little *ping*. The fog of war lifted, and she could soon see again.

She watched the Martyr jitter like a flea, pre-jump. It thrashed on the ground, kicking and gnashing its teeth. All at once, it collapsed in a heap of dark bones.

She lay beside it, dazed, staring into the skull's empty eye sockets.

The sudden, staccato clatter of thousands of bones caught her attention. Whether standing, leaping, lunging, or biting, all the hundreds of Martyrs scattered across the battlefield fell to pieces. Every last one.

Her gaze drifted to the chitinous plates of the slain greatworm in whose shadow she rested. The thing was as big as four buses stacked two by two, and it draped around the courtyard like a tacky scarf. Only now did she realize she was lying in a pool of its congealed, gray... blood? Bile?

Wobbly, she stood. Blinking through the smoke and ash, she took in the field of slaughter, avoiding the blank stares of the dead. Hundreds of living eyes were focused on her. Landsiders and Elementals. Human and Aelf soldiers. Prisoners of war. Survivors, all.

She looked up, then. High above, Authority blimps flashed their warning lights. Interrupting the unexpected stillness that had fallen over the courtyard was a siren.

Six clipped blasts. The signal to retreat.

Was this a trap? She'd lost her knife, so she grabbed the nearest Martyr femur and hefted it like a bat.

Mumbling, "Need a better view," she raced to the cracking wall, bumping against it, fingers fumbling on the rungs of a rickety ladder. The screws anchoring it to the stone squeaked unsettlingly as she ascended, but she reached the battlements. From there, she saw aircraft, convoys of tanks, and mecha, all turning away from Hexhall. Accompanied by thousands of soldiers, the vehicles were headed for Peregar's Grief. They were leaving.

Had The Authority been... defeated?

How? There'd been one hundred *thousand* of them. Sure, Cho had poached most of the vanguard—the ragged and smoke-scarred battalions surrounding her now—but they couldn't have made up more than a quarter of El's army. At most. And she wasn't arrogant enough to think her words, even broadcast by the news drones onto screens all throughout Ozar, had been enough to break the Elemental Empire's assault.

Yet, the signal to retreat echoed through the caverns of the Seventh Stack. That was really happening.

To the west, there fell a shower of stalactites, catching the fleeing army's flank. Next, with a grating of stone on stone followed by a deafening boom, a section of the rocky shelf collapsed, taking several buildings into the abyss with it.

Cho turned her attention to the stone bridge connecting the town with the fortress, and she choked at the sight of soldiers—hundreds of them—marching up to it. However, as they began to cross, they waved white flags. They stopped near the gatehouse.

At their head, a man in Hruvic colors removed his helmet, announcing, "Hail, she whom they call Cho-Zen. The unthinkable has been accomplished this day. I speak for all those present when I congratulate you on your triumph."

Leaning over the lip of the rampart, Cho cleared her throat. "What can we, uh, do for you?"

"You, my lady, have done enough. It is we who wish to serve you. We have deserted our masters in favor of pledging ourselves to your cause. Would you grant us asylum?"

"Uh." She considered this might be a trick, but she had no real way of stopping them even if she'd wanted to. "Alright. Whatever burps your baby." That probably wasn't the greeting they'd been hoping to hear, but she was too tired and shell-shocked to care.

The new arrivals walked right through the busted gate and met with what was left of the vanguard. A tense moment followed. Then, to smatterings of laughter and tears of exhaustion, the two groups became one. Among the Tranquilizers, arms opened to embrace; backs were clapped; hands were shaken. Even between the humans of El and the others, an uneasy peace held.

As she watched the mixing of Families, nationalities, and species, she thought that maybe—maybe—her words *had* made this possible. And, maybe, she could do more...

Everyone settled down. In the hush, the limping, huddled, white-eyed masses of turncoat Authority soldiers, Covenants, and rag-tag Ozari defenders again looked to her as if waiting for a sign.

Slowly, she raised her bloody fist.

And they cheered, a jubilant unison cry that shook the cave city from roots to roof.

In victory, the soldiers gave to their fury and their battle ecstasy *her* name, chanting, "Cho-Zen. Cho-Zen..." They climbed to the ramparts where were arrayed the flags of the Twelve Families and the Nation of El. With axes they broke the chains holding the poles in place, and the flags fell. Putting the cloth to the torch, all the while they recited, "Cho-Zen," as if her name were their mantra, as if she'd singlehandedly defeated the Empire today.

She had developed quite the large fan club, but paid their praise little attention. Instead, she scanned the still-burning buildings beyond the chasm, the smoke-screened air above, and the shattered bodies all around.

"Alina, where are you?"

78

ALINA

SHE RETURNED IN SOUNDLESSNESS—a quiet like honey rolling into the crevices of reality, filling the cracks of Hexhall. An inhaled prayer for the fallen. The grateful breath of a revived drowning victim. She returned to the mortal world, and she carried with her The Abyss.

Her spirit-form, like strands of a sweater catching on a hook, unraveled, and she didn't so much step out of the Revoscape as *drag* patches of it with her. The trillion threads of her being entwined, slithering like worms of light, like grasping fingers, encircling and enveloping each other. Then there stood a golden outline, almost human in shape.

Even in her ghostly form, her arrival was like an iron ball dropping onto a sheet of parchment. The weight of her raw, primordial power threatened to tear through reality itself. The boundaries of the physical plane bent backward, away from her, as if hand-cranked—bending, bending—until she was encompassed by a perfect sphere of empty air. There came a crackle and a rather troubling *pop* as material existence itself strained to hold her.

Concerned by the idea that reality might have a you-broke-it-you-bought-it policy, she hurried to her corporeal, curled body. Energy craves a container, and there her container lay, in the cracked and crumbling chamber of the Hextarchs, on the glass floor—that window into the endless Abyss, where swam the stars and planets like schools of fish. Encircled by the six hexagonal pillars, her unconscious body looked so small and frail. Appearances, however, could be deceiving. Inside that electric scooter of a body roared a thousand V8 engines.

She laid her spirit down. As she re-entered her crumpled form, two things happened: reality snapped back into place around her (for the most part); and, she felt a great deal of pain. Broken ribs, wrist bones, nose. Throbbing; bruises. Bleeding internally.

She was dying. That wouldn't do.

Turning the full force of her will inward, she disappeared these ailments. Her heartbeat stabilized as bone and sinew stitched together. The battered green and yellow splotches on her flesh cleared up.

Lifted by a pillar of earth, she rose.

Beside her, in the Hextarchs' silent and empty sanctuary, she saw Tolomond. Lying still, asleep. She left him there for now. He wouldn't wake until she let him.

Her feet led her past the bent metal double doors, her footfalls echoing along the stone hallway. For a time, she was alone.

Soon, she found others. Warriors clad in dark, shiny armor or yellow robes. Leaning against the walls, lying upon one another. Their knives bared, mouths open, they clutched their wounds. She felt so much pain emanating from these bodies around her, writhing—shot, stabbed, clubbed, crushed. Some approached death like inchworms; others galloped toward it like gazelles.

Abyssal, labradorite-green energy expanded from Alina—a pressure, firm but gentle. She did not discriminate in applying it. She had more than enough for everyone; she simply healed.

All around her, the bodies of soldiers—Authority and Plastick and Covenant and every other—were enveloped in a glowing, growing, revitalizing cocoon of Corpromancy.

In the span of a breath, she broke the limits of everything Mateus had imagined Corpromancy could be. It was as easy as wading into the deeper end of a pool. But she did not leave him behind. She took him with her, holding his hands—and those of the others inside her being—because she wanted them to see. The possible. The beautiful. Before, he had only ever used his healing power superficially, to numb and wash away the aches of the body. He'd erased tissue damage with his tremendous expertise, but he couldn't treat the underlying ills. She, however, could.

She wove a spell of Zoiimancy and Somnexiomancy for healing and restful dreams, working in notes of Terramancy for grounding and Igniomancy for purification of the spirit. With Divinumancy (the Deïmantic power indwelling small gods), she split herself into as many pieces as there were patients, and she stepped into each of their minds, one at a time but in such rapid succession that it hardly mattered. And she gave them all waking dreams… Of happy childhoods, of lost

lovers, of parties, of pets, of children on the way, of nostalgia and grief and ca-
tharsis. Of the old mill near the forest, the bend in the river where she said "yes."
Of burial grounds, where wild weeds may grow. Of the return home at war's
end. Of better days to come.

And where those wearied soldiers got up, gone were enemy combatants
who'd come to Ozar to kill or die or both. One by one, squad by squad, cohort
by cohort, they shook themselves awake, and from them fell away their fear.
Gazing upon her with naked awe, they parted to let her pass. From her, they felt
kindness and threat, hearth and wildfire.

They watched her move on until, as if each one of them were being pulled
by an invisible thread tethering their heart to hers, they decided to follow. They
trailed her farther down the corridor, whose end was clogged by more dead and
dying.

Nothing could be done for the deceased. Mateus's empty miracle could not
restore souls to flesh, only puppet corpses. This was the first step toward Mar-
tyrdom. And, powerful though they were, Alina, had no room for such abominations in the army she was building. So, she left the dead to their momentary
peace and wished she didn't know exactly where they were headed, and how
terrible a fate it truly was.

However, the dying she could save: Abyssal power and her Niima combined,
rippling outward from her, altering, restoring. The twisting, convulsing wounded
calmed, their breaths steadying. Blade shards and shrapnel slid from their muscle
tissue, tinkling on the ground. Slashes and bullet holes sealed. Burns cooled,
scarred, and smoothed over. The fighters opened their eyes, gasping.

She welcomed the healed back as they, too, stood. And they, too, followed.

Under an arch ahead, some others still fought. The hallway, here, was wide
enough to fit six adults shoulder to shoulder, and it was packed. Farther up,
honeycomb-like chambers and side passages were equally jammed with bodies.
The struggles within were up close and personal now, elbow to face, knife to gut.

Alina had her followers hang back. As she approached the rear of The Authority's forces, the back-most lines turned and fired a storm of bullets and grenades and magic missiles at her. The projectiles burnt up—hundreds of red and
yellow flares, like incinerating fireflies.

Hanging from the ceiling like a bat, surveying the skirmish, the Covenant in
command of the Ozari defenders ordered her battalion to back off and hold.

Alina looked to those who'd shot at her, then to those behind—whose soot-
and gunpowder-clouded expressions were lighter now, their chins higher. To the
ones still clinging to their guns and rocket launchers and riot shields and dia-
mond-edged swords—to El and to Ozar—she said, "It's over."

Neither side seemed convinced, and The Authority rear-guard rushed her.

She glared at them, flaring her Igniomancy. The alloyed metals of their weapons and the carbon nanotubes of their body armor super-heated, becoming un-

bearably hot within seconds. Mid-stroke, mid-reload, the soldiers shed their bay-oneted guns, their blades, their helms and bracers and bullet-proof vests. Sensing Alina's power, the Mages lowered their Niima-imbued hands.

Disarmed, they looked around and seemed to see something in themselves and their comrades, something to which they'd previously been blind. They were ashamed. And that shame spread like a virus, infecting those behind, row after row, until every one of them lowered their weapons.

The Covenant spider-climbed along the ceiling toward Alina, dropped down, and knelt before her. "Achemir," she said, bowing her head. "You are the shield of our people now. Our loyalty, until death and beyond, is yours."

Alina placed a hand on her shoulder.

The Authority soldiers also fell to their knees. "Forgive me," they were say-ing.

"I'm sorry."

"I was afraid."

"I just want to go home."

"The fight's over," Alina told them. "Follow me."

They, like their comrades before them, fell in line. The Covenant and her forces did the same. By the time she exited the ravaged fortress of Hexhall, there were hundreds behind her. Once she came to the center of the courtyard, that number had swelled to thousands. She kept walking, and the silent soldiers trailed behind, flowing into a single mass in her wake. Growing, growing, but never speaking.

Along her path lay the inert obsidian bones of the hundreds of Martyrs. Their Niimantic link to their master had been severed at the moment the Sevensin had banished him from Ozar. For the likes of Elwoch, this was only a temporary setback, but one he wouldn't soon forget.

Between a heap of the unbroken but inert tungsten bones lay the bodies of several Covenants. They'd been herded into a crumbling corner of the courtyard and torn apart.

Alina recognized one of them.

Sprinting, dropping, she slid on her shins to Vessa's side. She brushed strands of pink hair behind Vessa's ear, cradling her blood- and dirt-smeared face. Her eyes were covered by a strip of tattered yellow cloth. Her shoulders had been dislocated. Both knees, shattered. Repeated trauma to the skull had caused a se-vere brain hemorrhage. Another few minutes—minutes—and it would have been too late.

Alina's trembling lips smudged the grime on Vessa's forehead. She pulled the blindfold away and held her close. Tightly.

Vessa gasped and retched and contorted and, finally, screamed as her shoul-ders were relocated, bones reknit, cartilage resculpted.

She opened her eyes and, seeing who held her, closed them again with a con-tented smile. "Something different," she murmured, "about you."

Combing her fingers through Vessa's fine hair, Alina laughed quietly.

Squinting, Vessa noticed Alina's entourage. "There's a lot of guys behind you. Thought you'd wanna know."

"I've roped them into helping me take care of a few things. Right now, I've got somewhere I need to be. Can you stand?"

"Yeah, though I was kinda hoping to milk the injury a tad longer. You doting on me, I don't mind it."

"There's always tonight."

She helped Vessa up.

Vessa retrieved her whip, unraveling it from the spine of a nearby Martyr, and pursed her lips.

"What is it?" Alina asked.

"A weird dream. I was floating up, toward this swirling *spiral* of light. Thing was lifting me up to it. Then I heard you in my head, calling me back. You glided in between me and the light—like an eclipse. And I started to fall down, but you were there to catch me."

"What did you feel, when the light was pulling you in?"

"Peace."

"And when I brought you back?"

"Anger."

"Good. Remember that feeling. Because that light is the portal to hell—the *real* hell. A feeding trough. It's dinner for one up there, and he's never satisfied."

"Alina, *what* are you talking about?"

"I'll tell you everything I can, but it's gonna have to wait a bit. First, I kinda have to go end one war and start another." Alina pecked her on the cheek and swished off, edges of her cloak ruffling.

Her patient army followed.

"Alina!" Vessa snapped.

Alina turned.

"You're not gonna tell me how I'm still alive? How you saved me? I *saw the light*. I shouldn't be standing here right now."

Alina approached Vessa again. "It's a long story. The short version? I'm a mix of thousands of souls crammed into one body. When enough Abyssal energy binds itself to one being, you get what I am."

"And, that is?"

"A Dragon."

"What."

"A Dragon, I said."

Vessa's brow furrowed. She laughed, though uncertainly. "That right? Well, call me loopy, but I don't see any chitin or wings. Can you even breathe fire?"

"The fire thing is a myth."

"Damn. Woulda been dope."

"But, yeah, Dragons did take on beastly shapes. The last ones, from hundreds of years back, were kinda like hella big bugs. I'm… something different. Also, cards on the table, I'm probably immortal? Jury's still out on that one."

"Uh-huh. Uh-huh. I see." Cupping her chin, Vessa nodded thoughtfully. "This is a lot. You know?"

"I get it. If you want some space, no prob, I can—"

"Oh, what-*ever*. Shut up, already. We both know that I'm still so totally *in*. I've never dated a god before."

"I've never dated *anyone*, so." Awkwardly snapping her fingers, Alina blinked a whole lot, then swiveled and walked off. Well, she tried to.

Vessa caught her arm.

"What are you—"

"I was thinking we'd make out."

"Right now? Vess, I have to, like, go."

"Just a cool five seconds."

Alina laughed, a sound that rippled through the gathered thousands of soldiers. She could feel their hearts lifting, too.

Grabbing her by the hip, Vessa yanked her in close. "Your fan club—" She gestured toward the army around them. "—are they gonna be weird about it?"

"I don't care." Alina leaned in.

The kiss ended, the fastest five seconds of her life. But, however brief, the moment was a fragment of joy she'd carry with her through the many trials ahead.

As Alina walked away, Vessa shouted after her, "You. Are. So. Hot."

Without turning—if she turned now, she'd stay forever—Alina waved one hand high overhead.

Along her path, ever more rivers of soldiers flowed into her gathering sea.

Into her mind sprang a memory of the day she'd made the chemical element of tritium from bottled water. At the time, she'd thought little of the accomplishment. The task had been difficult, sure, but she'd always had a knack for manipulating matter.

Because she could only do it on small things and in small amounts, and because she'd heard of very few others who had this ability, she'd always figured it wasn't significant. In hindsight, that logic was laughable—the wicked work of her low self-esteem.

Now, she knew the truth: altering the elements was a gift of the Demidivine.

Her heritage had granted her the skill, but it was her determination that expanded it. With her six siblings' powers united in her, she couldn't yet imagine her limits. It was as if she'd been handed an insanely huge key ring, with a key to every door in the universe. Theoretically, all paths could open to her, but she'd have to put in the hard work of matching keys to locks. She had a lot of self-learning to do.

Leading the procession of healed soldiers, she thought again of Mezami. If only she'd been stronger sooner, she could have mended him, too.

She felt the motion of his spirit inside her own, flitting like a sparrow on the hunt for bees.

Their eternal union was ecstasy and tragedy: the full joy of him would be hers to relish forever, but it would be hers alone.

79

CHO-ZEN

TRAITORS, RESISTORS, TRUE BELIEVERS, mercenaries— united, the enemies of El cheered.

And then they prowled the grounds, sniffing out the Elemental officers who'd fled during the encounter with the Martyrs. These remaining loyalists, led by Kaspuri Walazzin, had executed a battle maneuver entirely unfamiliar to them—but one they'd soon have lots of practice with—the swift retreat. They hadn't made it very far, though.

They were discovered before too long, inside one of Hexhall's Coven temple storehouses, hiding in barrels of pickled fish and ritualistically prepared "seeing herbs." Coming into contact with the magically cultivated roots and shoots (which had been grown for Covenant consumption) had knocked many of the officers out cold. Upon waking, vivid, nightmarish hallucinations would plague them for three to five days. Those who had chosen the fish barrels fared better, with only the foul odor to contend with. Any who'd *eaten* the stuff, however, would soon find out just how big a mistake they'd made...

In both cases, the Cutcords swarmed and grabbed the enemy officers. One of the younger, hotshot Elementals drew his sidearm, which earned him a throwing knife to the meat of his leg. He went down, wailing. The others either took the hint or were experienced enough to know they'd been beaten. Plastic and metal cuffs were clipped around their wrists, and the Cutcords dragged them before Cho-Zen.

She gave the prisoners a once-over. Usually impeccably coiffed and fashionable, the present state of these sky-snobs brought to mind water-logged peacocks. Saggy-faced, soggy-bottomed. Unable to hide their mounting terror, some clung to each other like mice pups. Others glowered at her, muttering under their breath, grinding their jawbones. Kaspuri was in a league all his own; the man had been broken. He would not meet her eye nor answer her challenge. Picking at the skin on his knuckles until they bled, he said nothing.

She grew tired of the sight. Turning to the soldiers at her side, she said, "Cutcords. Coneys."

The dark-blue-armored, elite troops quickly scanned each other's barcodes (on the shoulders of their uniforms), determining which of them held the highest rank. One of them, a man, stepped smartly forward and saluted. "My lady?"

She considered what to do with the prisoners. She'd really wanted to say something cool like "Take them away!" but knew there wasn't anywhere to "take" them to. The Seventh Stack was in shambles. And those shambles were currently on fire.

She sighed. "Arrest them. Tie 'em up and leave 'em in a corner until I decide what needs to happen with 'em." As the Cutcord officer brought together a group of soldiers to herd the loyalists away, Cho pointed to Kaspuri and added, "And make sure that one *doesn't* fall down a whole bunch. Make sure his toes *aren't* stomped every other step. And be really, extra, especially careful he *doesn't* get kneed in the balls on the way. Not even *one single time*. Got me?"

The Cutcord suppressed a smirk, acknowledging the command with a salute before dashing off to fulfill it.

Rubbing her bruised throat, she returned to searching the courtyard, the tunnels, and the walls. Each moment that passed without any sign of her friends was a mixed bag of pure relief and stomach-clenching panic.

She kept going because it was all she could think to do.

Eventually, she found Tiberaira tangled in the ribcage of an inert Martyr. Looking like a creature out of a horror film, her robotic lower jaw had been hacked off, and little sparks of electricity flickered where her tongue should have been. Deep gashes in the artificial skin on her remaining arm exposed her subdermal nanoweave armor, severely scratched.

She said, "I'd stand if I could, but I think my ankles are broken."

Squatting on her haunches, Cho swallowed dryly. "At ease, captain. Sit tight. We'll get you outta there. You fought like a lion. Like a demon. Like—"

"Like a Coney." Pink sweat trickled down her forehead.

"That's right. Now, you just take a load off. You've..."

Tiberaira had passed out.

"Hey, you guys. Help me," said Cho, snapping her fingers at a nearby group of soldiers who'd been rifling through the pockets of the dead.

Over the next few minutes, Tiberaira was carefully extracted from where she'd fallen, laid down on flat ground, and covered with a yellow cloak. Biting her cuticles, Cho sat with the fallen soldier, working up the nerve to resume her search.

A gnarled, black tree burst from the ground, splitting down the middle. Broken human bodies rolled off its thickening roots. Tangled vines spilled from it like entrails as, out of its core, crawled Cbarassan. Leaking green blood, the *Fyarda* was met with fear and hostility until Cho arrived to help them to their feet. After that, the human soldiers offered them some space.

Clasping Cbarassan's forearms, Cho said, "This doesn't feel real. Like I'm wandering through a dream."

"What kind?"

"Not sure yet. Guess I won't know until I either wake up or... Thanks, by the way. For saving my life. Again."

The *Fyarda*, uncharacteristically, looked away, tri-pupils rotating downward. Quietly, they said, "Do you believe in reincarnation, Cho?"

"I don't know. Sometimes. Why?"

"I... had a child. Once. Long before you were born. My people believe there are eight planes of existence, and that each of these is a sphere overlapping slightly with the others. When someone dies, they pass from one sphere to the next. No punishment. No reward. Simply... movement. Left or right, up or down, it doesn't matter. Life is life, and death is a transition. Souls are constantly in motion, going round and round, experiencing the universe through many eyes, in myriad worlds. Learning, growing. We *Fyarda* also believe, however, that some souls—the ones that have bonded really, really strongly in a given lifetime—travel together. Destiny may bind such kindred spirits across dozens or perhaps hundreds of incarnations."

Cho squeezed Cbarassan's hand.

They said, "Maybe that's silly."

"No."

"It's only that—sometimes, when I feel my heart open—It seems to me— The strange magic-less magic you've wrought... You remind me of them. My child, Oshiseka. My joy, my pride."

Hugging the *Fyarda*'s waist, Cho gripped her own elbows behind their back. She clutched Cbarassan as if hoping to push her love for them right through their skin and clothes, straight into their core.

Shivering now, Cbarassan made a series of strange, reedy noises. Cho worried for a moment that she'd hurt them before realizing the truth: they were crying.

The orphan and the childless parent stood there awhile. Although Cho knew she'd never be able to hug Cbarassan fiercely enough to choke their pain into submission, that wouldn't stop her from trying.

A cadre of Coneys forming a loose protective circle around her, Cho sat alone on a crate, elbows on her knees, face in her hands. Her internal clock was busted, so she couldn't tell how much time had passed since the battle. It felt like too much time, though. Alina still hadn't returned.

As Cho's repressed doubt and terror resurfaced, she heard a familiar voice: "The Elemental leadership. You should have killed them."

She lifted her sights to find Ivion standing inside the Coneys' circle, five feet to her left.

"Sergeant," Cho said, pointing, "shoot her."

To the sergeant's credit, he turned, pulled, and fired almost as fast as Cho could blink. The bullet, however, passed through Ivion's head—its only effect a slight ripple in the projection.

"Of course," said Cho, noticing the spherical projector drone behind the woman's full-sized image. "Of course, you'd be too big a coward to show up in person. Well, *Ordin* Ivoir. You're here. What do you want?" Even knowing Ivion's true identity, Cho found it nearly impossible to think of her as anyone but Ivion. After all, she still looked exactly the same—white suit, wide smirk, and perfect symmetry in her every feature.

Ivion's earrings glimmered as she tossed her hair. "You're acting admirably restrained for once."

"No point getting into a tizzy. Your time'll come. Sure, maybe I can't get at you now, but I will. I swear it by Buthmertha and all the Seventy-Seven Gods. For what happened to Mezami, I will slit your throat."

"Prove it."

"Excuse me?"

"Prove that you are even capable of such bold action. Do what you came here to do: kill Walazzin and his toadies."

"Not that I really care, but aren't you working with them?"

"My dear infantile, naive Choraelia. War is coming to El. The Plutocracy fractures; the Families turn on one another. By eliminating your parents, the

Walazzins pushed us to the brink of civil war. They are a cancer and must be excised, or, like any noble beast, our Empire will die."

"Sounds like a *you* problem."

"Does even one liquid ounce of patriotic blood course through that runtish body of yours?"

"Newp."

"Were you not such a petulant reprobate, you would see how much we could mutually benefit from an alliance, sharing as many enemies as we do."

"You enjoy the sound of your own voice way too much. Use as many big words as ya like, you can't hide what you're doing: pretending your side didn't just lose horribly to a fourteen-year-old *misckie*."

"My dear, dear, little girl—"

"Boy, do I wish one of my guys could shut you up."

"Don't make me laugh. Even were I physically there with you, you wouldn't be able to do anything meaningful to me. I've died once already, remember."

"Yeah, yeah, your trillions of gelders will save you. We know."

"Almost a trillion in material costs, yes, but that pales in comparison with the true debt incurred."

"Oh my gods, what are you talking about? Could ya just skip to the part where you say something frustratingly mysterious and go away?"

"Though it's hopeless, I will try to impress upon you the folly of your actions. There is still time to surrender to the graces of the Enlightened One."

"*Hard* pass."

"Then you condemn thousands more to death. Why must there be more bloodshed? For all your bravado, you will fall. It's futile, Choraelia. Please. Listen to me, I beg you, and understand. I am in His debt. We all are. Even you. We all *owe* him, and there is no hope in disobeying. He owns everything, hears everything—*is* everything. All we can do is act in accordance with His will and remain in His good graces."

"This is pathetic."

"Can't you see, you selfish brat? You have no idea what He's capable of. Maybe, in your wildest fantasies, you believe you've won a significant victory here today. But let me be the first to confront you with reality: all your stunts have managed is to anger the one true God. Call Him The Author, the Lord, the Creator, Elwoch—it makes no difference. He's coming for you." Ivion raised her voice. "All of you, you're doomed. Damned!"

Looking around, Cho asked, "Does anyone have some kinda signal jammer or something? Shut this yipping dog up?"

"You'd best take my warnings seriously."

"Fine. I'll bite. If your god's really *so awesome*, why'd he send you? And why's he so worried about me?"

The projection of Ivion flickered.

Cho said, "Whoever or whatever he actually is, to me it sounds an awful lot like he's scared. And, seeing you shaking in your seal-skin booties, well… If you're the best he's got, I'm not too worried."

"Listen to me. Just listen. If you surrender now, shut down this insane revolt—you could still protect your friends, protect Alina."

Closing her eyes, Cho sighed. Suddenly, the full weight of her exhaustion draped itself across her shoulders like a length of heavy chain. She sagged, feeling like she could have slept for a week.

A notification *dinged* on her display.

INCOMING PACKET > UNKNOWN LICENSE

DOWNLOAD > Y/N?

The offer was wordless, given to the soundtrack of clinking chain links, echoing in her mind.

What did she have to lose?

She said, "Yes."

PATCHING

Something buried in the pit of her stomach stirred, and she blacked out. Her operating system rebooted, and, when she opened her eyes again, it felt like waking from an unremembered dream.

SOFTWARE PATCH COMPLETE

She experienced two conflicting sensations: the weight on her shoulders intensified; yet, she felt energized enough to run a marathon over hot coals—or play tug of war with a bear.

find me

and i will give you power

Something happened then, a thing that didn't make sense. She couldn't say what had possessed her even to try, but she'd grabbed at Ivion's wrist. A ridiculous, pointless move because, of course, Ivion wasn't physically there. Except, Cho's fingers *did* close around the projection—as if it were solid.

Ivion's narrow eyes snapped to the point of contact. "How are you—"

The soldiers around Cho gasped and cried out in shock.

Cho herself forgot to breathe, but, taking advantage of this impossibility made real, she jerked Ivion's wrist and noted with satisfaction the *pop* and *crackle* of joints and delicate little bones. She bent Ivion's hand back, forcing the taller woman to her knees.

"You'll listen to me now." Cho entwined her fingers with Ivion's perfect hair, wrenching her head close. Nose to nose. "Thank you for telling me about your boss. Consider him added to my list."

Twisting, unable to escape, Ivion yammered, "It shouldn't have happened like it did. Alina's phone wasn't supposed to explode. Please, it was a malfunction! I was only trying to end the war, to—"

"To puff yourself up, yeah? That's right, isn't it? You only care about you."

"He used me—no, *betrayed* me, like He did you all. You have to let me help you survive. I am doing everything I can to—"

"Sergeant," Cho called. "Your gun."

Hesitating for a second, the man did hand over his weapon, grip first.

Cho jammed the barrel under Ivion's chin. "Honestly, I got no clue how I'm pulling this off, so neither of us can be sure of what'll happen if I put a bullet in your head right now." Her thumb disengaged the safety, clicked back the hammer. "Let's find out together."

The projection of Ivion vanished.

"Thought so," said Cho.

She carefully returned the pistol to her sergeant, and—taking three steps back, trying to avoid the boots of her Cutcords—puked her guts out. She walked over to where the loyalist officers had been corralled. Squatting in front of Kaspuri, she wiped her mouth with her hand, which she then dragged across his uniform.

He gagged.

She patted his cheek. "Sooo, apparently, you and Ivion Ivoir aren't exactly besties. Go figure. How much d'you think she'd pay for you? Hmm. On the other hand, your daddy might appreciate getting you back in a fairly small number of pieces. Decisions, decisions… Well, for now, yer worth more to us alive. Till I can figure out what to do with you, you'll stay real close. In case anybody tries to get cute with me or my people."

"You delude yourself if you think I'd ever help you," he spat through his weirdly sharp teeth. He seemed to have found his fire again.

Cho chuckled. "Mr. Walazzin, this isn't a negotiation. It's hilarious, you thinkin' ya still got leverage of any kind. Good for you. But, one way or another, you'll either be our cash cow or our meat shield. The end. Ugh, what's with the grinning?"

"I am imagining your bloated, rat-chewed husk drifting down a sewer drain."

"Don't let fantasy run away with you. I'm not the one in cuffs."

"You're in for far worse before long. Wait and see."

"Know what, I hope The Authority does attack us, just so I get the chance to strap you to the closest warhead and launch your pasty butt right back at your friends. Look at ya, all the privilege in the world, the best education money can buy, dozens of cybernetic amps, and you wasted it on being a two-bit bully."

"What, then, have *you* accomplished, you little—"

She leaned in, speaking real low. "*I* grew up alone, in the house of my family's murderers. I learned to lie and steal and cheat. The hard way. Everything I have, I had to fight for. And look at me now, somehow back on top. I'm a survivor. As for you?" She ruffled his greasy hair. "Guess we'll see."

The fires in the courtyard and its surroundings had been doused. The dead had been brought to one side, covered for burial but, so far, unburied. Some men busied themselves lobbing Martyr bones into the chasm.

Enough time had passed that the soldiers were getting antsy. They couldn't stay here forever, Cho knew, but whenever she looked around, she shrank into herself a little more. The adrenaline had long since worn off, and now several thousand adults waited for her to make decisions for them, to command them. Where was she supposed to start?

Thankfully, one of the Coneys carried Tibby over. Her mechanical voice box emitted a grungy sound—a laugh. "My Lady, well done seizing control of the courtyard and apprehending the enemy's commanders. May I suggest your honor guard, the Coneys, lead the efforts to secure the remainder of this fortress and the Seventh Stack outside it? Perhaps, first, they could establish a multi-layered defensive perimeter and assume control of functional communications towers, to announce the news of your victory and sway any retreating Authority to reconsider their allegiances?"

"Uh." Cho turned to the sergeant from earlier, waving her hand, saying, "Yes, that. Do all of that."

His smile was slight, and he bowed his head to hide it. "By your will, my lady." He relayed her orders, and the Cutcords got to work.

Moments later, however, they halted. Cho then saw why, gasping at the horde marching across the courtyard.

Her first thought was, *Oh, here comes The Authority to squash us after all. That's a wrap, I guess. Nice while it lasted.* But several details seemed off about this new army:

it had come from inside Hexhall; it was made up not just of Tranqs but Ozari, too, with plenty of Aelf mixed in; and, all the fighters walked calmly, weapons sheathed or lowered.

Finally, her brain acknowledged the figure leading them. A young woman, her cheaply-dyed, red hair singed at the tips. A red crow mask hung from her neck, dangling, staring ahead blankly. Her black cloak flapped behind her oh-so-dramatically as her golden eyes flashed (also dramatically).

The sergeant, agitated, reached for his sidearm, but Cho placed a hand on his. He said, "Hold your fire, Cutcords."

The motley army slowed to a stop. Their red-haired leader strode forward until she stood no more than three feet from Cho.

They stared at each other.

Something lay between them. Thick, unctuous. Wordless, unnameable.

All Cho could think to say was, "Are you still Alina?"

Arms akimbo, the golden-eyed, black-caped mystic said, "Are you still Cho?" And her smile was one Cho recognized.

Cho ran into Alina's opening arms—a wet, warm pitter-patter of tears falling onto her bald scalp. Her friend whispered something she couldn't quite catch, and a wave of warmth flowed through her, dissolving her aches and pains. In fact, each of her own soldiers' faces, she noticed, now carried a subtle smile. Even Tibby's expression softened. An overwhelming sense of peace swept all else away, if only for a moment.

Alina broke the hug. Her smile burst, overflowing with tears, as she took three steps back and dropped to one knee. "Lady Cho-Zen, Heir of the Torvir, Primarch of Ozar." She hadn't raised her voice above a murmur, but it somehow carried anyway, rippling through the ranks of warfighters.

They, too, knelt. Row after row. Column after column. Young and old. Elemental, Landsider, and Ozari. Human and Aelf.

"Cho-Zen the rebel!" someone shouted.

"Long live Cho-Zen!"

"Long live the Primarch," said Alina.

Everyone was shouting her name again. She didn't dare bask in this feeling, though; didn't dare enjoy the adulation for fear of how it might change her.

The chanting died down after a minute. Then came the expectant stares.

She said, "Um. Could you all excuse me and my friend, please? Quick meeting. Be right back." She pulled Alina aside. Out in the open, surrounded by people, there wasn't really anywhere private to stand, so she simply spoke as quietly as she could. "That's a lot of dudes you got there."

"They're *your* dudes now."

"And what, pray tell, am I supposed to *do* with all these dudes?"

"Same things you were planning for all the ones you converted with that fiery speech. Nicely done, by the way. Meant to say so earlier, but I got a little distracted."

"You took a bullet for me."

"Three, actually. But who's counting? Anyway, seeing you up there, I was so proud of you."

Whenever Alina got mushy, it meant she was hiding something. Cho became afraid again. Just how had Alina pulled off her apparently super successful (and fast!) recruitment drive? Was she mind-controlling all these people?

Alina shook her head. "They're here because they want to be. I just... helped them let go of whatever was holding them back."

"You just read my thoughts again."

"Did I? Coulda sworn you'd said that part out loud. Whoops."

"So, just double-checking. This isn't, like, an army of zombies you've brought me, right?"

"No."

"Oh well then."

A moment of silence followed.

"Something's wrong," said Cho. "You're making that face again."

"What face?"

"The face. The one where you do this." With her hands, Cho squished her cheeks and brows together. "This one."

"Alright, alright. Stop that. No, *please*, stop. I promise, nothing's 'wrong.' I just wanna talk about you. About us."

"Gasp. Are you friend-breaking-up with me?"

Alina sighed. "Do you think you can be serious for one second?"

"No promises. Say your piece."

"Well, it's hard to explain. Every time I try to think about it, it's, like, there's this... feeling. A fog. Or a web. Like I'm being turned around and pulled in different directions. It's tricky. I have to tell you something now, but I need to choose my words carefully. If I say the wrong thing, even one wrong word, I'll lose the thread. I have to try, though. It's about the future. See, we're all... tangled, you and me."

"Li, you're giving me a panic attack."

"What I'm trying to say is, whatever we do next, we do it together."

"Don't worry. I'm not going anywhere, so—"

"You don't get it. I'm talking about the job ahead. I'm trying to tell you that we've already *done* it. Because we *will* do it. But, right now, we still have to choose to *have done* it. Does that make sense? No, no, I can see it doesn't. Agh. It's all a jumble in my head. I swear, I'm being as clear as I can be right now, and I'm giving you the truth. It's just not coming out right." She closed her eyes. Focused. Breathed. "Okay. One more time: there are an infinite number of realities, each with an infinite number of possible choices at any given point in time. With me so far?"

"Somehow, yes."

"Think of the choices like paths. You can't change where you've already come from, and you can't really know what's ahead. All you can do is decide to take the left, right, or middle way."

"You said we had unlimited options, though."

"We do. But, in our reality, only three of them give us any chance of making it through the next few months."

"Time out. The odds of us not dying are *three to infinity?*"

"*One* to infinity. Two of the three paths give us a couple years at most. That's why we have to win this battle."

"What battle? The fighting's over. We've won (I think)."

"But, it's not over." Alina seemed honestly confused. "Are we not in the Partykian Caves, helping the Faehn resistance? The Authority's attacking Yulche City. I can hear them, drilling down to us. Unless... What year is it?"

"I don't know what you're talking about. You're really scaring me." Cho took Alina's hand. "We're in Ozar. It's 3504. Did you take a hit to the head or something? What happened to you in Hexhall?"

Alina blinked her way out of her thousand-yard stare.

Cho asked, "How many fingers am I holding up? Do you know who you are?"

Swatting Cho's hand down, Alina said, "Of course I do. I am the Bane of New El."

"Okay... And who do you think I am?"

"Stop giving me that look. I'm not crazy, and I don't have a brain injury. I *know* who you are, Cho. You're the Primarch of Ozar."

"What're you saying? What does that mean?"

"It's what they'll call you."

"Who?"

"The Ozari, The Authority, the Sanctumites—everyone. Did I tell you about the paths yet? The infinite choices with—"

"Only three options that won't kill us. Yup, ya did."

"Then you should know you're the Primarch. And I'm the Dragon. And, together, we're going to invade the Elemental Empire."

8O

BARAAM

AS REVEALED BY RECENTLY discovered stone tablets, thousands of years ago, the Kadician desert had once been lush plains and forests. From air-conditioned libraries and offices, Elemental scholars wrote extensive research papers on shifting weather patterns, deforestation, and aggressive agriculture—all factors that had supposedly "erased a once rich and vibrant ecosystem."

The *Shem* Sahamans held a different opinion. Wielders of the "battle trance," an ancient combat art granting the warrior invincibility at the cost of consciousness, they claimed the desertification of Kadic's heartland had been the gods' greatest gift.

Scorching days and frigid nights tempered the land like steel. Sandstorms scoured the earth like a warrior might scour chainmail. And the dunes shifted as readily as the whims of men.

It was a hard world. In the intervening millennia, Kadic's flora and fauna had adapted to survive off only an inch of rainfall per year. Among other tricks, they had learned to retain water, shun sunlight, or drink blood.

The creatures of the desert had endured, for they had come to live by one law: their Maker willed them to be strong, and so they were.

At some point, he'd started to crawl.

Thereafter came the realization that he'd managed to drape Eva across his shoulders. Bleeding, broken-fingered, he shouldn't have been able to move. Yet, he did.

He dragged their two bodies—hers and his—over rock, through pools of blood and water, between the twisted carcasses of war machines; through rising smoke, falling ash, and the pounding of his own heartbeat in his skull.

He crawled, hands slippery with blood, eyes swollen shut, blindly.

He crawled, her frame weighing him down. Chin scraping through mud and gravel, skinned fingers protesting all the way, he crawled until he could go no farther.

81

CHO-ZEN

IFTY-TWO HOURS. THAT'S HOW long it took to uncover and force the surrender of the remaining Authority and Sanctumite holdouts on the Seventh Stack.

In total, Cho-Zen's army captured 3,787 prisoners of war. Of these, 3,155 would—eventually—switch sides. Even those who remained loyal to El (mainly high-ranking officers and dignitaries) were fairly treated. Kaspuri Walazzin and Gildmaster Ridect, for instance, were allowed a daily game of chess, if only because the guards enjoyed the way the Walazzin heir huffed when he lost (which was always). He pouted like a little boy sent to his room without his tablet.

During those initial fifty-two hours, a group of scouts had encountered a broken man dragging himself over oil-slick, charred barricades, between mounds of shattered wall and open mass graves. He'd had a bleeding woman draped across his shoulders. By the look of him, he ought to have died, and she fared no better. Horrific burns marred both their bodies and faces. When one of the soldiers recognized the wounded man as Baraam bol-Talanai, the scout party hurried the two survivors to the field hospital. The power surge when he awoke the next day fried nearly every monitor and device keeping him alive. It was touch-and-go for some time.

The woman—Eva—was laid down in the dungeons, opposite Tolomond Stayd. Both were kept isolated and under constant watch, in deep cells with steel doors, supervised by no fewer than ten guards at all times. Tolomond stared at the wall, never moving except to eat. Eva would not wake, her guards drawing straws to spoon-feed her and tend to her bedding.

Gossip began to swirl around Baraam's return, for many had witnessed the lightning storm that had torn through the Stack at the climax of the battle. The rumor-mongers claimed any man capable of unleashing and surviving such a force could hardly be called a "man." There probably didn't exist any thing that could kill such a person, except the unrelenting erosion of time. *Baraam the juggernaut*, the people said, *king of the skies; the higher he soared, the more devastating his eventual fall.* He was as a stone hurtling to earth; he'd shatter on impact, one day, but his trajectory was unstoppable. The tellers of tall tales were further emboldened when none other than the Bane of New El arrived to personally administer first aid to Baraam shortly after his retrieval. *Baraam bol-Talanai*, they proclaimed, *cursed by fate, blessed by the Bane.*

And, having restored him, the Bane moved through the rest of the hospital, curing ills small and great. Each life saved was another warrior pledged to her name.

Achemir, they said. *Heir of the Hextarchs.*

Terror, they whispered. *Dragon.*

The legend of Alina grew.

Burying the bodies—thousands upon thousands of them—was the work of nine days. Volunteers, digging 'round the clock. Cold, hard earth.

The remains had been laid out in the streets. Some were identified by loved ones, friends; many were not. Too large a number of them were unrecognizable, ravaged by fire and Martyr and more.

The priests and clerics of many gods worked together, taking sixteen-hour shifts to walk the rows and rows of prostrate dead, performing last rites. They grew increasingly glassy-eyed and stiff-muscled, yet always there were more bodies to tend to.

Cho and Alina searched for Kinneas and Calthin, but found neither.

The events at Hexhall in the year 3504 entered history and song under a slew of different names. Contemporary Elemental historians wrote of the "Fools' Defiance," "the Coward's Mutiny," "the Rebellion of the Few." They blamed the uprising on mass hysteria and ambient Niimantic poisoning caused by bad air and worse soil. Ozar's climate was rotten, they claimed; no Elementals could thrive there. El's national news networks spun The Authority's defeat as a "strategic withdrawal," assuring the public that the rebels would be summarily handled. With extreme prejudice. All in due time.

However, to the rebels who'd claimed the Seventh Stack, that fateful day generally became known as "the Battle of the Seven." Depending on one's faith, or lack thereof, other names might also have applied. The soldiers under General Tiberaira's command, who believed primarily in steel and strength, stuck to straightforward phrases: "the Holding of the Line," "Fortune's Turning," and so on. There were, however, many who were more poetic in their interpretations, throwing around phrases like "Alina's Anointing," "the Coming of the Achemir," and "The Rebirth of Rhin." (In the Iorian tongue, "Rhin" meant "Dragon," and "Dragon" meant "Overlord.")

In the aftermath, a tentative peace was cobbled together. Tiberaira's legions ruled the material world: enforcing justice; organizing breadlines and housing for the homeless; and, generally doing the thankless, daily work of maintaining order through fair governance. This was challenging because their small country—buried miles beneath the surface, beset by foes—had no name; its soul was split. In those early days, it seemed the only glue that bound the people of the Seventh in common purpose was their common hatred of The Authority.

This changed over time. A vocal but growing minority of speakers soon gave the masses another reason to remain united: faith in the Achemir, who was destined to shatter the chains, right the wrongs, etc., etc. Before forever departing the world of mortals, the Hextarchs had divinely appointed Alina as their successor. Therefore, to be ruled by the Primarch Cho-Zen—who in turn was guided by Alina—was the only way to live in accordance with divine law. Cho-Zen's government encouraged this belief through propaganda and the establishment of the Abbey of the Achemir.

For some months, this strategy worked. Kneeling side by side, humans and Aelf laid hand-carved idols—half crow, half woman—upon simple stone altars. They prayed for salvation by night. And, by day, they worked to shore up the defenses of the Seventh Stack.

Unfortunately, soon a schism occurred between two rival sects, the "Alinites" and the "Banelings." Skirmishes erupted fairly regularly, though there was only one fatality (ruled an accident). When Tiberaira's peacekeepers brought the scrappers in for questioning, the growing complexity of Ozar's newest religion was laid bare. The Alinites, comprised mostly of reformed Sanctumites, preached that The Savior had been a fraud and Alina was the true Avatar of The Author. They renounced the power structure of The Sanctum, calling for the skin-threshing of the heretic Hierophant Pontifex Ridect. The Banelings, on the other hand, were adamant about the apocalyptic nature of Alina's arrival: she would burn New El to ash, tear it from the sky, and water the soil of the world with the blood of millions so that new life could grow free and wild.

Alina herself frequently aired her disgust with both these philosophies and the existence of the Abbey, but Tiberaira forbade any public contradiction or comment. The furious passions of the Alinites and Banelings made them the most productive workers and boldest fighters. Already, hundreds of them had volunteered for the militias being raised. They were needed.

More and more frequently, Alina retreated into the catacombs of the fortress. Alone.

The Covenants, who'd fought with unparalleled courage, had suffered heavy casualties. As was their way, they'd led from the front lines, and—overwhelmingly outnumbered—had been decimated. The loss of so many of their leaders left Vessa Tardrop among the ranking officers. Under this new generation's direction, The Coven was reorganized to serve as palace guards, spies, and secret police. Their oaths bound them to Cho-Zen.

Regardless of religious or political background, those who swore allegiance to the Primarch were given respect and a place in society. They were fed, clothed, and housed. There was one notable exception, however. The Sanctumites who refused to recant their faith in The Author remained imprisoned with The Authority loyalists.

One day, all knew, The Authority would seek revenge. In the months that followed the Battle of the Seven, though, the rebels abandoned their *fears* of Elemental retaliation, replacing these with dread at the inevitability of the war ahead. Still, they labored: building shelters, rationing leftover food stores, and patching the walls of their Primarch's fortress (dubbed "Primehall"). Each citizen of this emerging nation was given a task, and Tiberaira made certain that non-cooperation was met with swift and harsh punishment. Cho-Zen was much more forgiving, but her rising number of councilors, advisors, and tutors dampened her voice somewhat. She told herself this made sense. She was fourteen, after all, and probably had no business being Primarch (whatever that even meant). For worse or better, though, she'd been handed *far too much* power. The least she could do was learn to use it well. So, she studied the people around her and, eventually, came to earn her title.

Every day, for hours, she would sit and listen to her Covenant and ex-Authority tacticians and planners as they laid the ground-work for supply lines and gambits to repel the Elemental Empire's eventual counterattack. They spoke of grim realities. The words "outnumbered" and "attrition" were thrown around an awful lot. Also, unless the situation changed dramatically, the people were going to run out of provisions. The Hextarchs had set aside prodigious amounts of food, water, and medical supplies, but these had been meant for the fortress's garrison only. Devoured by the few million souls now under Cho-Zen's care, these stores would be used up within a year. Or less.

Five months had fallen away since the Battle of the Seven.

Cho walked the halls of her fortress like an animal expecting a trap around every corner. Her back and arms ached from a morning of brutal combat training with Tibby, and her brain was a mushy puddle after hours of Ozari history lessons with Cbarassan. But she hadn't missed a council meeting yet, and she didn't plan to start now.

Alina found Primehall impossible to navigate without a map (drawn on the back of her hand). She often said the place had made way more sense in dreamland. Cho, though, had spent her first several sleepless nights wandering the twisting corridors, counting the stairways, building upon her understanding of the fort's vaults and alcoves. Its stone sighed at the touch of her bare feet, breaths stirring the dust of ages. Slowly, the fortress came to life again. Slowly, she began to feel it was hers.

With some exceptions, of course.

She took a deep breath before the stone double doors that led into the war room.

An irregular recess, The Coven's war room from above must have looked like an ink blotch or cracked, graying parchment. Its edges were sharp, its walls wavering like a line drawn by a hiccupping sketch artist. There were no chairs, only a long, rectangular central table. There were no torches either. How the place stayed so well-lit was a mystery no one had ever solved. The room was also *old*. If what Vessa claimed were true, it predated Ozar and the Hextarchy. It had been found, not made.

The Coven had insisted that all strategy meetings and discussions of matters of state be held in this creepy, dank corner of Hexhall—sorry, *Prime*hall. Since Cho preferred *not* to tick off the Covenants, she'd agreed.

She stood at the head of the table (nearest the blue, translucent, holographic map of the Seven Stacks), feeling stuffy despite the damp chill. Done up in her high-necked, thick, woolen coat, she looked like someone who took herself way too seriously. Her advisers even forced her to carry a sword—a straight-edged, gaudy, gilded letter opener—whose tip kept clanking against everything, knocking over vases, and scratching walls. She'd become a joke. ("It's a ceremonial symbol of your authority," Tibby had explained, to which she'd answered, "I hate that word." But she'd accepted that symbol on Tibby's urging. General Hael

Tiberaira, after all, was half the reason the Primarchy hadn't dissolved on day two. Really, *she* was Cho's sword. "Fine, I'll play dress-up. But I don't gotta be happy about it. Any minute now, you'll suggest something *really* dumb. Like a crown." Cho had stopped snickering once she'd realized Tibby wasn't laughing with her.)

Proceeding clockwise, at Cho's left was Cbarassan. The *Fyarda*, recovered from their burns and broken limbs thanks to Alina, had rejected the offer of generalship at first, but Cho had pleaded with them to reconsider. In addition to having been an integral part of Anarkey, Cbarassan spoke to the hopes of the Aelf among Cho's people, and strengthening those unstable alliances between species was absolutely crucial. However, most importantly, Cho and Cbarassan had bled and lost so much together. She couldn't imagine continuing without them.

Next, standing on the rim of a pint-glass was Pyct'Aks Ruire, a Coven bigwig and Vessa's direct superior. The scars crisscrossing her gold-furred back hinted at a horror story Cho wasn't sure she'd ever be ready to hear.

To the Pyct's left, a willow-limbed, genetically modified woman with gilded armor and long blonde hair swished the wine around her glass. Adaranser Niparagi Agad had previously been a resident of the Divitia District of New El, serving as military liaison for Domestic Command's Office of Obtainment. She was good at finding things, but better still at keeping them. Representing the concerns of the Elementals who'd sworn themselves to Cho, she seemed loyal—maybe to a fault. Every time Cho looked her way, Agad bowed her head, hand over her heart, her rings clinking against her ornamental breastplate. Cho distrusted the woman's showiness, but the needs of the rebellion came first. Agad was the highest ranking officer who'd switched sides, which made her invaluable. Necessary.

The next two were Ozari natives. One, a curly-haired human man named Gamabbeis. The other, a worm in a jar. That's right, a spiny, blue worm in a corked glass jar, swimming in clear, viscous liquid. It had a name only because everyone else insisted. So, it answered to Yudi, communicating its desires and intentions in a peculiar sign language—twisting in specific patterns which Gamabbeis interpreted.

Lastly, there was Tibby, who'd had new artificial limbs and joints appended to her body. (Well, *newer,* but the stuff was still battlefield-scavenged, second-hand Authority tech.) She called the meeting to order.

"Will the Bane be in attendance today?" asked Agad.

"Out of order," said Tibby. "And, as usual, that girl's comings and goings are impossible to track."

"'That girl'? General Tiberaira would do well to address the subject of the Achemir with appropriate decorum," said Cbarassan. "We must respect our savior."

"Is: where, she?" said Ruire, the light catching the whiskers of gray on her wrinkled face.

Cho-Zen grunted. "Somewhere." The members of the council stared at her, so she added, "You think she reports to me? Do I look like a clock-in/clock-out machine?"

Tibby slapped the table. "On to old business." She looked to Ruire.

"Proceeding: integration, units. Anticipated: fifteen weeks, basic fight-readiness."

"That's too long." Tibby lifted her hand toward Yudi. "Were the scrapper teams able to salvage any more hovercraft? What's the current count of our fleet?"

In its jar, Yudi spiraled erratically. Gamabbeis frowned at the worm, translating: "Three this week, but the chasms are now empty of operational vehicles. The rest of the junk down there is scrap only. With the recent refurbished additions, our forces number fifteen tanks, four mecha, and seven aircraft. Of the last, five are fighters, and two are troop transports."

Tibby shook her head. "So few."

"Trust: in machinery, too much you. Have faith: in the arcane, The Coven."

"While we all certainly appreciate The Coven's... contributions, to defend our tentative borders, we'll need more modern weaponry."

The Pyct scoffed.

The other council members chimed in, each with more bad news: shrinking resource piles, growing unrest among the people, and reports of The Authority mobilizing for a siege.

Tibby said, "They'll smother our nation in its cradle if we let them. We can't stay in our hole for good."

Bent over the table, Agad leaned on her elbows. "What does the general propose we do? As has been made abundantly clear by my colleagues, we are beleaguered. Tens of thousands of rabble militia, dwindling victuals, precious little fresh water (most of it probably laced with eldritch magics). Certainly, we have the General's Coneys, and the former Authority units under my own humble command... Yet, tenuous at best is our hold on all these Assets."

"Citizens," Cho corrected, "not 'Assets.' You're not in El anymore."

Agad bit back her knee-jerk reply. By her eye movements and rising heart rate, which Cho could of course clearly hear, she'd become upset. (Bristling at taking lip from a teenager, maybe?) Agad said only, "Of course, my lady. I chose my words poorly."

Gamabbeis cleared his throat. "While we're at it, what was that about our water being 'laced with eldritch magics'? Eh?" Yudi darted back and forth in a zigzagging pattern. Gamabbeis followed the motions, saying, "I disagree, my friend. In Commander Agad's bird-brained comment, there was more than an *undercurrent* of bigotry."

Everyone's blood pressure spiked. Resting her chin on her palms, Cho blew a raspberry, waiting for the adults in the room to simmer down. She said, "We don't have enough supplies. That's our biggest problem. So, why don't we go get more?"

Combing her blonde locks with her fingers, Agad said, "A lovely idea. From where?"

Cho pointed toward the ceiling. "From them."

The others looked to her, then each other.

Tibby said, "The Primarch is right. We must look to the Sixth Stack, and the other five above it. If we wish to eat, we must conquer."

"Not ready: militias, ours."

"Then make them ready. And, no, fifteen weeks simply won't work for our timetable. You have eight."

"Ask: impossible, you."

"Nothing is impossible," said Cbarassan.

Agad hid her smirk behind her beautiful hand.

"The main issue is integration. Regrettably, prejudiced as they have been taught to be," Gamabbeis said, looking pointedly at her, "few outlanders will accept an Aelf commander, I fear."

"The reverse is also true," Agad said. "You Ozari, you'd turn up your noses at a chest full of gold were it offered to you by an immigrant. We have all seen such nativist discrimination firsthand. Elementals are the most distrusted minority in this city."

"And whose doing is that? You've had centuries to prove us wrong."

Switching on her voice-amplifier, Cho said, "Stop it. If the people in this room can't work together, how can you expect the soldiers on the ground to? We need everyone—Aelf and human—to fight as one, or El won't get a chance to kill us because we'll have done it ourselves."

All eyes sank to the edge of the table. No one spoke for nearly a minute.

Gamabbeis held up his hand.

"Yeah?"

"The term 'Aelf' is an Elemental slur."

Cho flushed. "I'm sorry. I will do better."

A lengthy pause followed during which she wished literally *anyone* would open their mouths and say something. None of the councilors seemed capable of deciding where to look.

Then Gamabbeis said, "It's not my lady's fault. I praise her commitment to equality and justice. Indeed, I only point out the nomenclature concern to raise a larger issue. To become a unified people, we need to educate the masses and ourselves on how to show each other proper respect."

Agad licked her lips. "I completely agree."

Caught off-guard, Gamabbeis grinned. "It begins with labels. The 'Aelf' as you call them belong to myriad subcultures, each with a unique history and self-given name. However, if one isn't familiar with these intricacies, one may simply say 'Nobles' for beings blessed with sentience and 'Others' for the baser forms of non-human life."

Making a note on her holopad, Agad said, "I'll instruct my men to take care in their word-choices, but a training session or two would be helpful in making sure the lesson sticks."

Gamabbeis looked to Yudi, who swirled up and down. "It says, 'This can be arranged.'"

Agad bowed her head to Cho. "Let it be known that I and my forces are of a mind: no Elemental will be responsible for the breaking of this alliance."

"Nor shall the Ozari be," said Gammabbeis. To Agad: "Were the Elementals to acknowledge the dignity of co-equal species, it would go a long way. And the Ozari would return any such considerations given, of course."

Several minutes of setup ensued. New unit integration measures were brainstormed. The council members' cooperation had Cho smiling to herself.

As the meeting seemed to wind down, Cbarassan said, "Courage, my friends. The Authority has poisoned the minds of the people of this land for centuries. Yet, their hold is not unbreakable. Remember, with our own eyes, we have seen the Achemir perform miracles. Bound as she is to our Primarch, we share her destiny. With her as our spearhead, no peak is beyond our reach. Cho-Zen, you are her closest ally. I welcome your thoughts."

"If you're hoping to use Li as a weapon, you got another thing comin'. She's gonna do whatever she thinks is best. Sometimes, that'll be what we want— probably. But, overall, we should assume she's gonna be off on her own."

"Pursuing what agenda?" said Tibby.

"I wish I knew. She spends half her time catatonic in her room. And, the other half, she's unfindable."

Agad said, "I mean nothing by this, but... She's no threat to us, is she?"

Cbarassan glared at her.

Cho wanted to say, *I trust her more than you, Goldie,* but held back. "She's on our side, through and through. She's just... operating on a different level than we are. If we live long enough, maybe she'll clue us in to what she's been up to."

"So," said Tibby, "realistically, it's us versus the remaining Six Stacks."

"And then the surface world," said Cbarassan.

"Which is entirely controlled by the Plutocrats," said Gamabbeis.

"Not all of it." Cho tapped her chin. "Even in El, there are plenty of people so deeply unhappy that they'd join us in a second if they could. Where Alina and I are from, for example." She thought back to Rooster, broken in his cell. "But there are lots of other oppressed towns, too. Many of them would fight, but, first, we need to show them it's not hopeless."

"Is: unwinnable, this campaign."

"Maybe." Cho sighed. "Maybe we'll all be dead next year. But I don't think so. I don't think we've come all this way by accident. We already won an impossible battle, didn't we? Who in the world would've put their money on The Coven and a couple of kids from Truct versus *The Authority*?"

"Indeed," Cbarassan cut in. "We must not forget that, prior to Cho-Zen's intervention, The Authority faced no serious opposition on the Seventh Stack. It was she who turned Elemental officers like Ms. Agad, and the Landsider soldiers under their command, against their masters. I say again, we have witnessed miracles."

"Wars aren't won on faith alone."

"You're right, Agad," said Cho. "Still, faith's gonna have to be a big part of our operation. The Authority can afford to lose a battle or two—or ten—where even one loss could end us. So, we should only tango when we're the ones setting the tempo. But, if we play it too safe, we'll lose the momentum we've got going. We can't forget that faith built our army. Faith in Alina, in each other—"

"In you," added Cbarassan.

"We have to believe in what we're doing, especially when it seems hopeless. And people around the world have to see that we *can* win this thing—or we'll lose."

"A regrettable conundrum," said Gamabbeis. Yudi sloshed around its jar. "It says, 'The Elemental Empire is too huge, old, and deep-rooted to be burned out. We have to do the hard work of loosening the soil before any will be foolhardy enough to rally to us.'"

Cho nodded. "We have to prove we're the better choice. Don't get me wrong, we'll cut 'em down if they come for us, but killing can't be our main, long-term tactic. The Empire's got way more bodies to throw in this fire. They're counting on the advantage of numbers. But we can tip those scales." She had their attentions now. "It's already started with the Abbey and the religious cults worshiping the *grand mystery* that is Alina." She rolled her eyes. "She puts butts in seats. Or, in our case, dudes in boots. Why? Her power's a big draw, sure. But she can only bring people in. Do you know why they stay? Our promise. With us, they get a better deal than they could in any backwater town where they're from. In El, the only people thriving are the ones literally at the top."

Agad said, "Even many of us see the system for what it is—corrupt. The Plutocrats care nothing for their Assets—excuse me, their citizens."

"Which brings me back to my first point: we don't have enough stuff *or* people to throw at this war. So, we capture more of both. We take from The Authority the weapons we'll use against them. Like we did at the Battle of the Seven. Like we've been doing this whole time, with our salvage operations. But *more*." Cho stood, pacing around the table. "Towns, cities, fortresses… If we get our ideas out to them before we show up, it won't always come to a fight. It will, sometimes, but not always. So, we drop pamphlets. We blast our message from every broadcast station and loudspeaker. We make sure everyone hears it."

"And that message is?"

"Hope. Join me and Alina, and you get food, shelter, freedom. Even better—" She looked to Gamabbeis—"you get respect. And that's something no one squashed under The Authority's boot has ever really had." She put her hand on Tibby's metal shoulder. "We'll grow our country from the scraps of theirs. Converts, not corpses, yeah?"

"Converts, not corpses," said Tibby.

Agad lifted her glass. "To the Primarch, whose youth belies her wisdom. And to the better world we fight to leave behind." She drank.

The others toasted as well. Then they all leaned in, the meeting continuing another hour as plans were set in motion to unify all of Ozar under Cho-Zen's banner.

When the other councilors left the war room, Tibby lingered at the door. "You did well, Cho."

"I feel like a flailing idiot."

Tibby laughed. "If an idiot you are, what does that make the millions who follow you?"

Cho didn't answer. Tibby walked out.

Her feet on the table, Cho rubbed her eyes. Not for the first nor last time, she asked herself what she was doing here, locked in this damp cave. As she felt the teeth of the earth clamp down on her, she was a lost thing—drowned in sorrow, grabbing at shadows, strangled by her own tentacles. She'd be found out; her councilors and friends soon would see she didn't belong, and she'd be left with nothing. Alone again.

Then her mind served her an image of Kinneas's sunken, sallow face, and her self-pity was chased away by guilt. There was no one else around to hear her confession: "I bled you dry, Kin. And I'll never forgive myself."

She fidgeted with the three-dimensional holo-map of the Stacks of Ozar, flicking it around and around until she'd set it spinning so fast it became a baby blue blur of light.

The blur and the clammy air lulled her to sleep.

82

ALINA

GUIDED BY THE RESTLESS whisperings of a lost soul, Alina eventually found the unmarked grave in a ditch, at the end of a long road, just past a compost heap.

She'd known this would happen, but had hoped for better anyway.

Gazing upon the small mound of earth, she shut her eyes. "Kellfyute Erestes. I'm sorry. I didn't end your life, but I am the reason it ended. I should've known Ivion was lying. I should've found a better way to…"

She shook her head.

"In your case, I was no better than your god. I guess I came here to apologize, yeah, but also to thank you. What I learned because of you—" She sat on her knees. "Neither of us meant for it to happen this way, but you helped me find clarity. Maybe nothing I do can ever make up for what I've already done, but I will try."

There was nothing else to say, so she sat awhile in darkness and disquiet, and dreamed the troubled dreams of the dead.

83

CHO-ZEN

THERE WERE FILE CABINETS everywhere, drawers stuffed to overflowing with folders and note cards—yellowed paper. The cabinets towered so high they bowed at their tops, and Cho was amazed they didn't topple.

Slowly, she tugged one of the drawers open. A card drifted to the lime-smelling, linoleum floor. She knelt, reading, "*Know Thy Enemy, Know Thyself: A Treatise on Martial Affairs* by T. Crua." Looking up, she saw the drawers had been labeled: *Military Strategy, First Aid,* and *Things I Wish I Hadn't Said.*

To her left, *Banned Speeches by Forgotten Historical Figures* and *Myths of Berl.*

On the right, *Improvised Explosives and You* and *Wild Kitchen: Recipes for Forestry Survival.*

"Oh, I get it," she said. "I'm dreaming." She was inside her own mind. A sloppy, cheap, metaphorical version of it. How tedious. Still, in a way, it was kinda nice, this peace and quiet. Eventful dreams could be so tiring.

Since she had the time, she wandered between the rows of file cabinets—*Spoken-Word Poets of the 33rd Century, Reconstructed Administrations and Laws of the Ancient World, Dealing with Depression*—and shook her head at how cluttered the place was. Thousands of books. Thousands of memories. Categories crammed together in loosely organized sections. All supposedly here to serve a purpose.

Again, the question presented itself. The one she'd asked herself every night, when she got to thinking about her family and how, one day, she too would die—blink out, stop existing.

The question: why had her parents stuffed her brain full of all this junk, forcing her to phonetically read and memorize all these words long before she even could understand what they meant? A six-year-old, speed-reading ancient philosophy and modern political theory. A child who'd only wanted to play and harass the kitchen staff, to stuff buttered rolls in her mouth and run off, drooling.

The question had always been *why?*

She asked the silence, "Why did you make me this way?"

A spotlight fell upon an intersection of paths ahead, and a crow hopped into view. A crow with gold eyes. It said, "They were preparing you."

"Preparing me for what? They couldn't have known what I'd need."

The crow blinked.

All the knowledge she'd memorized, she could now access and use it thanks to her perfect recall. It was all there and ready to save her in these critical days, when the very earth around her seemed to teeter on the brink of collapse. "They couldn't have known. Could they?"

"The motivations of the dead are a mystery. Whatever their reasons were, you are what you are. What they had you learn, it's their legacy but *your* heritage."

On her shins, Cho cupped her hands to offer the crow a perch. It hopped aboard.

Together, they traveled her mind for some time until their path was blocked by an old, scuffed laptop. Cho picked it up, lifting the folding screen. The keys on its keyboard weren't normal; there were only six letters, arranged to spell "EI-LARS" over and over. The screen flared to life, white text burning into the bright blue background: "REVENGE."

Alina the crow gently tapped her beak against Cho's earlobe.

Cho sighed and hit the "Escape" button, and she closed the laptop, leaning it against the nearest file cabinet.

"That was a little obvious, wasn't it?" she said.

"Not all symbolism is subtle."

"I hope he's with his family now. His wife and son."

Tellingly, Alina said nothing.

As they moved on, Cho said, "Do you think we'll find Ruqastra in here, too? She was hitching a ride with me—haunting me, I dunno—for a while. But, then, during the battle, I felt her... go."

"When I used up the Chrononite." Alina paused to preen her feathers. "It untethered her."

"Is she... gone for good then?"

"I seriously doubt that was her last trick."

They passed the section called *Tools of the Trade*, with colorful headings such as *Improvised Entry, The Art of Creative Persuasion*, and *How to Go Unseen*. There was a home-movie-quality video, projected onto a white sheet, displaying a highlight reel of Cho's pickpocketing days.

Alina squawked. "From the moment we met, I knew you were special."

Cho stared at the images of her younger self. Stealing, running, getting caught. "This kid has no idea what she's in for."

"Greatness."

Chuckling, Cho ran her fingers down the sheet, rippling the image. "Well. I owe a lot to you believing in me, Li."

"And I'd be nowhere without you. Before I came to New El, I—" Alina the crow cocked her head. "You gave me—all of me—something worth believing *in*." Her pause unfolded between them, the quilt of all their shared memories blanketing their silence. Alina glanced at the home movie again. "Hey! Wait a second! So, you *were* the one who stole my—"

"Moving on!" Cho hurriedly carried her friend away, heading toward the darker, dustier section way at the back.

Alina looked up at the sign hanging from the ceiling by one chain (the other having rusted and broken). "'Loneliness,'" she read, taking in the stacks and stacks of loose-leaf papers. "You've felt trapped a long time."

"The Walazzins—" Cho swallowed—"they're just as much responsible for what I've become as my parents were."

Alina clucked in agreement. "Despite their best efforts."

"They tried to break me." Cho kicked over a pile of pages as tall as she was.

"And look at you now."

Watching the sheets flutter, Cho echoed, "Look at me now." She set Alina the crow on the ground. "I miss you."

Growing, beak transforming into a nose, wings becoming arms—Alina reverted to her usual self, although her hair had gone wild and gray, haloing her head like a crest of feathers. "I'm still here."

"Why did you make *me* 'Primarch'? What were you thinking?"

Alina answered only with a smile.

"It should've been you, y'know. The soldiers, you're the one who healed them. The people respect you. They like you better than me."

"No. I agitate them. Which is fine. They should be upset by me. To wake them up is my role."

"Your role, huh?"

"I've made my decisions about who I am. And you?"

Cho waved her hand dismissively. "Oh, never mind. Like you'd ever give me a straight answer."

Without warning, Alina swept in, sniffing the air above Cho's head. "Ruqastra's gone, but you've got a new passenger."

Her fingertips tingling, Cho backed away. "The Sleeper."

"'Sleeper'? Oh, Cho… How did you ever manage to cross paths with Ji'inaluud?"

"What's a Ginny-lute?"

"Once upon a time, she was three who became one. Now she's a prisoner."

"Gods, talking to you has only gotten more frustrating."

"Look, why doncha ask her yourself. You're the one with a piece of her in here." Alina tapped Cho's temple.

"Or, here's a crazy idea… you could just tell me what's up."

"I can't."

"Chuh."

"You don't believe me."

"Of course not."

Alina rubbed her eyes. "Easy for you to say. You're just one person with one set of problems and opinions. Do me a favor: imagine every thought and feeling that defines you. Got it?"

"Okay, I got it. Yeesh."

"Now, take all those loves and regrets and desires and fears and multiply them by a thousand. No, how 'bout a million."

"Uh. I don't know—"

"That's right. You can't do it. The human brain isn't built to contain that much… personality. Even yours couldn't hack it. So, since you can't begin to *imagine* the chaos in my mind, you'll just have to take my word for it: by Buthmertha, I swear, I'm telling you everything I can, as soon as it becomes clear. Most of what's rolling around my dome doesn't make any sense even to me. It's like… my thoughts and my memories of all my many lives are people locked away behind doors I don't have the keys for. But sometimes, those people sneak messages out to me. I want to set them all free, but I…"

Seeing Alina's shoulders climb to her ears and her face scrunch in distress, Cho patted her friend's back. "It's okay. Yer granddad was a riddle-loving coot, too. You just took after him more than you thought is all. It's fine." A weak little chuckle escaped Cho's lips, covering the worry that Alina was slipping away. "So, am I supposed to wake the Sleeper?"

"If you do, New El will be destroyed."

"That's a yes, then…?"

Dodging the question with a shrug, Alina started re-stacking the papers Cho had kicked a few minutes ago. She was clearly working up to something.

Cho gave her some space to think.

Finally, she said, "There's something I need to do. I'll probably be gone a while."

"Like, physically, or—"

"As usual, I'll drop my body in the crypts beneath Primehall. Don't be worried if I don't come out for—"

"How long?"

"Three weeks. Maybe three months. Time's a little screwy where I'm headed."

"You know what? I'm calling it. This is garbage. It's bad enough that you've been in-and-out since you dropped a title and an army in my lap, but now you're going on vacation?"

Alina snorted. "'Vacation,' she says. Well, I am going on a tour, sort of, but you definitely wouldn't envy me if you knew what kind. And, by the way, I didn't 'give' you an army. That was all you, girl."

"Li, what am I supposed to do without you?"

"Simple. Radiate hope, you shining, little beacon, you." Alina placed the last of the papers atop the stack, straightening it.

Trying to hide her tears, Cho turned away.

Alina wrapped her arms around Cho's shoulders, whispering, "You're so much more than the sum of your parts," before backing off.

Cho faced her again.

Holding up her mask, Alina stared with those molten-gold eyes, the edge of a fang poking between her lips. "You have your fight. I have mine. We serve the same end. But we each require *very* different weapons."

"There. Just there." Cho frowned. "You don't sound like you used to—like yourself—anymore. Sometimes."

Alina's smile became real, soft, and human again. "I never cared about the fate of the world. Not until I met you. My friend. You saved me. Remember that, during the hard days. And remember that I love you, and I will always come back for you."

Dragging a snail's trail of snot across her sleeve, Cho sniffled. "Don't make me say it."

Then Alina was a crow once more, taking wing, disappearing into shadow.

Alone among the file cabinets, Cho closed her eyes. "I love you, too."

On her fifteenth birthday, Cho-Zen was officially sworn in as Primarch of the Seven Stacks, signaling her ambitions. (Thankfully, there was no crown involved, only a shiny badge and shinier sword.) She addressed her people using the recently repaired radio towers (previously sabotaged by retreating Authority forces). Her face and voice were broadcast via pirated airwaves into every home in Ozar. Her speech laid the groundwork for the months and years ahead while acknowledging the fruits of cooperation harvested thus far.

The Covenant, Ozari partisan, and ex-patriot Landsider/Elemental military units were fully integrated and retrained under the guidance of a multiracial, multi-species team of drill sergeants, consultants, and more. All were taught to fight together using combinations of human and Aelf tactics. Traditional and guerilla warfare; machinery and magic; the warriors of Cho-Zen left nothing on the field.

Over time, a multitude of skills was shared in the areas of medicine, agriculture, physics, magic, and more. The *Fyarda* Cbarassan, with their encyclopedic knowledge base, was instrumental in initially bridging the language and culture gaps. Soon, others took up the charge. A new generation of warriors, doctors, and engineers was born. The quality of life on the Seventh Stack began to improve, slowly but steadily.

A long struggle lay ahead, but there were moments of excitement and even joy—shoots sprouting, pushing out of the dust of death. With the passage of months, bonds were forged between unexpected allies, among species that had hated one another for all their lives and beyond. Even after Alina herself retreated into the crypts, tales of her miracles yielded new fruit almost every day; an ever-increasing number of prisoners and citizens swore themselves to Cho-Zen's cause. Children were born into this chaotic, budding nation—including the first *Fyarda* to be spawned in decades, emerging from the pods Cbarassan had nurtured in solitude for so very long.

Many Seventh Stack natives breathed freely for the first time in their lives, and with that small freedom came renewed hope. When they greeted one another, they still said, "OSO."

"Ozar shall overcome."

Cho ended her first official speech with a promise: "We will bring liberty and justice to all the peoples of Ozar, on all the Stacks. What The Authority couldn't pull off in a thousand years, we will do in three.

"If you're listening to this, you are the resistance. Good hunting."

In and out of resource-budgeting and lawmaking meetings, every few days Cho still made time to break away for a visit to Alina's cold, breathless body.

Dug into a shaft beneath the foundations of Primehall, the crypts felt to Cho like the cellar of the world. They'd been built around a spiraling staircase of stone, a sort of vertical tunnel ending in a chamber not much bigger than an alcove. The chamber was empty except for a stone slab, and it was there that Alina had chosen to lie. With only the steady dripping of the stalactites for company.

Lying in near-total darkness in this claustrophobic space, her mouth slightly open, she seemed unsuited to the mantle of mystic goddess. Rather, she looked every bit the late-blooming woman on the cusp of her twentieth year.

In the corner of the humble shrine, a fat candle shed little light. It had been brought in by Vessa, who often enough held vigil over her girlfriend's empty shell. The pink-haired Covenant sat quietly, hands in her lap, staring at nothing.

On seeing Cho, she stood and bowed her head. "Primarch."

Cho nodded in greeting. Gesturing toward Alina: "Still freaks me out, seeing her this way."

"Haven't gotten used to it myself."

"So." Awkwardly, Cho snapped her fingers a few times. "What's it like, dating a zombie?"

"Frustrating." Vessa held her candle up to the dripping walls, the light revealing time-weathered runes carved into the long-sleeping stone. "Still amazes me that she found this place when no one else knew it was here."

"Well, you didn't know to look. She did because—"

"She's been here before. Yeah, she told me." Vessa cupped her hands around the candle flame. "Some kinda burial pit for Iorian Mages."

"Thaal," Cho agreed.

Silence. Then Vessa said, "Where do you suppose she goes off to, when she's like this?"

"Maybe, someday, if we're real good and she's feeling especially chatty, she'll tell us. But I wouldn't hold my breath." Cho placed her finger under Alina's nose. No airflow, as usual.

"Was that a pun?" said Vessa.

"Sure was. And, as your Primarch, I order you to laugh."

"I am sworn to serve. Hah. Hah. Hah."

Vessa's forced laugh was quickly subsumed by a real one, and Cho joined in.

She returned to the base of the stairs. Over-shoulder, she said, "Catch some winks, Captain Tardrop. I'll need you fresh for the fights coming up."

Vessa saluted.

Climbing the stairs, Cho called down one more time: "And don't worry. She'll be back."

84

ALINA

IN DREAMS, THERE ARE no "chance" meetings. The fork in the path reveals itself when it so wishes.

Alina was not surprised to find the black jackal-masked figure kneeling at the exact center of the crossroads ahead.

In unison, they said, "I was wondering when I'd see you again."

The figure stood, her midnight-blue cloak brushing a rough semicircle in the twinkling dust of the Revoscape. With her silver-gloved hands, she lifted the jackal mask from her head even as it morphed expressively, snarling.

Revealed, Ruqastra's freckled face was impassive.

Alina said, "I now know what you, in your own damaged way, were really trying to teach me about responsibility: some fights are necessary, and it isn't right to walk away from them. When I said I refuse to kill, you heard 'I refuse to fight.' Let me be clear. I'll never be exactly what you and Dimas wanted me to be. You chose me, raised me, but I have to find my own way forward. And, I've decided. I'll never take a life again—once was more than enough. But, in my own way, I will fight. As long as it takes, whatever it takes. I will fight."

"And?"

"*And?* Give me a tiny bit of credit, here. My results speak for themselves, don't they? Elwoch's armies, The Authority, were driven back. For the first time ever, he tasted *real* defeat. And, in history's craziest BOGO deal, I even managed to reunite the pieces of my soul *while* roping the Hextarchs in, too. I mean, come on. I am the Seven made One. Not half bad for 'an inadequate student,' I'd say."

"Are you fishing for a medal? A gold star?"

"If you're offering, sure."

"That fate deigned *you* a worthy receptacle for an ungodly quantity of power is—regardless of our respective personal opinions—the purest accident of birth. Well, in your case, an accident of 'creation.' Must I reward you for that over which you had—and have—no control?"

"None of use choose to be born, Ruqastra. What we do with what we're given, that's what matters."

The slightest nod from her teacher. It clearly took a lot of effort for her to say, "For your efforts, yes, I submit to you the requisite congratulations."

"Please, now you're smothering me with praise. Seriously, what would I have to do to get a 'good job, Alina' out of you?"

"For a start, next time, you might try to think before you act. I was watching you, you know. Every step like a drunk climbing icy stairs. You're sloppy and arrogant, and much of your success is owed to sheer luck."

"There a 'but' on its way?"

"*However,* for an immature, thoughtless, unsubtle novice—"

"Alright, y'know what—"

"You did well enough, Alina."

There, the conversation ended, and Alina stood in stunned silence.

Eventually she moved forward, Ruqastra striding at her side.

The teacher did not ask aloud where they were headed, and Alina was skilled and powerful enough now to rebuff her attempts at mind-reading.

Ruqastra's frustrated sigh was its own reward.

Distance is a measurement of physical dimensions, of space. In dreams, there are no boundaries, and a thing may be at once small and large.

Their progress couldn't be determined in steps taken. There were, however, landmarks aplenty:

The Sunken Temple, half-swallowed by marshlands, where the Revomancers were stalked by pale, long-limbed, fleshy creatures with hooked suckers for noses.

The Tomb of the Metrubulae, a colossal burial mound whose ever-burning flame was fueled by the souls of sacrificed servants. How strange to see that moon-crowned hill—a relic of a time when Demons had been kings—now merely a blip in the mythic landscape of the human unconscious.

And, there, just ahead now, the Cloudgrove. Its trees bore spherical fruit: the unripe ones were dark rainclouds, readying to burst; the rest, active thunderstorms with translucent peels. Occasionally, an overripe cloudfruit would strike the earth and burst in a boom of thunder or brief miniature tornado.

Beyond the grove lay Alina's destination. She waited for Ruqastra, who'd fallen behind a few paces.

"Tolomond Stayd lives," said her teacher.

"That bother you?"

"No, I only find it curious. You must have a plan for him?"

"I have some ideas." Telepathically, Alina shared her surface-level thoughts.

Ruqastra skated across them, spinning, reveling. "The Sleeper?" She smiled. "My, that is quite devious."

With a flourishing twirl of her wrist and fingers, Alina bowed her head. "The student has quite literally *become* the master."

"Ascended to near-godhood, and still you pun. Why venture to the grove, though, when there remains so much to do among the living?"

"This." Alina held *Ida* up to the light. The red mask's beak gleamed in the effervescence of the Cloudgrove's pollen—purple sparks of static. "I really appreciate it, and what you did for me. Honestly, I do. But it just doesn't fit."

"I... understand."

"Really? I had a whole speech planned to win you over."

"My apologies for depriving you of that pleasure. But I've seen that you're right. You've outgrown the Sisters. Yet, they are yours; the price has been paid. It cannot be undone. They cannot be returned."

"I'm not planning to return them." Alina smiled when she felt Ruqastra's mental claws scratch at the iron shell of her mind. "Nice try. You'll just have to be patient."

"Fine." Pouting, Ruqastra crossed her arms. "Have your fun. I will observe."

"This is killing you, isn't it? Not knowing everything?"

"It's an unpleasant change of pace."

Alina plucked a nice juicy storm from the branch above her head, taking a bite. Her tongue tingled before going numb, and then her feet lifted off the ground. A moment later, Ruqastra did the same.

Together, they soared straight up, into the stars and beyond.

Near the end of their long journey, they circled the crystal tower three times and left their blood-tithes (droplets from pricked fingers) on the stone arch beyond it. Thus, they passed through the flimsy barrier between human and demonic dreams, continuing their long flight.

At last, ahead, they saw the glowing green and red and orange gas clouds of the Loom, the transient home of the Sloth Demons. There, Abyssal energy was woven, given shape and purpose.

Ruqastra said, "As Dimas, you first brought me here when I was fourteen. It feels a lifetime ago. Though, now that I've died, I suppose it *was*."

Swerving left, sprinting across a comet before leaping into the infinite sky again, the student turned to her teacher and said, "I remember when Alina—the human Alina—and you met. Dimas was there, giving instructions and preparing his spell, but it was you who bathed the baby in the waters of Mount Morbin. You held her close as she died. And, after she was gone, you whispered something. What was it?"

"I don't recall."

"Liar."

Ruqastra grumbled. "It all happened so quickly. That night, Dimas—you—summoned me without warning, passing Zatalena's daughter into my arms. She was so fragile and small, and I... was terrified. You guided me through a baptism of sorts, had me reciting hymns to gods forgotten before the dawn of human-kind. Soon, the child stopped breathing. And that's when you, Dimas, forged *yourself* from the ether and drew *yourself* into the lifeless infant's body. At the time, I couldn't have known what we were doing. I couldn't have known that you were passing, through me, a piece of yourself into her—this *other you*. Only when it was over did I begin to understand what I had witnessed: *Egoskisma*, the splitting of the soul. Through this dark miracle, you—Alina—were born into both life and death; the baby serving as the deathly vessel; and I, the living conduit."

"But what did you whisper to me, Alina the Sevensin, in the moment I was made?"

"Does it matter? Some trite teenager nonsense, I'm sure."

"You're deflecting."

"Alright, fine. Since you have badgered me into confessing... yes, I remember exactly what I said to you that night: 'I'll die before I let anyone hurt you.'"

Spinning gently with the astral winds, Alina kicked her legs as if swimming. "You kept your promise."

Ruqastra shrugged, but the damage had been done: like a broken bone, properly set and mended, their relationship had calcified, stronger than before.

After an appropriately lengthy pause, Alina said, "We're almost there now, but, I've been dying to ask—Oh, sorry."

"No offense taken."

"Well, just wondering, what's it like being, uh, not alive? A few times now, I've come close to finding out, but you've got the inside scoop."

"Ah. For the most part, the differences are negligible. There are fewer distractions, like the body's constant demands for food and sex. Although, being wholly incorporeal does present some minor inconveniences. Very few can see me outside of their dreams, for example. And interacting with tangible objects requires an extraordinary amount of willpower."

"Being dead is a 'minor inconvenience' to you?"

"You prepared me well for it. Do you not recall?"

Iridescent bubbles floated in Alina's mind. They popped, the rush of air bringing memories…

The feel of young Ruqastra's slim throat, Alina's fingers pinching the girl's jackhammering pulse until it finally weakened, weakened, then ceased.

The brisk splash of spring water as Ruqastra, drowning, kicked and struggled involuntarily against Alina's grip.

Ruqastra's wet gray face as she lay, immobile, near the pond, shaded by the trees of Mount Morbin.

Landing on a meteoroid, Alina said, "I killed you."

"Many times." Ruqastra slowed, drifting closer. "And you resuscitated me just as often."

"What Dimas—what *I* put you through—"

"Was all for the sake of preparing me."

"For what? You were a kid."

"I am a soldier. I submitted myself willingly."

Alina's disgust was a slimy film covering her whole body. "I can still taste your fear—"

"Of course I was frightened. But I trusted you. Because you trusted me. You needed a pliable mind, a youth who could endure the repeated touch of death. For me to serve you well, you needed me to see. And *see* I did. I was twelve the first time you drowned me, the first time I faced Elwoch and the unending oblivion that awaits us all beyond the grave. That vision destroyed me, and yet I survived. Each time I died and you brought me back, a little more of my weakness died too—until you had your selfless agent, she who would not fail you."

Alina felt sick. She couldn't hide from the knowledge that what Dimas had done, she had done. "What I asked of you was too much."

"The noblest cause demands the greatest sacrifice."

"Enough," Alina shouted, gripping Ruqastra's wrist as if it were her throat. She noticed what she did and let go. "You've sacrificed enough."

"That's not your decision to make. I may have been a child when you recruited me, but you never forced me to stay. You gave both my brother and me the choice, and, when only I accepted, you left him free. And, you sheltered the two of us when we had no one and nothing left. You trained us, gave me my purpose. For you, I would do anything."

There passed a surreal moment in which Alina realized that the woman she'd come to think of as a pedantic, distant, self-righteous older sister now looked at her like a child would a parent.

"No teacher is perfect." Ruqastra smiled. "Your methods were extreme, but necessary to arm me for the war. A war that is far from over. Even now, the *wheel* still turns. You know the one I speak of: the charnel platter on which the souls of the dead await consumption by the most gluttonous parasite to have ever been vomited into existence. When that feeding wheel is broken, when Elwoch—slug of slugs—is no more, then and only then will I have kept my promise to you. Then, and only then, will I have done 'enough.' Now, lead on."

Alina lifted off the meteoroid, *Rego* rippling behind her like a sail. As she and Ruqastra drew nearer and nearer the Loom, silence became their third companion, gliding into formation between them.

Eventually Alina worked up the nerve to say, "I'm sorry. For everything."

Another long pause followed. Then: "I forgive you."

They arrived at the Loom, that nebula painted by the hands of the creators in every color real and imagined. Inside it floated the puffy, translucent, sack-like Sloth Demons who greeted the two Revomancers with curious roils of violet and aquamarine.

Sloth Demons, by their nature, had no need for social hierarchy nor a permanent address. They drifted wherever the celestial winds willed. Though their supercluster gas-cloud home could never be found twice in the same place, it would always remain open to Revomancers, who provided the Sloths with the only currency they craved: human souls. Souls, exchanged for a weaving of dreams—the power of fear, imbued in a cloak and a mask.

The trade was simple, ghastly. It had not changed since its beginning, but Alina would make sure she was the last Revomancer to ever strike such a bargain.

Dozens of gliding Demons gathered around their two dark visitors, greeting them with swirls of color inside their bodies. Scarlet politeness laced with electric blue threats. Their question, *What brings you here?*, was a reminder: there was always a chance that their appetites would overpower them. Accustomed though they were to deal-making with mortals who'd stolen into their dream-tossed home, the Sloths might not deem the offer worthy—settling instead for the instant gratification of inhaling the soul of the bargainer.

Alina, however, hadn't come with an offer but a demand.

She surveyed the camouflaging kaleidoscope of clouds, knowing that there were many more hundreds of Sloth Demons hiding just out of sight. A mortal would have known to be afraid, but what is fear to a ghost and a Dragon?

Alina tore off her cloak and mask, feeling suddenly a whole lot smaller and lighter, and held these up to the circling, undulating Sloths.

"These are useless," she declared. The Demons would understand her words even if they could not speak them. "You've known it all along. For thousands of years, you've been giving us dull blades. These Revomantic foci, these weapons, they were forged to shatter. To destroy. But pain and terror are harmless to the Revomancer's true enemy." She waited for this to sink in. Puffs of gray and white meant the Sloths grew restless. "Dreams are wishes for change. I was reborn to change the world, but I can't build on a foundation of fear." She threw *Ida* and *Rego* into the air, where they tumbled in the low gravity, rotating as slowly as the Sloths who'd woven them from the very fabric of the Revoscape. "Knowing Elwoch feeds off fear, you let us think you'd given us power, when all you'd really handed us was his favorite seasoning. You broke the agreement."

Angry, prideful explosions of emerald and mauve rippled through the Sloths like a wave. *All compacts were made in good faith. No dream walker ever expressly asked for the power to war against God. We did more than enough for you squalling mammals. Would you have had us court our doom by breaking trust with the Master?*

"No, no. The terms of the *original* deal with the first human Revomancer were 'one mortal soul, stolen in secret, in exchange for protection.'"

You speak as if you know. Begone, dreamer, before we drown you in the waters you tread.

"Well, I do know, actually. Because that original contract was mine."

The first human Revomancer? You would have us believe that was you?

Alina shook her head. "I was the weaver. Why don't you all scooch in, get a closer look?" She crossed her arms and floated straight up, slowly turning in place.

The Sloths drifted towards her, packing in, flashing an array of colors, signaling pangs of frustration and concern. Finally, they must have recognized her, for their sack-like skins rippled in alarm.

You cannot be.

"But I am."

You were lost to all worlds an age ago. Centuries, as humans reckon it.

"I've worn a lot of different masks the past five hundred years, yeah. Monster, mentor, mother, uncle, daughter—granddaughter. But, now that I'm whole again, I've come back to remind you that *I* am your boss, not Elwoch. Before you were Demons, before you were even apprentice sorcerers, you were snot-nosed, grubby-fingered children, barely able to string together two syllables of incantation, and it was *me* who taught you everything you know."

They puffed her unique color signature, then—mauve and lavender, flecked with gold: *Vranakvius'rin-erlin.*

"So, you do remember. Good. Now, you gonna remake my Sisters for me or what?"

Shivering, they huddled together, belching thick pockets of color. Quickly, they agreed. Though, confused, they asked, *How? How can it be done?*

Alina had given this a lot of thought. When it came, the answer was as obvious as only hindsight can be. In a way, everything she'd ever done had led to this moment—and what would come afterward. "Fear," she said, "it's so last-millennium. I want you to make me a mask and cloak from *hope*."

Impossible.

"I'll be the one to tell you what's possible."

They deflated, shrinking away.

"Listen up, then, because here's your new contract: you do as I ask, and I let you leave. You'll go far, far away—somewhere you'll never see another human being again."

Or?

"Or? Or? Well, honestly, I'm not going to Rave you. But there are worse humiliations for your kind than death. Just ask Osesoc'ex-calea."

Hope. An entirely unfamiliar element to any Demon.

Perhaps, once, in ages beyond memory, they'd touched it, but to them it had become as mysterious and fathomless as the depths beneath the ocean floor; as treacherous as a rotting bridge. But once the Sloths began to mold its rough and graceless edges into a suitable shape, they tasted of its bitter sweetness—the watering eyes of the abandoned child, the condemned man's seemly lies.

Hope.

The Sloth weavers encircled Alina. It would take every last one of them to tame her energies.

She drifted between them in meditation, calling to the souls within her, "Give me everything you've got. I can't do this alone."

In her heart lived Haba, Etia, and Gurm, her childhood friends. Stonoz, her earliest rival. Nasres, her conscience. And Aam, her first love. Each of them, in turn, contained a multitude of conquered spirits, fragmented and scarred—victims of their age-long feeding frenzy in service to Elwoch.

Beyond them rested Mezami, whose last words, his will and testament, she repeated now: "No fear."

She dug deeper, reaching further to touch those countless others who had shaped her soul in life and in death.

She thought of Ruqastra and Baraam, her adopted siblings; Ordin or Ivion, her complicated unfinished business; Calthin and Kinneas, the hometown friends of her latest incarnation; Ugarda Pankrish, who'd been kind to her just because he could; Cho, who meant everything; Vessa, her reason to dream.

Deeper and deeper within herself, she delved.

She found herself somewhere else then. A place of black sky, black earth, which broke away. And, through the cracks therein, she could see herself—a thousand of herselves, staring back. A shower of asteroids, burning up on impact, crashed upon her mirror images, which were struck down by the dozens—shattering, scattering shards of ice-touched glass. Each shard glowed, a star in this contracting darkness, until these winked out, one by one.

Only one shard remained, and it burnt like ice to the touch. Before she could lose her nerve, she grabbed it, held it like a knife, and buried it in her chest. The shard fractured inside her, burrowing deep. The cold suffused her entire being, and she choked. She coughed up a perfectly spherical marble of ice that melted in her hands. And what was left inside her was a purified, rarified mote of infinite possibility.

In her innermost dreams, somewhere between the waves of fear and the rocks of doubt, around the bend in the path leading away from despair, upon a hill built by determination—there, Alina found a tree called hope, and watered it with the sweat and tears of the millions who'd come before her and the millions more who depended on her now.

When she opened her eyes to the Revoscape, the Sloth Demons that surrounded her slumped, winded. Floating in front of her, *Ida* and *Rego* appeared unchanged, still a black cloak and red crow mask. However, reclaiming them, she felt the truth: they were hers.

She garbed herself in the raiments of the Revomancer once again, sinking to where Ruqastra waited.

"It's done," said Alina.

"I hope you know what you are doing."

"You and me both."

The Revomancers watched the supercluster gas-cloud brimming with Sloth Demons float away until it had fully departed the Revoscape.

No human would ever come to the Loom again.

Ruqastra said, "Sweeping changes. Tell me you're not stirring the pot just to see what floats and what sinks."

"You kept a lot of secrets. Now that I finally have more information, I'm acting on it. Sue me." Alina cracked her neck. "Out of curiosity, what're your plans for the next—oh, I dunno—several years?"

"My schedule has cleared considerably. What did you have in mind?"

"Elwoch can't be stopped while he's protected. Something's gotta be done about his guard dogs."

"The Order of the Enlightened. What do you know of them?"

"Elwoch-worshipers. An esoteric group of murderous nerds who secretly control most of the world's governments and corporations. Am I on target?"

"A bit of an oversimplification, but, yes. The Enemy has had thousands of years to bolster his defenses, the greatest of which is the Order. To strike at him, you will need to go through them. Each of the Scholars of the Enlightened holds a unique key. Without all of these keys, the door to Elwoch's sanctum cannot be opened."

Notes of familiarity chimed in Alina's mind. "Shake down the Scholars, get the keys. No prob. When do we start?"

"Not so fast. In addition to having a firm grasp on the reins of the Elemental Empire, the Scholars are proficient Mages. Even graver threats are their faithful protectors—the Knights of the Riddle. Talented assassins and warriors, all."

"High praise, coming from you."

"I mean every word of it."

"Think I can take 'em?"

"You will have to. Though, I've learned of no one else who has."

"Huh. 'Kay."

"The Scholars defend the keys; the Knights defend the Scholars. We must arm ourselves with knowledge before we strike. As of now, there are two items most pertinent to this quest: a roster of the Order's membership and a map detailing their locations."

"Awesome. Why is this the first I'm hearing of these things, and how can I get my hands on them?"

"I am getting to that. When you were Dimas, you had me research and spy on my own. I infiltrated the Order—briefly. Despite being discovered and nearly killed, I was able to recover what I'd been after. Upon my return, you ordered me to keep my discoveries secret from everyone. Even you."

"Seems pointlessly complicated and risky."

"And, thus, very much your strong suit."

"Ya got me, there."

"Dimas could not risk knowing, in case Mateus got to him before you did. Your uncle was always too bullish to be useful. If he'd learned of the existence and inner workings of the Order, he might have charged them and been killed, ending all hope for the Sevensin. Or, worse, he might have joined them. He'd already been deceived by Elwoch's minions once, unwittingly serving their aims. As you saw for yourself, his ill-reasoned attacks only aggravated his entanglement. He was a prisoner of his own emotions. A mere reactionary."

"Now that he's a part of me, I feel the need to tell you to back off a little."

"Regardless. Dimas had faith in you, Alina, and in my ability to get the information you needed to you when you needed it. Considering recent events," she said, smiling, "one might even say that he had *hope* you would succeed against all odds."

"You sneer at that word, hope. But, we'll make a believer of you yet."

"Over my dead body."

"Two jokes in one day!" Alina waggled her finger. "Careful, or you'll pull a muscle. So, where is this map?"

Ruqastra spread her arms. "You are looking at her."

"You memorized all the names and locations?"

"Not quite."

"Let's cut to the chase, please. I hate guessing games."

"Then use your damned ears and *hear* me. I *am* the map." She sighed. "It's a long story involving espionage, sex, and a spree of indelicate murders. The short of it is that, in order to secure the map, I had to swallow the Lorestone containing it."

"Hang on. Hang on. This is too much, and I can't deal. Sex and murder?"

"And?"

"You're not going to elaborate at all?"

Ruqastra smirked.

"Fine, fine. So, what, then? You *ate* Chrononite? How do we... Or, when will... Gods, there's no decent way to say it: how long will it take to... pass or whatever?"

"Excuse me? It *won't* 'pass.' I digested it. The cells of my body were crusted— battered, stained perhaps?—with billions of splinters of the stuff. My spirit, it seems, retains the information stored therein. It may be why I was able to withstand the pull of the beyond. But that hardly matters."

"Yeah, I agree. The fact that you're an unkillable time ghost is not at all fascinating. Definitely in no way worth a conversation."

"Hush. Listen. Once again, you blunder into the right answer by mistake. 'Time' is, in fact, the operative term. For, regarding the locations of the Order, it isn't so much a matter of *where* as *when*."

"Say what? Time travel? You're talking about *time travel*."

Ruqastra nodded.

Alina sucked on her teeth. "Kick. Ass."

"I can already tell this will require a lot of explaining."

"Well, I got nowhere else to be. Here I am, finally ready to face my destiny and all that junk. Blah, blah, blah. So, come on. Hit me."

"Ugh. We are about to embark on a time- and multiverse-spanning journey to unseat an immortal arch-demon. You will have to take this seriously *at some point*."

"Is that a challenge?" Alina wiped the smirk from her face. "For you, Morphea, I will try. Since we already have the map, what about the list of names you mentioned?"

"That invaluable information we will procure from a certain Scholar. Consider him the first item on our long to-do list."

"Do I know him?"

"You know *of* him."

Alina thought of Ordin.

"No," said Ruqastra. "His hour will come. The one I refer to now is an old man who has wasted many decades wreaking evil on our world. (Admittedly, his suffering will bring me considerable personal satisfaction, but that's just a bonus.) Before we make ourselves known to him, however, a more urgent priority calls for your attention."

"What now?"

"Our quarry will remain permanently beyond our reach unless you unlock the true potential of Revomancy. You must teach yourself, once again, to walk through time."

Alina had about five quips ready to fire off in reply, gems like *Is that all?* and *No pressure, then*. But she held back.

Ruqastra nodded approvingly. "For now, let's return to Ozar to make the necessary preparations. I can relay all I've learned of the Order on the way." She smiled, a rictus that tore across her face. "Finally, we begin the real work. Are you ready, *Aelfraver?*"

"By all means, *Aelfraver*. I got one more Rave left in me."

And, try as she might, Ruqastra could suppress herself no longer: she laughed, loud and long.

Coyote and crow, she and Alina donned their masks. Their cloaks swirled around them, gimlets of darkness, carving through unreality itself. Then, they were gone. Where they'd been standing, a silence lingered before it, too, was swallowed by the hum and reshuffling of the nebulous, vacuous eternities of the Revoscape.

Briefly, all that remained of the Revomancers was Ruqastra's gleeful cackle. The laughter of a shade, echo of echoes.

85

BARAAM

FRUSTRATED, HE TOSSED HIS trash novel at his feet. The book, a nonsensical swashbuckler entitled *The Old World Will Burn* by Juleas Trees, landed on the paper-thin blanket covering him up to his waist.

The field hospital—basically, a large cluster of tents spanning a parking lot—made it impossible for Baraam to read, sleep, or even think. The room dividers sectioning off his cramped little corner did nothing to give any real sense of privacy, and his rigid mattress had him fondly recalling the Saludbabni's straw cots.

He wished he could move about on his own again. The doctor had ordered him to remain immobile for at least another four days, adding that, when they'd found him, he ought to have been comatose. Dead, really. Yet, by the grace of the gods, he'd survived.

A constant stream of doctors, nurses, and other patients harassed him, chittering like frightened mice. Their voices crowded his every waking moment, stifling him. If only he could take a walk at least. Clear his head.

"Oh, come on, B."

"Ruqastra?" he whispered, but it wasn't her. He looked up to find Alina standing there instead, her arms crossed.

She said, "We both know why you wanna be up and out. It's about *her*."

"I can't imagine who you're referring to."

"Why are you so fascinated by her?"

He sighed. "Let's suppose I am. Call it 'professional curiosity.'"

"Are you always so curious about people who almost kill you?"

"I couldn't say. It's never happened before." He cleared his throat. "Where is she?"

Alina grinned pettishly. "She *was* locked in the dungeons, surrounded by Niima-nullifiers, in the cell just next to Tolomond's, actually."

"Was?"

"I had her moved. Here." Alina shifted aside the room divider behind her.

There, in a bed identical to Baraam's, lay Eva. Matted hair, her closed eyelids sunken and purple. She was breathing.

"The docs can't figure out why she's asleep. It's something supernatural. I told them to take away the devices blocking her Niima flow. That should help. The rest is up to her."

Baraam did his level best to mask his feelings.

Alina's grin remained static.

He said, "Why do all this? She's in league with your enemy."

"You don't believe that. You aren't even sure who *our* enemy is. As for 'why,' consider it a favor. From me to you."

"There is no such thing as 'a favor.' What do you want in return?"

"Join the Primarch's army. You can be a grunt or a colonel, it doesn't matter. Just fight with us."

"Your 'Primarch' is a twelve-year-old girl."

"There's more courage in that *fifteen*-year-old than both of us combined. Face it, she's got the backing of the Coneys, who happen to be in charge of the ex-Authority."

"Turncoats."

"Rebels."

"Under no circumstances will I bow to a child, regardless of lineage."

Alina cocked her head as if listening. "You're hesitating. Undecided."

"Do not gaze into my mind again. I'm warning you."

"Then start being honest with me, bro. This is war. You have to come to grips with the facts, like, *now*. Or, The Authority will take advantage of our in-fighting and wipe us out."

Baraam stared at the placid face of Eva, the one who'd defeated him. In recovering her body from the battlefield, had he saved or damned her? "Who is she? Where did she come from?"

"An Authority project gone terribly wrong."

Despite himself, he shuddered. "Are there others like her?"

"Cho-Zen has people looking into it. But there's not much we can do from down here. You want the freedom to investigate for real?" She let the question hang a moment. "Well, there's about fifty thousand Tranquilizers between you and the answers. Help us."

He met her eyes. For an instant, he saw the mischievous girl who used to try to surprise-tackle him at every opportunity—even though he'd always outweighed her by more than a hundred pounds.

"I need you," she said now.

"And I must remember my promise to my Master."

"Dimas is gone, but I'm still here. We're moving ahead with our plans, Cho and I, with or without you. What you do next, it's your choice and your responsibility."

His tone softened: "You're sounding like Ruqastra again. She used to say, 'Even doing nothing is a choice.' I shouldn't have left her alone with the Master. If I'd stayed..." The words wouldn't come.

"She forgave you, Baraam. A long time ago."

"I don't believe you."

Green again, Alina's eyes misted, her theatrical grin fading to a pitying smile. "When you do, then you'll be ready."

Baraam rubbed his face to hide his own tears. "Ready for what?" he asked. But he was alone.

Three days later, Baraam was discharged from the field hospital, though he'd still have to walk with a cane for some time. Upon his leaving, his nurse told him, "Merciful Nninithin, son. Both your legs were broken. The cartilage in your knees, shattered. The fact that you're standing here is nothing short of—"

"Miraculous?" said Baraam, knowing whom he had to thank for the favor. With a scowl, he hobbled away from the medical tent.

That night, a memorial service was held for those who had fallen in battle. They were given heroes sendings, one and all. Even the Aelf.

In many cases, there was no body to burn.

Attended by thousands, and watched from home by millions more, the ceremony took place in the courtyard, which had been swept clean. Scaffolding and wooden beams braced the walls in process of being reinforced. The scene was appropriately solemn. Alinites, Banelings, priests of the Elemental pantheon, and many older, heathen faiths were each given an opportunity to speak their blessings.

The Pyct, Mezami, was singled out for having traded his life for the Primarch's. And it was the Primarch herself who gave his eulogy, her Aelf and human entourage fanning out to give her space. Beside her stood Alina, who waved. Baraam nodded curtly.

As Cho-Zen spoke, Baraam admitted to himself that her appearance was significantly more impressive than that of the urchin he barely remembered meeting the once. That day, he had thrown her and Alina and their Pyct friend onto the first private shuttle out of New El. She'd been a wisp of a thing, then, dressed in rags and in the company of fools. Now, he appraised her garb: a long, brass-buttoned, midnight-blue jacket; cerulean vest; gray breeches; and tall, laced, leather boots. The darkness of her uniform contrasted with her pale skin and gleaming, hairless head. Although diminutive in height, she cut a striking figure. Stately, even.

Her words were simple, straightforward. Therein, her power. She spoke with such emotion and, dare he say, eloquence that he forgot for a moment that he was standing in the midst of a crowd of mingled humans and Aelf. It was a strange, almost out-of-body experience for him.

When she'd finished speaking for Mezami, Cho-Zen turned to the subject of the many thousands who'd died in the months that had followed the battle. Soldiers who'd succumbed to their war-wounds, peacekeepers killed in brawls and riots, rioters and looters shot down by peacekeepers, civilians lost to fire or earthquake. For all of them, she ordered a moment of silence. Finally, she said a few words for someone named Eilars—an android? How was that possible?—and for Ruqastra bol-Talanai.

The Primarch's sending was respectful, rife with details of their time together on Mount Morbin. Alina held up a fist and said only, "Morphea, Queen of Dreams." No one else contributed, for no one else had known Ruqastra. She had been too talented a spy.

Baraam wept.

He remembered little else of the dignified event (and he'd declined to speak beforehand). All he could think was how little his sister would have cared for the trappings and "theatrics," as she'd have called them. After all, she'd never been especially tied to the world of the living. And he was one of the few who knew why: though she'd been physically unharmed, something of hers had burned away in the wreckage of their childhood home.

Maybe, now that she was well and truly gone, she'd find that part of herself again. In another realm, wherever it was that the spirit went upon outgrowing the body.

It was a comforting thought that he would cling to through many long, cold nights in this alien, underground city. In this country choked by death. Surrounded by Aelf and the humans who—until a month ago—had been trained all their lives to hate them. Trained, as he had been, to hate.

Wherever Ruqastra was, he had to hope, must be fairer than here. Ozar was a disaster inching, each day, toward apocalypse. Holding the Seventh Stack together would be an impossible task. That made Alina a perfect fool, tangled with scores of other fools, striving for an insane, impossible dream.

Baraam ought to have focused on his recovery until he was strong enough to escape this place. However, when he looked to this Cho-Zen girl now, he lost his nerve. He saw something in her. What it was, exactly, he couldn't tell, but it surely was a thing he lacked.

In many ways, though half his age, she seemed to have achieved what he so desperately desired: self-reinvention. If he followed her, could he too be so profoundly transformed?

As songs of praise were sung for the fallen Aelf, including Mezami the Pyct, Baraam stayed respectfully silent. He could not bring himself to sing—not yet—but he could see why others did.

Humans and Aelf, harmonizing. It should have been impossible.

Perhaps nothing was impossible.

But, preserving the Seventh Stack...

When Cho-Zen had finished speaking, Alina stood and announced, "This one's for Taru, and for all the children of two worlds." She began to sing, her voice shaky at first but growing gradually in confidence and poise.

Baraam had forgotten how beautifully she could sing. He hadn't heard her do so in a long, long time. Though her choice of song was nothing special—a lullaby known by every parent and child in Truct—she captivated his attention. The simple, sad lyrics and somber, minor key returned him to his teenhood visits to Dimas and The School. The memories, and the lilt of Alina's voice, haunted him.

Child of two worlds.

Perhaps Cho-Zen's struggle could ease even the weight of his loss, give him purpose again. Yes, a reason to wake up, to rise. Getting up in the wake of a beating, surely, was a victory in itself.

If he died, he would be freed of his suffering. And, if, against all odds, the Primarch's ragtag army conquered the earth, he could return to the sky. Either way, he supposed, there was hope. Purpose and hope.

Perhaps they were the same.

He listened to the end of Alina's song, and then he watched everyone else leave. Finally, he sat a while alone, thinking.

Over time, the swelling lessened. The aches dulled.

Baraam broke his cane over his knee and tossed the pieces into a ditch.

"I will never lose again," he vowed.

Wincing with each step, he made the long walk to Primehall.

He barged past the guards, who looked at each other, stunned at his brazenness, unsure if they had any right to challenge him. To their relief, he stopped in the entrance hall, and waited.

Cho-Zen came out to greet him, though she stayed at the top of the wide, open staircase.

"I would like to contact the surface world," he said, adding "my lady" a beat too late.

General Tiberaira, the girl's apparent mentor and confidante, glowered down at him. "We owe you no favors, Mr. bol-Talanai. We've already given you your life. And what you ask will put us all at risk."

But Cho-Zen said, "What's the problem? What do you think is gonna happen? Our location ain't exactly a secret."

"He could reveal sensitive information."

"Send some dudes with him, then. I think the Primarchy will survive Captain Thunderpants's phone-a-friend."

Overlooking the nickname, Baraam bowed. "Thank you."

Within the hour, he was escorted by three Cutcords to the repaired communications center (little more than a metal box buried in a cliff-face). The steep climb was agony, and he required frequent breaks which he spent huffing and puffing over the metal railing. Finally, he arrived at the top and was let in. Groaning, knees popping, he lowered himself onto the plastic chair in front of the radio, phone, and computer terminal. These devices were connected to a bundle of cables as thick as a subway car, fed through the ceiling to a satellite dish that could beam a signal almost anywhere on the planet—through more than a mile of solid rock.

The soldiers spread out from the console, giving him some space while remaining within earshot. Catching his breath, Baraam did his best to ignore his escort's presence.

He knew exactly whose voice he most wanted to hear. The dial tone sounded three times before that very man picked up. Even with the slight mechanical stutter, when Baraam heard the Kadician words of greeting, to him, they were the most beautiful music.

"Ah!" Jija laughed on recognizing Baraam's voice. "The wayward beast-head lives! You froth-mouthed ram. You twice-blessed rascal."

Baraam smiled. "I'm glad I caught you, my friend."

"By the gods, how are things, lad? We've all fretted over you for months. Wherever have you landed?" He listened soberly as Baraam told him.

"And, Jija, I must humbly ask something of you."

"Anything."

"Would you hold a place at the table for me?"

"As long as thistle graces the daughter's crown, the Saludbabni, your home, will welcome you into her bosom. Yet, if I'm understanding your situation, some considerable obstacles bar your path back to us."

"It's true. I will be delayed." Like shifting sands, static distorted the call for a moment. Baraam watched a blue spark of electricity dance across his knuckles. He made a fist. "But I am coming home."

TOLOMOND

"... a deal..."

Drenched in sweat, Tolomond opened his eyes.

He was in his solitary cell, still. Lying on a cot tucked in the corner opposite the bucket. He'd covered his face with his arms—his blackened, spindly arms, charred to the shoulders.

He went limp-limbed, quickly closing his eyes once more. Perhaps, if he slept again, he would dream. Perhaps he would wake somewhere better. Or, better still, never wake again.

As his consciousness slipped into swirling, empty darkness, he knew for certain that God was a lie.

Were God real, were there any mercy or justice left to this world, Tolomond would be allowed to die after all he'd suffered through.

On the other hand, perhaps God was real, and this was hell.

Why had they healed him? Why had the young crow witch mended his bones and restored his soul to his body?

Torment. "Yes, that must be the answer," he whispered to himself, and he laughed at his own pitiful reasoning.

Every second, a reminder. Of what he'd lost. Of all he'd taken.

Later, the steel door to his cell scraped open. His head slipped from his pillow. He curled into a ball, his twiggy fingers cradling his skull.

He risked a peek.

A backlit silhouette occupied the doorframe.

The figure stepped forward, the low light revealing her curly, graying hair and dark skin, the drape of her dark cloak, and the golden gleam of her inhuman eyes.

"Tolomond Stayd," said she who looked *almost* like Alina K'vich, but whom he knew to be the devil. "I have a deal for you."

In the ashen gloom, her golden eyes glowed like embers.

IVION

The woman with the straight white hair and artificially symmetrical face had taken shelter for the week in an undisclosed location. She'd hidden herself among the steel and glass towers of New El—that sky-bound city tethered to the earth by the three great chains of Concordia, Libra, and Consortio. She watched hovercars and drones zip past her penthouse. On that crisp summer's midnight, the single, wall-width, bulletproof window of her cloud-kissed miniature fortress provided a clear view of the Eleru District as it burned.

The penthouse was comfortable enough, all things considered. The woman sipped her wine, spread a gooey piece of cheese onto a cracker, took a bite. Chewing, she waved at the inferno outside, muttering, "Goodbye, Wodjaego."

As the fires spread, she pressed a button on her holopad. Sheets of metal slid down to cover the window. The bars and locks on the only door clicked into place.

Next, she removed her clothes and slid into the king-sized bed. She read for exactly sixty minutes (half of the time devoted to the news of the day, half to managing her family's rapidly expanding financial portfolio). "Lights, off," she said afterward, and the lights obeyed.

Despite the total darkness, she snapped her sleep mask over her eyes. Before long, she'd drifted off.

Something woke her. A feeling. Like a fingernail, raked along her spine.

She pulled off her sleep mask, listening. As expected, she heard nothing and no one. So, feeling quite foolish, she laid her head back onto the fluffy, starched pillow.

Then someone said, "Consul Ivoir, congratulations on your appointment."

The white-haired woman tumbled out of bed, shouting for help.

"I just have one question. Did you get a kick out of it, using your sister's face to get to me?"

Ivion tried calling out. She got the distinct feeling that no one was coming.

"And you'd be right, Ordin," said the voice in the darkness. "Your security team can't hear you."

Ivion fumbled for her holopad, slapping the button that raised the blinds. Slowly, they ground upward.

Awash in rising moonlight, occupying the chair opposite the bed, Alina crossed one leg over the other. "Hard to find reliable help these days, isn't it? They always seem to be asleep on the job."

Pulling a sheet over herself, Ivion quivered.

"Relax. While you can. I'm just delivering a message. Ready? Here goes: you thought you could control me. You thought you could use my connections to the Hextarchs to give your gilded world a spit-and-shine job. You were wrong. The days of the Plutocrats' forcing everyone to fight their battles for them are done. I just gotta ask, Ordin, how does it feel, knowing that—in trying to have me do your dirty work—you personally steered me into becoming your biggest headache? Does it help to think of this whole ordeal as... a nightmare?"

"Alina, I never—"

"The question was rhetorical. Anyway, I also came to warn you that my friend is coming, and she doesn't have my same hangups about taking lives. You'd drop your bloody crown and make a run for it, if you knew what was good for ya."

"If you're here, why not finish me now?"

"Because I'm not done with you yet." Alina's grin was ninety percent fang.

"What do you want? Name your price."

Out of nowhere, it began to rain. The staccato pattering drowned out Alina's laughter.

Ivion pushed: "I can offer you money, amnesty, alliance. All you have to do is—"

"Trust you?" Alina shook her head. "I'm not for sale." She stood, jerked her thumb toward the window. Despite the rain, chemical fires continued to ravage Walazzin Manor. "You and your pals can keep playing your little war games a bit longer—keep knocking each other off for all I care. But your reckoning's on its way. In the meantime, I'll be watching you and stopping by whenever I can. Oh, there's no use running, nowhere you can hide. As long as you dream, I'll find you. And my visits won't be fun."

"Torture, then."

"Encouragement, more like. Don't worry too much yet. As I said, I'm going to let you ripen a while. You need time to really think on what you've done." Alina advanced, step by step, as Ivion tripped over the leg of a chair and tumbled. "Ruqastra, Eilars, Mezami. I won't have you dying on me until I'm sure their names are etched into your mind. I'm going to burn their faces onto the backs of your eyelids so that you'll never blink again without reliving the pain you've caused." She leaned over Ivion, who'd backed into a wall. She sniffed the air and sighed. "Only when you can't take it anymore, when you're tap-dancing on the edge of madness and ready for that final nudge... then, I might just let Cho have you." She took a big step back and pressed her palm against the window. "Until then, 'Badnight.'"

Kneeling, naked at the foot of the bed, Ivion shivered. She shrank at the sudden three-burst flash of lightning.

Alina had vanished, leaving only her handprint on the glass.

86

JEJUNE

MAYBE YOU CAUGHT A glimpse of it, out of the corner of your eye. You could be forgiven for imagining that, at first glance, it was only an animal of some kind. A sick dog that's lost all its fur to the ravages of disease. Or, maybe, you thought it was a lost person, wasted by starvation, ignored and turned away from every doorstep. For this mistake, too, you could not be blamed.

Indeed, the pale thing that fled through the alleys of the Sixth Stack's lake district, that scurried into the vents—it was a most pathetic sight. Too large and owning too many limbs to be dog or man, it moved with the awkwardness of a creature that had grown unused to its own true form. As it dragged itself through dusty, dingy vents, its spiky, clumsy body dented the metal siding. It searched for some semblance of safety, its blue, ridged tongue flicking to taste air and ground, testing the way forward. Through abandoned radioactive plants and acid-flooded basins, wind tunnels and vacuum-sealed garbage chutes, it slithered along.

Eventually, after perhaps hours or days of feeding on man-sized rats and roaches and the oily residue of discarded fast food wrappers, the creature exited the vents onto the ice fields of the Fifth Stack. Above, snow fell from the inverted mountains hanging like crusted snot from God's own nostril. Massive furnaces were fed, day and night, to prevent the magical ice from encroaching on the city below—and flash-freezing every living resident.

Still, the creature pressed on. Haggard, weary, burned, broken limbed, but very much alive and *enraged*, it crept through darkened streets (rolling power outages) toward the local Patriot's Watch broadcast station. The billboard-sized digital clock above proclaimed the hour—4:30 a.m.

The night guard in the lobby looked up, seeing the creature's pale, three-pronged, dew-clawed appendage tap on the glass. He gagged, and he cursed to himself. But, with the press of a button, he did let the unannounced visitor inside.

Crossing the lobby, it crammed itself into the elevator, which it rode to the fiftieth floor.

With a ding, the doors opened. The creature gave a start when it saw the host of *The Fix with Kert Sonnenkarl*—New El's favorite nightly talk show—standing there. The man himself, red bow tie and all.

He looked like a doll stuffed into a cheap, blue suit two sizes too small.

"Sonnenkarl?" The creature's voice was the squeal of a hundred bleeding pigs. "What are you doing here?"

Sonnenkarl plastered onto his face that dopey, slack-jawed gape of pure ignorance that had endeared him to elderly human Watchbox viewers the world over. His brows formed an upside-down vee, stretching his surgically tightened, artificially tanned skin to its limit. Was he completely baffled or merely constipated—with Sonnenkarl it was impossible to tell for certain. Finally, he said, "Jejune. Nice of you to join us. I came to meet you."

Jejune hadn't had eyes for centuries (not functional ones, anyway). But, if he had, he would have narrowed them now. He chose his words with care: "I have urgent news for the Order."

"It can wait."

Even hunched and hobbled, Jejune stood two heads taller than Sonnenkarl. The barbs of the Demon's bowed limbs scratched the drywall on either side. The man standing in his shadow checked the time on his antique brass pocketwatch.

"Crew will be here soon. Show's starting in ninety. So, let's make this quick, huh? Is it true that you, personally, failed to end the threat posed by Choraelia Torvir, a.k.a. 'Cho-Zen'? Well? (Actually, don't answer that.) What does your abject, brutal failure mean for your job prospects? (Don't answer that either.) Could it *be* that this is the end for you, that the last of your fumbles will finally put you out of commission for good? Or will the Big Man give you one last chance? Is that likely, I wonder?"

How dare this bipedal rodent speak to Jejune this way? The Demon bit back his wrath. "Can't you see the state I find myself in? Get me someone to eat. Then we'll talk."

"Waste valuable human resources on the likes of you? No. No, I don't think so. Actually, isn't it funny? I was just thinking how *funny* it is that the tables have reversed."

"Turned."

"What?"

"'The tables have *turned*,' you mean."

Sonnenkarl blinked. "An-y-way. Used to be, I was the one begging favors from you. Do you remember that? When I was a page, doing coffee runs for you? Abducting homeless people for you to rip open? And, now, here we are, with *you* in *my* house. What turn of events, do you suppose, led to this circumstance?"

"Shut up already," growled Jejune. He had to stay in control. Had to. Ah, but if only he were a little stronger, he would have torn Sonnenkarl and his quizzical smirk into irretrievably tiny bits. Wrath oozed from the Demon's wounds, slipped between his angular fangs. "Simpering ape. In my day, I'd have—"

"But, isn't it clear that this isn't your day anymore? Why, if it were still your day, we'd all be surrendering to the Ozari rebels by now, wouldn't we? No, I don't need you to speak. I need you to listen. What's it going to take for you and the rest of the old guard to realize that you've had your time?"

Thoroughly done, Jejune shoved past him, sliming the talk show host's slightly-too-short-and-tight sleeves.

"Hang on. There *was* something else," said Sonnenkarl. "A message I'm meant to deliver. Seems your antics have made some waves with management."

Jejune stopped. "They're reviewing the case?"

"This case, and several of your priors, sure."

"Looking for... what, exactly?"

Sonnenkarl shrugged. "Connections? Who can imagine the Scholars' motivations? I'm just the man they pay to ask questions. So, Jejune, what did you expect? That girl you couldn't take care of? Do you have any idea how much of a threat she could become to the Order? Did you stop to think *for a second* about the wellbeing of our entire operation? Without us, civilization will collapse. But you don't care. You only care about you. See, me? I'm all about family. And, the family is concerned. Have you seen what the Torvir punk's been up to lately? You haven't? Well, you must have been under a rock the last few weeks because they're calling her 'Primarch' and giving her armies. If it were left to you, she'd somehow be queen of the world by now. Luckily, it's *not* anymore. Up to you, that is."

Knowing Sonnenkarl to be a man in love with his own mediocrity, Jejune decided to humble himself. "I can fix this."

"No, no, no. Management disagrees, and who would I be to disagree with their disagreement? Besides, quarterly reviews are in, and you've been swept out. I'm the guy they called in to close up after the disasters you left behind, Jejune. I won't call myself 'hero,' but, really, who better to be a fixer than the number-one-rated-host and The Capital's sweetheart—Mr. Fix? (Don't answer that; I'm talking about me.)"

"Your claims mean nothing. Without an official memorandum, you're only—"

"Oh, you mean this?" From his breast pocket, Sonnenkarl pulled a crumpled envelope.

Jejune recognized the cursive immediately. "Lord Omadan?"

"Straight from. Handwritten."

"Terminated…" The Demon imagined his essence, wracked upon the wheel of souls, stretched until it tore—to be consumed, bleeding, by Great Elwoch. He could accept this fate. There was much honor in feeding the Master.

"You're not being let go, Jejune. Just demoted."

"De…mo…ted?" Staggering, Jejune spun in that narrow hallway like a rat trapped in a bucket. Facing the man, he fell to his many knees (well, knee-like joints). "I entreat you, Sonnenkarl. I beg! Intercede on my behalf. You—you owe me. Yes, I've—"

"Listen, pal, buddy. It's out of my hands. If an exception was made for you, where would it end? Huh? Would we have to forgive all the blasphemers against Elwoch, give them pats on the back, and send them on their way? Maybe write them all fat checks for their trouble because everyone deserves a fair shake? If we went around pardoning all the radical, anti-El activists out there (like you're suggesting we should), we'd be bankrupt before noon tomorrow. Before you know it, those anarcho-atheists would be running rampant, spreading false gospel, holding high court as our eternal empire burned to cinders, and we'd all be out on the streets, out of jobs too—all because we had to make an exception for poor old Nergali-irra'cuthirgal, a.k.a Mr. Jejune."

"What in the Seventy-Seven *Hells* are you on about?" In that moment, Jejune changed his mind. If his only salvation lay in the hands of Sonnenkarl, he'd accept damnation with two thumbs up.

Sonnenkarl smiled as if he'd just defecated in his neighbor's well. "Let me dumb it down for you, old-timer: do you honestly think I'd do anything to save you, even if I could?"

Pincers poised, venomous stingers extending, Jejune lunged for the kill. He bore down on the puny man with all the speed and might his failing body still possessed.

Sonnenkarl slapped the letter against Jejune's thorax, and the Demon was immediately paralyzed. Then his flesh caught fire, plumes of white smoke curling like horns from his sizzling, gristly frame. He tried to retreat, but the parcel anchored him. So, he burned, and could do nothing.

"Demons." Sonnenkarl snickered. "Aren't you just so predictable? You only have the one mode, doncha? Trapped by your own vices, see? But, me? Well, I'm a real boy. I'm the future. And I can be anything I want. Never send an ageless parasite to do a man's job, I guess? Hah!" Fingers flapping up and down, opening and closing like a puppet's mouth, he added, "'Please, please. It's not fair.' You sound like all the other inferior scum, always complaining when they should be thanking their lucky stars that the Order is willing to protect them from terrorists like Cho-Zen. Your problem? You got too comfortable with luxuries, Jejune. I'm different, a man of the people. Are you worried, Jejune? Don't be. You had your chance, didn't you? But now it's our turn. The Order of the Enlightened has shielded civilization from the darkness since the beginning of time. I think we are ready for one little girl playing dress up. Even if you weren't."

"Talk all you like." Despite the stink of his cooking flesh, Jejune laughed. "You weren't down there, human. You didn't see Cho-Zen's allies. I did."

"A gaggle of handicapped vets led by a child? Why, whatever will we do?"

"Careful now. One of the *Rel'ia'tuakr* you are not, but your sin may come to rule you yet. Had you faced the Adversary as I have, you would indeed be afraid."

"Aw. Are you scared, buddy?"

"Yes, for I have felt *her* arrival. As a great rippling, she brings with her the illimitable dark." Pieces of him flaked away as wisps of white ash.

Sonnenkarl pressed harder, and the paper's flame grew. Ash burrowed into Jejune's flesh like ticks. The Demon cried out, and the man said, "Do you expect me to quiver because of your superstitions? 'Illimitable dark'? What, are you suggesting she's—"

"The Dragon?" Jejune's laughter, a distorted warble, could just as easily have been a stuttering scream. Most of him had burned away now; the ash of his own destroyed corporeal form choked him.

"Are you finished yet?" Sonnenkarl snapped.

"Almost. But I go in bliss, for I will revel in your failure," Jejune rasped. His cocoon of ash collapsed on itself, a cloud of the stuff wafting outward, coating the walls.

The letter from management crumbled into black flakes in Sonnenkarl's hand, which he wiped on his too-short pant leg. A puddle of gelatinous essence—all that remained of Jejune—began to evaporate. Sonnenkarl covered his mouth.

Backing away, he pulled out his phone and tapped number 5 on his speed-dial. "Yeah? Mr. Head Janitor or whatever? You speak Ellish? Great. Gonna need a clean-up team on the 50th. That's right. Yes, *another one*. Were you hired to yap or to scrub? You got fifteen minutes. Chop-chop." He hung up. Then he straightened his bow-tie, ran a hand through his helmet-like brown hair, and strode into the studio to prepare for another ten-hour day of delivering the highest quality infotainment money could buy.

Steering a trolley of industrial grade sanitizers and stain removers through the hallway, a dozen cleaners in hazmat suits arrived and got to work.

Sonnenkarl tapped his foot. Soon they'd finished, and he was left alone—in a spotless, freshly-painted hallway—with his thoughts. As he reminded himself that hundreds of millions of fans tuned in to his show every day, tuned in to see and hear *him*, his faithful crew arrived.

The stage was prepped. Lights, camera, and...

He focused on the red light as the countdown began.

"We're live in five, four, three…"

Like an animatronic doll at a haunted carnival, he turned on. "Good morning, Assets of the Empire! Boy, oh *boy*, have we got a great and historic show for you to-day. In a short while, the pure-hearted and purely delightful Sanzynna will be joining us to promote her newest chart-topping album *Author of My Life, I Am Your Instrument*. But, first, our top story in our long-time recurring segment 'They're At It Again.'" He paused for the graphic of a faceless mob of torch- and pitchfork-wielding rioters to scamper past on-screen. "Well, folks, there's no easy way to say this. Outrage in the streets as the rebel government in the Seventh Stack of Ozar *barely* holds onto power. Casualties of this disturbing coup are estimated in the tens of thousands, and rising astronomically every day. To make matters worse, in a sick, demented move, these cowardly, pro-Aelf terrorists have taken countless hostages—effectively using Gods-fearing Assets of El, just like you and me, as human shields. Our hearts go out to the many, many loved ones of these hostages, who no doubt are desperate for relief from this waking night-mare." He stared earnestly into the camera. "Listen, folks. I want you to know that, even with these dark times we find ourselves in, we here at *Patriot's Watch*, well, we are 'Watching Your Back.' And I promise you this"—lowering his voice, speaking intimately—"your Authority will keep you safe. Law and order will pre-vail, never fear. The righteous will triumph because we are protected by the Gods and each other. Together, we will wipe this stain from our world." Louder again: "In just a few minutes, we'll have 'Operation Ozari Liberation' front line com-mander, General Ishonz, on for an exclusive interview—after a word from our sponsors."

During commercial breaks, normally, Sonnenkarl switched off. Micro-breaks kept him able to go, go, go all day, seven days per week. But, today, he was restless; the tattoo on the underside of his tongue itched. He hadn't felt this excited in a long time.

Someone powdered his face. He switched on again for the cameras.

He interviewed Sanzynna, pretended to be impressed by the animal trainer's monkey, and discussed the impending success of The Authority's campaign against the Ozari rebellion.

All the while, in the back of his mind—just like the motivational podcasters had instructed—he visualized success: his fingers, crushing Cho-Zen's stubby little throat.

At the end of the broadcast, Sonnenkarl retreated to his dressing room to wash off his makeup. When he was sure the crew and superfans had left for the day, he locked the door. He walked over to his closet full of too-small suits and identical red bow ties, and he shut that door as well.

He waited a few seconds, feeling the crackle of energy pass through him and into the handle as he opened it again. On the other side of the portal, there now awaited a very different scene. He stepped through into the vault beneath the mountain.

In that great chamber, under the colossal statues of Thaal and Kuura, he greeted his colleagues—souls from all over the world, from all manner of places and times—and found his assigned seat. Numbering one hundred and fifty-four in all, they sat in a big circle, smiling and nodding at each other.

The Scholars convened, intoning a prayer to the Enlightened One, to Elwoch. Even the new girl—Ivion—was there, dark circles under her eyes, looking like she'd seen a ghost. What a sweetheart. Sonnenkarl knew firsthand how tiring ambition could be. Good for her, by the way, stealing old Wodjaego's spot. Certainly, the Enlightened could use more of that kind of initiative; it was only natural for the young and sturdy to replace the old and brittle. (He thought, once more, of Jejune and chuckled.) Speaking of *old and brittle*, the Ridect brothers took their seats and proceeded to frown judgmentally at just about everyone else present. High-and-mighty, senile codgers. Look at them, sucking all the life right out of the room.

The meeting was called to order.

Lord Omadan took the floor, wild black hair tied back in a tail that brushed his ankles, his open robes exposing the slash of white scar tissue that ran from his collarbone to his navel—his death-scar.

Muttering broke out. Omadan hardly ever spoke, and never first.

"Settle, children. Settle. We have a critical first item on today's agenda." He raised his hand, and all chatter immediately ceased. Beside him appeared the full-sized, shimmering, magical image of a young woman in a long black cloak, the tips of her graying hair touched with remnants of red. Underarm, she carried a crimson crow mask.

Someone near Sonnenkarl stage-whispered, "That's her."

"A unique adversary has slithered its way up from forgotten depths." Omadan snapped his fingers, and the image transformed from woman into gray-fleshed, razor-feathered behemoth. "The topic of the day—" He smiled— "is Dragonslaying."

Alina, Cho, and company will return in

THE AELFRAVER TRILOGY BOOK III

THE RUIN

ELEMENTAL GLOSSARY

For more lore of the world of El, visit *blankbooklibrary.com*.

Achemir, The –

> *... For it is written that,*
> *one day, the Achemir*
> *shall wreak vengeance upon the world*
> *in the name of the enslaved/created,*
> *whose champion/undoing shall be*
> *master of eight,*
> *killer of death*

Prank or prophecy, these words became the death-knell of a destroyed race. Many Iorian legends are well-documented; by contrast, this one survives as a single four-thousand-year-old scrawl memorializing the lost hopes of a damned civilization—graffiti, knife-etched into walls by the shaky hands of ritually blinded priests, even as their empire crumbled around them.

Aelf (also, "Others" or "Nobles") – A blanket term denoting all those creatures that are neither human nor animal. Each species is endowed with a magical attribute. Over millennia, human scholars and hunters have organized the Aelf into nine distinct categories: Liliskur, Raccitan, Uardini, Mythidim, Legionari, Collosi, Ushum, Demidivines, and Uult.

Aelfraver (a/k/a "Raver"; archaic: "Reaper of Elves" or "Reaver") – Those whose profession it is to hunt the Aelf. The term "Aelfraver" is an adaptation of the poetic "Reaper of Elves." Originally, it was believed that all Aelf were the magical creations of the Elves, an assumption proven false centuries ago. The name "Aelf," however, has survived scholarly correction.

There are a wide variety of private training programs designed to transform a young mage into an Aelfraver. However, anyone seeking to become a full-fledged member of the profession must take the grueling final exam at The Gild-hall in New El. Only then may one (legally) hunt Aelf for pay.

Aetherthreads – The state-run and state-monitored information network that facilitates all manner of digital communication, from sharing images with friends via digimail to tracking the real-time location of every single Asset of El. It is common knowledge that, using the Virtual Intelligence "ViiCter" (see below), The Authority keeps a close eye on the everyday activities of everyday people via this medium. For this reason, some have turned to the "Darkthreads" (see below) as a means of avoiding unwanted attention.

Anarkey – Ozar-native, anti-Elemental terrorists. Their base of operations is believed to be located on the Sixth Stack, though they have launched attacks throughout Authority-controlled Ozar. Violence is the first and last resort of these militant partisans. Xenophobic fanatics, they are suicidally devoted to their "divine" patrons, the Hextarchs.

Auggie (a/k/a "Licksy" a/k/a "Ability Augmentation Elixir") – Alchemical concoctions created through a blending of the medical and arcane arts. Only a mage can brew an Augmentation Elixir. The severity of the effect (and side-effects) depends on the strength of the brew and the ingredients used. Generations of trial and error resulted in many failed attempts and deaths—often by disintegration of the skeletal system, liquification of the muscles, or spontaneous human combustion. However, after many sacrifices, a wide variety of performance enhancing drugs have been engineered, the most common of which are: *Corpraega* (enhances the drinker's physical capabilities); *Synethesial* (allows the drinker to taste or smell colors or see/hear smells); *Chronolastic* (stretches time from the perspective of the drinker, elongating one second into ten, or a minute into two, depending on the strength of the brew); and *Chronomora* (alters the drinker for corporeal movement through time).

Author of Creation, The – The One True God according to the doctrines of The Sanctum, a rapidly growing religion whose principal place of worship is the Mountain of the Mendicant in downtown New El. Overseen by the Hierophant Pontifex Ridect, the zealous adherents of The Author (called "Sanctumites") have done their utmost to spread their beliefs—both in New El and in the Twelve Provinces. In three short centuries, their work has grown the organization from a marginal cult, worshipping an esoteric and long-forgotten deity, to an officially recognized religion with ties to many major political families (within the Nation of El and abroad).

Authority, The – Organized in 1630 in the wake of political unrest in Cantus (just seven years after it was conquered by El), The Authority was created in order to suppress riots and maintain control of the Nation of El's contemporary acquisitions of territory and resources. Having grown in influence over the centuries, The Authority presently boasts headquarters in every major city within El (and many outside it). A special division of The Authority, the Jaandarmes (also called "Dragoons") serves the Consul personally as a private security and police force.

Bane of New El – A creature of unknown origin and ability, responsible for the slaughter of several members of the Xaveyr and Reautz Families (and other members of the minor nobility) in 3502. Though the beast is believed to have been a Draaken-class Aelf, this detail has yet to be confirmed by either Authority investigators or Gild experts. Regardless, the Bane's fate is certain: it was destroyed during the "Battle of City Hall" (see below).

Battle of City Hall (a/k/a "the Pluto Panic") – In the year 3502, a ragtag mob of some 500 disgruntled Landsider Aelfravers attacked the Elemental Bank (also called "City Hall"), the seat of Plutocratic government. The Battle of City Hall, as this event came to be known, caused millions of gelders in damages and loss of life. Although The Authority valiantly defended the bank, the damage done to the structure proved irreparable, and the building was condemned and demolished. At time of writing, reconstruction plans are still in process of approval.

Despite the setback, the "Pluto Panic" has since abated. Our government remains secure. The people have been reassured by The Authority's massively successful efforts to capture the rogue Aelfravers. Additionally, the outcome of the battle led to one immensely positive result—the slaying of the so-called "Bane of New El" (see above).

Buthmertha – "Holy Buthmertha," goddess of hearth and family, patron of the lost and downtrodden, protector of orphans (see also "Gods").

Chains of El – The magic keeping New El aloft—woven by the Twin Dragon Kings—is so immensely powerful that the planetoid would drift into the cold reaches of space were it not for the three great chains tethering it to the earth: *Consortio* ("Fellowship"), *Libra* ("Balance"), and *Concordia* ("Harmony").

Chronology, Elemental – In El, time is counted from the slaying of the Twin Dragon Kings—that day beginning the year 0. The year as of this tale is 3504 "After El" (A.E.). Prehistory is reckoned in years "Before El" (B.E.).
As El goes, so the world must follow: the Elemental Calendar is the international standard.

Chrononite – An element of unknown origin discovered as early as 300 B.E. by explorers of The Elder Isle. If the hieroglyphics of long-dead civilizations are to be believed, the use of Chrononite grants dominion over time, space, life, and death. Although, this has yet to be confirmed.
Upwards of 99% of the world's Chrononite supply may have been consumed in previous millennia—though, again, this comes to us from ancient, somewhat dubious sources. The means of consumption (and the reasons for it) remain unclear.

Ciirimaic – The long-dead language of the Ciirima, ancient humans predating the Elemental Empire. "Ciir" translates to "Yoked Man" or, less poetically, "slave." Records indicate that Ciirimaic originated as a pidgin of the human serfs laboring under the Twin Dragon Kings' tyrannical regime. Over time, it grew in complexity, branching into many different continental languages—Kadician, Kantusian, Sentasi, Svenian, etc. In the 36th century A.E., of all the off-shoots of Ciirimaic, Ellish is of course the dominant one. Any hope for upward mobility in Elemental business and society requires fluency in Ellish.
Curiously, evidence indicates that the written forms of Ciirimaic and Iorian (see "Iorian Precursors") share a common linguistic ancestor, albeit one forgotten to time.

Colonies of El – As the world's undisputed superpower, El commands dozens of client kingdoms, puppet monarchies, "neutral" territories, and colonies. The largest of this last category are Agadur, Glasku, Oronor, Sicacor, Tinoch, and Zinokla.

Consul – The head of the government of El and the tie-breaking vote on the Council of Plutocrats (see also "Plutocrats"). Every ten years, the Plutocrats of the Twelve Families elect from among their number the next Consul, whose servants enjoy even greater social and financial privileges.

Coven, The – The elite guard of the Hextarchs. Virtually nothing is known of the Covenants (as members of The Coven are called), their aura of mystery maintained by two factors: they are brutal, merciless killers; and, none have ever allowed themselves to be taken alive.

Darkthreads – A magically enhanced series of digital networks that feed into sub-universes maintained by a shadowy collective known only as "Gnosis." The identities and motivations of Gnosis remain a mystery, but many Assets of El have turned to the Darkthreads for transactions of all sorts, some more nefarious than others. Not *all* users of this service are career criminals, but the simple act of logging on represents a criminal offense in the eyes of The Authority. Users of the Darkthreads are often called "ThreddHedds" or "Thredders."

El, Nation of – The Capital at its heart, El is divided into twelve nearly equal-in-size Provinces, each named after its governing Family. Beginning in the north, and proceeding clockwise: Xaveyr, Ivoir, D'Hydromel, Kracht, Malach, Walazzin, Torviri, Denadon, Hruvic, Reautz, Udutetta, and Caelus.

- Xaveyr Province has as its capital the harbor city of Xalagavna, the primary port of entry for goods flowing into El from its eastern colonies. Other sources of wealth for the Xaveyr faction include desalination of seawater—fresh water being in short supply in recent decades—as well as the refining of biofuels and the processing of waste products for recycling, which happen to be two of the largest industries worldwide. Also, the Xaveyr control access to the island chains of Rudu and Tyar, forty miles off the mainland; these islands are sources of immensely valuable raw materials, such as exotic animal hides and ginger, and the importation of these resources to any part of El is *heavily* taxed by the Xaveyr.

- Ivoir Province also claims an extensive coastline, allowing it to share in the profit yielded by desalination efforts. In addition, the Ivoirs control the production of steel and—most importantly—the creation of cement, granting them the monopoly on concrete.

- Once, D'Hydromel's vast lakes practically overflowed with fish. However, in recent decades, local marine life has declined precipitously. The Provincial government adapted to this blow to the fishing industry by doubling down on its promotion of tourism. Famed for its shipbuilding (sea and air), the region is home to a multitude of museums celebrating the D'Hydromel ship-wrights, carpenters, and metalsmiths who have equipped the navy and air forces of El for centuries.

- Kracht Province is most well-known as the birthplace of numerous heroes of antiquity. In imitation of these myths, over time, many mercenary companies have sprung up. Thanks to popular, syndicated Watchbox dramas, two such mercenary bands—the Myrrevuam Company and the Iron Feet—have risen to fame. The law requiring guns-for-hire to display their weapons in plain sight (see "Plasticks") originated in this Province.

- Timber, tobacco, and several cash crops are the primary revenue sources for Malach Province. It is estimated that its vast plantations rely on the labor of three million souls—over half of whom are indentured servants working off a colossal personal debt. Most of its southwestern border is straddled by the primordial Malachi Forest, whose oldest trees predate El.

- The main product of Walazzin Province is oil, mostly used to power the oldest machines—too costly to replace, too important to ignore. This mountainous territory was once home to many rich mines of copper and silver. The mines have long-since run dry—and, with them, a great deal of the Walazzins' fortune.

- Many of Torvir Province's cities were built in the last two-hundred years—bleak, utilitarian sprawls whose main offerings to its non-wealthy residents are telecommuting jobs and illicit substances. Half of Torviri Province is immensely wealthy due to the diamond mining operations centered on the Torvirius Mountains. The other half is depressed beyond belief: in the wake of an economic boom three generations prior, rapid expansion and gentrification resulted; new money flooded into the cities and towns, pushing the locals off their land—or rezoning their districts to include landfills, fully automated factories, and toxic waste dump sites. When the Torvir Family fell from grace, the lesser nobility and industrial magnates moved on; their economic and social impacts, however, proved to be permanent.

- Denadon Province is home to the four largest industrial agribusiness giants the world has ever seen. Millions upon millions of heads of cattle, chickens, pigs, and other farm animals are born, raised, and slaughtered there. Without a doubt, the Denadon Family holds the key to the nation's pantry.

- In Hruvic Province, textiles are produced with the highest degree of efficiency using the cotton and synthetic fabrics sourced from Ciuriath, its capital. (Most of the wool it processes, however, comes from the animals of Denadon.) The HQ of Goga Drop is also housed in this province, the corporation being a subsidiary of the Hruvic branch of ELCORP. At the last corporate census, Goga boasted 17 million Employee Assets (counting part- and full-time).

- The Province of Reautz has two claims to fame. Firstly, the massive and untamable Denudrevic Forest that it shares with Hruvic and Denadon attracts many adventurous college students each spring break. Secondly, in the remote Tzur Valley is housed the single most crucial supercomputer cluster in El: the official backup mainframe, the failsafe in case of massive data breach of the nation's communication and financial networks, under heavy guard by the most elite soldiers. It is common knowledge that these computers are in Tzur, but the last prankster to get within three miles of the military compound was obliterated by drone-strike within thirty seconds.

- Udutetta owns by far the most significant marble, quartz, amethyst, topaz, and tourmaline mines in the world—with the exception of Zinokla. From the 1300s to the 1900s, this Province's metalsmiths outfitted the soldiers of El with arms and armor of the finest steel (using iron mined in Torvir, refined in Ivoir, and forged in Udutetta). Now, this Province's most important contribution to the GDP of ELCORP is its pioneering research into and production of cutting-edge bionic organs, limbs, and other vital human components. These revolutionary products have saved millions of lives, both Authority and Asset, and are the result of research related to the short-lived but destructive Androids—a product line that ended with the Android Revolt of 3445.

ELCORP – The corporate-political mega conglomerate that owns, operates, and profits from almost all the doings of the Nation of El. In many ways, EL-CORP and El are indistinguishable from one another, as the masters of one are the masters of both: the Twelve Families own ninety-nine percent of the company's shares, and the Plutocrats (selected by each of the Families) also serve as board members of ELCORP.

Elemental(s) – The name for the inhabitants of New El, a reminder of their privileged status as dwellers of the sky.

Elemental Bank, The – Formerly, the biggest bank in the world and seat of government of the Nation of El, located on Pluto Plaza, Divitia District, New El. It was commonly called "City Hall" because, from the twelfth floor of its clocktower, the selected Consuls serving on the Council of Plutocrats weighed, measured, and controlled the business of the country. The Elemental Bank was the political and economic heart of ELCORP—until it was destroyed in 3502 (see "Battle of City Hall"). Since then, members of the Council have conducted their affairs via telecommunication, from the safety of their mansions or undisclosed locations.

Gild, The – The premier, government-sanctioned school for the study of magic and the Aelf, founded in 1507 A.E. It is also the international organization responsible for licensing and policing all Aelfravers, all over the world. Headquartered in The Capital, its first Grandmaster was Uzimsar Kwurdla.

Gildhall, The – The headquarters of the foremost school wherein aspiring Aelfravers are taught the theoretical and practical aspects of their trade. Located in the Perium District of New El, The Gildhall is the only institution legally permitted to administer the Aelfraver licensing test. It is comprised of six distinct structures set within two layers of isosceles-triangle-shaped walls: the Azurite Alchamer, the Iron Wheel, the Stone Keep, the Adamantine Manor, the Labradorite Dome, and the Crystallarium.

Gods – Of the seventy-seven sanctioned deities, twelve chief gods and goddesses make up the most widely worshipped pantheon in El: Plutonia, Buthmertha, Caï-ana-eïa, Daïshr-og, Ononsareth, Ka-Yehrost, Yarilo, Sulla Mazdahur, Nninithin, Rinakvi, Skrymga, and Zo. Official Elemental Doctrine dictates that Plutonia, the Goddess of Fortune, is the head of the pantheon.

Only a handful of divinities are specifically outlawed, including Ëétion (primarily worshipped by the seminomadic Kadician desert-dwellers) and Mydras'shymm (ancestor-god of the Ozari).

Hextarchs, The – Six living gods of a dying nation, the Hextarchs govern the affairs of the Seventh and Sixth Stacks of Ozar, an underground City-State locked in war with El. According to reputation, the Hextarchs are immortal and omnipotent. However, it has been centuries since any but the Covenants have laid eyes on them. This fact leads many to question whether Ozar's theocracy has already crumbled from within. Poised to conquer the final Stack, The Authority will soon have the answer.

H'ranajaan – Perhaps the most awe-inspiring reminder of The Authority was H'ranajaan—the Machinamantically powered, artificial dragon. It had watched over The Capital for a century before its untimely destruction at the hands of dissident Landsider Aelfravers during the "Battle of City Hall" (see above).

Iingrid – It moniker short for "Integrated Intelligence National Grid," Iingrid is the built-in organizational assistant in most Asset-use personal mobile devices.

Iorian Precursors – Before humanity arose to primacy, before the apocalyptic rule of the Twin Dragon Kings, the Iorian Empire was the world's sole super power. The Iorians were a barbaric, bloodthirsty, backstabbing brood of Mythidim Aelf, employing their sentience in cunning self-aggrandizement. Their civilization was watered with the blood of their neighbors (and built on the backs of the earliest humans). Once there were no more worlds to conquer, they naturally turned on each other. Some have claimed their fall a cautionary tale from which modern humanity could stand to learn.

Independent Raver Schools – Aelfraver training facilities officially recognized by the government but not directly affiliated with The Gild (see above).

Landsider – The more politically correct term to distinguish between Elementals (sky-dwelling natives of The Capital, New el) and everyone else.

Maggo (see also "Magic") – A widely used informal term for "Mage"; an individual possessed of magical ability.

Magic – Studied throughout the world by every human culture, magic is divided into eight principal Disciplines (and sixteen sub-disciplines):

- Terramancy
    - Geomancy
    - Phytomancy
- Aquamancy
    - Lacomancy
    - Tempetamancy
- Machinamancy
    - Engeniomancy
    - Partumancy
- Revomancy
    - Somniomancy
    - Somnexiomancy
- Deïmancy
    - Divinumancy
    - Daemoniomancy
- Ignimancy
    - Caloramancy
    - Conflagramancy
- Caelomancy
    - Luxomancy
    - Umbramancy
- Corpromancy
    - Necromancy
    - Zoiimancy

Misckie – Informal: a "miscreant" and/or "committer of miscellaneous crimes and misdemeanors"; worn as a badge of honor by the ne'er-do-wells of impolite society.

National Anthem of El, unabridged –

Dragons' blood,
Dragons' blood

At dawn we bathe in Dragons' blood

Scale the chains, leap the walls
Through wind and hail and fiery rain,
By wetted blades, through cracking halls,
Ascend, arise, and bleed your veins
Or die as crawling, wretched thralls
Awash in Dragons' blood, for Dragons' pains;

A thousand men, a thousand more
By curse of mage and spear erased;
It cannot be as was before:
A stair of bone and flesh is raised
Each yard is earned by comrades' gore—
'Tis Dragons' blood they thirsted for

And, in hell, they bathe in Dragons' blood;
Dragons' blood,
In hell they bathe in Dragons' blood...

Blades now pierce both hide and scale
Look ye on, ye cowards—Knaves!
There, winged tyrants flag and fail,
Now trampled by the heels of slaves;
Upon our spears, cruel hearts impaled;
Ichor flows in darkest waves

From ruin, liberty attest,
A temple to our rage we lift
And when we lastly go to rest
Shall rule the Twelve, our virtue's gift;
Champions risen at gods' behest,
Their strikes were true, their smitings swift

Glory be, 'twas they first spilled the Dragons' blood,
Dragons' blood,
'Twas they first spilled the Dragons' blood

Fear not the dark nor wicked things
Ye fledgling sky-born child of El;
Fear not the claws, nor fangs, nor wings,
For, tested 'gainst all shades of hell,
Thy princedom earned by bow and sling,

Was quenchèd in that deepest well

Where, in the dark, there festers still
The Dragons' blood,
Dragons' blood
There festers still the Dragon's blood

And, come the dawn, bathe we will
In Dragon's blood,
Dragon's blood
Bathe we will in Dragon's blood

Nehalennia (see also "Sanctum") – Bordered by the glassy Shearing Sea, an ocean petrified mid-storm, Nehalennia is the Promised Field of White at the center of which lies the Tower of The Author. It is a place of utmost stillness: there are no birds or beasts to cut the silence. There is no sun, the sky perpetually a blank sheaf of paper upon which The Author writes each day anew. It is His land of perfect concentration, in which all words and deeds and songs and moments are His and His alone. According to Sanctum belief, only the most righteous of the faithful are rewarded with this endless life after death, granted the privilege to wander the infinite fields, forever silently praising their Lord.

New El (see also "The Capital") – A city built upon a sphere of earth suspended ten thousand feet above sea level, the seat of power of the Twelve Families and the Capital of the Nation of El. According to legend, the planetoid and the temple atop it were constructed by legions of human slaves some four thousand years ago. It was lifted into the sky by the combined powers of the Twin Dragon Kings, the contemporary tyrant rulers of the world. Following the rebellion of the enslaved, the Dragon Kings were overthrown by the "Twelve Champions" (see below), who claimed the sky-city as their dominion, naming it "New El." The city is divided into twelve districts: Decus, Divitia, Dyrex, Esperant, Eleru, Fidae, Iuscat, Lexat, Negotopus, Perium, Tilitatem, and Triditio.

Niima (See also "Magic") – When first discovered, Niima was believed to be an internally generated essence that powers the casting of magical spells. This is partially true. Niima, in some ways, is similar to physical stamina; for example, overexertion quickly leads to exhaustion, and rest will replenish one's Niimantic reserves. Also, one's Niima pool can be expanded through stress training of the body and mind. However, there are at least two crucial differences between Niima and stamina: while everyone has some amount of physical stamina (and the capability to increase that amount), Niima is a resource possessed only by Mages; and, this energy—while created inside the body—is also present *outside* of it.

Additionally, Niima is radioactive, and, although the body of the Mage naturally regenerates cells destroyed by spell-casting, *excessive* expenditure of this energy can result in Niima Deficit Sickness (or NDS; colloquially referred to as "the Nids"). Symptoms include slower and less effective cell regeneration, leading to organ failure; accelerated cell reproduction, causing certain cancers; or, in extreme cases, instant death.

Ozar – Enemy of El, a sprawling underground city-state comprised of seven layers, called "Stacks." As the name implies, the Stacks are organized vertically, one atop the other. The Seventh and lowest of these holds Hexhall, seat of the Hextarchs' power. The Hextharchy is a theocratic government, controlled (according the heathen Ozari) by literal gods. Only accessible through a hexagonal shaft carved into the earth, Ozar is located southwest of Kadic.

Pinkojack – A derogatory term for anyone in the employ of the Elemental government, either local or national. The word refers to the standard pink sheets of paper on which the bureaucracy's physical written records are kept and "jack," which is roughly synonymous with "lapdog." Essentially, to call someone a "pinkojack" is to accuse him of utterly thoughtless servitude to the government—at the cost of his honor.

Plasticks – A blanket term for the Elemental mercenaries most often in the employ of the Twelve Families. The name derives from their habit of wearing translucent jackets, a concession to the national law forbidding soldiers of fortune from concealing their weapons (see "Nation of El, Kracht Province").

Rave – An officially sanctioned hunt of a specific Aelf or group thereof. The bounty for a successful "Rave" may be lawfully cashed in only by a Gild-licensed Aelfraver (also called a "Raver")—a professional hunter of Aelf.

Raver License – Students of The Gild, usually at fifteen years old, are issued a provisional Raver-T License. Following graduation, the completion of a two-year probationary period, and the successful closing of a Gild-assigned bounty, this Raver-T License is replaced by a Raver-X, which designates the owner as a full-fledged Aelfraver. The third type of License, and by far the most difficult to acquire, is the Raver-S. Only through extraordinary service to The Gild, or by becoming a high-ranking member thereof, may a Raver-S License be granted. Even then, the matter is put to a vote by the Council of Masters. The top *quarter* of one percent of Aelfravers are the proud owners of Raver-S Licenses, and as such they enjoy untold benefits throughout the nation—merchant discounts, free meals in many restaurants, corporate sponsorships, and more.

Revoscape, The – Realm of dreams and the dreamer; a liminal space to which the sentient imagination applies physicality, but which has no heft whatsoever. Practitioners of Revomancy being so rare, reliable information about this extra-terrestrial dimension is exceedingly unreliable—and almost solely the purview of science fiction peddlers.

Sanctum, The – An organized religion devoted to The Author of Creation, whose members are called "Sanctumites." Having drastically increased in popularity over the past three centuries, Sanctum hierarchy is as follows (from least to greatest importance):

- Porters, who walk the streets and spread the word
- Lectors, who organize and command the Porters
- Exorcists, who slay infidels
- Acolytes, who oversee the operations of the entire church
- … and The Hierophant himself, whose word is synonymous with the Lord's

Sisters, The – According to Gild records, centuries ago, "The Sisters" were the tools of the Revomancer, taking the form of a cloak and mask—*Rego* and *Ida*, respectively (terms which, in Ciirimaic, translate to "control" and "chaos"). A notoriously mysterious and esoteric art, Revomancy is a discipline of duality, ex-emplified by the contradictory natures of its tools. Graduates of The Gild's Revomancy program have long-since shed the archaic practice of utilizing "The Sisters," relying on their hard-won skills rather than mysticism.

Terrie – A pejorative abbreviation of "Terrestrial," used by Elementals to reinforce the social divide between themselves and those born and raised on the earth below New El.

Twelve Champions – Leaders of the human rebellion against the Twin Dragon Kings, they became the founding fathers of the Nation of El. Their descendants—the Twelve Families—helm the Plutocracy, a government that has held firm for more than three and a half millennia (see below).

Twelve Families – a/k/a **The Plutocrats** – The descendants of the Twelve Champions who led humanity to victory against the Aelf and the Twin Dragon Kings more than 3,500 years ago. Ever since, El has been led by the representatives chosen from each of the favored Twelve Families.

The **sigils** and *mottos* of the noble Twelve Families are as follows:

1. Xaveyr – **Midnight-blue dragon pierced by a white spear on a field of lavender**; *"Victory is Ours"*
2. Ivoir – **White tower on a field of black, crested by three white stars**; *"Through Knowledge, Transcendence"*
3. Malach – **Red, three-branched tree on a field of green**; *"From Deep Roots"*
4. D'Hydromel – **Three white ships on a sea of green and blue**; *"Tested by the Storm"*
5. Walazzin – **Gold lion, rampant, on a crimson field**; *"Piety, Humility, Honor"*
6. Kracht – **A red net and spear on a black field, crossed with crimson slashes**; *"Death Spurns Us"*
7. Torvir – **On a field of cobalt, two bright orange dragons, entwined above a crossed orange hammer and key**; *"Ours Shall Endure"*
8. Hruvic – **Purple hornet, stinger poised, on a field of gray**; *"Beware My Sting"*
9. Caelus – **A gold chisel and sword, crossing on a sky-blue field**; *"Heaven's Fury Unveiled"*
10. Udutteta – **Upon white field, a red hammer and anvil, crowned in yellow flames**; *"Harder than Steel"*
11. Reautz – **Three emerald wolves' heads on a field of checkered black-and-dark-green**; *"The Pack Prevails"*

12. Denadon – **Yellow scythe above a boar's head, on a tan field**; *"Eternal Bounty"*

ViiCter – Like Iingrid, ViiCter ("Virtual Intelligence Interface Control Terminal") is an Integrated Intelligence. Unlike Iingrid, however, ViiCter is military-grade, possessed of both vastly greater capabilities and responsibilities. The hub of operating software built into all government devices, it polices El's information network (see "Aetherthreads"), industrial and financial sectors, supply chains, national defense, and more.

Zero-One – The "splitting" of one's consciousness into (usually) two pieces, the larger part controlling the physical body while the smaller interfaces with nearby smart devices. This separation results in the "Hackerdox," the simultaneous experiencing of two different rates of time.

Zinokla (see also "Colonies of El") – In many ways the breadbasket of the Elemental Empire, Zinokla's plantations and farms have claimed millions of lives over the past several centuries. Historically, most plantation workers succumbed to some combination of exhaustion, disease, dehydration, and malnutrition. As their population dwindled to dangerously low levels, the local Zinoklese were granted exemption from working on the El's plantations. The Plutocracy, accordingly, instituted a humane solution: the use of prison labor.

Those serving time for serious and/or violent crimes were commonly presented with a choice: remain in prison for the full duration of their sentence, or work in Zinokla (reducing said sentence by up to half its length). Many took the offer, a practice colloquially called "getting Zinokled"; almost none of them survived the full term of their contract.

Today, machinery has largely replaced both colonial and prison labor. However, individuals designated as "special cases" by The Authority—traitors, usually— are still "Zinokled" from time to time.

BESTIARY

The nine types of Aelf, ranked by threat-level, from lowest to highest:

1. Liliskur
2. Raccitan
3. Uardini
4. Mythidim
5. Legionari
6. Collosi
7. Ushum
8. Demidivines
9. Uult

Below are described each of these categories and examples thereof.

Liliskur – Sometimes called "Worms" due to this category's including only non-sentient and (relatively) harmless species.

- *Chernoboggle* – Barely even a nuisance, *chernoboggles* are miniscule parasitic creatures that feed on the dreams of humans and, sometimes, animals. Long believed to be myth, the existence of *chernoboggles* was proven in 1778 in what has been called the first-ever sleep study.

- *Filcher* – Prehensile-tongued, many-limbed creatures with a penchant for pilfering jewelry and other portable metallic items. The *filcher* derives sustenance from metals, consuming some unknown component thereof (and, in the process, rusting and degrading the material itself). Studies have yet to show how this occurs—or what, exactly, the *filcher* is "eating."

- *Jittuch* – A mysterious creature native to the Revoscape, appearing in our world only while it is asleep. Since capturing a *Jittuch* before it wakes (and returns to the ether) is nearly impossible, only one successful study has been conducted on them. The *Jittuch* are furry, glowing white "worm clusters." Each cluster is believed to number between ten to fifty of these "worms," all of which share a single consciousness and body-sense. They move in perfect concert, a fact proven time and again by how quickly and synchronously they disappear from our plane of existence.

- *Ka'a'tee* – Commonly known as "Katy Tears" because of their distinctive mewls (*"Kay-tee, kay-tee"*), the *ka'a'tee* evolved over the centuries to appear nearly indistinguishable from feral cats. Their harmless appearance provides them a significant advantage when hunting their preferred prey—cats and dogs. The fur of a *ka'a'tee* is most often black or orange, leading to a great deal of superstition concerning breeds of actual cats bearing the same coloration. The most notable feature of the *ka'a'tee*, however, is its ability to teleport across short distances—between one and thirty feet—allowing it to quickly climb or escape even the most treacherous areas with ease.

- *Marlok* – Known for their strong herd instincts, when spotted in the wild, the *marlok* can frequently be seen migrating in a wedge formation—safety in numbers.

- *Pevool* – A rainbow-colored, shiny-plumed bird, long extinct. Historical record indicates the *pevools'* temperament was unusually effervescent for a species of Aelf.

- *Vippersnüp* – Winged, omnivorous, meerkat-like. Most frequently sighted in larger human towns and cities, especially those of the northern hemisphere and on the waterfront, these creatures scavenge human offal, and they are able to metabolize everything from banana peels to plastic containers.

Raccitan – This category belongs to the small-to-medium-sized pack-hunters and other dangerous Aelf-fauna—be they clawed or spiked, flying or land-bound.

- *Einharthrak* – A white-furred dire wolf native to icy mountaintops. Fire is its principal weapon against its rivals, its prey, and its frigid environment. With its lightweight skeletal system and flying-squirrel-like skin flaps, the *einharthrak* can also glide from rock to rock. Because of the relative flimsiness of its bones, this beast hunts in large numbers for safety and prefers to run its prey to exhaustion before closing in for the kill.

- *Hrilliuk* – A dog-sized, rotund herbivore able to launch heat-seeking spines from its back when threatened. In small doses, the paralytic venom coating the darts is non-lethal. However, anyone foolish enough to hold their ground after being pierced by a *hrilliuk's* spines will receive a second—fatal—volley.

- *Iurk'et* – A slow, lumbering beast that walks on four legs, the *iurk'et* grow to a height of four to five feet. Each of the three "mouths" on its bulbous head performs a specific function: the first ingests and masticates food; the second blasts super-heated steam capable of melting flesh to the bone in under a second; and, the third passes excrement—highly toxic and acidic.

- *Hyndun* – A legless lizard native to deserts and steppes. A small dose of its venom could kill an elephant in less than a minute.
- *Onshorun* – The saber-toothed, camouflaging bats found in and around the cavernous reaches of Ozar.
- *Quixiil* – Two feet tall and beaked.
- *Utch-Aharan* – Also known as "Kadician war dogs," these long, lean, and powerful desert beasts are synonymous with Kadician religious iconography of the Grand Dynastic Period.

Uardini – Spirits of forests, mountains, lakes, and rivers, the Uardini are as varied as the natural world.

- *Gighifnol* – Dwellers of the briny depths, the *gighifnol* protect their amber or orange exoskeletons with chalk shells—natural armor which they themselves construct. Resembling crustaceans, they have several primary limbs and sets of mandibles, and many smaller "arms" running the length of their abdomens up to their necks.
- *Fyarda* – Also called "Moon Dryads," this species was romanticized by Ellish novelists of the Nouveau View Movement. The *Fyarda's* popular depiction as noble, melancholic savages takes inspiration from their tradition of ancestor- and tree-worship. They are a unique hybrid of flora and fauna. Accordingly, their offspring are not born but *grown*. It has, however, been centuries since a *Fyardan* "budling" has been captured and studied. This fact, coupled with the lack of adult *Fyarda* sightings in recent decades, has led the scientific community to surmise that this species teeters on the precipice of extinction.
- *J'kugn* – According to ancient Cantusian texts, it was once common practice for powerful warriors to bind, inside special stone totems, the souls of those they had slain in battle. Carved from living rock, the totems would be placed on their property to protect their homes and families while they were off fighting. Should intruders cross the threshold, the spirits of the dead would awaken, take the form of indigo tigers with red eyes, and fight ferociously until every enemy was killed—or every warding stone was shattered.
- *Paoph* – Toad-like creatures with flat backs, the *paoph* stack themselves upon one another for warmth and safety. Native to swamplands, they are fiercely territorial.

- *Raea* – A species made extinct during the Extermination War. The only hints at the appearance and characteristics of the *Raea* survive in song and ancient temples. Some stories claimed they were formless air spirits; others provided a far less flattering sketch of lumpy, sightless, squawking chickens missing their feathers—clumsy, oafish things reeking of fish and blood.

- *Vlindra* – A giant moth-like creature native to the deciduous forests of eastern Kadic. It sheds once per year, its husks sought after for their powerful neurotoxin used in most pest control. Touching the husk with one's bare hands can lead to hallucinations, followed by a messy death (usually within minutes). A *Vlindra* that has freshly shed emits spores that cause blindness when inhaled in even trace amounts.

- *Yuspinggr* – Sentient light beings taking the form of glimmering orbs or, seldomly, humanoid outlines. Frequenting forests, jungles, and bogs, they delight in leading unwary travelers into quicksand and other natural dangers.

Mythidim – Sentient. Terrible. Cruel. Cunning. These are a few of the politest descriptors of the Mythidim.

  o *Crûb* – Preferring to dwell in areas with high yearly precipitation or, failing that, damp caves, the *Crûb* are amphibious humanoids. They shun sunlight, rendering their flesh milk-pale. Slightly shorter, on average, than humans, these hairless, saucer-eyed creatures have no known verbal language. How—of if—they can "talk" to one another is unclear. Any contact with outsiders involves a complex somatic communication system—hand signs, in which the angle of the elbow and bend of the knee serve as indicators of inflection and emotion.

  - *Elves* – From the Elves, humankind derived the term "Aelf," which eventually came to be associated will all non-human, non-animal denizens of the world. This was most likely due to the Elves' being the most visible and cleverest foes of early humanity. The Elves are divided into two subspecies: *Iorian* ("Children of the Stars") and *Rioan* ("Children of the Deep")

  - *Lords and Ladies* – Animated by an ethereal inner glow, these spirits are "born" in places that have endured a high concentration of suffering and death—battlefields, for example. Also called Widows-grief, the Lords and Ladies may appear as beautiful humans wearing nightclothes or the attire of a noble man or woman, but they are nothing more than hungry sprites feeding upon the echoes of human pain. With their mind-altering magics, these beings are able to naturally confuse and lead astray the careless battlefield historian or graveyard walker. Such field trips often prove hazardous.

- *Pycts* – The Pycts range in height from seven to eleven inches. Their features are distinct: they have dragonfly-like wings, mouse-like faces, badger-like claws, and goat-like hooves. The males' fur is most often a shade cobalt or navy blue, while the females' is silver or gold. The Pycts' social structure is tribal, each tribe aware of others but entirely self-sufficient. The tribe is typically comprised of between twenty and one hundred individuals. Possessed of a hive-mind, these sentient Aelf have developed a most peculiar trait: if not eliminated all at once (within the hour), any who survive the deaths of their fellows will absorb the psychic and physical energy of the fallen, making them much harder to kill. This variation of the peculiar (and extremely rare) ability known as Egogenesis is the subject of vigorous study and debate.
- *Thaal* – A subset of Iorians (see "Elves") that evolved to survive through parasitic Corpromancy, feeding off the blood or psychic energies of their victims (hence the terms *Sangothaal* and *Psychothaal*). Some biologists have contended that the *Thaal* would better be classified as *Legionari*.
- *Ziv Rodoji* – A many-tentacled creature, as ferociously intelligent as it is fatal. The *Ziv Rodoji* is noteworthy for the manner in which its limbs may act independently from each other (and its brain) when entering the state of fight-or-flight.

Legionari – Dangerous parasites and miscellaneous abominations make up this category.

- *Chimaerae* – The term for those who, although born human, have blasphemously fused themselves with Aelf parts—either through perversion of the arcane or scientific disciplines. Driven beyond all reason by their lust for power, in mutating their bodies, such individuals necessarily forfeit their souls. Thus, they relinquish their humanity—and their right to live.
- *Demons* – There are as many varieties of demons as there are human sins—Greed, Apathy, Wrath, Vanity, Sloth, etc. Their own name for their kind is "**Rel'ia'tuakr**," which translates loosely to "Undermoon and Overstar."
- *Gahool* – An enigmatic race, predating the Iorians and the Rioans (see

"Mythidim, Elves"). Leading Elemental archaeologists believe that some *Gahool* ruins are tens of thousands of years old.

- *Hybrids* – The offspring of tabooed unions of human and Aelf; in academic circles, they are called "Homonculi."

- *Jallantope* – Sentient frog people with ape-like, hairless arms. Supposedly the result of a careless experiment by a deranged and power-mad hermit mage. Not to be confused with the *paophs*.

- *Lamiae* – Driven to extinction several centuries ago, *lamiae* possessed the bodies of apes and the heads of serpents. They were notorious hunters and formidable archers: using bows carved from a type of as-yet unidentified wood, they could shoot down a fast-moving target—on starless nights, from impossible distances. Reputedly, *lamiae* reinforced and strung their bows with human gut string.

- *Mil'iggini* – Ape-like, brick-fisted, silver- or white-furred. The males sport blue or black stripes on their lower backs.

- *Razenzu* – An all but extinct, subaquatic species native to the Bay of Caelus and its environs, the *Razenzu* breathe sulfur rather than oxygen.

- *Shifters/Hidelings* – Origin unknown, these creatures' namesakes derive from their ability to magically transform their physicality. Some weave spells of deception and illusion to beguile the onlooker into *believing* a shape-change has occurred; the more powerful among them are able to actually manipulate bone structure, flesh tone, eye color, hair color, vocal pattern, and much more. Such beings are truly dangerous, insinuating themselves in the unlikeliest places; therefore, wherever uncovered, they have been ruthlessly exterminated.

- *Umbrites* – Shadow-born shapeshifting parasites, Umbrites are formless while unattached to a host; when feeding, they meld with its shadow. Umbrites survive off the fear of their hosts, and the former stoke this fear through the careful trickling of anxiety directly into the consciousnesses of the latter.

- *Xyloph* – Typically eight feet tall, these bipedal, muscled feline beasts range in color from black to purplish silver to gray. They are ferocious, terrifyingly strong, and brutally territorial.

Colossi – All those Aelf that are larger than the average city bus but *non-sentient* belong to this category.

- *Dan'yn'daup* – Train-sized worms that burrow huge tunnels in the earth. They use the saw-like bony protrusions on their backs to grip rock while navigating the magma-laced chasms miles below the surface.

- *Giant* – Denizens of the poles, the arctic, and high mountain peaks of the northern hemisphere. The last proven specimen of this mammoth-sized species was slain in 1889 by an anonymous Igniomancer.

- *Góra'cień* – With a 30-foot wingspan, the scaly, long-necked *góra'cień* is a carnivorous predator predominantly found in the westernmost regions of El. Early settlers of these territories, pressing ever deeper into the untamed wildernesses of the continent, needed to contend with flocks of these beasts.

- *Kraken* – Former scourge of the sea trade, in the 2020s, these tentacled monstrosities were hunted to extinction—at a terrible cost in human lives—through the combined efforts of Authority vessels and Gild Aquamancers.

- *Lemlar* – Also called "cave ape" because its facial features are vaguely reminiscent of a silverback gorilla's. There, however, the similarities end. The hairless, fleshy *lemlar* has no arms nor legs but boasts ten muscular tentacles which it uses to navigate its preferred environment—forgotten lakes, deep underground.

- *Schildkrahe* – A mountain-sized turtle, an active volcano having grown upon its back. Only one has ever been confirmed to exist—on an island in the Suur-al-Swalpan, the Sea of Dreams. It was accidently killed in 2122 by a fracking operation that shattered its shell, infecting its flesh.

Ushum – Included in this category are all those Aelf that are massive, brutal, and sentient.

- *Dragons* – By far, the most infamous example of this subcategory are the Twin Dragon Kings, H'ranajaan and Ji'inaluud. Together, they ruled over armies of sentient Aelf foot-soldiers and millions of human slaves. From an academic standpoint, their partnership was noteworthy because Dragons were, in every other case, solitary and preferred to keep well away from human beings. After the deaths of the Twin Dragon Kings, Aelfravers spent centuries ruthlessly hunting down and destroying every last Dragon.

- *Drualoniok* – A species gone extinct during the reign of the Iorian Empire. Details unknown.

- *Yuorgith* – Same as above.

Demidivines – Ancient, patient, their true natures are often obscured by the erosions of millennia.

- *Sevensin* – The sole surviving account of these mysterious beings is an old (and dubious) Monraïc legend claiming they were born of the same seven-sourced magic that brought all Aelf into the world.

  According to the story, seven Iorian sorcerers combined their dark powers to exterminate all of humanity with one final spell. Seven mystical gates were built and opened, and through these poured legions of Aelf, led by the newly spawned Sevensin.

  Each of the Sevensin supposedly bore the face of a man but the hideously deformed and monstrous body of a squid, a hawk, a spider. The last of them faded from history in the earliest years after the slaying of the Twin Dragon Kings.

Uult – Believed by most to be mere superstition, the only evidence for the Uult's existence lies in scraps of myth and ancient epics.

About the Author

J.R. Traas is an author, editor, and tutor who has published over twenty books, as well as various short stories and poems.

With well over a decade of teaching experience, it has been his privilege to instruct dozens upon dozens of young people in a plethora of subjects. Some of his students have won awards and scholarships for their writing. One of them calls him "Gandalf"—the highest compliment he has ever received.

Gandalf lives near Atlanta with his wife and their animal friends.

Heading over to *Blankbooklibrary.com* is the simplest way to reach him and join the conversation. If you liked this story, please leave a review and spread the word. Cat food, after all, doesn't grow on trees.

Made in United States
North Haven, CT
28 May 2022

19614521R00452